Doorway 54

James A Lyons

Doorway 54

First Edition

August 2018

ISBN: 9781717895400

Doorway 54

Oh l'amour, broke my heart and now I'm aching for you.
Mon amour, what's a boy in love supposed to do?

- Erasure, Oh L'amour

Doorway 54

This book is dedicated for all in the LGBTQ community and its true allies.

Thank you to David Brown for correcting my spelling, grammar and everything else that made no sense when I originally handed the draft across.

This is also for Mum, Dad, Chris, Liam, Benjamin and Thomas. Big thanks to Josh Baldwin and Mark Bishop, without their books, this book wouldn't exist. Thanks to Joey Lewin for letting me inadvertently steal his name.

Finally, I'm sorry to the friends who I forgot to text back whilst writing this novel.

Contact the author

www.twitter.com/jalwrites
www.jamesalyons.co.uk

This book has been self-published. I have tried to correct any minor errors, however a couple of small ones may exist. Apologies if this happens. If you notice mistakes, please feel free to email

james.a.lyons@outlook.com

Doorway 54

This book is a work of fiction. Any similarities to a specfic person, living or deceased, is purely coincidental.

15% of the profits from the sales of this book will be donated between Young Minds UK, The Attitude Foundation and Pride in London who work towards supporting youth mental health, youth homelessness and the LGBTQ community.

Doorway 54

One

Three weeks. Just three more weeks and I will be free. Twenty-one days. About five hundred hours. Around thirty-two thousand minutes. One point eight million seconds, give or take.

I should have a plan. I can do a plan when I'm free. I say free, by that I mean I'll probably head off to work some hours in the supermarket, secretly hatching my master plan whilst putting tins of beans on a shelf. Maybe I should start a plan now? Is it so much of a plan or is it just being who I am now but in a different setting? Who knows. At least I'll be earning more money I guess.

"Joseph". My nonsensical train of thought is interrupted. "Joseph Eaton, are you listening to me?"

I can't lie. I'm not listening. I haven't really been listening for the best part of a month to be honest with you. I am currently sat on a grey sofa in the school library. It's not at all comfortable and it has definitely seen better days. The foam on the cushions is slowly disappearing where it has been picked at by other bored students over the years. It was probably placed here when this particular teacher was a student here at Greenwood Academy. Dwindling budgets mean that it will probably be here by the time that I reach her age. She always ALWAYS goes on about how she was more alert and engaged "when she was a student at this school". The 'she' I am referring to here is Miss Moxley. It's a strange name that makes her sound like she should be about sixty years old with her hair in a bun, but in reality, she can't be much older than twenty-five. Her short dark bobbed hair frames her mouse-like face, which is complimented (Wait. Complimented is definitely the wrong word – What is the opposite??), her face is *paired* with a set of round red-rimmed glasses. They make her look a bit more evil than she actually is. Miss Moxley is quite laid back as far as teachers here at Greenwood go. This doesn't make this situation much easier for either of us though. Younger teachers are regularly seen as easy targets by some of the more unruly students. She knows that I'm not listening to her. It's the second time today she has broken one of my trances.

"Sorry miss" I mumble.

"I know it's a Monday morning Joseph, but you still need to listen"

She carries on with her talk and once again my thoughts slowly drift to the very near future. It is a Monday, and the first 'lesson' of each week is always dedicated to 'Tutor Time'. We are 'officially' on study leave at the moment. I use inverted commas here because we were told that this hourly period per week was to remain mandatory. The blame for this lies in the hands of those in the year above us at this school. During study leave last year a group of kids got involved in a drinking game in the town centre that got out of hand, and somehow ended up with arson. No one knows exactly how it happened, but it ended with the local coffee shed on fire. As a result, students are now forced to attend these sessions, and sign in to ensure attendance, every single Thursday morning.

Tutor Time used to be interesting, and we learnt the very basics of politics, sign language, nutrition and a variety of other things during these sessions over the last two years. These lessons used to be quite good fun as they provided things that would be useful in future life. Now though we are into our GCSE's, which continue next Monday. All of tutor time is therefore dedicated to things that will apparently help us succeed in life. That is how it is sold to us, but sadly they aren't very useful to me. One of the things that sets me apart from ninety-five per cent of the people in this room is that I have no interest in going to university. None at all. I'm not sure why it is exactly that I don't wish to go, but it's never been something that I have been keen on. Today the topic is filling in UCAS forms, and how students can do extra-curricular activities to really make them stand out when they apply in about eighteen months' time. There is a lot of talk about the Duke of Edinburgh scheme, about how we can volunteer at charity shops throughout Sixth Form, or help with local community groups and that kind of thing. As mentioned, I won't need to bolster my UCAS application because I won't have one that needs submitting. The Duke of Edinburgh Scheme sounds awful enough. I don't enjoy sitting in this library with many of these people, let alone having to go through the endless task of putting up a tent in the rain whilst trapped on the Gower Peninsula in South Wales with them. Volunteering at a charity shop sounds dull, although I bet there are some fabulous grey-haired women there who could bore me to death. Community groups? Why would I want to be involved in the community when the community subconsciously tries to reject me at every opportunity? You will never catch me running a community project.

Why do I dislike these people so much? Well, they have never really wanted to engage with me in all honesty. I don't really fit in with most of them and I think the fact that I am gay means that some subconsciously distance themselves from me. My school friends know about my sexuality, despite me not actually going through any official coming out parade. In fact, I have never even confirmed it, but everyone has great delight in telling me how obvious I make it. Why do people feel the need to tell you how obvious you are? Some of the girls seem to use it as a way to become my friend as if I am a big glittery unicorn shaped accessory to add to their outfit. This is just as frustrating as those who go out of their way to bully me. The ones who call me a 'faggot' or 'gay boy' in the long white corridors. Being the token 'gay friend' and being the 'token queer' are both just as offensive to me. I just want to crack on with my own life to be honest. To most in this school, the abuse comes because they only think of the sexual acts involved, rather than the fact that gay people go through all the same emotions as straight people. Honestly, I don't know why homophobes are so obsessed with talking about it. It's not as if sex is the pot of gold at the end of the LGBT rainbow. Anyway, I know that in three weeks I will not be required to see these people ever again if I so wish. Three weeks. Just three more weeks and I will be free. Twenty-one days. About five hundred hours. Around thirty-two thousand minutes. One point eight million seconds, give or take. I keep repeating this to myself over and over again, much more than you imagine. I am completely done with this school.

The stress of school life has taken its toll on me over the years, and the lack of support has meant that I have also struggled with my mental health. I find family life quite hard sometimes, and it sometimes feels that whatever I do never improves a situation. It's quite hard to describe. It probably is in part to my sexuality, however my parents do not know about that, so I am unable to explain my problems to them. Recently I have made some online friends, mainly in forums that discuss gay things. I'm a bit behind in terms of the internet as my parents have an overly strict policy with using it at home. They have even put restrictions on my phone so I can't access anything that has been classed as 'adult content' by the militant in-built parental lock. These friends tell me that I will know when I am ready to let people know, and the time isn't right with the parents just yet. I just know that when I tell them things will be very hard for a while. I wish I had a brother or sister who could help support me through it, but I have been cursed as an only child. I know some other only children and they think it's great that they get all the attention, but I would love a sibling who I could share things with, someone who I would be able to speak to about anything.

Now, I bet by now you have a picture of me in your mind. You have a picture of what I look like, how I sound, what my interests are, that kind of thing. I think you are wrong. Being gay does not mean you are effeminate and camp. I'm not saying that there aren't effeminate and camp people, and there is nothing wrong with that. Nothing wrong whatsoever. A lot of my online friends are like that, just as equally that a lot of my online friends talk about Top Gear and rugby. See, being gay does not mean that you dance around in a pink crop top to Britney Spears or Lady Gaga or Ariana Grande. Being gay does not mean getting an erection every time a boy in shorts walks past. Being gay does not mean that you describe everything as fabulous, as a-maz-ing or beautiful whilst flinging your arms around in some grand gesture. Most people assume this is the case as this is how we are portrayed in most mainstream television shows. Gay people are not just your new best friend and someone to gossip with or to help you choose an outfit. We are doctors, nurses, firefighters, police officers, politicians, business CEO's, retail workers, Olympians, teachers, physicians, engineers, astronauts, IT consultants, butchers, bakers and candlestick makers. Being gay means that you are gay. It has no connection to what you listen to, what books you read, which films you watch, which famous people you aspire to, which sport is your favourite, what career you want. Literally no correlation. One common connection is that we have all had our own struggles with being gay. People assume it is easier if you are 'straight acting'. What a horrible fucking phrase. Each gay person has fought, or is fighting, their own battle, most likely inside of their own mind. And let me tell you this, it isn't easy. You can't leave your mind and conscience to one side whilst you take a breather. Your mind, your battle, follows you EVERYWHERE. It's with me in this library right this second. It's with me when I'm walking on my own through town past a group of men. It's with me during Sunday lunch with my family. It will be with me when I hit eighteen and I'm enjoying my first legal pint. It will be with me in the workplace when I do have a career. It's with you when you wake up sweating at 3am wondering why you were chosen to fight this. Older friends tell me it gets easier and I hope that they are right. The first step for me will be walking out the double doors of Greenwood after my last GCSE and into my future whilst all the 'fag hags' and hormonal boys slowly disappear behind the sun that will be reflecting off the glass. This is why I can't wait. Three weeks. Just three more weeks and I will be free. Twenty-one days. About five hundred hours. Around thirty-two thousand minutes. One point eight million seconds, give or take.

I've digressed, sorry. As I was saying, you're probably wrong about me. Now before I go on I need you to clear your mind. Whatever picture of me you currently have is something I need you to flush out. Breathe in. Breathe out. You don't know what I look like. You don't know my interests. You don't know my height, my weight, my hair colour, my eye colour or anything. You don't know what this library looks like. You don't know what my school friends are like, or even any of their names. Breathe in. Breathe out. Forget everything.

Two

I'll start again. I am sat in this week's 'Tutor Time' in Greenwood Academy's school library. The library is quite big, with about three-quarters of it set aside for the books, and the rest separated into desks for studying and a computer area. The most enthusiastic readers tend to be the newer students, and they can often be spotted in here at lunchtime in the fiction sections. As you progress through the years though you shift across to the more factual books as you start to do some last-minute revision and research for the exams. It's a shame really that when you get nearer to those exams the time you can spend reading fiction dwindles. I hardly do any reading these days, whereas when I first started I went through all the Harry Potter books, and various other collections. I know you're not meant to judge a book by its cover, but come on, at least make the front of text books a bit engaging even if the content inside is dire. All the pictures inside look like they were taken in the 1970's too. All beige slacks and sensible pale blue pullovers. At the computer desks I can see four sixth form students doing prep work for essays. It won't be long until I spot one of them procrastinating and ending up on social media or down a Wikipedia black hole. To the right is the desk where the librarian Miss Earnshaw sits. She looks like a librarian. Can I say that? Green jumper, green cardigan (hand made by the looks of it) and straight brown hair which is slowly turning grey at the roots. All school librarians probably go grey by the time they move to a different job. Working in a place surrounded by students would probably do this to you, especially in a department where you're not really seen as a proper member of staff by the pupils.

The far end of the library looks across to the school playing fields. Form my position I can look directly past Miss Moxley and out of the floor to ceiling windows opposite. Outside are a few dishevelled trees, with a concrete square to the right where outdoor sports take place. I can't look at that square without the thought of the 'bleep test' springing into my mind. Every year we must do it. I'm not bad at it, but I don't enjoy it. The only people who enjoy it are the PE teachers who see the bleep test as an uncomplicated way to waste an hour. To the left of the trees is the main sports field. A slightly derelict pavilion stands at the far end, with cricket nets beside it. There is a long jump runway with sand pit and a javelin area. In the large gap in between here and the square, the 400-metre running track is marked out. This takes the place of the rugby pitches during the summer term, and it's hardly likely to inspire the next Mo Farah. It's on bumpy grass and the lines are about as straight as I am. Apart from this, you can't really see much else from here.

Now then, on to me. As Miss Moxley pointed out when I wasn't listening, my name is Joseph Eaton. Joseph Jobe Eaton if you'd like my full name. I'm known as Joey though to my friends here. I am fifteen years old and will be sixteen on June 10th. I am about five feet eight inches tall, ten stone with size nine feet. My eyes are hazel, and my hair is light brown in colour. I have fairly short hair apart from my fringe, which is a bit longer and rests just above my eyebrows. I do not wear glasses, but probably should. I am right-handed, right-footed and apparently right-eyed. I can ride a bike, but I am unable to swim. I am a fan of garlic bread but despise anything that tastes of ginger. I am scared of unsecured heights and also weirdly have a phobia of wet bread. It's a strange one but it makes me feel weird and the reason why I am unable to eat trifle. I am sat on this battered grey sofa in my Greenwood uniform of black trousers and shoes, white shirt and a horrendous green and gold striped tie. If I am being totally honest I would say that my trousers are a little too short for me these days. You can see my socks (one blue, one white) quite clearly when I am slouched down like I am today.

Doorway 54

I realised I was gay when I was thirteen. Despite knowing that I was different, it was confirmed during a break time in year nine. It had been raining heavily on that January day so rather than let us outside we were forced to all eat our packed lunches in our tutor rooms. Everyone would prefer to be outside, especially as there was always one kid who would bring egg sandwiches, which made the classroom smell horrendous. Our teacher during this time in Year 9 at the time was also the Head of Year 10 so left us to our own devices whilst she went to sort out a fight that had started in the tuck shop between two boys. One of those school fights where people had fallen out about something stupid. As with any group of school children, once the authoritative figure is removed it will soon descend into a free for all. Within about a minute of being alone, my classmates were soon free of their designated tables and were sat randomly around the classroom, swinging on chairs and perched on tables. I was sat next to Sarah Vickers, who most of boys in our year were obsessed with. I had never seen her like this and I often wondered what I was missing. Due to her being beside me, there was soon a group of boys sat on my table whilst I tried to finish my bag of Monster Munch in peace. They were discussing the girls that they fancied, and one of them pulled a magazine out that opened suspiciously straight onto a page of some reality TV star reclining on a beach. Their discussion was very primal to say the least, and it wasn't long before the magazine was put in front of me.

"What do you think of her then Joey?" asked Gavin, whilst jabbing a finger onto the picture of Ms Monét, the bikini model and reality star who was spread across the sand in his tattered magazine.

"Yeah, nice" I replied, trying to be as convincing as possible.

"Nice? She's perfect mate" he responded.

To me though, she wasn't perfect in the sense that Gavin was getting at. In fact, she didn't stir up any emotions in me whatsoever. The light in Gavin's eyes did match the light that was probably in mine when I became obsessed with my own magazine hero though.

Now this is a bit embarrassing but for your benefit I will be honest with you. I had gone through a similar set of emotions to those that Gavin was experiencing, around two weeks prior to this classroom incident. I can hear you asking which famous person it was who had convinced me that I was gay. Well, they weren't famous, and I will never know his name. He was a model in an Argos catalogue who was horizontal and shirtless whilst demonstrating the "Super Ab Workout Device". I told you it was embarrassing. There are seven billion people in this world, so let's say that's about three point five billion men, and the one that will forever get credited with starting my lifetime entry into the glittery world of homosexuality was a fucking model for Argos. I still have that page in a locked box in the drawer under my bed. I don't have the heart to get rid of it.

I have anxiety attacks about that locked box at home. I sometimes panic and think that my parents will find it whilst doing some cleaning. I have the key to it in another locked box though, and the key to that box is on my keychain in my school bag. Parents can be suspicious though. My mother Ann is a verger at the local church, St Frideswide's. She has worked there for around ten years and her whole career has been based within religion. She used to be a teacher of Religious Studies at a local college, and something that she adored. I told you earlier that I am an only child. This is only partly true. Ten years ago, mum fell pregnant with my brother Matthew. There were many complications with her pregnancy and Matthew passed away at just two days old. To me, he is still my brother. I think this is why I still crave a sibling to be at home, someone who will share the blame for things I do or just someone to hang around with if I ever feel lonely. The reality is that I am an older brother, but without the younger sibling being able to talk to me. I often visit the area where he was laid to rest and talk to him. I like to think that he can hear me. Despite this, I am not as religious or as spiritual as my parents, however the thought that he is with me through life is something that I find guides me at the tough times. My mum took two years from work after the loss of Matthew, with my Dad switching to part-time after spending six months alongside her. Despite the issues between us, I hope that I inherit the strength that they have. My Dad, Peter, runs a charity bookshop which raises funds for St Frideswide's and has owned this since his father died twenty-five years ago. The loss of Matthew added a lot of strain to my parents' marriage, and there many times where it became close to splintering, leaving them to be another notch on the country's divorce statistics. Once my dad returned to work though things did start to settle, and the sense of routine started to reappear. On the anniversary of Matthew's birth, they renewed their vows.

It's quite clear from what I am telling you that religion is something that has been a staple of the Eaton family for many many years. It also explains my irritating middle name. This is also why I cannot tell them about being gay. I may do one day, but I know that it will cause a lot of friction. I honestly don't know how they will react, and I know that I won't be the first to be made to feel like an outcast because of being gay. I wish there was someone who has been through the same to give me reassurance that everything will be OK. Without this unknown figure though I am not ready to be open with them. I'm not ready to be open with anyone about it, not even my closest friends.

My closest friend is Angelica. Her parents are second generation immigrants, having originated from Jamaica. Angelica is one of the most natural learners that I have ever met. She is guaranteed to get an extensive collection of top grades from these exams, and she is sat opposite me furiously taking notes to ensure that she will get into the top university of her choice. It wouldn't surprise me if she studied one of the sciences at Oxford or Cambridge. She is a natural. She is also a natural beauty. Her black skin is always perfect, and her bone structure is high on the list of things which make me jealous. Over the last few weeks she has written her own revision plan and has not wavered from it for one minute. It has meant that we haven't had as much time to hang around together over the last few weeks, but we have made some very loose plans to do some day trips as soon as the exams are over.

The most concrete plan so far is a visit to Harrods. It's just a shop, I know, but when you don't live in London and are not overrun with money it is like the Emerald City (A Wizard of Oz reference. How stereotypical eh?!). I'm obsessed with seeing Harrods. I want to have afternoon tea there, sat amongst women with facelifts laughing over nothing with their equally rich friends. After that we will go to the V&A museum as they have an exhibition on with a lot of historical dresses from the golden age of Hollywood. Apparently, it will have the Breakfast at Tiffany's dress, and others worn by the ultimate cinematic icons. I've already researched the tubes and trains and know exactly how to get around a big city. I've even been on streetview to see what it will look like when we arrive at Marylebone station and get spat onto the streets. It will feel like an entirely different world. In my head I can picture walking around. I can picture which café I will go to first. I can envisage the sounds, the smells, the people. I would go this second if I wasn't stuck in this school for exams. Three weeks. Just three more weeks and I will be free. Twenty-one days. About five hundred hours. Around thirty-two thousand minutes. One point eight million seconds, give or take.

My sexuality is not something that me and Angelica have talked about either. I do want to discuss it more with her, but I always get the feeling that she changes the subject each time she knows that I am getting close to mentioning it. It's heart-breaking and isolating that this is a subject that even she, perhaps inadvertently, makes a taboo area. We know that we can discuss anything else and neither side is judged for their opinion. She has told me many things first that she has been too afraid to talk to her parents about. Some of the things make no sense to me and I've had to Google them, so it has led to my search history resembling that of a maniac. Still, I can't wait to get her back from revision.

I have just realised that I have completely left this Tutor Time mentally again and bought you with me. My head and heart are not in it and I've given up listening. I think even Miss Moxley has realised that I won't be coming back to the discussion. According to the clocks on either side of the library there are just five or ten minutes to go until we can have the daily fifteen-minute morning break. The two clocks have never shown the same time as each other. You notice the trivial things when you're on your own so much.

Three

It turns out the slower clock in the library was correct. The last ten minutes dragged on longer than you can imagine. As it goes, Miss Moxley had noticed me not listening for the third time and she pulled me aside at the end to give me a talk on how listening to her would make things 'so much easier once I have finished sixth form". She knows I am not going into sixth form but if you're not interested in continuing at Greenwood Academy the teachers are less interested in you. It's a sad fact that I'm used to unfortunately. I do have career ambitions, it's just that I don't know what they are yet. Miss Moxley also used the following sentence to try and hammer home her points; "You can't just flaunt your way through life hoping that things will come to you". Flaunt. I do not flaunt. I don't think that she, or any other teacher who casually refers to my sexuality, intend to offer some low level homophobic language into the way they speak to me but hearing it used time and time again does more to demoralise me than it does to engage me. You may think that I am being paranoid, but trust me, it happens.

Breaktime is going to be spent indoors again today. Even though it is mid-May the showery weather seems to be back and the windows all along the length of this long corridor are streaked with rain that does not look like it is slowing anytime soon. I get to my locker and pull out my wallet as I need a sugar hit to keep me going today. When

I enter the tuck shop the queue is massive, but I spot Angelica near the front, so I tactfully slide up to her to get nearer the front.

“Hey Joey, how’s it going?” she asks.
“Not bad. The same I guess”
“You seem a bit vague today”
“Might be exam nerves” I reply. I want to tell her I need her, but at the same time she deserves just to focus on the next few weeks. “Are you staying here for break?”
“I’ll be here for a few minutes” she replies, “but I do want to get to my French class a little early as there is something I need to speak to Monsieur Garrett about”
I hate the way that the clever kids call him by his preferred French title even when they aren’t anywhere near him. Bloody Monsieur Garrett. He grew up on a rough estate near Bolton and he is the least French person I know. He’s only ever been to France when he has had to take a group of schoolkids across to Le Harve every October.

“Grab your food Joey and come sit with me. I need to speak to you”
“Will do”. At least she wants to talk about something.

The dinner staff are never the quickest here, and it takes me three goes to explain to the elderly lady serving me that it’s a cream bun that I want. It’s not exactly the most complex order. With bun and serviette in hand I walk across the small white walled room and sit opposite Angelica on the rickety metal legged table.

"How can I be of service?" I ask as I shove at least a quarter of the bun into my mouth in one go.
"It's about London" she says
"Oh my God, I cannot wait. Have you seen the reviews of the preview show?"
"I have yes, but, well Joey I'm not sure if I can do it anymore"

We have been talking about this so much for at least ten weeks. She was keener than I was, and that's saying something.

"What? Why not? It's going to be wonderful!"
"I know, it looks great, just the thing is my parents have decided to take me away on the Saturday after the exams finish"
"Well that's OK, it's on until the middle of June so we will just delay it until you're back"
"That's the thing. I am going to be away for at least a month"
"A bloody month? Where the hell are you going for a bloody month?"
"Jamaica"

Of all the places it had to be there. Because of her ancestry it's really the one place I can't get angry at her for. I am angry though. I feel like I have already lost her for the last month, and now I have another month after the exams without her. No Angelica, no Hepburn dress. I can't go to London on my own. I was relying on her as being my security blanket. I am nowhere near confident enough to go on my own. On top of that my parents wouldn't let me anyway. They barely trust me to walk to school on my own without getting into trouble.

"What are you going to do out there for a month?" I ask, exhausted, accidentally spitting bits of bun onto the table

"My parents have organised it as a surprise for me. It's my Granny's 85th birthday soon and they want to get as much of the family together as possible. We only really had to pay for the flights as we will be hopping around the various Caribbean islands staying with many uncles and aunts. Jamaica, Trinidad and Tobago and St Lucia. Everywhere! It's going to be such an experience"

"It does sound good, I'll let you have that, but what about me?"

"I know, I am sorry, but you don't have to go into work full time straight away so I'm sure there are things that you can do whilst I'm away"

"I get bored at weekends already Angelica. I'll be a recluse after a month without you"

"It'll be OK I promise. Look I'll speak to you more about it later, I have to go to French now". I wanted to protest but when she was determined there was no point in trying to distract her.

Angelica got up and left rapidly, and I sat on my own now finishing the most depressing cream bun that I've ever had.

After a couple of long quiet minutes, a voice pops up from behind.

"Anyone sat here?"

I turn around and Gary Tanner is stood there. I hate Gary Tanner. Of all the people making snide comments to me, he is the king. He has a couple of his friends with him, Abdul and Ian. They're always with him. I've seen warts cling to people less than these two idiots cling to Gary.

"You can have the table" I say as I sweep the leftover bun crumbs onto the floor. "I was just going anyway"

"Come on now Joey, you don't have to go". He says this with a firm hand placed on my shoulder, and given his weight, it makes me immobile.

"I want to go Gary"

"Look just sit with us, it won't hurt you to be friendly for a change will it?"

I don't want to be friendly. I'm nearly at the end of Greenwood and I can't even begin to feel friendly to anyone, let alone these three. I've done quite well to keep myself away from a lot of the people here in my year group. We all only know each other through circumstance of being thrown into the same school at the same time. There are probably some great people at the other school in town, yet we never really mix. The other school is known as Askey's, but it's official title is Lord Askew's. I'm not quite sure where the rivalry started but some people would defend their school for everything they own. Football matches have been known to be abandoned between the two schools due to fighting breaking out. The fighting isn't always isolated to the pitch either. I attended one of these matches, but it didn't last much past thirty minutes. One of the girls on the sidelines who is in the year above threw a choc ice at a girl from Askey's and before you knew it there was a bundle of bodies scrapping with each other. As our Head of Science was also the referee he was in the most senior position to try and break it up, and you can't really play a match whilst the referee is dragging someone to a classroom. It's exciting at least, and something you'd never see in the Premier League.

"We just want to know your plans for the summer, that's all" continued Gary.

"Really? As if you care"

"'course we care" Abdul chips in. "We wanna know what kids like you do"

"Kids like me?"

"Yeah y'know, queer kids. What do you do when you're not here"

"Fuck off Abdul, I'm not here for your amusement"

"Look mate" continues Ian, picking up from Abdul, "It's the World Cup this summer, it's meant to be decent weather, and it's the last before some of us leave everyone to go to college and work and stuff. What will you do?"

"I'll be watching the World Cup, Ian"

"Hang on though, I thought"

"Well you thought wrong" I interjected before he could claim that being gay and liking football was mutually exclusive.

"OK sorry Princess, no need to get defensive" Ian concluded

It wasn't long before Gary started to try another intimidating conversation.

"Joey do your friends mind you being a queer?"

"Can you stop calling me that?"

"Why, there's nothing wrong with being a queer, is there lads" he said, looking to his friends to get their confirmation

"Nothing at all, nothing at all" they both said in unison

"Gary listen" I said, trying to get out of the conversation and out of the room "whatever you think is fine to call me, you are wrong"

"Why are you always so defensive?"

"I'm not, it's just that I don't need to explain my life to people like you. You never used to care about me and only talk to me now to try and take the piss"

"Have it your way then you queer. I recommend you stop being so defensive and stop trying to make me look like an idiot"

"But you are an idiot sometimes Gary, you just don't realise it yet"
"He could destroy you Joey" said Abdul, chipping in again
"No one can destroy me"
"Do your parents know?"
"About what?"
"About you being a queer"
"Stop calling me that" I say again, knowing full well he won't stop.
"Do they know though?"
"It's none of your business. Nothing about me is any of your business"
"It'd be a shame if they found out wouldn't it. Suggest you play nice"

I should have left it there. I should have kept quiet. They were getting up to leave when I finally snapped. I couldn't control it.

"Three weeks and I'll be gone Gary. Three weeks before I can finally tell you to fuck off and never have to put up with you again". I didn't even give them eye contact, that would have been far too decent of me. Gary stopped dead, sort of halfway between standing and sitting. He was large for his age and always had been. I think it was the reason why he felt he had some masculine power over every other boy in the school. He had to always take someone down to make himself feel superior. He had a heavy frame, permanently angry expression and was nearly as wide as he was tall. When he first started primary school, he was bullied himself due to his size. I don't condone any bullying and was never an instigator, but some of the other kids used to claim that he ate curry for breakfast and that's why he was bigger than everyone else. This thing is, he maintained this large body mass so once he hit puberty he could use it to his advantage and take out the years of being a target onto anyone who he pleased.

"Tell me to fuck off? Is that what you just said?"
"Just go Gary, I'm not in the mood"
"I don't appreciate being told to fuck off Joey, I don't think you understand that I don't like being treated like that, especially by a fag"

Rather than argue, I thought it would be a clever idea to say it again.
"Gary. Fuck. Off". This time I was looking straight at him. Then, without thinking, I picked up a half-finished cup of juice from the table next to mine and threw it at him. It was an instinctive reaction and not something that I have ever done before. I have never crossed a line by quite this far before. Despite all the arguments and fights that I have had in my head, I'd never turned one into reality before. I think this is the moment. This is that moment when I snapped. It was a moment that was the culmination of all the rejection and homophobia that had been bubbling

underneath the surface of my skin over the last four years or more.

I have never been someone who excelled in any sport involving elements of throwing, and on this morning my aim was as bad as ever. I once nearly managed to spear a friend with a javelin even though they had been stood behind me. The memory of this popped into my head when I was looking out across the playing fields from my seat in the library earlier. Back in the tuck shop, the glass that I threw caught Gary on his left shoulder before ricocheting on to the wall and shattering to the floor. The orange liquid inside was deposited over the left side of his face, and also across a group of Year 11 girls and their textbooks. I wanted to run, but my actions had even shocked myself and I couldn't get my legs to move. The whole room had frozen around me and an array of emotions, headed by anger, powered through my body. It must have only been a few seconds before things started moving again but, in my mind, it felt like an eternity. What I hadn't realised before was that the Deputy Head of the school, Mr Shepherd, was nearby. As Gary lunged towards me he was pulled back by Mr Shepherd and told to go and clean himself up. Mr Shepherd was an ex-rugby player and had no trouble in issuing his authority over Gary and his gang despite being smaller in size. What he lacked in size he made up for in muscle and it would be a stupid decision to even try and protest. In another life Mr Shepherd was definitely someone of high rank in the army. One of those men with a strong moustache who would bellow at the poor new recruits from across a drill yard. Gary continued to stare at me as he made his way towards the door. I've never seen someone go so long without blinking before. I'm not sure if it was shock or anger that made his eyes stay permanently open. His noodle like blonde hair was damp on the left-hand side and was starting to matt together from whatever ingredients were in the juice. Hopefully the bastard would get chased by bees all the way home.

Once Gary had departed Mr Shepherd turned his attention to me.

"Joseph Eaton follow me" he said, turning around towards the door before I could even utter a reply. I slowly followed him from the room and every pair of students' eyes were fixed upon me. The Year 11's started calling me an idiot as they mopped up juice from their books. Mr Shepherd's office was located at the far end of the main corridor and the walk there seemed to take forever. I could hear my own heartbeat and my chest felt tight. The rain was still pounding against the long windows. I wasn't looking forward to how he would react, and I made an effort to delay the inevitable by dragging my feet so that the walk took twice as long. He held the door open for me as I approached, finally telling me to get a move on when I was about ten metres away. You could always tell when Mr Shepherd was angry because he became monosyllabic.

His face also reddened easily which made his ginger eyebrows stand out prominently.

"You. Sit" he said firmly.

I slinked into the room and perched on the edge of another foam-vomiting padded chair. He then closed the door with him outside and I heard his footsteps pacing up and down outside. It was like he was a cricketer preparing himself to run up to release a fast ball at an unsuspecting batsman. I couldn't see him, but I knew exactly what expression he had. His trainers struck the tiled floor outside time and time again. He was that angry that he would still make noise if he was just pacing around in his socks. I had no idea how long he planned to be out there, and I wanted to keep my mind occupied to take myself away from this situation. Mr Shepherd was head of physical education at Greenwood, however his office resembled that of a geography teacher, but much smaller and untidier than the actual geography teachers here. On the wall opposite to where I was sat was a large world map surrounded by the various nations' flags, and weird pie charts about the different continents' GDP, population and landmass. To keep my mind elsewhere I tried to correctly state the name of the country that each flag represented. I would get as far as two or three guesses before I got dumped back into the reality of my situation. Regardless of how much I tried there was no escape. I sat back with my eyes closed and used the ticking of the clock on the left-hand wall as a metronome to calm my breathing. It was no good trying to fight now, and as I sat there, eyes shut to the world, the tears began to form and roll down my cheeks.

Mr Shepherd entered back into the room and I quickly wiped my face with my right sleeve. His pacing had done nothing to calm him down either it seemed, and he was a lot redder in the face than it was when he had mentally dragged me down the corridor. I had spotted a pack of cigarettes poking out of his leather bag that was slung loosely around the back of his chair and I bet he was dying to have one right now. It's always weird when you find out your teachers do something....un-teacher like. He was always known as the one who would walk around the school border at lunchtimes catching smokers and confiscating their goods. I bet he only did this to save himself from having to buy his own. He drummed on the table with the knuckles of his left hand as he walked round the desk before taking a seat opposite me. PE teachers always felt the need to dress as if they may be called into the field of action at any moment. Along with the trainers he wore the Wales national rugby top, and shorts that bordered on the edge of common decency. He leant forward to prove to me that he meant business. His shoes squeaked on the floor as he put weight on them and a small amount of spit shot across the table with each word.

"Joseph. What the hell do you think you are doing?"

"I....I...Sir I'm sorry. I snapped. I don't normally do things like that. You know I don't"
"You tried assaulting a student with a glass. Do you not realise how dangerous that is? If that had hit him, we could have been on our way to the hospital"
"I know sir, but it didn't hit him"
"Oh well that's okay then. As long as you didn't blind him that makes everything okay" he said sarcastically, still spitting. "Not only did you assault him, you've also affected other students who are now sat there covered in orange juice. The wall will probably need to be repainted and they will have to close the tuck shop whilst they clean up the mess you've made. There's glass everywhere".
"I can help, Sir. I can go back and help them clean"
"You've done more than enough already Joseph Eaton. More. Than. Enough. Why the hell did you think you could act like that?"
"It wasn't my fault"
"Oh really. And how do you come to that conclusion?"
"He started the assault Sir!"
"I was there, remember that Eaton".

I hate it when I get called by my surname by the teachers here. I think it makes them feel like they have further power over you, as if it is back in the Victorian era. No doubt they would use the cane also if they could.

"If you were there Sir then you must have heard what he was saying to me"

“It’s school break time. I’ve been working in schools for over a decade to know that kids will be kids. If you think that this is the first time I have had a conversation like this then you must be more stupid than I thought. All the hormones in one place is never a good recipe so it’s more than natural to see people argue, but we must make sure that no lines are crossed. Unfortunately, you have crossed that line by quite some distance”

“Did you actually hear the argument Sir?” I asked hopefully

“It’s not my job to listen to every conversation in the room Eaton, I’m just there to make sure that people don’t start throwing glasses about at each other and damaging school property in the process”

“He called me a queer and a fag Sir. He and his mates are always like this”

“Sticks and stones, Joseph, sticks and stones”

“But it’s not sticks and stones. We are not at primary school. We are bordering on being adults. Sticks and stones is what we are told when we are five and someone says that they don’t like your new shoes or something. It’s not the same as being verbally attacked is it?”

“Come on Joseph, if you are saying that someone mocking you is the same as a physical assault then I’m afraid you are not nearly as much of an adult as you expect. You’ve only got a few weeks left here so do everyone a favour and try and contain your anger for once”

I'd had enough. I'd had enough of being stuck in a school with a group of people who I couldn't connect with, and now it was assured that the teachers didn't even care enough to take things seriously, and instead were more concerned about stained paint on a tuck shop wall. I had been becoming more isolated over time and needed to break free.

"It's not just sticks and stones Sir" I pleaded again. "It's bullying. He's been doing it for years"

"Just walk away from it"

"Seriously? Walk away? Is that all you're going to offer me? I've been wanting to walk away for years from this place. Not just walk, but full on sprint away from here. I've spent my morning counting down until the moment until I can go through those doors and never have to come anywhere near this school, these people and these teachers ever again"

"I must remind you who is in charge here Joseph" he said, leaning even closer. He was so close that I could smell the cheap value coffee on his breath that was failing to be masked by an awful earthy smelling aftershave. "There is no place in this school for assault. With all due respect, throwing a glass at a student's head is not comparable with banter"

"With slightly less respect Sir, that is bollocks and I'm not afraid to use that word in front of you. It's absolute bollocks". I'd given up trying to be polite about the whole affair. "You have no idea what it is like to get part of you chipped away mentally every day for years both in school and at home. None at all. You haven't got one single idea at all and don't you say that you do. Banter is nothing like being called a fag. It's homophobic and it is not just words. As a teacher you should practice as you preach and do some studying if you think otherwise. You can pretend to be the best school in the county all you like, but all you care about is the grades that we get and how they make you look. You don't really care for me at all. None of you do"

"Our students' safety is our priority Joseph and that's why I had to drag you down here. We can't have incidents like this happening"

"Look Sir, you obviously only care about one side of this. You don't care for me and you certainly don't represent me. You're no better than bloody Gary is. Considering you have been in teaching for so long I'd expect you to at least consider what has happened from both sides of the situation, but instead as always you just do the bare minimum to make your life easier. It's pointless even trying to talk to you"

"Go"

"What?"

"Go. I want you to get out of this school today whilst we sort this mess out that you have created. Wait here whilst I call your parents and tell them what you have done. I'll need to discuss this with the Head and then decide what we are going to do. We will let you know when we have sorted this and we can welcome you back"

“No need for discussions. I’ll be back for my exams and that’s it. I can’t take this anymore”

Mr Shepherd was already leaving the room before I had finished talking and was off to call my parents. I stayed sitting for a couple of minutes at a loss to what had just happened. It was no good talking to Mr Shepherd anymore about it. I’m not sure if he was expecting me to calm down, and if anything, I was angrier than I had been when back in the tuck shop. I decided that it was no use waiting for him to return. As soon as I had heard the sound of his footsteps on the tiled floor filter away, I picked up my bag, slung it over one shoulder and left his office and his school. My days in the classroom were finally over.

Four

It should have taken me around twenty minutes to walk back to my house from the school, but that walk was the best that I had experienced, and I decided there was nothing to rush back for. For the first time in many years I felt so free, but I knew it would be short lived. Behind me was a school that was full of failing teachers and failing standards, ahead of me would be my parents. By the time I got home I knew that they'd have been told about what had gone on that morning and there was no way in which I could explain to them exactly why I had thrown that glass. They, like Mr Shepherd, were very much from the 'sticks and stones' camp.

The rain had eased off a bit by the time I had started the walk, and the fields had that scent that is common when rain has fallen onto the grass. Two months ago, I would have been struggling with my hay fever on this walk but now summer was here, and the rain had just fallen I could finally smell the oncoming summer in the air. I was feeling strangely happy and dragged my feet through the small piles of cut grass as I trudged across the school fields and onto the dirt track that led back towards the estate where I lived. I took my time to make the most of the freedom. As I passed the old dairy the front of my shoes had a wet semi-circular patch around each toe, with some blades of grass clinging on. I kicked my toes against a low brick wall to knock off the dirt before sitting down for five minutes to delay the upcoming lecture from my Dad. I stuffed my tie in my backpack and untucked my shirt. Even just loosening the uniform had made me feel that I had shed some of the school away from me and part of me wished to toss my tie into the stream as some kind of symbolic gesture.

My plan for the next few days was to lock myself in my room and revise for the rest of the exams next week. I'd break this up with a few walks around the fields nearby. My house was on the edge of town and the farms that lay just east had a lot of land to explore. Having lived there all my life I knew the tracks well up there and knew which were the best if you were in the mood to avoid people. The old railway track provided a long straight path into the distance; however, it was the trails through the woods that led from here that interested me more. In the summer you could walk for hours without seeing a soul, yet at the same time not venturing too far from your home. In early Autumn you could collect blackberries from the bramble bushes that bordered the ditches, and as a child I used to collect these with my mum which were then turned into jams, crumbles and pies for our family and others on the estate. In winter I would take my camera to the woods and try to capture the changing shadows bouncing off the thorny branches. I did have dreams of becoming a photographer one day, but school always tried to nudge you to a more generic career. In another life I would be off to university to study photography before embarking on a career taking pictures for nature magazines. Sadly, the standard academic subjects took over more and more of my time, and now my camera would only be used as a hobby.

Revising for my remaining exams at home would be a lot better than having to sit with my classmates going over things I already knew time and time again. The next exam was maths, which was at 9.30am on the Thursday. This gave me nearly three whole days. The timetables for the exams are weird this year and I'm not sure how we ended up with nearly a half week gap between them, but I wasn't going to argue. Before starting my plans for my unexpected free time, I just had to get past the lecture from the parents. I thought the best thing would be to get it over and done with as soon as possible. I jumped down from the wall and continued on the second part of my journey home, passing through a maze of back alleys that formed the bottom of the housing estate in which I lived. As I turned into my cul-de-sac I saw my Dad's car was there. I'd completely forgotten that he wasn't at work today. We were getting a new extension built you see, and today was an exciting day in my parents' world as a new sofa was arriving. It's amazing what mundane things brighten the days of others isn't it. Hopefully the excitement would lead to me not having to listen to their ranting for too long.

I was wrong. Very wrong.

Doorway 54

When I opened my front door, I realised that the new sofa had already been delivered and stood in our hallway covered in enough plastic to kill most of the world's ocean life. It had that weird unused furniture smell that's a mixture between carpet shops and glue. Both of my parents were already waiting for me. I was summoned into the kitchen by my Dad. He was using his spare time this day to help decorate the extension and was dressed in a distressed white t-shirt and light blue denim jeans. He looked a bit like Bruce Springsteen and he had a similar haircut to the one he called 'The Boss'. He could have passed as a lookalike; however, I have never seen Bruce Springsteen covered in splashes of pale green paint like the state my dad was currently in.

I entered the kitchen and pulled one of the high stalls from under the breakfast bar as my parents moved across to sit opposite me. They were both drinking coffee from the cafertiére which had been poured out into vomit inducing 'husband' and 'wife' mugs. Dad had black no sugar, yet Mum dropped at least three sugar cubes into hers before stirring the drink without making eye contact with me. They were both so generic. They didn't even offer me a mug before it started. The content of the lecture was as expected. It involved talk on how I brought shame to the family, and how that we must learn to forgive and forget rather than retaliate. It was a little bit rich of my dad as I know that in his youth he had been in far more scrapes than I had myself, and often recounted stories of incidents involving other boys in his town. As these incidents took place over forty years ago it was all looked back on with rose tinted glasses so that it was more of just a unique piece of history rather than trouble that my own family had been involved with.

My Dad often dropped stories from his childhood into conversations. Most of the stories have been sugar coated over the years however, and it's sometimes hard to relate to them. As I said, he still lives in the same area from where he grew up. There are other men his age around town who have also stayed here. They are all very similar to one another, including having underlying bigoted and outdated views on the world. Men of a certain age in this town also have a funny habit of being informative and helpful, but adding odd examples to illustrate what they mean afterwards. If, for example, they are talking about the weight of something they will always say something similar to *"it's X kilograms.....that's the same as thirty-two bags of sugar!"* as if we know what it is like to carry more than two bags of sugar at any one time. I think it must be a generational thing as even middle-aged journalists say certain things like it as well. Pick up the nearest paper to you now and have a flick through. I bet there is some story in there that talks about an *area "...which is the equivalent to sixteen football pitches"* or *"...three times the size of Cumbria".* Who knows why this is so common in Britain. We all just nod along, breathe out through pursed lips and go "Three times the size of Cumbria. Blimey" in a way that seemingly makes us think we understand. I wonder if my parent's preacher friends use this technique at church?

"Jesus split the loaves and fishes and fed 5,000 people. That's the same as the population of Tenby"

(Disclaimer: I don't know the population of Tenby. It may be more. It was just the first place that came into my head as Mum did this weird jigsaw of boats on the seafront there recently).

The one good thing that my parents have from their time in the church is that they never tend to raise their voices when berating me for something that I have done. It's more of the "we aren't angry, just ashamed" type approach. I didn't see the point in telling them exactly what was said, and whatever reason I had would not be good enough or make my actions justifiable in their eyes. I wish I could be open and say that I was gay and that I am sick of being isolated and outcast by literally everyone in this town, but I knew their reaction would lead to all sorts of trouble. It wouldn't surprise me at all if I was taken down to see the vicar if they knew or enrolled in some kind of youth volunteer programme that the parish ran, aiming to flush anything seen as negative out of the young people in the area. They had never been homophobic to me directly due to their lack of knowledge about it, and they hadn't gone out of their way to really ask me in detail about a love life of any type. The closest it got was when mum would talk about her friends' daughters, and how lovely they are as if to hint that I will grow up to marry one of them like some kind of romance from the fifties. If they knew about my sexuality they would probably not believe that they could produce a homosexual child themselves. They had gossiped in the past about other people who they knew were gay and they had some underlying internalised homophobia that became a key point of not liking someone. It's England, it's 2018 and yet my parents, the ones who preach about compassion and love for others are up there with the worst offenders. I know other people in their church lives are not like this. Their friend Margot actually attended the Pride in London parade last summer. It raised many eyebrows at the next parish meeting, let me tell you. Some assumed that she had gone there to offer forgiveness, but she had told them in no uncertain terms that she had nothing to forgive. She left the parish the day after their annual Harvest Festival service. Apparently when the older generation were creating food parcels, a debate about a donation of a tin of pineapple slices somehow got out of hand, words were spoken and the next thing I'd heard is that Margot had told everyone present to piss off. I wish I was there. It sounded brilliant! Margot had never returned to the church and instead was settling in with another group in the village that neighboured our town. I saw her around quite a bit, often riding across the common on her bike, and she would always stop and talk to me, asking about school. One Christmas I blew up one of the pictures that I had taken of the town from high up on the hill and gave it to her to thank her for doing some research for an essay that I had due in my religious studies class. Margot was also a dinner lady at my primary school and in my head, she had always been elderly, yet in reality she can't have been much older than sixty even today. It's weird how you sometimes assume someone is old when you are just a kid, and that this sticks with you throughout life, thinking that they must already be retired and living a life of pottering around their garden.

Anyway, the parents' lecture went on for a good fifteen minutes and only came to an end when an electrician arrived to put the new spotlights in. Together they could go on at me for hours, but individually they were weaker. I was given the usual punishment of no mobile phone for two weeks (apart from when I was at school for exams) and given a stern warning that I should not produce exam results that would let them down. I'm not sure exactly if there were specific results in mind, but they probably would base it on what their friends Linda and Rob's son achieved. Despite being best friends with Linda and Rob, both sets of parents felt the need to try and outdo each other all the time. It was quite a weird relationship. The two couples cared for each other but behind closed doors my parents would make sarcastic comments. I'm certain they spoke about my parents this way also. Last year Linda and Rob had an extension put on to the side of their home, and within months my Dad decided that that was what our house also needed. It was a constant battle back and forth about which family could have the newest and biggest thing. New cars, new furniture, better holidays, they had all come to both sets of adults within a few weeks of each other. Despite all this, there was a great level of care and my parents were godparents to their children Gene and Katy, and Linda and Rob were my godparents. Gene isn't too bad as a person, although he is a bit nerdier than I am, and without an interest in sports. Because of this we have drifted since being in secondary school.

My parents had a timetable already written for my studying and I was to be stored away in my room between nine and six each day with three short breaks. In the evenings I could have some free time, but I was not allowed out to see any friends outside of school time until the exams were over. Oh, and I also had to write a letter of apology to both Gary and Mr Shepherd. For fuck sake. I'd use the evenings to go for my walks. I couldn't spend that time in my room as well.

Once the lecture was over, I handed over my mobile and headed to my room. I'd deleted any incriminating apps from my phone before the confiscation took place. I'm not stupid. There's nothing dodgy on there, it's just the phone needs to remain unlocked at all times when stashed away and I don't want them going through my social media in case I haven't hidden some clue about my gayness (is that a word?) well enough. Even if I did have something on there they weren't clued up enough to find it anyway. My Dad is the kind of parent who asks things like "Joseph, what is the Snapchat?". They can barely work the TV remote despite having the same TV for nearly a decade.

~

You now join me in my bedroom an hour later. I've done no revision for Maths yet. I have a couple more days remember. Instead I have laid out books and some pre-written notes that I had done at school last week, so it looked like I had been very attentive and busy. I had doodled a list of things that I might want to do as a career. None of them excited me. I was far too interested in the near future. One way or another, I will get to London next month and see the exhibition at the V&A. I can't wait to step from the train at Marylebone and start exploring. Three weeks. Three weeks. Just three more weeks. Twenty-one days. About five hundred hours. Around thirty-two thousand minutes. One point eight million seconds, give or take.

My family have lived in this house for many years. I am never sure of the exact duration, however I know it was shortly after my parents married. Houses are a weird thing. At their bare bones they are just four walls and a roof, but the most important material contained within a house are the memories. Between these four walls there have been several highs and an equal number of lows. I recently redecorated my room, deciding one day that I wanted to lose the childishness of its old design. I have had some painful memories in here. I didn't take the change between primary and secondary school very well at all, and during year nine I had become particularly reclusive, and developed issues which stifled my ability to interact with people. Looking back on it this was the first time that I feel that I developed depression. There came points when I would get home from school and sit on my own for hours. I would keep my PlayStation on pause so that if my mum came in it would look like I was playing. In truth though I felt at a loss and I'm not afraid to tell you that there were a few moments that I thought it may be best for me to just disappear completely. I don't know precisely if it was suicide that I was contemplating, or if I just wanted to be transported elsewhere, wherever elsewhere could be. My lowest point came when my parents and I fell out over an apparent lack of effort on my part at school. There has not been a visible example of depression in my family, so I don't think my parents were equipped to deal with the issue, and if anything, they probably believed that depression wasn't something that would affect this family. It's absurd when you think about it as there were clearly some effects on my parents' own mental health when they lost Matthew. I truly believe that the close-knit society which they grew up in led them to think that it was just a case of pulling your socks up and trying to struggle through rather than realise that you were in fact ill.

Doorway 54

My lowest point came just as the summer holidays had started when I was fourteen years old. I can't even describe what it was that day that made me feel so low as nothing had happened that was out of the ordinary. That's the worst thing about depression and anxiety. You just don't know *why* you have these peaks and troughs with your mental health. It may have been something subconscious that took my brain to a tough time from the past, such as a smell or a song or something, but something that day knocked me down. I lay on my bed for about five hours straight without wanting to pull myself away. As the afternoon turned to evening I sent a text to around five different friends hinting that I needed someone, yet no replies came within the next thirty minutes. I felt as if I was alone and of no use. I left my phone on my bed and left the house, taking a walk to the lake on the edge of town. The lake was an old gravel pit that had been filled in during the seventies and it was known to be a very dangerous body of water. Swimming was banned there due to strong currents which could pull you under without a moment's notice. Once there I walked around its perimeter until I found the small bridge that passed over an outlet stream. Here the water flowed fast down a concrete slope, and where it hit the main channel the water churned violently. I jumped up so that I was sat on the metal railings with my legs hanging above the flow. I have always found that water brings me this calm feeling, and despite the water flowing fast and dangerously I still felt at peace on this metal ledge. I sat on that bridge for about two hours. It was just far enough off the main track that people never really ventured down there. One man did pass by, but he was too busy trying to control his chocolate brown Labrador to notice that I was so young and contemplating something stupid. Did I want to really jump though? Well at times, yes, I did. There were a few points where I would talk myself into thinking that dropping into the rapids would be the best option for me. After all, it would end the loneliness and I wouldn't have to force myself into social situations any more. Despite wanting to drop, something stopped me from doing so that day. It was only looking back on it that I realised how it may affect my parents, and after the loss of Matthew could I really put them through the loss of a second child? I thought of Matthew and how he would have reacted to my problems. I wish he was there through my childhood, and I often thought how my life would have turned out had he been. I left the bridge just as the twilight turned into darkness and walked slowly back home. When I got back to the estate I was mobbed by worried neighbours who had joined my parents search party for me. Instead of sympathy that night I received a stern talking to from my Dad and warned that I mustn't 'pull stunts' like this because of how worried it made my parents feel. They were interested in where I had been, but not so much why I had been there. I tried telling them that something wasn't right with me but rather than seek a professional opinion they thought the best form of action was to force me into being more social over that summer. I spent the six long weeks taking part in activities, including some with the church summer camp, and also helping out with some work in the church. It was as if my life was being shaped to the one that my parents believed I needed, and not what I wanted myself. There are times when my mind wanders back to that bridge. When at my lowest I can lay and close my eyes and see the water rippling underneath, waiting for me to plunge into its depths.

Returning to school after that summer was tough, and word had got around that I had 'lost the plot'. The bullying intensified after this and I started separating myself from many other pupils at the school. The moment on the bridge was the lowest point that I had experienced, and I often daydreamed about how those around me would be different had I decided to fall forward into its waters.

For now though, I am sat in this bedroom half looking at notes for the maths exam instead of the river. It's only been a few hours, but I am bored of it already. I'll be happy to never do trigonometry or statistics again in my life. All the test questions make no sense. The one I am currently staring at involves a window cleaner. He is four metres up a ladder, and the ladder is two metres away from the wall. It says that the owner of the house wants to find out the angle between the ladder and the ground. I mean, come on, who gives a shit? I want to go out and explore and I do worry that being locked up will lead to a decline in my mental health again. I want to be able to explain this to my parents however I feel as if they would see it as me using an excuse to rebel against their ground rules.

Five

Good morning. I've skipped forward three weeks. I could have kept you abreast of all the daily on goings in my life since being banished to my room but to be honest, what exciting things are there to tell you about a student sitting their GCSEs? There were a couple of high points however. In the evenings I did manage to leave the house and go for the planned walks up to the nearby farms.

In order to take a mental break from the studying I decided to open my photographic equipment and take some shots out in the wild. Having this hobby back was key in keeping me sane. Suffering from mental health issues restricts you from a lot of things, and many people often take solace from the darker side of their mind by investing in a hobby. There are many who have taken up sports such as running, and the release that they get from the endorphins that flood their brain helps to steady their ship. It doesn't just have to be an active hobby though, and that's quite good considering my poor record of success within sport. In life you need that one thing which can spark something inside of you. Something that, to you, is not just a hobby, but a way of controlling your thoughts and emotions, something that can detach you from the realities of life. For my parents this is probably the church, and whilst I know that the church and its teachings have led to my isolation at times, the way that it has helped my parents through the tough times in the past means that it can work for some. I know people who have turned to painting, to music and even fishing as a way to distract themselves from the elements of everyday life. These hobbies may not seem all that interesting to even those closest to you, but rather than mock them, these hobbies should be celebrated. A world without release would lead to a world full of people that have pent up anger, or a world of people who would slowly lose the inability to interact in an understanding and humane manner. Mental health is much less a taboo subject these days, but there is still work to be done. It isn't a common fad of the modern age as the media would have us believe. It is more spoken about these days because more people are becoming less afraid to say when they are not okay. Sadly, we are far from a time where mental health is seen as real as physical health by many, yet as the generations get older I hope that this will change. Too many people assume that mental health is tied up to a person's success or wealth. Recently a top footballer took his own life after his career was cut short by a knee injury. When the news broke so many people reverted to the clichéd phrase of "he was rich and successful, what did he have to be depressed about?", and that's the thing. Mental health issues do not correlate to how much money a person has, how many friends a person has or how successful someone is. It is a non-judgemental beast which can attack and choke every single person, often without any notice. The most beautiful buildings in the country are subject to the same shadows when the clouds pass in front of the sun, in the same way that metaphorical shadows can cloud over every single one of us. When the clouds come we do not love these buildings any less, but instead we see them in a new light, noticing elements which have been previously hidden in plain sight. With people, we need to adopt the same approach. The shadows that fall on those around us should not be seen as a chance to neglect. We should adapt our thinking to love these people in a new way, engage with them and to remind them that they are still the same person. There is not one single person on this entire planet that doesn't have highs and lows in their lives, yet many are quick to distance themselves from those who may be struggling, no matter how close they have been in the past. It may not be a conscious decision, but a subconscious fear that may have been bought on through the lack of education of how to talk to someone who is experiencing poor mental health. For me, I wouldn't want people to go too far with their compassion, but instead just reassure me that they are there where I need them. We are often told that it is okay to not be okay, and that speaking out is key, but I feel that speaking out should not always be at the feet of the person who is struggling. As a society we should make those around us feel comfortable to talk to one another, even when you are feeling good. Too often we act in hindsight, adopting a reactive rather than proactive approach.

Being trapped in my room for the last three weeks has at times been troubling, and my parents' focus seems to have been more on the extension than myself. The revision itself didn't help a great deal and hearing about it is probably the only thing worse than having to do it yourself so I will not bore you with the details of my flashcards and revision techniques. The exams have mainly been and gone and I would say that I am quietly confident that I have matched my expectations at the bare minimum. Maths was the worst, and I can't see how much of it will be of any use in the future (a question about a man up a ladder came up again). The sciences were probably the best for me as questions about the areas I have the most knowledge in were in the papers. As for the others? They're done and were a bit of a mixture. I am expected to get a C grade or above in nearly all, with the exception of German. For some reason I just can't get to grips with languages. I know a lot of the words but putting them in a sentence is a completely different matter.

On a positive note, today is June 7th and the final day of my school life. At 11.30am I will be sitting a Geography exam, the final time I need to be sat in that school hall with my classmates. The last time I will have teachers invigilating. The last time these teachers will ever have any authority over me. This is an exam that I am fairly confident with as well, so it should be straightforward. It lasts one and a half hours and involves your standard questions for half the paper, and then an essay question at the end. If the essay involves discussion on National Parks in Sierra Leone, then I will smash through it. It's amazing how much I know about places like the Gola Rainforest. I'm not convinced that this knowledge will be any more beneficial in life than the equations I had to learn for the maths exam but at least geography is a subject I enjoy. So anyway, the last three weeks happened and nothing exciting really took place, it was just more of the same. I'll fill you in on a couple of edited highlights however.

Angelica.

She has continued to be a bit weird and I'm not sure exactly what it is that I have done wrong here. We used to be much closer, but now she is obsessed with filling everyone in about her amazing upcoming trip to the Caribbean. I'm sure it'll be great for her, but the subject does tend to bore me now. I think I know her travel plans just as well as she does with the amount of times I have been near her whilst she has enthusiastically gone in to detail with anyone who is unfortunately close enough to hear. One thing that did upset me was that she felt the need to also give me a talking to in regard to the glass throwing incident. I honestly thought that she would be the one person who would understand, the one person who would speak up in my defence and support me. Sadly, this wasn't to be, and I am certain her parents have told her to keep her distance from me as a result due to be being a potential bad influence. They know that she has a chance of getting into a top university, and they don't want anything to distract her or to intervene to stop this from happening. She will be the first one from her family to achieve this, and to be honest I think that it has gone to her head a little. I want things to go back to how they were and hopefully after she has returned we can do some day trips together and become close again. I would love to still go to London with Angelica one day, but this will probably have to wait until she has some time off from her A-Levels. At the end of the summer she will be back to school whilst I will be working. I still need to work out my next step. I'm not looking forward to spending the first few weeks after exams going through application forms and interviews for jobs that I won't really care for. I'm scared that this September will mean things change for good.

My Parents.

We have existed in the same space, but they still haven't fully forgiven me for what I did either. I've had various bits of text given to me to read, but they are all from their church and Dad's bookshop so there is always an underlying moral of taking the consequences of your actions and letting the light guide you to redemption. None of them involved Matthew, Mark, Luke or John being called a fag or a queer so sorry, I just couldn't relate.

The extension with our house is just about finished now, and the sofa made its way in there from the hall after a stressful hour of lifting and heaving with dad and Ian who lives over the road. There is also a new smaller TV in the room and various plants potted around the window sills.

Doorway 54

Despite not wanting to like the extension due to my parents seemingly spending more time on it than helping me, it is quite a nice area to lie down and get some peace in, especially when they are out of the house. When they were out I could also stray away from their revision timetable a bit, but not so much to risk leaving the house. Getting caught doing that simply wouldn't be worth it and would lead to a lock on my bedroom door knowing them. Whilst laying on the new sofa I've become a bit addicted to a show on one of the Sky channels called "Dream House". It's as trashy as it sounds and involves middle-class couples having their front rooms done up. I have no idea why I have become so addicted to it. The presenter is this strange man with a lazy eye and a northern accent but there's something about him which makes you unable to change channels. Another thing that my parents made me do was to send apology letters off to Mr Shepherd and Gary. They were written through gritted teeth and the one to Gary had to be rewritten at least three times in order for it to be approved by mum. I got a 'thank you for your apology' letter from Mr Shepherd. Being forced to apologise for being verbally abused is ridiculous but that man is now less than three hours away from being out of my life. The same goes for Gary. I sent the letter via school and received a reply. He didn't accept my apology (he may have hinted the sarcasm used, unlike my parents when they proofread it). The reply I got was as follows:

Joseph.

Doorway 54

It isn't over.

Gary.

That was all. It did make me worry to be honest and it has been playing on my mind quite often whilst I have been sat here these last three weeks. I don't know if he will carry out any further verbal attacks but just the thought of something coming my way makes me a little nervous. Once school has finished there is the chance that he could do something more serious and as it will no longer be a school issue, it could even be a physical attack. Since the incident in the Tuck Shop I know that the staff at school do not take the abuse I get seriously, and my parents always seem to respect what they are told by the teachers also. The whole thing makes me feel isolated, and sometimes I get short of breath. I thought I was having a heart attack the first time it happened. I even searched the symptoms online, which I know is often dangerous territory. You can convince yourself that the slightest issue with your health is in fact some major medical trauma. After a few articles of thinking that I may need a heart transplant, I related to stories of people suffering from anxiety and depression. I tried talking to Mum about this and yet even this was dismissed. She told me that it was just exam stress. She also said the typical "Depression? What have you got to be depressed about?" before telling me to stop being silly. It's true though, something just isn't right, and I can't put my finger on it. The smallest things can lead to me losing my breathing rhythm and before I know it I am pacing up and down my room worrying about everything. I just need to get through today. Writing this is even making me feel a little uneasy. Maybe I do need to just stop being stupid.

On Sundays I have been taken to church to help set things up, like put out the bibles and change hymn numbers, that kind of thing. It's sort of my parents' form of community service. I feel uncomfortable being in the church these days and feel that the eyes of the statues along the walls are looking down and judging me for my sexuality. I don't feel that the church is there for me, and I'm not fully convinced my parents are either.

KFC

Okay this bit isn't important, but our town got a KFC! We have never had any of those fast food type places here, so this is kind of a big deal. As I say, not important at all but I found it cool and wanted to tell you.

Six

My morning has been unremarkable but knowing that this will be my last walk up the track to school is making me feel good. Thursday 7th June. The day I leave school. I keep telling myself this over and over to keep my mood buoyant. I had quite a bad night's sleep and kept waking up throughout. This is the first time it has happened this week and I don't know why it had to happen on the last night. It's my last exam. The last day. In less than two hours I will begin the rest of my life. I have agreed to go for lunch with my parents this afternoon. They feel that I have repaid them I guess and seemed quite chirpy themselves when I set off. They are both off today to do a trip to a garden centre. Apparently my Dad wants to find something for the trellis fence that 'matches mums clematis' (not a euphemism I hope).

The weather has also become a lot more summery. Flowers are out and there are a lot of bees flying about. I should really be in the best mood possible but there is still something inside that is eating away at me. I don't know if it's the threat from Gary or if I am subconsciously being attacked by a hidden worry. I've been thinking a bit about the whole 'gay' thing too. Aside from my feelings being dismissed, I have done a bloody good job at making it all the way through school without any physical attacks, but what will it be like in the real world? I know a lot of other people my age have had it a lot worse when they come out, whether the decision to was their own or if it was forced out. I thought maybe coming out to my parents would make things better and I entrusted my good friend the Internet to get advice. My online friends said that only I will know when I am ready to be more open with it, and not to do it hoping that everything will be great at the end. Other sites I googled had mixed messages. Time will tell I guess. I need to stop thinking about it. I'm in a good mood yet again tears have formed in my eyes. I'm happy today, I tell myself. It's true, I should be, but I can't stop this spontaneous crying. I have my shades on so at least no one near me will be able to spot it until I manage to pull myself together. I'll blame any red eyes on hay fever and pollen if anyone fancies pointing out to me just how awful I look.

I idly continue on my journey to school, and the track starts getting busier as we approach the bottom of the main playing field. I have to walk the long way around as the running track is being used by the Year 7's and I don't fancy getting trampled by them yet. Once I have avoided them successfully the main back door of the hall is close, and for the final time my walk to school is complete. I take a deep breath and head on in.

~

"You can turn over your papers now"

This is it, the final exam. It's typical that Mr Shepherd has to be the one to invigilate and act as spokesman. It's also typical that on this last occasion in the hall that Gary is sat on the desk to my right. We are on the back row of the entire group. There are eighty students taking GCSE Geography today. I've counted the 1960's style wooden desks nearly every exam I've sat. If I believed in a God then I'd say that this is the ultimate test, not the questions in front of me. He's put my enemy next to me, with another enemy watching over me. Being in this situation makes it a bit uncomfortable and it is harder to concentrate than I'd have liked. I turn over the paper and start (NB. The case study is on the Gola Rainforest!). I know this subject almost spontaneously and without even thinking I have written over three pages about how different techniques can be used by park rangers to ensure the National Parks of Sierra Leone continue to flourish. I always start with the exam questions. If you crack these then you are basically guaranteed a C Grade. The rest of the exam is about the Amazon River basin, the effects of deforestation and 'Coastal Processes'. If you ever need a public speaker to do a talk on Long Shore Drift and anti-cliff erosion techniques, Joey Eaton is your man (ignoring the fact I am rubbish at public speaking).

Before I know it, I am done with the shorter questions on this exam also, and I'm surprised to see that there is still twenty minutes to go. I have a quick flick through and decide there is nothing left to add so just lean back and daydream whilst staring out of the long row of wall to ceiling windows that provide a view out to a small grass area. There is a piece of modern art that stands in this area and despite being at this school for five years I still am unsure as to what it is meant to represent. It kind of looks like two thin stone figures reaching up into the sky, but from other angles it can resemble just a jumbled circular mess. I don't think I'll ever understand modern art.

My studies are over, my exams are over. I would leave the room now if I could, but I doubt Mr Shepherd would entertain that. I look across towards Gary out of curiosity. He's only just started the essay questions and there is no way that he can get much down in the remaining time. He catches me looking and turns around with a grimace. I respond with a grin. To anyone else this would look fine, if not a bit smug. I know, and more importantly Gary knows, that my smile is code for a big "fuck you". I continue to smile as I lean back in my chair and close my eyes.

Once the exam clock had finished its countdown and the papers collected, Mr Shepherd takes a change from the normal process and gets the students to leave the hall from the front to the back. I'm sure that this is his last final swipe at me. He wants me gone as much as I want to go I think but making me wait will make it seem like a final act of power. It also means that Gary will be behind me as we filter out of the hall and into the rest of our lives.

As we get out of the hall into the reception it has already descended into carnage. Through the double doors students are destroying their reading materials, screwing up pages from their revision books and throwing them at each other like snowballs. It seems that I am not the only one to be pleased that they are free of this school, albeit many of those outside will be returning in a few months for another two years. More fool them. Despite the feeling of joy, I'm also disappointed in a way, as marching through those doors was to be my grand departure. I had played it over in my head many times, however in that fantasy there were never any other students visible. Instead though, this way might be better. All the commotion will mean that I can slip out quietly, turning left straight away towards home and forgetting about this place.

Just as I am about to speed my walk up into a trot, a hand is placed on my shoulder. I turn around to see Mr Shepherd standing over me.

"That's you done then, Son" he says, a bit too familiarly for my liking. "Let what happened before just be water under the bridge".

He doesn't deserve an answer for this. He has brushed the verbal abuse off once before, and now he thinks by doing it again I will forgive him. He has no power over me now, and without responding I walk to his right and towards home. I take one final look back and see him stood open mouthed looking in my direction. It seems as if he wants to say more, but his chance has gone. As I pass the staff car park and the outside swimming pool, I am stopped again. This time Gary and his gang are stood three abreast across the path. I know they are stupid, but surely not stupid enough to attack me somewhere so open. I quicken my pace and try to walk past.

"In a rush are you Joey?" asks Gary
"Just off home. Go and enjoy yourselves somewhere" I respond. I've lost all the will to fight back now.
"That should be fun. Let me know how that pans out for you"
"It will be better than having to be here"
"You say that now"
"Just because you fucked up your geography exam doesn't mean you have to take it out on me"
"I didn't fuck it up" he responds.
"I was sat next to you Gary. I know that you only wrote about two paragraphs for the essay question"

With his stupidity stifling his ability to respond with anything of note, he comes closer to me and pushes me with both hands on my chest. Abdul seems to be a bit more reserved than Ian as they watch their ringleader in action. He's stood back a bit further than the other two now and is concentrating on kicking a crushed coke can between his feet.

"Come on Gary, let's just go downtown. It's too hot to stand here and mess about with this prick" Abdul says, making them both turn and look at him.
"You've gone soft lad" says Ian

"We've all finished school now, so I can't be bothered to stand here anymore. I'm bored of this place" he replies
"Come on then" says Gary. "We'll go and see J down the shop"

Despite being sixteen already, Gary still does a paper round at the newsagents, something which he has done since he was thirteen. The owner, known as J, hasn't got an alcohol licence but does have some stored in a back corridor that he sells on the sly to teenagers. I've utilised this before, mainly when I have had to reluctantly head to parties of others at the school. Angelica is normally with me when we have to go here. The alcohol that you get from J's is always a mixed bag. He seems to have collections of things that you don't tend to find in any other shop. The last time I got some from him I ended up with bottles of something called Jammin. This was a kind of alcopop which tasted of coconut. We collected them and took them back across the rivers to our friend Matt's house. The bottles were stored in those fluorescent bags that paperboys were often weighed down with. We thought it was discreet, but the clinking of the contents must have given the game away. Matt's parents were off on holiday on this particular Saturday afternoon, so we sat on the grass just around the corner from his house. We had full view of the driveway and once we saw his parents' car leave we carried our goods in. When these things happen, you feel like you are an adult, but in fact you are just an annoying teenager. I'm never comfortable at parties but as it was the summer and the weather was good it was actually quite nice. It's probably the last social occasion which I felt truly happy at, but that was nearly twelve months ago now.

I've no idea what weird drinks J would have in his shop today, but at least it was more appealing to Gary, Ian and Abdul than bullying me anymore. The three of them laugh and stood aside to let me pass by.

"Let me know how you get on" said Gary over his shoulder as I jump over a small wall that separates the car park from the fence around the cold and greenish school swimming pool. I have literally no idea what he means by this. I'm just glad that they didn't give me a good kicking across the car park to be honest. I wouldn't have totally ruled that option out. Alternatively, they might have thrown me in the pool, but they decided against that as well. For a group of lads who were adamant that they were going to destroy me, they didn't put much effort into it.

~

The walk home was somehow no more enjoyable than the walk to school that morning, but I only cried once this time. I always imagined it to be the most blissful walk of my school life. Maybe I had used up some of positive feeling on the walk home after being suspended. I passed over the fields again and down the track for the final time.

Before the dirt track turns to concrete you have to pass over the stream through the trees. I was crossing a small wooden bridge that goes over the narrow, but fairly deep, water filled ditch by the old dairy. I must have crossed this bridge over a thousand times. As a mark of respect to my final journey, I took off my awful tie and pulled it into a knot firmly around one of the beams. To me it felt that leaving this here meant leaving my issues behind. That chapter of my life is over. Onward and upward. It was at this point the tears came. I kept telling myself that they were happy tears, but deep down I knew that they weren't, however the exact reason why they came at this point was lost to me. It wasn't that I was feeling upset, but perhaps it was because I was lost. That school had broken me. It hadn't supported me. It hadn't listened to me. Instead of being happy at leaving, I was mourning the chances that were taken away from me so many times. Being picked last in PE, being asked to speak aloud in class despite being a crap public speaker, being judged and mocked and verbally abused just for existing. Not one of those bastards, students or staff, bothered to help. They all washed their hands of me.

Looking over the edge of the bridge, I decided to throw every bit of paper that I had relating to that place into the water below. I opened my bag and tore the pages out of all the textbooks that I had left with me. My English poetry anthology, my revision notes for geography, my German textbooks and finally the planner that had been with me for the last five years. I wanted this bridge to be the dividing line between my past and my future and wouldn't leave until my school life had been washed away. No one was in as much of a rush to leave school as me and the path that led to the bottom of Greenwood's playing fields was deserted. I stayed and watched the debris as it became sodden, waiting for the pages to grey and sink below the surface. I paused until the final piece had disappeared around the bend downstream, put on my shades and walked home for the final part of the trip.

Seven

Ok something is different. I’ve just got into my cul-de-sac and Dad is off work again, and this time it wasn’t planned. I know for sure that he was meant to be in work today as he has not stopped talking about their stocktake all week. He has parked his green hatchback car close to the house rather than in the designated space at the end of the road. He must have got home in a rush and he is still on the step by the front door. I don’t know what has happened, but Mum is with him, and she has her head buried into his shoulder whilst he strokes the back of it. Even from this distance I can tell that she is crying. All thoughts about what it could be rush through my head. My best guess is that one of my grandparents has been taken ill. I only have two grandparents left, both my nans. I have always thought that they would live forever, and both seem to be made of stern stuff. My dad's mother grew up on one of the farms at the top of the estate, one of those that I explored with my camera during the revision imprisonment. Her father was killed during the second world war when she was only six years old. She has spent a great deal of her life learning about his involvement and often tells me stories of what it was like to live through that era. It’s a shame that these parts aren’t taught in history classes. He was killed on 7th September 1940, one of the first to die during the blitz. He was unloading cargo from an area near London Bridge when a bomb struck the depot nearby. He was crushed under the falling debris. Nan still carries his ID card in her wallet. Her widowed mother remained on the farm and encouraged other widows to join her to help grow and cultivate produce for the war effort. My nan, Maggie, encouraged those who had lost husbands in the county to move in with their children and a community soon formed. I can't imagine how hard it must have been to not be broken by the awful things that were happening. The ladies on the farm soon helped further by welcoming child evacuees as apart of Operation Pied Piper. Children from London were brought up by train to spend the war time helping my own nan pick fruit. There are films that are waiting to be made of the stories of women like these. There must be so many people with stories of survival in adverse times. Despite now being eighty-two years old, nan is still very active, much more so than the other ladies who live nearby to her bungalow.

One of these neighbouring ladies is my other nan, Enid, who is a bit more old fashioned. She is ninety-eight years old and actually worked in offices during the war. She is less energetic than Maggie, mainly due to her age, but still has all the sharpness of mind. It sounds awful to say but I don't enjoy spending much time with her. Her stories are told with less animation, and her house is cluttered and small. I think my dad has inherited this trait as he stores a lot of things in the loft of our house. I would bet a good bit of money that he doesn't actually know what is in half of the boxes. I think it secretly drives my mum mad. She is in the loft more than dad and I think she spends most of the time rearranging his items and putting them into the furthest corners. I assume this is the case because she tends to wait until he has left the house to go up there. I really hope my Nan's are both okay though, as although I don't spend as much time with them as I should, I would hate to lose them.

As I approach my mum looks up and catches me with her gaze. Her mood shifts quickly. She moves both hands to Dads shoulders and physically turns him around to see me. They both stand side by side, holding hands. Mum looks absolutely terrible. They do not say a word, so I break the silence when I am about five metres away.

"Are you okay? What's happened?" I ask, getting worried about what I will hear
"Come inside Joseph" Dad says, leading the way and dragging Mum behind.

It's one of my grandparents, it has to be. Of all the days it has to happen. I follow them down the hallway and into the kitchen, where we all take a seat around the pine kitchen table.

"Do you want a drink?" I ask. "I can put some coffee on?"

They seem to ignore my offer and both stare down. "Is it nan?" I ask, without specifying which one it may be. Again they ignore me. I go to the sink and fill a glass with water whilst I wait for them to let me in on the secret. My Dad is the first to relinquish his gaze from the table. He stares at me for a few seconds without blinking.

"Why, Joseph? Why?"
"Why what?". I am genuinely baffled.

Dad takes a piece of paper out of his pocket, unfolds it and pushes it across the table towards me. I look down and everything comes crashing down around me. The letter is printed on official Greenwood Academy headed paper.

"Dear Mr and Mrs Eaton,

As you may know Joseph has recently been acting strangely here at the school which led to his suspension. This has involved him physically attacking a fellow student, as well as defacing school property and playing truant. Despite the schools' efforts to engage with him he has decided to not attend any meetings with us over the weeks leading up to the exams. As his parents, and as hes leaving us now for good we want to inform you that we believe that he is struggling with being gay more than he has let on to you. I know he has talked to you about this and we as staff agreed that the issue would be passed on to you once he had left.

Best wishes,

Graham Barrington
Head Teacher
Greenwood Academy"

I don't know what to do. I don't know how to react or what to say. Without even realising I start shaking and it's not long before tears follow, dropping on to the top of the table.

"Is it true Joseph?" asks Mum, still choosing not to make eye contact with me.
I do not answer.
"Is it true?" she asks again, this time more firmly.
"Answer your bloody mother" demands Dad. What I had thought of as sadness was in fact anger.

Everything inside me feels twisted. My stomach, my nerves, my mind. Everything is being torn apart inside me. I feel myself sweating and I try to stand as I think I am going to be sick, but my legs seem to have forgotten what they do.

"Are you going to tell us what the hell is going on, Joseph?" says Dad firmly. For someone so heavily involved in the church he often forgets the rules about blasphemy when he is angry. Again, I chose not to answer as I struggle to find the right words to reply. I look through the letter again and that is when it dawns on me. This letter is not from Mr Barrington. Our head teacher is also the head of the English Faculty. He has been teaching English at the school for twenty-eight years and even taught Dad. The letter is filled with mistakes that I know he would give the cane to students if given half the chance. There are missing apostrophes and commas, and I know for certain he would use the phrase "struggling with being gay". This is all Gary's doing. That is what he meant in the car park. "Let me know how that pans out". The words are now bouncing around my skull. I manage to stand and lean against the sink, looking out the window to our back garden.

"Joseph. Please just tell us. Is it true?" asks Dad, taking over the questioning.
"The letter is not from him Dad" I say before throwing up into the kitchen sink. I turn the tap on and wash it down the plug with the help of a bit of stirring from my right index finger.

"The way you are reacting Joseph makes us think that what it says is true though. Is it true?"

I focus again on the garden. I have three options. To flat out deny it. To admit it. To stay silent. Staying silent is basically the same as admitting it so let's rule that out. I didn't want to do this here and now. I've spent five years putting up with so much shit from people at school and in life who have tried to break me. I am exhausted and at the moment I am ready to give up. What's the fucking point?

"It's true" I say quietly, still staring outside.

Silence.

"Come and sit down Joseph" says Dad finally. I am sick into the sink again and start the process of getting it flushed down the plug.

"Just bloody leave it Joseph and come and sit down" continues Dad. I turn off the tap and stumble across towards them and retake my seat.

"Why?"

"Why what" I reply slowly, not making eye contact.

"Why you? After all we have done and how we have bought you up. Why?"

This is what I had been fearing.

"It's nothing personal against you two" I say. "It's just....it is what it is". Tears are still raining down my cheeks and my breathing becomes irregular. They remain silent for another couple of minutes. The clock in the room ticks by loudly, echoing into my ears as I bury my head into my arms. I picture myself back on the bridge looking down into the water. Maybe I should have escaped back then. Maybe that would have been better for everyone.

"Can you imagine what people at work will say about this?" says mum, speaking for the first time. By work she means both hers and dads as their parts in the jigsaw of the church community are so strongly linked. But could I imagine what their colleagues would say? I can. I imagine they'd just be like Mr Shepherd or Gary or every other fucker who has thought about my effect on their lives rather than the other way around.

"Fuck them" I say. I should have thought of something more tactful here, but as I said, I had given up completely. I wanted this to be over and be away from people for a while. The look in Dad's eyes proved I definitely should have been more tactful. He looks ready to explode. Mum has started crying again and has slumped over the table.

"We taught you better than this Joseph. Have some bloody respect" he bellows, standing up halfway through speaking to pace around the kitchen. For the first time ever, he has found something to raise his voice over. "After all we have done to give you the best start in life; you repay us by bringing shame on the family. I have to face people from the church tomorrow and you know how quick these things spread around this town. We have always been there for you and offered you support and could have gotten you some help to make things right for you"

"By 'make things right for me', do you mean for you? Do you think that this is a choice that I have purposefully made?"

"Look we can still get you someone to talk to, son, someone who can offer friendly advice on how things can be okay"

"Dad, it can't be changed. You say that I have let you down despite the support you have supposedly offered, but have you really offered support? Where was the support over the last four years? You and Mum are so bloody invested with keeping up your false reputation of being the golden couple of the town that you haven't even noticed your own son crumbling away in front of you. I have barely any friends left here, and I have just walked out of a school that didn't give a single fuck about me"

By this point I am completely at rock bottom. I don't want to stay in this house right now. I get up and go to leave.

"Where are you going?" asks Dad.
"I don't know" I reply honestly. Where can I go?
"It might be best if you crash at a friend's house this evening Joseph whilst we figure this out" he says. He isn't listening to me. It's not their place to decide how I should feel.
"Are you kicking me out?"
"No, no it's not like that. Me and your mum just need to process this. Look, we can see if we can get you involved in some of the church programmes again over the summer. I know that it is in fashion these days to be quirky, and to make yourselves stand out, and I'm sorry that we missed things that led up to you making this decision"
"It's not a decision. How many times do I have to tell you that? You two are no better than anyone at Greenwood. This is why I haven't spoken to you about it. You are both

in this weird bubble that you have formed, only concerning yourself with people who are in that bubble with you. It's no wonder nobody my age is going to church these days"

"Don't you dare talk about our church like that Joseph" says mum before dad can continue. "Our church is here to help and support everyone and with the right guidance I am sure that we can help you still be part of it"

"Damage limitation is it?" I ask sarcastically

"No. We just need to work this through. We've lost one son and it's feeling like we are losing another"

This is a step too far. Being gay does not compare with what happened to the loss Matthew all those years ago. My parents don't understand a single thing. I want to be out of this house just as much as they currently want me out of it.

"Have you got anything to say Mum?" I say through the tears. She doesn't say a word. She hasn't said anything for a few minutes. She doesn't reply.

"Look Joseph, go around a friends, stay there for the night and have a think okay" Dad says again

"There is nothing to sort, Dad. Nothing at all. I have been rejected enough to know that there is no purpose in fighting it. In five minutes I'll be gone and you two can do what the fuck you like. I'll just be a series of blurs"

"Joseph, look. Call me tomorrow morning and let me know where you are, and I'll come and pick you up and we can see what happens"

"Tomorrow is too early. I am going to Angelica's and will stay there until you are ready to accept me". This was only partly true as Angelica will be heading off to the Caribbean within hours, but telling them that I was with a friend would mean that they would not be chasing me for a while. I'm hoping it is not too late to catch her before she goes though. Regardless of where I would go, I just needed to be gone. In ten minutes I will be out this house and off to, well, somewhere. I hadn't thought that far ahead yet. The one thing I was certain of though was that this town no longer held anything for me. In that one conversation I knew that the relationship between me and my parents had shifted forever. I could never be happy living under that roof again. Today was the first day of freedom from school, and now it is the first day of surviving on my own. I would be sixteen in a week and the chains were slipping off. I went up to my room and packed as much as I could into my largest holdall. I had about twenty pound, four sets of clothes and a mobile phone to my name. Before leaving I remembered that there was some money on the window sill of the landing that was put aside for the window cleaner who would be coming around tomorrow. I walked out and saw it was still there. It was only thirty pounds, but it would come in handy at some point. I don't condone stealing, but today I was desperate. It was time for a break.

Eight

“The train now approaching Platform 4 is the delayed three fourteen service to London Marylebone, calling at High Wycombe and London Marylebone”

Why have I ended up here, I hear you ask. Well, I had to get away from the town and not just the house. I think I have managed to pack the essentials in my bag, and I will probably be in London by the time I realise what I have forgotten. That conversation with my parents was the lowest that I have ever felt. In my head I keep going over what I could have said that may have made things different, but each time the different scenarios play out they still result in me packing my belongings up and leaving. It felt like there was some invisible force pushing onto my temples, and another anxiety attack hit rapidly. I wish things could be different, but in that moment, I realised that my house was no longer my home. There is a difference.

Once I had packed my bag and left the house I suddenly felt very alone. As I said before, this town doesn’t hold anything for me anymore. My first port of call was to Angelica’s. She lives about a twenty-minute walk from mine, and I wanted to see her before anyone else. I didn’t have much time, but I wanted to let her know everything. She lives in a decent sized detached house on the outskirts. It’s one of those houses that is symmetrical in appearance, and with a clean gravel driveway. Her father's 4x4 was parked on the drive, and the suitcases for their big adventure were already loaded into the back. I rang the doorbell three separate times. It felt like I was stood there for an eternity. With each ring, no answer came. Ringing and waiting made the sense of rejection feel stronger, but this ended when I gave the letterbox a firm bang. Through the glass I saw the large figure of her father appear, and I quickly pulled on my shades again so that he wouldn't notice that I had been crying. I'm not sure what I was expecting him to say, and I was secretly hoping that he had realised that the glass throwing incident wasn't a reflection of who I am. Three weeks had passed since I covered the tuck shop in orange juice, but some people tend to hold grudges for longer. I crossed my fingers behind my back hoping that I would be welcomed into the house. Sadly, as is usual, this wasn't the case.

In the past he would open the door fully and welcome me with a bellowing "Joey, my boy!" greeting. This time though, the door opened only far enough for him to poke his face through. The frame and the door rested on his cheeks. I took a step backwards and felt very small. He towered over me and didn't say a word.

"Hey. Is Angelica there please?" I asked, desperately.
"She is out, sorry Joey. I'll let her know you called" he replied, moving back from the gap as if he was about to

close it in my face. I reached out and place a hand on the central glass pane.

"Please do let her know, I need to speak to her" I pleaded.

"I will, I will". This time he definitely was going to close it on me.

"Thank you, oh, and enjoy your trip!" I said, trying to sound blasé, however the door was shut on me without him acknowledging my well wishes.

I didn't believe that Angelica was out, however she was refusing to answer my calls. I felt paranoid, almost as if she was watching me from behind the curtains that hung behind one of the many bay windows of the house. She was getting ready to head off on holiday, and as the car was already prepared for their departure it would be odd for her not to be around. Part of me wanted to hang around until she came out but that may anger her dad even more. Hopefully a month-long trip in the sun will allow him to calm down and let me be welcomed back into the house.

I trudged back down the crunching driveway and started walking along the road outside which led away from the town and into the countryside. I didn't really have a plan as to where I was going to go now. My bag was starting to cause my shoulder to ache. Despite it not being heavy, I didn't really have much upper body strength, so it's pull on the right side of my body was starting to affect me quickly.

I followed the road for around half a mile, kicking stones along the pavement as I went. Between our town and the next village, which is only about two miles away, stood a stone-built bus shelter. It smelt of urine and there were empty crisp packets and cola bottles scattered around the floor. There were still remnants of dead leaves in one corner that must have been blown there in the Autumn, a good eight months ago. They had turned into one damp pile. It shows how often this small spot of salvation was cleaned. I sat on its broken wooden bench staring out to space, fighting my thoughts. Despite being close to my town, it was remote enough to allow you to have some time alone. I can't imagine anyone really used this bus stop anymore. When it was built it can't have served more than a dozen houses, but these have long gone. Behind the shelter is a small area of woodland. I left my bag in the bus stop and walked around the back.

The houses were down a short track, around three-hundred yards from the main carriageway. I don't know why they became derelict. There were many rumours which had been passed around about what it could have been, but the truth ended up buried under the exaggerated stories that previous generations of school children told. The most famous one was that a young boy was killed in the woods one winter by a man who lived in a kind of underground base, and that this drove the residents away. This is probably the most far-fetched of the stories also but as children you always get drawn into anything that's slightly creepy, especially when it involves somewhere in your own town. Because of this rumour the area is known as Dead Ken's Wood to anyone who is under forty-five years old. I don't even remember the boy being called Ken in the stories. It goes without saying that as kids we were banned from going up to these woods, but when you are told you can't go somewhere it just makes you want to go there more. One Saturday during a past summer break at school a group of us did visit. The houses at the back were bordering on collapse by this point and even we didn't risk going inside. We played in the woods for a short while but were never visited by the ghost of the boy who supposedly died up there. I remember feeling a bit sad at the time after we had got back home. Some of the mystery of the area had been lost. We never did go up there again. I think that sitting here now is actually the nearest I have been to Dead Ken's Wood since that day. I can't see any of the houses through the trees though due to their foliage, however I imagine they will probably be long condemned or knocked down. Deciding that now was not the best time to re-explore the woods, I headed back to the bus stop and hid myself from view as much as possible.

After about twenty minutes of sitting and thinking of where I could head, a bus pulled up outside. One passenger alighted, and the driver held the electric doors open.

"Are you waiting to get on?" the driver asked me. I wasn't, in fact I wasn't waiting for anything. I asked him where he was heading.
"Goes 'round the west of town and then ends up at the station" he replied.

When he said the station, I made the spontaneous decision to jump on board. The driver looks to be in his early sixties, but there is still evidence of his wilder days from his youth. He has a mid-length beard which is now grey, and this is matched by a grey ponytail. Due to the summer weather he is in short sleeves and this reveals numerous tattoos up both arms, all of which have started going that green colour that is common with old ink. I don't know what they all mean but I do recognise a tattoo of the Rolling Stones logo. I'd like to think that this driver still heads out to a small and sweaty back room of a pub to watch similarly aged men play in bands, bands which cover all the kind of songs that you would find on compilations called things like "The Greatest Rock Driving Album". The bus that I had boarded served the local villages and was one of those routes that only had about one bus an hour, if that. As it was a quiet route I managed to get the front seats on the top deck. I have no idea why they sent double decker buses on this route as there would never be enough people needing the service to fill all the seats. This particular bus had around a dozen older ladies on it, each with their small tartan covered shopping trolleys. I used my position on the top deck to take a good look at my town, and not one drop of nostalgia passed through me. Now, when I talk to my friends online there is this meme that crops up frequently. (NB. For those who don't use the internet in the same way, here is the dictionary definition. Meme - an image, video, piece of text, etc., typically humorous in nature, that is copied and spread rapidly by internet users, often with slight variations). So yes, there is a meme where a short video of something bleak or exasperating is shared, with the Simon and Garfunkel lyric "Hello darkness my old friend" playing over the top. On this bus journey we past the market square and through the High Street. For no reason whatsoever, or without warning, "Hello darkness my old friend" popped into my head and continued on loop. I couldn't stop it, and before I knew it I was chuckling to myself. It was the first time I had laughed for a good few days and with the situation I was currently in there is no explanation for why it was that moment that laughter came back into my life.

The rest of the journey was uneventful, and once clear of the traffic at the two main roundabouts we pulled up outside the station. I got off the bus and opened my bag to get my wallet. The driver was looking at me through his reaction-lensed glasses, and his greying beard moved more than expected when he told me to take care. He reminded me a bit of Harold Shipman, but friendly.

Without a destination, I sat in the window of Costa Coffee and fiddled with a wooden stirrer whilst checking out the departure board. Some of the places I hadn't heard of, and many seemed many miles away. When the name London Marylebone popped up at the foot of the electronic board my decision was made. As you know, London was always top of my to-do list this summer, so why not now? I jumped up and headed over to the ticket queue. The station was quite busy, and I had to wait for around ten minutes before I was called forward. The lady in the ticket window seemed very uninterested in actually providing any decent customer service, but I came away with a one-way ticket to the capital. It cost £16, which isn't too bad but only left me with about £35 to make use of at the other end. I stuffed my wallet back into my bag and headed outside to find the way to platform four. Typically, this platform was on the other side of the station and I had to drag my holdall up over the bridge. There were a few people waiting for the London train, and all the benches along the platform were occupied. I threw my bag on the floor near the fence that separates commuters from the car park and sat down beside it.

This now brings us back to the beginning of this part of the story. As the robot lady announced, my train is now approaching the platform.

This would be the first time that I had ever been on a long train journey, and definitely the first time I had been on any journey of note on my own. It was a popular route judging by the amount of people on the platform, but I managed to claim a table and two seats just for myself. The couple opposite were German and even with my recent GCSE knowledge of the subject, I couldn't understand what any of the words they were using. The timetable said that I should arrive into London just after 5pm. Once there I would pop across to the Italian café that I had seen on streetview and watch the world go by for a bit before trying to find a cheap room where I could crash for the night.

There were two sideways plug sockets near the window of the carriage, so I took the opportunity to charge my phone and try and get some sleep before I arrived. Today I truly believe that I had hit rock bottom, but the capital would surely provide unlimited opportunities. As we started to roll away I put on my headphones and tried to think about how things will be better from now on. Goodbye town!

Nine

I was woken by the sudden jolt of the train coming to a standstill. I can't remember how far into the journey it was that I had fallen asleep, but I barely recall leaving the station. My left arm is dead after having used it to prop my head up for the entire duration of the trip, and pins and needles shoot down my arm as I clench and unclench my hand to get the blood flowing. I unplug my phone and check the time. It is just coming up to ten past five. I stuffed my cables into my holdall and followed the row of people off of the train and out onto the main concourse of Marylebone Station. I knew London was a busy city, but I wasn't prepared for this. Marylebone Station was absolutely packed. I scan myself through the ticket barriers and try and find somewhere to sit. There must be a lot of offices around here as there is a plague of men and women in suits and business wear milling about. The small coffee shop in the centre of the station near the timetables has a queue which snakes back towards the entrance of the underground, with those waiting all engrossed in their mobile phones. Every few seconds the queue would shuffle forward, and they would kick their bags forward a few feet. The station isn't big, and it's no surprise that all the benches are currently fully occupied. I stand on the spot, slowly turning around trying to take it all in. Within seconds I feel a sharp pain on my right ankle and notice that I have been caught by a lady wheeling an oversized red suitcase. She is oblivious though and is far to engrossed in a call to realise that she has walked into me, and therefore no apology is forthcoming.

The amount of people in here is making me feel a bit uneasy, and I won't lie, I am feeling a little scared also. I've searched pictures of this station so many times, however all these never gave me the notice as to how busy and claustrophobic it would feel once I had arrived. I wandered through crowds trying to find the toilets, following the badly placed blue and white signs hanging from the high ceiling. When I eventually did arrive, I saw that they wanted me to pay 30p for the privilege to use the facilities. I didn't have spare change, and I couldn't face joining the crowds in the queue for one of the fast food stands. Instead, I would head onto the streets and find my café.

I bustled through the commuters, being forcefully knocked left and right on the short journey to the exit, and it was here that I was spat out into the city. Marylebone Station is housed behind a large symmetrical red bricked building, and I found myself leaning up against the side of one of the tall arched doorways. Clouds of cigarette smoke drifted across to me from the small smoking area that was to the left of the main entrance. This was not the clean, fresh start that I was expecting. I tightened my bag strap and strode out of the station and across the taxi rank. The Italian café that I had seen online so many times was now stood in front of me across the zebra crossing, no more than thirty yards away. Closed. Why would it be closed at this time of day? They could make a fortune from all these people. I'd been looking forward to a cup of coffee here for so long and small things like this made me feel that the world was truly against me. Now what? I don't know where I should go first. Definitely not Harrods. I'm not confident enough on my own to try and find it yet, and I don't even know if I would be let in. I'm a young kid, sweaty from the train journey and not exactly looking like the type of customer they are wanting to attract. Once again, I am alone. A young, teenage gay kid in a big city. In hindsight I should have used the train journey to plot out exactly what I would be doing when I arrived, and there were maps available at the station when I came to board. I guess the tiredness from the stressful day affected my judgment back then, so my decision making wasn't at its sharpest.

I move away from the crowds and stand just down the road opposite the café for a few minutes, watching the people come and go. I lean against the railings that border a small square of grass which the road sign tells me is called Dorset Square. Trees tower over me from inside, and it's nice to be shaded from the sun, although sweat forms on my forehead due to how muggy it is in central London. The tall buildings must be trapping the heat at street level, and the cars that pass by do nothing to alleviate this. People watching has always been an enjoyable hobby, but the anxiety of feeling lost means that it is doing nothing to improve my current mood. I've always found that another way to clear my mind and make me feel better is to go for a walk. Back home when walking around the fields, I always felt much calmer after exploring the random pathways through forests and countryside. I have, or I should say had, a collection of items that I had found on my walks which I kept stored in an old plastic cookie box underneath my bed. It had all sorts in there, such as pieces of old broken pottery, small glass bottles, weird shaped stones and everything in between. I don't think there is any countryside of note in London however, but there are a few parks which I will explore tomorrow. If I get the chance I will try and get to the banks of the Thames at low tide to see if any treasure has been cast upon the banks. As for today, I will walk to clear my mind, but remain vigilant for any B&B's that might have a cheap room to house me overnight. With my back to the square I set off to the left and walk among the tall white buildings. The roads are heaving with rush hour traffic, but it's nice to be surrounded by people who don't know me or my story. I've got a fascination for the big city and the street names all sound very grand. Within five minutes I have passed a Gloucester Place and a Glentworth Street. Just past here is where I come across the first of the famous landmarks. I glance up at the road sign as I bear to the right and realise that I am on Baker Street. THE Baker Street. The Sherlock Holmes Baker Street! I know there is a statue around here somewhere, so I head off to find it. I love the Sherlock Holmes stories and must have read through the complete collection at least five times. I don't know what it is about them that attracted me more than other books that are popular with people my age. Having a slightly different taste to others is quite useful as it meant that my preferred choices of book was usually in the library when I needed a new book to start.

My first experience of crossing the road in London is an interesting one. Despite the signal for us not being green, people are pushing past me and dodging between the traffic. I have nowhere near that level of confidence yet so stand patiently until the green man tells me to go. I don't fancy getting run down on my first day. The drivers that are passing seem to communicate with constant beeping of their horns and a variety of hand gestures out their windows, and it all seems very impolite. The smell of the traffic is a lot stronger than it is back home, and there is a distinct aroma of petrol fumes drifting across to us.

Despite the stress of being near so many other people, I do find the statue eventually. I had to walk quite far down Baker Street until I found it. On the way I passed the offices for the London Underground Lost Property office. They had a window display of assorted items which I presume had been accidentally discarded on one of the many routes. Some of the items seem pretty usual, children's toys, notebooks and that kind of thing. What grabs my interest though are the more peculiar items towards the rear. There are at least three sets of false teeth, as well as crutches and even a fake limb. How on earth can you leave these on the train and not realise? I'm pretty certain no one will come back and claim their false teeth. How would you know which set is your own? I imagine the last thing you'd want is to pick up a set and then realise during your evening meal that you're chewing your food with teeth that have been in another person's mouth. If they haven't made a museum out of all their items yet, then they really should. I'm certain there must be other people like me who are curious about a collection of weird and wonderful items. I make a mental note to come back to this window in the future to see what else has been added. After leaving the window it only took a couple of minutes to reach the statue of Holmes. I wanted to get a picture but decided against it. Firstly, I need to save the battery on my phone in case I need it later. Secondly, everyone had the same idea as me, so the statue is partly hidden behind hundreds of tourists. I'm not even exaggerating. Well, OK maybe I am a bit, but there are a lot of people jostling for a photo opportunity. It's one thing ticked off my list though and I will come back again soon when I have more of a plan. From Baker Street I follow the dual carriageway until the buildings start to get boring. A lot of it becomes offices and the smell of pollution in the air is even stronger here. The white facades of the building appear to have a grey film forming on them due to the particles that have been spat out of exhaust pipes and into the air. Deciding that polluted air may not be the best should I suffer an anxiety attack, I venture off to find somewhere greener.

I head east across the capital before turning to head towards the very centre. I pass the British Museum, Soho Square and Leicester Square before finally coming across the river Thames. I hadn't realised how close everything was in central London, in terms of notable places I mean. I had always imagined that you would need a train to get around this vast metropolis but many of the underground stations seem to be very close to each other. Sorry about the pointless fancy words I keep dropping in here, I've done a geography exam this morning remember! You get bonus points for saying things like metropolis rather than 'city centre' hopefully.

As I sit myself down on the wall near the banks, I take some time to just sit and reflect on my day. I'm quite tired by this point. Also, it has now past 6pm and I'm starting to get hungry and a little cold. The sunshine has disappeared behind large clouds and the wind speed has started to pick up a bit. I pull my jacket tighter around me to stop the breeze heading down the back of my t-shirt. The Thames is at high tide and even in the light it appears to be a dull blue and grey colour. It's a bit bleak. My stomach rumbles and churns so I quickly pop into a small newsagent and pick up a chicken and stuffing sandwich before heading back to the river, finding an unattended bench on the Embankment. I decide that once I have eaten that I will go for a wander to find a room. On my walk from Marylebone I found myself losing my attention to some of the surroundings, so I am certain that I have passed many B&B's but not noticed. Even if that is the case, they were probably too expensive to be covered by the small amount of money I have on me. My thirty-odd pound budget would never get me anything decent, plus I would need to try and save some for tomorrow morning.

As I am sat looking at the boats passing by I notice a figure come and sit at the other end of the bench. I turn to look, and his seating position is similar to mine, and he too is staring out. He has a black woollen hat and a green hoodie. He looks a bit like a gardener who has just finished his shift as there are patches of what looks like mud on his elbows. His boots are sturdy and brown, and his grey jogging trousers are tucked into them. Without looking away from across the Thames he reaches into his pocket and pulls out a pouch of tobacco before rolling a cigarette slowly. It sort of slips my mind that he is a real person until he notices that I have been staring at him without blinking for about two minutes.

"Yer alright?" he asks in a slight Glaswegian accent. I wasn't expecting that for some reason. He also appears much younger now he is focussing on me also. I'd say mid-twenties at most.

"Yes sorry" I mumble.

"Did ye want a cigarette?"

"No, no thank you. I don't smoke"

"Ah yer a good wee lad. D'ya live 'round here then?"

This seems quite forward. I was always told that no one in London talks to each other.

“Nah I’m just visiting”
“So where are yer from?”
“Um.. Denmark. I’m on holiday”.

Your guess as to why I said Denmark is as good as mine. I panicked! I neither look nor sound like your standard Danish kid.

“Denmark? Aye. Yer sound English son”. He knows. Fuck.
“Yeah, my parents are English speakers, so I guess the accent hasn’t really stuck”

He remains silent for a bit.

“Do you live here?” I ask
“Aye. Been here for about a year. Moved down from Glasgow”
“Cool. Where do you live?”
“Anywhere. I don’t have a house son. I am a nomad”
“A Nomad? Makes you sound like one of the Avengers”
“Ha. Aye, without any of the powers, unless having a strong smell is a power”
“It could be. I hope you don’t mind me asking, but do you sleep on the streets?”

"You have a curious mind, son, but aye, most of the time. I try for hostels but yer can't always get the room"

"Are there many hostels?"

"Aye a few, but some are 'orrible places yer see. Full of drugs. I may not look like one for guidance, but I try and avoid the drugs. No one has ever improved their life with them"

"Whereabouts are they?"

"What the drugs?"

"No sorry, the hostels. Are they near here?"

"Why yer asking?"

"As you say, just curious. I've not seen any"

"It's cos they don't make a song and dance of them. They hardly bring the tourists in do they. The ones I don't mind are down by Vauxhall. Have to know the right ones though"

"How can you tell the difference from a good one and a bad one?"

"The only real way is spending the night in one. Until you've been in one you don't really know what it's gonna be like. They try their best to help you, and if it wasn't for the many people who give their time up to help there I probably wouldn't be sat here speaking to you"

"How come?" I ask, half thinking that I knew the answer already.

"Well, the streets are dangerous. Many a person has been lost on the streets round here. You don't hear about that though. Aye, the papers know that it won't sell"

"Have you lost many people that way?"

"To the streets?"

"I guess, yeah"

"A few. Over the last year there's been many that have come and gone from my life. Some bought it on themselves. Felt that their life wasn't worth living y'know?"

"Like suicide?"

"I presume. People just often disappear and yer never hear about them again"

"Maybe they just moved away?"

"It's a nice thought. Hopefully wherever they went they found peace and happiness there"

"Do you think you'll find happiness again soon?"

"You're presuming I ain't happy now"

"God, sorry. I didn't mean to be horrible"

"Ha don't worry. I am kinda happy now I guess, but I think ye expectations change"

"I don't follow"

"Well, a year ago, happiness may have been getting a new place in Glasgow y'know. Being settled up there, finding work etc. Now though? Happiness might be sleeping anywhere that has a roof and where you don't feel threatened by everything around you. It might also be having three meals a day. It's hard, but more often than not I guess I'd say I'm happy. Actually, not happy, but content"

"I understand"

"Don't be like me son. If you ever have trouble in life, don't wait for the opportunities to come to you. Go out and find them. Once you start spiralling it's hard to change course"

I didn't really know how to respond to this, so I just nodded and turned back to the waters. The Nomad continued to smoke his cigarette, flicking ash onto the paving slab between his feet.

"Look anyway son, I best be heading off. Enjoy your holiday". He winked when saying holiday. My lies were obvious to him, but he seemed kind regardless. The Nomad stood and threw the remains of his cigarette to the floor before extinguishing it with the heel of his boot.
"See you around" I said as he turned to head away
"Aye, maybe" came his reply through a small smile. He turned away from me and headed off down the Embankment.

I'm not sure why, but I kind of liked The Nomad already. Once he was far enough away I stood up and walked in the same direction. I didn't want him to think that I was following him. The idea of a hostel to stay in this evening seemed quite appealing, as I'm sure it was something which I could afford. I pulled out my phone and searched Vauxhall on the maps app.

It took me ages to navigate my way to Vauxhall. On the map it looked simple and I try my best to follow the main roads. In reality though the whole area is very built up and quite intimidating. The brief summer-like weather had now completely departed, and the rain started to fall again. The sound of the cars and lorries powering down through the puddles in the road lead to me becoming covered in a shower of dirty water a fair few times and I was becoming colder by the second as a result. None of the buildings seem to match each other around this area, and it appeared that many of them had been forgotten. Pubs stood boarded up, a long way from their heydays where they would be overflowing with locals grabbing a pint. It makes me sad to think that buildings which formed the centre of many people's lives were now just a shell. I guess that my love of the nostalgic clouds my thoughts on this, and that maybe these pubs were on the decline long before they finally shut their cellars for good. Elsewhere, nearly every small patch of empty land has had a tall building erected on it meaning that the area is quite dark where the daylight struggles to break through fully to ground level. The railway bridges overhead provide shelter from the storms but the thundering noise from the trains above echoes out loudly. Nearly every corner I turn makes me feel more and more claustrophobic. Without realising, my anxiety has started to bubble to the surface again and I am finding it hard to locate the street signs. It isn't long before I am really struggling for breath and need to take some time out. I slump into a shop doorway to recover. At least it is a bit sheltered here. I try to get my bearings. The building that I am leaning against is a cheap fried chicken shop on Vauxhall Street. With the street and the area both having the same name, it makes things that little bit more difficult. I need to find a hostel. Walking is no longer providing any calm, and each step seems to chip away at me, however I must carry on in order to find somewhere that will allow me to be safe for the night.

Sitting in this shop doorway isn't very comfortable, but I remain there for around thirty minutes whilst I wait for my anxiety to calm. The people who pass by look down at me, but no one stops to talk. I don't know if I would have preferred people to stop and have a chat, but in this situation, it was maybe for the best. If I was them, I would have probably walked past also. I'm not sure what time this shop opens but I need to make my scarce before it does. When I sat down I hadn't noticed how dirty it was on the floor, and my trousers have a layer of beige dust on them on the underside. I stand up and pat myself down, before picking a direction to walk in. I have no idea which would be the best road to take, so I just put my trust in fate and head off away from the road that brought me here.

For the next hour I am wandering. I can't seem to find any hostel despite my best efforts. A couple of times I spot a sign hanging from a building at the far end of a street, yet when I reach them it is just a sign for an opticians or similar. I am wary that the time will soon pass by and it will be too late. London wasn't meant to be like this. London was meant to be a celebration of finishing school. It was meant to be the place where me and Angelica got to see where the rich people hung out. I could not be further away from afternoon tea in the Harrods restaurant as I am now. If I thought that I hit rock bottom earlier, I'd definitely hit it now. I've lost count of the times that I have cried today, and once again I have spontaneous tears forming. If The Nomad was here at least I could get some more directions. I wish I didn't lie to him now and instead asked for the name of somewhere safe. I made a promise to myself there and then that I would be honest with anyone who gave up some of their time to talk to me. I think when I met The Nomad that I feared that he would cause me harm if I went with him. Having these preconceptions can help you remain safe, but in situations like the one I now find myself in, being honest and asking for help is far more beneficial. I left home as no one understood me, and yet here I have chosen to ignore the first person who genuinely could have offered support. As it stands though, nothing feels safe about this place now. The clouds have continued to get darker and the rain has been coming and going. On top of this, the sun has started to set. In midsummer it tends not to get fully dark until nearer 10pm, however the taller buildings cast their shadows over the city long before this. I decide to find someone, anyone, who might be able to help. The people walking around do not look like the type to know which the best hostel is. They're all youngish looking couples, the men with well-trimmed beards and the women with cool hairstyles. They all walk and laugh arm in arm down the streets to the many bars and pubs that are scattered here, each one full of revellers.

Another few minutes are spent walking around with no direction, and I unbelievably find myself turning a corner only to see the same fried chicken shop that I crashed by earlier. There is a difference this time though, and this is that there is a bright yellow delivery van parked adjacent to it on the street. I walk up to it but there is no one in there, but I decide to wait until the driver returns. If anyone knows the streets it will be a postal worker surely? I was in luck, as ten minutes later a large black man appeared. He wasn't best pleased to find a kid leaning against his van.

"Can you get off my van mate?" he said in a deep voice. I noticed he was wearing a Bluetooth headset, and appeared to be on a call to someone.

"Sorry to interrupt. I know you're busy. Um, I'm just wondering if you know where the hostel is please?"

"Which one?" he asked

"Any. Any one will be fine". This is the truth. By now I didn't care which one he pointed me to. I just wanted somewhere with a bed and a roof.

"Go down here" he said, using small parcel to point. At the end there is a red door with "Gold's" written above it. That's the closest. If that's no good, then they'll be able to tell you one that is good enough for you"

"Thank you that's very kind"

He silently nods at me and I shift away from his van. He gets in and drives off quickly, giving me a small signalling wave with his right hand as he passes.

Ten

How did I not spot Gold's? It's obviously a hostel when you know it exists. It is located at the other end of the road from where I met the delivery driver. It is a large corner house with tarmac outside rather than any garden. It's only two stories, but it looks like there may be a basement also. Outside stands a tall iron post, where a rectangular sign stating the hostel's name hangs. This, and the style of the building, makes me believe that it used to be a pub. It's good to see that not all the pubs around here are just boarded up shells, but some have been reimagined into something that will be beneficial to those in the area. The black front door is on the left-hand side of the building, although it looks like a second door has been bricked up a few years ago. It is set back up a couple of steps. I don't know what the protocol is here, so I take my chances and knock on the gold lion knocker that is towards it's top. I wait for thirty seconds but there is no answer. I take a step back and can see that there is light emanating from an upstairs window. I head back to the door and try the handle rather than knock again. The door clicks and opens inwardly.

As I step inside, a weird smell hits me. It's quite musty and every time I take a step on the beige carpet a cloud of dust rises up. The hall that I have found myself in is narrow, and two more doors, on either side of me, have also been bricked up. I could just about see their outline from the plaster that had been placed over them. At the end of the corridor it widens, and on the left-hand side is a straight staircase. Next to the stairs another hallway leads back a further ten to fifteen feet, with two fire doors on the right, and a third at the far end. Each door has a green emergency exit sticker, with brass numbers screwed on. They're all at different angles and the whole place doesn't feel cared for. The wallpaper is dappled and has been painted over with magnolia paint, the same shade that my Dad had splattered across him the day I got thrown out of school. In places, the wallpaper has started to peel, revealing stained walls behind it. The smell reminds me of an old library. It smells generally a bit damp but at least it is somewhere with a roof and walls so tonight I hopefully won't have to sleep outside, which is at least one positive.

I don't know what the next thing I have to do is. There doesn't seem to be any bell to press for attention and no signs give any indication of where I am meant to head. I decide to busy myself by reading the information on the small noticeboard that is behind the main door. After a while I kind of wish I hadn't. There are many official notices about drink and drug policies, and also the reporting processes if you're attacked. This is the reality. I felt unsafe and vulnerable enough outside, and this was meant to be my haven, but it's not. I'm scared and still feel unsafe. At the moment I am the lowest of the low here.

I am young.

I am gay.
I am vulnerable.
I have no contacts in the city.
I currently have no family.
I don't know my way around.
I am not strong physically.
I am not strong mentally.

Surely all these, whether combined or separate, will make me a target. I thought all my studying of London that I did in preparation for my day with Angelica was enough, but everything is so different in reality. To be fair to myself, I would never have predicted that I would be in a situation like this so suddenly so there was no research into hostels to be done when planning our trip to the V&A.

I wait around the hall and continue to read everything on the board over and over, unsure whether anyone will come and help. As I lift up a leaflet to read the one underneath I accidentally knock the board from its nail and it falls to the ground before I can move quick enough to catch it. The noise alerts someone from one of the back rooms and I can hear steps coming from the far end of the hall. The door furthest away creaks as it swings open and a lady with a heavy necklace and smoky lensed glasses stops and looks at me.

"Can I help?" she asks. Her voice is a lot softer than her appearance would suggest but it has a gravelly quality that makes me think that at least twenty cigarettes a day are placed between her pale lips. She must be in her mid-fifties (if I am being kind), and her hair has been badly dyed a dirty sand colour. Although the haircut is short, the grey roots are showing through. It looks as though it has been stained by the cigarette smoke.

"Hi. Um. I just wondered if you had a room for this evening please?"
"Let me have a check for you. Come through to reception"

She steps back through the door, holding it open for me as I shuffle nervously down towards her. She stands with her back to the door and allows me to squeeze past. There isn't much room and I feel uncomfortable when I feel my back brush against her chest. I'm not sure if she is doing it deliberately. As I turn back towards her I realise there is clearly a sign saying reception on the door, just below the number. In my panicked state I hadn't noticed this, and I feel a bit stupid.

"What's your name?" she says coldly.
"I'm Joey. Joey Eaton" I say, holding out a hand. I'm not sure if a handshake is appropriate but I want to appear polite.
"Hi Joey Eaton. I am Gloria". She takes my hand and gives it a weak shake. "I am the hostel manager. How old are you?"

"I am sixteen, seventeen in a couple of weeks". This time the lie is deliberate. I wasn't sure if under-sixteens would be turned away and referred to somewhere else, so on this occasion I felt that not telling the truth was justified. It was too late in the day to start another search for a room.
"I see. And how have you ended up here?"

Whether Gloria wanted to hear all the details or not, I tell her about the last twenty-four hours of my life. It feels good to say it out loud and makes me take notice of how much has happened in such a short space of time. I don't mention the gay bit just in case she is homophobic. I've had enough rejection for one day. She does seem to listen to my story, and even poured me an orange juice halfway through when my throat dried out from speaking in a smoky room. I think the smell from those out the back smoking was drifting in through the outlets in the kitchen. After I have wrapped up my story, she consults a diary for available space. It's odd to see someone using a large paper diary as the sole means of organisation these days but I leave Gloria to it. After many page turns and taps with a pen on her teeth she has some good news.

"We have a bed if you'd like it?" she says smiling
"Yes please, thank you!" I reply immediately. "How much is it?"
"It's £4 for the night, but I need to go through the details to make sure you're okay with it?"

I've already made up my mind, but I nod for her to continue.

"First things first, despite what you may have heard, we are not a hostel. We are a night shelter. You've come at an appropriate time luckily, as we give our beds out on a first come, first served basis. We only opened the door about half an hour ago. We open at 8pm sharp each night, and each person who stays has to vacate their room by 8.30am the following morning"

"That's fine" I say.

"For your £4 you will get a bed, and a warm meal this evening and some breakfast. Tonight, it will be Mediterranean Soup and crusty bread"

"Sounds lovely thank you"

"As you are taking our last bed I must inform you that it is in one of the shared rooms"

"That's okay, I just need anywhere tonight. I don't mind sharing with someone"

Gloria lowers her glasses and looks at me. "When I say sharing, it's not like a hotel room. You will be in a dormitory with seventeen others"

I wasn't expecting that. It goes to show just how little I know. "That will still be fine thank you" I respond without showing my fear. "How many people do you have staying here?"

“Each night we are full. In total there are two eighteen-bed dorms, and three four-bed dorms. The four-bed rooms are for females only. Forty-eight people each night. It breaks your heart, let me tell you”

“Do you get the same people each day?”

“A few regulars yeah, but the addicts tend to be less consistent. As much as we want to help, we can’t save a space just on the off chance that they will make it back here”.

“I understand. Thank you again for this. How can I pay?”

“All I need you to do is read and sign this, and then you can pay by cash or card”

I take the clipboard that she offers me and sign it without reading it fully. I dig out my wallet and hand the clipboard back along with a five-pound note. Once done I slip the change into my pocket and wait for Gloria to show me up to my room.

“You’re all wet boy” she says, noticing my wet jeans

“I got caught in the rain” I say sadly.

“We have showers on the landing that you’re welcome to use. There’s towels here if you want one. Also, and I’m not being funny, wear this”.

Gloria hands me a black baseball cap with NYC written across the peak. “Your fringe makes it look like you’re gay. If you want to stay safe, then this might be a precaution. Come, let me show you up”.

As much as I hate wearing caps, the way that Gloria offers me the cap makes me think that the people in the dorm will be even more intimidating than I imagined. I know lots of people with floppy fringes, but it doesn't mean they are gay. I conclude that she is only trying to help, but it makes me nervous again. I thought that sharing a hostel would be better as everyone here needs somewhere to stay. The thought that people would turn on each other hadn't even occurred to me and I guess it proves my naivety. I pull my fringe back and place the cap on my head in a way that completely hides it and then follow Gloria.

We move back to the hall and then up the stairs that I spotted when arriving. They creak loudly, and they are all at slightly different angles. The smell of damp gets stronger the higher we go. As we ascend Gloria points at various doors. She must do this tour many times a night and is visually bored by the whole thing. "Showers here" she says tapping on a door as we reach the first landing. She doesn't stop though, and we continue up and up until we are nearly in the attic.

"This is where I leave you. Feel free to pick any bed that's available. If I were you though, I'd say a top bunk is better as a newbie. We'll bring the soup up in a bit. Take care". She turns almost immediately, and I mumble my thanks to her back. She waves her left hand in the air in response. I stand and face the door building up the nerve to enter.

Part of me wants to run, but the other part of me knows that there isn't anywhere to run to. I focus on the door trying to ensure no anxiety or tears show now. This is reality and I must appear strong in order to survive. I breathe in and out slowly to compose myself. I pull the cap down on my head firmly to ensure no hair is hanging through, and with my left hand I reach towards the door handle and slowly push it open.

Eleven

You will have been on a school trip where you've been placed in a dormitory. It's a rite of passage for every school kid in the country. I remember the first time I stayed in one. We were on a school trip in Year 7 and visiting Chepstow. Being away from family and having the opportunity to share a room with a few of your friends felt fantastic. The teachers would prowl in the corridors outside, but it felt like you were on some big adventure where you were independent for the first time. Looking back that wasn't the case as any teacher can hear a dormitory whisper from around fifty metres and peak through the door to tell you to be quiet within seconds. This dormitory was different. There would be no one stalking the corridors waiting to tell you to sleep here, and no one would be looking after your safety. What's more, the people that I would be sharing the night with were no friends. They could be anyone of any age, of any background and with their own coping mechanisms. The one thing we had in common was that on this night none of us had somewhere to call home.

The room was very basic. There were five bunk beds on the left-hand side, and four on the right. Each one was identical. They had blue painted metal frames which looked rather weak, and they let out a small painful squeal each time any movement was made. On each bed lay a plastic covered mattress, all of which had slightly yellowed from their original white state. In the far-right corner of the dorm was a small sink with a cracked bar of soap behind the tap. The mirror above the sink was also cracked, and a few pieces of glass were no longer present. As unhygienic as it looked, it was probably cleaner than me, so I took the opportunity to wash my face, tossing my holdall onto the floor beneath. Despite it being less than eight hours since I left my town, my face already appeared to have a slight haunted look to it. My eyes were puffy from the stress and the crying which I had experienced. My hair had become greasy and I had dirt patches on my forearms. I ran cold water over my head for about ten minutes. It felt fresh and cool and the sound of the water had a calming effect. Drying my face on the front of my t-shirt, I looked up and then jumped back as I saw a face in the mirror looking at me from behind.

"Hi. I didn't mean to startle you. I'm sorry" said the soft voice. They were dressed in an oversized blue jumper and had a peach silk style scarf tied around their neck. Their hair was thin and limp and ran down to their shoulders. It was blonde in colour, apart from the last few inches which were dyed in a way that made them appear aqua-blue.

"That's OK" I answered, smiling.
"You must be new here" they said, smiling. "My name is Mimi".
"Nice to meet you Mimi. I'm Joey" offering my hand, much like I had to Gloria upon arriving.

"So, what brings you here?" they ask

"I've just moved to London for a bit. I needed somewhere to stay, and this place was kind of recommended to me. Do you stay here a lot?"

"On and off. I prefer other places but if they are full then I make do with coming to Gold's. A roof is a roof at the end of the day"

"Yeah, I'm happy just to be inside for the night if I'm honest. I've never stayed in a hostel like this before"

"A lot of people haven't. Most people don't even know they exist. Most people don't know WE exist. By 'most people' I am of course referring to those who have never found themselves homeless like us"

This is the first time I have ever been described as homeless, and despite only being so for a few hours, I guess that I am. I mean, I certainly wouldn't be welcomed at my actual home this evening and there are no friends who would be willing to take me in. It's an odd feeling. In my head it has felt more like I have been away for a couple of days already. I try to explain this to Mimi.

"Joey dear, there are so many people in this country who thought that after a couple of days they would be able to get back on their feet. It's a common problem. It is naïve to think that. I'm talking from experience as I was the same as you. I left the comfort of my father for a couple of nights on my own, and suddenly, here I am a year later in the same night shelter where I spent my first night alone.

I'm not blaming you for being naïve. It's just part of the process you go through. Naivety will be followed by fear which is followed by helplessness. It's a vicious spiral. How old are you?"

"I'm fifteen. Well. Nearly sixteen. Gloria thinks that I am already sixteen though so please don't tell her"

"I won't, I promise. You do need to be careful though. Stick with me if you like and I'll make sure you're okay"

"Thank you, I don't want to be a burden so let me know if I get a bit annoying. Sometimes I talk too much, or panic and say the wrong thing"

"Understandable, just make sure that you don't say the wrong thing to the wrong person in here. Some of them have been known to get a little violent"

"I'll be as quiet as I can all night" I say, unsure as to how violent my roommates may turn. "How old are you, Mimi, if you don't mind me asking?"

"I'm twenty-two. I feel about forty though". Mimi's eyes seem a bit distant as if she is not fully present in the room.

The door to the dormitory opens and three men walk in. They seem to know each other. Two of the men throw bags onto nearby bunks as if claiming their territory, and they join the third on the bottom bunk nearest to the door.

"Come sit with me Joey" says Mimi, holding my left arm lightly near the elbow. She guides me to the furthest set of beds. I put my bag on the top bunk just as Gloria had advised. I sit next to Mimi and discover the mattresses are a lot firmer than they looked. I'm worried about how much sleep I will get, but for some reason Mimi seems to have calmed me. I wouldn't go as far to say that I now have a friend, but I seem to have someone who can let me know what to expect.

Perched next to Mimi, she pulls out two bottles of water and hands me one. I accept gratefully and as I swig she turns to me.

"Gloria told me that I was the last person to claim a room for this evening so how come it's so empty?" I as Mimi.
"It may appear empty, but these people have probably already staked their claims to their bunks before heading out to pick up some gear down the road"
"Gear as in drugs?"
"Gear as in drugs, yes"
"What kind of drugs?"
"Joey, all I will say is that if you have never seen anyone inject themselves, and wish it to remain that way, make sure you try to sleep facing the wall. Did Gloria tell you to take the top bunk at the back?"
"She did yeah"
"It may not seem like she cares that much, as she can be quite short with people, but her telling you that is her way of trying to make sure you are safe. I have the bottom bunk here, so you will be above me. All I will say is to try and remain quiet even if you feel nervous. It can be very

tough at times, and some people will attack the weakest in order to get what they want, a bit like how lions attack the slowest gazelles"

"Do you get attacked often?"

"I have been occasionally, and the severity depends on the attacker. Normally it's just verbal abuse and you slowly build this immunity to it. Hopefully you will be safe in here this evening though. Tomorrow morning, I will take you around and show you some of the better places that I have stayed, just in case you are in need of another shelter. It'll save you having to search the streets on your own again. I've also got some numbers I can give you. Do you have a phone?"

I tell her I do. I pass it to her and she types in some numbers into the contacts so that I will have access to these easily. She also puts her number in the phone and asks me to call her if I ever need anything. By the time we are done the room has filled up a bit more, but I follow her lead and decide not to engage with the others. So far, no one has paid any attention to us either.

After a couple of minutes she takes another sip of water and asks me what my story is. The feeling that there is someone who is willing to listen makes an incredible difference. I start from the beginning, much as I have done with you. I tell them about my upbringing, my family and the church, I tell them about Gary and his gang and about how I came to be sat next to Mimi on this mattress. Mimi listens to everything I say and nods and smiles throughout. After I have finished I ask how she ended up here.

Mimi starts off by telling me she is transgender. "Do you know what that means?" she asks. I tell her that I do, as I don't want to offend. The reality is that I know of the word but have never had anyone to really educate me on the subject. Mimi can tell that I am not being entirely truthful so kindly fills in any blanks that I have.

"Transgender is when a person whose sense of personal identity and gender does not correspond with their birth sex. That's basically the dictionary definition. I know it off by heart as I have had to say it so many times."

As you know I am slightly blinkered to the real world, and I ask Mimi to explain more.

"I was born male. My birth name was Roger, named after my father. I identify as female and like to be referred to as 'her' or 'she'" she explains.

"If you don't mind me asking, and I don't want to offend you as you're kind, but why are you in this dorm too?"

"Jesus Christ. You're only fifteen and even you get it. The thing is Joey that because I am transgender, I am kind of rejected by both sides. In this dorm I am vulnerable and feel as if I am always going to be the first one who is attacked. On the other hand, Gloria has told me that I am not welcome in the female dorms as she has had complaints from the ladies there, saying that I make them uncomfortable and as if I would attack them. I'm a kind person and would never hurt anyone. It's absurd to think that people think that I am just a man who has put on a dress and has gone out looking for trouble. If I was to be that way inclined, I think there are many easier ways of doing it. I am located in some kind of gender purgatory and there is no in-between area for me. My choice is either to stay in this room and put myself at risk, or sleep on the street where the risk is equally as high, if not higher. Even walking down the road during the day can lead to insults being slung at me from people in cars. If I had a pound for each person who has stepped to the other side of the road or pulled their child away from me then I would be a very rich woman indeed".

I don't know how to respond to Mimi really. I like her, and yet I know so little about her situation. I've never met anyone transgender before, let alone had the opportunity to sit down and talk to them. Before continuing to hear Mimi's story, Gloria enters the room and rolls a trolley of soup and bread through. I don't know if it's just because I am expecting it, but Gloria seems a lot colder towards Mimi than she does to me, maybe it's just because I am young, but her feelings towards Mimi are apparent whether she is putting on a kind face or not. I think that she doesn't even realise she is treating her any differently. Gloria takes the soup around to the others in the room, and there are now nine other people in here. They're all different ages, and some look a lot worse than others. It strikes me that now I am in this bubble, I notice these people. I don't just mean recognise they are there. I have always been aware that there are homeless people. It's more that I am now starting to see them as people with backgrounds, with stories, with mothers and fathers rather than just a nameless person asking for spare change on a high street.

We sit and eat our soup in silence. It's a nice meal and once finished I am thankful of having had something warm. Mimi takes my empty bowl and rinses it in the sink before placing it by the entrance to our dorm. Once she has sat back beside me I ask her how she ended up here. Her story has connections to mine, but the route of how it happened was different. Mimi's mother passed away from cancer when she was just three years old. She has no siblings. Her parents had met in the late 1980's at an army barracks in Oxfordshire. Her mother was an Army Dental Nurse, whereas her father was often on active service. He had been to many countries across the world and taken part in conflicts as well as humanitarian relief work. She explains how that she felt that she wasn't like other people when she was around twelve years old. The mental battles and fights that she had fought with herself mirrored those that I had been experiencing recently. She told me about anxiety and panic attacks, and I started to learn that what is happening with me happens to others too. Mimi left home when she told her father about being transgender. By all accounts he was a terrifying man, and having spent so long in a masculine environment, including homelife where he no longer had his wife, he found it hard to accept. His non-acceptance turned to anger quite regularly, and Mimi showed me scars on her arms where her father had beaten and burnt her. She would be fearful each time he would return from the pub, not knowing which version of her father would come home. If he had been in an argument, or if his team had lost the football he would take his frustration out on her. At one point he locked her in their cupboard under the stairs before passing out. She didn't manage to escape until the following morning.

"To be honest, I think he was suffering from PTSD but was too proud to seek help"

"PTSD?"

"Post-traumatic stress disorder. He saw some awful things whilst on duty, things that would affect even the strongest of people"

"Did he confide in anyone at all?"

"No one. I used to hear him cry sometimes from the neighbouring room but I knew that he wouldn't want to talk to me about it. Our relationship wasn't close enough for that to happen. Me being transgender might have been the straw that broke the camel's back and he took his frustrations out on me"

"Do you still speak to him?"

"Not for a few years now. How can I? I hope that he has found help but alcohol seemed to be the answer for every question that hung over him"

"Would you try and get back in touch?"
"I did once. I sent him a letter to try and rebuild but I never received a reply"

Mimi continued to tell me more about her family, and how her mum's sister had moved to Canada, meaning they had lost touch too. She found one of her cousins on Facebook recently but was too worried about what would happen if she tried to get in contact. Once her story was over I spontaneously clutched her hand. She brushed this off quickly and turned and smiled at me.

"Not many people have sat and listened to me before Joey. I'm sorry that you have ended up in this situation, but it's nice to meet someone who actually cares. You do need to be careful in here though. I know you held me through sympathy, but even a gesture like that could lead to one of us becoming the target this evening".
"I'm sorry" I said
"Don't be silly. There's nothing wrong with it, it's just these may not understand why someone is friends with the freak"
"The freak? They call you that?"
"Them and a million others"
"Have you had trouble here before?" I ask her
"A lot yeah. It's normally just a case of being verbally abused, but there have been times when I have been dragged from my bed"
"I'm so sorry"

"It's become part of life I'm afraid. As I said though, there are places better than Gold's. One day I will have somewhere safe"

"Are the other hostels like this, in terms of looks and set up and that?"

"Night shelters are all very much the same. You never know what will happen during your time there. This one is self-referral, so it does differ from some of the others in London"

"What's the difference?"

"Self-referral means you can call or drop in yourself. There's not always enough room though so I'd say you're lucky to be in here tonight"

"Gloria said I took the last space"

"There we go see. Tomorrow may be different. Most offer hostels require you to be referred by a council or something. Many are run by the church, but from what you told me I feel that the you might feel the church won't accept you. You might be lucky and get referred though, but on your first evening in London that'd be a miracle quite frankly"

"Where else do you stay?"

"On the streets is the only real option. Because of the way I look it's hard to fit in with groups in the homeless community, so I try and find somewhere quiet and blend into the background. The City is the preferred location for that. Most of the people there are lawyers and bankers so once it hits 6pm it gets a lot quieter"

"Where is the city?". I ask this as I've heard of it, but no one has ever told me where.

"Aim for St Paul's Cathedral. To me that's the best landmark. You've got St Pauls, Bank and Fleet Street. All good places to hideaway if you need. Hiding in plain sight".

"Cool, thanks. I'll go tomorrow and see it. I've never been before. Will you come and show me?"

"I'd be delighted" replies Mimi. "Now though, I am going to get some rest. I barely slept last night, and I want to hide away in case any of the drunks come in and need someone to take their frustrations out on. I'd recommend you do the same"

I check my phone and notice that it's nearly half nine at night. The artificial lamps and the lack of natural light through the windows makes you lose track of time. I guess in this other world time doesn't really matter anyway. I look round for a plug socket but there doesn't seem to be any in this room. The beds squeak loudly as I clamber into my top bunk. After throwing my bag at my feet I lay back and try to forget where I am.

~

Forgetting where you are is harder than you imagine when you are surrounded by unknown people in an unknown room. I have managed to drift off to sleep briefly, however I am woken up by the raised voices nearby. I shift my weight so that I am leaning on my right-hand side, and partially open my eyes. I know that I was warned not to do this, but I'm feeling more vulnerable with my back to people. I poke my head over the corner and look down to see Mimi asleep below, hibernating under all her blankets. As well as being bright, the room is also incredibly hot. There is no breeze coming through and being the middle of summer the mugginess is quite uncomfortable. Looking through my squinted eyes, I see that the room is full of people now. Half of the people are in bed, with one man shifting around uncomfortably on the bunks opposite. He seems to be thrashing about a fair bit. The main noise though is coming from the men nearest the door who were the first to enter after Mimi.

It takes me some time to figure out what's going on as they are huddled close, but when one man moves the answer becomes obvious. They have kept one of the soup spoons and are now using a lighter to heat it from underneath. One subject that we learnt in a Mrs Moxley tutor time was about the effects of drugs. I remember it clearly as I was shaken by the documentary which was shown. There was footage of drug dens, and pictures of people who had been found unconscious, surrounded by drugs. It was meant to shock us into not falling into that way of life, and believe me, after watching it I definitely didn't want to take them myself. Watching a programme about heroin and spice is one thing but waking up and seeing a group of strangers twice your age cooking heroin in a makeshift manner absolutely terrified me. I felt sick and wanted to run away, but I was trapped. When a needle was produced to suck up the liquid I couldn't watch anymore. I turned over to face the wall instead as I had been advised to do. I should have never have turned around in the first place. Once again, I had found a new rock bottom.

The drug taking went on for over two hours, and for the whole time I faced the wall, trying to hide the movement caused by my crying. There were also some very drunk people in here and arguments broke out spontaneously every few minutes. The whole situation is terrifying, and I can't wait to make my escape in the morning.

The voices continue, and the atmosphere gets even more unsettling. I can't rest so peer down the side of the bed nearest to the wall. There is just enough room to be able to get a view of below. Mimi is staring up and spots me straight away. She puts a finger to her lips to remind me not to make too many movements.

"Why don't they do anything about the drugs?" I ask quietly. She slowly sits up so that her face is only around a foot away from my own.

"There's no regulations on alcohol Joey, and this has led to people exploiting the rules even further. Others are so much better than this one. The landscape is changing" she replies, continuing to stare straight at me. She even seems too afraid to blink.

"Why do they do it?"

“To escape. It’s the one thing we all want to do. You might escape by walking, or by trying to sleep through. Others escape through narcotics and whiskey. John over there is on pills to control his psychosis and trembling. The problem is, drinking may seem like a solution, but it is in fact making their anxiety and situation worse”. I assume John was the man shaking nervously on his bed earlier. He has since calmed.

“What you need to remember also Joey is that drugs are the reason why some people have ended up here. Addiction is a massive cause of homelessness, whether it is drinks, drugs, gambling or whatever”

“Why aren’t they being helped?”

“They are, people are trying to connect, but a click of the fingers won’t solve the problem overnight. There’s more of us each year, and for every successful rehabilitation there is probably another two people entering the system”

I’m not sure what to say. I think my questioning is making Mimi feel uncomfortable, so I lay back and close my eyes hoping to get a bit more sleep before the morning. I imagine this is what prison feels like. It’s noisy, it’s bright and I don’t find it welcoming. Of course, I am free to leave, but feel that this would be a more negative alternative. If I am going to prepare myself for more nights like this I really need to at least try and last through the first night. After about twenty minutes the noise quietens slightly and I drift off back into a light sleep, however it isn’t long before I get woken by some movement from nearby. I open my eyes and can feel something hit my feet. I turn over and open my eyes. One of the men from in the dorm has come across and has my holdall, tipping it upside-down and pouring the contents out onto my blanket. I sit up quickly and try and pull it away from him.

“What are you doing?” I shout at him.
“Go back to sleep” he says, snarling at me. I try and take things back from him, but he already has my phone and my money in his hands. I should have stuffed it under my pillow and I hate myself for being naïve enough to leave it so open.
“You’re new” he says, with his arms held out of reach.
“So?”
“If you’re new then you don’t know how things work. You’ll understand eventually though”. He steps closer and smiles at me. “You’ll be fine. Young boy like you will be able to earn a few bob”
“By doing what?”

I notice Mimi has stood up and she grabs the man from behind.

“Give him his stuff back. You don’t need to do this”
“Oh, fuck off you freak” he shouts, overpowering Mimi and pushing her to the floor. As she tries to stand he kicks her stomach and she winces to the ground struggling for breath. I jump down off of my top bunk and try and pull him away, but a second man is now grabbing more of my items. It’s impossible to fight off both of them, and the

other people in the dorm are silently watching, either unable or unwilling to offer support.

"If you wanna survive kid I know a few men who'd spend good money to spend some time with you" says the first attacker again.

"No way am I doing that. Give me my stuff"

By now my phone and wallet has been passed to the second man. He has also taken my charging cables and is heading towards the door. I stand in front of him and try to grab my items, but he is taller and much stronger than me and easily pushes me to the ground. The other man is crouched down with one knee on Mimi's back, and he has her hair in his right hand, pulling it back so that her head is pulled into the air. She is trying to say something but is unable to get the words out.

As I reach forward again my attacker grabs my arm and throws me hard against the wall. The sink strikes me on the lower part of my spine, and my head is thrown back and hits the broken mirror with a thud. Some more shards become loose and fall towards my feet and I can feel blood running down my face. I become disorientated and can't focus properly. I try to stand but am pushed back down. The man on top of Mimi stands up and gives her another firm kick to the stomach. She curls into a ball and screams out in pain. Both men are now exiting the room but I can't gain the energy to stand up and chase them. I lay on the cold floor praying for someone to save me. I daren't move for the fear of more blows being thrown at me. Blood is now staining my t-shirt and my cap is on the floor a few feet away. I lay flat on my back with my eyes closed waiting until I have heard their footsteps disappear down the stairs.

Once I am certain the coast is clear, I slowly stand and hold the sink to steady myself. I turn the taps on full and rinse the cut, holding a paper towel to it until the bleeding stops. I have the beginning of a black eye appearing already and the skin is red and glistening under the water. I lean down and take some sips directly from the tap, and then go to see if Mimi is okay. Upon turning around I notice that she has gone. I call her name but she doesn't seem to be near. My holdall has also been taken so the only money which I have to my name is that which was in my trouser pockets. This amounts to about seven pounds.

The other residents in the dorm are pretending to be asleep. I don't know why these people attacked me as I didn't engage with them at all when they were entering. The three who took the heroin earlier are still around, with one in particular looking very fragile against the wall. Why didn't any of the others try to help? Deciding enough was enough, I had to get out of Gold's. With no belongings left apart from the clothes that I am in, I head out of the room in search of Mimi. My head is throbbing and my balance still hasn't been fully restored. I stumble down the staircase to the ground floor. I head into the reception area but Gloria must have gone home a long time ago. I am not sure who is in charge of the shelter during the small hours but the room is deserted. Through a frosted window at the rear I can see two figures smoking cigarettes. They both look male, but I am too frightened to head out in case it is our attackers. Instead, I turn myself back into the hall and head straight for the front door. I want to find Mimi but her knowledge of the streets around Vauxhall are much stronger than mine so I know my chances are slim. I pull my cap over my head and wince at the pain as it makes contact with my cut. At the front door I pull a leaflet off from the noticeboard which has been re-nailed to the wall after my mishap last night. I needed something with the shelter's address on just on the small chance that I would need to return here in desperation. I could hear some more movements from upstairs and knew that now was the time to head back out into the open. I pulled the door, stepped out and slammed it hard behind me.

Twelve

The artificial light and the terror in that dormitory room have made me lose my sense of direction and purpose. The thought of having to spend any more time in there made me feel frightened so I had to head to the streets to escape. In that dormitory room it still felt like the dead of night but leaving the night shelter I noticed the heavy traffic passing through Vauxhall. I asked someone for the time and they dismissively told me that it is just before 7am before walking on quickly. My head was throbbing from the attack, and I have no money or phone. I tried to report it to Gloria, but there was someone else there as I left, and they told me to write it up in an incident book. I don't think any good will come of it, however I obliged. I was too scared to stay for breakfast.

For the next hour I wandered around the streets trying to figure out where Mimi could have gone. She knew London far better than I, and it felt like I had lost her for good. I liked her and hoped that I would bump into her quickly. I needed her guidance. On my travels I passed a few new places that I hadn't seen yesterday, but there was no excitement. Elephant and Castle was nowhere near as intriguing as I thought and was just an urban sprawl of offices. The Imperial War Museum was equally as disappointing. These are the things that should be exciting me, but instead it feels like a dream state. I am physically here but mentally drained. I continued to walk aimlessly, trying to ignore the hunger. I felt dirty and unwanted. I pick up every lose coin that I find, and by the time I reach the London Eye I have eighty-seven pence. I really don't want to lower myself to beg, but I feel like I have no choice. Sitting in Jubilee Gardens, under the shadow of the eye, I place a discarded coffee cup on the floor and sit next to it. There must be thousands of people around, despite it being so early, and yet I am ignored by nearly every single one of them. Across the water stand the Houses of Parliament. If there was ever a metaphor needed for class divide, then this would be it. Within two hundred metres you had prominent people claiming expenses, making the decisions about my life. I just want to be treated like a human but I'm getting less attention than the nearby dog tied to a lamp post. It's not even a nice dog and its left ear is all haggard.

I'm feeling very exposed here and decide it will be best for me to move on. I'm devastated about being assaulted last night. A few people have given me change though and I have just less than four pounds so hopefully this will be enough for a coffee and something to eat at least. It's a surprisingly warm day in London today, and the Thames is a lot bluer than when I first saw it. I'm glad that I have still got the cap that Gloria gave me as I don't want to add sunstroke to my growing list of problems. I'm thankful for her allowing me to stay last night, but this evening I am going to try a different approach. If it stays warm I may shelter in a park overnight. The one good thing that I have discovered this morning is that bus stops have maps. They only cover the immediate area; however, you can get a sense of direction from them and at least know where you are. This morning though I feel that sticking by the river is the best option. Trying to find a distraction from my plight, I lose myself in the street entertainers on the South Bank. It's as Mimi said last night, we all just need something to help us escape. I am fearful I may have another panic attack if I do not keep myself calm, and despite being in the worst situation possible I need to try and keep myself composed. The entertainers help with this for a short while, however after a while I start feeling very self-aware. I have a sense that the crowds are watching me rather than the person doing juggling tricks at the front. I wander to the river and lean over the railing to look down into the water. Small waves lap at the shingle covered bank, and I use them to time my breathing. I feel very small in this city, and in each direction the skyscrapers appear daunting. The main ones are to my right. The Shard is on the same side as me, hidden partially behind the OXO Tower. On the opposite bank you can see mismatched glassed buildings glinting in the sun. And then I spot it. St Pauls' Cathedral stands prominently nearby. Why didn't I remember this before? Mimi said this was one of her favourite areas, and I know now that this is where I should head. I put the change in my pocket and loosened my cap slightly so that it stopped putting pressure on my cut. I'm a bit worried that I need to shower and that I'm starting to smell a bit so make a mental note to try and find somewhere this afternoon.

~

I reach St Paul's at around midday, having slowly meandered there via the Millennium Bridge. I'm feeling incredibly lonely, so I am glad to see that there is a crowd at the bottom of the cathedral steps. There are barriers set up to keep the public back, and every inch is taken up of by the crowd which must be at least five people deep. I decide to remain close as I am intrigued as to what is going on. I sit down on the flagstone floor, leaning back against a lamppost. My empty coffee cup is again sat out in front of me to collect any change that may be offered. A helicopter buzzes overhead and there are many TV crews present. It's hard to figure out why all these people are here, and I don't feel confident to ask. I am not looking my best and have dried blood still on my head around the cut. My clothes are dirty, and I feel very unclean.

After a few minutes, a familiar voice comes from behind.

"Good to see yer again" it says. The accent is unmistakable, and I turn around to see The Nomad leaning over me.

"Hey! It's good to see you too! How's things?"

“Aye the same, the same. What’s going on here?” He said, nodding towards the throngs of people.
“Absolutely no idea”
“It’s probably nothing yer know. There’s always a crowd here when something is going on. The power of human curiosity. One person is intrigued and stands and waits. More start to join to see what the first person is looking at, and before you know it, it looks like that’
“But the TV people are here too”
“It’s London. Everything in London is exaggerated”.

I sit with The Nomad for ages. The conversation doesn’t always flow but I go into full detail about the night I spent at Gold’s. He tells me that similar has happened to him, and he knows of many who have had their possessions stolen in a hostel or night shelter. He tried to compare me to a new born lamb in a field of sheep. The thieves, or foxes, will always go for the weakest and most vulnerable. It’s an easy win for the fox, and the fox doesn’t care what mess is left behind. I tell him about Mimi also, and he seems genuinely sad that she has disappeared from my life so soon.

“She sounds like one of the good ones. She’ll be back, son, she’ll be back”. I admire his optimism, although for some reason I am surprised that they have never met. I just assumed that all homeless people sort of knew each other. It’s odd that I am now the common connection between the two.

Doorway 54

The crowd start cheering, and I excitedly stand up to see what is happening. At the top of the stairs I can see someone waving to the crowds. I'm too short to see who it is, and The Nomad laughs as I push through people like a maniac. People mutter as I push past them, but I fight my way to the front. At the top of the steps a few members of the Royal Family are leaving the cathedral. Prince Harry is here along with his wife. William and Kate aren't about though but I recognise some other royals but can't remember all their names. Rather than getting straight in to their cars, they make their way around the semi-circular crowd shaking hands. I manage to grab a handshake off Harry but within moments he has gone again. Others are trying to take selfies and hand out flowers.

I slope off back to The Nomad.

"How the other half live, eh" he says, rolling a cigarette. "I knew you weren't on holiday by the way"

I'd completely forgotten that I told him I was from Denmark.

"Sorry. I don't quite know why I told you that"
"That's OK. I've met so many young people that I can see the fear of being new and alone in their eyes. So, what's your story?"

I'm losing count of the times that I have told people about why I am here over the last twenty-four hours, but I want as many people to understand so spend twenty minutes telling him. By the time I have finished the outside of St Paul's has started to clear and workmen in high visibility jackets are sweeping the area around us in formation. At the end I thank The Nomad for listening.

"I may not be able to offer more than an ear so it's my pleasure" he says smiling.
"I'm sorry by the way. I've been so focussed on myself that I don't really know anything about you. I don't even know your name. All I know is that you come from Glasgow"
"Let's find somewhere to sit and I'll tell you everything. I know a nice wee place not far from here. I'm meeting people outside there later, so I can give you a tour on the way"

I stand up in unison with The Nomad and let him guide me away from the dispersing crowds and across the City. We pass down Ludgate Hill and onto Fleet Street. The Nomad points out one of his old resting places. It's the door of a private dentists. It's not set back far from the street, but he says the warmth from the extractor fan of the café next door means that it's more comfortable than other places nearby. I make a mental note in case I ever need it. Fleet Street is full of grand buildings, with most ground level areas owned by cafés, sandwich shops and sushi takeaway places. Each building has at least four floors, and the names on the windows suggest they are all owned by law firms, stockbrokers and banks. Some old text is still visible on a few of the buildings, remnants of the time when this was the centre of the media. The area is heaving with city workers during the lunchtime rush and many seem oblivious to the two of us walking between them. The small side streets see vans and taxis pulling into them from all angles, and I nearly get knocked down on at least three occasions.

"If you keep going straight up that way you'll get to The Strand, I assume you know of it?" asks the Nomad.
"Only from Monopoly. It's one of the red ones"
"Right. Well anyway, there are some good spots to collect money up there. Lots of theatres up that way and when people are in a good mood after a show they tend to me more willing to give. Be careful though, especially as a new face on the block. It's competitive y'see and they may try and drive yer out. Best to try and get to know some of 'em"

I thank him for this information and dodge a cyclist who swings by unexpectedly in front of us. We continue walking for about fifteen minutes before we come across a pub with an outside seating area. It's called The Old Cheddar Cheese and looks like it has stood here for years. It is filled with a few office workers but is quiet enough for us to not really stand out. It's set back down a side road off of where Fleet Street and The Strand meet.

"Here we are" he says, taking a seat on one of the wooden tables out the front.
"Are we OK to be here?"
"Aye, I know the landlord. I, er, helped him with some stock once"

The Nomad doesn't strike me as someone who would be a key part of a supply chain, but I chose to ignore this as it's probably best not to ask. He asks me to keep the table whilst he goes inside. He reappears shortly after carrying two drinks and two bags of pork scratchings. I've never had pork scratchings before, but I would eat anything solid right now. They're a bit weird, and somehow soft and crunchy at the same time. There's a lot of salt on them so once finished I find myself gasping for a drink. I pick up my cola and take a large swig. Instead of a refreshing cold drink I get a mouthful of something that tastes a bit weird. I instinctively pull a weird face.

"You okay, son?" he asks.
"Yes, thank you. Just it tastes a bit different"
"Oh aye, there's a bit of rum in there. It'll help to keep you warm"

It burns my throat, so I'm not convinced how small the 'bit' of rum is, and if anything, it makes me thirstier. I am grateful to The Nomad though.

"You were going to tell me how you ended up here" I remind him, whilst scratching at the loosening paint on the table.

"Ah aye, sorry. Where do you want me to start?"

"Wherever you want me to know from"

"OK, I'll be brief as if I tell you the lot you'll probably run a mile"

This makes me a bit nervous, but I smile politely and ask him to continue.

"I got married at twenty. I met a girl on a night out on my eighteenth birthday and she was magic. She worked in the same office building as me as well, which was lucky, and we got on well. We moved in together about six months later. Now, when you get comfortable you start living outside of your means, and we started spending too much on credit cards. I was afraid to lose her though, so I got into more and more debt. Just before the Christmas she announces that she was pregnant, and that reason was enough for her to want to get married. Our daughter was born in the July, and we had set a date to marry in the November. I'd never really been keen on marriage but making her happy made me happy. Y'know what lasses are like. They plan their wedding for years so rather than something small we got married in this massive castle in the Highlands. It cost a bloody fortune, and her family didn't really have the means to pay much so more went on credit cards. We honeymooned on a cruise ship around the coast of Spain. It was all very quick but once it was all over I went back to work and tried my best to support her"

"What's your daughter's name?"
"Holly. She's five now. Not long started school"
"When did you last see her?"
"I've not seen her since she just turned four. Y'see, the week after her birthday party the company I worked for went into administration. As I was one of the lowest on the ladder I was one of the first to be let go. Didn't get hardly any redundancy pay, and what I did have went on paying the credit card bills. I tried finding work again but could never hold anything down, and it caused a lot of troubles between us. I started drinking and one night I went too far"
"You didn't hit her, did you?"
"God no. I ain't one of them. I just started shouting at her. It wasn't her fault, but I needed someone to blame and she was just there. The following morning, I woke up to find her Da' standing over me. He was a giant. Before I could even apologise, he had picked me up and thrown me out of the house. I thought he was going to kill me. He told me not to come back and I never did. I wanted to. I wanted to still be near Holly, but it was just too unsafe"
"So why London?"

"Just chance. After leaving the house I went to the service station on the outskirts of Glasgow and started begging people for a lift. As you can imagine, no one really wanted to help, but one lorry driver offered me a trip down to London in return for some lifting of his goods"

"What did you do when you got here?"

"Pretty much the same as you. I was a bit older of course, but at the end of the day you're still the new kid in London. I only knew Glasgow and was completely lost. Spent some time in hostels, went through the same experience you did a couple of times. I have been robbed, beaten and abused on numerous occasions. I was told there were some places that could help but the sheer number of people meant that places were often full or had waiting lists. Most of what I've learnt is from the homeless network. It's a fragile community, but a community all the same"

"I'm sorry" I said again. I'd only been here a day and I can't imagine what The Nomad must have gone through to be here with me. Her daughter deserved a dad but it's never easy for things to be okay.

"Aye, you're alright, son. Shit happens, as they say. I pray that yer have better luck than me. You're far too young to have been rejected so much"

This hit me hard. The Nomad was right and the realisation that a lifetime of rejection was to blame stunned me to silence. Rejection. That's all it is for all of us. With each rejection you lose your grip on normal life, down a seemingly endless slide.

I had been so engrossed in The Nomad's story that I suddenly felt very self-conscious during this silence. The Nomad has a very animated face, and when he talks you kind of get lost into his world. The downside of this is that when he stops you are suddenly thrown back into the real world. I have never had an alcoholic drink in a pub before, and this is down to the fact that I would almost certainly get asked for identification if I even thought about trying it. Despite approaching sixteen, I have always looked a bit young for my age. Today though no one seems to be raising eyebrows in my direction, so either nobody actually cares, or I have become so dishevelled in the last twenty-four hours that I have aged considerably. This doesn't stop me feeling uncomfortable though, and I suggest to The Nomad that I might head off for a bit. I need to walk to clear my head again as another wave of anxiety has swept across my mind. It feels as if I am developing a mild form of agoraphobia or social anxiety. I hated my night in the night shelter and I am still physically and emotionally beaten. I don't want to return to an enclosed space, yet I also don't want to really interact with the people around me here. I mention my concerns to The Nomad.

"Aye, that sounds about right. People think it's a slow slippery spiral to the bottom, but as you now know, it's more like stumbling over a cliff edge"

"It feels like every decision I make is the wrong one"
"At times there isn't a right decision, and it's about picking the one that will cause the least damage"
"I wish I had picked that one last night rather than have to suffer the abuse"
"But what would the alternative be like? If you weren't in there then that person wouldn't have beaten you, but you may have been in an underpass instead. The same could have happened there and the consequences worse"

The Nomad had a weird way of looking on the bright side, and it is probably a self defence mechanism that has developed within him over his year of living rough. I tried to smile and thank him, but my tank was empty.

"Son" he said as I stood, "I know it doesn't seem like it, but things will be alright. To most you may seem like a faceless boy but to me you are a human with a story. I'll be back here again tomorrow afternoon and I want you to join me. It might be best if you're not here when the people I am meeting soon arrive. I want to keep an eye out for you and not put you in any danger"

I am not entirely sure what he means by this, but I appreciate the caring nature in which he said it. I decide to leave The Nomad for the day and head off in search of a park to lie in. He tells me to head north, gesturing with his drink in the direction of Chancery Lane.

“See you tomorrow” I say as I head towards the nearby zebra crossings, across to the front of the Royal Courts of Justice. There is some sort of protest happening outside. I’m unsure as to what it is but seems to involve Donald Trump visiting Britain.

“Aye, see you tomorrow” replies The Nomad from behind.

As I cross Fleet Street and head up Chancery Lane I start to feel a bit lightheaded. Maybe alcohol isn’t for me, and even though I only had a small amount it isn’t doing me any favours. The fact that I haven’t eaten properly also doesn’t help. I have now completed my first full day in London and it hasn’t been the fairytale that I expected. I don’t know why I thought it would all be so easy, and I hate that I was so naive. Chancery Lane is surprisingly busy, and I am paranoid that I do not fit in here. I can sense everyone staring at me, so I look down to the floor and shuffle on as quickly as possible. I am missing having my phone to use for directions. Thinking about my phone brings on the realisation that I did not receive any notifications on it for the entire evening before it was taken. My parents may have still been working it out between them, but how can they not even try and communicate? I had nothing from my friends either, but those bridges were probably burned during the glass throwing day in the Tuck Shop. Even when I went back to sit my exams they barely spoke to me. I'm stood on the corner of Holborn and contemplate my next move. As it stands, the only person who cares for me is The Nomad, and even he seemed to suggest that I was better off away from him for the afternoon. I might try and find him this evening though. As of this point in time though, I had no one.

~

I had continued to walk for a further half an hour before finally stumbling into a grassy area where time seemed to stand still. The central park area was surrounded by tall grand looking houses, many of which had been converted into offices. I walked around the outskirts looking through the windows at the lofty ceilings and chandeliers. Inside, secretaries and administrators are furiously tapping away at keyboards, their desks laden with files and paperwork. When I was at school I always fancied the idea of working in an office eventually, mainly as they all seemed to have weekends off, yet looking at these people made me lose a bit of faith in that idea.

I walk around the buildings slowly, thinking of what must be going on in each one. Many have oil paintings on the wall and large marble fireplaces. It's all very grand. On one occasion I end up getting a little too close and do not notice that I am being watched by a male worker from the inside. At the desk behind him sits a lady in a fantastic green and gold Caribbean-style dress, and the sight of it reminds me of Angelica. By now she will be somewhere on the other side of the Atlantic, oblivious to my plight. I must have given these two a shock. Imagine being at work and looking up to see a dishevelled boy with blood visible under the peak of a dirty baseball cap looking back at you through the window. I hadn't expected any sympathy from them and when the man approached the window I backed away. He was quite short and plump, and he had small metal rimmed glasses on. His royal blue suit fitted perfectly and must have been custom made. He wore a white shirt underneath and his pocket square and tie were a matching deep red. I heard him bang on the glass as I dashed across the road, and as I turned back at the entrance of the grass square he was still looking out. He stood glaring at me from behind the glass with hands on hips. He reminded me a bit of a stereotypical ex-army major who had not lost his idea of authority and power over others. Another one added to the list of people who don't seem to care about my life.

The square I had found myself in was Russell Square. I only know this from the noticeboard situated just inside the entrance by the lawn. The sun was hitting only about half of the park, so it seemed the perfect place to lay on the grass. I could switch between the sun and the shade depending on the intensity of the heat. The notices informed me that the park would remain open until 10pm, so I planned to spend a good few hours here. Finding a patch of grass in the sun, I took off my cap and placed it over my face as I lay down. My hair felt greasy and tangled and my skin oily. Laying in a park with your eyes closed is a pleasant experience, and I would recommend it if you need some time to recuperate from any troubling thoughts. For me, I am in a small park in central London, yet with my eyes closed you can shut away so much of the world. Instead, your mind focuses on the noises around you. From my patch I can hear songbirds in the trees, and snatches of conversation from people passing by. I don't understand much of the conversations as many focus around areas of which I have no knowledge or interest. Someone is talking about the DOW Index, which I think is something to do with banks or similar. Another lady is talking to her baby in that weird high-pitched voice that parents always use. Laying here I start having deep thoughts about how funny life can be. Each person I hear has their own story and could have been born anywhere in the world; They could have gone to a variety of schools and universities, and held down all sorts of job; Every decision that each of us has made has led to us all being in the same small park at the same time on the same day. If I was a strong believer in fate and karma I would probably be less anxious than I am, and I could be content in the fact that something good will come. As it stands though, for the next few hours as I lie there, drifting in and out of a light sleep, nothing changes.

I decide to leave the park just after the sun has set as the air has started to get cold. I have no idea of the time, but I guess it must be around 9pm. I dig around my pockets and count the change I have left. It amounts to just under four pounds, so I pop into a coffee shop on the corner of the square to get a snack and a cheap drink. I polish both of quickly and it still leaves me feeling rather unsatisfied. I need to decide about where to stay tonight. I cannot face another night in the shelter just yet. The thought of leaving myself open for another attack terrifies me. I am not strong enough to be around drug taking, and the aggressive residents there really make me fear for my safety. I've heard stories so far about people who have experienced worse than me and feel that the next attack could be more vicious and with longer lasting effects. Part of me wants to find The Nomad but this carries its own risks. I wonder where Mimi is? I hope she is OK.

In the end I wander back towards St Pauls until I find myself stood back on Fleet Street. There is a stand full of evening newspapers, so I take a handful to use for warmth if I find myself outside overnight. Would a subway be the best bet? I don't know but decide to try and find the nearest one. I pass down towards Blackfriars and consider hiding away in a corner near the station there. The station is odd, and the platforms span the river. Inside, there doesn't seem to be a space where it would be acceptable to stay, and the station staff eye me suspiciously as I pass through. This isn't good enough. I want to be warm and safe, but I don't want to be somewhere so obvious. I think back to the walk with The Nomad earlier and decide to take his advice about the doorway of the private dentists that we passed this afternoon. With any luck he will also be there tonight so at least I wouldn't be alone.

It only takes a few minutes to arrive in front of the daunting building. The doorway has a floor of small red tiles and I set my stack of newspapers down to one side. Before settling I need to confirm to myself that this is safe, so I cross the road and watch for a few minutes. Some revellers from the nearby pubs pass by me, but the alcohol in their blood seems to distract them from noticing that I am here. I look across to my home for the night. The firm names on the upper windows all sound very upper class. Just from my viewpoint I can see many lawyers' names that sound as if they are from period dramas. Forsythe & Belcher Chambers and Bates & Bishop LLP are present, as are Montague, Blythe, Harris and Stone, all in the gold writing across the higher windows. Despite doing nothing all afternoon, the stress of my situation has made me feel the need to switch off from today. I cross back over the road and slump into the doorway. I read the posters in the dentists' window and wonder how people have so much money to spend on the things I've never even considered. There's all kinds of whacky therapies being offered, like laser teeth whitening and 'Hollywood' caps. The prices are eye-watering.

Doorway 54

Fleet Street has completely quietened down, and the buildings glow with an orange coat that is spreading from the street lamps that are evenly spaced down the gradually sloping road. The floor is hard, and despite the extractor fan blowing warm air, it is still quite cold. I unfold some newspapers to act as a makeshift mattress however they do little to soften the surface. I open the remaining papers and place them on me to try and generate more warmth, but the breeze causes them to blow out of position quickly. I am hoping I see a turn in fortunes tomorrow, but I am not feeling positive. Tomorrow is the day before my birthday and yet here I am, in the doorway of number 54 Fleet Street with very little hope. My family have gone, my friends won't notice, and I will be dismissed by the passing public in the blink of an eye. I start to cry once more and wonder if any of this is worth it. What is the fucking point? Having found a new rock bottom, I close my eyes and try to sleep.

Thirteen

I am awoken seemingly early the following morning. I feel more rested today, and the doorway of 54 Fleet Street was much more bearable than the night in the hostel. I think I could have stayed asleep for a couple more hours, but the City was already a hive of activity. Police cars and ambulances were passing down towards Blackfriars Station, and the pavements were full of workers hurrying themselves to the many surrounding offices. I asked the nearest person the time, and a tall man in a suit informed me that it had just past 8am. He looked down at me, tried to smile, and then stepped over me and through the black door behind me, nearly catching my head with his umbrella.

Before I went to sleep I had placed another empty coffee cup at the edge of the doorway, and I was surprised that people had been so generous without me having to do anything. I poured the change onto an opened newspaper and was happy to see that I had been given over six pounds in loose change, mostly coppers however a few pound coins and silvers were included. I remember passing a MacDonald's on Fleet Street when walking with The Nomad so pulled my cap down tightly and got ready to set off to find it. The newspapers that I had placed over me were long gone, blown away in the overnight breeze that powers down between the tall buildings on either side of most London streets. The remaining papers had worked well as a pillow and mattress and stopped the cold from the tiles passing onto me. I was feeling okay, however a coffee and some hot breakfast was all I wanted right now.

Despite being desperately hungry, I decided to drop into the chemist next door to pick up some cheap deodorant and a pack of mints. I felt disgusting and desperately needed a shower and a toothbrush. As these weren't available, I'd just have to try and mask the odours that were no doubt lingering around me.

I ordered as much food as I felt I could eat in McDonalds and sat with my breakfast of hash browns and bacon McMuffins for over an hour. Taking a window seat, I watched the world outside, and thought about the stories behind the people passing by. It's easier to think about the tales behind the people when you are at the bottom yourself. When I was living back at home I would notice homeless people, but at that time that's all they were. They were just a figure in a doorway and I assumed they were all heavy drinkers or drug users. I made a promise to myself there and then that if I ever got out of this situation I would make it my mission to give something back to help those in need, despite not having the help myself. My train of thought was constantly being interrupted by sirens as vehicles continued to head down the road sporadically, clearly dealing with an incident nearby.

I needed to decide as to what to do with my day today and hoped to spend some of it in the same way as yesterday. The weather was bright, and I could feel the warmth on my face through the window. I picked up a discarded map from the table next to me and studied for a new park. The map was from one of the many open top tour bus companies that operates around the capital and it was as full of adverts for attractions as it was for the map itself. I had never realised how close some of the river landmarks were to me now, and I decided on a plan to walk down to the Millennium Bridge, going past the Tate Modern en route, and onto Tower Bridge. These would be tourist hot spots, especially as today was a Saturday, and hopefully I will be able to collect more change whilst relaxing in a clearing. Wiping my mouth of ketchup, I folded the map into my pocket and headed back to Blackfriars bridge. I passed number 54 and the dentists was now open. There was no indication that a vulnerable boy had called that home last night. I'd return there this evening, and ultimately wake up there on my seventeenth birthday.

~

Blackfriars Bridge isn't my favourite, I'll tell you that now. At this hour you must have your wits about you unless you want to be mown down by a group of joggers, or even the cyclists who pass as if they are in the Tour de France. There are also high numbers of businessmen on hands free calls that obviously can't wait until they actually get to their office. It leads them to weave across the paths without any consideration of others. Others are busy looking at their screens typing and nearly walking straight into the middle of the road. They are probably tweeting articles about how millennials are addicted to technology. I reach the centre of the bridge and look out across the Thames in the direction of the London Eye, wondering how many miles I must have covered on foot since my arrival. The water is again dirty and failing to reflect the blueness of the sky. The Oxo Tower is now on my left, and the South Bank is busy with tourists taking photos on its jetty. To my right I can see some commotion on the northern bank of the river, and the reason for the police presence earlier. An incident tent has been set up on a road that is just a few yards from the main Victoria Embankment. It has been cordoned off with blue and white tape. Officers stand at all corners, and the public are being kept well away from the scene. There are building works taking place on that side of the Thames however it seems that the workers have been sent away from the area. I am intrigued to have a look, but as I am feeling a little uneasy I decide to continue on my journey.

The Tate Modern is located just behind Blackfriars Station, and I am there fairly quickly. Set back slightly from the barriers between path and water, the Tate is a huge building that towers across the area. It's only when you get up close that the full scale of it hits you. The people outside seem to shrink when close to its walls, and many school groups are sat patiently along the outside waiting for it to open. I'd quite like to go in and have a look around but there is not a chance that I would want to be near large groups of children right now. It will probably bring on an anxiety attack, and I might not be the most patient if they decide to get in my way either.

An Ice Cream van is already outside the gallery despite it being so early, and there seems to be a constant queue for it due to the ever-increasing heat from the sun. I would love to join them but decide that I need to use my change sparingly in case I fail in my attempts to secure more. I go back to watching the world go by and take my place on a metal bench outside the art gallery. Due to the heat, I have removed my cap, and this is now my coin collector. This is the busiest place that I have sat yet, but the money is not forthcoming. An hour later and I have only made a pound. I notice someone has put a Euro coin in as well, which isn't much use as I won't be travelling abroad anytime soon if things continue the way they are. Every couple of minutes a riverboat passes by. I always enjoyed trips to the harbours of southern England when on holiday as a kid, and again the water seems to relax and mesmerise me. I don't know if there is a name for being hypnotised by something natural, but seeing the high tide lap up against the concrete walls is akin to meditation in my book. It's weird to think that both my darkest and brightest moments involve water. Being back in my hometown and looking down into the churning river seems a long way mentally for me now, however the consequences that led to that time are far less worse than they are for me now. I hope that the Thames does not change it's meaning to me and I get the suicidal thoughts again. Coming to watch the waters pass has saved me this week I feel.

Fourteen waves a minute hit the banks. When a boat passes this rises to twenty. I count every single one. Each time they hit, a small splash of water is thrown up, but it never reaches the paths.

After around twenty minutes (judging by the three hundred and fifteen odd waves that have hit the wall), a large black lady with a wide smile and chunky gold necklace comes and sits next to me. I heard her arriving before I saw her due to her jewellery clinking. It was a bit like when we put a bell around the neck of our old cat to warn birds that they were on the hunt. This analogy is a bit unfair actually, as this woman looks kind. I turn to her and I am surprised that she is holding an ice cream out in my direction. She seems familiar, but I have no idea why.

"Foy you, honey" she says, waving the ice cream nearer to me, whilst simultaneously biting into the top of a Cornetto. Seeing people bite ice cream makes my teeth feel funny, but I'm salivating at the thought of the sweet treat.

"Thank you so much" I say, taking the cone in my right hand, "that's very kind of you"

"I'm sorry I didn't help you yesterday" she says solemnly. "I wanted to, it's just the timing just wasn't right"

Yesterday? I try to think where I may have seen her before. After the alcohol the day was a bit of a blur, despite it only being a very small amount. I hope I hadn't offended her somewhere. I try to reply tactfully.

"Oh, honestly don't worry. You being here today has made me feel a bit better already"

She smiles again, and I'm warmed by her kind face. Forget tactfulness, I'll ask her outright.

"I don't want to sound rude" I say, "but I can't recall where I saw you yesterday. It had been a stressful day you see so I'm sorry if I asked you for some money or was rude to you"

"You're a sweet boy. We didn't speak but you were in Russell Square in the afternoon"

"Yes, that's correct" I reply, still unsure who she was.

"You seemed in a bit of a daze and went around the streets looking inside all the houses. I was at a meeting with my solicitor, and when you came to our building he startled you and you went"

It suddenly clicked.

"You're the lady in the green and gold dress!" I say excitedly

"Yep that's me honey" she said, laughing. "I'm not surprised you don't remember me though, sat here in my shorts and sandals". She smiles again.

"It was a beautiful dress" I tell her.

"Thank you. I always wear my best when I am trying to seal a deal"

"What kind of deal is it that you were doing?"

"I'll tell you very soon, it's very complicated. In a nutshell though? I owned a failing café and am trying to reinvent it, change its purpose, and my solicitor is helping with all the legal things as that's not my strong point. No one wants to come and try my food anymore, and you can't run a business these days when it's making such a loss. I'm more of the Food Queen type anyway. I do some killer chicken dishes". She is laughing again. I bloody love her already.

"Whereabouts is your café?"

"It's down in Marylebone, just near the station there"

"Not the Italian one?" I ask, knowing that it probably wouldn't be

"No no, that's not mine but that is lovely there. Mine was on Bell Street, sort of in the other direction. I had to close the doors last month, but I want to keep the building and try something new"

"I hope it all works out. Do you know what type of thing it will be yet?"

"I have a few ideas baby, a few ideas"

We sit and eat the rest of our ice creams in silence. I use my sleeve to wipe the remnants from my chin. Some has dripped onto my trousers.

"Aside from the Food Queen, what name do you go by?" I ask, wiping off even more ice cream, this time off my jumper.

"Diana, officially, but my friends call me Dee Dee"

"Well, Diana, it's lovely to meet you. I'm Joseph, but my friends call me Joey"

"Honey, you will be Joey to me, and I'll be Dee Dee to you. Deal?"

"Deal!".

I can't stop smiling. Not only did she read my mind and buy me an ice cream, but she has shown more kindness to me than anyone has in a month. I mean, there is The Nomad, but I've only met him twice, Oh and Mimi of course. I reckon Dee Dee would love Mimi. I'm still wary of the other homeless people. After what some of them did to me, I don't trust anyone from my community fully just yet.

"You're such a sweet child. How old are you?"

"I'm sixteen tomorrow"

"No kidding! You poor thing. That is no age. My son was still just a baby to me when he was that age"

"I bet you think he's still your baby now though"

"I'm afraid he is no longer with us, but he will always be my baby"
"Oh, I'm so sorry, I didn't know"
"How were you to know? I'll tell you all about him someday. He was such a beautiful soul".

For one moment her eyes show a glimpse of sadness, but she appears well practiced in controlling the pain and snaps back towards me and places a hand on my knee.

"How did you track me down today, Dee Dee? London is a big place"
"It was simply by chance. Well, I say that, but do you believe in fate?"
"I'm not sure. Do you mean like horoscopes and things?"
"No not quite. I mean, sometimes things happen by chance, but as if they were always *meant* to happen?"
"In my situation I don't see how being made homeless was meant to happen, but meeting you is good"
"Your situation is not the result of you being a bad person. What I am saying is that maybe I was meant to see you again today. We often walk past the same person two days in a row, even in a city like London, but unless we recognise that face we may never know about it. I couldn't believe it when I saw you again"
"So, there is someone out there who made sure we met again?" I asked nervously. I was a bit apprehensive that Dee Dee was referring to religion and a higher power, but my family's connections with that landed me here in the

first place so I am not sure that I'd agree that only the good things can be attributed to a God.

"Not someone, but something. I don't know what"

"Maybe. I dunno"

"Anyway, and I need you to listen to me Joey, I am just on my way to Euston as I have to be somewhere this afternoon, but I couldn't pass you by, not for a second time. How about we meet up again tomorrow and I can try and explain some more about what I am doing, and where you come in. We can go for a birthday lunch if you like?"

"Oh my God, are you sure?"

"Of course, baby. Do you have a number and I'll give you a call?"

"It got stolen a couple of nights ago" I say sadly

"Not a problem. Tomorrow morning meet me here at about the same time. Shall we say 10.30? Don't worry if I am a few minutes late, I sometimes get too engrossed in my magazines on the tube and miss my stops. I'm a bit ditzy like that, as you will get to realise. Now, before I head off, are you okay for somewhere to stay today?"

"Yeah I will be fine. I will find somewhere". I don't know where that somewhere will be, but I feel that I would become a burden to Dee Dee if I am honest this early.

"As long as you are sure. Have you got enough for food and water?"

"I have a bit, I should be okay hopefully"

"You shouldn't have to hope for food, Joey. Here take this"

She opens her purse and passes me a twenty-pound note.

"Get yourself some hot food for lunch and dinner, okay, and make sure you are safe this evening"
"I will do thank you. And thank you for being so kind. You don't know how much it means to me"

Dee Dee smiled even wider and pinched my left cheek. "I shall see you tomorrow Joey, you take care baby, okay?"
"I promise. Have safe travels!"
"I will. B-bye honey"
"Goodbye Dee Dee"

I watch as she walks off into the distance, and stare at her until she disappears into the bowels of Blackfriars Station. Having suffered so much rejection, all it takes is one act of kindness for the future to appear brighter. I start to wonder what she had meant when she said "...and where you fit in". How can I be part of her plans? She's only known me for five minutes. I'd be no good working in a kitchen or a café. I'm not even old enough to buy a kitchen knife for another twelve months. Anyway, I decide not to dwell on it as my anxiety will only cause clouds to pass over the memory of our chat, and I don't want to make myself worry so much that I decide not to come back to her tomorrow. I'm feeling in a much more buoyant mood after my encounter with Dee Dee, so decide to head back to Russell Square to laze the afternoon away. I get a little lost on my way up there, but eventually get my bearings. On arrival, the square is much busier than yesterday, and there are many families having picnics. The sight of the various spreads of food and drink make me hungry, so I set off for the local Sainsbury's before finding a place to sit. I'm still desperately in need of a shower but apply another couple of sprays of deodorant to mask any unwanted odour that is seeping through my clothes.

Using my new twenty-pound note to pay, I leave the store with a cheap but filling meal deal, and also treat myself to some extra snacks and a bar of chocolate. I feel a bit like Charlie Bucket, hoping that Dee Dee is my golden ticket to a place that I never thought could exist. Only time would tell. Returning to the square, I look across to the office where I first encountered Dee Dee. The solicitor is again stood staring out the window, as if waiting for me. As he glares I give him a brief wave, which to my surprise, he nervously returns. His expression doesn't change. Maybe people in that profession are trained to keep a poker face regardless of the joy inside them.

I settle down on a patch of grass and tuck into my sandwich, pork pie, scotch egg and crisps. It reminds me of picnics from when I was younger, and the nostalgia makes me uneasy. At times like this I feel I should contact my parents, but I weigh up the possibility of them still being angry, and there is a chance of them rejecting me again, so decide against it.

Fourteen

I must have fallen asleep without purpose not long after I had finished my lunch, and when I wake up the park is near enough deserted. I've no idea how long I was asleep for, but it was long enough for both my arms to turn a slight shade of red. It's a bit itchy so I pour some of the remaining water I had over them, and even this liquid is lukewarm. When it hits my skin it becomes irritable quickly. By tomorrow this will probably be too painful to wear long sleeves over. Hopefully Dee Dee carries some kind of aftersun lotion in her handbag with her. There are a few people scattered in the far corners of the square, and there is a surprisingly high amount of litter strewn over the well-cut green lawns. I've never understood how people can come to an area, enjoy their time there, and then leave it in such a disgusting state. You walk past bins on the way out, it's not hard to take the rubbish with you. It's one of the problems with so many people in this country. They expect other people to clean up after themselves.

It must be past 5pm as I sit up and brush myself down, as traffic around the perimeter is at a standstill, with taxis, buses and vans all beeping at each other. You can even see the haze from the exhaust of the vehicles rising past the Georgian style houses on the eastern side. I turn onto my knees and stretch my upper body as far as I can, hearing cracks from my shoulders as they try to return to their natural positions. I lean back with my palms on the ground and let out a large yawn, the type that forces your eyes to close. When I finish I blink into the sunlight and notice two figures approaching me. Without stereotyping the two of them, I know that they are both also homeless. Their clothes are dirty, and they have that look about them where the skin appears oily. I'd put the male at around fifty years old, but his female companion can't be much older than twenty-five at most. She is carrying a large beige material sack over her right shoulder, and they appear to be arguing. I kind of hope that I am just being paranoid, and they don't want to speak to me, as I am still weary of new people approaching regardless if they are part of the community or not. The male figure removes a large brimmed hat to reveal greasy blonde hair that now falls down to his shoulders. He has the look of an Australian in the outback, especially as he is dressed in clothes that resemble those worn by an explorer in the desert. I'm trying to think of the name of that man who discovered Tutankhamun's tomb as that is who he reminds me of. I think back to school history lessons, and think it might be Harold? Or was it Howard? This is irrelevant I know.

It turns out the couple were approaching me. When they were a couple of metres away they both crouched down, as if they were staring at a creature at the side of the road or something. They didn't say anything for a few seconds and I felt a bit like an animal in a zoo. I decided to break the silence.

"Hullo" I said, putting on my best smile
"Are you Joey?" asked the lady
"Um, yes. I'm not sure if I recognise you. Sorry"

It's odd how many people have seemed to know me without me knowing them. Rather than address me, the lady turned to the explorer.

"I told you it was him. It's the cap, it's just like Baz said" she said. The man nodded back to her.
"You should come with us Joey""
"How do you know me?" I ask, concerned. "And who is Baz? I don't think I know him either?"
"Look, Joey" says the man, speaking for the first time. I notice he has a slight Welsh accent. "My name is Pete, and this is Jenny. We need to speak to you, but we will need to find somewhere more private"
"What's it about? I haven't done anything. How do you know me?"

I'm getting a little worried and just need to get through today. Once tomorrow comes I will be back with Dee Dee and just know that everything will be OK. My anxiety kicks in and many thoughts race through my mind. What if tomorrow isn't okay though? What if Dee Dee has sent them and I'm a pawn in a big game of chess?

Jenny reaches out and touches my arm. It stings a little on the sunburnt area. “Don’t worry Joey, you’ll be safe with us. We need to tell you about Baz. It’s a serious situation and we just need to understand if he said anything to you, that’s all”. She does her best to look kind but I’m feeling a little sick at the situation.

“But I don’t know a Baz” I plead. The two of them stare at each other as if talking telepathically. In order to get me to go with them, they take the matter into their own hands. Pete grabs my carrier bag of possessions, whilst Jenny tugs on my arm as she stands. I have little choice but to go with them.

“Where are you taking me?” I ask

“Just ‘round the corner. Don’t worry, we’ll look after you. Jenny’s got some food if you want some?”

“I’m okay thank you”. I’m feeling far too sick to eat right now. There isn’t any more small talk for the rest of the walk, and Jenny doesn’t seem able to let go of my arm on the journey. I think they know that I am uncomfortable and fully expect me to run off if given the chance. They wouldn’t be wrong if honest, and I looked down every street for a place to sprint should the grip on my arm loosen.

Eventually we turn a corner and head down a quiet back street. It appears to be the rear entrance to one of the larger shops on Oxford Street as there are a few ‘Goods In’ doors marked out in the narrow street. Litter lines the kerbs on both sides, and at the far end a large pile of cardboard forms a small mountain. It smells awful too. The air is heavy and you can virtually taste the pollution. The road is a dead end and is blocked by a huge multi-storey building. Towards the far end is a doorway which is set back slightly from the street. Pete picks up a bag that has been left there and I assume that this doorway is the one which they are currently calling home. It's definitely much more secluded than my doorway at number 54, but it's not as clean. The white walls of the building have a layer of grey dirt on them, and pigeons fill the window sills above. Their droppings streak down the walls and some parts resemble a Jackson Pollock painting. It's amazing how snobby I seem at this thought but being hidden away would make me feel too vulnerable.

"Take a seat, Joey" says Jenny, and I oblige by perching on the edge of a stone step. She crouches down again and stares straight into my eyes. "We need to tell you something, OK. We saw you with Baz so feel it's best that you are told before you find out from the newspapers or something this evening"

I am now terrified. I would hope it was mistaken identity however them knowing my name means that I must somehow know this Baz. I need this confirmed though.

"Who is Baz?" I ask again.
"We saw you with him yesterday sat in the pub. We were coming to meet him and watched the two of you

talking. We were going to join you both but you got up and left quickly before we had made a decision"

Baz was The Nomad. I felt bad that I had listened to his story for so long yesterday and still not asked him his name. Maybe he likes being a sort of unknown character? Maybe it made him feel special in a way. I still should have asked.

"Is he coming here too?" I ask them, but they both fall silent. Jenny holds onto my arm again, and Pete put his hand on her shoulder. She seems upset.

"Joey, listen, I hate to have to tell you this, but we found Baz unconscious this morning, and we got the paramedics who tried to save him, but it was no good. We'd got there too late".

I was stunned. I couldn't comprehend it at all, and the sick feeling in my stomach grew stronger. Within moments, tears came, and I felt guilty that I didn't do more to help him. I noticed that Jenny was crying too, and she moved from my arm to lean in and hold me. She was squeezing me, and I could feel the sobs from deep inside of her.

We sat there hugging in silence for a while. It seemed that none of us knew exactly what to do next. Over the last two days I had feared for my safety a few times, most notably during the night at Gold's Night Shelter, and the fear continued to appear each time I realised just how precarious my situation was. Pete was the first to break the silence, offering around a bottle of drink, I think it was whisky. I politely declined as I didn't feel like alcohol was the best way for me to gather my thoughts right now, although the lightheaded feeling that the rum had given me earlier did make things seem okay for a short while. Jenny also declined and suggested a walk instead.

"Maybe we should go and lay some flowers" she suggested.

I always found the laying of flowers a bit strange to be honest. Around my hometown there had been a few areas where flowers had been laid in order to remember someone who had been killed, mainly road accidents and that kind of thing, and they always made me feel uneasy. I'd never actually laid flowers myself. I told Jenny that I wasn't sure.

"Joey, the thing that you have to remember is that if we don't, then no one will. The homeless are an invisible community to so many people. Some ignore us as they think we are just wasters who want drink and drugs, others ignore us as they think we will cause them harm, and others are so used to seeing us that we are just part of the background of their life. Whichever way, we are cared less for than a lot of the rest of society. If people read about what happened today in the papers later they will probably forget about it by the time they have finished the next article. If we go there, it may only be a small gesture, but many small gestures make a statement. Every flood starts with a single drop of rain"

I liked Jenny, and she certainly had a way of conveying her thoughts much more eloquently than myself. I guess I am no different to the people she is referring to. I wouldn't have thought that someone living on the streets could have that passion, and to be so well informed in order to make a change. I felt guilty. I was guilty about not wanting to lay flowers, and I felt guilty about all the times I walked past someone sleeping rough without a second thought. If you do the same, please don't feel ashamed. I'm not telling you this in order to guilt trip you. All I will say is that the next time you walk past someone in a doorway, stop and think for a few minutes and make up a story for their background. Why are they there? What went wrong? Who failed them? Doing this will bring the human element back to that sleeping bag on the floor in front of you. The next person you walk past could be Pete, it could be Jenny, it could even be me. I'm glad I got to spend some time with The Nomad, but I am upset and angry that it was all too brief.

I wasn't sure if I wanted to know exactly what had happened, but a sense of where we may be heading would be good. I asked Jenny if she can let me know where she had found him.

"Baz used to spend a lot of time in the City" she started, correlating with his knowledge of Fleet Street and St Paul's that he had passed onto me yesterday. “I don’t know quite why he preferred it there, but there were often various streets where he would hide away. Over time these became less and less and recently we could narrow it down to two streets, both leading to the Victoria Embankment”

“What did he say to you yesterday, when you met him in that pub?”

“Not a lot really, we agreed to meet as he said he was concerned that he was being followed”

“Who by?”

“I’ll tell you that later. Now isn’t the time. He’s been concerned before, but it normally comes in waves. Yesterday though he was definitely more agitated than he had been before, so we said that he could spend today with us. We did offer to stay with him yesterday also, but he was adamant that he would prefer to be on his own for a few days and maybe get away to a different part of town. It’s why he sent you away too. If his concerns were correct, and ultimately it turned out they were, he didn’t want to put you into unnecessary danger as well. He had a kind heart and genuinely cared for people. This morning we decided to go and check up on him, on the off chance that he had stayed local. He was at the first street out of the two. It was only when we reached him that we couldn’t wake him up and….”

Jenny tailed off before putting her hands inside her sleeves and bringing them up to cover the lower part of her face. I decided not to push the subject any more for now as she was grieving in the same way that anyone would when they've lost someone close.

A few minutes later, the slight breeze that was whistling down our alleyway had started to pick up, and I decided that I did want to go and lay flowers. The alternative was to go somewhere else on my own, and I really didn't want to spend the afternoon coupled only with my own anxiety. Jenny gave me a hint of a smile and took my hand to help drag me up off of the step. Pete took another swig of his whisky before offering it around the group again. He had remained quiet for a while now. Me and Jenny declined his drink once more, and we all headed down towards the Thames, to where The Nomad's journey ended.

Fifteen

Despite having known them for a very short space of time, I felt as if I could trust both Jenny and Peter. I think this is my naivety coming through again. I have still not learnt to allow myself to get to know new people before making a decision on trust, and this is something which I need to do now that the new people I meet have not been connected to my life before.

For the first part of the walk I told them all about how I ended up being in this situation. They both seemed genuinely sympathetic. I'd learnt a lesson from The Nomad, and now needed to find out more about other people straight away as you never know when the last time you would see them would be. It would help me to know who I needed to be more cautious around also. It seems ridiculous to think how many people I will get to know whilst on the street who would then disappear out of my life again just as rapidly. The chances of seeing The Nomad again had gone, and it made me want to find Mimi again desperately. I wanted to find her, engage with her and let her know just how thankful I was for her taking me under her wing on my first night alone. I made a promise to myself during this walk that the next time I see her I will ensure that she knows just how much I want to be around her again.

The walk to the river would take about forty-five minutes, however I wanted it to last for much longer. I needed to know about Jenny and her story. The majority of that walk was done in silence however, as we weaved our way down Oxford Street, Tottenham Court Road and then the Strand. Eventually we passed by 54 Fleet Street down towards Blackfriars Bridge.

"I'm just going to nip in here and get some flowers" said Pete as we reached a Sainsbury's Local. The large clock on the building opposite showed the time to be just before 5pm, which wasn't as late as I had thought. Not having anywhere to go meant that time mattered less. The nap in the park had further disorientated my perception, and the overcast skies which had arrived made the whole city feel a bit darker. It was heaving with people in business wear, and despite not checking the time all afternoon, I assumed it was closer to 6pm as many looked to be picking up a sandwich for their train journey home. As Pete entered the shop I asked Jenny to tell me about her life. We both sat on a small wall outside the shop.

"Jesus, where do I start?"
"Wherever you feel comfortable" I replied
"I'm not comfortable with any of it, but I've told it a million times to a million counsellors and social workers and yet I'm still in the same position, so telling another person won't make much difference" she said, with a hint of a smile. "Basically, I had just sat my A-Levels at my

school in Liverpool. I'd been offered a place at Durham University and on the outside, everything seemed like it was perfect. Friends felt that I had it easy as I was somehow naturally gifted at school. I would have been the first to go to university and everything"

"I didn't realise you were from Liverpool. You don't have the accent"

"My mum moved up there just before meeting my dad, and because I spent more time with her I never picked it up, despite spending twelve years in schools there"

"How come you didn't go to Durham?"

"My Dad had been on a downward spiral for many years. He was born in raised in Liverpool and had worked there all his life down the docks. In the nineties though things changed and my Dad, along with many of his friends, lost their jobs. I won't go into the details of the situation but it caused a national outcry. The dispute went on for a good few years, and although some got redundancy packages, issues meant that not everyone came through it well. Dad used to work up to eighty hours a week sometimes, and the job was hard going. He lost so many of his friends through illness that was bought on by the stress. Not only this, but the whole situation affected the community. I always thought he was strong, but everyone can be broken. Everyone has their limit. In fact the whole of the nineties broke many people in that city. Have you heard of Hillsborough?"

I'd heard of the name, and knew it was to do with football, but it wasn't something I was familiar with, so I asked her how it linked in.

"Well, at Hillsborough ninety-six fans were killed when there was a crush in the stands during the game. Our street lost two boys that day, and at that moment things were different. We wanted to rally as a community and rise, but we were isolated. The media blamed the fans and we were made to feel like criminals. Some of the stuff that was written about the people like those who we grew up with was disgraceful and we felt like we were fighting for our name and our neighbourhood as well as fighting for the justice of those who never came back that day. This hung over my Dad like a heavy cloud, and him losing his job a few years after made him feel completely worthless. At this time he started drinking heavily, and it ended up with him and mum getting divorced. Growing up in that era in Liverpool seemed to be a constant battle against horrible situations. Just after I was born a young boy was kidnapped and killed, and the sense of injustice that was being dealt to our city had effects on its people far greater than I can even try and convey to you Joey"

"Was it this alone that stopped you going to university?" I said, somewhat ignorantly. I tried to put myself in her position but couldn't see the link clearly.
"It was a combination Joey. I won't patronise you as I know how much affect a parent's attitude can have on life.

It if had no effect, then you wouldn't be here. For you, it was religion and antiquated views, for me it was divorced parents and alcoholism. Plus, the divorce meant that I couldn't fund the course properly, or at least it felt that way. I felt guilty about leaving these people behind, guilty that I would be spending money on something that wouldn't matter in the long run. I wish I had gone now, obviously, but I made that decision at that time, so I can't regret it".

"Why not?"

"Regret is such an easy thing to have in hindsight, but in that moment, in that environment, I felt that not leaving was the best option. Everyone would change decisions in hindsight but you have to learn to trust your past self. Whatever made you make that choice at the time is hard to remember in many situations".

"Was your mum still in Liverpool after the divorce?"

"Sadly not. My mum moved over to Ireland after their divorce, as her sister lives in Kilkenny. I wanted to go with her, but I had already started secondary school by this point, and it was decided that it would be best for me to stay there and finish studying. For the first few years I was able to cope, but Dad went into a very rapid decline when I was fifteen. He started drinking more heavily, and also gambled away a lot of the money that he had. University was my dream but I struggled to cope with my home life and didn't know where to go for help. This then eventually led to me having a breakdown of my own. In the lead up to my A-Levels I had started to hang about with what people would call 'the wrong crowd', and looking back, I guess they were. They used me in ways you don't want to imagine, yet I didn't want to escape as I felt that they did genuinely care. The truth is that they didn't though. This then led to petty crime, drink and drugs. It was a few nights after my last exam that I was arrested one night"

"I'm sorry. You can stop if you want"

"Nah, it's too late to change things now. It's all part of who I am. So yeah, with the arrest, it was on the cards for a while I think. We'd gone down into the centre and some of the lads had started trouble with another neighbourhood, and before you knew it a fight had broken out. One lad ended up with a broken jaw, and there was a fair bit of criminal damage to shop fronts and cars from stray missiles that were thrown. I'd love to tell you that I wasn't involved but that wouldn't be true. I was released without charge as there was no real evidence against me, but it didn't end there. I went home a couple of days later after staying at a friends and found that Dad had been drinking heavily. I'd often take some of his spirits when heading out because of his alcoholism; I became a target for him. I'd heard rumours that he had hit my mum, but never wanted to believe them, yet on this night he threw me down the stairs and launched an attack on me. I had to leave that house and I did the same as you and came to London. Been here ever since".

"Why did you choose London?"

"Another of our group was arrested too, also released without charge, but he was tired of having to go around the city on edge, always on the lookout for someone who might want to attack him. People sometimes do want to get out of the vicious circles they find themselves in, but all the exits are blocked. He decided to get in his car and drive down here so I jumped in too"

"Where is he these days?"

"I don't know. We lost contact. He got out from the gangs up there but fell back into them down here. I have no idea if he is even in the city anymore"

At this point Pete came out of the shop carrying a small bunch of flowers and the three of us set off down towards the river. I liked Jenny, and I sympathised with her for all the events that led to her becoming homeless. I wanted to find out more about Pete as well, however now didn't feel like the correct time to do so.

"Do you think there will be many leaving flowers?" I asked as we turned towards Blackfriars Bridge. I hoped that there would be, however I already knew that he probably only seemed important to us rather than London as a whole. Looking around me, the street was full of people in suits carrying on with their lives oblivious to the tragedy that had happened just a few hundred metres away. They probably didn't even know that a young man lost his life last night, and even if they did it would just be a statistic rather than anything deeper. The way that society is means that they may read about it in the evening papers on their commute home, but once off their trains, they would have already forgotten about it. Within twelve hours his whole life will be reduced to a small column in a paper that is discarded into a bin on a platform.

“We’ll probably be the first to lay flowers” answered Jenny, “I doubt that there will be many more. It’s sad, but it’s a fact. This won’t be the first time that we have done this, and it’s not even the first time this month. It definitely won’t be the last. Once done though, it may be best for us to head off just in case we are seen by people who may have harmed Baz. They might be looking out for people he associated with as well”

“But why would they harm us?”

“Joey, if someone here has a grudge, they may look to harm those in that person's network as well”

“But he hadn’t done anything had he?” I asked, worriedly.

“He hadn’t, but that doesn’t mean that people think the same. Look, I’ll tell you everything after we leave there okay?”

I felt a bit deflated but agreed.

We don’t quite reach the Thames before we take a right, moving onto Victoria Embankment. Pete stops and pulls out a slip of paper.

“I can’t understand this, Joey have a read will ya?” he says.

I take it from him. It is a small envelope, and on the back a crudely drawn map has been sketched in blue biro. It’s quite hard to read, and not in great detail at all, but it has a large X on a street named "JC" and I assume this is what he has shoddily marked down as the place where The Nomad had been found. There are a few water marks on the envelope which has led to some of the ink running, meaning other street names are quite hard to understand.

"It's the first right down here" I say, nodding in the direction upstream. "Just 'round the corner. Hang on, I thought you said that you found him? Why have you got a map?"

"I wasn't entirely honest Joey, sorry. Sometimes we have to bend the truth to protect others".

I was now unsure on what to believe. Was Jenny as innocent as she had made out? Yes she had been involved with the wrong crowd, but how much did they influence her? Was it a case of her influencing them instead? I started to doubt whether she was even from Liverpool. As I had asked, she didn't even have a hint of the accent.

We approach the junction highlighted on the small map, and the come across John Carpenter Street. I assume this must be what the JC stands for on the bit of paper. As we turn, we realise that this is definitely correct. A short distance ahead we can see a fair bit of police activity still. A white tent has been erected, and there are a few officers milling about. You can only access this street from the end furthest away from ourselves, however it is currently closed to traffic. Police tape has sealed the street off at our end also and a lone female police officer is stood centrally to ensure no one approaches the area. The three of us slowly approach the officer, and she smiles sympathetically to us. Jenny seemed most confident and acted as spokesperson for our small group.

Whilst Jenny heads forward, I hang back with Pete. He decides to sit on the floor and seems a bit distant by the whole scenario. Next to where I am is a statue facing out across the Thames. I am always intrigued by statues, although art has never been my strong point, so I don't really understand who it is of, or what its purpose is. It's a bit taller than me, and depicts a man in a shirt, suit and tie, with his right arm raised as if trying to flag down a taxi. He has a briefcase in his left hand, partially hidden under a large coat that has been draped over his forearm. I find it weirdly reassuring. In this city there are thousands of people just like this man, rushing around to or from offices. I said earlier that these workers are the ones who ignore the people on the streets, but this statue makes me realise that maybe we are all as guilty as each other in not recognising what is around us. We are all guilty of living through our smartphones or getting caught up in our own journeys to realise the stories that are around us. It's only when I see this statue that I realise that everyone has lived an interesting life, full of problems both large and trivial, and made decisions their whole life, to end up next to you, and yet we never stop to think. Could this man be hailing a taxi? Maybe. He could also be shouting down a work colleague. He could be alerting someone to danger. I'll probably never know to be honest as Jenny was walking back towards us with the flowers hanging upside down from her right hand.

"Are you okay, Pete?" I asked before Jenny reached us
"I'll be alright son" he replied wistfully. "I just find this kind of thing a bit strange"
"Does it worry you, y'know, that it could have been you or Jenny?"
"This one is different Joey. Jenny will tell you about it all once we're done here, and after that it's probably best that you head away for a bit"
"Head away? Why?"
"To keep yourself safe"
"But where can I go?"
"Do what you normally do I guess. Us three being together won't ever bring you anything good"

I don't know what to make of this. Although still a bit sceptical of the pair, Jenny had seemed very open when I was speaking to her earlier. Pete has always been a bit more reserved though, and did seem to be numbing something with the whiskey earlier. It could be the grief of today that he is numbing, or just his whole situation. I don't know if whiskey was part of his daily routine, but I know he didn't flinch when he drank straight from the bottle. That said, they have lied to me about how they found him unconscious. If they didn't find him, someone must have told them. But who? Also, I'm feeling more anxious about the fact that they were watching me with The Nomad whilst in the pub yesterday. What if someone was watching me now? Someone waiting to follow me and harm me.

"We aren't allowed through" said Jenny when we reached us. "They're still doing some evidence stuff over there and don't want anyone going near, which makes sense. She said that we can leave the flowers at the end of the street though. We're the first ones to do it. Where would be best?"

"How about the statue?" I ask. It would seem fitting that our tribute is left to the anonymous figure. Jenny nods and walks past me and places the flowers at the bronze man's feet. Me and Pete walk towards the statue also once the flowers have been laid. There is a small plaque on the floor. It turns out the statue is called simply 'Taxi'. It's incredibly detailed, and quite beautiful in its own way when you are up close to it. I've warmed to it. Jenny and Pete don't seem too bothered by the artwork and are instead looking up the road to beyond the tape. I look up there now myself and the sight of police moving things in small clear bags makes me feel a bit ill. How can someone's life end so suddenly in a place so unremarkable. The Nomad had never mentioned this street to me before, or indeed pointed it out when we had passed it yesterday. Maybe the part about this being one of his sleeping spots was also untrue. I started to trust the couple less and less as the minutes passed by. I wanted to leave straight away but this would make me look suspicious. If Jenny and Pete did want to somehow cause me harm, leaving rashly would have aggravated them. Instead, I stand alongside them at the statue for a short while before Pete suggests that we should move on. He definitely sounds on edge for some reason.

"Can you tell me what's going on?" I ask as we reach the junction between Victoria Embankment and the bridge across the river. I was going to ask it more gently, but my anxiety was going into overdrive. I felt the beginnings of a panic attack coming on so focussed on the flowing water to calm me down. I had timed my breathing with the waves hitting the now visible shingle banks.

"What you have to realise Joey" starts Jenny, "is that nothing is ever straightforward. We've tried just letting you know the basics but you're inquisitive and probably deserve to know more. After though, you should make yourself scarce from us for a bit, okay?"
"Okay I promise. Pete said the same"

Pete and Jenny look at each other, before Pete gives a silent and small nod. Jenny holds on to my right arm gently and leads me across the bridge until we reach a small seated area about a third of the way across. The bridge has deep red and white painted metal railings across its entire length, with the only breaks in them coming from two of these seats. At these points, small stone horseshoe shaped seats push out slightly above the water flowing below, and the three of us sit close to each other. The view from here is quite nice now and seems a bit clearer than when I last looked out from here this morning. Traffic is flowing heavily across behind me, and behind this the train station on the bridge adjacent is picking up the commuters, everyone oblivious to the investigation that has started less than three-hundred yards away.

I'm feeling vulnerable again now. I don't know what the deal is with these two, or why they have brought me here specifically. Many things are going through my head. It seems somewhere which could be used for a setup, as if they have taken me somewhere easy to find. I'm not sure why exactly, but it just seems, well, a bit odd. Alternatively, they could easily pick me up and drop me into the Thames. I'm not the strongest swimmer so could be lost to the current within seconds. Jesus, why am I thinking like this? They probably just think that this area is discreet but in reality, it really isn't. I kind of want to remove myself from this situation as I have started to feel very uncomfortable. I don't want to be dragged into anything dangerous. In fact, all I want is for it to be tomorrow, and to sit again with Dee Dee. That is the only time that I have felt at ease since leaving home. I know it hasn't been long, but maybe I wasn't as cut out for this as I thought. I thought it would be easy. In order to get away from here, I needed to get through this conversation with

Jenny and Pete. If things got out of hand I would dive of the bridge myself. The cool waters would drag me away, where hopefully someone would spot me and pull me to safely. No. I can't think like this. Concentrate.

"Can you please tell me what's going on?" I ask.
"Do you know of Michael Banton?" asks Jenny
"Um, it doesn't seem familiar" I answer, "Where would I have met him?"
"You wouldn't have, but do you know of the name?"
"No, not at all". I'm being honest here, I have no idea who they are on about.
"Fucking paedo" Pete chips in. I'm not sure if he is talking about me or this Michael character, so I presume, and hope, the latter.
"There was a thing in the papers last summer, Joey. The Stirling Childcatcher they called him. Do you not remember?" said Jenny, now taking over the narrative.

"I really don't, I'm sorry. What was it about?"
"It started last July. Stirling is in Scotland as you probably know. Anyway, a kid went missing up there. Young kid, I think he was about nine years old, called Graham Mountford. He went to a school about three-hundred yards from the house where he lived with his parents, just a short walk across the park between the two. He left school on the Thursday afternoon but never made it back. Took them nearly a week to find his body"
"That's awful" I say, shocked.

"It completely ruined the community. He was from a place called Raploch which is on the outskirts of the town. No one came forward to say that they had seen him taken by anyone, or even talking to anyone and it wasn't quite clear how he managed to go missing in broad daylight. Five days the police and locals searched the area for him, looking in all the woodlands and trails that surrounded the place, and they weren't even sure if he would still be in the area. At the end of the week someone out walking called the police to say that they could see something in the water near where the football ground was. The police came down and pulled the boy out of the River Forth. They couldn't tell how long he had been in there for, but there were marks on his body that made them open up a murder investigation. Sadly, there are a fair few people who go missing for various reasons, and a week later the whole thing started over again. This time a twelve-year-old boy was found in a ditch, partially hidden under branches. Same injuries"

"What were the injuries?" I asked

"That's not important right now, you just need to know that there was a bastard out there free to do these terrible things. Obviously security was stepped up, parents collecting their kids from school, that kind of thing, and it stopped for a short period. Not too long after though, maybe a month, the same thing happened, but this time near Derby. Three kids in two months, in two parts of the country. On this one though, the killer made a mistake. There had been more of a struggle this time, and on the body they had found a piece of material that didn't seem to fit. They did the investigation and some digging and realised that it came from inside the cab of an HGV vehicle, and the travelling around the country fitted the story as obviously truck drivers go all over the place"

"It wasn't Baz was it?" I asked, extremely worried, thinking of the times that I had been there for the taking if it was.

"It wasn't, no, Baz didn't have that in him. But he came down to London in a lorry"

"yes, he told me that. Jumped in at some service station"

"Yeah, that's right. Well anyway, the lorry he got in happened to be driven by a bloke called Michael Banton. Just so happened that Banton lived near Stirling and worked for a haulage firm, so when the police did checks on the journey records for the area, his was one that would have been looked at. Guess where he had been delivering to a couple of weeks before?"

"Derby?"

"Precisely. He was arrested in London whilst on another job, the job that Baz had jumped into the cab on. It didn't take them long to charge Banton with the murders, as there was a stack of evidence against him, including a match to his DNA on the material found on the third boy. His stature also matched the bruising on the first kids body. The thing was, Baz was also looked into heavily. It's understandable; if you're with a killer for such a long journey then they have to y'know?"

"Did they charge him with anything?"

"Baz? No. His story checked out. He was a good person and it was just bad luck that he ended up in that situation. Anyway, after it was all over, Baz stayed here in London, but a few people recognised his face and didn't want to believe that he had nothing to do with it, so it was as if he would always have a vigilante mob after him trying to take revenge. This is why it's dangerous to all stick together. These people are the ones who did this to Baz this morning, and who knows who else they are watching. They may think that we are involved too. They could have seen you down the pub with him yesterday or seen us all together today. They know that me and Pete hung around with him a bit"

"Do you think they will come after me?"

"I'd like to say they won't, but I can't guarantee anything. People are bastards Joey. Since it happened, every time Baz got talking to a young person, that person seemed to receive threats. Baz hadn't done anything wrong whatsoever, and I think that he engaged with young people because he lost the chance to be there for his daughter. Hearing that he was talking to you made us feel like you were in danger too"

"What happened to the other young people he spoke to?"

"To be honest, I don't know. A few of them haven't been seen again. We like to assume that they somehow got away, but Christ knows where they would go. This city will spit you out as quickly as it took you in"

"I assume Banton got put in prison?"

"Life. Not the first time he had abducted people. First time he had killed though"

"So what should I do? Do I need to leave?"

"Just be vigilant. Don't put yourself in any danger and try and stay near other people where you can. I know that's not easy"

"By people, this doesn't include yourselves right?"

"We want to look out for you, but I don't know how safe it is. How about we arrange to meet somewhere discrete once a week?"

I was unsure about this. For some reason it made me feel as if they wanted to meet me only to keep track of me, maybe in case I went and said something that would land them in trouble. My trust of the pair had lessened over the course of this evening, and something didn't sit right with me. Despite this, I agreed, but my intentions were to not actually attend. Agreeing seemed the sensible option for now. My anxiety was coming back strongly and I tried to get a view of the river in order to calm myself.

I hated this. I hated everything about this. I wanted to escape and hide away. I had lost Baz, Pete and Jenny were a bit of a mystery and also about to leave, I had lost Mimi, I had lost my friends, I had lost my family, I had lost my possessions and was actually about to lose all hope. I needed Dee Dee. I was shaken by the story that Jenny had just told me, and I actually felt nervous even being near them now, so asked if it was okay for me to leave. They didn't really say much but it was clear that they would rather I went.

I headed back towards Fleet Street and picked up a coffee from the same McDonald's that I had spent the first part of the day. It was just past 7pm now but I'd had enough for one day. I crossed the road and slumped into the doorway of number 54, reading a discarded paper. The Nomad's killing wasn't even mentioned. The door next to me opened, and a tall man looked down at me. He gave me a small smile and dropped a couple of pounds into my empty cup before tucking an umbrella under his arm and heading off into the distance. It was a different man to the one who had stepped over me this morning, but they must have been in the same line of work. They had a similar appearance, and both been dressed in expensive looking suits.

The sun had yet to set, although the shadows from the buildings around me had started to lengthen. Slowly but surely, Fleet Street started to empty for the evening. A few groups were heading to the bars nearby, and those who had been in late meetings were walking quickly to the station at the foot of the hill in order to catch their trains home. Even the traffic on the road had eased considerably. I couldn't sleep for a while, so read the paper from cover to cover. The first half was mainly politics, and the second half seemed to be in depth analysis of every team for the upcoming World Cup. I formed a pillow out of copies of the newspapers once more, and laid down. Folding my arms into my body, I closed my eyes, feeling a little sick.

Sixteen

You now find me the day after, sat in an Italian owned café in an Aston Villa shirt. It's mid-morning and I am drinking a decent cup of coffee and feeling okay. How I got here was anything but simple though, but I needed to get my head back in a good place before I could update you. In order for me to help you catch up, I will go back to the beginning.

Before doing this however, I want you to try and understand that mental health is a hard thing to explain to people who have never suffered with poor mental health. That's a clumsy way of starting this, but I will try to elaborate. As you know, I suffer from anxiety, and have had moments of depression also. The worst bout that I had led to that time being sat on that bridge back home. Mental health is seen as a completely different beast from physical health, and whilst there are differences behind each type, both are very real, and inextricably linked.

Many say that these days it's too easy for young people to claim to have poor mental health, rather than "suck it up and get on with it", and that the figures of those claiming to be affected are rising because the millennial generation and younger can't cope with an environment where they aren't in 'their safe space'. Rather than accept that mental health issues are real and extremely important, people and certain strains of the British media attack those suffering all too often. The word 'snowflake' now is probably more known for someone who speaks out than as an actual flake of snow these days. Support, not attack, is the only way to change things. It would be wrong for me to claim that everyone's mental health issues can be resolved, but as a society we could all act in a way so that poor mental health can be controlled.

Mental health has always been a thing. It is not a modern phenomenon. Over the last decade more organisations of support have appeared, giving people who are suffering the effects a place to go, a place to open up, a place to be listened to and a place to be helped. Because of these opportunities, more and more people are willing to discuss their mental health and how it affects their life. Even the Royal Family help promote the idea of trying to gain courage to talk. Many say that it is okay to not be okay and it's true. The elder generations didn't have the support that we have these days, so there must be so many who still carry guilt with them throughout their later years, blaming themselves for things that were not, and are not, their fault. Not everyone is comfortable with opening up, and no one who is uncomfortable with doing so should be disregarded as ignoring help. Many have grown up into an environment where it is still a taboo subject.

My mental health lows (normally anxiety, occasionally depression, sometimes both) are very real, and to me they are the mental equivalent of unexpectedly stepping on a piece of Lego with no shoes on. Rather than a piece of Lego, it can be a place, a sound, an experience, a smell or something that has been said that causes the pain. Whatever it is, the time difference between feeling healthy and feeling unwell can be a split second. When you step on a bit of Lego you are not thinking that it will happen. You are just going about your day. Then BAM, out of nowhere you are sitting on the floor, pain shooting up your leg, swearing obscenities at the nearest person to you (or the wall if you are alone). After a certain amount of time (could be a minute, could be weeks) you are no longer in pain, but it does not mean that you will never step on a bit of Lego again. It's the same with my mental health. I know after a few times that things will be better, but then out of nowhere I crash and wonder if it ever will. The process repeats over and over. Saying things such as "Why don't you cheer up? Life ain't that bad" is the same as me saying to you "Why don't you just not step on Lego?". We don't want to feel this way.

So why am I telling you this? Well, since coming to London a couple of days ago I feel that I have been mentally kicking bits of Lego, but since leaving Jenny and Pete yesterday, I have been thrown into a box of it from a great height. I will take you back a few hours and explain how I ended up sipping a latté.

Yesterday evening in the doorway of Number 54 was all a bit of a blur. Nothing of any note seemed to take place whilst I sat there, and despite trying to stay alert, I was tired and weary, and I fell asleep. I started to think that maybe I should just give up and head back home, hopeful that my parents would take me back in and I could restart my life back where I had left it, however too much damage will have been done. There was nothing for me back home, Angelica was still away for a while yet and all I would be doing would be transferring my problem to a different place. The people back home wouldn't care about a young kid being on the streets, just like they didn't seem to care here.

If I thought it wouldn't get any worse, I was wrong. I don't know if it was a type of Stockholm Syndrome kicking in, but part of me wanted to go back to the Night Shelter and try again. I had become accustomed to sleeping in this doorway despite only being here for a second time, yet the divide between the haves and the have-nots proved itself once again on this night. As usual I had left a coffee cup near me in the hope that sympathetic coins were tossed in my direction. This night though, I somehow became a target. I had been nervous anyway, thinking that at any moment my connection to The Nomad would lead to me being dragged off and abused. All I had been trying to do was survive. I was woken during the night by the sounds of voices and laughter, and soon realised that I was the target of the abuse. I always slept facing away from the street, feeling that I was safer if my face was not visible to anyone who happened to be passing. I could hear three, maybe four, different voices nearby, with one particularly close by.

"Go on do it!" yelled a voice towards the back of the group, struggling to get the words out through the laughter

"Stop shouting, I can't do it when I know you're all watching" came the male voice from nearby. I wanted to get up and run but was paralysed by the fear of what could be about to happen. It was at this point that a shout of "Wahaaay" went up from the group in unison, and I soon felt warm liquid seep through my jumper. I moved sharply and turned to face them, and once the initial shock had worn off, realised that the ringleader of the group was urinating onto me.

"Get the fuck off" I shouted, trying to lash out and take cover at the same time.

"Calm down princess" came the voice. There were three in total, and all were male. I'd put them in their early thirties, and wearing suit trousers with shirts, all of which were now untucked. They looked like they were on their way home from some kind of office party. They continued to laugh as the one pissing on me stopped and tucked himself back in. The only thing I could think to say was "Why?". They never did answer, and when I tried to retaliate I was overpowered by one of the bystanders and thrown back into the doorway. I wanted to follow them but I just couldn't bring myself to rise up again. I simply had no energy left. Instead I watched as they headed up Fleet Street in the direction of the Strand. They were all much larger than I was, and reminded me of the students who formed the rugby team from the university back home. They were pricks too. Everyone was a prick. Every single person back home is a prick. Every single person in this fucking city is a prick. Apart from Dee Dee of course. Dee Dee was now the only person in the world who could make a difference to me, but why had I built my hopes up that she will be any different. What if she doesn't show up today? I can't go back to Jenny and Pete as I don't know if they are all part of this weird criminal world or not, and after the incident last night I no longer felt safe in that doorway. At that point I was suffering from severe anxiety, and the thought that came into my mind was "maybe not being here at all would actually be best for everyone". If I was gone, would there be anyone out there to miss me?

Fighting back tears I picked up my coffee cup, which had been knocked over in the incident. There was probably a handful of coins in it, mainly copper, and I had to collect these from the piss covered tiles around me. More had been kicked into the road but I didn't see the point in trying to collect them. For now, money wouldn't save me from what I wanted to do.

It was still fairly early, and the sun was only just slowly turning the sky from black into dark blue, and there was a chill in the air. I couldn't keep this jumper on, that's for sure, it was smelling awful already. My t-shirt underneath wasn't much better so I decided to discard that as well. I threw them into the corner next to the door of the dentists, and headed away from Fleet Street for the last time. There were not many people about at this time, and the ones who were seemed to cross the road to ensure that they didn't have to interact with me. If I was in their position I probably would have done the same. What would you do if you were faced with a dirty shirtless boy walking towards you, blank expression on his face? I wouldn't blame you if you didn't help. Whilst you were weighing up your choices in your head I probably would have passed by and then it would be too late. I think there were only about three people about at this time though.

This state of mind I was currently experiencing hadn't come on overnight as you know. Or you may think it has? I've kept you informed of everything that has happened to me over this week, and the time sat doing my last GCSE seemed a world away the moment I am describing I guess, when the reality is that it has only been a few days. The situation I am now in has not come from a few days of being kicked around, it's come from years of it. I didn't realise this myself until I sat there. 'There' by the way was on the edge of Blackfriars Bridge, on the top of the concrete structure where me, Jenny and Pete spent that time yesterday afternoon. In order to try and get you to fully understand how I felt, I will put you on the ledge with me.

My back is to the road, and my feet are hanging over the edge. It's currently a low tide, and small waves are lapping at both banks. No matter how many times I count the waves, it doesn't seem to be calming me. It feels now that I have reached a low and I am unable to climb up away from the bottom. I'm sat here watching the waves hit the shingle, watching the ripples and the eddies directly beneath me whirl around in their circular way. The mud from the floor of the river is being picked up by the current, and it forms coffee brown swirls on the surface. The more I looked down, the more appealing it seemed to slip off over the edge and disappear. I don't believe in a higher power as you know, my parents' dismissal of me put paid to that, but there was something that gave me comfort. The thought of me being in a state of unconsciousness in the water, floating down stream and out into the North Sea. I wondered how long it will take for people to notice that I was no longer here? I'm feeling as if the dark waters would form a blanket around me, somewhere I could lay back and drift into a neverending dream-like state.

In GCSE English we had to do a module on poetry. I guess you probably did too when you took yours (Or your O-Levels if you're older like my parents). We studied a fair few poets, and I'd gladly never have to read anymore Seamus Heaney or John Donne. One part of the module was to study and then write poetry from a certain topic.

This was decided in a very highly technical manner; basically pulling a slip of paper out of an old green fruit bowl that happened to be on the classroom's window sill. Anyway, our group of five got the topic of "The Coast". For the next three weeks we had to produce a booklet of our favourite coastal poems, as well as contribute our own efforts. The best one from each group would then be read out at the annual Literature Conference that our school insisted on hosting. This conference was well liked, mainly as it meant not having to do proper lessons for half a day. Over those weeks we looked at poems by Lewis Carroll and Edgar Allen Poe and the like, and they were alright. I didn't win the competition for our group luckily, I hate public speaking as you know. The winner was Lucia Hawkings. Lucy's poem was awful but she had just been in hospital with some kidney infection and I feel that our teacher unfairly took this into consideration when handing out the prizes. It's not that I'm bitter, of course. I was proud of my effort though and sat looking down into the Thames I start to recall my own words to myself.

I am the boat upon the sea
I leave the land and now I'm free
I see my sailors upon the quay
I wonder 'are they missing me?'

I never said it was good, and I guess it is clumsy in the way that most teenage poetry is, but I feel it sums up exactly how I am feeling. When I am passing over the waves and through the storms, will those I leave behind really miss me? Why should I even care what they think? They've given me nothing and aren't here to comfort me when I really need it. Mesmerized by the water, I decide that my words would make a nice thing to leave behind. People may read it but not understand why the words were written, or what was going on in my head when I wrote them down. I've been troubled for such a long time now, and the more I contemplate, the more I want to be that boat drifting off towards the horizon, finally free from the troubles that were present on the shore.

I swing myself around and look around the floor until I find a piece of stone, and spend a few minutes carving the words in a chalk-like manner onto the stone bench that encases this part of the bridge. The sky continues to get brighter, and once done, I move back to my ledge. I'm starting to have doubts as to whether plunging into the cool water is the best option, but what else do I have to stay dry for? They say closing your eyes heightens your other senses. It's the same way people think that blind people suddenly develop some kind of hearing superpower, where in reality they are probably more just tuned in to the sounds around them. Sitting here, it does seem like I am listening to a completely different city. With your eyes closed you can go to whichever place in the world that you wish. I listen to the small waves colliding with the stone pillars below, and I am transported to a rocky beach, all alone and without a care. It's sort of a hypnotised state I guess? Whilst serene, I am battling myself about slipping forward. I keep swaying from wanting to disappear and wanting to fight on, like there is a massive moral pendulum swinging inside of me. Although the sun is rising fast, I am feeling cold and having no clothes on my upper body is the main cause of this.

I sit with my eyes closed for a good while, dreaming of being on the beach, arguing with myself whether I should topple forward or back. I start to weigh up all the things that have happened in the past, before quickly stopping as I make myself agitated very quickly, before repeating this process over and over. I can finally leave everyone and everything behind and admit defeat, admit that they were right, admit that I am of no use. I also want to know what might have been. What would Dee Dee have done? What had Mimi been up to?

I was probably only sat there for around fifteen minutes, but the sunlight had yet to fully break over the city. I continued to think about what road to take. I listened to the water flow below, I listened to the silence of the road behind. Forward or back? Forward or back? My breathing was becoming much shallower and I could hear my pulse as the blood pumped around my head. Despite being cold I was sweating, and my throat was becoming dry. I needed to choose. Sitting on the edge was doing me no good. Second after second another part of body would speak up to try and make me decide. It seemed deadly silent but terrifyingly loud at the same time. I tried control my breathing with the sound of the waves but by this point this was no use.

I made up my mind, closed my eyes and toppled from my seat.

Seventeen

I'm not sure what caused the blood. It might have been the seat, it might have been the floor. Either way, the backwards fall down onto the concrete bridge had caused a cut on the back of my head, and blood trickled down my exposed neck and left shoulder. The sun still wasn't fully risen, so despite feeling like I had been knocked out, I can't have been on the floor for long before getting my bearings back. Whilst sat on the ledge I had made a decision to jump forward into the Thames, and then this disappeared, and I thought maybe not everything is lost. I did this a few times before finally gaining momentum and deciding to fall backwards. I wish I thought it through a bit more though as my head is bloody killing me. Many thoughts went through my head during that moment of swaying. I think what made me fall back and continue though were the words to that Death Cab for Cutie song that I listened to on loop on the train to London earlier this week. "I know your heart belongs to someone you've yet to meet. Someday you will be loved". This has been my favourite lyric since the day I heard it. It is one of those that just resonates with me, where the lyrics and the music aren't just a song, but a moment which can make you transcend to an entirely new place. Music often has that effect, and a lot of the time you probably don't realise it. I bet there is a song that you have sort of forgotten about, but once you hear it again you are transported back in time to an insignificant part of your past. Taken to a moment that would generally be pointless to remember. An example of this is that song that goes "we built this city on rock and roll". You might know it, I don't know. Anyway, it's one of those cheesy rock songs from the 80's that's always found on random compilations. Every time I hear it I get a flashback to sitting in a brown Volvo Estate car outside the local newsagents, waiting for my mum to jump in and drive us to the cash and carry. Her friends owned the little shop just near to our estate, and after her friend gave birth to a son, mum worked there for a bit to help them with the odd bits of work. That car wasn't ours and I guess it belonged to her friend. I can't have been more than five years old when I heard that song coming through the tinny speakers. Now every time I hear it, I am back in that car. When it plays I can see the row of shops outside of the Volvo's windows, and I can smell the scents of match boxes and chocolate that have been bought in bulk and stacked upon the back seats. Orinoco Flow by Enya is another song that brings back a certain memory from my youth, but that's a story for another time.

Music has this magical power, sort of like mental time travel. I have mentioned this to people before, and some people get it. Others say they feel the same but through a certain smell, or a certain image or a certain word. Smells and images and words that we think have been resigned to history, yet somehow are kept subconsciously alive somewhere deep inside our brains.

Christ, all this reminiscing is making me so glad I chose the concrete and not the dark waters. It pains me that I can't go back in time properly and see if my life could have worked out differently. Maybe it's the bump to my head that is making me feel like this. I decide it's probably best for me to leave the bridge for now. It will start to get busy again soon and I don't want to freak all the commuters out. The last thing they probably want to see this morning is me looking confused and covered in blood. I don't fancy going back to the doorway much, so head across the bridge in the opposite direction. I never realised just how long this bridge is, and it takes me a good couple of minutes to reach the bank on the south side of the Thames. At the far end of the bridge is a pub. I'm assuming it is called Doggetts judging by the ridiculously large gold letters saying as such which run down its outside wall. It's a weird little place, and has that weird angular architecture that was common in the 1960's. The kind of building where it looked like it was designed by using whatever Lego was left in the architects' kids' toy box. It juts out at weird angles and looks like three light stoned buildings fused together. Outside the pub, steps fall down to take you down to the lower level, and the walkway along the river in the opposite direction to the Tate. At the base of these you can go right into an underpass or left towards the wide promenade of the South Bank, and it's this way that I choose to go. The Thames is still at low tide, and although it looks incredibly dirty, I can at least use some of the water to wash away the blood that is now drying on my skin. I look over the railings but it's too far to jump down. Not far enough to kill you, but far enough to break an ankle at the very least. The beach is mainly shingle, although it is interspersed with litter from a variety of years. Up ahead I can see a sort of ladder that connects the shingle and sand to the footpath. It's not the sturdiest structure, and I imagine it has been here at least one hundred years, probably built to help fisherman reach their boats when that industry was stronger. I can't be sure that this was the case, I've never really studied London industries.

The sun is now rising fast and the sky has gone from dark to royal blue. On one horizon to my right you can see it starting to bronze. I reach the steps and climb down to the banks. Underfoot I clamber across all kinds of debris. There is sand and pebbles, but also old bottles, random plastic, bottle tops, fishing wire and crisp packets. I've no idea how long these have been subjected to the water but judging by the design of the can that I kick into the water, it is quite a long time. I've never even heard of Tab Clear Coke. It makes a satisfying splash as I kick it back into the river, and I watch for a moment as it rises to the surfaces and starts bobbing away.

The water looks even dirtier now that I am up close, and I lean over and dip my right-hand in. It's cold and grubby, but I use it to rinse my body. I decide against using it on the cut itself, who knows what I would catch from pouring it into an open wound. The coolness of the water makes me feel a bit more alert though, and once cleaner I walk further along the bank, passing the OXO Tower until I find a sandy section in the shadow of the TV studios that face out across to the rest of London. I could do with a sleep but decide resting will do just as much for me, and I lay back on the sand, propping my body up on my elbows. The tide seemed to be on its way in now. If you look to the wooden jetties you can see which parts are still damp on their support beams. If you can see moisture above the water line, the tide is going out. If you can't, it's coming in. The pillars above the water were bone dry, with limp remnants of seaweed clinging onto them. It's something that we studied during a topic on coastal erosion at school, in case you were ever trapped on a beach. I never thought that I would put this knowledge to use. There isn't a chance of me getting stranded here though. I'm only a few metres from being able to climb. The only danger would be if I fell asleep accidentally, but my head was throbbing far too much for that right now.

Sat on the bank I thought to all those who have been offered the same choice as I was this morning. Those who saw their momentum carry them the other way. Those people who have felt such utter loss in their life that the only way out was to fall into their own metaphorical Thames. If you had asked me six months ago whether I understood why people might do it I'd have probably flippantly said yes, that ending their own life was because they believed they had nothing to live for. Now having been there myself, I felt the pain that these people experienced. That time on the bridge back home that I told you about earlier seemed to me to be as close as I had ever come, but after feeling even lower this morning I know it wasn't event nearly as close as I thought. The choice not to jump in a couple of years ago was much easier than the choice this morning. There were a couple of times where I did lean forward to go, before managing to grapple my way back to the midpoint. It's a fine line. Being on the edge is not just a case of feeling low, it's a feeling of being completely useless. It's a feeling that no one else out of the seven billion people on the planet could help you. It's an accumulation of many feelings and I wouldn't wish it upon anyone. I look across the Thames to the buildings opposite. Despite it being early, there are many lights on in them and I can see the small figures of people inside, silhouetted against the windows by the artificial light. I don't know their stories and probably never will.

Take one of the buildings I can see from this position as an example. It is a modern red brick building attached to a much older style building. It looks as if a new block has been built to create office space, one of the types that will probably be rented out for a large amount of money because it's next to the water. The right-hand side of the building is made up of around thirty large rectangular windows. My attention was taken to this building as the strip lighting on the top floor flickered into action, and a man in a shirt and dark tie wandered in. It looked like he might be on the phone, but it was hard to tell for sure from this distance. Now, what is this man's backstory? He is in the office very early. Is he here to take part in a conference call maybe? For all I know he could be speaking to a colleague about an important deal in Japan. He could have a deadline to hit by lunchtime and has come in early to ensure his figures are all in order. What if the reason he is here isn't work related though? He might have spent the night in a hotel with a mistress, and he has got to the office early in order to clean himself up before the day starts. He could be on the phone to his estranged wife to tell her he has just landed back in the UK after a fake business trip abroad. But what of his mood? Is he happy? He might be feeling upbeat as he has exciting plans at the weekend. He could be stressed from work. He could be feeling the lowest he has ever felt. See? It's impossible to understand exactly what everyone is going through, how they are feeling and what they plan to do next. How many times have you heard people say "But he was always the life and the soul of the party" or "He didn't seem depressed" when someone has taken their own life? Or how about when a famous person overdoses or is found in a hotel room? The papers will be filled with how it is a tragedy, and commenters will say "he had all the money in the world. What did HE have to be depressed about?" Life simply isn't that easy. I always remember my Nan saying something to me when I was younger when a young man on her street jumped into traffic one day. “Joey” she said, “you could go for a walk and pass the most beautiful house in the world, with the perfect garden with perfect symmetry, but you’ll never know what is happening behind the front door”. She was right y’know, she always was. Whatever you can see on the outside of a person doesn’t always reflect what is happening on the inside. I wish my Nan was alive today. If she was I would be waking up today in her back bedroom to endless cups of tea and rounds of toast. She never judged anyone. If she knew that her son had forced me out of the house just for being who I am she would have been round like a shot. My dad was always terrified of his mother even when she was slowly being lost to dementia.

I love the summer months, however the one thing I always forget about them is just how quickly the sun rises. Since sitting back here, the sun has risen behind the skyscrapers of the city and the rays are now bouncing off the choppy Thames in front of me. Whilst thinking about my nan and watching the people opposite, I had been throwing small stones at a milk bottle that was stood at the water's edge. The bottle has now been knocked sideways by the water and will soon disappear off into the depths. I don’t really know how long it takes for the tide to come in on the river. Despite being excellent at Geography, this was something that we didn’t cover. I could explain the litter on the shore and how it links to longshore drift, but I wouldn’t want to bore you with these details. The site of the river swallowing my target bottle made me aware that the tide must come in much faster than I expected, and I start to think that if I sit around here any longer I will probably be trapped after all. Two wide work barges have moved down the river and are now moored directly in front of me. I jump up and climb back up the ladder onto the walkway above. There are a few more people around now too, and a coffee shop owner looks slightly confused by my shirtless appearance. Early morning joggers are passing in fluorescent bursts, all focussed on their routine. It's very rare to be able to come to this area when it is so quiet yet none of them seem to be taking the time to appreciate the beautiful surroundings. Due to their tunnel vision they don't seem to be taking any notice of me, so perhaps it is a good thing that they are so oblivious. I sit down again as I still have some time to waste before I have to meet Dee Dee. Shit. I don't actually know how long I have. I can't remember what time we agreed to meet. I know she said "the same time as today" to me yesterday, but so much has happened in the last twenty-four hours that I have forgotten exactly when that was. I'll get there earlyish as I have to make sure I see her. I also need to find some clothes so that I am somewhat presentable when she arrives. I hope that she does arrive. I catch myself being doubtful again and try to reassure my own mind that of course she will be there. Sitting with my own thoughts will still lead me to become pessimistic, and having the bridge where things nearly ended earlier in my sights is not helping. I decide to stand and go for a walk away from the area. Once I get back on to Blackfriars Bridge I continue away from central London. Cycling commuters are now passing thick and fast, and the builders working on some of the new tower blocks are already at work. It must be nearing 8am now surely.

I arrive in Southwark not long after. It's a nice area and the buildings appear clean. I imagine it's an area where a lot of the richer people come to drink after they finish for the day in their financial jobs. Many of the buildings look like they have been renovated from warehouses, and I walk along the sandy coloured structures on Webber Street, and before long find myself near Waterloo East train station. I like discovering new areas, but I can't venture far as I need to be able to find my way back to the Tate Modern easily. I stop and monitor a traffic sign to try and get a sense of where I am in relation to the rest of London. Many of the names seem familiar, however I have only become accustomed to a few localised areas in my time here.

"Are you okay?" comes a heavily accented voice from behind. I turn around and see a café owner looking at me in a peculiar manner.

"Yes. Thank you" I reply, smiling politely. I dig my hands into my trouser pockets and see what change I have on me. It's now only about £1.50. I must have lost some in my tumble from the bridge earlier. "Are you open for coffee?"

I ask. “I don’t have much so whatever you can give me will be fine”.

The owner waves me over to him and I follow him into the shop. It’s a small café with a heated food cabinet and coffee machine on the left-hand side. Beyond the back white wall I can see silver kitchen units that are used to cook the food here. They haven’t been ignited just yet, however once the rush hour hits they will probably working overtime. There are four tables on the right-hand side, each with four white chairs on them. They are covered in black and white chequerboard style plastic table cloths. I love this kind of café. The type that has its ketchup poured into plastic squeezy tomato shaped bottles. The far wall has a large mirror, and on the other wall are retro metal signs advertising coca cola, Guinness and Cadbury’s chocolate. The advertisements are the type that would have been used during the wartime I figure. The Cadbury’s one has a large cherub faced boy on it with the area around his mouth covered in chocolate remains. They probably wouldn’t allow it these days as a celebrity chef would probably say it promotes unhealthy lifestyles.

“What can I get for you?” asks the owner, breaking my thoughts.

“What’s your cheapest coffee?” I ask.

“For you? Anything you like”

“Are you sure?”

“I am sure” he says, gleefully. “We like to help people here. We will make plenty from the greedy bankers don’t you worry". He's laughing now, and I spontaneously burst out into a grin. It looks like he has worked in kitchens for a while. His skin has that Mediterranean olive appearance, and his accent matches. Above his lip is a bushy moustache. I would definitely say he is Italian.

"That's very kind of you to offer this" I say. "Can I have a latte if that's not too much trouble?"

"Nothing is too much trouble" he continues, still smiling. "My name is Mario. Mario likes to help"

I wonder how many times he gets told how he looks like the Nintendo plumber. It's so tempting to make a joke, but I luckily resist. Instead I opt for "Hi Mario, I'm Joey"

"Lovely to meet you Joey. Do you live near here?"

"I do, yes" I reply. It's not strictly a lie is it? I mean the doorway of number 54 Fleet Street can't be more than a mile away.

"Well, anytime you need a coffee, come and see Mario and Mario will sort you out"

"That's very kind of you. Thank you again". I always repeat myself when someone is offering me something.

He waves a hand at me in a don't-worry-about-it manner. He passes me the coffee and I hold out my change to him.

"First one free for you" he says. He's still smiling. "Now wait here one moment"

He disappears off out the back and I can hear his footsteps rising up an unseen staircase. I sit at one of the tables, ensuring that I don't cover his chair or his table with dirt. Thank God I washed the blood off my body. I have a look in the mirror and the cut has stopped bleeding, but there is still some red on one side of my face. Whilst Mario is away I take some of his napkins, spit on them, and try my best to freshen my appearance. Along with the blood, a layer of dirt is starting to be removed too. Cleaning your face with spit is not the most hygienic, however I do feel I look better for having done so. I toss the napkins in a silver flip-lid bin and sit back to my coffee. I sit there for a good five minutes before I hear him coming back down towards me.

Does this man ever not smile? His grin appears to be permanent. He walks towards me from the back room and is holding out a carrier bag. "Joey, I want to offer you this. You look like you may need something. It is nothing much, but Mario wants to help". I find the way he talks in both first and third person, often within the same sentence, quite endearing.

"Thank you" I say, taking the bag from him. I open it and see that inside are two items of clothing. One is a black sweatshirt, and the other appears to be a football shirt. I pull it out and hold it up.

"Aston Villa!" exclaims Mario. I smile, it is thoughtful of him to look after me like this.

"Put it on, put it on" he says excitedly. I oblige.

"Up the Villa!" he says smiling even wider than before.

I'm not an Aston Villa fan, but it's good to finally have clothes on my upper body again. "Are you sure I can have these?" I ask

"Yes of course. My son no longer wears these. He will want them put to good use"
"You're very kind thank you"
"The least I can do. If you need anything, come and see Mario"
"Thank you again. I've had a rough night"
"I understand. I like to help. I like to help"

It has taken me a bit longer than expected to get you to this point, and I apologise for that. But here I am, back where the mini story started. It's the day after the night before, and I am sat in an Italian owned café in an Aston Villa shirt. It's mid-morning and I am drinking a decent cup of coffee and feeling okay.

I sit in Mario's café talking to him about a whole range of subjects. He asks if I am watching the World Cup this week. I explain that I will try to. For the next four weeks he will be an England fan apparently, mainly due to his home nation of Italy failing to qualify. He says he also wants Panama to do well, but only because he loves an underdog (He actually calls them the 'small dog' so I am assuming this is what he meant). He has no hidden agenda for helping me. He genuinely cares for people. I learn that his son, confusingly also called Mario, is studying medicine at Nottingham University. He is in his second year and is currently finishing his exams before coming back to London for the summer. I ask if Mario (the son) would be helping in the café whilst back. I would like to thank him for the shirt. I'm told that he will only be here briefly as he has a two-month volunteering role in Eastern Europe. Compassion must run in the family. Mario (the café owner) tells me about his life, and I tell him more about mine. We are worlds apart in terms of background. He is originally from Genoa and moved across to England when he was just seven years old. His father worked in the motor industry and got transferred. They originally planned to move back to Italy but, like many people, life threw up a series of new avenues for him. He met his wife Mary at school, and they married when they were both twenty-two years old. Mario Junior was born five years later, and a daughter, Sofia, arrived two years after that. I ask him about his café, how he came to own it, and whether he lived in the rooms on its upper storeys. Still smiling, he was more than happy to answer.

"No no. We have a family home in Croydon. It is nice there. If I lived here I would always be working. You need to keep work life and home life separate"

Mario has owned this café for ten years, having previously been an assistant manager at a greasy spoon style establishment. He tells me that he used to see homeless people in the doorways near this old place. The sight of them made him feel guilty for not being able to help more, so for what he couldn't donate in money, he donated in compassion instead. He would invite them in for breakfast and coffee to ensure they had one warm meal a day at least. He hasn't changed since this time, and always does his best to help those facing struggles around him. “To be rich in the heart is more important than to be rich in the bank” was something that he said a few times over the course of our meeting. I start to wonder if fate was real. Was I destined to come down this street this morning? Was I destined to meet Dee Dee yesterday? It could be fate, but it could also be pure luck, or it could even be that there are many genuinely caring people in the community that we just don’t know about.

“I have to go and prepare some breakfasts now” says Mario at the end of his story. “You can sit and wait here if you wish, I can get you scrambled egg and toast?”

I really want to stay for as long as possible, but part of me feels that I am abusing his kindness. I tell him that I need to leave but will be back later.

“That is okay. Come and see Mario later when you are nearby. You are a good kid. You promise you come sometime?” he says.

“I promise” I say. “Thank you again for the clothes. And say thank you to your son as well”

“I promise” says a beaming Mario.

By the time I have left the café and walked a bit further, I find a clock and check the time. It is now just past 9.30am and the streets are filling with commuters. Out of the hundreds that I see passing, none of them seem to show me any compassion. In fact, Mario showed more care than all of these people combined. They are mainly glued to their phones, checking the online newspapers, or tweeting about train delays and the like. If I head towards the Tate now I will be incredibly early to meet Dee Dee, however I feel that getting there very early is a better option than arriving five minutes late. Feeling somehow buoyant, I walk back to the river and find the bench where I sat yesterday morning. The sky looks gloomy and the top of St Paul's Cathedral opposite is not it's normal bright white self. Today is not as warm as it was yesterday either, and there is no queue for the ice cream van yet. It's probably too early to be eating all that sugar anyway I guess. A slight breeze is coming across the Thames, and I slip on the jumper that Mario gave to me to protect me from the cold. Content, I slouch back and close my eyes. Aside from the footsteps of a few joggers bouncing past and the odd plane flying overhead it is virtually silent.

Eighteen

I drifted off whilst sat on that bench outside of the Tate, however I was awoken suddenly by a large clap of thunder. Summer storms had been predicted for a few weeks now, but they hadn't materialised until today. The rain was coming down gently, but the clouds above the bridges downstream were heavy and dark. You could see grey streaks reaching out from them to areas in the distance, and the odd bit of lightning was visible every few minutes. There were reports that after this week we would have a month-long heatwave. I can't remember a summer with hardly any rain, so it would be interesting to see if the weather presenters would get it right. For now though, I needed to ensure that I didn't get my new clothes damp straight away so I stood up and looked for shelter. It is quite an open area around the Tate Modern, however I found sanctuary underneath the Millennium Bridge. It didn't stop the effects of the wind that was rattling along the banks of the Thames, however it was dry and still allowed me to see both directions clearly, meaning that if Dee Dee did appear I would be able to spot her. There was no bench to sit on here, but there were some steps which led up to the walkway. These were sheltered by the bridge itself. It would probably allow some water to leak though onto me, but it was satisfactory.

It wasn't long before the sound of heavy rain could be heard on the far side of the bridge, and it moved rapidly to the south side and started chiming off the metal bridge above. The ice cream seller had closed his windows, although there was no one brave enough to weather the storm to get a cold treat anyway. I sat in a ball shape up against the foot of the bridge to try and stay warm. The thunder above was now much stronger, and fork lightning was breaking through the dark skies and striking some of the taller buildings in the city. I sat and counted the time between the lightning and the thunder. Lightning. One Mississippi, two Mississippi. Thunder. I used to sit and watch storms as a kid out of the upstairs window of my childhood home. Dad used to sit with me and taught me that for every second that passed between a lightning strike and a thunderbolt, the storm was about a quarter of a mile away. If my Mississippi's were accurate, the storm is currently just over half a mile away. I counted again. This time it was just over one second. The eye of the storm would be overhead soon. I don't know if you have ever concentrated during the eye of the storm, but I recommend you doing so if you have the chance. It's such a serene and peaceful moment. The rain that has been growing heavier and heavier for the last few minutes will slow right down, and you can hear rivers of rainwater fighting their way down to the drains nearby. The wind will die down, and it feels as if you are in some kind of purgatory. Everything is still, everything is quiet. It's as if the weather has been turned off for a moment. This will only last for a few seconds though, and the silence is broken by a crack of thunder and a flash of lightning simultaneously. The rain will then appear, and the skies darken again.

I am under the bridge still when the eye of the storm is overhead. I plan to sit there and take in the silence, but in the distance I can make out a figure power walking towards me. I can tell straight away from the colourful dress that she is wearing that it is Dee Dee, despite not being able to see her face properly due to her holding a cardigan around her head tightly, sort of like a nun's habit. The sense of relief that passes through me when I know that she has come back for me is massive. I stand up and wave and she starts walking even faster, resembling those you see in the Olympics. Once standing I realise that I had sat on a step where ants had been coming in and out of a small crack, immediately making me feel uncomfortable. I get the feeling that they are all over me, but I can't see any. I keep patting myself down as Dee Dee approaches. I'm not sure if it the thought of spending time with me or the rain that is making her pace so quickly towards me. Before long she is right beside me. Taking a seat next to me, she removes her makeshift headwear and gives me a massive smile. I immediately find myself in a bear-like power hug and can virtually taste her perfume. It smells a bit like white chocolate.

"Happy birthday Joey my boy" she says, still with me in her grip.

My birthday! Today is my birthday. All the commotion of last night and this morning had made me forget. How can you forget your own bloody birthday? Especially as I have had fifteen previous ones.

"Thank you" I reply, feeling a bit more upbeat than before. "Is it wrong to say that I had forgotten?" I ask

Dee Dee does her trademark laugh. "When you start getting older you're meant to forget your age, not your birthday dear!"

"I'm only sixteen though" I say, trying to justify myself

"You've probably lived more in the last few days than many have in a lifetime" she replies. I love the way that Dee Dee thinks.

"So how have you been?"

"I had a rough night if I'm honest Dee Dee"

"I'm here to listen. Before you tell me though, do you think we could go somewhere, y'know, a bit less on the wet side?"

It was more of an instruction rather than a question, but I would love to be inside now.

"There's a café inside the Tate I think" I say, pointing in the general direction of the big building next to us as if somehow Dee Dee didn't know what it was.

“Come on then” she replied, taking my hand and dragging me alongside her. “I hope you don’t mind me saying Joey, but you sort of smell a bit...well”
“Of piss” I say, interrupting.
“I was going to be a bit more eloquent than that, but yes”
“I’ll get to that in a minute”

We walk into the Tate through the main doors. When you enter you pass through the side of the gift shop, separated from the shelves by a large glass window. Other areas can be seen through the glass walls on the other side also and it makes it feel very open. Once you have passed these you enter into a spectacularly large main room. The sign on the wall tells me that this is the Turbine Hall and was once one of the main parts of the building in its previous life as a power station. Dee Dee is studying the map next to one of the lifts.

“Says here that the café is members only. I ain’t no member of this place I’m sorry”
“Me neither, but I don’t feel like heading back out in that rain just yet”
Dee Dee laughs again
“If you don’t mind sitting on the floor Dee Dee, we can perch just down there?”
‘Down there’ is the floor of the Turbine Hall, and half of it is a long slope that rises to a side entrance. A few people are down there, and despite wearing an oversized jumper

and dirty jeans, I don't look any less underdressed than some of the people currently in that area.

We walk down and sit on the slope, facing into the main hall. There are some steel structures at the far end, but I have no idea of what they are or what they are meant to represent. I had always wanted to visit the Tate one day. I heard they had slides in here at one point and that would have been great fun. I won't count this as a proper visit however. I will come back and have a proper look around when I can.

"As it's your birthday, I have got you a couple of little things Joey" said Dee Dee, pulling out a small box and a carrier bag from her seemingly bottomless shoulder bag.

"That's very kind of you, thank you. You didn't have to do that"

"And leave you on your own and with nothing on your birthday? Don't be silly!"

In the bag are two new sets of clothes from H&M. There are jeans and t-shirts, and more importantly, new underwear. Sorry if you are eating breakfast, but I've been unable to change mine for the last few days. Would it be wrong to get changed straight away in the toilets here? As much as I want to, it's definitely best that I somehow get a shower beforehand. I'm not sure where I can do this, but I'll figure something out. I thank Dee Dee for her kindness, yet she seems to be smiling wider and nudging the smaller box across to me.

I take the neatly wrapped box and tear off the rainbow coloured paper. I like that Dee Dee has even thought through what wrapping paper to use, as she knows that it will please me. I feel guilty for tearing it to be honest, yet she is watching over me closely, still grinning widely. I slide open the white box inside and find myself presented with a brand new mobile phone. I immediately feel myself overcome with emotion, and I give her the biggest hug that I have ever given. I thank her, but my words are slightly lost in the tears and cracked voice that seem to be leaving my body. I have no idea what I have done to deserve such kindness, and the feeling of genuinely being loved and cared for is miles away from the emotions that I have been experiencing at the other end of the scale over the last forty-eight hours. I sit there on the floor of the Turbine Hall for at least five minutes, wetting Dee Dee's shoulders with my tears. After a while she carefully nudges my head off of her and looks straight into my eyes.

"I said to you yesterday Joey that I would tell you about my plans, and I really think that you could be a big part of them. You don't realise how much you have changed my perspective, let me tell you that. Over lunch, I want you to listen to me and hear me through okay?"

"Okay I promise" I replied, although still slightly apprehensive just what she had in store. It was Dee Dee though, and I did trust her, and felt it was only fair to try and help her too. I have trusted people too quickly before since arriving to London as you know, however Dee Dee seemed different. It turned out that the main reason that she got me the phone was so that I could always contact her if I needed to, if I was in any trouble and that kind of thing. It wasn't a fancy iPhone or anything like that, but having a device where I could speak to someone or text someone who cared for me was the biggest thing in my life.

"Thank you, Joey" she said smiling. "Now, why don't you fill me in on what has happened to you? I can tell by the way you are acting today that there are things on your mind".

For the next quarter of an hour I told her everything. I told her about The Nomad, about Jenny and Pete, and also that moment on the bridge. She held my right hand tightly throughout and kept telling me that she is here for me now. She had a way that allowed me to open up, and I thought that maybe her losing a son may have been a factor in this. Had she lost her son her son to suicide like so many others? It felt the wrong time to ask her this, but I wanted to know all about her past, as much as she wanted to know about mine. The whole process felt as if the pressure that had been building up inside me had been released. Once I had finished, she continued to hold my hand. We had become so immersed in what had happened that I had forgotten that I was sat on the floor of one of the largest galleries in the country.

"I hope baby" said Dee Dee after a short silence, "I hope that you see the hope that there is. I am so sorry that I wasn't there for you this morning"

"But you are here for me now though" I replied, as if to reconfirm what she had told me earlier.

"I am here for you now. Life is full of hope, life is full of fear"

"Do you live in hope, Dee Dee, or do you live in fear? I'm guessing hope?"

"Joey my boy, one can live in hope *and* live in fear, they're not mutually exclusive. I think it's natural for humans to experience both emotions simultaneously and would think it odd if a person did not hope and fear for something. Life is about seizing the situation when hope is high. Take love for example. I know it's a bit different and may sound a bit odd, but it's the example which highlights both. Say you've known someone for a long time, or that a person you care for has come into and out of your life many times, yet you have an emotional connection to them. You may not know exactly what it is, but something taps away in your mind about it. You live in hope that something will happen, that this person may return your love, yet you also fear that you may be wrong. You both don't know if the other person feels the same way and rather than one of you seizing the moment you both just wonder what might be until the time is too late. I know how hard it can be to reach out to seize what you want but failing and learning is better than not knowing how life could have been without them being a part of it. Do you get me?"

"I do. I think. I don't think I've ever been in love though"

"It doesn't have to be love. Right now, at this moment, are you hopeful or fearful?"

"Well, I'm worried that things won't get easier"

"Yet you hope they do?"

"Of course, yeah, I don't think they can get worse, but at the same time I am fearful that they might"

"Well there we go. You're living in hope and in fear. You need to seize on to the hope. That's why I think you should listen to me and help me through with the idea. If you walked away right now, I will know that I had tried my best, whereas in a day or a week you may regret not knowing what might have been"

~

From the Tate, me and Dee Dee travelled across London on the tube, ironically heading back to Marylebone where this whole adventure had started for me. It only took around twenty minutes to get there via the Circle and Bakerloo lines, however the journey seemed to take longer due to feeling self-conscious about how I looked. Dee Dee had promised me a shower before we went for lunch, although I wasn't really sure exactly why we were heading in this direction. I knew I'd feel much better once I had got into the new clothes that she had kindly given me. Not only did I have a few days of dirt and sweat on me, the rain that fell earlier had made the football shirt from Mario smell a little musty. I think he must have stored it in the loft above his café.

As we exited the station, I felt a little awkward. My naivety upon arriving here before made me wish that I had been better prepared for life in the capital. I was told to wait for a few minutes as Dee Dee needed to use the cashpoint, so I took this as an opportunity to look inside my favourite café. The Italian café across the road was open this time, and I made a mental note to ask Dee Dee if we could go there this afternoon as a birthday treat. I stared through the window, noticing how very busy it was inside, a mixture of tourists with suitcases and railway workers in bright, yet grubby, orange Network Rail overalls. They all seemed to be tucking into various different breakfast meals, all based around a fried egg. Without wanting to put them off their food, I moved back away from the café windows and sat on a bench nearby, watching from a distance. I found there to be a bit of charm in the plastic tablecloths and throwaway coffee cups. I've always been a bit of a sucker for nostalgia and am often intrigued by seeing things which in the past were the epicentre of people's lives. Take those buildings you see around London for example which have the faded advertising slogans painted high on their outside walls. Or seaside towns. About sixty years ago Bournemouth or Brighton may have been the ultimate holiday destination for families in Britain, but they have been left to battle the elements on their own in many places. If you visit them now you can see amusements and hotels with paint slowly removing itself from the walls and signs. I'm not sure what it is exactly which makes me love this so much though. I spent a fair number of family holidays down on the South Coast of England as a child, so maybe there is a part of me that still wishes that I was young and innocent, sat on the sea wall looking out from Herne Bay or Christchurch as the sun set, with a jacket potato on my lap for an evening meal. Me and my mum used to love the jacket potatoes you used to get from the seaside vans. Those days are now long gone for me. A lot of the coast now is being rejuvenated and the buildings that you'd find nearest to the sea are being given a new lease of life in the forms of small takeaway places. These are mainly fish and chips, but the invasion of the hipsters has also taken over in some places, so the food is more expensive because it is served to you in a quirky fashion.

I was knocked out my nostalgic day dream by Dee Dee returning.

"Come on then, let's go get you a shower" she said, as she came past. I stood up and followed her down a road to the right of Marylebone Station.

"Where are we going to?" I asked her

"My plan revolves around the place that we will end up at in about five minutes time" she replied, smiling.

We took a left hand turn onto Bell Street. I had never been here before, but instantly loved it. On the left were tall red-bricked buildings that I assumed were owned by rich lawyers or doctors. On the right were the kind of houses that you saw Sherlock Holmes living in on the TV. All symmetrical with black or red doors, and two neat stories above them. We continued down the street, and it seemed Dee Dee was on a mission. She pointed out a church at the next junction.

"I know your thoughts on religion, Joey, however I want to take you in there later" she said, pointing to the large sand coloured church. "It is where my son is, and I want to introduce you to him"

"Of course" I replied. She was right, religion definitely wasn't my thing, especially after this week, but I owed it to her to do this. I still didn't know exactly what had happened, and I really should ask. I need to find the correct moment, and maybe when we visit her son later she will explain.

"Okay Joey" said Dee Dee, standing in the centre of the road just a few yards past the church. It was a quiet street so no risk of getting run over just now. "This is what I wanted to bring you here for"

I was failing to see what she wanted me to see if I am being honest. "What is it?" I asked.

"I want you to look across the road at the building"

"Which one? The glass one?" I said, still a bit confused. There were two buildings directly ahead of us. One was a glass fronted four storey building, which looked like giant white blocks stacked on top of each other.

"No, not that one, the one next door"

I assumed she was not on about the building that was on the left of the glass monstrosity, as that was being demolished. I'd be very surprised if Dee Dee's plan was for me to rebuild something from scratch. The one to the right of the first building was lovely, however in need of a fair bit of love. It was also four storeys in height, however rather than being covered in glass, it was a much older building. It had white stone work, complete with some nostalgic peeling paint, and a light coloured wooden door. Bizarrely, it also had a second door on the right-hand side of the front facing wall. For somewhere so narrow, this seemed odd. The two floors above had a pair of windows each, both rectangular ones that slid up from the bottom, and way up the top there were two further windows which looked as though they provided a view from a loft conversion.

"What is this place?" I asked

"This was where my business used to be, until last month anyway"

"This was your café? But, it's empty?"

"Although the café failed Joey, I wanted to keep hold of the building and reinvent it, hence why I met with that solicitor"

“You own this building?”

“I do indeed. It makes me sad to see it so empty. It used to be the centre point of this areas community. We had big gatherings after things at the church, like receptions for christenings, wedding breakfasts and even the odd wake. Time always moves on though Joey, that’s the problem. When time moves on, people move on. The young people who grew up here all moved away and that left no one to keep the community alive. It’s now surrounded by people who moved from out of town. Don’t get me wrong, they are nice people, but their hearts lie elsewhere. You never really see any of them at the weekend. Even the church is struggling here these days. I was lucky to get this place at the right time, but it has sometimes been hard to pay off. I used to have tenants on the top two floors as a way to help me pay off the mortgage. Once that was sorted though, I never replaced them. In a way I wish I did get more as they were always interesting people. One is an actor now, he has been in some big films over the last few years”

“What’s his name?” I asked, being nosey. I loved celebrity spotting, and this was as close as I had got since moving to London

“Martin van de Molen. I’m sure you’ve heard of him”

“Of course I have, he’s won about fifty Oscars”

“Bit of an exaggeration baby” said Dee Dee laughing, “he’s won two. He lived here when he was just starting out in theatre. He took me down to the West End a few times to see some of the top plays”

"I can't believe you know van de Molen" I said shaking my head. Nothing about Dee Dee could surprise me anymore.
"I don't know him anymore Joey, it's been over ten years since I last saw him"
"Still cool though!" I said excitedly.
"Anyway, do you want to come inside and get showered?"
"Yes please, thank you"

Dee Dee opened the left door of the two on the front of the property, and I followed her down a small hall before turning right up a long straight staircase. It was very clean inside, however the walls were painted a deep red which made the building seem very dark inside. Wooden bannisters stretched up on either side, and a tall potted plant was located at the very top. The window behind the plant was clear, however the buildings at the rear of Dee Dee's property meant that not a great deal of natural light found its way into the hall on the first floor. It was surprisingly big inside this flat, and there were five rooms which led off from the hall. To the left was a small kitchen, with a bathroom in the room to its right.

"You should rent this out Dee Dee, you'd make a fortune on this as a flat here"
"I could, that's true, but I have other plans for this. Come and sit with me and I'll explain"

I peered into each room as I followed Dee Dee, and all had the same dark red walls, and it seemed to make them seem a bit intimidating. The building had a narrow front, but what it lost in width it easily made up for in depth. The whole of this floor didn't seem to have been lived in for a few years, and the beige curtains were showing signs of decolourisation at their bases.

"How do you get to the other flats?" I asked Dee Dee, as there didn't seem to be any further staircase from the one that we were in.

"There is another entrance through the old café. It's a spiral staircase which leads up to the upper two floors"

"Ah OK, so is this your flat we are in now?"

"Technically, they're all mine" she replied laughing, "but I spend most of my time on the top floor as you get the best view. This one we are in now needs a bit of decorating, and that's where you come in".

Dee Dee can't have bought me all this way just to make me decorate her flats, can she? We enter the room on the far right of the landing, and it's a small sitting room. It's much lighter in this room than the other parts of the flat, mainly due to the large window that looks back over Bell Street. There are two double sofas, situated on the left and right of the room, and facing each other. In the middle is a glass coffee table. Apart from that there isn't a great deal in this room. I study the paintings on the wall. The artwork is inspired by many different regions. Directly opposite is a painting of an elephant charging, dust being thrown up from its pounding feet. On the left-hand wall is a copy of a lady from the Orient stood near blossoming trees. It has the feel of somewhere an elderly person would be happy.

"Would you like a coffee?" Dee Dee asks me.
"Yes please, thank you"
"Well, while I go and make that, why not go and have that shower. There is a towel in the bathroom at the end of the hall"

The water comes out of the modern looking shower steaming. I can't wait to get myself cleaned off, and I spend the next fifteen minutes soaking under the hot water. I could have stayed in there all day, however Dee Dee asking me if I had washed myself down the plug made me realise why I was here. She wanted to tell me her plan, and I wanted to hear it. I put my old clothes into the large metallic bin in the corner of the bathroom and changed into the new ones that had been bought for me this morning. Feeling a million times better, I headed back to the front room and asked Dee Dee if I could hear what she had been planning. She poured me a cup of coffee from a tall brass coloured pot and smiled gently.

Nineteen

"Now listen to me Joey" says Dee Dee, turning more serious than she has ever been since I met her yesterday. "I don't want you to build your hopes up okay, but I want to inform you of my plans for this building. What I need you to do is to keep it a secret for the time being, because if more people find out about it early, the more chance there will be of it not being approved"

I agree to this.

"First things first, this is now your home. You can have part of the top floor of the building. There is a bedroom up there for you already set up, and also a kitchen and bathroom which we can share"

"That's amazing, thank you. I don't really know what to say. Are you sure I won't get in your way?"

"No, silly, I have always had a spare room up there for guests. I'd rather guests stayed with me as this floor and the one above are not as nice looking, and Dee Dee has a reputation to uphold".

She is smiling again. I can't wait to sleep in an actual bed this evening. No sleeping in doorways, no sleeping in hostels. I wonder if I will be able to enjoy. When you spend a few nights sleeping in a different place, your first night's sleep back home always feels strange. I know that I haven't returned home as such, but it will be a bed on my own. I fully expect to have some realistic dreams where I am being urinated on by a passer-by, but hopefully these won't force me to have anxiety attacks or to run somewhere else. I really don't want to ever be in a situation where I am on a bridge again, looking down contemplating whether to jump. I did say this after the first time however, so I will not take anything for granted.

Dee Dee was continuing with her plan. I had missed a couple of sentences through the excitement (or worry) about tonight.

"Now, the main part of the plans. I have been in talks with my solicitor for a while since my café closed, ironing out my options for how best we can move on. There have been talks of selling the building for it to be turned into flats, but I have worked very hard to have this place. This is my home. This street is my home. The community may have disappeared, but this is where I belong. As I said to you yesterday, helping people is how I want to live my life. I may not have wealth in the bank, but I have a wealth of happiness in my life, and that is sometimes more important"

"So, you are thinking of turning it back into some kind of a community centre?" I ask impatiently.

"No, the space isn't quite right for that here now"

"Okay"

"Joey, this building has three floors which I do not use. WE do not use" she continued, emphasising my resident status. “What I have asked for is to turn the building into a centre for those without a place to stay, people like yourself”

“That’s incredible! Was that just because of me?”

I was genuinely excited by this. I knew that Dee Dee always put other people first, but her love and compassion for those in need almost seemed unreal compared to those in my hometown. Even my own parents hadn’t cared enough.

“It is not solely down to you, not that part anyway. I had been thinking for a while on how I could utilise the space to help people in need. I must admit that I didn’t know as much about shelters before speaking with you about the night you spent in one though. So much is unreported. All you normally hear is that these places exist, and they provide you with this and that. You rarely hear from the people who use them. The people who have seen the rougher side of life in them. I’m not saying that they are all like that, of course not. And most of the people who stay in them are wonderful. It’s like that girl that you mentioned to me. I forget her name sorry”

“Mimi?”

“Yes, Mimi. That was her. There are so many people like her in our society, people who look out for others despite being in a disadvantaged position themselves. Those people do not sell newspapers unfortunately, so most of the media and the television programmes focus on the small proportion who take drugs or commit crimes. It brings in the viewing figures and it sells the newspapers. The privileged people who are in a safe environment watch and read it and have a thirst for more. You could say that thisn side of homelessness is being exploited by our media. Hopefully what we can do can help change attitudes from others as well as help protect the most vulnerable".

This made a lot of sense to me and made me think to how many people didn't offer me any help at all. Some people definitely passed me when I was preparing to jump but none of them approached and asked if I was okay. That is all it would have taken for me to step back onto the pavement. Did anyone see The Nomad as he lay unconscious? Perhaps, but if they did, they didn't even phone for help. I ask Dee Dee if we can start to prepare for visitors straight away. I know this will involve a lot of repainting but I'm willing to keep myself occupied by doing it.

"Setting up a shelter is a bit of a longer process than that I'm afraid. I've already put in for planning permission to make the necessary alterations, however it has gone to a public consultation"

"What does that mean?"

"Basically, we need to listen to residents nearby who may have concerns. It has been ongoing for three weeks already, and it will finish with a public debate in the town hall in July sometime. I'm just waiting to hear about exactly when that will be. Anyway, before I get into all that, I haven't finished telling you everything yet"

"Sorry, I'm excited"

"That's understandable. So am I if I am being honest. I was originally planning to make it into the shelter for the homeless, and as I have a kitchen downstairs I could provide those who arrive with some hot food each night. When I met you yesterday that all changed. The night that you spent in the night shelter terrified you, I know it did. I know also how much it affected Mimi also. I tried finding her yesterday by calling around a few places, but no one had seen her. What both you and Mimi needed was a place where you could feel safe. After speaking with you I went to my meeting with the solicitor again and told him to help me change the public consultation so that it read it would be a shelter for those in the LGBT community. I tried to find you again in the short space of time I had but you were not in the few places I checked. It made my heart sink. I am so sorry that I couldn't let you stay here last night"

"Dee Dee you don't realise how much you have done for me. You never ever need to apologise. I can't believe that I have found someone who genuinely cares for me, despite having no reason to"

"I have lost one son in my life, and the feeling that I had let you down bought back so many emotions to me. I was away yesterday evening visiting old friends and told them all about you, and about all the young people out in this

city just like you. We don't even know how many there are like you here, and that's why I need to help"
"You should become an MBE or something. You probably do more than some of the people who get given that title"
"Honey I don't do it for awards. I do it because I love people".

I was a bit lost for words and didn't know quite what to say to Dee Dee. I offered to help as much as possible with everything she needed to help make this work. I asked her what I needed to do.

"There are a fair few things, Joey. In fact, there are a great deal of things that we need to do. Firstly, we need to decorate this place, source all the beds and equipment that we may need and all at the same time keep fighting our case to ensure that it gets the approval of the local residents"
"But why would they be against it?"
"Because they may not understand. They may assume that all the people on the streets are there because of drink and drugs"
"Do you want me to go and talk to them all?"
"That would take you all month and we don't have the time. You will be at the public meeting I hope, and maybe you could tell them your story?"
"Of course, definitely"
"We also have a reporter coming around this afternoon also. I called in a favour as one of the local journalists

owed me a favour. He is going to publish our plans and take a couple of photographs if you want to be in them?"

"But no one knows me"

"Not yet they don't, and your time of being anonymous is over"

"But what if my parents see somehow? I'd hate that"

"That is something else you should do. You need to write to them, and that friend of yours"

"But my parents hate me"

"It may seem that way, and I know it is partly their fault that you ended up here, but I want you to write and tell them that you are safe. You don't need to go into detail. At the end of the day they should know. You're legally allowed to move out now that you are sixteen and if they know that you are not in any danger that will be some comfort, whether you think they care or not. One day Joey I believe they will accept you for who you are"

"I could never move back to there. I guess I should though. Anyway, have you looked into getting beds and those kinds of things for here already?"

"I have yes, but we need the funding before we can even think to start to transform the place. Without the funding we will be unable to start even the smallest part of the project. Hopefully though, someone will see our article if they publish it and we can get the ball rolling"

"How likely do you think it will be that we will get the money?"

"I'm hopeful not fearful" she said with a wink. It's as if she knows something has been confirmed already, but when I question her on this she swears that she has now got any financial backing confirmed at all. She also tells me briefly about all the training and legal items that need to be completed also. The list is quite exhausting and involves everything from health and safety right through to managing volunteers, first aid, mental health training and safeguarding. It seems that I may have to do some more studying after all. I agree to help out where possible. Dee Dee decides that we have discussed enough of what she calls “the boring side” of the shelter for now and asks if I would like to get some lunch and discuss how we are going to transform the look of the building inside. She mentions that we need to be back by 3pm for the journalist and asks if there is anywhere special I would like to eat.

Fifteen minutes later we were sat in Zappi’s Italian Café opposite Marylebone Station.

Dee Dee was on her second cup of coffee when she reached down into her bag and pulled out an A4 notepad and two pens, one black and one red. I put down my knife and fork and momentarily stopped eating my full English all-day breakfast. It wasn’t Michelin starred this place, but it wasn’t bad. It was nice to finally be sat in here. The baked beans were a cheap variety, I could always tell, but the sausage, bacon and eggs more than made up for it. We also had slices of banana bread for afterwards that we were sort of forced into buying. Apparently it was homemade by Mr Zappi's wife and we would really be missing out if we didn't have some.

Picking up the notepad and black pen, I felt a little uneasy. "I don't really feel comfortable writing the letters in here. I'm sorry. Can I do it later when we are back in your house?"
"This isn't for the letters Joey, I wouldn't make you do them here. This is for us to draw up our master plan. We will make a list of everything we need, and also a list of people who might be willing to help"
"You could ask your film star friends" I joked
"You laugh, but there is no harm in writing is there?" she replied seriously

I took the pad and put it to the right of my plate, using the fork in my left hand to continue eating. I licked the nib of the pen before I started writing; I've no idea why, and wrote the words "DEE DEE AND JOEYS MASTERP LAN OF ACTION" across the top of the page, underlining it four times. I actually spelled it 'master pan' to start with. It's weirdly hard to spell correctly when writing in big letters. I squeezed in the missing 'L' and was then stumped. I'd never done a proper plan before. Maybe I should have listened in those bloody UCAS sessions we had in those school Tutor Time sessions after all.

"So, what first?" I asked, desperate for help.
"How about we make a list of all the things we need for the rooms?"

"So, beds and bedding?" I said, whilst scribbling down the same thing on the pad.

"Well, yes, that's a start Joey, but we need ideas of where we can get these economically"

"As long as they aren't plastic lined mattress covers"

"This is why you'll be great with helping to set this up. You've been in a shelter and know what makes things comfortable and what makes things worse"

We stayed in the café for nearly two hours, only leaving to get back in time for the journalist to hear the plan and take some photographs. The list that we had made now spanned over ten pages in our notepad, and it seemed a daunting task to get everything done by the time we would open, if the plans were approved (and whenever 'open' would be). Dee Dee promised to make sure that all our needs would be added to the article and would put out a call for help to anyone who wished to volunteer to help. On our way back up Bell Street to our four storey, Dee Dee pulled me aside into the church. The front of the church is quite daunting and seems much more intense when up close. It has four large pillars at its front, with more in a square turret above. It's much bigger than the church my parents dragged me too back home. We head through the black metal gates, and up the four stone steps. Upon entering there is a large blue sign with gold writing. It informs me that this is the Christ Church of England, and underneath has a list of all the upcoming services. I feel odd about being in a church again, however

I owe it to Dee Dee to be here. She takes my right arm, and slowly we walk down the right-hand side of the church, passing the lines of pews that were once filled every Sunday, but now probably struggle to reach half capacity.

When we get to the far corner, Dee Dee takes a seat in front of a small bronze plaque on the wall. “Joey” she starts, “I want you to meet my son Marcus”. Her voice is cracked with emotion as she speaks, and nods towards the wall.

This plaque commemorates the lives of

Michael Webster
Marcus Ashton

Taken from our lives to sit with our Lord
6th November 2010

I sit silently staring at the plaque, before trying to comfort Dee Dee. “I’m so sorry” I say twice, unsure how to find the right way of consoling her.

“Thank you” she replies, taking my left hand in her right. I feel her nudge across the pew slightly towards me until our upper arms are touching.

“They shouldn’t have been there” she says finally. I ask her where ‘there’ is.

“I had Marcus in 1982. It was during the late Spring. I remember going into labour as the television news showed coverage of the Falklands War. Me and Marcus' father Danny didn't plan to have a child together and were not really together as a couple. Back in those days, and with my parents' strong connections to the church, I was convinced that keeping the baby was the correct thing to do. I don't think I would have been emotionally strong enough to have an abortion, and once he was born I loved him straight away. I was maybe too young, I was only twenty years old myself. His father was slightly older. I think he was twenty-six at the time. I met him through a friend on a night out at the cinema in June of the year before. A couple of my male friends who I had known since school were big James Bond fanatics. We saw For Your Eyes Only and I happened to be stood next to this man when we were getting food before the showing. We got on instantly and stayed sitting next to one another for the entire movie. After this we went on a few dates. Danny used to sing the theme tune to the film to me. It was quite romantic back in the day. Things didn't work out however, and he was often getting caught up in trouble near the area where he lived. He came from North London, and there was a lot of political tension between the police and the black community for a few years. After Marcus was born I wanted to keep his father as part of his life, and he did try hard to be there for him. Danny lived on the same estate as his brother and mother, and he used to get Marcus along to play football with the other children in the area. Michael, the other boy on the plaque, that was Marcus' cousin.

"Does Marcus' dad still live up there?" I ask

"No, he unfortunately became involved in some trouble a few years ago. After Marcus died he sort of lost his way. I tried helping but he got caught up in gambling and alcohol addictions. We thought he had turned a corner at one point, but he was then arrested on suspicion of armed burglary. I sat through the court case. It went on for six weeks. In the end he was found guilty and was sentenced to twelve years in jail. I hope to God that prison has acted as some kind of rehabilitation for him"

"Will you be there for him when he is released?"

"I don't know. At first I will offer support from a distance, communicate through his brother maybe. I want to help, but I need to protect myself too"

"I understand. Do you mind me asking what happened to Marcus and Michael?"

"You need to know. It's one of the reasons why I couldn't leave you, as I said"

I noticed that Dee Dee was squeezing my hand a bit tighter now. Despite eight years passing, it was clear that the pain was still raw.

"They were both up in North London one day. There had been some charity event for bonfire night. It took a long time for the truth to come out, but the reality was that some people from a gang mistook the boys as their rivals. I know my child wasn't a saint, but I know for certain that he wasn't involved in the gangs. He never stayed over at his father's because he never felt safe. He removed himself from any potential situation as soon as possible as he just didn't want to become involved. He was only up there that night as some of the money that was being raised from the firework display was going to help fund new facilities at the local recreation ground where the boys played their football. As things escalated that night, the gang chased the boys as they started to run. There was footage from CCTV cameras of them running along Seven Sisters Road with a group of about six or seven not far behind. They only made it as far as Finsbury Park station"

Dee Dee stops and bows her head. I tell her that she doesn't have to go on if it is too hard. She sits silently for a brief period, before continuing.

"They were beaten around the side of the station. Some people tried to help, but the gang had weapons and fought them off. Eventually the police arrived, and the paramedics shortly after that, however it was too late. Both had been struck by bats, and Michael had been stabbed in his side. When I got the call, I went across to the hospital, meeting Danny and his sister-in-law there. We stayed all night in that corridor, pacing up and down praying that they would be okay. I lost my boy just after 3am. Michael lost his fight less than an hour later".

Again, Dee Dee falls silent. I can't see her face but I know that she is crying. She doesn't say any more about the events that took place on the 6th November 2010. After a period of quiet reflection, she stands, and pats me on my shoulder.

"Come on, lets head back and meet these reporters. We owe it to the boys to do good".

I stand up behind her, and she kisses her hand before placing it on the plaque. It leaves a small damp mark on the top right, and we head out the church together.

Twenty

Dear Mum and Dad,

I hope that you are both well. I am doing fine. I am just writing to tell you that I am safe and well. I have currently moved away for a bit, however I am living with a friend named Diana. She is wonderful and caring and has done a lot for the church. I need time to work myself out.

Yours,

Joseph.

~

Dear Angelica,

I hope everything is good! You won't get this until you are back from your time in the West Indies, so I hope that you have had an amazing time.

A lot has changed for me, in fact too much to put into one letter. Anyway, I will try and summarise. I went to London like we had planned after having a bit of a fall out with the parents. Can you believe that Italian café was shut when I got here after all my planning?! Anyway, I stayed in hotels for a couple of nights before meeting a lovely woman named Diana. I think she might be from the West Indies too. She did tell me earlier this week but I'll be honest and say I have forgotten. It feels a bit rude to ask her again now.

Anyway, I've moved in with Diana. I know her as Dee Dee and she has this amazing house in Marylebone and we have some amazing plans for it. I want to tell you about them but I've been told to be quiet about it. Anyway, you won't be back to read this until after we know either way so I'll tell you. We are planning to open and run a hostel for LGBT homeless people. It will have beds, bathrooms and Dee Dee will cook some amazing chicken (apparently. I've never tasted it). Anyway, we have to go through loads of boring planning meetings and things but hopefully it all works out.

Anyway, I won't keep you, I want to fill in the gaps to you IN PERSON when you are home. We have lots to catch up with. I might write again before you're home anyway as I'm too excited. I have a new phone so will text you from my new number. I hope you get it. Anyway I have to go. Dee Dee is downstairs talking to some journalist. I might get my picture in the paper.

Anyway, have to go

Love ya and miss ya!

Joey
xx

PS. I say 'anyway' too much! X

PPS. I am forcing you to come and visit me when you get home! Xx

It didn't take me long to write the letters, and I knew that Dee Dee wanted me to do them. I was genuinely excited about seeing Angelica again. My parents? Not so much but I thought it was best to keep it civil. I did genuinely miss Angelica and felt a bit ashamed that I wasn't more enthusiastic about her trip away. I know how important it would be to her to visit her relations in the West indies, and also to get a sense of the culture that her parents and extended family were a part of. Everything is easier in hindsight, and the problems that I was going through at the time had led me to become selfish. This is something that I am slowly overcoming though, and I am in a much better place now. I am still cautious however as I know my state of mind may not always be like this. If the plans for the night shelter are not approved it will put me back a few steps I believe. On the other hand, I need to have belief that they will get approved. I must live in hope and not in fear.

Anyway, I'm off to post them now and then start my media career!

Twenty-one

I'll apologise now as I have skipped forward a day. It's currently 6pm on Tuesday 12th June. The rest of my birthday was nice, and I spent some time with Dee Dee in the evening watching bits of the soaps on the television. It was great just to have a normal kind of evening for a change. I also managed to have the most relaxing sleep of the year. No exam worries, no risk of being urinated on and no chance of being mugged. My worries about being restless after sleeping in odd places were unfounded, and I think I fell asleep after about five minutes at most. Before settling down for the evening together, I helped Dee Dee with the journalist. He had a lot of questions, and she took a politician-style approach, avoiding answering some of the trickier ones. This wasn't because she didn't know, but more the fact that she didn't want to spread too much detail across the pages when the public consultation was still ongoing.

We both were not sure how much he would take away from our discussion, or if he would even fully understand why. Also, I didn't expect the journalist to be from a big publication so became very nervous when he told me he was from the Evening Standard, the same paper I slept under in the doorway of 54 Fleet Street earlier this week. Every commuter in the city had access to this for free so a good article would really push things in the right direction. I never did ask why the journalist owed Dee Dee a favour, but sometimes it's better not to be nosey. He was a nice man though and sat with us for a good while listening to various things that I had to say too. He asked a lot about my background, but I decided to be a bit coy about the whole thing. I also lied about my age. For some reason I panicked when he asked, and I didn't want my young age to lead to any repercussions on either me or Dee Dee. I told him I had just turned eighteen and he didn't seem to give me any looks that questioned this. I definitely look younger than eighteen, but in my new clothes I may have just about convinced him. I also didn't give him a surname as the last thing I wanted was for my parents to somehow be shown it and then them get involved. After talking to him for a good couple of hours, he led us outside to take some pictures that he would use in the paper "if the light was right". Cut to me and Dee Dee stood in various poses outside on the street, sat on the sofa or sitting on the stairs. I felt a bit of a knob, I won't lie. I hate having my photograph taken and always look a bit odd when I try and smile so I sat looking like a moody and jilted teenager (not a hard act to pull off, I'm sure you'll agree).

I don't know who was more excited to see what they had written. When it got to 4pm today Dee Dee asked if I could go and collect the paper. She really didn't have to ask. I pulled on my shoes and ran outside. I wasn't sure which station is nearest to Bell Street, but I knew how to get to Marylebone and thought that'd be as good as anything. I sprinted past the church. And turned the corner to the station. It was getting busy inside with commuters heading back to High Wycombe and Oxford and I bustled past people, probably causing a few people to spill their coffees. In my head it looked like that scene in Willy Wonka where Charlie finds his Golden Ticket. Who knows, they might even make a film of me one day. I need to calm down, the shelter might not even get approved yet I'm already dreaming of some big-name producer wanting to turn my rags to riches story into the feel-good film of the summer.

I found an Evening Standard seller (are they a seller if the paper is free?) and asked if I could take more than one. She didn't seem to mind and motioned towards the stack of them without saying a word. I picked up about ten and hurried my way back outside. Impatient, I put nine of them on the curb, sat on them and started flicking through the remaining copy. Nothing on pages one to six. To be honest, most of the front pages were full of American and North Korean politicians at a summit. I would try and read this later as I have not really seen the main news properly this week. I kept flicking through the paper. It must be in here surely? I turned and turned each page until eventually, there it was. A double page spread. Pages fourteen and fifteen. Under the headline of "Marylebone Residents LGBT Dream" were four pictures of Dee Dee and me, alongside a lengthy piece about our plans for the ex-café. I think Dee Dee must have let on more information than she thought as in the column inches were talks about what our shelter would offer, information on the public consultation and also a small bit of background about me. I'm glad it didn't go into the details too much about the darker sides of my week. Since meeting Dee Dee I feel that I have made so much progress, and now hope and fear are split about eight per cent to twenty per cent in favour of the 'hope' side. If details about being beaten in the shelter, or being urinated on, or indeed contemplating ending my life on Blackfriars Bridge were printed I feel that I may have slipped backwards a few steps. I'm a bit concerned that I will become burnt out by everything that is happening. I've never felt so low as I did this week, and yet today I have something to challenge and inspire me in a safe environment with someone who cares. This process doesn't rarely happen within a year, let alone a week. This time just over a week ago I was doing a Drama exam. Mad.

I read the article in the paper twice and hoped that someone out there would read it and come to offer their support. Me and Dee Dee are on a mission this afternoon to try and get hold of supplies to start decorating the rooms. We mentioned this in the paper too. "If there are any businesses who would like to form a partnership, please contact us at Dee Dee's Café, Bell Street, Marylebone". Hopefully this tactic will work. It also means that we best not remove the fading red sign announcing that it is indeed Dee Dee's building until the very last minute, despite the fact that it is barely readable due to being bleached by the sun.

The pictures in the paper haven't turned out too bad. I look like I have been pulled out of some 1990's teen drama, or a background member of a rubbish boyband. All moody, arms folded, staring deep into the camera. I actually find it quite funny that I am pictured here, rather than cringing. I have been in the paper once before. It was back when I was in Year 7 at school. The local paper did a 'National Environment Week' and being a geography nerd, I tried getting involved in everything. The next week there I was on the front page no less, pretending to dig holes to plant trees, holding a shovel that was obviously too big for me. I looked a complete knob. Still, this Evening Standard more than makes up for it. I became excited to show Dee Dee and ran back all the way from Marylebone Station to the house. Needless to say, that she was absolutely thrilled by it all also, and we got to work right away going through the plans we made in the café. We decided that all the walls would be a pale blue if we could get the paint on the cheap. Failing that we would have to go with magnolia. I really didn't want magnolia. It would be too similar to Gold's Hostel, and after my night there I feel those negative images could be brought across. No, this would be our place. This would be different.

Dee Dee was so excited about the article that she immediately had a copy was pinned to the wall in the hall leading up the stairs, and also on the wall in the kitchen of our flat. The reason behind this was to ensure we remembered why we were doing all the hard work, in case we became tired from trying to convert the building. She was pleased at how well we had both come across and was due a call regarding an update on the feedback so far from local residents. It was publicised to local people yesterday that it will be for the LGBT community as part of the consultation. You always hope that people would show compassion, but many will only support it if it wasn't to be on their own doorstep. A hostel in another borough of this city would get support from them no doubt. Many support providing facilities like this, but only at an arm's reach.

Now, this brings us up to date. There was no real news from the consultation yesterday in regards to comments, however the public meeting had been set for the morning of Wednesday 4th July, and a decision to come through on the following Saturday. Dee Dee has asked me to talk at the meeting on behalf of the shelter, so you now find me lying on my bed with the notepad trying to write a five-minute speech. I think I'm on about my tenth draft. A pile of screwed up paper is scattered around the bin in the corner. It's all very stereotypical. I was planning on getting this speech down quickly and then taking a nap but two hours in and I have about two paragraphs, both of which are rubbish. Dee Dee tells me to just write from the heart, and I kind of know what I want to put down, but it all just comes out a bit crap.

"JOOOOOEEEEYYYYY"

I sit up. I've never heard Dee Dee shout before. It's weird and catches me a little off guard. She is calling from at least two floors below. I jump off the bed and bounce down the stairs. She is stood at the foot of the last flight.

"You okay?" I ask her
"There is someone here to see you" she says with a small smile.

I immediately worry that it's my parents. If it was Angelica that would be better, but I know she is still away. I nervously make my way into the front room. Sat on the far sofa sits Mimi.

"Want a hand with some painting?" she asks. I immediately run over and hug her.
"I can't believe you're here" I say excitedly
"It's good to see you Joey, I'm sorry that I went missing"
"I didn't think I would see you again after, y'know" I said, tailing off.
"That wasn't a rare night for me Joey. Every time it happens I just need to spend some time elsewhere for a few days. It's like an endless cycle"
"But you're okay, right? They didn't hurt you?"
"A few bruises, couple of cuts on my legs. Other than that, all good"

I can't believe that Mimi is back. I need to tell her everything and anything but decide that bombarding her with information may not be the best idea. She also looks different from when I saw her last. The make-up has been toned right down, and her hair is shorter and darker.

"How did you find us?" I ask
"I saw you in the paper. It took a while to work out where the place was once I got to Marylebone though. I was walking around like a tourist as I couldn't find how to get to Bell Street. I put Bell Road in my phone like an idiot and that showed me some car park near Hounslow. Most of the people I asked weren't from London so didn't know where it was either. But hey, I got here in the end"
"It's great to see you. Like, actually amazing. Are you keeping okay?"
"I'm okay thank you sweetie. I was a bit shaken after what happened when you were with me earlier this week"
"Where did you run to?"
"I think it was Southwark to start with, and then up near Farringdon. I've been sleeping on the streets for the last couple of nights as the shelters were full".

I moved across and sat next to Mimi, putting my hand on her shoulder. She leaned across into me. It's good that we could keep her safe. I'll ask Dee Dee later if she can stay for a while, help us do the place up.

"So, what's the plans here then?" she asked me, pulling out a tissue and wiping her nose.

“We have a meeting on the 4th July where we have to put our points across about exactly what we are doing here. About who it is for and that kind of thing” I explained, before going into too much detail about decorating and renovating. Most of the background of why we are doing it was in the article, and Mimi has more experience than me, so I felt it would have been patronising to explain a hostel part to her as well. “The plans are currently in some kind of consultation stage. We haven’t heard much so far, but no news is good news isn’t it?”

“I’d be careful. It might seem that way, but people may be holding out until just before the meeting. Did you want me to come along to that meeting?”

“That’d be great if you were free, thank you! I’m doing a speech at it, so a friendly face will always be a welcome sight. We find out on the 7th about whether we can go forward and plan an opening”

“I’m definitely free Joey. I can’t see myself having any other plans, eh. Also, that Saturday, when you find out, that’s London Pride day. Do you want to come to that with me?”

“Would I be allowed? Like, I’m too young to drink”

“It’s not about alcohol Joey. It’s about being together with those like you, celebrating our community, raising awareness of charities and things. Of course, you’d be welcome”

“In that case, yes please. I’ve never been to a Pride before. Will we be in the parade?”

"I'll be watching it this year, so if you want to join me to do that that'd be really nice. I'm not great in crowds but watching is less stressful for me than having to march"

"That's fine. Definitely. Do you mind if I ask you something?"

"Of course not"

"You've changed a bit since I last saw you. Your hair is different and, a bit, y'know"

"A bit more masculine?"

"I guess, yeah"

"After what happened I didn't feel as safe. I know it has happened before, but it really does knock you when you're feeling low anyway. I just thought maybe it was best that I hide myself away. I guess I just feel as if I have been defeated a bit. You know how unsafe the hostels are now, and I did try anyway the night after, but they were full. Because of this I just tried to find somewhere discreet to stay. I thought maybe having my hair extensions in and a face full of makeup might invite more trouble, especially when you are crouched in an underpass"

"You can be yourself around us Mimi" I say. I hate the thought of her having to pretend to be someone else again. That's one of the things that would scare me if I ever have to return home. I would have to be a watered-down version of myself, especially around my own family. It's so common for others to try and decide what you should look like or be like in order to make their lives easier, so they don't have to face awkward questions. They don't think how their actions are affecting that person. It's selfish and unjustified. Why should we have to make changes to our appearance and lifestyle to make other people happy? So many parents think they know best for their children, but in reality, they can do more harm than good. All the newspapers these days are full of articles that label every part of the young society as a problem. Whatever the younger generation do, it gets knocked. We are labelled as useless, as snowflakes, and as having no clue about the world. We continuously get criticised by the elder generations and then they act surprised when there is a rise in Mental Health issues. Even then we are called throwaway names by ignorant and pompous journalists (using the term very loosely in certain cases), as if for some reason that suffering from mental health means that you are too weak to survive modern life. One day they will realise that it is support and not criticism that will help make things right.

From the outside it is far too easy for other generations to criticise, and from inside their little thought bubble of friends they feel as if they are correct. Inner city communities? Gay people? Poor people? Black and Asian communities? All dismissed far too easily. When these parts of society are embraced, and those outside those groups take time to learn about the background and cultures of others, community and love grows. All have been kicked and dismissed so much and little if any progress has been made. It's time that people actually took a step back and approached each other and cared for each other with at least a shred of humanity.

Me and Mimi sit on the sofa going over plans for how to get hold of materials when there is a knock on the door. Dee Dee pokes her head into the room.

"Sorry to interrupt you two, but there is a man here who would like to have a talk with us all. Am I okay to bring him through?"

"Yes of course, we're just getting carried away with over the top plans"

Dee Dee nods. "Mr Belcher, would you like to come through? I'd like you to meet Joey and Mimi"

Twenty-two

Mr Belcher is an older gentleman in a black suit with white pinstripes. His shoes have been polished to within an inch of their lives, and his tie is of a rich blue silk that looks very expensive. He is carrying a brown briefcase in his right hand. As for the man himself, he has a slightly wiry face. I'd put him in his late sixties. He has thin black glasses, and is nearly completely bald, except for a few long hairs that have been slicked back across his head. Even from a distance I can see that there appears to be more hair growing out of his ears and nostrils than on the top of his head itself.

Both Mimi and I stand and shake the guests' hand, before settling ourselves back down.

"Please take a seat" says Dee Dee. "Tea, coffee?"
"Thank you, yes" says the man in a voice that sounds as if he is a stereotypical old Etonian. "A latte with skimmed milk please" he continues, smiling.
Dee Dee gives me a blank look outside of the man's eyesight, causing me to snigger quite loudly. I know for a fact that when Dee Dee said tea or coffee, she really meant PG Tips or a spoonful of instant. Her rented coffee machine went as soon as she closed the café. Regardless of machine or no machine, Dee Dee tells Mr Belcher that it wouldn't be a problem as he takes a seat diagonally across from me, and next to Mimi,

We sit and make small talk with the gentleman whilst we wait for Dee Dee to arrive back. We chat about the weather, and he mentions something about politics which I don't quite understand, but Mimi seems engaged. I remain quiet, nodding along in the correct places so as to not appear rude. Dee Dee comes back after about ten minutes and hands the visitor a latte in the nicest cup we have.

"Here you go, now let me take a seat" she says as she hands him the cup and comes to sit with me on the sofa. "I had to pop round to Starbucks for that, don't tell him" she whispers to me as she makes herself comfortable.

Once we were all seated, we turned and faced our guest. He took a long sip of his coffee and placed it on the table that separated us. I don't think he noticed that the coffee had been bought in a panic. He then opened his briefcase and pulled out a graduation photo of a young woman, placing it silently in front of the three of us.

"My name is Herbert Belcher. This here is my granddaughter Helen Timms" he said, tapping his right index finger on to the picture. He took a sip of his coffee again before continuing. "I'd like to tell you a story. I am a lawyer, currently working from my chambers in the City. I have been a lawyer for nearly fifty years. I think it's forty-seven years to be precise. It was a career that my own father took great pleasure in, and the chambers were set up by his close friend Hugo Forsythe. They had met through Middle Temple, the Inn of Court where they were both members. It was luck that lead them to becoming tenants in Erskine Chambers after they had qualified and decided to branch out and set up on their own after a few years. This was way back in 1936. As you can tell, our Chambers is very well established, very highly regarded and very much respected"

He stopped and took another sip of the coffee. It was if he was doing it for dramatic effect, like he was part of a film or a book. I didn't think people ever acted this way in real life. I was fascinated by him. I wasn't quite sure what he meant by Chambers, but I am assuming it's like a lawyer's office? I recognised Middle Temple too. I couldn't place why at this time though. Was it a temple temple? No, he said an Inn of Court. It must be like the Old Bailey. Where had I heard that name before though?

"Once I had been called to the Bar in 1971, I eventually took up tenancy in my father's' business. I believe the stress of the job had negative effects on both his, and Hugo's, health and they both deteriorated fairly quickly. They were both Queen's Counsel, so under a very large amount of pressure. We knew that they both were in poor health, however it was a shock when they both passed away within a week of each other just after Christmas of 1979. Despite their illnesses they continued working as much as possible. I was given the honour of becoming the Head of the Chambers, a role which I still hold to this day"

He stops again and drinks more coffee. Two sips this time. I hope he doesn't want a second. I'm not convinced Dee Dee has the energy to run to Starbucks again, and I don't fancy it much myself.

"I met my wife at a Summer Garden Party at Lincoln's Inn in 1972. Lincoln's is another Inn of Court, and my wife was a member there. It was a very brief romance before we became engaged, and we had a daughter in 1976, getting married the same year. We lived together as a family in Church End, near Finchley in North London. For a while life was blissful, however my wife fell ill herself in 1982. She had developed cancer and sadly there was nothing to be done. She passed away less than six months later. It was hard juggling work and looking after my daughter, but she was always my priority. She always came first"

Another sip of coffee. Dee Dee is thinking the same as me, I can tell by the way that she is glaring at the ever-decreasing liquid in the cup.

"My daughter grew up to be just like her mother, both in terms of looks and motivation. She graduated with a first-class degree in Marine Studies and secured a role working on the Galapagos Islands. One Christmas, when she was back home for a month or so, she fell pregnant after a night out with friends, giving birth to this wonderful girl here" he says, tapping the photograph once more. The baby's father was a great chap named Michael Timms, and he would do anything for Helen, and for my daughter. They were due to marry for a short while in the late nineties however for one reason or another things just didn't work out. Despite her parents never marrying or living together after her birth, Helen grew up in a happy environment, but this all changed when she went to university. She studied Sports Science at Loughborough. This photograph in front of you shows a happy and loving woman, but behind the scenes her life had started to unravel. She had told my daughter that she was a lesbian, however, and please do not judge me for this, both myself and my daughter believed it to be just a phase. We believed that as a successful family, with a firm that had been passed down the family, that this was a non-traditional way of life. I am sorry to tell you that I was not there for her during this time. It caused a lot of tension in the family, and ultimately led to both myself and my daughter becoming estranged from Helen. We tried a few times to reconcile our differences, but eventually we would let her down time and time again. Helen lost her job as a sports physiotherapist due to one moment of negligence and this is what made her completely collapse. Although we weren't close, we would hear the odd piece of news every month or so. We were due to meet Helen to try again on the 6th August 2016, and despite her not really being in touch often, we hoped that we could finally live together as a normally family again. A family where you have meals together or visit each other's houses in the summer for a barbecue. Just normal everyday life. We didn't hear from Helen on that morning before we travelled, yet thought that she would still be willing to let us into her house and to discuss the issues that lay between us. I say between us, but it was all the fault of both myself and my daughter. I had realised how awful I had been to her and was ready to beg for forgiveness. I hate myself for it more than I could ever explain to you all. Upon arrival to Helen's we encountered the scene that no parent or grandparent should ever want to see. Her car was on her gravel driveway, and she was sat in the passenger seat unconscious, poisoning herself with the fumes from the exhaust"

Another sip of coffee. The three of us listening hadn't spoken a word in over five minutes and left these coffee breaks as silent also.

"Of course, me and my daughter called the paramedics, and I broke through the window on the drivers' side of her car and turned off the engine, opened all the doors and everything, but we were too late"

The gentleman appeared much more weak than when he first arrived. It was hard not to be critical of someone who had treated his own granddaughter with the same contempt that my parents had shown me. I could tell from the way Mimi had shifted her seating position that she was also felt uncomfortable in the presence of the man.

"What is the purpose of your visit, Mr Belcher" Dee Dee asked, firmly. I am not sure if it had angered her also, or if somehow, he was here for forgiveness from us, but the kindness from Dee Dee's voice had been removed slightly.

"I am here because I know that I was wrong. I was an idiot who let down his own family at the time when they needed him. I let down my granddaughter. I let down my own daughter. She should never have held the same views as me too, and she inherited them from me. I made a promise on the day Helen died that I would do everything within my powers to turn things around for as many people in that situation as possible. That is the purpose of my visit. I am here to work with you. I saw you in the papers last night and if I passed on the opportunity to help other young people in need I would never have been able to live with the guilt. Guilt is cumulative in my world. I have done a lot for the LGBT community over the last eighteen months. I do not believe in God, so it is not a holy redemption that are fuelling my actions. I am angry, no, I am disgusted at myself that I have lived my life out in such a bubble that I have not fully lived a life at all. Life is nothing if you do not live alongside others. We are all brothers and sisters under the blue sky. Whatever your race, religion, upbringing, gender or sexuality. We are all one. That is the purpose of my visit, and I will get down on my knees here and now and beg the three of you to let me be here with you through this"

He made a movement off the sofa, and fell to his knees in front of us, knocking his remaining coffee onto the table top.

“Now, come on Mr Belcher” said Dee Dee immediately, “there is no need for you to beg to us on your knees. Come, come sit back on the sofa”

Mr Belcher was agitated through the anger at himself, and the pain of losing his granddaughter was still very clear. We gave him a couple of minutes to compose himself. He held the picture of Helen in both hands, occasionally releasing with his left to dab his eyes with a handkerchief.

“Do you know what really hit home?” he asked quietly. We didn’t answer, but Mimi relaxed slightly in order to confirm that it was okay for him to continue. I was still very sceptical myself however.

“I know the boy” said Mr Belcher softly.
“The boy?” asked Dee Dee

Mr Belcher’s bony hand lifted, revealing an expensive looking watch, and pointed at me.

“Me?” I asked shocked. “How do you know me?”
“When I saw the picture of you last night in the Standard I left work immediately. You have been at my offices”

“Mr Belcher, I am sorry but I think you must be mistaking me with someone else. I haven’t visited any offices during my time in London. I’ve been in cafés and galleries, but not in an office”

“Not IN them, AT them”

“I’m not following. I’m sorry”

“My Chambers. I work for Forsythe and Belcher LLP. We are located at 54c Fleet Street. You looked up and asked me the time a few days ago”

“The last days have been a bit of a blur Mr Belcher, but I do remember you now. I recall you being one of the many who stepped over me whilst heading into your office”

“I came back down not five minutes later to offer you a warm drink, but you had already vanished. I was working away for the last two days so was unable to return to see if you were spending another night there. When I got back to the chambers yesterday evening you had not returned. I contemplated staying in the office overnight so that I could be there for your return but seeing you in the article made me think of my Helen again and the pain that this caused me led me to head home”

“I’ve been to various places, that is true, but your doorway was where I spent my first night on the streets, curled up outside of 54. I think when you saw me that was my second night in the city”

“When I saw your face again I couldn’t believe it. It was as if it was a sign. It was as if I was meant to find you, Joseph”

“Joey, please. Joseph is my parents name for me”

"Sorry Joey. And sorry for the other day. I should have been with you quicker when I saw you outside of the doorway of fifty-four"

"What is it you are looking to do Mr Belcher, how are you wanting to help?" interjected Dee Dee

"I will do anything that I am of use for. I do a lot of Pro Bono work for LGBT charities and individuals"

"Pro Bono?" I asked. Another term I didn't know

"Pro Bono is carrying out legal work for no charge" he answered. "So yes, I do as much as I can with the legal side of proceedings. "If that is of no use I am happy to try and engage those within my network to offer support also, especially those based around the Marylebone area. A sizable number of close friends who I have known for many years live nearby to the building we are sat in now, and I am more than happy to try and influence them to give positive notions in regard to the public consultation. I do believe a few of them are on the council itself"

"Isn't that a bit, well, underhand Mr Belcher?" asked Mimi

"A friend convincing a friend is all above board. I currently have no financial input into the venture, and I am not receiving any payment for trying to get your plans approved. I am just doing it to support you, if you would allow me to?"

Dee Dee jumped into respond first, keeping her voice fairly monotone. "Well thank you Mr Belcher, we would definitely need to discuss this offer. Will you allow us a moment please?"

He waved his hand, and Mimi and I followed her out of the room. The three of us gathered in the bathroom at the end of the hall, out of earshot of Mr Belcher.

"So, what do we think?" asked Dee Dee

"I think it would be silly not to" replied Mimi. "I mean, we all want this to get approval, and if we have someone in a position of power who can help convince those voting to vote in our favour, I can't see any downsides"

"I agree with Mimi" I said. To me, it would be awful not to use this opportunity, it was an open goal.

"My only concern is that he wants something in return. Lawyers can be cunning people"

"But what would he want? He said he has no financial interest"

"I may regret this, but I genuinely believe that he is sorry for what he has done in the past. As awful as it was, he has taken time to try and educate himself. He may not be there yet, and the amount of guilt he has inside him means that he will never get over Helen's suicide. Shall we be blunt with him?" asked Dee Dee

"But not too blunt that we upset him" Mimi responded hesitantly

"I am tactful, don't you worry. It appears to me that he's using this as an opportunity for redemption for the errors that he made in his granddaughters' life, and we should allow him to prove that he's a changed man. It's no use holding a grudge against someone when they willingly want to change. He didn't have to come and see us today, and he does seem genuine. Let me do the talking when we go back in, and if we are all agreed, we will shake his hand now and then work as much as possible over the next few weeks until the public meeting. We will work on our speeches, gather facts, gather everything we need. If, after that, he puts a foot wrong, we can cut our ties with him. There will be no signing of contracts or anything like that"

Myself and Mimi both agreed with Dee Dee, and we headed back into the room.

"Sorry about that" said Dee Dee softly to Mr Belcher
"Oh, do not worry, I know how important this venture is for you all"
"We just want to confirm, Mr Belcher, that your kind offer of helping us gain permission is solely down to compassion, and not financial gains"
"I can confirm. I run a very successful chambers in the city, and have seen many people fall off of the rails by trying to benefit from charitable causes, lining their pockets with hidden agendas, and I would be horrified if there was any financial gain to be made by this for myself or indeed my family. As I spoke about before, I have done wrong in the past, and the pain of losing Helen has led me to wake up and act like a human. I am here for you whenever and wherever you need me"
"Thank you, Mr Belcher, that was our only question, and I believe we are all in agreement that we would love to

have you on board going forward, aren't we" Dee Dee confirmed, turning to look and Mimi and myself. We both nodded in agreement. I still had some doubts in the back of my mind, and I believe Mimi and Dee Dee did too, but time was passing by quickly and we needed to get the public on board. Approval of the night shelter was the key to everything, and weighing up the options, having Mr Belcher on our side would bring more positives than negatives.

"That means a lot to me, thank you" said Mr Belcher, standing and shaking all of our hands. "You said that the public meeting is on 4th July, didn't you?"

"That is correct yes"

"Well, I shall be there. I will leave you my business card also, please feel free to get in touch with any questions you have. I will be having meetings and dinners with various friends nearby and will tactfully promote the good that you are all doing here. Now, if you will excuse me I have to head off. I am travelling to Birmingham early tomorrow morning to see a client"

"Thank you, Mr Belcher," I said, shaking his hand once again. Mimi did the same and offered to show him out.

Once he had departed, the three of us returned to the front room and discussed the plans for the next three weeks. We had a lot of painting and decorating to do, and also had to source the materials needed. We would use Mr Belcher to utilise his contacts whenever we felt they could be of assistance. Although nothing was confirmed, and despite the underlying doubts about his intentions, we all had a good feeling about our venture.

I went to pick up my notes from the bedroom that I had been working on with Mimi.

"Joey, before you go" said Dee Dee, as I headed towards the door, "I have it"

I returned and sat down. "You have what, sorry?" I asked, confused.
"The name"
"What name?"
"For the shelter. Something you said to Mr Belcher stuck with me instantly"
"I'm all ears" I said. I hadn't even thought about what we could call the shelter, and was intrigued as to what Dee Dee would come up with. I just hoped it wasn't anything too stereotypical. I don't know why I thought that, but it deserved something better than a lazy name. I allowed Dee Dee to explain.

"When you came to London you had an awful time at Gold's, but the first night you spent after that was in the doorway. It provided you with a sanctuary, even just for a short while, and if you hadn't chosen that spot then Mr Belcher would not have been here to support us either. Doorway 54 was the key for your survival, and if all others in your situation had a Doorway 54 available to them then they would be much safer from the outset. I propose that this building is now known as Doorway 54. It is a safe space, it is a loving space, and it will be a space that young people in the LGBT community can come to when they feel that everyone else has given up"

I sat silent for a moment. I really liked the name. Although I did encounter the darkest parts of my mind on the morning after a night in that doorway, it had helped me survive. It had led Mr Belcher to us too and for some reason, the name did fit. Dee Dee was a great listener, and she understood the emotions that people like Mimi and I had. It made me proud to think that between us we could make a change, and now it had a name. I turned to Dee Dee and Mimi and raised Mr Belcher's empty coffee mug in a mock-toast.

"Welcome to Doorway 54"

Twenty-three

Goooood afternoon! I would like to welcome you to Joey's very exclusive tour of Doorway 54. Two and a half weeks have passed since Mr Belcher's visit to see us and the three of us have been working stupidly hard to make sure everything is set up and ready to go. We were lucky in the fact that no structural work was needed in order to modify and change the building so it would be fit for purpose as a shelter for homeless lesbian, gay, bisexual and transgender people. Although Dee Dee had the café on the ground floor, two flats above that and her own flat at the top, the doors were still in place inside, just hidden behind wooden panels. It was like some murder mystery apartment, but without all the death. I'm going to take you round quickly and show you what we have done.

We will start on the street. We are stood in the spot now where I saw the building for the first time. Mr Belcher happened to have some friends in good places, so much of the work has been done with the help of them, notably Barrett and Barrett's who are a local building merchants based about a mile away. Mr Belcher knew the original Mr Barrett, and they have allowed us to purchase things at the lowest price possible. They also threw in a lot of the items for free in return for one of their signs being displayed in our windows. This was a good deal for us, and we still have their marketing on both the ground and first floors.

When we last looked at the outside there was a faded café sign, with the majority of the white paint on the building itself either peeling off or stained by the elements. What we have now is something much fresher. The walls are now back to pure white, and the window sills are a pale duck egg blue. It looks a lot more modern and fits into the aesthetics of Bell Street. There are still a few bits to do, but we will have to wait until we have approval for Doorway 54 to run before we can go ahead with these. We felt that making the building look newer, and less of an eyesore, would do our campaign to open the hostel a large amount of good. If it does happen to be declined, the building will be more appealing to potential buyers also. Although she has not specifically said so, I believe that Dee Dee will sell the property and move to somewhere smaller. I just hope that I can go with her. So, all that is left to do is install the signage and put in a new kitchen. We have reserved a brand new cooker, freezer and fridge, and these will be situated in the same downstairs room where Dee Dee ran her café from. All the electrics are still in place so it would make no sense to move it elsewhere. The sign has been designed by the three of us, and we have put a call out to local firms who may help us build it and then fix it in place (Barrett's were unavailable for this). It is a simple white sign with a red border, and the name Doorway 54 in a large deep red font through the middle. We do not want anything too brash.

I'll now take you inside. The main entrance is still the door on the left-hand side of the building, the one that leads to the staircase that Dee Dee first took me up. I was told to be brutally honest when explaining my first thoughts of the building. It took a bit of time to build up the courage to criticise as I didn't want to hurt anyone's feelings, but then if we want to be successful changes needed to be made. The one thing that struck me originally was how dark it seemed inside. It needed to change from the red walls of before, but definitely not replaced with the magnolia found at Gold's. Mimi had found an old copy of the yellow pages that Dee Dee had been using to keep an old table upright, replacing it with a brick stuck inside a cereal bar box, and gone through every single painter and decorator that she could find within its covers. The idea behind this was to try and source as much paint as possible for free. It turns out that the Yellow Pages was actually delivered in the summer of 2005 so well over half the firms were either no longer in existence, or their contact details had changed. She did have some luck though, and as a result we had received six pots of duck egg blue paint, and a few brushes and rollers. We had a painting party on the Saturday of last week and managed to get the entire of the downstairs done with the paint donated. Mimi is quite good on social media, so she uploaded some pictures and asked if there were any more supplies available. As the day went on, more people dropped their old cans of paint off to us, and by the end we had far too much. It was great to have a routine with some actual work to do. I would get up at 7am, have tea and toast, and then start painting from where I had finished the night before. It took nine days in total to get it all done. It was a bit sketchy in patches, but it was definitely an improvement. Mimi and Dee Dee left me to do it on my own for the most part as they were better at negotiating than I was, and we had so much to get for the place.

The best thing about Mimi is her ability to talk to people. There hasn't been one person yet who she hasn't been comfortable around and is a very engaging woman. She looks into your eyes when you speak, and it genuinely seems as if she is listening, even if she has little or no interest in what is being said. We decided that we all needed roles in order to get the work completed efficiently. We drew up the plans of what needed to be done, with these split between pre-council decision and post-council decision. Dee Dee acted as project manager, which was only fair considering this is her building and the project was her idea. She was still regularly in touch with her solicitor in Russell Square and he had put everything in place for us to open as soon as possible once we got approval. She seems the most nervous out of the three of us about the council's decision, although she does have the most riding on it. In her spare moments she has pulled together lots of facts about LGBT homelessness for me to use in my speech. I still haven't got very far with it, but I do have an arsenal of figures that I can use if I get stuck for words.

Mimi's role was to be 'Personnel Recruitment and Product Negotiator'. She chose that job title herself. As well as sourcing paint, brushes and pretty much everything we needed, she was also in charge of spreading the word to those who will need us. It turns out that Mimi is very talented with designing leaflets. She would have gone on to art school had she not left home. She has many designs all ready to be printed should we get the green light and has been in contact with the metropolitan police to ask if they can be distributed at train stations on their billboards. They have asked her to return if we open. Having Mimi back has been fantastic for me, and it has made me feel much more at ease again. Dee Dee also loves her and has been equally as kind to her as she was to me. This is reflected in Mimi's appearance. The long hair is back, and they both went to see a friend of Dee Dee's in Croydon who runs a shop that sells ladies wigs. Her look is more feminine again, and she now has a few assorted styles to choose from each morning. It has restored her confidence and has led to her being instrumental in our progress. Whilst the work is taking place Dee Dee agreed to my request that Mimi move in. It's as if we have our own new family now. We have all taken on these roles as volunteers, and no rent is expected from us. Mimi still dreams of gaining her own career also and has said that she will continue to look for work whilst also helping us.

Having an address is a massive step for people to be able to rebuild their lives.

My role is basically “Everything Else”. I paint, I build flat pack furniture, I carry stuff and I run errands. I am completely fine with this set up. I’d rather leave the technical stuff to the ladies.

Anyway, on with the tour. I’m not sure why I am making this sound like a grand tour, as the first and second floors are basically identical, and not that much different to what we had before. The bathroom at the top of the stairs has been cleaned to within an inch of its life, and we have put some reed diffusers to make it seem a bit more like a hotel. I had to ask Dee Dee to swap the first batch she bought. Currently we have ‘Cotton Fresh’ scent, which is kind of pleasant, however originally, she bought home lavender, but it ended up smelling like an old people's home within five minutes. I know a few people who like the smell of lavender, but it made me feel a bit nauseous, and I could smell it over the paint and bleach. Anyway, on the shelving unit in the bathroom we have bottles of shampoos and body lotions, and there is a cupboard full of sanitary items that we can give away to those who need them. It’s important that we have systems in place that cater for all, and that everyone has access to everything they may need. Mimi has told me stories of homeless women that she has met who have been getting caught and charged with shoplifting as they simply cannot afford to buy things like tampons and towels. Society really does like to kick people when they're down, and to not offer advice to these women is just as much a crime as the shoplifting. In the kitchens next door we have removed some old units and updated the facilities. The residents who were here before had their own means of cooking, but they took them when they left. What we have now is a large work surface where food can be prepared, along with microwaves on a shelf above. On the right is the sink, with a cleaning cupboard underneath. The other cupboards have space for dry goods, and on the window sill, Mimi managed to get hold of some wooden trays, in which she has placed small plants to make it seem less clinical and more like a home. In the left-hand corner is a small fridge. This layout is repeated in the kitchen on the floor above.

On the first floor there were the three other rooms. The two bedrooms, and the room that acted as the meeting point between us and Mr Belcher. We decided that all rooms on the first and second floor should act as bedrooms. With the space available we could fit three bunk beds into the larger two rooms, and two into the smallest. This means that when up and running we could potentially host thirty-two people in need where possible. We have concerns about how to split the rooms, as it's not as straightforward as it seems. Having to watch the way Mimi was treated back in Gold's was awful, and we want to ensure that we eliminate this behaviour as much as we can. If we get the go ahead we are going to see if we can employ volunteers who can help with the first few weeks to ensure that everyone is being able to stay with respect. After all, Doorway 54 is designed to be a place welcoming to all and we need to get it right immediately. If a young gay man whose story is similar to mine comes in and we fail to help, and they then go back to the street, surrounded by all the dangers, I would feel as if I have failed.

Another volunteer role that we are currently seeking is for that of a counsellor or two. My mental health seems to have plateaued for the moment, but this has only been because I feel safe. If I lose this I know that I could quite easily find myself sat on the edge of Blackfriars Bridge again, counting down to a fall. Last time I hit the pavement, but next time it may be the dark waters. There are people out there who need a counsellor, need someone to help them through the darkness, and becoming a place where this could happen is something we are keen to implement.

Now, these bedrooms. So far two of the rooms on the first floor have their bunk beds built. Dee Dee invested some money to buy new ones so that all the beds were matching across the property. The small bedroom on the second floor is currently acting as a store room for all these flat packs. And whose job is it to build them? That would be me. The first one took a whole day, but by the end I managed to complete a sturdy bed that wasn't in danger of collapse as soon as any weight was bestowed upon it. The main struggle was getting the mattress onto the top bunk. I'm not quite tall enough to manage it, but I was determined to do it myself. This was a bad decision as within five minutes I was on my back on the floor with the mattress pressed on top of me. With broken pride I enlisted the help of Mimi. She is surprisingly strong and had no trouble passing it up to me. Once each is built we will keep them covered until we open. Each has a set of fresh bedding to add each day and not a plastic mattress cover in sight. Dee Dee has managed to secure a deal with Barry the Laundrette owner. This is only about four doors down and he and Dee Dee have been friends for a good few years, so she used her charm so that we can now do three loads of washing a day for free. This should allow us to clean all the sheets that we have in the hostel easily. All the spare sheets will be stored in a locked cupboard at the bottom of the main stairs.

This kind of brings us to the end of the tour. As I said, there isn't a great deal to show you, but it's so much more brighter and inviting than the time I first visited. I am keeping everything crossed that we can push on to prepare for a grand opening, or if all our efforts were wasted. We just hope that Mr Belcher has been true to his word and has spent time influencing key people in the neighbourhood. I do have a good feeling though. The public meeting is taking place very soon and I still have a speech to prepare. I have kept plugging away at it but it's still a bit crap. When I read it back I'm not even convincing myself that the shelter is a good idea. It's Wednesday now which means that I have a week to prepare the most important speech of my life.

I have no idea how many people will be present at the meeting. I am hoping for a small number, however seeing many people who support us will make my job a lot easier. I need my speech to be honest and I hope that those in attendance learn to put the stories into the people that they see on the streets.

Twenty-four

I wake up suddenly to a knock on my bedroom door. I was in a deep sleep, and it was one of those noises where you aren't sure if you have dreamt it or not. The more I think about it, the more I think that I did dream it, until the knock comes again.

"Joey, are you up? Breakfast is ready" comes Dee Dee's voice from the other side.
"I'll be down in a minute" I respond.
"Don't be long. Big day today remember"

It dawns on me that today is Wednesday 4th July. It's the day of the council meeting. I turn and look at my alarm clock and notice that it has just past 8.15am. I had set my alarm last night for 7am so I must have subconsciously turned it off when it rang and fallen back to sleep. There are pieces of note paper all over my bed, and I have slept on a pen which has caused a small blue stain on my bed sheets. I have still been struggling to write my speech for the last week and it's obvious that my attempts last night ended in failure also. I pick up a couple of crumpled pages, and what I have written is either illegible or doesn't make any sense. I have had offers to help me write this from many people, but I want it all to come from me. That may sound selfish, however Dee Dee will be talking also beforehand and I want my words to be real and to reflect the struggles that I have felt since coming to the capital, and also the reasons behind why I ended up here in the first place. We think that I will have only five minutes to talk so it's not too bad and I do have a few facts to go on. If all fails I will just tell them the story that I have been telling you.

London, and nearly all of the country, is in the middle of a long heatwave at the moment. There are rumours that it is going to last for another month or two. I enjoy the hot weather, but it makes sleeping difficult. It has been so humid over the last week that I can only sleep if I am stripped to my boxers and laying on top of my covers. I have the window constantly open and a fan on in the corner of the room on top of my small bedside cabinet. Each night the heat makes me wake up at least two or three times, and the anxiety that I have about having to do some public speaking has not helped at all. Despite it still being relatively early, it must be close to twenty-five degrees already. I climb out of bed and pull on a red t-shirt, deciding not to get changed into my formal clothes until we are until just before we are due to leave. I don't want to spend the morning covered in sweat.

The meeting starts at 11am so that gives me around two hours before we have to leave the building. It will be held at Marylebone Old Town Hall. Apparently, this is only a ten-minute walk away. I'm feeling stupidly nervous right now and I'm not sure I am really in the mood for food. Walking into the bathroom I lean my hands on the sink and stare at my face in the mirror. I'm looking a bit better again now. My face is less gaunt than it was a few weeks ago, and the bags under my eyes have definitely reduced. Dee Dee has all these moisturisers in the bathroom cabinet so I have been treating myself to face masks and ointments when she isn't around. You often hear how bad the pollution is in London, but you never realise how bad until you have lived here for a bit. I don't know if all cities are as bad as this, but I imagine people from Manchester and Birmingham at least can relate. Each night my skin feels as if there is a layer of oil on it. My hair also becomes greasy within five minutes of being outside. There are some major roads through Marylebone, and when you add the pollution from the trains as well it makes it a pretty disgusting place at times. You can smell it on your clothes when you take them off at night. Add to this the constant sunshine and it's clear why my skin has been so hard to keep in good condition. I lift my fringe and it reveals a spectrum of colour from red through to white, covering every shade of pink in between. I was hoping that finally having a long hot summer would mean that I would look healthy and tanned, but currently I am closer to looking like a beacon. Talking of my hair, I should really get it cut. It has been on the agenda since I moved in with Dee Dee but I have been so focussed on building furniture and painting rooms that I just haven't had the time. My fringe can now reach my top lip if I pull it down straight. As a result, today I will have to style my hair in some kind of volumatic quiff. It will look a bit silly, and I always feel uncomfortable with gel and hairspray in, but it's not the kind of situation where I can easily get away with throwing a baseball cap or beanie hat on is it? As I mentioned, I will be wearing formal clothes for the event. Mimi saw a suit in a charity shop last week and picked it up for me. Apparently, it was reasonable and despite my protests she wouldn't allow me to give her anything in return for it. Not that I have any money still, however I will pay her back when I start earning if she wants me to or not. It's only fair to give back what you have been given, whether this is money or compassion. Having not been one for suits before, I have to say that I absolutely love the one that has been given to me. It is a deep royal blue colour and fits perfectly. I've never looked smarter in anything before. We picked up a white shirt from Oxford Street, along with a royal blue tie. I can see the suit in the mirror hanging on the bathroom door behind me. I've heard of people talking about dressing to impress so I guess this is what I will be doing.

I wash my face with cold water and rinse the sleep out of my eyes before heading to the breakfast table. On arrival it feels as if I have entered the scene of a sitcom from the 1970's. Both Dee Dee and Mimi are sat at the table in matching purple dressing gowns, with white towels around their heads. They each hold a cup in their left hand and are gossiping about a lady who lives at the end of the street.

"I obviously didn't get the memo about uniform" I joked as I took my place nearest the window
"Some of us like to be ready with time to spare, unlike some" joked Mimi back, pointing a butter knife in my direction.

The lady they are talking about is called Violet and owns one of the flats on the corner. Whatever the weather, and whatever day of the week it is you will nearly always see Violet passing down the street in a long purple padded jacket. Occasionally she will wear a fleece which has pictures of wolves woven into it. There is a certain type of person that wears those fleeces, and it reminds me of the market stall back home which had a wide range featuring all sorts of animals, but mainly dolphins. Violet also wears bright green crocs and you can normally spot these from fifty yards, even when it is busy. The only other constant is the red dog lead that she carries in her right hand. It will swing loosely with each step. This wouldn't be so unusual except the fact that no one has ever seen her dog, and we are certain that she doesn't own one. Every city, town, village or hamlet has their own version of Violet. Back home it was Jumble Sale Lil. Jumble Sale Lil, or JSL as all the kids knew her, would stalk around the fields complaining about every single child on the estate. We lost many footballs over her garden wall as we were too afraid to knock on her door to ask for them back. When we were at primary school a rumour started that she was a witch and that terrified us for at least ten years. It wouldn't be uncommon for her to come into the school to complain about one of the pupils. JSL always seemed to be very old, yet she never changed, and I think she's actually still alive today.

Back in the kitchen, I shuffled into my chair and Dee Dee bought across a plate of breakfast. On it were three boiled eggs in and two slices of buttered bread which had been cut into soldiers. She placed it on the blue and white chequered tablecloth and tapped me on the head with a teaspoon.

"We will need to leave at about 10.30 Joey, so after breakfast we will go through the facts that you need again, and then get ourselves dressed and ready to walk down. How is the speech?"

"It's all okay" I lie. I'm confident that I still have time for a moment of inspiration.

"Well if you need to practice it, me and Mimi will be more than happy to listen"

"I will practice in the mirror again before I go"

"If that works for you then that works for me too" smiled Dee Dee, as she ruffles my hair on the way to the kettle. "Coffee?" she asks.

I politely decline as I know if I have too much liquid I will be distracted by wanting to rush to the toilets during the discussions. The nerves have started to kick in already. I think my main concern is how many people will be present. I hope that there will be a mix of people on both sides of the debate, but I worry that it could also just be us three against the room. Dee Dee has sent a message to Mr Belcher to remind him, however we have yet to hear back. He will be there though. He has to be.

~

'Ladies and gentlemen. Thank you for inviting me to talk'

No. That makes it sound like I am doing a TED talk. I cross through it five times with the pen. I have an hour before we leave, and I am still not happy with the first line, let alone anything else. How do you address a group like this? Why am I so unprepared? I've often heard that a lot of people come up with the best ideas whilst sat on the toilet or in the shower, so I decide to leave the speech writing again to go and do both. I have the fact sheet with some figures on it, so surely, it's just a case of telling them whilst weaving my story through the middle of them.

I'm in the shower now and plotting through the journey that I have taken over the last month. If I get this I will be fine. I make a mental note of the key things that I must remember and repeat them over and over in my head.

The break down with my parents.
The train journey.
The night at Gold's.
Meeting Mimi.
Meeting The Nomad.

My first night on the streets.
The Nomad's death.
Jenny and Pete.
Meeting Dee Dee.
The humiliation of being urinated on.
Feeling helpless on the bridge.
Feeling rescued.

These are the key things that I need to say. I stop the shower and half dry myself so that I can write them down whilst they are still in my head. I then tear the page out and pin it onto the small cork board that hangs off the back of my bedroom door. This way I can keep going over it whilst I am drying my hair and getting dressed. I keep staring at the words and repeating them to myself. The nerves make me think that I will forget them which is ridiculous considering that I have lived these words.

I must have been in the shower for much longer than I thought as it is now coming up to five past ten, which only leaves twenty-five minutes. In under an hour we will be in the town hall fighting to make Doorway 54 a reality. I put on a pair of red boxer shorts (red has always been my lucky colour) and pull my shirt and suit off the hanger on the bathroom door. The shirt is a bit too big, and when on it looks a bit odd under the suit jacket. I decide that a t-shirt underneath might solve the problem so tip up my drawer with my clothes in onto my bed. I don't have many and need to look smart so in theory it should be an easy choice. Instead, I pull the one from the bottom. No one will be able to see through the shirt to what is underneath, so the colour of what I choose shouldn't matter. Out of all the clothes I want to wear the least smart. It's not because I want to be a rebel, or to 'keep in touch' with my real self. It is because the least smart item I own is the football shirt that Mario gave to me when I stumbled into his café bloody and shirtless. Many people would have pushed me back out of the door, but it was the first step to getting myself back on track. The shirt no longer just represents Aston Villa. It represents hope and belief. If I have this on during my speech I know it will go well. That's how it works doesn't it? I hold out the shirt and give it a quick sniff, and it isn't as musty as I thought it might be. I put it on and place the white shirt over the top. Looking at it in the mirror, some of the design was showing through on the shoulders, however my jacket would hide this, so I'd definitely be able to get away with it. My only worry is that I will melt in the heat.

I head back to the kitchen after finishing getting dressed and sit at the table ready for Mimi to do my hair. Both Dee Dee and Mimi don't trust me enough to do it myself when it is this length. They witnessed my effort earlier in the week and said I looked like I had fallen in a vat of grease. As I sit down, Dee Dee throws a newspaper in front of me.

“Have a look at this” she says, tapping the front cover. I stare down at it but don’t understand what she is getting at.

“What am I meant to be looking at?”

“The main story. The one about the councillor. Y’see him?”

“I do” I say nodding

“That is Crawford Samuels” she says. “He owns two houses, one here and one in Camden. If you read the story it goes into detail about how he has been trying to claim expenses for a lot of the items that he has been buying for them. Apparently, it has cost the taxpayer over ten thousand pound”

“What a robbing bastard” I reply, quickly altering my response. “Sorry, I mean, that’s hardly fair is it? What a fool”

“Do you know what the best bit of this is though, baby?” she asks with a smirk on her face

“There’s a good bit?”

“Oh, there is. Crawford Samuel’s just so happens to be the leading opponent to our application for Doorway 54”

“Are you serious?”

“One. Hundred. Percent”

“Will he be there today?”

“He is down to talk just before you. If you need some ammunition, this is it”

“Am I allowed to take this article in with me?”

"I'm not sure to be honest, but maybe mentioning that someone with two homes is criticising those without a home at all won't do our cause any harm at all"

This newspaper is definitely coming with me today. It eases the pressure a bit knowing that the person I am up against is the smug looking git who only cares for himself. I'll be more than happy to call him out in front of everyone in that room today and show just how awful he has been.

Dee Dee winks at me and walks off to find Mimi, shouting her name as she leaves the kitchen.

"I'm here, I'm here, don't panic" says Mimi immediately, entering the kitchen from the opposite side. "Are you ready for your hair appointment Joseph?"

"I will be as long as you never call me Joseph again" I reply. She laughs and punches me gently on the upper arm.

"Right I need you to sit dead still. We only have one go at this because we need to leave shortly, and you won't have time to wash it again"

"I won't move a muscle"

Mimi dumps a small purple bag on the table and opens it up to reveal a salon's worth of hair products. I ask her for a mirror but she tells me I need to learn to trust her. This somehow makes me trust her less.

"Now, sir, what I am going to do is a swept back style, reminiscent of James Dean, using a collection of mousses, gels and spray. Please tilt your head back". I do as I am asked. It feels as if some of my hair is being ripped from my head and I am worried that I will resemble an ice cream cone when she is done. I mean, I do have a lot of hair to tame.

"Jesus, how can one person's hair be so knotted?" she said shortly after. Her impression of a top hairdresser didn't last long.
"Shave it all off if you have to, as long as I look smart"
"Nah you wouldn't suit that look. Grit your teeth as this may hurt a little"

For the next five minutes she dragged a comb through my hair and it felt like it was being ripped from my head. A further five minutes after that and we were done. To be fair to Mimi, she had done a very good job. What was a bird-nest style mess beforehand now had been turned into something acceptable.

"We need to go, we need to go!" cried Dee Dee re-entering the kitchen. "Get your shoes on"

We still had a few minutes before we due to leave but I think the nerves had started kicking in for her, which in turn made me nervous. I dashed back to my bedroom and pulled on my shoes, tucking my notes into the inside pocket of the suit. I took one final look in the mirror and barely recognised the boy looking back at me. I seemed to have matured a lot since taking my GCSE's, although this is probably down to cramming in a few years' worth of life experience in this time. Seeing myself like this made me feel a bit of pain that I had become estranged from my parents again. Most parents would take a photo of their child when they were looking smart and display it on their mantelpieces or in their halls, however mine may never know that it happened. They may never know that the shy boy who they raised was about to head to a town hall and talk in front of a large group of people about something that he was passionate about. I hoped that one day I would be able to show them what I could do, however this would require them to step up. I contemplated writing to them again.

"Are you ready?" asked Dee Dee, poking her head round the door. As I turn to her a wide grin appears across her face. "Oh baby, look at you" she said cheerfully, coming across and giving my cheeks a squeeze. "How will anyone be able to go against you when you look like that!"
"Are you sure I look okay?" I ask, despite knowing that I look the best I ever have since meeting her
"Of course, baby. Now, come along we have to head to the town hall now. Have you got your speech?"

I tapped my top pocket to confirm that I had, although speech was a bit of an exaggeration, and then followed her down the stairs to where Mimi was waiting at the bottom.

“Let’s do this!” she exclaimed as we reached the ground floor.

“Oh, one second” I say, before dashing back up the stairs to the kitchen. I flick through the paper until I find the main article about Crawford Samuels, pulling these pages out and folding them into my jacket also. As I was about to head back down I noticed a story which had been revealed by the missing pages. My heart raised itself into my mouth and I felt a little sick.

“No, not now” I said to myself as I pushed the paper onto the floor. I had recognised the mugshot staring out from one of the pages. Now was the worst time to have seen it, and I decided that I needed to not read the story until we were back home later. I felt sick very quickly and tried to push the image to the back of my mind. I took a sip of water directly from the kitchen tap and went back down to the front door.

“Are you okay Joey?” asked Mimi. You look a bit pale.

“I’m fine, just a bit of nerves” I lied. “Come on, let’s head on”.

It was one of the hottest days of the year so far, and they predicted it could even reach thirty degrees this afternoon. Walking out of the house into the sunshine led me to be partially sighted for a few minutes until my eyes had adjusted. On the walk we discussed everything that we needed to say and went over some of the questions that we felt may have been asked. I kept instigating the conversation so that it solely focussed on the job we had to do over the next hour. Talking about the short term was a way of dealing with what I had seen. The area surrounding Marylebone was absolutely full of tourists, and our journey was slowed by having to follow a group of school children in matching yellow caps and backpacks. This area was often this busy due to its proximity to Madame Tussaud's and Baker Street, two of the main attractions for a day out in this part of the city. I tried dodging through some of the children, but in the end decided that the stress that this added wasn't worth it. The kids were extremely excited to be in a different country and had no grasp of walking in an organised fashion. They were definitely French, and I wish I had listened more to Monsieur Garrett's classes back at Greenwood so that I could have at least them to move a bit snappier. I let out some audible grunts of frustration a few times before Mimi started mocking me for being too easily angered by them. She was stood at the rear of the group and was acting out wielding a whip as if rounding up animals.

Despite the delays caused by the kids, we arrived at Marylebone Old Town Hall ten minutes before the meeting was due to start. I had seen this building before as I stopped on its steps within the first hour of being in London. Knowing this would be the building where I made or broke my future made my nerves go into overdrive. I thought that I had been nervous this morning and struggled to eat all the soldiers that Dee Dee had presented to me with my eggs, but this was now a different level. Marylebone Old Town Hall is intimidating. It is a very large structure situated on the south side of Marylebone Road, just down from where it forms a junction with Gloucester Place. The front entrance was formed of large wooden doors which stood at the top of ten wide stone steps. There were also ten stone columns which reached as high as the second-floor ceilings. And these were complemented by two daunting lions which were located on the left and right of the building. The windows were large, and each was split into small glass sections by thin iron work.

At the top of the stairs the door was open, and an official looking gentleman dressed in a suit stood at the entrance with a clipboard. Dee Dee asked us to wait whilst she went and informed him that we had arrived. She was wearing the same dress that she had worn when I first saw her through the window of her solicitors on Russell Square. She claimed that it was her lucky dress. I hoped that she was correct.

"Are you okay, Joey?" asked Mimi. She was dressed in a black skirt, black shoes and a white blouse. She looked like she meant business. Her hair had been re-dyed to blonde, and the length was added to by extensions which faded into a pastel blue at their tips.

"I'm a bit nervous Mimi" I responded. "What if it doesn't happen?"

"Now, you can't go on thinking like that. You know that Doorway 54 will add so much to both the LGBTQ community and the community in Marylebone itself"

"I know, but what if I mess it up?"

"I have faith in you. This is your chance to give people the opportunity that you should have had yourself. Although we won't be the first people to offer this, it doesn't make it any less important. We can start up Doorway 54 and work to ensure that those who need us hear about either ourselves or one of the other LGBTQ shelters as soon as possible. I have every faith in you Joey. I know once you stand up you will ensure that the right thing will happen"

"Thank you, Mimi, that means a lot. I'm just worried my speech may not be as good as it could have been"

"Speak from the heart. That's all you need to do"

Mimi pulled me in for a tight hug before we ventured up the steps to join Dee Dee.

"They're all ready for us" said Dee Dee when we reached her. "There are reserved seats in the front row on the left-hand side. Most of the council are present so we should be starting on time"

"Are there many people in there?" I asked

"Around seventy apparently. I think there will be many on our side though so don't go worrying yourself. You'll do us proud"

"Thank you, Dee Dee. I think I need some water"
"Let's go in and get you some baby"

We entered into a large marble hall which had staircases leading off to both the left and right-hand sides. There was a main room just ahead which had the name "Lord Mayor's Room" written above the door in stone. This was where our fate would be decided. Corridors ran away from either side of the door to smaller rooms. The doors to the Lord Mayor's room were closed until we were around two feet away, when they were opened by an official looking porter from the inside, revealing a large wood panelled chamber with raised desks at the far end. Between the front of the room and ourselves were at least ten rows of chairs, with each row twelve seats wide. The back rows were empty aside from a couple of older gentlemen, however the front seven were packed, save for the reserved seats for those who would be debating. The man who had opened the door for us led us down a central aisle until we reached the front. Each chair was made of deep oak, with a green leather cushion to sit on, which matched their backrest. Me, Dee Dee and Mimi took our places and nervously waited for events to unfold.

We sat there in uncomfortable silence before a noise from the back of the room alerted us to the fact that the chairman of the meeting was arriving. He was a large gentleman with a pink face and receding grey hair, dressed in a dark suit. He walked down the central aisle towards us followed by a second man. I recognised the second figure as Crawford Samuels. Samuels looked smaller than he had on the front page of the newspaper that Dee Dee had shown me this morning. Both were carrying takeaway coffees from the café opposite the old town hall and it was clear that they had met prior to this morning's meeting. It proved that, as with a lot of things in life, that it could be a case of who you know rather than what you know. The meeting and debate now seemed even more of a challenge and something about this fired up something inside of me.

Twenty-five

"Ladies and gentlemen, I welcome you all today to Marylebone Town Hall, and welcome you all to listen and engage with the points raised today concerning the proposed opening of a new homeless shelter to be situated in nearby Bell Street. My name is Colin Burrows and I will be the chair for today. I have been on the council within Marylebone for fifteen years and it is my duty to ensure that we conduct today in an open environment, and one which no bias is shown by the panel made up of my colleagues"

I am sat in the front row no more than five metres away from Mr Burrows. He is the pink faced rotund gentleman who entered with Crawford Samuels before we got underway. This alone made me sceptical about how unbiased the entire day would be. The colleagues that he had mentioned were sat on a raised area away to the right-hand side of the chamber.

"As with other debates that we have had in the past, today marks the final part of the consultation period for the submission for a new business in our area. We hope that all present have had a chance to look over the proposals that have been submitted by the legal representatives of Ms Diana Hall"

Ms Diana Hall is Dee Dee's full name by the way. I only found this out myself less than a week ago. Mr Burrows continued to introduce the meeting.

"After the discussion has been completed today, my colleagues will retire to discuss the proposals, before announcing a final decision on this upcoming Saturday, the 7th day of July 2018. Please may I ask all those in attendance to listen to the points raised by both sides, and not to interrupt the speeches that will be made. We will start with a speech from Ms Diana Hall, who has put forward the proposal for the debate. This will then be followed by Mr Crawford Samuels, who is in opposition to the new night shelter, and finally we shall hear a brief talk by Master Joseph Eaton".

I feel very sick when my name is mentioned in such a formal manner. I repeated to myself that I could do this, despite my speech seemingly lacking in substance. I look around the room to see who is attending. I do not recognise any of them and hope that many are in support of Doorway 54.

"The meeting will last no longer than thirty minutes, and I have advised those speaking that they must stick to their five-minute time limit. Due to these time constraints, we will start the formal part of the discussions now. Please can I invite Ms Hall to the lectern please".

There is some low-level noise emitted from people shuffling in their seats as Dee Dee walks up to face the room. Mimi shifts across to take her unoccupied chair so that she is now sat next to me. We both remain silent as we sit their squeezing each other's hands with anticipation.

Dee Dee places her notes down and looks out across the whole room. She is showing no sign of any nerves.

"Good morning. As Mr Burrows has mentioned, I am Ms Diana Hall. I was previously the owner of Dee Dee's Café that was situated on Bell Street, the location for which we will be discussing today. I have lived on Bell Street for many years, and class it as my home in more ways than one. I have seen many changes over the years and seen the identity of the street change from year to year. When I first opened my café in 1988 I was still young, but the support of those around me allowed me to create a successful business when so many people thought it would fail. To many it was not just a café, but instead the heart of the community. It would be a meeting point. It would be an area for celebrations and it would be an area where we all could come to support one another.

Over the last year the people who have lived there for most of their lives have been priced out by out of town landlords who care more for money than they do for the area. Many of my closest friends have now not only left Marylebone, but London as a whole, with some in areas as far away as Luton and Slough. What we now have on this street are people who rent a property so that they have a base during the working week. Every weekend they depart leaving it virtually deserted for two days. This is even more noticeable over the Christian holidays. We used to run many events over the Christmas period especially, events which allowed residents to make it a special time of the year for the younger children who lived nearby. We had fetes, grottos and many other schemes that really brought everyone together, often introducing many religions to celebrate together. Not celebrating Christmas itself in all cases but celebrating the community. This community has now been torn apart by people who simply do not care for those less affluent.

My proposal is to bring back something for a community and create an area that will benefit those who have been less fortunate than ourselves. I met a young man last month whose story is one that shows just how susceptible every single one of us can be to changing circumstances in life. It is my pleasure that I have been able to get to know this boy, and very happy that he is here to share his story with you all as well.

Now, to the proposal. As Mr Burrows mentioned, we believe that you have all been able to look over the plans for my building in Bell Street, and I am here to show you just why it will be needed. I will be happy to answer concerns afterwards, concerns about misconceptions regarding homeless people, and concerns about people in the LGBTQ community. It is 2018 and I am sorry to say that many people still do not understand this community and make inaccurate and downright offensive accusations about them. The proposal, at its bare bones, is to provide a night shelter exclusively for those in the LGBTQ community. It will be able to welcome up to forty-eight guests per night, and it will be an environment where they can experience a night in safe accommodation. We also propose to provide the residents with access to hot meals, washing and changing facilities and also sanitary products. Further to this, we are in discussions to have volunteer counsellors who will be able to provide support in promoting positive mental health initiatives.

I would like to introduce some facts for you.

Nearly twenty-five per cent of homeless young people identify themselves as part of the LGBTQ community.

Over three-quarters of these say that coming out to their parents was the main factor.

Homeless LGBTQ youth are significantly more likely to suffer exploitation, substance misuse and physical and mental health problems.

If these stats do not shock you I will be very surprised. Whilst there are support areas out there for LGBTQ youth, many do not know where they can get help, and Doorway 54 will be there to help and alleviate this. You will hear from Joey later today. Joey stayed in a shelter for all homeless people, and over the course of that night alone he saw first-hand heroin use and was also beaten. Our dear friend Mimi stayed in the same shelter that night and was also beaten due to being transgender. As a collective we have worked hard to introduce a place which will remove the fear that people like them face. It will not be an exaggeration to say that on another night the consequences could have been a lot worse. Many young LGBTQ people lose their life through violence on the streets when homeless. For many more it plays a strong part in their mental health issues. Nearly half of all transgender people under the age of twenty-six have attempted suicide. I know that both Mimi and Joey have both contemplated it themselves also. They want me to tell you this to try and make it seem realistic to you. The figures can be so high that it becomes too hard to comprehend to some. Look at them now. They are both sat here but in different circumstances those chairs could well be empty. These facts are not just statistics on a page. They are real people, with real lives and real experiences. I urge you all to think of those who are in, or who will enter, the homeless population and help us to help them. This is not about point scoring. It is about protecting those who need our help.

Ultimately, the decision for Doorway 54 will be made by these councillors sat in this room. I urge you all, every single one of you, to make the correct decision. Together we can be stronger".

With that, Dee Dee stood back from the podium. The applause started slowly, but before long a clear majority of the room had joined in as she returned to her seat. I rose and gave her a hug before she took her place next to me again. I could feel her heart beating fast through the adrenaline that had been prominent during her passionate speech. I knew that she would be wonderful, but she blew me away completely. The way that she had spoken, and the reaction from those in the room, had given me hope that we may just win the approval. There was still work to be done however, and we still had to hear from Crawford Samuels before I had to stand. Mr Burrows was back at the lectern again.

"Thank you, Ms Hall, for your contribution there. Before we move on to Mr Samuels, I just wanted to clarify the voting procedure. Each proposal that is similar to this one has to gather an approval by a simple majority. My esteemed colleagues and myself will meet at the end of this week to discuss the matters arising from today, and from the support and concerns raised by the public during the consultation period. As you can imagine, we have had a lot of interest surrounding this. The final vote will involve twenty-three people. They will be asked the question "Do you support the motion for a homeless LGBTQ shelter to open in Marylebone". Councillors are allowed to abstain from the vote if they wish. The Yes votes and No votes will be counted, with the most popular going through to be approved. I hope that this is all clear, however I will be happy to discuss with you anything that may seem unclear. Right, we will now move on and hear from Mr Crawford Samuels"

Again, people shifted in their seats audibly as Mr Samuels made his way to the front to talk. I was hoping that his connections with the council would not lead to questionable voting patterns.

"Good morning to you all" he started, in an accent that you hear from those who have attended public school. An accent that didn't drop any letters from a word when spoken. "I have been involved with councils in the past, and for the majority of the 1980's I worked on the planning committee of Sussex County Council. During those years we had many applications come through the system that were a similar nature of the one that has been put forward to the council today. It is a common misnomer that those who work for councils simply do not care for the residents in their area, instead approving options that benefit only themselves. This is completely untrue and can lead to some friction between us as a council and the residents that we represent. Over the course of this consultation I have heard some interesting points from both sides, however sometimes opinions are mislabelled as facts, with people basing their thoughts on heresy. I have, however, listened to the views of others who live in Marylebone, as well as forming my own opinion based on the proposal put forward by Ms Diana Hall for her property on Bell Street.

Having weighed up the options I have come forward to represent objecting the plans for the hostel"

A few jeers came from those seated behind me.

"I appreciate that many in the audience may not agree with me, however we do have to take into consideration those who currently reside in Bell Street. As you well know, Marylebone Station has seen some changes over the last two years, meaning that the number of people who use the station has risen. We have now got links with other major locations in the Thames Valley, such as High Wycombe and Oxford, and have seen numerous improvement works to the station itself. With these high numbers arriving to London through this area, we need to work towards implementing procedures that will reduce the impact to the quality of life of those that live there. Bell Street itself is traditionally a residential street with a few business properties spread along its distance. Cuts that have been handed down to our council by the government have been slashed, and the number of police officers on the street has fallen to virtually zero. If you combine this with the local public houses and bars in the area, there has been an increase in the number of reports of antisocial behaviour, leading to area being seen as less desirable than before.

I take on board Ms Hall's comments regarding the issue of homelessness in London, however I feel that Marylebone is not the correct area for a hostel such as this to be set up. Many other boroughs in London have a more serious number of people sleeping rough and therefore I feel that the hostel would just be a hollow gesture away from those who need the support of a place such as the one proposed.

Resident safety and wellbeing ranked highly in a survey that we conducted with local residents last year, and their concerns highlighted how anti-social behaviour had led to a lower quality of life. During the consultation period I met personally both in my office and at resident's homes, with those who had concerns about the proposal. Many raised the point that the shelter could lead to a further rise in anti-social behaviour, and also may lead to noise pollution on Bell Street. Noise from nearby licenced premises is already audible in the neighbouring streets and having a new set of premises which could add to that is a grave concern. Another issue that has been raised to me is the potential rise in crime that could result. We have seen in the past that members of the homeless community engage in substance abuse and small thefts such as shoplifting and presenting an opportunity for this to happen should be grounds to rule against this proposal alone. I understand that the shelter is for a specific section of the homeless community, however we know from studies that drug and alcohol misuse is high regardless of someone's gender or sexuality. Many who are in attendance today would not appreciate these activities taking place in their residential areas, so to expect this to be accepted elsewhere is both hypocritical and dangerous.

Although I am against the proposal for Bell Street, I believe that help should be given to those who find themselves on the streets. I feel that hostels act as just a temporary fix for that community, and instead we should invest in the education of those without a home in order for them to integrate themselves further, and also to learn about the dangers that they face. London has a large number of hostels spread across many areas of the city, and creating a chain of information from Marylebone to options for shelters would be a more beneficial proposal in our opinion. The costs that could result from the shelter being approved could lead to a further strain on the resources of an already underfunded council.

I am more than willing to enter discussions with Ms Hall going forward if the proposal is rejected and work together to find a solution that is safer, more viable and with long term benefits rather than the one that has been put in front of us this month. I acknowledge the compassion of Ms Hall and appreciate the hard work that she has put into her argument, however I urge that the council see, on this occasion, that the plans to open a hostel on Bell Street are rejected".

After Mr Samuels had finished, there was a small round of applause from some people present, and I don't know if it was just my bias, but it definitely felt flatter than the one that Dee Dee had received. I didn't have time to contemplate this however, as I was next to address the room. My heart was going a hundred miles an hour, and despite not having a full draft of what I wanted to say, something which Crawford Samuels had mentioned had given me the platform to hopefully ensure people would be in support.

Mr Burrows was now introducing me, but it was as if I wasn't there. I could see him talking and could hear the words, but I couldn't make sense of them. It was only when he had stepped away from the lectern that I knew that I was up. I pulled my brief speech notes and the newspaper out of the inside pocket of my jacket and walked up to face the room. I needed time to gather my thoughts and to calm myself down.

Once I was at the front I placed my materials down and looked up to see everyone staring at me. I closed my eyes for a few seconds and imagined the River Thames. I timed my breathing with the imaginary waves hitting the shingle, trying to push back on the forthcoming anxiety attack. I told myself that in less than five minutes time this would all be over. I reopened my eyes and looked at Dee Dee and Mimi in the front row. They were both smiling kindly, and Mimi gave me a wink. I surveyed the rest of the room to see if there were any familiar faces present. I recognised no one who was sat in the main area, however at the back there was the unmistakable figure of Mr Belcher. He was dressed in the same suit as the one he wore when he came to visit. He nodded his head in a silent act of encouragement. I became conscious to the fact that I had been stood at the front in silence for about a minute now and knew that I had to start. My first words came out nervously from my dry mouth.

"Good morning" I squeaked. The room felt even more silent now that I had said something.

"My name is Joey and I am working with Dee Dee, sorry, I am working with Ms Hall on the project for the homeless shelter. I have been trying to write a speech for you for the last few weeks, but I overthought it too much and was scared that I couldn't convince you. Luckily though, I only need one word to describe why it is needed, and I thank Mr Samuels for saying it".

I was beginning to get into my stride, but I knew my speech would only be about two minutes at most. I was certain that this would be enough.

"Rejection. Hearing Mr Samuels say that today has brought back a lot of memories for me today, and it is the sole reason that I am stood here now. I am only sixteen years old however I have been rejected by friends, rejected by my school, and most importantly rejected by my parents. I left home with a plan to come to London to escape my old life and start again. I was naïve and thought it would be easy. Instead, I have been rejected here as well. I have met many homeless people since finding myself on the streets. Out of those, one was beaten in front of me simply because of who they were. Another was killed. When I met Ms Hall, my life was spiralling and for the second time of my life I was seconds away from committing suicide. I wouldn't be stood here before you today. I would just be another statistic. I chose to fall away from the water, but many other people like me fall the other way. With our project we will do everything possible to try and give hope to those who live in fear. As Ms Hall mentioned, the figures for homeless LGBTQ youth are terrifying. We might only be one small hostel, but as a whofriend once said, every flood starts with a single drop of rain.

I am tired of being rejected, and tired of people accusing homeless people as solely being trouble makers and drug takers and thieves. I want to be humble, but instead I will literally beg the councillors to approve the plans for our hostel. Voting yes will save someone's life".

I don't know if there was applause for me. I was there physical but not mentally. I can't remember walking back to my seat, and I can't remember Mr Burrows final address to the room. I was shaking from anxiety, and in disbelief that I had managed to speak to the room. Although it seemed okay in my head, I think my speech was a bit more of a mumble than profound, but I think that Dee Dee and myself had both done as much as we possibly could. I decided not to use the newspaper to highlight the hypocrisy of Crawford Samuels, but as I left the Lord Mayor's Room I left it on the table by the doors so that people passing would be able to see it.

~

It is now midday and the three of us are sat in a café on the corner of Bell Street and Cosway Street. We are here to meet Mr Belcher, who Dee Dee invited along at the end of the meeting. The town hall was busy and she though it would be good to reconvene somewhere quieter in order for him to provide an update if he had one. Even though the talks were over, I was still feeling on edge and couldn't quite relax. Due to my age I couldn't have an alcoholic drink like the other two, so while they drink prosecco I am making do with a freshly squeezed orange juice. I keep drifting out of the conversation due to lack of concentration, and my paper straw has softened so much that it's unusable. I end up ditching it and gulp the rest of the juice down in one go.

Mimi reassures me that my speech was fine, and she says that she is proud of me for keeping it on point. I keep thinking of more things that I could have said but the nerves, anxiety and adrenaline were not a good mix for allowing me to be succinct. I ask them what was said at the end, and Dee Dee informs me that Mr Burrows had just reiterated the dates on which the announcement would be made. We should know by midday this Saturday, with us finding out before the result is made public. All we need is for thirteen of the councillors to support our proposal, and I was hoping for once that this would be a lucky number for us.

Before long, the bell above the door rang, and Mr Belcher entered still in his pin-striped suit. He was smiling widely and seemed to have more bounce in his step than before. I have never met a person whose emotions were reflected so heavily in their body language. When he had been discussing his granddaughter, he had been more hunched and weaker in appearance. Despite our concerns about his intentions I was happy that he had offered to help us out. Our inclination that he was genuinely remorseful for his previous actions turned out to be true, and he went above and beyond in supporting Doorway 54. He approached our table and kissed Dee Dee and Mimi on the cheek, before turning to me and shaking my hand.

"Please sit" said Dee Dee, and he duly obliged.

"You lot were fantastic this morning" he said. "I am not just saying that because you are my friends, but I really believe that your speeches today were of the correct tone, and with the correct content"

"Thank you" I said. "I was a little nervous, and still am. I hope the council agree"
"I would like to think that the proposal will be passed, however it is a waiting game and I do not want to build up your hopes just in case it gets blocked"
"Did you speak to your friends on the council Mr Belcher?" asked Mimi
"Out of the twenty-five present today, I lunched with four of them. I sent correspondence to a further two, however their diaries led them to be unavailable to meet. I have tried my very best to educate them on the background of your project, and I hope that they will be voting in favour"
"Are you confident?"
"Quietly so, yes. I think we all should be. And you should all be very proud of yourself for your work this morning"

This was the last that was said about the meeting over lunch. Mr Belcher treated us to food and more drinks, over which we discussed other topics. We were all mentally tired after the long preparations for the events at the town hall and this was the ideal opportunity in order to switch off. The plan for the evening was to head back to Doorway 54, get some rest and then maybe do some painting in the evening. I needed some time alone from the group however, mainly due to what I saw in the newspaper this morning before setting off.

~

I am sat on my bed having napped for the past hour. It is approaching 6pm now and I can smell the curry that Dee Dee and Mimi are preparing for our evening meal. We've decided to have a film night in, and the plan is to watch a comedy to end the day on a bright note. I'm not sure what they have chosen but I'll happily watch most things. I still have the remaining parts of the newspaper in my room (the bits that weren't taken to the town hall) as I saw a picture in there that shook me a little. I've now read the article fully, and it wasn't as bad as I had feared, however I am even more grateful that Dee Dee gave me a safe space to stay. The article in question was headlined "Three Arrested in Thames Murder Enquiry". These types of headlines are common in London sadly, and often I will only take note briefly of what the article involves. With this one, the three men were pictured, and their names had been released due to a trial starting at the Old Bailey next Monday.

The murder victim in question was Barry McKenzie. The Nomad. I thought that his death would go unnoticed, but now it had reached the trial stage it was gaining more and more column inches. The three men pictured were the accused. Two were being charged with carrying out the act of murder, and the third with conspiracy to murder. According to the report, two men attacked The Nomad as he slept under an archway of Southwark Bridge, before taking his body to John Carpenter Street, where we laid the flowers later that day. The third person has been accused of planning to murder The Nomad, however was beaten to it by the first two. I'm sorry if this is confusing. The third person, as in the one who planned to kill but didn't, is Peter Newburn. Peter Newburn is Pete. I had spent the day with him and Jenny and knew at the time that he appeared awkward and nervous when laying the flowers. They had told me about his connections to the Sterling Childcatcher from Scotland, and despite saying that they didn't think he was involved, Pete obviously thought he was. There is no mention of Jenny in the article and I would like to think that she genuinely didn't have any involvement. It makes me think to how things could have been different. Why did they both meet with The Nomad on that day when I was there having the drink with him at the Cheshire Cheese pub? They both said to me the day after that it may be best if I didn't hang around with them in case I got caught up in something untoward. Seeing Pete's picture in the paper made me realise just how easy it had been to get caught up in the darker networks of London, and how I could be in serious trouble if I had been recognised that afternoon. I was scared to think how much Jenny knew and scared to think that they easily could trace me to where I was napping in Russell Square. How long had they been watching me that day? Was coming to speak to me quietly always the plan? What options had they discussed whilst they were watching me sleep? Did they think about a way to ensure I kept quiet when they took me down the back alley before telling me The Nomad was dead? I was shaking from the fear of what might have been. I was safely out of this for the time being, but I would always need to remain vigilant if it was ever mentioned to me. Seeing Pete's face stare from the pages with a blank expression made me feel uneasy and I took a ballpoint pen and scribbled over it as much as I could before tearing it out and throwing it into the bin with my failed attempts at speech writing.

The rest of the article went into some details about The Nomad and confirmed that he was an innocent party to the work of Michael Banton, the one who carried out all those awful crimes. At least I knew that he was genuinely a good person. I am not religious as you know, but I hope that he has found peace.

~

I needed an evening away from my thoughts after today. The curry that the ladies had prepared was great, and was served with bhajis, naan bread and mango chutney. Dee Dee had been correct when she told me that she was handy in the kitchen all those weeks ago. Once we had eaten, we washed up together and settled down to watch the film. We may be unconventional, but we are still family.

Twenty-six

Friday July 9th. The pressures of speaking to the council and the public is over, and tomorrow is the day that we find out the result of the vote. I am also going to Pride with Mimi, and she is taking me to meet a friend of hers who is performing at a charity drag show at a pub on Chancery Lane. The act goes by the name of 'Honey Latté' and is quite popular around Soho. I should be in the best of moods today, with so much to look forward to with my favourite people. Instead, today I am low. Depression and anxiety are horrible things as I explained to you previously. I am not sure what has caused them to be so prominent today however. I've not had the energy to do anything around Doorway 54, and have spent a lot of time in my room. I had a cry earlier today and hoped that once that was over I would feel better, but the feeling has yet to shake itself away. I have also stood with my head in the sink, running the cold tap over the back of my head. I again found some calmness in the water, but this also hasn't pulled me from this bout. The only thing that I can take for today is that I must never take anything for granted. Despite having new opportunities ahead, and new friends to share them with, I still need help to stay afloat. I might go for a walk.

Twenty-seven

"You've got it on back to front you daft bastard"

I'm in the kitchen preparing to head down to watch the Pride parade with Mimi. She has given me a present. It is a black t-shirt with the words Doorway 54 splashed across it in a white typewriter-style font. Underneath are the outline of footsteps which lead up to the name. It's a nice design and seeing the name of our project brings home the reality of just how important this day will be. Mimi had the t-shirts made as a surprise, and Mr Belcher was actually the one who paid for them. I thought the words were to be displayed on the back, hence why Mimi had called me a daft bastard. We wanted to wear the t-shirts around today in order to promote what we are doing and to gather some further interest. We were hopeful of positive news from the council, and we would find out before 1pm, all being well.

Dee Dee had been summoned to a meeting at the town hall at 12.30pm, and she would be attending with both Mr Belcher and her solicitor, who I have now learnt is called Mr Oake. Having this hanging over us made us all feel nervous, but we will hopefully keep ourselves occupied by activities in central London. We don't have a concrete plan once we arrive, and our only commitment is getting to the bar to watch Honey Latté at 4pm.

I am in a much better place than I was yesterday. I did go for a walk and followed a similar plan to that of which I used to use at home. The best way to discover new places is to just walk, and that is what I did. For four hours. I had told Dee Dee that I was off to explore, and I think she knew that I was experiencing a low. She is protective of me, however does not restrict my freedom. She just ensured that I had my mobile phone with me in case I needed to call her. This conversation was simple and brief, but that is all you need sometimes. Someone telling you that they are there for you, without actually using those words, is so important. All I need sometimes is someone to text me "Hey, I saw this and it reminded me of you" and I feel better. Knowing that someone is thinking of you, even if that is because of something trivial, means an incredible amount to some people.

With my t-shirt now on the correct way around, I run to my room to pick up my phone and wallet. I have kept the phone plugged in all morning as I don't want to risk missing a call from Dee Dee when the news comes in. Mimi enters my room afterwards and asks how she looks. She is stood there in knee high silver boots, with heels that are at least six inches. It makes her tower over me, considering she is about six foot tall without them. Her thighs have been spray tanned and contrast her white denim shorts. With the Doorway 54 t-shirt she has a large pair of rainbow fairy wings that protrude a foot either side. To complete the look she has chosen her largest wig.

This adds another couple of inches to her height, and is platinum blonde in colour. Her make-up is incredible too. Dark eyeliner gives her a piercing stare. In fact, she looks phenomenal, and I tell her that too. She compliments my look as well, even though it is just the t-shirt and a pair of black shorts that I picked up with Dee Dee earlier in the week. I still haven't had my haircut so I allow Mimi to do style it the same way as she did on the morning of the Town Hall meeting.

"Shall we go?" asked Mimi
"Ready when you are. Are you sure you can get down the stairs in those heels?"
"You'll be surprised by how much I can do in these heels young man" she replied.

We shouted good luck to Dee Dee and said that we would speak to her later. She was in the shower and preparing to leave shortly. Dee Dee did say something back, but it wasn't fully audible. Mimi and I headed down the many flights of stairs, through the bright corridors and out of the front door.

~

As it turns out, our planning was a bit out. The parade itself doesn't start until later this afternoon, so we may not be able to catch much of it before heading to Chancery Lane. It's okay though as some of Mimi's friends are in town already and have invited us to join them. They are people that she has got to know over the last couple of weeks, but they have been more than happy to welcome her, and now me, to their group. We walk down to Soho Square and sit with at least ten others. Names aren't important, which is lucky as I can't remember them all. They are all drinking and offer some rhubarb and apple flavoured cider to me. I'm feeling good and the weather is again glorious, so I decide a small amount wouldn't do any harm.

"Are you heading to watch Honey this afternoon?" Mimi asks the group

"I think we might head down for a bit" replies a man with blue-dyed hair. "I like her, but I always find that cabaret nights are the place where I bump into ex-boyfriends that I have been avoiding. To me, going to cabaret is Russian roulette, like a man with a peanut allergy eating a bag of Revels"

This brings a laugh from the group. A couple of others mention that they will come down for the later part of the evening as they have friends in the parade who they want to see. One is apparently dressed in a fifteen-foot unicorn costume with the other LGBTQ members of their banking company.

Sitting in the square is lovely, and I find myself fully relaxing for the first time in a long time. I lay back with my eyes closed just listening to the conversations around me, both from our group and others situated nearby. Being around these people on a day which celebrates diversity quite literally fills me with pride. I am no longer ashamed of my sexuality, and couldn't imagine a life without being the way I am. Yes, I have had my troubles, and they aren't over yet, but so has everyone else. As Dee Dee said in her speech, together we are stronger.

I decline a second bottle of cider in case I experience any side effects but sit up to try and learn more about the group. A few are already on the way to becoming drunk. A couple of others have just got up to leave also. They are part of a musical act called 'Bi Bi Baby', which is a choir made up entirely of bisexuals. They're outfits are made up of the blue, pink and mauve bisexual flag and look amazing, however I feel they may melt judging by the material that has been used to make them. I'd quite like to watch them to be honest but this would have to wait.

Due to the excitement of the day, it's hard to break into a conversation with many of the people here, but I know that I will see them with Mimi again in the future. She has been fairly quiet however and I ask if she is okay.

"It's midday, Joey" she says. "Dee Dee will be in that meeting soon which means that we could find out any moment now if we have done it"

"I feel a bit sick" I reply, truthfully too as the reality of the decision being so close has made me nauseous.
"You and me both" replies Mimi.
"I need to keep myself distracted"
"More cider?"
"That probably won't help" I laugh. I have no idea what I want to do. I am so nervous to find out that I am unable to concentrate on anything else now.
"I can't concentrate" says Mimi, as if reading my mind. "Fancy going for a walk?"

I agree to this. Mimi stands first and lets the group know that we are going. They are kind and wish us luck, and we promise to tell them when we see them next.

As we leave Soho Square there is a vendor selling pride flags on the corner. Mimi buys two large ones 'for luck". She wraps hers round her waist whilst I wear mine like a cape.

"Where do you want to go then?" she asks me.
"Is it too early to go to the pub where the drag thing is?" I ask. She says that although it won't start yet, it might be a chance to catch up with her friends. Apparently, they are excited to meet me, which still makes me feel weird. The walk to Chancery Lane takes about thirty minutes, and we still haven't heard from Dee Dee when we arrive. Hearing the news today is both a blessing and a curse. On one hand we have plenty of things to see on the journey, but

on the other hand we are so worried that we don't take any of it in. They say that no news is good news, but we worry in case it is bad news and she is afraid to tell us. The nerves get the better of Mimi more and she drops into a newsagent to pick up some small cans of Gin and Tonic.

"For the nerves" she says as she pulls back the ring pulls on both and hands one to me. I don't know how anyone can drink gin, it tastes disgusting, but believing it will help me settle I down the contents of the can quickly.
"You don't have to down every drink in one go Joey, you'll be on the floor by 2pm if you do"
"I'm too young to be drinking anyway" I reply
"I keep forgetting you're so young. You're lucky"

I don't feel lucky, but I know that she is only being kind. Once we arrive on Chancery Lane we are greeted by hundreds of people. Both of us had forgotten that England were playing in a World Cup semi-final today and therefore we stupidly expected this to be a quiet area. We sit down on the pavement near to the pub whilst Mimi finished her gin. You can hear the supporters singing about football coming home from about to hundred yards.

"This is where I used to sleep" I say to Mimi. "The doorway that I called home is just around the corner"
"I remember you telling me that it was Fleet Street. It must seem a lifetime ago"

"In a way it does, but being back here now makes it seem like only yesterday"

"I know what you mean. So much has happened since that night I met you in Gold's. But hey, we've done alright since. Eventually"

"I guess so. It feels weird being back here. Part of me wants to see it again to remind myself how far I have come"

"I'll come with you if you want to see?"

"In a weird way I do think it will help me"

"If you want to show me I will come. If you feel uncomfortable at any point though just say and we can move away"

I help Mimi up off the floor and we start walking slowly down towards Fleet Street. The streets are quieter than I have ever seen them, and I assume this is because of the football. Everyone seems to be out to watch either the football or Pride, with many people trying to do both judging by the amount of people we see with a St George's cross on one cheek and a rainbow on the other. It's made the atmosphere quite good as everyone seems to be in a great mood. The blistering sun shining down has also helped, although it has made me a bit sweaty. This might be in part to the nerves again though.

Fleet Street is a different world now. All my memories of it are of a grey road with daunting buildings. Now though it seems brighter and more vibrant. I hope that I never have to spend another night out here. I have security for now, but you never know what is around the corner.

We continue walking down the slope and cross onto the southern side of the street. Some scaffolding has been put up in front of some of the buildings and we are forced to walk out into the road to avoid it. From this viewpoint I catch a glimpse of number fifty-four for the first time in weeks. I was expecting to feel sadness when I saw it, but instead found my strides quickening. I was near enough dragging Mimi down the street by this point, her heels making her less manoeuvrable than she had claimed when back at the house. For all the low points that I had experienced in its doorway, I remembered that if it wasn't for here then Mr Belcher wouldn't have been part of our project. And without that? The chances of getting approval from the council in Marylebone would have been much slimmer.

The doorway seemed much smaller than I remembered, and I was unsure how I even managed to fit in it to sleep. The back corners near the black door were covered in litter, and the smell or urine was quite strong. It transported me back to the morning where I contemplated jumping from Blackfriars Bridge. I felt uncomfortable and told Mimi that we needed to continue. She didn't question this, and we linked arms and continued towards the river.

The further we walked through these old areas, the more I couldn't believe that I had survived my time here. I felt that seeing the bridge would be hard, however after having a bad day yesterday in terms of my mental health, I wanted to see it, if nothing more to remind myself that things can get better. The junction at the end of Fleet Street was virtually deserted, with the only real noise coming from taxi's flying past from south of the river, many complete with England flags flying from the back window. We took a right and passed the closed café where I used to sometimes got my morning coffee as the river came into view. The building work taking place on the edge of the river itself had nearly doubled in size since I was last here and the sound of drilling and metal work being lifted around ruined any chance of finding the moment peaceful.

I took Mimi to the central seat on the bridge.

"This is where it was" I said as we got there.
"And you're okay being here?"
"I am yeah. Weirdly it seems as though it's giving me closure on the previous chapter of my life. So much has changed since I was sat on the edge here"

I climbed up onto the steps and looked into the water below. It was similar to how it was on that morning, but the bright sunshine was making the water much less intimidating. There were still swirls of mud dancing around the surface, but that's all they were to me now. There were no longer metaphors below me, and there wasn't a single part of me now contemplating diving down into the currents.

"You get quite a nice view from up here" said Mimi, holding onto her wings as the breeze across the bridge picked up.

"Yeah, I like it here. It's even better when it's this quiet"

"Seems the perfect place to stop and have a drink before we head back to the pub to see Honey" she said, pulling out a further two cans from her bag. "Gin and tonic?"

"Is that wise? I'm not great at holding my drink you know that" I laughed.

"It has cucumber in it"

"And that's meant to tempt me how?"

"It's nice! This will be your last today though. You're too young to drink in the pub anyway so you will be sticking to orange juice in there, okay"

"Okay" I said, deciding to have the second gin after all. It was only a small can anyway.

I was enjoying my time with Mimi, and it was liberating to be able to sit with a friend on a Pride day, being the real me. It felt like the real Joey Eaton had finally arrived. Me and Mimi discussed anything and everything for a while, including a game of 'Snog, Marry Avoid' with any group of three who happened to pass us. At two points Mimi was laughing so much that she was on her knees struggling to breathe. We were sat there for close to an hour before the sound of Mimi's phone broke through the conversation.

"It's Dee Dee" she said, grabbing my arm. "Are you ready to find out?"
"As ready as I can be" I replied, feeling instantly sick again. Mimi grabbed my left hand and answered the call.

"Hi Dee Dee" she answered, nonchalantly, turning her head away from me slightly. "How did the meeting go?"

I kept leaning closer, but she swatted me away each time. I sat back against the wall and tucked my legs up onto the stone bench in front of me. I closed my eyes and just repeated 'please' to myself over and over. It seemed as if Dee Dee was doing most of the talking, with Mimi adding 'I see' and 'yep' at regular intervals.

The conversation went on for about five minutes before it appeared to draw to a conclusion.

"Yeah, we are all good here thanks. We're sat on Blackfriars at the moment to avoid the crowds. What? No no, it was his idea. He's in good spirits" she said whilst turning to look at me, her tongue poking just out her mouth. "Yes, we will be at the pub at around three. Thanks for letting me know. I'll let Joey know. See you in a bit babe. Yep. Yep. Okay, yep. I won't. Yep. No he will be fine to go in. Yeah, yeah of course, he will stick to the orange juice. Okay Dee Dee, I will speak to you in a minute I'm sure. B-bye"

Mimi slid the phone back into her short pockets and came back to sit next to me. During the call she had let go of her grip on me and had wandered around in circles and by the time she hung up she was about five metres away. I was almost too scared to ask about the vote.

"Have we done it?" I asked apprehensively.

"Six councillors abstained from voting"

"Six. Bloody hell. It was only a yes or no vote. What are they scared of? What does that leave?"

"That would leave nineteen"

"Did we still get the thirteen we needed in our favour?"

Mimi turned to look at me before grinning widely. "We got seventeen of them".

Twenty-eight

"This is for the ladies and the gentleman, for the boy and the girls, and for the L's, the B's. the G's, the T's, the Q's and everyone in between. I am Miss Honey Latté and I am about to BLOW. YOUR. MIND"

Honey Latté entered the stage at the Knight's Templar amid the bang of glitter cannons and loud music. Confetti was raining down from the old-style architecture, and she was belting out a cover of Proud Mary with two fellow drag queens (Pumpkin Spice and Mocha Chocolaté to give them their stage names) acting as her backing dancers. She had put the afternoon together to raise money for an LGBTQ charity and had a number of acts on until mid-evening. Alongside the drag queens there was a nun-themed dance duo, an all-male gospel-style choir performing their Abba based acapella act and a dance music act whose name escapes me. There were also some non-performance-based things too, such as a painting competition (where you are only allowed to use your body parts to paint) and 'Naked Bingo', which thankfully I won't be around long enough for to find out exactly what that is.

Honey Latté is in full swing on stage and is firing small jets of silver glitter from the breast plate of her silver armour style outfit. She is lip-syncing to various chart songs, and by the third re-enters the stage astride a full-size paper maché cow. She is pulled around stage on this fake farmyard animal by four shirtless men whilst she sings You Spin Me Right Round. When it comes to the finale she jumps off, pulls out a phallically shaped baseball bat and smashes it like a piñata. As safe sex is one of the messages of the day, sweets inside have been replaced by condoms and packets of lube. These are then scattered across the room from the stage by the drag queens present.

The whole afternoon so far has been well received, and there have even been football fans coming in from the pub opposite to join in the fun, buoyed by the fact that England had beaten Sweden less than half an hour previously. Mimi has introduced me to many people, and a few have snuck ciders onto my table, so my mind sometimes feels as if I am observing the whole scenario on a television. As you can imagine we are in extremely good spirits after hearing the news that we have approval to go forward and open Doorway 54. Dee Dee may come down to join us later, however she has said that she wants us to stay and have fun after all the hard work we had put in over the previous month. If she decides not to come, we will head back to Doorway 54 to celebrate together. It wouldn't be right be separated from each other after everything we have been through.

~

When Mimi had broken the news to me on the bridge that seventeen councillors had voted in favour of the plans we both didn't really know what to do for the first few seconds. It was a mixture of relief and overwhelming joy. We had both been through so much to get to that moment in our life. To finally have confirmation that we had achieved this great thing, a thing that will help so many in the positions we had found ourselves in at the start of the summer, was hard to get our heads around. Once the news started to sink in we had both screamed and danced along Blackfriars Bridge. I had called Dee Dee back shortly afterwards but could hardly control my excitement in order for the conversation to be of any worth. Alongside the dancing, there were also lots of tears of course. It just seemed that we had reached the end of something, and for us both to come through it together just became too much. I thought back to all the things that had happened to me, and how one different choice somewhere in this journey would have started a chain reaction along another path. I was scared even just thinking about this.

One person who I had wanted to tell the good news to was Mario. I know his café wasn't too far from here, but we didn't have enough time today to visit it so instead Mimi agreed to come with me in the morning to see him. I wanted to thank everyone who had tried to keep me safe. Some of them have probably helped more than I realised, whether that is the postman who directed me to Gold's, or even its manager, Gloria. I may not be able to find them all of course, but I will pay forward to others all that has been paid to me. Like Mario, what I do not have in terms of money, I have in terms of compassion. We were still on the bridge as 4.30pm approached and we needed to get going in order to get a good seat for the rest of Honey's afternoon. Before departing, Mimi turned to me.

"Do you feel at home here in London now?"

I thought about it for a few seconds. "I think I do, yes. More so than where I was".

"I'm glad. We can both restart our lives fully now. You'll never forget this day"

"You can say that again"

"Here, come and give me a hand".

Mimi turned and was walking to the railings in the middle of the bridge. She untied the large rainbow flag from around her waist and waved it from the bridge.

"In my bag are some hair ties" she said, just audible over the wind that was now striking our faces directly. "Take them out and bite through them".

I did as I was told. Once I had completed the task I helped her fasten each corner of the flag to one of the vertical posts on the bridge, allowing us to leave the flag to fly and look out over London from the spot where I had nearly committed suicide not so long ago. It was only a small symbol, but to me it meant the world. I followed suit and tied my flag nearby.

"These flags are for the ones who didn't make it" said Mimi, leaning her head into my shoulder, despite her being so tall in heels.
"For the ones we lost on the way" I said.

We leaned against the barrier looking into the waters in silence for a moment. I wondered how many people like me didn't get the chance to be saved. I didn't even have names to put to these people, but I knew there were many that existed. I thought of all the families that they had left behind, wondering what the reasons were behind their decision to fall the other way. I wish I could have spent five minutes with each of them, just to talk and learn from them.

Eventually the conversation picked up and we started to discuss more things we wanted at Doorway 54. Dee Dee had warned us not to get too carried away, but we were both young and excited so dreaming big was no harm. We would only put forward the sensible ideas though. As we were talking, a man, I'd say aged in his mid-thirties, approached us. He was wearing a white V-necked t-shirt, and pale blue skinny jeans. His eyes were covered by shades and sweat had formed in beads on his forehead.

"Hey, how's it going?" he said in a welcoming and friendly tone
"We are very well, thank you" replied Mimi

"Are you heading towards Pride?"
"We are off to a cabaret, how about you?"
"Meant to be meeting some friends in Soho. A friend has hired out a whole bar this evening. If you're about you should come down. I'm running late as always though, it's too hot to get the tube at the moment so thought I'd walk it from London Bridge"

It struck me how open the man was being with us, and I'm not sure if this was just because it was Pride day. I have found a lot of people in the LGBT community to be very open though. If they weren't then I'd probably not have become friends with Mimi. I had become used to ninety-nine per cent of Londoners ignoring each other. Mimi told him that we wouldn't be about but thanked him for the invitation. He told us that the reason he had stopped was to ask us why we were hanging the flags off of this bridge in particular. I didn't really feel comfortable opening up fully, so we told them it was just a symbol to remember absent friends. It seemed to strike a chord with him, and he told us that he had lost a friend named Brian at the start of the year to suicide. We sat and talked for five minutes about how he had felt, and it was upsetting to hear the guilt that he still bestowed upon himself. He told us that he was called Richard, and that for the first few months after Brian's suicide he became reclusive for a short while.

"I thought I was too busy to take his call that week" he said sadly. "You never expect that missing one conversation, however brief, could lead to something so tragic. It took me a long time to even begin to try and come to terms with what had happened. I was ashamed when I saw his parents and felt as if everyone was blaming me for his death, despite them saying that it wasn't my fault. It really affected me. Do you know those days where you just can't be bothered to be around people?"

Mimi and myself both knew these days well, and even now there were times when I would feel like that. We asked if he wanted to join us for a drink but unfortunately his other plans meant that he didn't have time. We did swap numbers though, and we invited him to come and see Doorway 54 on the day it opened. We said that there are other people like him out there, who feel guilt for something that they are not to blame for, and that being around others may help him. He was more than keen to be involved and said he would mention it to his other friends who also knew Brian. Before going our separate ways, he asked if he could add to our small display.

"Of course you can" replied Mimi. "This way Brian can be here with us looking out towards the city".

Richard lifted up his t-shirt to reveal a rainbow belt. He unbuckled this and slid it out of his jeans. He proceeded to fasten this around another of the pillars of the bridge.

“Here you go Brian, this one is for you” he said as he stepped back. It was nice to have someone else understand our gesture straight away, and I hoped that no one would remove the display today. “Do you mind if I take a photo of you two please? Just with the things in the background?”

Neither of us minded, and we posed whilst he took a few snaps of us near the rainbows, with the London Eye and other landmarks in the background. Once complete the three of us walked together back up towards Chancery Lane, where he would jump on the underground to meet his friends. Despite the warmth he said that he couldn’t be over an hour late and the tube was a necessary evil. On the journey we told him more about Doorway 54 and he said that he would try and volunteer for us if time, and his mental health allowed. We told him to tell as many people as possible about it also. Despite having approval, word of mouth would be essential. Not only would this allow it to be shared to people who may need it, it might also lead to some extra funds being sent our way. Richard suggested that we also set up a crowdfunding page whereby people could donate to support the shelter. I had never done crowdfunding before so we made a note of it so we could mention the idea to Dee Dee later. Hopefully she would be better at that kind of thing, or even Mr Belcher will be able to do that for us if he had time. I’m sure he mixes in circles with some wealthy lawyers that would be willing to donate a small amount to help us.

~

All of these events now lead us to where we are now, sat in the Knight's Templar at the end of Honey's set. Dee Dee has text saying that she has more exciting news for us, but news that will prevent her from coming down. Naked Bingo will be starting shortly so we decide to say goodbye to those in the bar and head back home. Saying goodbye isn't a quick process when you have been getting to know so many people, and each person offered to buy us a drink which we had to decline. We were making our way around the room towards the doors at the same time that Honey was handing out bingo cards and glitter pens. We stood near to her to grab her attention as we wanted to thank her for making the afternoon even more memorable. I was still a bit giddy from the cider and was a bit concerned about having my first proper hangover. I didn't want to have to make Dee Dee nurse my self-inflicted illness in the morning so told Mimi to make sure that I didn't accept any more alcohol off anyone, even if I thought it would be okay to have one more. She told me that she didn't even realise I was drinking.

After what seemed like an hour, Honey finished handing out the items and approached us.

"I am glad I have caught you" she said, in her mock-American accent that she uses when on stage.

"We wanted to wait and thank you" said Mimi. "It's been perfect. I hope it raises a lot of money and the rest of the afternoon is just as good"

"That's very kind thank you, but that's not the main reason I wanted to grab you. Have you seen what you have started?"

"With Doorway 54? It's just the beginning but hopefully it all works out"

"Oh, that definitely will, but what I mean have you seen what you've done on the bridge?"

"Oh, the flags, yeah we thought it might just be a nice gesture"

"Do you use Twitter?" Honey asked.

Neither of us really did. We did know about it though, of course, but my phone wasn't advanced enough to have it installed, and Mimi always said she 'couldn't be arsed' with social media. When we told Honey this she became excited and dragged us out to the front of the building. Out the front of the Knight's Templar was nearly as busy as it was inside, with many people on the step outside smoking in the burning sun.

"You need to see this" she said as she pulled her mobile phone out from between her fake breasts. She opened it up and spent a few seconds scrolling before holding it up for us to see. "You've gone viral" she said proudly.

The picture on the screen was the one that Richard had taken of us. The caption underneath said "I met Mimi and Joey from Doorway 54 today. We put up our rainbow flags up on Blackfriars to remember those that we have lost".

"Wow, that's really kind of him" I said, feeling proud that he found comfort from our small gesture.

"But look at the retweets!" she said, turning the phone back to us. "Nearly five hundred people have shared it already, and it's getting more and more every second".

We were surprised just how many people appreciated what we did, and it was a great that Doorway 54 was being shown in a positive light less than three hours after we got the approval to open. Honey was still excited.

"In the replies many people have said that they are going to do the same. Some people have even shared pictures of themselves hanging their own items from the bridge already. Look at this one"

She turned the phone for a third time and a user had tweeted a picture of a flag being tied up with the message "For Michelle. Here in spirit whilst we are on spirits" written in blue across its yellow stripe. "You two have tapped into something. People are following your example. I think there might be a fair few things down on that bridge now. You should probably go and have a look".

We were surprised that more people were following our lead, but I felt a warmth inside me that the whole community had started to share their own tributes. I really wanted to go and see the bridge again before we headed home, and Mimi was basically ready to drag me down there now. We called Dee Dee and told her, and she told us that she felt proud of what was happening and told us to take lots of pictures to show her.

The journey back to the bridge took no time at all, mainly as we were virtually running back down there. I wanted to see the bridge from the river side first, so we headed down the back streets to the Victoria Embankment. I wasn't prepared for the sight we would see as the bridge came into view. A few weeks ago, I was sat on this bridge feeling alone, ready to end the darkness. Now, it couldn't be brighter. There must have been at least thirty flags hanging over the Thames, along with balloons and even t-shirts. The whole central part of the bridge was entirely covered, and there were small groups of people still scattered across its length still tying their tributes up. We took a picture and headed off to read some of what had been left.

Up close, the tributes were very moving. Photos had been left in some places, and even people who had passed away from many years ago were being celebrated.

The whole experience was humbling. Both Mimi and myself spent some time talking to people, asking about their stories and learning about the lives of those in our community who were no longer with us. So many people came together at that moment, laughing and crying at the memories of those who were missing from this year's celebrations. It shocked us to learn just how many people told us that those they were hanging flags for were people who had taken their own lives. Despite knowing why we wanted to open Doorway 54, hearing so many stories first hand confirmed that we were doing the right thing, and made us more determined to ensure that we would do everything we could to reach out to those who were in need.

~

It had gone 8pm by the time we got back to the house. Dee Dee was overwhelmed by the pictures of the bridge when we showed her. It was the first time that we were all together since she had been to meet the council.

"It seems that Mr Belcher had helped our cause by highlighting the positives" she said, whilst pouring out two glasses of prosecco and one of lemonade. "Some of those who were originally against the proposal compromised and abstained. Even if they had voted, we still would have had the approval due to the yes votes"

"So, what are our next steps?" asked Mimi

"I think the first thing to do is celebrate properly" replied Dee Dee. "I have a table booked at a restaurant nearby, and I would like to take you both to dinner. When out I will talk to you about funding Doorway 54. I spoke to my solicitor this afternoon, and have meetings planned the rest of the week. We will finalise bank accounts soon also, and then see if we can start the process to get ourselves registered as a charity. This will take time though, so we will need to try and get some sponsorship in the meantime. That's a discussion for later however, so go and get yourselves changed and we will head for food"

Up in my room I sat on the edge of my bed trying to process everything that had gone on today. I was somehow unbelievably happy, slightly sad, extremely energetic and absolutely knackered all at the same time. With not much time spare before having to head out, I showered and changed into a clean set of clothes. I hung my Doorway 54 t-shirt on a hanger from the back of my door, a reminder that this was real and I had done it. Not alone, in fact far from it, but I had done it. I had survived.

Epilogue

It is now late August and Pride seems a long time ago. So much has happened since that day, and Doorway 54 is nearly ready for its grand opening. I have tried to keep myself occupied over the last two months, and I am mentally and physically in a better place. This doesn't mean that I haven't been having low days though. They have been more infrequent, however sometimes I am still finding things overwhelming. I am coping with this by heading for walks around London and have discovered many new parks this way. I would like to say that I would never find myself sitting on the edge of a bridge again, but the human mind is a complex thing, so you never know what it will lead you to do. Dee Dee has been approached by four different volunteers who have experience with running therapy sessions, and I have been seeing one in particular on a weekly basis. I was reluctant to open up at first, but as the time moved on I revealed more of my inner thoughts and demons to her. I may never have perfect mental health, but I now live more in hope than I do in fear.

One part of the therapy involved trying to reconnect with those that you had lost contact with along the way. For a second time I had written letters to both my parents and Angelica. I am still yet to hear from Angelica fully, but she did send a short note to say that she was well, that the Caribbean was incredible, and that she will come to visit me when the time is right. I still think that her father is still reluctant to let her be closer to me. I also received a letter from my parents. As it turns out, my mum had been seeing a therapist also. She described how she had suffered a similar set of emotions to those that she encountered when Matthew had passed away so young. She said that at first she was in denial, and that all the blame was on me. Over time though she realised that the blame was actually an underlying guilt that she did nothing to help. As a result of all this she hoped that one day in the near future we could try and reconcile our differences. She was still involved with the church but had scaled down her duties there in order to try and get herself back on track. I wasn't ready to meet with her or my dad yet, but we both wanted to keep in touch to see what would happen. I may have lost the bond with my birth family, but I had gained a new family thanks to Dee Dee and Mimi. I don't know what I would do without them.

Something else that has happened is GCSE results day. This was last week, however there was no way that I would head back into Greenwood Academy to collect these in person. Being back in that environment may have a detrimental effect on me, so instead I asked that the results be sent here instead. Last Friday over dinner I opened them alone in my room. One 8, four 6's, four 4's and two 3's (This is One A, four B's, four C's and two D's in old money). The 8 was in geography of course. A-levels and university are still out of the question. There is nothing that will make me go back into that kind of education again, and instead I discussed the idea of enrolling in a business management course at the local college in Marylebone sometime next year. I think this will be fantastic to learn more about how to help run Doorway 54, and also more about the legal side of it all. I am sure Mr Belcher could help with parts that aren't taught during the formal lessons.

As for Doorway 54? We are due to open on September the 18th. We are all slightly nervous as to what will happen on that first night, but even if one member of the LGBTQ community stays with us on that evening we will be happy. It will be one person who won't be hunting for an underpass to shelter in, at risk from those who stumble across them. Mimi explained about the crowdfunding idea, and Dee Dee had set this up whilst we worked towards gaining charity status. We were given a boost during the meal that we went out for on the evening of Pride in London. As I mentioned, Dee Dee told us that she had some exciting news to tell us. Unbelievably, the news was that the actor (and now director) Martin van de Molen had responded to our letter to him. He apologised for the delay, but this was due to filming commitments in Brazil. He wrote fondly about his time in the flat that he had rented from Dee Dee, the second-floor flat which now would provide shelter for up to twelve gay men. He said that when he was back in the country he would like to come to visit us. On top of this, he sent through a payment of £20,000 in order to cover the costs of setting up Doorway 54. His generosity had ensured that there were no delays in completing the works to transform the building into a place fit to function. Mr Belcher has also still been involved and has called upon friends to provide legal support for all the times that we have needed it. The locals in Marylebone have been another group to offer their services to us, mainly in the form of volunteering. Over the previous six weeks many of those who live on Bell Street and the roads nearby have been up ladders painting ceilings and door frames. Some of those helping originally objected to the plans for the hostel during the consultation stage.

The spontaneous display of flags on Blackfriars Bridge reached an audience far greater than we expected, and national newspapers even included pictures of it in their Monday morning editions. We received some apologetic gifts from a few Marylebone residents on the basis of this picture, and some who owned businesses had provided materials such as sanitary products, cleaning materials and even a laptop. Dee Dee could not be any prouder to finally bring the community feel back to Bell Street. The tweet that Richard had posted which had kick-started the whole thing had now been retweeted over fifteen thousand times, and so many people who had passed away were remembered through stories and anecdotes. There is even talk of making the displaying of rainbow flags on Blackfriars Bridge an annual memorial during Pride to ensure that those who we have lost can still be part of the day. Richard has also confirmed that he will be down for the grand opening.

The building which houses Doorway 54 itself looks fantastic. We have tested the kitchen equipment numerous times to ensure we have hot food available, and I can now confirm that Dee Dee's chicken dishes are incredible. The rooms inside have been fully decorated, the beds have been constructed (a few had to be redone due to my poor DIY skills), and the front of the building has been cleaned up. If you now stand on the street and look across, Doorway 54 is a reality.

There are just a few more small bits to do here now until we are ready to open our doors to the LGBTQ homeless community of London. Mimi is trying to set up more media appearances (including the BBC and Sky News), and I am going to spend some time in the rear garden clearing weeds and cleaning off the patio. It will be entering Autumn by the time that we open, but the evenings should still be warm and light enough for residents to enjoy some peace in their safe environment. This has been a long road for Dee Dee, Mimi and myself, and I love them more than I can explain. In just three weeks we will have completed the first part of our journey together.

Three weeks. Just three more weeks. Twenty-one days. About five hundred hours. Around thirty-two thousand minutes. One point eight million seconds, give or take.

Doorway 54

Contacts

This book is a work of fiction, however the issues that Joey faces are a familiar story to many people in the United Kingdom. Across the next few pages are some organisations, along with their contact details, that can provide help and support.

The Albert Kennedy Trust (www.akt.org.uk/) are the national LGBTQ+ youth homelessness charity; focused on prevention and early action they provide: safe homes, mentoring, training, advocacy and support to young people who are homeless or living in a hostile environment after coming out to their parents, care givers and peers.

Mental Health and Suicide

NHS Choices – Suicide

www.nhs.uk/conditions/suicide/

Samaritans

Tel: 116 123
samaritans.org

Samaritans is available round the clock, every single day of the year. We provide a safe place for anyone struggling to cope, whoever they are, however they feel, whatever life has done to them. Please call 08457 90 90 90 (UK) 1850 60 90 90 (ROI), email jo@samaritans.org, or visit samaritans.org to find details of the nearest branch.

YoungMinds

Helpline: 0808 802 5544
youngminds.org.uk

Parents' Information Service gives advice to parents or carers who may be concerned about the mental health or emotional well being of a child or young person.

Mind

MindInfoline: 0300 123 3393
mind.org.uk

The MindinfoLine offers thousands of callers confidential help on a range of mental health issues. Mind helps people take control of their mental health. We do this by providing high-quality information and advice, and campaigning to promote and protect good mental health for everyone. They also provide a special legal service to the public, lawyers and mental health workers.

Campaign Against Living Miserably

Helpline: 0800 58 58 58
thecalmzone.net

The Campaign Against Living Miserably (CALM) works to prevent male suicide and offers support services for any man who is struggling or in crisis. CALM's helpline 0800 58 58 58 and web-chat are for men in the UK who need to talk or find information and support. The services are open 5pm–midnight daily and are free, anonymous and confidential. For access or to find more information visit thecalmzone.net

ChildLine

Helpline: 0808 11 11
childline.org.uk

ChildLine is a counselling service for children and young people. You can contact ChildLine about anything - no problem is too big or too small. If you are feeling scared or out of control or just want to talk to someone you can contact ChildLine.

Students Against Depression

https://www.studentsagainstdepression.org/

Students Against Depression is a website offering advice, information, guidance and resources to those affected by low mood, depression and suicidal thinking. Alongside clinically-validated information and resources it presents the experiences, strategies and advice of students themselves – after all, who are better placed to speak to their peers about how depression can be overcome.

Homelessness

Centrepoint

https://centrepoint.org.uk/

The UK's leading youth homelessness charity. Together with their partners, they support more than 10,000 homeless young people each year. At Centrepoint, they help vulnerable young people by giving them the practical and emotional support they need to find a job and live independently.

Shelter

https://www.shelter.org.uk/

Shelter helps millions of people every year struggling with bad housing or homelessness by offering advice, support and legal services. They campaign to make sure that, one day, no one will have to turn to them for help.

LGBTQ+

Attitude

https://attitude.co.uk/

Attitude was founded in 1994 and is the UK's best-selling gay magazine. As well as a print edition, Attitude is available as a magazine on tablet and mobile and is renowned for its high-profile celebrity events.

Pride in London

http://prideinlondon.org

Pride in London is wholly run by a group of volunteers who are passionate about equality and diversity. They are a not-for-profit organisation, and any surplus funds raised are used to support the LGBTQ community and improve the event.

Together, they run the UK's biggest, most diverse pride, and their job is to make sure they provide a platform for every part of London's LGBT+ community (lesbian, gay, bisexual, trans*, queer, questioning, intersex, non-binary, asexual, polysexual, genderqueer and gender variant people) to raise awareness of LGBT+ issues and campaign for the freedoms that will allow them to live their lives on a genuinely equal footing.

Stonewall

https://www.stonewall.org.uk/

Stonewall are here to let all lesbian, gay, bi and trans people, here and abroad, know they're not alone. They believe we're stronger united, so they partner with organisations that help create real change for the better. They have laid deep foundations across Britain - in some of our greatest institutions - so our communities can continue to find ways to flourish, and individuals can reach their full potential. They are here to support those who can't yet be themselves.

LGBT Foundation

https://lgbt.foundation/

Established in 1975, LGBT Foundation exists to support the needs of the diverse range of people who identify as lesbian, gay, bisexual and trans. They believe in a fair and equal society where all LGBT people can achieve their full potential. #EqualityWins underpins much of what they do and they aim to be; 'here if you need us.'

They are a nationally significant charity firmly rooted in their local communities of Greater Manchester and provide a wide range of evidence-based and cost effective services.

Each year, they serve over 40,000 people, as well as providing information to over 200,000 individuals online. Throughout all of their work, they support LGBT people to increase their skills, knowledge and self-confidence to improve and maintain their health and wellbeing.

Doorway 54

PS. The population of Tenby was just shy of 5,000 in the 2011 census.....

Doorway 54

Doorway 54

Doorway 54

28303873R00235

Printed in Poland
by Amazon Fulfillment
Poland Sp. z o.o., Wrocław

The Trump Effect in Contemporary Art and Visual Culture

The Trump Effect in Contemporary Art and Visual Culture

Populism, Politics, and Paranoia

KIT MESSHAM-MUIR AND
UROŠ ČVORO

BLOOMSBURY VISUAL ARTS
LONDON • NEW YORK • OXFORD • NEW DELHI • SYDNEY

BLOOMSBURY VISUAL ARTS
Bloomsbury Publishing Plc
50 Bedford Square, London, WC1B 3DP, UK
1385 Broadway, New York, NY 10018, USA
29 Earlsfort Terrace, Dublin 2, Ireland

BLOOMSBURY, BLOOMSBURY VISUAL ARTS and the Diana logo are trademarks of Bloomsbury Publishing Plc

First published in Great Britain 2023

Cover design: Tjasa Krivec
Cover image: The "Trump Baby" blimp, designed by Matt Bonner, now in the collection of the Museum of London. Photo: AP. © Mike Kemp/Getty Images

A catalogue record for this book is available from the British Library.

A catalogue record for this book is available from the Library of Congress.

ISBN: HB: 978-1-3502-8728-0
PB: 978-1-3503-4659-8
ePDF: 978-1-3502-8729-7
eBook: 978-1-3502-8730-3

Typeset by RefineCatch Limited, Bungay, Suffolk
Printed and bound in India

To find out more about our authors and books visit www.bloomsbury.com and sign up for our newsletters.

To Dr David McNeill

ILLUSTRATIONS

ACKNOWLEDGMENTS

This book is part of the Art in Conflict project, led by Prof Kit Messham-Muir (Curtin University), in collaboration with Prof Charles Green (University of Melbourne), A/Prof Uroš Čvoro (UNSW Art & Design), Ryan Johnston (University of Melbourne) and Prof Ana Carden Coyne (University of Manchester), and Partner Investigators Dr Anthea Gunn and Laura Webster (Australian War Memorial). The Australian War Memorial and National Trust (NSW) are Partner Organisations. Art in Conflict is a three-year project funded by the Australian Government through the Australian Research Council. Art in Conflict (LP170100039) receives a Linkage Project grant of $293,380.

We wish to note here that many of the artists and galleries we approached in the production of this publication did not grant permission or respond to our requests, much to our surprise. This is perhaps an indication of a reluctance to be associated with the topic of this book. While we respect their decisions, we also give very special thanks to the artists, galleries and agencies who did grant permission for use of the images that appear in these pages. These include Stephen Manka, Mladen Miljanović, Adrian Paci, Cornelia Parker (as well as the British Museum and Frith Street Gallery, London, Hellenic Parliament + NEON), Raqs Media Collective, Kara Walker, as well as the photographers credited in the image captions. We also thank Australian Associated Press, Associated Press and Getty Images for their very valuable assistance in including so many excellent news media images in this publication, which are of equal importance as the contemporary art works included.

Sanja Iveković, *Triangle*, 1979 is reproduced by permission of New York, Museum of Modern Art (MoMA) and Scala, Florence.

A short section of Chapter 5 draws on the ideas from Uroš Čvoro, *Transitional Aesthetics: Contemporary Art at the Edge of Europe* (London: Bloomsbury, 2018). The argument in that section is substantially further developed and updated for the present discussion.

We wish to express our thanks to the staff at Bloomsbury, London, particularly Alex Highfield and Ross Fraser Smith, and past personnel April Peake and Yvonne Thouroude. Thanks also to Elena Knox and Rhubarb for copy editing of the manuscript, and special thanks to Dr Monika Lukowska-Appel for her research assistance.

As ever, we both give the deepest gratitude to our spouses—Uroš's wife Marijana Čvoro and Kit's wife Loretta Tolnai—for their continued love, support and tolerance of our rants. Thank you.

Finally, we dedicate this book to Dr David McNeill, former Senior Lecturer at the University of New South Wales, where we both completed our PhDs and then worked alongside Dr McNeill. Thank you, David, you have been an inspirational mentor and good friend to both of us.

Introduction

The Trump Effect

A lean, well-dressed, youthful white man walks through a courtyard in front of the white walls of the US Capitol Building in Washington, D.C., at 12:35p.m. on January 6, 2021. The man in the image is Senator Josh Hawley, junior Republican Senator for Missouri. In a buttoned-up blue suit jacket and Republican-red tie he strides across the scene, hair swept up by the cold winter breeze, lips resolutely pursed, brow furrowed, gaze fixed; in the background, a row of black government cars, a white van and two masked-up security guards. Hawley's left hand is raised in a tight fist, his elbow bent: he is gesturing beyond the right edge of the frame to an angry mob of QAnons, Proud Boys, and other Trump supporters as they fought with police and security in their attempt to forcibly overthrow the certification of the election of President Joe Biden. The violent insurrection led to five deaths on the day.[1] After the riot, President Biden would assert that Hawley was equally as responsible for the violence as President Donald J. Trump and Senator Ted Cruz.[2]

Hawley and Cruz had led the Republicans' attempt in the Senate to overturn the election result. That raised fist was both a provocation and a validation to the crowd. Francis Chung, the photographer from E&E News who took the photograph, says that the crowd "got as animated as I'd seen at that point."[3] The Senator's raised fist, on that day, at that place, may well have empowered the mob with a deeper sense of legitimacy: for their movement, for their sense of being on the right side of history, for their assurance that a vast criminal conspiracy had taken place involving corrupt electronic counting machines, colluding election officials, and complicity of mainstream media all at the behest of nefarious liberal elites, aimed at stealing election victory from President Trump.

Two days later, after Chung's photograph had circulated widely and the Senator's raised fist had become an iconic image of the Capitol Hill riot,

FIGURE 0.1 Senator Josh Hawley at the United States Capitol Building on January 6, 2021, shortly before the Capitol Hill Riot and attempted insurrection. Photo: Francis Chung/E&E News and Politico via AP via AAP.

Simon & Schuster, who were due to publish Hawley's book *The Tyranny of Big Tech* in June 2021, canceled the deal.[4] Hawley tweeted:

> This could not be more Orwellian. Simon & Schuster is cancelling my contract because I was representing my constituents, leading a debate on the Senate floor on voter integrity, which they have now decided to redefine as sedition. Let me be clear, this is not just a contract dispute. It's a direct assault on the First Amendment. Only approved speech can now be published. This is the Left looking to cancel everyone they don't approve of. I will fight this cancel culture with everything I have. We'll see you in court.[5]

To Hawley, the attempt to overturn the outcome of a legitimate presidential election based on claims of conspiracy (unfounded, of course) was an act of democracy in the name of "voter integrity" and representation of his constituents; cancelation of a contract by a publishing subsidiary of the multinational conglomerate ViacomCBS was an assault on freedom by the "woke" scourge of the Left and their "cancel culture."

Perhaps most Orwellian, however, is Hawley's raised fist. It is the gestural and aesthetic expression of traditional leftist radical resistance, which manifested in such historical moments as John Carlos and Tommie Smith's civil rights protest on the dais at the 1968 Mexico City Olympics, anti-

FIGURE 0.2 Honore Daumier, The Uprising (L'Emeute), 1848 or later, oil on canvas, 34 1/2 × 44 1/2 inch; 87.63 × 113.03 cm. Acquired 1925. The Phillips Collection, Washington, D.C.

fascist resistance in the Spanish Civil War of the 1930s, and Honoré Daumier's painting *The Uprising* of a revolutionary in the streets of Paris in 1848; it figured in a spate of revolutions that tore across Europe and pressed Karl Marx and Fredrich Engels to write the Communist Manifesto. This image—Hawley's fist raised in solidarity with the insurgents at the Capitol Hill insurrection in 2021—lies at the nexus of the complex, relatively recent and rapidly evolving political, social, cultural, and aesthetic conditions that this book seeks to understand: the "Trump Effect."

The Trump Effect

The Trump Effect can be characterized in many ways; in this book we focus on four key features. First, while the Trump Effect is centered on the politics of the United States of America, it is a global phenomenon whose trajectory precedes the Trump presidency, and the resonance of US culture war politics at the "peripheries" such as Australia and Eastern Europe is vital to its amplification. Second, the Trump Effect is marked by ideological confusion, and contemporary visual culture articulates this confusion whilst being an important site where ideological and iconological collisions take place. Third, key to the Trump Effect (and emanating from the first two mentioned features) is something we describe as the "balkanization" of American politics.[6] Fourth, the Trump Effect is a manifestation in the political mainstream of an underlying "paranoid style" that has been sustained in America's underbelly as conspiratorial thinking since the beginning of the Republic.[7] Important to us, as theorists of contemporary art and visual culture, are the ways in which these features of the Trump Effect operate through aesthetics and visual culture, and the moments at which contemporary art intervenes in or collides with the Trump Effect, providing valuable insight into the current political context.

The presidency of Donald J. Trump is a symptom of the Trump Effect, not its source. The politics of the Trump Effect were already emerging in around 2011—even earlier in some parts of the world—and will long outlive Trump himself. It took Trump's announcement of his Republican presidential election primary run in 2015 to discern the Effect more clearly and attach it to an easily identifiable public persona, yet if events had played out differently, we may well have seen a similar but earlier "Palin Effect." As we have argued in our previous book *Images of War in Contemporary Art* (2021), the politics of our times are biopolitical, affective and ontological.[8] Right across the political spectrum (insofar as there is still a coherent spectrum), politics are expressly performative, public, and declarative. In the US culture war politics of the last few years, we may frequently hear terms such as "cultural politics" or "identity politics," yet the Trump Effect arises from politics *as* culture, politics *as* identity. Whereas Walter Benjamin warned that the aestheticization of politics is a property of fascism—a claim which has frequently been recalled in discussions of Trump[9]—we argue that these conditions, of the aestheticization of politics, also create the grounds for artistic practices to intervene into the public sphere of politics.

A more expansive inventory of characteristics of the Trump Effect might be articulated via many seemingly contradictory and contestable statements, each requiring much complex and critical unpacking. That inventory could well include further aspects such as the following claims: the old world of fact-based systems of representation has been overwhelmed by the politics of affect and emotion—on the Left and on the Right. Politics are framed in the negative—political position is no longer about having a vision of the future, but rather promoting a caricature of your opposition's vision and aiming to derail it. Thus, political contestation is not very concerned with the persuasiveness of genuine and earnestly held ideas, but is instead a pitch battle of different regimes of truth/propaganda. Populations of Western democracies are not becoming more politically engaged but rather that political subjectivity is becoming central to identity constructed in the declarative and simplified space of social media, with little room for nuance and manifold opportunities for conflict; it seems that political alignment in the present culture war politics has become a central element to "how" we now identify. Republican politics have shifted from traditional conservatism to "anti-wokeism" and radical paranoid conspiracism that indulge in caricatures of evil and fantasies of persecution. Leftist politics, arguably diminished and degraded, are pictured by the Right as dominant and engaged in an authoritarian ideological take-over of culture, public institutions, and corporations deploying ideas around social justice that—depending on your perspective—aim at either recognizing and addressing historical and systemic injustices or undermining the legitimacy of Western values. To the Trumpist Right, the *progressive* Left is engaged in a communistic identity politics that have abandoned civil rights liberalism (which, we suggest, has been cynically taken on by the Right as an anti-progressivist cause), while the more materialist *egalitarian* Left is losing their claims on class and economic politics to the Right, now diverting them into a conservative morality frame. While these are not our primary concerns in this book, our analyses glance across many of these other features to varying degrees, and no doubt other writers are at this moment buried in their laptops, books, and reams of online materials, attempting to make sense of them.

Post-Ideology

One of the most important features of the Trump Effect, around which we organize this book, is that it is a global, not merely an American, phenomenon. Indeed, as non-American authors, we bring an outsider perspective to its reassertion of America's political centrality even in decline. We reject outright the exceptionalist idea that Trump, as either villain or savior, is a political aberration; rather, we regard the political phenomenon of Trump as the crystallization of deeper and longer-term philosophical shifts. America is fundamentally important in this analysis of the Trump Effect, yet our focus on its effects is as deeply involved with where *we* are "from." Your authors are a migrant and a refugee: straight, white, middle-class males from working-class towns in historically subjugated nations. We are living in the wealthy global periphery that is Australia and are privileged to be well-paid research academics in an industry in possibly terminal decline, under sustained attack from government, media, and circumstances arising from COVID-19. As thinkers of visual culture, contemporary art, conflict, and politics we have worked mostly in Australia and researched in the US, UK, and Europe, and consequentially we bring to the work an intimate knowledge of those centers, as well as of this and other peripheries. Through our discussions here of visual culture and contemporary art, we explore the Trump Effect as a circulation of ideas and images throughout the US and also a broader global sphere of influence.

While the Trump effect is a term framed through still developing and malleable power relations, other terms used in this book are positioned within specific histories and fields of study. Terms such as delegated performance and turbo sculpture belong to art history and speak about the relation between visual culture, aesthetic pursuits, and audience engagement. These terms speak to the long and complex relation of art to everyday life, marked by desires to distinguish between true and false culture, between complacency and critical thinking. To work effectively, we move between contemporary art and visual culture, maintaining that all disciplinary divisions are arbitrary and porous. What we maintain throughout is the ability of art to intervene into the ideological field of the present by mobilizing images. In this sense, we are not simply interested in works that are overtly critical of Trump—and if fact we don't discuss several of them—but works that demystify the appeal of the Trump Effect.

Another principal feature of the Trump Effect is that it is a condition of twenty-first-century post-ideology politics. It is the present evolution of the conditions of post-1989 post-historicism. Trump Effect post-ideology politics are complex and arose outside the US. In the Introduction to *Images of War in Contemporary Art*, we sketched out our thesis that the twin narratives (often held in irreconcilable tension) of neoliberalism and nationalism that characterize the former Yugoslavia have become established more broadly throughout the rest of the world. Building on Francis Fukuyama's idea that the end of the Cold War marked the end of the grand historical dialectic, culminating in the final resolution of capitalism versus communism, we assert that this "post-historicist" post-1989 was not the end of history in the sense that Fukuyama suggested. Rather, it was the beginning of a new, unresolved historical process of tensions between the triumph of *ahistorical* universalistic neoliberalism (characterized by the European Union) and a growing *retroactive transhistorical* nationalism that ignores modernity. This three-decades-long tension between neoliberalism (abstracted, technocratic, globalist, post-ideological) and identitarianism (embodied, experientialist, regionalist, biological, biopolitical) has formed the politics of the 2020s—an inversion of twentieth-century utopian politics. The Trump Effect is the hang-over of the age of ideology, of twentieth-century communism, fascism, and technocratic neoliberalism, no longer driven by an idealized vision of the future but by discontent, resentment, fear, and paranoia. The politics of the Trump Effect are the politics of our post-ideological, post-historicist condition. The model leader is perhaps Vladimir Putin, the ideologically bankrupt President of a Russia in which, "with no idea of the future left," as Peter Pomarantsev says, "facts become unnecessary."[10] As we write, Russia's euphemistically-named "Special Military Operation" is underway in Ukraine, launched following Putin's lengthy diatribe, denying the sovereignty of Ukraine and weaponizing history with the combined mythologies of a pre-modern ethnonationalist Malorossiia (Малороссия, Ukraine as "Little Russia") and the re-establishment of a Soviet-era buffer zone against NATO. Most of the following chapters were written in the months preceding Putin's 2022 invasion of Ukraine, yet they presage much of what has played out thus far: the ideological perplexity of a fascistic aggression in the name of "denazification"; framing a war of aggression as "peacekeeping" to stop genocide and oppression of Russian minorities; the adoption of culture war tropes with Putin comparing anti-Russia sanctions with the "canceling" of JK Rowling, and conspiracist pro-Russia accusations that civilian victims of war crimes are "crisis actors." Many of the peculiarities of the current war in Ukraine are foreshadowed in our analyses here of the Trump Effect; and, we fear, are likely to shape and dominate domestic and international political discourse throughout the 2020s.

The politics of Trumpism performatively favor rhetorical potency over ideological coherence. Panayota Gounari argues that Trump's presidency was pervaded by "ideological confusion." She asserts that the epitome of this ideological confusion is the slogan "Make America Great Again," which appears on baseball caps and as #MAGA on social media platforms. The slogan contradictorily unites "people across the lines of class, race, gender, ethnicity, an imagined community of Americans under the umbrella of patriotism, most specifically the white European Anglo-patriotism."[11] In one 1990s episode of long-running cartoon sitcom *The Simpsons*, the character of McBain, a parody of Arnold Schwarzenegger, pilots a UN military cargo plane attempting to deliver "UNICEF pennies" to disadvantaged children. He suddenly comes under attack from "Commie-Nazis" in jetfighters emblazoned with Hammer/Sickle/Swastika livery and piloted by monocled cartoon villains.[12] When the episode first aired in 1998, its comedy played off an intersection of movie tropes of fictitious villains and loose plotlines, and was funny because it was both hilariously dumb and smartly ironic, crystalizing the 1990s post-historicity, post-grand-ideologies moment, not seven years after the dissolution of the Soviet Union.[13] In the 2020s, it is no longer so "dumb" and its irony has disappeared. Even at the time of first airing, real "Commie-Nazis" were emerging as a marginal party in post-ideology 1990s politics: Eduard Limonov's National Bolshevik Party (initially founded in 1992 as the National Bolshevik Front) whose standard is a Nazi flag on which the Swastika is replaced by the Hammer and Sickle. In the three decades since the collapse of European communism in 1989, "NazBols" have risen as a serious political force in the Eastern European continent, and include the Bulgarian Attack party, the Greater Romania Party, the Serbian Radical Party, and the Slovenian National Party. Today's "Commie-Nazis" are populist, white-supremacist ethnonationalists favorably disposed to elements of state socialism, who often romanticize their Cold War communist past. Their political tendencies are often opposed to the European Union's multilateral, post-national, technocratic, neoliberalist, liberal democracy and, conversely, in favor of the unilateral, nationalistic, autocratic authoritarianism of Putin's Russia.

Characteristics of this surge of "Commie-Nazis," or of the real-life NazBol politics in Eastern Europe, have emerged in the US politics of

FIGURE 0.3 National Bolsheviks with the Party's flag during a rally to commemorate the Bolshevik Revolution, Moscow, Monday, November 7, 2005. Photo: Ivan Sekretarev via AP via AAP. Blurred with permission of AAP.

Trumpism, and resonate back in interesting ways to Eastern European politics. In *Turbo-Folk Music and Cultural Representations of National Identity in Former Yugoslavia* (2014),[14] Čvoro analysed Maria Todorova's notion of "balkanization," and we return to that analysis in this book. Todorova is less concerned with the divide-and-rule splitting of states that followed the First World War, and more with perception of that area of Eastern Europe during the twentieth century as a variation on Edward Said's idea of "orientalism"—the West's essentializing construction of an exotic yet dangerous Middle East, which is actually the West's projection of its own values onto the Middle East as its converse.[15] Todorova critiques and retools Said's postcolonial theory,[16] arguing that the Balkan region of Eastern Europe began losing its identity as it Europeanized, commercialized, and industrialized in the twentieth century[17] and that, unlike the "Orient," the

Balkans, "with their unimaginative concreteness, and almost total lack of wealth, induced a straightforward attitude, usually negative, but rarely nuanced."[18]

Already regarded as devoid of exoticism, during the Cold War the Balkans became a "synonym for unreliability, lethargy, corruption, irresponsibility, mismanagement, blurring of the competencies and borders in the order of law and much else."[19] Whereas the apparent ideological confusion of the 1990s NazBol may have been read in the West as an Eastern European misreading of global left–right politics—inept, corrupt, and just as laughable as cartoon "Commie-Nazis"—2020s mainstream politics in the US can be seen to have become increasingly balkanized. In *Images of War*, we considered the extent to which 1990s Balkan-style enthonationalism seeped into the political fringes of the dark web, within the far-right online subcultures of the "chan" boards, only to spill into real-life terror; a few years later, the Trump Effect established this balkanization within the US political mainstream. When Trump made a vague threat to challenge the legitimacy of a win by Hillary Clinton in 2016, it could be read along a relatively benign spectrum of shocking to playful to outright trolling; when he challenged the legitimacy of Joe Biden's win in 2020, it was evidence of a malign willingness to burn the mechanisms of democracy in an attempt to hold onto power. It whipped up existing conspiracy theory, culminating in deadly violence and insurrection at Capitol Hill on January 6, 2021. (This event at Capitol Hill is critiqued in Chapters 5 and 6, and underpins much of the discussion in this book.)

Working Class Hero

Trump's well-documented appeal to the working class and the working poor in the US is vital to the ideological confusion characteristic of the balkanization of US politics. During the 2010s the American Right, which is usually fundamentally concerned with protecting corporate interests and imposing a particular suite of conservative values, moved in on poverty and class as a central cause, albeit in a very particular way. Let us take the example of the one-hour-and-fifteen-minutes-long documentary that America's PBS aired just seven days before the 2020 presidential election, Christopher Rufo's *America Lost* (2019).[20] Rufo is one of the minor stars in the Trumpist media constellation. He features in parts of this book, having played a small but pivotal role in lighting a particular firestorm in the US culture wars. Rufo is politically conservative and, with his influence in rallying the President against critical race theory, he is by definition a Trumpist. *America Lost* clearly demonstrates how Trumpism has co-opted class. The documentary focuses on the lives of a handful of Americans living in collapsing post-industrial America. In Youngstown in the "rust belt" of Ohio, Rufo follows Jennifer, who grew up in a violent home with a father who dealt drugs and was eventually murdered. She talks of the "mean disease" of poverty that keeps spreading in her town. The town's steel mill has been long closed and Todd, a former steel worker who has struggled with addiction and crime, now collects scrap metal. He is also an artist and finds his art materials while cleaning out abandoned homes. The documentary moves to Memphis, Tennessee, where Contrina, an African American single mother, is struggling to feed her daughters whose fathers are both absent. In Stockton, two hours' drive inland on Californian State Route 4 from San Francisco, are Michael and Marlene: he is looking for a job in the hope of better supporting the family; she is about to give birth to their second child. The stories of their lives and hardship are truly heartbreaking.

Rufo's voiceover commentary is clear on the apparent causes of these tragedies: industrial centers like Youngstown had been prosperous, but "then came the reckoning": "the reality is that cities like Youngstown failed to make the transition from the modern to the postmodern world." Later, Rufo tells us that "the public bureaucracy has taken over as the dominant institution of Youngstown"—it has "taken over the town" and now "people find themselves trapped in a web of social programs." At the conclusion of *America Lost*, Rufo leaves the audience in no doubt that this American tragedy is the result of a decline in "traditional roles" and the family, that public policy, the bureaucracy, and "top-down public policies" have failed, and that the only viable solutions to this "fractured postmodern world" are faith-based community groups.

America Lost mentions nothing of the series of corporate takeovers that led to the demise of Youngstown Sheet and Tube steelworks in the 1970s, or the lack of worker protections that allowed the 5,000 "Black Monday" layoffs in 1978.[21] Neither does it consider the larger structural shifts of globalization and unregulated free market ideology that led to the demise of industry in Ohio's Mahoning Valley or the American Midwest in general. Rufo does not once mention the 2007 Global Financial Crisis caused by the deregulated financial sector, that led to the flood of empty foreclosed houses in cities like Memphis and Stockton.

Rufo echoes the broader Trumpist performative instrumentalizing of class and poverty, reorienting them away from the specifics of the profound and widescale social failings of the unregulated free market economics that have been central to conservative politics for decades and increasingly normalized in American politics since the 1960s, and reframing poverty and class within popular and nebulous culture-war talking-points of "small government," "traditional roles," decline in Christian values, and the "fractured postmodern world." Rufo's short documentary *Homelessness* (2020) makes a similar argument, whilst also dismissing the "hard times narrative," propagated by "activists," "that capitalists, landlords, real estate developers, and systemic racism have conspired to put people on the streets. Activists say that homelessness is a manifestation of income inequality." The real problem, argues Rufo from a barely concealed culture-war stance, is the ideology of public policies of compassion, and the cure is greater public order.[22]

The Trumpist uptake of the issue of class ignores the damage that the free market economy has wrought in places like Youngstown; as Jeff Sparrow says, in his analysis of Trump-era shifts in both left and right politics, "[n]eoliberalism normalised market relationships in every aspect of life, deliberately breaking down traditions, customs and sentiments deemed economically irrational."[23] By refiguring each citizen as a corporation of one, it overturned "deeply held ideas about the nature of humanity."[24] Melissa Macauley, in the *Washington Post* shortly before the 2020 election, observed that "[u]ncompromising zealotry paradoxically empties ideology of meaning . . . [T]he Republican situation is exacerbated by the class contradictions of a party that promotes the economic interests of wealthy elites while inflaming the racial and religious resentments of a White, working-class base."[25]

The Left

This cynical Trumpist appropriation of class politics is the counterpoint of a larger rupture that occurred on the left in the 2010s, between what this book characterizes as the "egalitarian Left" and the "progressive Left." The egalitarian Left is characterized by social equality, government oriented to economic regulation, higher taxing to pay for social welfare, freedom of expression, and a civil rights-based universalistic humanism; the progressive Left is characterized by social equity, government oriented to promoting and regulating in favor of diversity and inclusion, regulation of expressions deemed harmful, and social justice for oppressed groups. Both definitions are painted here in broad brushstrokes, but these are generally accepted representations. The egalitarian Left was dominant from the 1960s to the 1990s, when the progressive Left began to dominate. The rise of the progressive Left correlated with broader paradigmatic changes in the Left's establishment, particularly the 1990s rise of the "third way" post-socialist Left. Notably, the post-socialist administrations of US President Bill Clinton and UK Prime Minister Tony Blair tended towards an ideal of small government (as conceptualized by Friedrich Hayek or Milton Friedman; Clinton's 1996 State of the Union Address used the phrase "the age of big government is over") and use of military force toward promoting liberal democracy and for "humanitarian" purposes (Clinton used such force in Kosovo in 1999). As the mainstream leftist establishment abandoned labor politics and embraced free market economics and neoconservative foreign policy, a grass-roots progressive Left developed out of the Civil Rights social justice dimension of leftist politics into more complex formulations for thinking about systemic oppression and activism.

The advent of social media, and its increasing dominance throughout and since the 2010s, doubtless had a profound impact on the foci and the language of the Left. In Angela Nagle's 2017 analysis of the shifting politics of social media and the internet, *Kill All Normies*, she employs a similar division to ours to explain the ways in which social media fractured and reoriented leftist politics during the previous decade. She applies the labels of the "liberal left" and the "materialist left."[26] By Nagle's account, the present progressive Left grew out of the online culture of platforms such as Tumblr, as much as the alt-Right grew out of 4chan and Reddit (as mentioned, we discuss alt-Right online politics in depth in *Images of War*). She says, "the once obscure call-out culture of the left emanating from Tumblr-style campus-based identity politics reached its peak during this period, in which everything from eating noodles to reading Shakespeare was declared 'problematic,' and even the most mundane acts 'misogynist' and 'white supremacist'."[27] One particular milestone in the escalation of this fracture into an increasingly intractable war within the Left was Mark Fisher's 2013 article "Exiting the Vampire Castle". Fisher, very much a leftist, characterizes what at the time was becoming the dominant strand of leftism, marked by an ongoing tendency for internet pile-ons and "cancelations" that are less aimed at conservatism and more concerned with policing the boundaries of leftist politics. "[C]lass has disappeared," argued Fisher, "but moralism is everywhere . . . solidarity is impossible, but guilt and fear are omnipresent—and not because we are terrorised by the right, but because we have allowed bourgeois modes of subjectivity to contaminate our movement."[28] A decade on from Fisher's article, the progressive Left are frequently characterized by calling-out and "canceling" by self-professed leftists such as Dan Kovalik recent book *Cancel This Book: The Progressive Case Against Cancel Culture*[29] and former trade unionist and a member of the UK Labour Party, Paul Embery's *Despised: Why the Modern Left Loathes the Working Class.*[30] As left-leaning Australian news presenter Waleed Aly puts it, "it is a border war within progressive politics."[31] This "performative vulnerability, self-righteous wokeness and bullying," Nagle argues, plays directly into the hands of the Right, who cast the Left as pedantic and infighting.[32]

To Trumpists, the progressive Left are now a familiar caricature—out-of-touch cappuccino-sipping cosmopolitan political and culture "elites"—while the Right frame themselves in contrast as defenders of ordinary people. Indeed, partly by populist intuition and partly by design, this formulation has been central to Trump's politics at least since Trump announced his run for the US presidency in 2015. In the relatively brief and recent timeframe that is covered by this book, the Right's war on the progressive Left's "wokeism" has become central to Republican politics in the US. We will discuss the fracturing of the left only tangentially as it relates to the 2021 critical race theory moral panic, and the subsequent rise of the Right's interest in leftist critical theory in its attack on universities (Chapters 2 and

3). The specific focus of our concern here is the ways in which the fracturing of the Left intersects with the Trump Effect. This fracturing of the Left is in and of itself a seismic shift in the current rapid overturning of the structure of the political spectrum, of which the Trump Effect is an integral part. It mirrors to some degree the overturning of the structure of conservatism, which at this point has split between a radical post-truth conspiracism and a more recognizable traditionalism. The fractured formulation of "progressive Left" versus "egalitarian Left" emerges on occasion through our discussions, for instance when discussing the Left's buying into the performative hyper-individual politics of aestheticized emotion. Further, in the adoption of leftist aesthetics by the American Right, such as the Trumpist Right's adoption of aspects of civil rights liberalism as part of its assault on the "progressive Left" (e.g., "color-blind" racial politics versus critical race theory which we touch on in Chapter 2), it has also hijacked the economic arguments of the "egalitarian Left." And, of course, this is one of the undercurrents percolating through the image of Hawley's raised fist in this entanglement of post-ideology politics. In his recent analysis of the upheaval of the political spectrum post-2016, Adrian Pabst's *Postliberal Politics* notes, "Across the West, the old opposition of left versus right has been supplanted by a new polarity of liberal versus populist, but neither appears capable of defining a new position except negatively and by demonizing the other."[33]

Conspiracy

The idea of a vast, deep state, conspiratorial "steal" of the 2020 US presidential election, which the Capitol Hill insurrection intended to prevent, may on its surface appear to be a new element in mainstream politics. Among the Capitol Hill mob were followers of Q, or QAnons, who believe that America is run by a Satanic cabal of pedophiles from the ranks of the Democratic political establishment and Hollywood, who are engaged in a global child-murdering conspiracy. They believe that Donald J. Trump will save the ritually abused children with "The Storm" of mass arrests and martial law.

Arguably, before Q and the "Stop the Steal" movement, conspiracy theories were for most people an entertaining curiosity, the stuff of *The X-Files* and Dan Brown novels, or the obsessions of an unhinged fringe who believe that Earth is flat and the moon landings were faked in a Hollywood sound stage. However, in 1964, Richard Hofstadter wrote an essay called "The paranoid style in American politics,"[34] in which he traces conspiracism in the US back to the very early years of the Republic. For Hofstadter, writing in the years immediately following the assassination of US President John F. Kennedy, a decade after McCarthyism, conspiracism, has a significant aesthetic and affective dimension. "When I speak of the paranoid style, I use the term much as a historian of art might speak of the baroque or the mannerist style. It is, above all, a way of seeing the world and of expressing oneself."[35] He borrows from the clinical definition of paranoia,[36] and suggests that in his use, the word "paranoid" is less about individual pathology and more about a cultural tendency within the body politic to see the world as hostile and conspiratorial, "directed against a nation, a culture, a way of life."[37]

Although his focus is on American politics, Hofstadter acknowledges that the paranoid style is not an American exception.[38] As an aesthetic, the paranoid style involves a view of the world as iconologically multifaceted, deeply layered and interconnected: a world of patterns and invisible connections that only reveal themselves to the "critical thinker" who does their *own* research. Hofstadter argued, half a century before the widespread use of the internet, that the paranoid style is not characterized by the absence of facts but by their over-abundance. And, of course, "[i]n the paranoid style . . . the feeling of persecution is central, and it is indeed systematized in grandiose theories of conspiracy."[39] Since January 6, 2021, the hold of QAnon has waned in the US in favor of COVID-19 deniers, anti-vaxxers, anti-maskers, and a conspiracist web of beliefs variously that SARS-CoV-2 does not exist, that the virus was grown by the Wuhan Institute of Virology, that the vaccines contain toxic heavy metals or nanochips developed by Bill Gates, that the disease is little more than an influenza, and that it can be treated with hydroxychloroquine or the horse de-wormer Ivermectin. It is in Hofstadter's sense of "paranoid style" that, in this book, we will use the term "paranoid epistemology"—a worldview that inverts conventional research epistemologies by distrusting information from any official systems of government and institutions of record, regarding them as inherently corrupt and, instead, regarding a source's outsider and outlier status as proof of its reliability.

The argument that we present in this book plots an arc from this newly-established and now-normalized conspiracism in conversative politics, fuelled by the notion of a stolen election and culminating with the Capitol Hill riot, through the 2021 critical race theory moral panic and populist paranoia surrounding critical theory, into the consideration of monuments in contemporary art, and the overidentification with the strongman authoritarian, to arrive at a playfully radical re-reading of the January 6, 2021 riot as a form delegated performance. At each point throughout this arc, we consider particular aesthetic expressions that manifest the shifting and fragmented politics of the Trump Effect. As art theorists, we have both, in our past collaborative and single-authored works, taken a particular visual culture approach, perhaps a legacy of having both emerged from the University of New South Wales's former School of Art History and Theory. As UNSW's Jill Bennett says, "Art does not just raid popular culture or science for its own ends—for 'ideas' to which it might give aesthetic form." Rather, she argues, "It becomes entangled with other forms of practice and knowledge, other ways of seeing and perceiving."[40] Thus, aesthetics is always integral to the political, and vice versa; hence our choices of the foci of our discussions arise from where we find the political and aesthetic to be most mutually animating. It is perhaps a bias, we acknowledge, that in framing the problematics we draw often from the internet, social media and mass media, and in searching for solutions we look towards contemporary art. To be clear here, we do not necessarily look to art with the expectation that its display can intervene in some way, directly, through moving its audience; more that contemporary art sometimes presents disruptive and counter-intuitive ways of conceptualizing the present.

On this trajectory, then, our first chapter focuses on the ways in which the Trump Effect manifests this undercurrent of conspiracism in American politics, and emanates outward beyond the US. We argue that it is important to understand the aesthetic dimensions of QAnon, because in many respects it is aesthetics that powerfully draw people to QAnon and keep them mesmerized, locked in an interminable temporality, awaiting The Storm. This particular aesthetic is simultaneously the gamification of propaganda and the weaponization of a game; it takes the vast, ever-expanding, mostly unrelated information of the internet and weaves it through processes of guided apophenia—tendency to find meanings and connections—within a hypnotic montage. It feeds on its own findings in a degenerating epistemic feedback loop. The aesthetics of QAnon, particularly its "mega-archive" and its hypnotic juxtapositions, relate to both an enduring tradition of paranoia in American politics, and the increasingly established post-ideological, post-historicist condition of twenty-first-century politics: QAnon is just one symptom of the growing distrust of authoritative systems of knowledge, a manifest assertion of a hyper-individualized, post-truth worldview in which nothing is true and everything is possible. Central to QAnon's game-turned-cult is its "deciphering" of the art of Marina Abramovic and Biljana Đurđević, whose work has been enlisted to play an unintended role in the conspiracist iconology of the movement.

Our second chapter concentrates on two points in time at which the politics of race in the United States became the focus of conflict. The first is the controversy surrounding the display at the 2017 Whitney Biennial of Dana Schutz's painting *Open Casket* (2016), a semi-abstract painting "based on one of the most iconic and charged photographs of the civil rights era—a picture of a fourteen-year-old black child, Emmett Till, horribly disfigured from a brutal and lethal beating that occurred when he was falsely accused of whistling at a white woman in 1955."[41] The second is the controversy, heavily live-streamed and consumed online, at Evergreen State College in Olympia, Washington State, which centered around the "deeply progressive" professor Bret Weinstein.[42] The Evergreen Affair put universities and critical race theory on the agenda for the mainstream Trumpist Right media, particularly Fox News, and Weinstein became part of the "intellectual dark web" and a favorite of the online alt-lite, spruiking against the notion of equity and also against universities, supposedly in defense of free speech and academic freedom.

We pick up on the 2021 critical race theory panic in the following chapter, exploring in greater depth the ways in which the Trump Effect and US culture war politics resonate between the "center" (USA) to the global "peripheries." The latter half of Chapter 3 takes us from Fox News, right-wing TikTok, and YouTube to an analysis of our own world as authors: humanities departments in Australian universities, which have been directly impacted by American culture wars politics in very material ways. We explore the Right's co-opting of the word "woke"; "anti-wokeness" and "anti-wokeism" emerged as central to the Trumpist Right's political platform. We discuss how in 2021 "anti-woke" sentiment combined with the overarching Trumpist disdain for university education resulted in a rising interest among the Right in humanities' critical theory. In keeping with the "paranoid style" in American politics, it seemed to many on the right that they had uncovered a vast, century-long conspiracy involving Marxist academics; suddenly, right-wing YouTubers and commentators were talking about Michel Foucault, Jacques Derrida, and Herbert Marcuse.

As we move into the fourth chapter, we approach the topic of post-truth from a slightly different perspective, that of historical memory and its representation in public spaces. At the beginning of the third decade of the twenty-first century, public monuments and statues became lightning rods for significant political conflict. Debates surrounding historical representation and the troubling legacies captured by public monuments were heating up throughout the 2010s, and in 2020 we saw a series of "statue wars," spanning clashes over Confederate statues in the US, colonial statues in the UK and Australia, and public commemorations in Canada, Germany, and New Zealand. These events highlighted the shifting public sentiments over monuments symbolizing colonialism and white supremacy, but have also led to increasing resistance from the Trumpist Right. Our discussion of the "statue wars" draws on insights provided by contemporary artists whose work deals with public monuments: Kara Walker and Raqs Media Collective, who address the colonial and racist legacies embodied in monuments, and Adrian Paci and Mladen Miljanović, who approach monuments through the prism of shifting post-socialism. Chapter 4 frames these "statue wars" as symbolic and symptomatic of a shifting historical horizon in the present, reframed within the politics of the post-ideological condition (including the Trump Effect) of the 2020s. While monument controversies are not by any means unique to the twenty-first century—consider the toppling of Nazi monuments at the end of World War II, colonial monuments at the end of South African apartheid, and monuments to Saddam Hussein in Iraq—1989 was the last time we saw this kind of convergence of big historical questions played out through debates over monuments. In the wake of the fall of the Berlin Wall in 1989, monuments seemed to epitomize communist authoritarianism, and images of their public demise were among the most prominent symbols of the collapse of those oppressive regimes. The Wall's fall was reinforced by media images of monuments being pulled down, destroyed, and transported to peripheral areas. In 1989, as now, monuments were viewed as time-keepers and time-dividers: material markers that divide time into "before" and "after" significant events. So, in addition to identifying the subjects of our monuments, we need to consider how monuments divide time and assign value, and the roles they have played in neoliberalism as a global economic and social framework from 1989 to 2020.

In the fifth chapter, we set our sights back on contemporary art and the ways in which it can intervene in the balkanized politics of the Trump Effect through strategies of over-identification. To this end, Chapter 5 discusses the work of artists Sanja Iveković, Adrian Paci, and 'Janez Janša, Janez Janša and Janez Janša' in relation to authoritarian leadership in present-day Eastern Europe and what Slavoj Žižek describes as the "obscene strongman" political persona of Trump. We are interested in the role of Trump in triggering the 2021 Capitol Hill riot, which we assert was the defining moment of Trump's presidency. The rioting of thousands of supporters of the outgoing—and out-voted—President, based on the big lie of a big conspiracy, marks a watershed in American political life, when fact-based systems of representation were well and truly overwhelmed by the politics of performative and aestheticized emotion. It was the culmination of Trumpism: a choreographed public performance of Trump's public rhetoric by his followers. But it was

FIGURE 0.4 Insurrectionists loyal to US President Donald J. Trump riot at the U.S. Capitol in Washington, D.C, following the Stop The Steal, in an attempt to prevent the certification of President-elect Joe Biden's electoral college victory. Photo: Jose Luis Magana, STAR MAX File Photo, via AP via AAP.

also something that seemingly happened without his knowledge, or at least for which he is unwilling to accept any responsibility. We argue that the Capitol Hill riot remains the most successful subversion and critique of Trumpism. We will examine the incident through Iveković, Paci, and Janšas' work to draw out unacknowledged aspects of Capitol Hill and Trump the strongman: how Trump's political power enunciated itself through Capitol Hill twice in different ways, how Capitol Hill performed loss ("stop the steal") while attempting insurrection, and how protesters overidentified with Trump's rhetorical and half-articulated message.

In varying degrees throughout these five chapters, the performative character of today's politics becomes clear, and it is fitting that our last chapter brings us to a final important aspect of the post-ideology politics of the Trump Effect: we consider the fact that the Capitol Hill riot was a way for the President to gain support by performing for the cameras, garnering both media and amateur broadcast footage. Building on our discussion we examine Capitol Hill through the art theoretical lens of delegated performance art, drawing out its key themes through analysis of Jeremy Deller's *Battle of Orgreave* (2001), Milica Tomić's *This Is Contemporary Art* (2001) and Vladimir Nikolić's *Death Anniversary* (2004). This chapter is intended as a theoretical experiment: a clash between a white-nationalist violent event and a socially progressive theory of performative art. In forcing an encounter between two things that seem incompatible, we seek to evaluate the continuing interchange between strategies on the left and on the right. Through this encounter, a new understanding of the Capitol Hill riot and delegated performance emerges. On the one hand, the Capitol Hill riot is a delegated performance that failed for the right reasons—it does not hold up to ethical standards but it shows up the injustice and racism of the system of power and exploitation it represents; on the other hand, delegated performance is a flawed approach to social relations that provides the right answers—it is performed social antagonism as the only way of showing injustice and exploitation. Aligned with our notion of the balkanization of American politics as key to the Trump Effect, our experiment views the encounter between the Capitol Hill insurrection and delegated performance "from the periphery." It is framed through the cultural and historical experience of the mythical Balkans as an imagined space full of political manipulators, liars, and bloodthirsty mobs. In other words, this chapter "balkanizes" the performance of Trump and his supporters at Capitol Hill on January 6, 2021, to demystify his hold on the imagination of many Americans. We place Trump in the context of corrupt nationalist demagogues from the Balkans to show that his political strategy has clear precedents, and we place his supporters in the context of "turbo-culture" from the Balkans to show that there are important historical lessons to be learned from the Balkans as a region with lived and historical experience of toxic nationalism.

Behind the carnivalesque façade of the Capitol Hill riot—red MAGA caps, Trump flags, cardboard "Q's, Boogaloo Bois in Hawaiian shirts—is a post-ideological reduction of politics to the level of sport, in which voters pick their colors and publicly demonstrate loyalty to their political team. Benjamin, in the epilogue of his most influential essay, 'The work of art in the age of mechanical reproduction," says that "[f]ascism sees its salvation in giving [the] masses not their right, but instead a chance to express themselves."[43] The ubiquity of internet connectivity and social media has created the firestorm conditions for fascism in our present world. And within those conditions, the power of the masses is proving not to lead to greater equality and democracy, to empower us, in Benjamin's words, "to change property relations."[44] Instead, on a global scale, we trade those potentialities for the narcissism of a performative aesthetic politics, or, as he terms it, "expression while preserving property. The logical result of fascism is the introduction of aesthetics into political life."[45]

While this book was prompted by the seismic political shifts that occurred during the Trump presidency and reached their violent crescendo on Capitol Hill on January 6, 2021, the questions it raises extend far beyond that spatial and temporal frame. Our approach to the Trump Effect is an acknowledgement of its complexity and breadth, and an attempt both to map it out through specific instances and to point the way forward. We don't pretend to have solutions to the toxic political tangle in which the world finds itself in the 2020s, but we believe that in understanding and demystifying the appeal of the Trump Effect, by pointing out its historical precedents and its resonances from the periphery, we may start to undo some of its potentially imperiling damage to democracy.

CHAPTER ONE

QAnon

"Shall We Play a Game?"

A video begins with a cacophony of shouting and the motion-blurred image of a small black baton laying on a yellow tiled floor next to white steps.[1] The unsteady, portrait-oriented image tilts upward to show a stockily built African American security guard silhouetted in a doorway, his right hand gripping the butt of his holstered firearm. Behind the guard is a handful of agitated, mostly middle-aged White men in red hats, scarves, and puffer jackets. Their numbers swell as a bearded man in a knitted hat, black hoodie, jeans, and sneakers pushes forward and repeats to the guard, "We're here for *you*! We're here for *you*!" The security guard backs up, turns, and reaches for the baton on the floor while the growing mob advances led by the bearded man in the hoodie, who follows the guard up the marble staircase as a press photographer snaps the oncoming crowd. Reaching the top of the stairs, the guard turns to repel the mob, but they push forward, and he runs from them up another flight of marble steps. He stops, glances left down a hallway, then walks backwards, drawing the mob in the other direction and into a vestibule where they are met by more uniformed guards shouting, "Leave now!" The bearded man in the hoodie, who has led the mob up to this point, stands at the center of the vestibule with hands defiantly on hips, and members of the mob trickle in behind him.

This video, recorded by *Huffington Post* reporter Igor Bobic, was one of the first news images to emerge from the Capitol Building on January 6, 2021. It was later realized that the lone security guard led the mob away from the entrance to the Senate Chamber at the top of the second set of stairs, where he had momentarily glanced left, and into the vestibule in order to stall their invasion of the Chamber. Photographs from the vestibule, taken for Associated Press by Manuel Balce Ceneta, show the bearded man defying the guards, arms outstretched. His hoodie is emblazoned with a large letter "Q"

FIGURE 1.1 Doug Jensen, center, and other pro-Trump protestors confront U.S. Capitol Police in the hallway outside of the Senate chamber at the Capitol in Washington, D.C., on January 6, 2021. Jensen's hoodie is emblazoned with a large "Q," and the words, "Trust the Plan" and "Where We Go One, We Go All." Photo: Manuel Balce Ceneta via AP via AAP.

printed in Stars and Stripes, encircling an American eagle with outstretched wings, and the words "Trust The Plan" and "Where We Go One We Go All." He is Douglas Jensen and would be arrested the following Saturday at his home in Des Moines. "Jensen later told investigators," American *ABC News* reports, "that he 'intentionally positioned himself' toward the front of the mob so his T-shirt would be visible to cameras and 'Q' could 'get the credit,' according to an FBI affidavit."[2] "Q," of course, refers to the anonymous online poster whose followers are known collectively as QAnon.

QAnon

The 2021 Capitol Hill riot was for many people their first introduction to the cultish QAnon movement, which had been growing on the fringes of politics since late 2017. One of the most iconic images of the breached hallways of the Capitol included the "QAnon Shaman," initially identified as Jake Angeli and then later by his real name, Jacob Chansley. A Google Image search for "Capitol Hill riot" will yield images of Chansley in the crowd at the Stop the Steal protest, climbing a scaffold on the Capitol and chanting in its hallways, in the galleries of the Senate and from the Speaker's chair on the dais. He is bare-chested and wears a large fur hat with horns, reminiscent of *The Flintstones*' Grand Poobah ceremonial lodge headwear. His face is painted red, white, and blue with stars, and he carries a bullhorn megaphone and a spear with the Stars and Stripes attached near the bladed tip.

Images of Chansley lent the aesthetic of the riot a veneer of the carnivalesque that was instrumental in initially masking the deadly seriousness of an insurrection and attempted coup that resulted in five deaths that day, including US Capitol Police Officer Brian Sicknick and protestor Ashli Babbitt, "an alleged QAnon-supporter" who was shot by another officer.[3] The QAnon Shaman became an instant viral internet meme. Within hours, the meme skipped across social media, joking "Steal His Look" and unpacking his dress code. Far more troubling images—a photo of a man in military attire with a batch of "flexcuffs" in the Senate Chamber, videos of a Capitol Hill policeman crushed in a door, and the mob chanting "Hang Mike Pence"—only emerged in the days and weeks following the insurrection.

The Capitol Hill riot so decisively thrust QAnon from the periphery into the center of mainstream news media that it is not necessary to provide much detailed background to the movement here.[4] However, a brief-as-possible summary is as follows: QAnon is an online movement that emerged in late 2017 in response to anonymous posts on the right-wing /pol/ message board on 8chan by a poster by the name of "Q." Q claims to have high-level security clearance in the federal government. From the first post on

FIGURE 1.2 Jacob Chansley, the "QAnon Shaman," at the Ellipse outside of the White House, on Wednesday, January 6, 2021, in Washington, D.C. Photo: Jose Luis Magana via AP via AAP.

October 28, 2017, to what was possibly the last on December 9, 2020, there were 4,953 "Q drops." Many of these posts are coded riddles, sometimes asking "shall we play a game?"; many more are reposts of memes and (mostly false) information. Taken together, Q's nearly 5,000 posts assert that Democrat politicians, led by Hillary Clinton and her 2016 campaign manager John Podesta, are involved in a Satanist cabal of pedophile celebrities and political elites, who rape and murder children so that they can extract an addictive compound called adrenochrome from their blood, which they then ingest.[5] This corrupt "Deep State" is, the posts allege, bankrolled by left-wing Hungarian Jewish billionaire George Soros.[6]

However, according to Q, under the presidency of Donald J. Trump, America was undergoing "The Great Awakening": the President was working with General Mike Flynn, the military, the National Security Agency, and the un-dead JFK Junior towards The Storm, when martial law would be declared, the Emergency Broadcast System activated (removing all the mainstream liberal "fake news"), and the Clintons, Obamas, Podestas, and their satanist cabal finally arrested and sent to Guantanamo Bay. The story's roots lie in the previously disproven "Pizzagate" conspiracy theory. Pizzagate arose in 2016 from creative interpretations of emails hacked from the Democratic Party's email server and released by Wikileaks. In those emails, Podesta made several mentions of pizza, which Q followers believe are coded references to procuring sex with minors. Furthermore, the Pizzagate conspiracy theory holds that Podesta, Clinton, and other members of the political elite are running a pedophile ring from a secret "kill room" in a basement beneath the Comet Ping Pong pizza parlor in Washington, D.C.

QAnon remained a fringe movement until the COVID-19 pandemic began in 2020, when it expanded on mainstream social media. "Facebook data since the start of 2020 shows QAnon membership grew by 581 per cent—most of which occurred after the United States closed its borders last March [2020] as part of its coronavirus containment strategy."[7] COVID-19 shelter-in-place orders in the US, and lockdowns across much of the world, placed masses of fearful and disoriented people at their keyboards, looking for answers, during long hours that they might have otherwise spent out of their houses. There is certainly an overlap in the timeframe and subscribers to the QAnon and COVID-19 anti-vaxxer movements, although the latter has become more dominant since what seems likely to have been the last "Q drop" on December 9, 2020, and since global vaccine roll-outs' picked up pace in 2021.

The Trump Effect: Conspiracism

In this chapter we explore the emphatically conspiracist dimension of the Trump Effect, which we identify as one of its four main characteristics, with a particular focus on QAnon, though QAnon is just one manifestation of what Richard Hofstadter in 1964 called "the paranoid style" in American politics.[8] A vital aspect of the Trump Effect is the way in which Trumpist politics moved the paranoid, conspiracist style from the fringes to the center of American politics and society. As well as sparking the perfect storm of idle time and social control, the COVID-19 pandemic fueled anti-vaxxer conspiracies about a "Plandemic," about 5G mobile technology causing the virus, and/or about a putative connection to Bill Gates, who is supposedly intent on injecting the world's population with a vaccine full of tracker nanochips or, more extremely, on depopulating the planet. While Trump seemed to know very little about QAnon when quizzed at a press conference in September 2020 (despite Q supporters having had a significant presence at his rallies and that he had, numerous times, re-posted QAnon materials on Twitter), his outrageous claim that Democrats stole the 2016 presidential election with the collusion of corrupt election officials, Venezuela, and Dominion voting machines aligns squarely with the QAnon conspiracist narrative.

As Hofstadter himself explains, the paranoid style is comparable to the baroque, or the mannerist, or another aesthetic style; it is a "way of seeing the world and of expressing oneself."[9] Our purpose here is not to aggregate now-common knowledge about QAnon and the core beliefs of its followers, but rather to focus specifically on the aesthetic dimensions of the QAnon movement as the most visible manifestation of this paranoid style to date. The aesthetics help us understand, connect and relate the various dimensions of the Trump Effect internationally. While the paranoid style has perpetuated throughout American history, it has become increasingly well-established in the balkanized, post-ideologist, post-historicist conditions of 2020s politics. In eastern Europe, Trump Effect paranoid conspiracism pervades the politics of leaders such as Hungary's Viktor Orbán, Romania's Liviu Dragnea,[10] or Slovenia's Janez Janša (who refused to acknowledge Trump's election loss and supported his Stop the Steal narrative and was himself recently voted out of office in what Slovenia's new Prime Minister said was a "referendum on democracy" (see also Chapter 5). The paranoid style exemplified by QAnon and its particular aesthetics can be seen as part of a larger pattern that goes back far and wide, as well as continuing in the COVID-19 anti-vaxxer movement that, at the time of writing, has gained enormous momentum throughout the world, leading to thousands of preventable deaths.

QAnon's Mega-Archive

It is important to understand the aesthetics of the paranoid style of QAnon, because in many respects it is this aesthetic that powerfully draws people to such movements. In both QAnon and COVID-19 anti-vaxxer cases, and also Trump's Stop the Steal conspiracy, the idea of a mega-archive of evidence is central. That is, vast amounts of relatively unrelated and often random information on the internet become woven together into the fabric of a conspiracy. As we will see looking at QAnon, this happens through processes of guided apophenia, the tendency to find meanings and connections, within a hypnotic aesthetic of montage and juxtaposition, keeping conspiracists mesmerized with the mega-archive of information and with "doing their own research." As with other conspiracies, QAnon's archive feeds off its own findings in a degenerating epistemic feedback loop. QAnon is a symptom of the growing distrust of authoritative systems of knowledge, an assertion of a hyper-individualized post-truth world in which nothing is true and everything is possible.[11]

For QAnon, part of its archive of "evidence" for conspiracy is "weird art" (as it is termed on "QMaps," which we will discuss shortly). In particular, the work of artists Biljana Đurđević and Marina Abramović has been appropriated by the QAnon conspiracy, particularly featuring in Q Drops. The opacity and conceptual complexity of contemporary art is ripe for adoption by a movement that ironically views with disdain the intellectual and cultural "elite" who follow, collect, and participate in contemporary art. As we will explain in Chapter 3, discussing the popular right-wing notion of a century-long conspiracy existing within the world's universities, there is a sense among conspiracists in which the art's conceptual complexity is deliberate obscurantism, hiding in plain sight the most nefarious of intentions.

The evidence collected by QAnon followers and posted on public Q discussions is overwhelmingly vast and even now is still expanding at a rate impossible to track in real time. The core of this material is the 4,953 "Q drops" posted on the right-wing /pol/ "Politically Incorrect" message board on 4chan, and later on 8chan and 8kun, which have been archived at https://qanon.pub. Many of these comment upon or intersect tangentially with the 25,000+ tweets by Trump during his presidency, and with his speeches, press conferences, and off-the-cuff comments. Some of Q's earliest posts make specific predictions of imminent events—the very first post asserted that "Hillary Clinton will be arrested between 7:45 AM– 8:30 AM EST on Monday—the morning on Oct 30, 2017." John Podesta would be imminently indicted (Q drop #15) and arrested (#34), and would flee the country (#67). Indeed, the overall thrust of Q's "drops" is the always-imminent arrest of key members of this Satanic cabal: "a state of temporary military control will be actioned and special ops carried out" is first mentioned in drop #34; "the calm before the storm" is declared in drops #38 and 48, referring to these high-level arrests; drop #55 claims that Trump will then announce, "My fellow Americans, the Storm is upon us."

Since its beginning, QAnon has been locked in a seemingly interminable temporality, awaiting The Storm that never came and never will. When none of these predicted events occurred, the posts became increasingly nebulous, and imminent events were no longer given a specific time of occurrence, as had Clinton's impending arrest within a 45-minute window; rather, they would be "next week" and "soon." The exact nature of events became vague:

"events about to happen" (#82), "about to drop" (#87), and "about to break" (#318). As the predictions became ambiguous, Q's revelations became more coded: "connect the 'markers'," "connect the dots," Q urged many times. Rather than reveal anything specific, "information" was drip-fed in puzzling "crumbs," that followers were urged to pore over again and again, to "[r]e-review all my crumbs" (#66). A fairly typical Q drop (#316, December 10, 2017) reads:

> Expand your thinking.
> Re-read crumbs.
> Re-listen to yesterday's speech.
> Connect the "markers."
> News (in all forms) unlocks the map.
> Expand your thinking.
> The Great Awakening.

Julie Ebner observes that like "investigative journalists and intelligence officers, the anons *[sic]* are collecting alleged 'evidence' day and night. Their sources of information and inspiration are cryptic poems shared by Q."[12] During her investigation into online extremism, Ebner spent two years undercover, adopting several online identities and infiltrating extremist groups from jihadists to QAnon.[13] She reports, "[t]he QAnon archiving system, I have to admit, is impressive. QAnon adherents might be better sorted than some government bureaucratic divisions. I scroll through archive after archive of fake news, nonsensical graphics and absurd allegations, all numbered serially and categorized into different sections."[14] Philosopher Steve Clarke notes that conspiracy theorists are primarily driven by the need to expose, and "are typically quite dedicated in their search for evidence relevant to their favorite conspiracy theory and are usually able to overwhelm you with a deluge of evidence in favor of that theory."[15] Another philosopher, Jenny Rice, similarly notes that "archives of conspiracies grow to unfathomable scales,"[16] and, in fact, that the process of constructing archives actualizes an aesthetic coherence that might well elude the logic of the theory.[17] The accumulated evidence gathered to support the theories is expansive yet thin: in QAnon's there are "hints" in old episodes of television shows, coded predictions in movies from the 1980s, the timing of tweets by Trump, his number of taps on the handrail while descending the steps of Air Force One. "Q gave open-source researchers a framework in which to 'dig' for data on this system of criminality," writes Q follower Martin Geddes. "The result is a vast trove of vetted data collated by anonymous citizens working in collaboration worldwide."[18] If the Deep State is everywhere, as is the movement to take it down, then quite literally everything has potential to be seen as a coded clue. To followers of QAnon, the "crumbs" are potentially everywhere. There is paradoxically overwhelming evidence and no solid proof.

Ebner describes a QMap, a complicated flow chart that connects "Pizza" to "Clinton" to "Weird art" to "Human trafficking." Similar "Great Awakening Maps" can be found throughout the internet: vast and continually changing diagrams that connect thousands of points denoting the usual suspects—the Illuminati, the Vatican, Satanists, JFK, 9/11, WTC7, Area 51, the faked Moon landings—along with less obvious actors in this global conspiracy such as CERN, Google, and the Myan calendar.[19] These maps, vast and complex slabs of text interlinked with lines, triangles, and circles, are a visual representation of the obsessive *horror vaccui* of QAnon's research method. As Ebner notes, "solving enigmas has taken over the life of many committed anons, sometimes consuming all their spare time."[20]

To many Q followers, perhaps it is the sheer scale of this mega-archive and the activity that it represents, possessing an aesthetic quality, that substitutes for the veracity of the claims made on its behalf. The complex Great Awakening Maps denote the sense of beauty that may be experienced in building an archive. Rice argues that the very act of accumulation is the source of their coherence.[21] In other words, in its capacity for the theory to accommodate its various pieces, for example connecting the disparate narratives that JFK Junior faked his own death alongside faked moon landings and a triangulation of stories about the Rothschilds, the Saudis, and George Soros, lies its "beauty" in the sense of its aesthetic coherence. Q follower Geddes claims in his personal treatise that "not only are many 'conspiracy theories' true, they are interlinked as part of a single plan to destroy freedom and bring on global totalitarian rule."[22] We will return shortly to this capacity of QAnon to absorb other, often contradictory, conspiracy theories.

"Research for Yourself"

Cass Sunstein and Adrian Vermeule argued in 2009 that conspiracy theories propagate as the result of a "degenerating research program,"[23] due to a "'crippled epistemology,' in the sense that they [conspiracy theory followers] know very few things, and what they know is wrong."[24] In particular, Sunstein and Vermeule argue that societies that lack civil rights and civil liberties are more prone to conspiracy theories because of restricted access to information. QAnon, and the COVID-19 anti-vaxxer movement that followed, categorically refute this. On the contrary, the seemingly endless expanse of information accessible via the internet is the "breadcrumb" hunting ground of QAnon. Moreover, the immense and dynamic incoherent heterotopia of the internet shapes the QAnon aesthetic. Indeed, Sunstein and Vermeule's 2009 solution to conspiracy thinking—that is, for governments to enlist independent groups to rebut degraded epistemology with better information[25]—now seems naïve given the present context. If QAnon is the result of a "degenerating research program," it is not one of constricted information in which truth withers on the vine because of the short supply of information, but rather one of an information hemorrhage, a plethoric overabundance of minutiae that has only become possible in the current internet age, networked amongst devotees using social media and content sharing. Tom Nichols, in *The Death of Expertise* whose 2017 first edition predates QAnon, opines that believers in conspiracy theories are often educated and intelligent people: "conspiracy theories are horrendously complicated. Indeed, it takes a reasonably smart person to construct a really interesting conspiracy theory," and the theories are "frustratingly precise because they are so intricate."[26]

"The Q drops frequently use the Socratic method," says Q follower Geddes, "encouraging learning via asking questions, rather than providing packaged answers. Q incites people to think for themselves."[27] Q drops urge followers multiple times to "research for yourself" and employ "critical thinking." Alongside its mega-archive, this belief that the movement as a whole is a crowd-sourced independent program of critical research underpins QAnon followers' steadfast rejection of the suggestion that it is a conspiracy theory.[28] It is, however, based on a fundamental of conspiracist epistemology. This is not a simple confirmation bias in which claims are tested by selectively seeking facts that confirm the claim while ignoring facts that contradict the claim, although this is certainly pervasive for QAnon. Rather, as Keith Harris, Steve Clarke, and Brian Keeley individually argue, conspiracy thinking is not simply based on lack of access to measures of the quality and verifiability of information.[29] Harris argues that conspiracy theorists do not lack intellect, that they "exhibit a sort of intellectual diligence, a motivation to uncover the truth, that seems downright praiseworthy."[30]

Instead, QAnon, like much conspiracism, engages in what Sunstein and Vermeule, Clarke, and others says is a "degenerating research program." That is, according to Clarke, it is built around a core theory which exponents are dedicated to protecting "from the effect of apparently contradictory evidence by making modifications to the 'protective belt' of auxiliary hypotheses and initial conditions."[31] Those modifications are, in turn, accommodated on the unwavering premise that any authoritative facts or accounts of events can be dismissed as part of the conspiracy: "Q has helped us understand what kinds of data we can rely on," says Geddes.[32] Some posters on Q forums upload links to philosophy videos on YouTube about critical thinking,[33] while others take the mention of "critical thinking . . . at this time" in Q drop 4,281 as a clue exhorting them to analyze in detail Burt Baccarat's 2005 album *At This Time*. One poster says, "I thought about doing a deep dive annotation of each of these songs, but there was just too much to deconstruct."[34] Official accounts of 9/11 are to be distrusted, while the lyrics of "What the World Needs Now" are a rich source of hints and clues about the Deep State. Rather than the Socratic method, in which hypotheses are interrogated by identifying consistencies and contradictions and accordingly verified or rejected, QAnon begins from a hypothesis that is a fundamental core belief, then accepts or rejects evidence on the basis of its consistency with that core. Harris argues that this tendency "often seems to be due to the exercise of a probabilistic, and fallacious, extension of *modus tollens*."[35] *Modus tollens* is a propositional logic, or a rule of inference, in which a premise infers a conclusion. In the logic of *modus ponens*, a particular premise infers a specific conclusion. (If it rains, I will put on my coat. It's raining. I will put on my coat.) *Modus tollens* is the negative form of this logic. (If it rains, I will put on my coat. It's not raining. I will not put on my coat.) The "probabilistic, and fallacious, extension of *modus tollens*" infers the premise from a conclusion. (If it rains, I will put on my coat. I have not put on my coat. It must not be raining. Or—a worse still inversion—if I put on my coat, it will be raining.) The example Harris gives is this: "If any given lottery with many participants is fair, it is improbable that any particular entrant will win. However, it would be absurd to conclude, once a winner is named, that the lottery was probably unfair."[36]

The Trumpist Fallacy

This fallacious form of *modus tollens* is the hallmark of the Trump presidency. At his June 2020 campaign rally in Tulsa, Trump applied this flawed logic to testing for COVID-19: "You know, testing is a double-edged sword. We've tested now 25 million people . . . Here's the bad part. When you do testing to that extent you're going to find more people, you're going to find more cases. So, I said to my people, 'Slow the testing down please'."[37] Moreover, this fallacious extension of *modus tollens* is at the heart of his claim that the 2020 election was stolen. (If the election is fair and legitimate, I will win the election. I have lost the election. The election must not have been fair and legitimate.) Following this illogic, one poster on a QAnon board writes that "evil traitors . . . committed a *coup d'etat* against our country," and that the fact that the courts found no evidence of this is only proof that "the courts are in on the scam, right up to the Supreme Court."[38] Variations of flawed logic are found throughout QAnon's research epistemology. (If the Deep State is real, then it will cover up its existence. There is no proof of a Deep State. Therefore, it has succeeded in covering up its existence.) In fact, fallacious logic underwrites QAnon's entire research epistemology, and so, contradictory evidence is co-opted as either further evidence of the perpetuation of a lie by the all-powerful conspirators that control society and the media, or it "is absorbed into the larger structure of the overall theory."[39] Psychologists Michael J. Wood, Karen M. Douglas, and Robbie M. Sutton argue that the monological nature of conspiracy beliefs in general is not based in consistency between conspiracy theories, that Theory A verifies Theory B; conspiracist thinking is "driven not by conspiracy theories directly supporting one another but by broader beliefs supporting conspiracy theories in general."[40] That is, Theory A can absolutely contradict Theory B, but both theories "prove" the greater truth that official narratives are false.

The overall effect for anyone tackling conspiracy theory with logic is that, once established, anything one throws at a conspiracy theory becomes absorbed. Rather than a critical epistemology, then, we might call QAnon's approach to research a "paranoid epistemology," in which assumptions around the veracity and reliability of sources of information are inverted: official accounts, authoritative facts, and expert consensus are assumed to be suspect, while discredited evidence, tangential and even random relationships, and outlier minority positions are assumed to be more reliable by virtue of their exclusion from the official consensus.[41] And any unintentional incorrect data in the official account is taken to indicate that the official account is false in total.[42] As Rice notes, "[e]ven through competing narratives, paradoxical claims, and unwarranted beliefs, conspiracists create a coherent ideology, namely, the ongoing boosterism of conspiracy thinking."[43]

The Paranoid Style and Populism

Hofstadter's essay "The paranoid style in American politics" traces conspiracism in the US back to its earliest times.[44] This paranoid style is a tendency within the body politic to understand the world as hostile and conspiratorial, "directed against a nation, a culture, a way of life."[45] "The feeling of persecution is central," says Hofstadter.[46] Drawing from this idea, we use the term "paranoid epistemology"—a system of knowledge in which the weight of consensus is inverted and the implied veracity of information is the inverse of the officiality of its source. In other words, governments, institutions, representative systems, and any bodies that accumulate and confer legitimacy are seen as inherently corrupt and their claims to neutrality as a mask for self-serving and nefarious intent.[47] At an aesthetic level, the paranoid style expresses a world deeply interconnected in ways that are counterintuitive and multifaceted yet that reveal the truth of these connections in slips of aesthetics, through interconnected iconology. In popular culture, the TV show *The X-Files* in the 1990s, Dan Brown's novel *The Da Vinci Code* in the 2000s and, in more recent years, the Netflix series *Stranger Things* all appealed to this tendency, playing on the idea of a dark, twisted netherworld hidden just beneath the surface of the mundane everyday.

The paranoid style sees the world as revealing patterns, invisible connecting lines in the spaces between all things. The *horror vaccui* of the QMaps comes to mind here, as both a literal visual aesthetic and a metaphor for this worldview; as we will see later in this chapter, this aesthetic pervades the visual culture of QAnon. Hofstadter argues that the paranoid style is not generally characterized by the absence of facts, but by a hyper-abundance of facts.

> The plausibility the paranoid style has for those who find it plausible lies, in good measure, in this appearance of the most careful, conscientious, and seemingly coherent application to detail, the laborious accumulation of what can be taken as convincing evidence for the most fantastic conclusions, the careful preparation for the big leap from the undeniable to the unbelievable. The singular thing about all this laborious work is that the passion for factual evidence does not, as in most intellectual exchanges, have the effect of putting the paranoid spokesman into effective two-way communication with the world outside his *[sic]* group—least of all with those who doubt his views.[48]

Similarly, we see from Q followers a laborious and meticulous accumulation of evidence, the scale of which effectively substitutes for the veracity of its many claims.

Hofstadter offers a history of conspiracism in the US that mentions some of the Internet Age's usual suspects: Bavarian Illuminati,[49] the Pope,[50] "Freemasons, international capitalists, international Jews, or Communists."[51] This history illustrates "the central preconception of the paranoid style—the existence of a vast, insidious, preternaturally effective international conspiratorial network designed to perpetrate acts of the most fiendish character."[52] He goes as far back as Jedediah Morse's 1798 sermon, which warned that "[s]ecret and systematic means have been adopted and pursued, with zeal and activity, by wicked and artful men, in foreign countries to undermine the foundations of this Religion [Christianity]."[53] Evangelical Protestantism is found in QAnon's disdain for "the massive hypocrisy of the Catholic Church,"[54] frequent references to God, Jesus, and Evangelistic memes in Q drops (e.g. #109), lengthy prayers (e.g. #4,739), and instruction to read the Bible (#1,603). QAnon's core beliefs echo some of the outlandish claims against Catholicism made nearly two centuries ago. Maria Monk's *Awful Disclosures* (1836) is a supposed account by an escapee from a nunnery in Montreal where, as Hofstadter describes it, "infants born of convent liaisons were baptised and then killed . . . so that they might ascend at once to heaven. A high point in the *Awful Disclosures* was Maria Monk's eyewitness account of the strangling of two babies."[55] There is not necessarily any meaningful connection between such claims, but they demonstrate a wish to undermine those they oppose as inhumane and depict as an abominable cabal of child murderers.

It is clear that QAnon arises from and is aligned with the American far Right—its brand of America-first flag-waving patriotism, its pro-gun militarism, its pro-life Protestant fundamentalism, not to mention its framing of the Democratic political establishment as the center of a pedophilic conspiracy and Donald J. Trump as its savior. QAnon's paranoid epistemology is embedded within the populism, anti-elitism, and anti-intellectualism of Trumpism. Matthew Hannah sees the rise of QAnon as an almost inevitable consequence of an "information dark age," characterized by "a synthesis of distrust in news media and mainstream politics, ubiquity of information access, and public inability to parse online truth from fiction."[56] He too finds QAnon to be driven by a fundamental rejection of official accounts, verified accounts, and "corporate media and academic expertise, which far-right blogger Mencius Moldbug dubs 'the Cathedral'."[57] Steve Clarke writes that "[c]onspiracy theorizing has long been favored by Populists, who are almost invariably antielitist, and therefore generally anti-intellectual as well."[58] Its rejection of academia's critical epistemology is ideological, part of a broader populist repudiation of enlightenment systems of record and representation; as William Davies argues, it is a dismantling of the Hobbesian systems of abstraction and institutions of objective expertise which arose during the Enlightenment.[59] Twenty-first-century populism favors how we feel, and what we believe as a result of that feeling, as "true" above any expert consensus on objective fact.[60] We see this in the United Kingdom's 2016 Brexit campaign, in its rejection of technocratic government, suspicion of representative democracy, and contempt for the authority of experts: it was widely demonstrated during this period that "people in this country have had enough of experts"[61]—"experts built the Titanic."[62] Expertise, according to John Clarke and Janet Newman's analysis of Brexit, "symbolized 'elsewhere'; international institutions, EU bureaucrats and those seeking to protect global free trade."[63] And, of course, throughout his 2016 presidential campaign Trump frequently attacked "the elites."[64]

Plandemic

The *Plandemic* online movie series is an exemplar of populist rejection of government authority, expertise, and official accounts. Added to the QAnon mega-archive while the COVID-19 pandemic hit the world in the early months of 2020, and aligning directly with Trump's positions, it promotes the unproven treatment of COVID by hydroxychloroquine and the conspiracy theory that SARS-CoV-2 was grown by the Wuhan Institute of Virology. It further develops the right-wing demonization of Bill Gates, who it suggests was involved with child sex trafficker Jeffrey Epstein and, through development of COVID-19 vaccines, is attempting to inject the global population with microscopic tracker chips. The populist, paranoid epistemology of QAnon is clear in these movies, which center around interviews with Dr Judy Mikovits, whose work linking mouse retroviruses to chronic fatigue syndrome was discredited in *Science*, one of the world's leading scientific journals, in 2011.[65] *Plandemic: The Hidden Agenda Behind Covid-19* turned Mikovits into, in the words of *The New York Times*, "a new star of virus disinformation."[66]

The *Plandemic* movies build upon Mikovits' claims that Dr Anthony Fauci, Chief Medical Advisor to the US President, was responsible for millions of HIV-related deaths, and that during the COVID-19 pandemic face masks "activated" the virus. She claims that influenza vaccines helped spread COVID-19 in Italy, and that the new vaccines will "kill millions."[67] At the time of the debunking of Mikovits' *Science* article, she speculated that the government was attempting to discredit her work;[68] in 2020's *Plandemic* this claim ballooned into: "for exposing their deadly secrets, the minions of Big Pharma waged war on Dr Mikovits, destroying her good name, career and personal life." Mikki Willis, narrator and "Father/ Filmmaker," continues, "now, as the fate of nations hangs in the balance, Dr Mikovits is naming names of those behind the plague of corruption that places human life in danger."[69] In the paranoid epistemology of conspiracism, Mikovits' outsider and outlier status are proof of her reliability, her discrediting is her prime credential, and even her arrest on charges of theft from her employer is offered as further proof of conspiracy.

Within the closed-off paranoid epistemology of QAnon, the level of unbelievability of the theory itself only magnifies its truth and the tragedy of its denial within the mainstream. As Michael A. Peters observes, "the more improbable the claim and the less it is open to any form of testing, the more it incites false belief."[70] Indeed, new and increasingly improbable QAnon theories come thick and fast on forums such as http://greatawakening.win, for example, that current US President Joe Biden is actually the product of computer generated imagery (CGI), evidenced by pixelation[71] or a poorly rendered shadow.[72] In the latter example, another camera angle shows clearly that the supposedly poorly rendered shadow of Biden is actually the shadow of someone else standing to the left,[73] yet despite this being pointed out in the forum discussion several times, the general opinion remains that "this is a hastily-done green screen where the background was not properly vetted." As Peters argues, another epistemic feature of conspiracy thinking is that "sometimes these conspiratorial beliefs cannot be easily dismissed without elaborate argument and testing."[74] In a curious and asymmetrical inversion of the onus of proof, the overwhelming scale and flow of "evidence" is impossible, and exhausting, to discredit case-by-case.

For some QAnon followers, the improbability of their theories provides further evidence of their inherent truth. One QAnon poster asserts that the whole conspiracy is

> [d]esigned to make you sound crazy if you describe it to someone. Like "The world is run by Satanic pedophile cannibals who trade children as currency and literally skin babies to make shoes out of, which they proudly wear to parties and to rituals of human-sacrifice and blood-drinking in places like Catholic cathedrals, Buckingham Palace, the halls of Congress, and the Vatican. We learned all about it from an anonymous guy on the Internet whose name consists of one letter."[75]

Peters explains, "[o]ften the more improbable the claim and the less it is open to any form of testing, the more it incites false belief."[76] The sheer scale, dynamism, and dubious connections of the QAnon mega-archive reinforce the "beauty" of its internal consistency to the fixed point of its core convictions.

Out of Shadows

Similarly to the *Plandemic* movies, the 2020 documentary *Out of Shadows*[77] demonstrates the enfolding of the "degenerating research program" of QAnon within its mega-archive aesthetic. The video was originally posted on YouTube amidst the first wave of international COVID-19 lockdowns, briefly taken down, then reposted in April 2020. At the time of writing, the video is freely available, despite claims in its comments threads that it is "shadow banned," that "google censors the truth," and that "they do not want people seeing this video."[78] *Out of Shadows* begins with a monologue by director and narrator Mike Smith. "Why do you believe what you believe?" he asks, and then answers, "because at some point in your life you trusted the information that somebody was giving you." His voiceover accompanies a quick-cut montage of moving images, often layered: a 1950s classroom, Mr Rogers, sweeping aerial shots over mountains, TV news images, JR Eyerman's famous 1952 *LIFE* magazine photograph of an audience wearing 3D glasses at the Paramount Theater.[79] An ominous, discordant drone raises the emotional intensity. Smith then appears on camera, speaking to an unseen offscreen interviewer, lending a sense of objectivity: "so, we've all heard the term 'conspiracy theory.' Personally, for me, I've never really had time to get into that because frankly I'm working all the time." Smith narrates over the following 77 minutes of an exquisitely curated, hypnotic, fast-cut juxtaposition of movie scenes, logos, nostalgia, cityscapes, Ken Burns effected screenshots of websites, old documents, and violent scenes reminiscent of the aversion therapy montage in Stanley Kubrick's *A Clockwork Orange* but accelerated and hyperbolic.

Out of Shadows' narrative winds initially through some of the US government's more off-the-wall actual and well-documented programs, such as the experimentation with mind controlling psychedelic drugs in the MK-Ultra Program, and a memo from the Office of Strategic Services, a forerunner to the CIA, titled "The Motion Picture as a Weapon of Psychological Warfare" from the 1940s (declassified in 2004). The narrative becomes increasingly infused with shakier conspiracies around "Operation Paperclip" and "Operation Mockingbird," both favorites amongst QAnon. From its mid-point, having primed its viewers, *Out of Shadows* ramps up its hyperbolic speculations with flow charts connecting Hillary Clinton, Barack Obama, and media networks, old clips about Satanism, and narratives about "false flags." Statements of fact about media ownership and monopolies that have been widely researched by academics for decades are presented as revelations that no one has previously dared speak about.

The structure of *Out of Shadows* recalls Hofstadter's discussion of eighteenth-century Scottish conspiracist John Robison's 1797 volume *Proofs of a Conspiracy: Against All the Religions and Governments of Europe, Carried on in the Secret Meetings of Freemasons, Illuminati, and Reading Societies*. According to Hofstadter, Robison's book provides a conscientious and laborious account of Adam Weishaupt's founding of the Illuminati in Bavaria, until it takes a particular turn. "For the most part, Robison seems to have made his work as factual as he could, but when he came to estimating the moral character and the political influence of Illuminism, he made the characteristic paranoid leap into fantasy."[80] The conspiracism in *Out of Shadows* is advanced slowly but steadily, through verifiable facts, then suggestible connections, then rumors, until finally it launches into QAnon territory of "an elite paedophile ring," and familiar Internet-age Conspiracies about the Illuminati's connection with Jeffrey Epstein, reinforced by "true, honest journalist" Liz Crokin, a key proponent of the Pizzagate conspiracy.[81]

"Weird Art"

At this point in *Out of Shadows*, into the narrative enters "weird art." Crokin breathlessly urges, "no one has ever explained why John Podesta has literal pedophile cannibalism paintings all over his office and his home," while the film shows images of artworks apparently owned by John and Tony Podesta, such as sculptures by Australian artist Patricia Piccinini and paintings by Serbian artist Biljana Đurđević. Đurđević's series *Living in Oblivion* (2006–9) has featured among Q's "crumbs" (#1,901 August 15, 2018), and has been taken up with eagerness by Q followers in innumerable posts and reposts across multiple social media platforms since 2018. Đurđević's paintings are figurative paintings that, taken as a whole, address the horror she experienced in the 1990s during the disintegration of Yugoslavia. Many of her paintings feature hollow-eyed children, often emaciated and bound, in tiled institutional rooms that the catalogue essay *Aesthetics of Violence* from the Haifa Museum of Art allude to as "public showers, operating rooms or morgues." The essay says, "these paintings bespeak the politics of fear haunting a society that has experienced too many images of dead bodies."[82] Drawing from Christian iconography and art historical references, they are unsettling images of raw humanity that would not be unusual in any contemporary art museum or international biennial exhibition.

However, for many of the followers of Q, the strangeness of Đurđević's work presents clear "evidence" of the allegedly pedophilic desires of the brother of John Podesta, who is said to collect her work. The more complex and unlikely the connections, the more appealing they appear to be. A YouTube video by "James" of the "Research Revolution" points to a 2015 article: "I want to show you something. I want to connect some dots for you guys." A *Washington Life* article about Podesta's house and art collection mentions Đurđević. "I'll show you who this is, thank you to 4chan," says

James, clicking through to the far-right wing /pol/ anonymous board to reveal two paintings by Đurđević. "Right there! Look at it! There's another one. See that one? It's in a pool! . . . Jesus do you see this? . . . Is that enough proof for you?" he asks.[83] Comments below his video include: "The kid in the first photo is the CNN anchor, Anderson cooper [sic]. It's in the film plandemic," and "Very sick creepy and Evil." One foolhardy commentor defends Đurđević, saying "that art or the art world it's not always flowers and Mona Lisa," and is rebuked as being "sick" for defending it: "Do what you want but leave kids out of it!"[84]

Nothing in the images suggests Đurđević's tiled backgrounds are a drained pool; that inference comes from two Q drops, which juxtapose one of Đurđević's paintings with a photograph of the drained pool at Biltmore House, Gloria Vanderbilt's mansion and childhood home of CNN's Anderson Cooper. Further QAnon memes claim that a child shown bound against a tiled wall in a Đurđević painting is the juvenile Cooper depicted in the Biltmore House pool. On the same day that Q posted images of Đurđević's art, he also posted an image of Gloria Vanderbilt reading to her sons in bed, with more "weird art" behind them, and mentioned "red shoes" (#1,895), which are later seen in Đurđević's art. Q's followers then made the connection, as though something profound yet hidden had been revealed, and they had each discovered it for themselves.

Marina Abramović features heavily in the climactic conclusions of *Out of Shadows*, and her work has been broadly co-opted into the QAnon archive due to a mention of her hosting a "*Spirit Cooking* dinner" in an email from John Podesta to his brother Tony, released by Wikileaks. Conspiracy theorist Alex Jones latched onto that email, citing it as proof that Hillary Clinton was "the antichrist personified" and asserting that Abramović was a Satanist linked to occultist Aleister Crowley.[85] Abramović initially said that the accusation was "absolutely outrageous and ridiculous," and laughed it off.[86] However, by April 2020, as QAnon hit pandemic proportions, Abramović was overwhelmed by the escalating harassment. "I really want to ask these people, 'Can you stop with this? Can you stop harassing me? Can't you see that this is just the art I've been doing for 50 years of my life?'"[87] To QAnon thinking, that Abramović has publicly dealt with aspects of spiritualism and used occult symbolism in her art for half a century is only further proof—of her hiding in plain sight. "I learned that Satanists believe that they have to reveal who they are in some way, shape, or form," explains Crokin in *Out of Shadows*, accompanied by images of Abramović and rapper Jay Z in which Z is making a pyramid sign with his hands, "so that is why we see a lot of these occult members in Hollywood constantly flaunting symbolism."

As Rice says of (pre-QAnon) conspiracy theorists, they "collect evidence, carefully archiving pictures, news stories, maps, interviews, and other texts that seem to offer perspective on the 'truth' that is hidden in plain sight."[88] This practice is central to QAnon's commonly held belief that "symbolism will be their downfall," a phrase repeated in multiple Q drops. In other words, the Satanic cabal of pedophiles, and the Deep State that they control, blatantly flaunt power through scarcely-hidden symbols, which are hidden in plain sight throughout mass culture. Q drop #4,627 (August 26, 2020) claims that a Satanist pentacle appears in the Democrat National Convention 2020 logo; Q drop #2,968 (March 4, 2019) suggests that the Gmail logo is based on the Masonic apron, the Google Chrome logo is a Satanic 666, and the Google Play logo is the Seal of Satan.

The Q drops, the QMaps and the videos *Plandemic* and *Out of Shadows* represent only a fragment of the archive of QAnon. This demonstrates something of the enormity of its "degenerating research program," driven by a conspiracist paranoid epistemology, which selectively harnesses the internet's vast and dynamic heterotopia to cherry-pick fragments of evidence that build upon each other and feed into an ever-tightening loop of mutually reinforcing, self-confirming knowledge, so that eventually the archive is too elaborate, the dots too creatively connected, the connections too manifold to argue against: how could it not all be true? In turn, the time and effort spent in its accumulation is so overwhelming that the mega-archive creates the additional bias of a sunk cost: how could these innumerable hours of obsessive searching and connecting, and throngs of people becoming "awakened" and joining the Q Army, all mean nothing?

Join the Dots

Q drop #1,895 on August 15, 2018 mentions "red shoes." Q followers enter "Tony Podesta red shoes" into Google. The search quickly delivers a 2010 *Huffington Post* article about Tony Podesta's sixty-fifth birthday party, to which guests were invited to come wearing red shoes.[89] Under the headline is an image of Podesta and a group of other men dressed in suits and red shoes. Twelve minutes later, another Q drop urges, "Compare pool of V w/ painting of kids in pool (red shoes)" (#1,898). Within minutes, a Q follower posts "PODESTA ART"; this is reposted by Q (#1,899). Then another follower posts the image of the Biltmore House pool, which Q also reposts (#1,900). Almost immediately, the same image is posted next to one of Đurđević's paintings by a follower who asks "this?," to which Q immediately responds "confirmed" (#1,901). Q then reposts another image of one of Đurđević's paintings of children wearing red shoes (#1,903). It is never stated, but the suggestion is that the red shoes are profoundly meaningful and that something has been uncovered.

The suggestion of the significance of red shoes then converges with an earlier article published on the far-right fake news site *News Punch*, which claimed to quote from Hollywood actor and former child star Macaulay Culkin that Hollywood executives "wear shoes, belts, and wallets made out of the skin of children that have been ritually murdered," and that one executive met him wearing shoes made from the skin of Heather O'Rourke, the deceased child star of the movie *Poltergeist*.[90] The quotes are entirely fabricated and the article has since been deleted,[91] but the fabricated Culkin quotes still circulate on social media in internet memes and Q followers continue to dig for clues, often within each other's posts, for confirmation.[92] Indeed, the book by Q followers Michael Knight and Martin Geddes, *QAnon and The Great Awakening*, dedicates four pages to red shoes, describing paintings of children wearing red shoes "hanging by their necks on a tiled wall," further perpetuating the suggestion that this wall is that of the Vanderbilt's indoor pool.[93]

This is but one cluster of "crumbs" dropped by Q, amongst numerous others in the nearly 5,000 posts. The timestamps on these posts convey something of the frenetic alacrity with which the crumbs are consumed, each an incremental "discovery" falling into place, confirming the last. An extensive QAnon archive of "evidence" has since been curated around red shoes, mostly reabsorbing pre-digested evidence and adding further seemingly random crumbs. Posters on Q forums continue to search for red shoes—on the Pope, on comedian Bill Maher, in an episode of *The Umbrella Academy*. The crumbs are seemingly everywhere and the hunt is still on.

Guided Apophenia

QAnon is simultaneously the gamification of propaganda and weaponization of a game. "When I saw QAnon, I knew exactly what it was and what it was doing," says Reed Berkowitz, a designer and researcher of games. "I had seen it before. I had almost built it before. It was gaming's evil twin. A game that plays people."[94] Berkovitz designs games that are intended to be played in reality, rather than mostly on a game console or computer—these span interactive theatre experiences, Live Action Role Play (LARP) games such as "Dungeons and Dragons," Alternate Reality Games (ARGs), and Experience Fictions (XFs). He explains how, in an XF game he designed, he set up one particular clue in a basement that, despite being quite obvious, was missed because participants became fixated on some scraps of wood on the floor nearby, which appeared to be an arrow pointing at a blank wall. The "arrow" was completely unintentional. Berkowitz had to quickly and creatively intervene, "before these well-meaning players started tearing apart the basement wall with crowbars looking for clues that did not exist."[95]

The term Berkowitz draws upon to explain this tendency to over-read clues in a game is "apophenia," something that plagues game designers and players of games set in any extended or unlimited world. In psychology, the term was first used in a German text by Klaus Conrad in 1958 in relation to schizophrenia,[96] but it has been used in recent decades in discussions and experiments around the common human tendency to recognize patterns in random formations and attempt to assign significance to them.[97] In 2001, Peter Brugger drew on Conrad's idea of "a heightened awareness of the 'meaningfulness' and personal relevance of any event," and applied it more broadly to paranormal thinking such as belief in ghosts.[98] Joining the dots, reading and re-reading the "crumbs," looking for patterns and connections in random distributions of data—that is, apophenia, or rather what Berkovitz calls "guided apophenia"—is the principle methodology of QAnon's paranoid epistemology: "QAnon grows on the wild misinterpretation of random data, presented in a suggestive fashion in a milieu designed to help the users come to the intended misunderstanding."[99] Former Q follower Melissa Rein Lively explained in an interview on CNN that "whatever your specific fear is, you can find essentially what is like a 'choose your own adventure' down a doomsday rabbit hole of whatever you are most afraid of."[100]

QAnon is the guided gamification of ideologically driven disinformation in which the players feel that they have discovered "truth." They have all followed the exact same "crumbs," which led each individually in the exact same direction; given the same evidence, they each independently came to the same conclusion, "without anyone telling them what to think": *I did my own research*. The pay-off, argues Berkovitz, is the thrill of the "eureka" moment of solving a problem or cracking a code, alongside a sense of exceptionalism, of belonging to a community of the awakened. Unlike the "normies," who lack "critical thinking," the players align to reject mainstream and official accounts and facts. "Solving puzzles together is a great way to form community and to join community," says Brugger.[101] QAnon is an ongoing Experience Fiction game of near-boundless possibilities that rewards obsessiveness, a game in which you, the ordinary, disempowered, and disenfranchised individual, armed with Google and YouTube, can outsmart and expose the world's most powerful elites, for no less noble a cause than to save the children.

Berkovitz's suggestion that QAnon is in essence a game controlled by guided apophenia intersects with recent conclusions by the social psychologists Jan-Willem van Prooijen, Karen M. Douglas, and Clara de Inocencio. In their appositely titled 2018 paper "Connecting the Dots,"[102] Prooijen, Douglas, and Inocencio tested Conrad's and Brugger's theories via a series of five experiments, designed to determine the extent to which pattern perception may correlate with conspiracy thinking, supernatural beliefs, and magical ideation. Each of the five experiments involved between 250 and 450 participants, was run online, and progressed in increasing levels of complexity. Study 1 asked participants to rate the extent to which they believed in conspiracy theories, ranging from a general, "the US government deliberately conceals a lot of information from the public," to a specific, "the US government had advance knowledge of the 9/11 attacks." It also measured participants' belief in fictitious conspiracy theories that the researchers themselves had made up, and beliefs in supernatural ideas such as certain numbers having special powers. Participants were also presented with a sequence of 100 coin tosses ("HTHHTTTTHH," etc.) and asked to "rate how random or determined the outcomes are."

The first experiment found a significant correlation between belief in conspiracy, belief in the supernatural, and perception of patterns in random coin tosses. In Study 3, Prooijen, Douglas, and Inocencio switched out the random coin toss task for a task involving the unstructured marks of Jackson Pollock paintings. Similarly, perceiving patterns in the Pollock paintings significantly predicted participants' belief in existing conspiracy theories, fictitious conspiracy theories, and supernatural powers.[103] In Study 4, participants were first given one of three texts to read, from either a "paranormal," "conspiracy," or "skeptic" [sic] perspective, and then again asked if they perceived patterns in random coin tosses and Pollock paintings. Results found that participants who had read the paranormal and conspiracy texts demonstrated greater pattern perception than those who read the "skeptic" text. "These findings suggest that only reading about paranormal or conspiracy beliefs is sufficient to cause a slight increase in pattern perception."[104] Of course, as theorists of art and visual culture it is not our place to comment authoritatively on the social psychology methods or conclusions of Prooijen, Douglas, and Inocencio. However, their research not only gives credence to the notion of "guided apophenia" as central to the methodology of QAnon's paranoid epistemology, but it also suggests that apophenia begets greater apophenia. Conspiracy thinking creates the tendency to see further connections; further connections reinforce conspiracy narratives.

Nothing Will Stop What Is Coming

The day before the Capitol Hill riot, Ashli Babbett, the Q follower who would die the following day, posted on Twitter, "Nothing will stop us . . . they can try and try and try but the storm is here and it is descending upon DC in less than 24 hours . . . dark to light!"[105] When January 6 turned out not to be The Storm the next date was set at January 20, the inauguration of Joe Biden; this was when the military would seize power, the cabal would be arrested, and Trump would be sworn in for a second term. "The next 48 hours will be like the entire Revolutionary War and the fall of Berlin compressed into two days. I have called off work so I can witness history in the making," wrote one Q follower.[106] January 20 turned out not to be The Storm either. Following the departure of Trump, his political resurrection has become rolled-into the concept of The Storm, and yet the lack of eventuality of either leaves Q devotees undeterred: March 4 became the next moment of reckoning (prior to 1933, March 4 was Inauguration Day), and when that did not eventuate, Mike Lindell, the "My Pillow Guy," high-profile supporter of Trump and major proponent of the Stop the Steal conspiracy, promised that the president would be reinstated on August 13, and yet, lo and behold, he was not.[107]

QAnon combines this perpetually suspended temporality, a sense of foreboding and imminence, with the addictive high-octane gamification of

American politics on a massive scale. "In the last few weeks, my thoughts have drifted towards the events of this autumn that are going to shake the world. We have seen all the pieces being put in place for a mass justice event in the USA—the like of which has never been encountered before," wrote Geddes in 2019, before detailing how it was all going to go down.[108] Mike Rothschild, in his astute and sustained analysis of QAnon, says, "[t]o any reasonable person, the failure of a long-foretold event erodes the belief that it will happen. But belief isn't reasonable."[109] Hofstadter says:

> The paranoid spokesman sees the fate of this conspiracy in apocalyptic terms—he *[sic]* traffics in the birth and death of whole worlds, whole political orders, whole systems of human values. He is always manning the barricades of civilization. He constantly lives at a turning point: it is now or never in organizing resistance to conspiracy. Time is forever just running out. Like religious millenarians, he expresses the anxiety of those who are living through the last days and he is sometimes disposed to set a date for the apocalypse.[110]

More than fifty years after Hofstadter's writings, QAnon's doomsday worldview is one of its more troubling features, and the Capitol Hill riot is one in a growing list of violent and lethal incidents inspired by QAnon. But beyond this immediate potential threat, QAnon signals something even more troubling in the longer term. Its paranoid style has moved out of the shadows in American politics. The election of Q-follower House members Marjorie Taylor Greene (Georgia) and Lauren Boebert (Colorado) to America's Congress, closely followed by the ousting of Liz Cheney from the Republican national leadership, is the concrete realization of the paranoid style into the mainstream.

Indeed, Trump's Stop the Steal conspiracy—enlisting fanciful narratives about corrupted voting machines, complicity of the FBI, Department of Justice, the Department of Homeland Security, thousands of electoral officials and others—is effectively an extension of the QAnon conspiracist narrative. While early pizzagate-related stories were initially given some credence on Fox News, the channel has largely played-down Q conspiracy theories, with their leading culture war pundit Tucker Carlson commenting after the Capitol Hill riot, "We spent all day trying to locate the famous QAnon, which in the end we learned is not even a website. If it's out there, we could not find it."[111] For Carlson, instead, the mega-archive of the internet has exposed the scam of mainstream media, comparing "doing your own research" with owning a car that can be repaired at home, without the expertise of a mechanic. Fox was much less reticent about buying into QAnon's paranoid conspiracy narrative, however, when Trump tweeted multiple times about Dominion voting machines deleting Trump votes immediately following the election, Fox News weighed in heavily for several weeks on the Stop the Steal conspiracy. Fox began propagating the narrative about Dominion's machines from the day following the 2020 election, when Maria Bartiromo interviewed Sidney Powell,[112] herself a lawyer for QAnon hero General Mike Flynn and someone who has retweeted QAnon material.[113] When Bartiromo asked about Dominion and "voting irregularities," Powell responded, "That's putting it mildly. . . That is where the fraud took place, where they were flipping votes in the computer system or adding votes that did not exist." When Trump gave his first interview following the election it was with Bartiromo on Fox, launching straight into Dominion's machines: "we had glitches where they moved thousands of votes from my account to Biden's account and these are glitches, so they're not glitches, they're theft, they're fraud, absolute fraud, and there were many of them. . . they did these massive dumps of votes and all of a sudden I went from winning by a lot to losing by a little". Trump centered the fraud narrative on, what he termed, "Garbage machinery, Dominion."[114]

At the time of writing, Dominion is suing Fox Corporation for $1.6 billion, for "verifiably false yet devastating lies about Dominion . . . outlandish, defamatory, and far-fetched fictions," arguing that Fox knowingly repeated these false claims.[115] The complaint suggests that Fox was experiencing a fierce Trump supporter backlash for calling the election for Biden, with Trump tweeting on election day that "#foxnews is dead."[116] The network was losing viewers to Newsmax and OAN Network, so doubled-down on the big lie: "that the election had been stolen by vote-flipping algorithms in Dominion machines that had been created in Venezuela to rig elections for Hugo Chávez."[117] Smartmatic, a company that Trump's lawyer Rudy Giuliani claimed "was founded in 2005 in Venezuela for the specific purpose of fixing elections,"[118] is suing Fox for $2.7 billion. The Stop the Steal stolen election conspiracy theory plugged into and fed from the same paranoid epistemology of QAnon but, importantly, shifted the paranoid style from the fringes into the mainstream. Dominion's suit claims:

> These lies did not simply harm Dominion. They harmed democracy. They harmed the idea of credible elections. They harmed a once-unshakeable faith in democratic and peaceful transfers of power. They harmed the foundational idea, as stated in the Declaration of Independence, that our country derives its "just powers" from "the consent of the governed." This lawsuit is about accountability.[119]

In our next chapter, we turn our attention to Fox News in the months that followed the January 6, 2021 insurrection, and its amplification of Trump's targeting of critical race theory during the final months of his presidency. Again, we consider the confluence of Trumpist racial politics with visual culture, as it crosses social media, network news and contemporary art, and consider the rise within the larger Trump Effect of a post-ideology right-wing liberalism.

CHAPTER TWO

The Critical Race Theory Moral Panic

Dana Schutz's *Open Casket* and the Evergreen Affair

At the moment in 2015 when Donald J. Trump, in Trump Tower, was announcing his run for the US presidency, African American artist William Pope.L's artwork *Trinket*, an enormous Stars and Stripes flag with an extra star, was being whipped around by industrial fans in the Geffen Contemporary exhibition at the Museum of Contemporary Art (MOCA) in Los Angeles. Just months after Eric Garner gasped the words "I can't breathe" before dying at the hands of the police, Pope.L's work spoke about having, or being deprived of, the freedom just to breathe in America. Five years later, George Floyd would repeat Garner's words before he died, sparking the 2020 Black Lives Matter riots. However, this time, BLM would become a target of white resentment and the obstinate retort, "all lives matter." When the mob of Trump supporters attempted insurrection on Capitol Hill on January 6, 2021, many commentators noted the contrast between the official response to the Trumpist mob versus the official response to BLM protestors six months earlier. On June 1, 2020, at Lafayette Square in Washington, D.C., The Metropolitan Police Department used tear gas and rubber bullets to clear BLM protestors so that the President could walk to St John's Episcopal Church for a photo opportunity.

Three months later, Christopher Rufo, the documentarian responsible for a film we discussed in our Introduction, *America Lost* (2019), ran a series of moral panic stories on Fox News' *Tucker Carlson Tonight*. In an episode broadcast on September 1, Rufo breathlessly explained to the visibly befuddled Carlson that "critical race theory has pervaded every institution in the federal government and what I've discovered is that critical race theory has become in essence the default ideology of the federal bureaucracy and is now being weaponized against the American people."[1] Rufo explained how this "cult indoctrination" had now taken hold of the US Treasury Department, the Sandia National Laboratories, and even the FBI, which "is now holding weekly seminars on intersectionality, which is a hard-left academic theory." Rufo reminded his audience that Sandia National Laboratories creates America's nuclear weapons arsenal: critical race theory was nothing less than an "existential threat to the United States," "weaponized against core American values."[2]

Rufo directly called on US President Donald J. Trump to immediately issue an "Executive Order and stamp out this destructive, divisive, pseudo-scientific ideology"; "it's something that he's denounced, this kind of Black Lives Matter and neo-Marxist rhetoric in places like Portland and Seattle."[3] The following morning, Trump's Chief of Staff Mark Meadows called Rufo, and three weeks after Rufo's plea, the President signed an Executive Order that would purportedly "combat offensive and anti-American race and sex stereotyping and scapegoating," and which in actuality banned any kind of diversity and inclusion training in all US federal agencies.[4] "I ended it because it's racist," Trump said a week later at the first Presidential Debate, held at Case Western Reserve University in Cleveland, Ohio. "It was a radical revolution that was taking place in our military, in our schools, all over the place."[5] And during the days following the 2020 US presidential election, with the outcome still unknown, Trump issued a proclamation for National American History and Founders Month asserting that "theoretical frameworks like 'Critical Race Theory' have corrupted our United States history and civic education courses in public schools, board rooms, the military, and government agencies, promoting racial division and discrimination."[6]

Six months after the Capitol Hill riot, and less than a year after Rufo's plea for an Executive Order, "critical race theory" (CRT) had become the bogeyman of America's Summer of '21 moral panic. Trump had left the presidency, but after incoming President Joe Biden rescinded Trump's Executive Order, the panic spread to the state legislatures. In mid-2021, *Media Matters* found that on Fox News, an average of around four mentions of critical race theory per month during the previous summer (with a blip of 69 mentions in September following Trump's Executive Order) had grown following Biden's election victory to 23, 21, and 29 mentions in December, January, and February, to 107 mentions in March, 226 in April, 537 in May, and 901 in June.[7] Fox's narrative resonated with an existing Trump pet hate: "Too many universities and school systems are about radical left indoctrination, not education," the president had Tweeted only weeks before Rufo's 2020 plea, "[t]herefore, I am telling the Treasury Department to re-examine their Tax-Exempt Status . . . and/or Funding, which will be taken away if this Propaganda or Act Against Public Policy continues. Our children must be Educated, not Indoctrinated!"[8] Also in June 2021, Keith Whittington noted that references to critical race theory in Republican Party social media posts and in conservative media had "exploded" in recent months: "Republican lawmakers across the United States have introduced bills seeking to curb the teaching of critical race theory. Some have already made their way into law."[9]

In the early months of the Biden administration, Republican-controlled state legislatures, such as in New Hampshire, were proposing laws that would ban state government entities from doing business with any companies that conducted diversity and inclusion training.[10] By mid-2021, nine US states had introduced similar legislation.[11] At that point, the debate had taken on a *Simpsons*-esque quality of "won't-somebody-please-think-of-the-children?!"

Loudoun County, Virginia, became a particular flash point of the 2021 CRT backlash, and Fox News aired a series of stories on a group of parents protesting the teaching of critical race theory in schools. The parents began running a TV advertising campaign warning other parents and teachers about the radical Left "infecting our schools with critical race theory, training teachers that Christians are oppressors."[12] One of the mothers, Elicia Brandy, says, "I really believe that our school board has really lost their way . . . I don't want critical *theory*—not just critical race theory, but critical *theory*—taught in our classrooms. Our schools are not for ideology. Our schools are for education."[13] Carlson also gave the same local moral panic a decent airing:

> Public schools in Virginia, like so many schools in this country, have gone insane in the last year. They've essentially stopped teaching; instead, they're indoctrinating children with creepy and poisonous racial theories, master race stuff. Scary. In Loudoun County, kids are not allowed to read *To Kill a Mockingbird* anymore. Instead, they're assigned pornographic novels and told that America is an evil, racist place.[14]

"Conservatives are not the only critics of diversity training," writes journalist Adam Harris.

> For years, some progressives, including critical race theorists, have questioned its value: *Is it performative? Is it the most effective way to move toward equity or is it simply an effective way of restating the obvious and stalling meaningful action?* But that is not the fight that has materialized over the past nine months. Instead, it is a confrontation with a cartoonish version of critical race theory.[15]

America's critical race theory moral panic of 2021 has undertones of the "paranoid style" in American politics: the idea that hard-Left, neo-Marxist theory is being taught to American children, surreptitiously slipped into the curriculum between the Pledge of Allegiance and nap time.[16] Richard an earlier modernist generation of black female artists, may have seemed "blithe and uncritical."[26] Three days after Black's letter demanding of *Open Casket* that "the painting must go," Walker posted on Instagram Artemisia Gentileschi's *Judith Beheading Holofernes* (c1599), commenting:

> The history of painting is full of graphic violence and narratives that don't necessarily belong to the artist's own life . . . a lot of art often lasts longer than the controversies that greet it. I say this as a shout to every artist and artwork that gives rise to vocal outrage. Perhaps it too gives rise to deeper inquiries and better art. It can only do this when it is seen.[27]

Similarly, on March 27, Coco Fusco wrote an article for *Hyperallergic* saying that she welcomes strong reactions to artworks, and has learned to expect them when art deals with issues of substance. However, in response to demands to remove and destroy *Open Casket*, and to D'Souza's suggestion that not to comply with the demand would be to defend Whiteness, Fusco said, "I find it alarming and entirely wrongheaded to call for the censorship and destruction of an artwork, no matter what its content is or who made it," and that "presuming that calls for censorship and destruction constitute a legitimate response to perceived injustice leads us down a very dark path."[28]

Conflicting Perspectives on the Left

Following Fusco's article, possibly wanting to reclaim some control of the debate that was raging mostly online and on social media, the Whitney invited Claudia Rankine (like Walker, a winner of the MacArthur "genius" grant) to convene an evening event at the museum in partnership with the Racial Imaginary Institute. Over two and a half hours, *Perspectives on Race and Representation* brought together fourteen speakers and a large public crowd at the Whitney Museum on April 9, 2017. Rather than finding common ground, the evening powerfully emphasized these conflicting perspectives.[29] The introduction by the Whitney's director, Adam Weinberg, reinforced the museum's assumption of the systemic neutrality of an institution that, through sometimes difficult art, opens up a space for difficult conversations. Weinberg opined that, in that respect, Schutz's painting and the Biennial had done their job and, moreover, that Black's letter and Bright's "Black Death Spectacle" protest had been "crucial in bringing us together tonight."[30] Biennial co-curator Chris Lew's defense of the inclusion of *Open Casket* began by framing the exhibition as tackling urgent, difficult, and polemical issues:

> artists with differing practices, from various parts of the country and from a range of backgrounds, were thinking hard about inequities, trauma, race, history and memory. The works they made speak to these

> issues as shared concerns as American ones. Ones to be tackled not by division, but by coming together.[31]

This perspective was reinforced by LeRonn P. Brooks, a member of the Racial Imaginary Institute, who concluded, "this is a necessary discussion."[32] The underlying message was that *Open Casket* and the ensuing controversy were actually liberal democracy in action.

On the other hand, reports D'Souza, Weinberg's promise to listen was understood by many of the protestors as "a refusal to allow the institution itself—its allocation of resources, its structural biases, its decision-making processes and management—to come into question."[33] During the discussions, a Black female audience member likened *Open Casket* to a snuff film, a warning that "this is what's going to happen to you in the white space," suggesting that *Open Casket* itself had asserted the museum as a White space. She continued, "the Whitney does some controversial shit, and they weren't prepared for the controversial shit-storm that came afterwards."[34] Rankine read aloud a statement from Christina Sharpe, author of *In the Wake: On Blackness and Being*, which argued that as a contested arena of representation art is not immune to systemic racism that manifests "most visibly in policing and mass criminalisation; less observably, but no less potently, in education and art."[35]

The conflicting perspectives were perhaps most clearly laid bare during Rankine's closing of the event, in which she poignantly cited James Baldwin: "artists are human beings and their greatest responsibility is to other human beings." She thanked the audience for "starting this discussion,"[36] at which point photographic artist Lyle Ashton Harris interrupted passionately, "I don't want to have, like, a kumbaya moment. Let's deal with the problem of cultural amnesia, not just with the Whitney, all institutions. My students are somehow saying "we don't want cultural sensitivity, we want cultural authority, [that] is what we want right now"."[37] In essence, the division lay between a perception of the *Open Casket* controversy as a successful exercise in liberal democracy and humanism, within a healthy discursive public arena, demonstrating empathy and universal humanity, versus seeing the painting's inclusion at the Whitney as a toxic assertion of White supremacy, under the flimsy guise of neutrality within the White institutional space.

D'Souza argues that this division was made all the more acute by Clinton-voting liberals who, only weeks after the inauguration of Donald Trump, "doubled down on the idea that empathy was the key to a more progressive political arena."[38] Indeed, Schutz's own defense of *Open Casket*, which was circulated to the press and quoted in *The New York Times*, emphasized a gendered empathic alignment between artist and subject: "I don't know what it is like to be black in America but I do know what it is like to be a mother . . . Art can be a space for empathy, a vehicle for connection."[39] Schutz's appeal to a liberal humanist universalism, according to D'Souza, simply did not wash with many of the protestors.[40] Josephine Livingstone of White supremacy. To the progressive Robin DiAngelo, for instance, well-meaning "good" White liberals leading "good" lives, whose color-blind models for understanding racism largely spring from the same well as the egalitarian Left, *are the problem*. To the progressive Left, racism cannot be resisted by simply being good citizens and maintaining the system, rather, systems of Whiteness must be actively resisted.[56] Racism is understood as ambient, systematic, and systemic: socially constructed but with concrete manifestations.

Perhaps it is a little too simplistic to map egalitarian Left and progressive Left along generational divides—rather, this faultline occurs more convincingly along the paradigmatic cleaving of post-ideological ontological politics from liberal humanism. We can maybe think of the former as represented by the approach of American Frank B. Wilderson III and the latter by that of British theorist Paul Gilroy; both Black men, both born in 1956. Gilroy's *The Black Atlantic* (1993) has had a formative influence on American critical race theory over the last three decades, arguing that the system of North Atlantic slave trade shaped both Black identities and their double-consciousness, in relation to Whiteness and nationalism.[57] However, Gilroy maintains an emphatically humanist frame, which he makes clear in *Against Race: Imagining political culture beyond the color line* (2000), in which he argues that "almost banal human sameness . . . present an opportunity where it almost points towards the possibility of leaving 'race' behind."[58] For Gilroy, it is a knowing, strategic humanism, but one that is preferable, he says, to the problems of in-humanity that raciology creates."[59] Since Gilroy wrote *Against Race* in 2000, his universalistic humanism has become only more radical, or conservative, depending on ones perspective. A recent article in *The Guardian* in 2021 notes, "He is an untimely figure. His ideas don't correspond to the vogueish pieties of identity politics or even cutting-edge studies of race."[60]

The work of Wilderson, on the other hand, represents a very different framing of race, and particularly of Blackness, reflected in the title of his book *Afropessimism*. The term precedes Wilderson's 2020 book, in his 2015 analysis of Steve McQueen's *12 Years a Slave*,[61] and in the work of scholars such as Shanara Reid-Brinkley, deriving from the Orlando Patterson's idea from 1982 that slavery renders a "social death";[62] as Kevin Lawrence Henry Jr. and Shameka N Powell summarize, "Within a historical US context, Blacks were neither human nor citizen. Rather, they were property to be traded and owned."[63] As Wilderson says, "the Human Other is Black":[64] Blacks are not Human subjects, but are instead structurally inert props, implements for the execution of White and non-Black fantasies and sadomasochistic pleasures."[65] Henry and Powell argue there is a "paradigmatic kinship" between Afropessimism and critical race theory, in that both emphasize the dehumanization of Black people.[66] And Wilderson's *Afropessimism* resonates with Parker Bright's Whitney Museum protest: "the *spectacle* of Black death is essential to the mental health of the world—

we can't be wiped out completely, because our deaths must be repeated, *visually*."[67] For Gilroy's liberal humanism, positionality, and biography is not fundamentally connected to political subjectivity. Indeed, at multiple points in the *Guardian*'s article, Gilroy resists connecting his life and his politics, stating even that "politics requires the abandonment of identity in a personal sense."[68] Meanwhile, Wilderson's *Afropessimism* combines memoir and theory, novelistic dialogue, and scholarly references, that emphatically embed his politics within biographical lived experience, in what Vinson Cunningham calls "auto theory."[69] We will return to this paradigmatic split shortly.

Systemic Racism

In our previous book, we discussed Arthur Jafa's video installation artwork *The White Album*, and particularly a section of the work in which Jafa includes a YouTube video of a young, blonde, White woman repeating the familiar, White, color-blind trope: "I've had best friends who are Hispanic and Black people . . . family, whatever, who are all different races. I can't stress enough that I do not care, I have no problem, whatsoever, what color skin you are. I do not care." Jafa then cuts to the rapper Plies saying, "you big mad!" as if in response to her, followed by Dixon White, a heavy-set White man who, in his Deep Southern accent, lays bare Whiteness as a field of power. He says:

> We [Americans] are a white supremacist nation, and we always have been. We have white supremacist institutions, culture, structures, power, psychology, everything. Politics. White-washing is in everything, the media, education, history is white-washed and biased, education is white-washed and biased, entertainment is white-washed and biased . . . Our white culture is racist. I ain't saying *all* white people are racist. I'm not saying that, but it's all that indifference, it's all that inaction, it's all that turning a blind fucking eye, that's the real fucking problem.

Lifting from social media, particularly Instagram and YouTube, Jafa's *The White Album* lays out the tension at the center of this conflict between the persistent invisibility of Whiteness in America and a critical challenge to that invisibility which, while having been developed and long accepted in academic theory, has only recently gained any wider purchase amongst American liberals; that is, the notion of systemic racism. One of the ways in which the notion of systemic racism has become established in recent years is through best-selling books such as Reni Eddo-Lodge's *Why I'm No Longer Talking to White People about Race* (2017) in the UK,[70] and in the US Robin DiAngelo's *White Fragility: Why It's So Hard for White People to Talk about Racism* (2018)[71] and, in the midst of the critical race theory panic, *Nice Racism: How Progressive White People Perpetuate Racial Harm* (2021).[72]

A watershed moment in the United States in 2020, the last year of the Trump administration, was the police's murder of George Floyd. Recorded on video and so undeniably callous and public, Floyd's murder hit America as a bare demonstration of systemic racism. It was the catalyst needed to jolt at least some Americans to the recognition that racism goes beyond individual attitudes and actions, that American racism lies within the structures of a system founded on stolen Indigenous land, the stolen labor of slaves, and the Jim Crow laws. Ongoing synergisms with poverty perpetuated through degrees of normalized privilege or oppression mean that—this is the biggest conceptual challenge to majority White America, and the core of DiAngelo's argument—to merely maintain the status quo is to perpetuate unchallenged a system of Whiteness. As Daniel Bergner noted during the Black Lives Matter protests throughout the US in July 2020, "as prominent as DiAngelo was then [when the book was released in 2018], she has become, since Floyd's death, a phenomenon."[73]

DiAngelo's idea of White fragility is based on a critical race theory approach insofar as it recognizes that White supremacy is baked into the social, cultural, and institutional structures of the United States, but it is also based on an activist pedagogy approach that has become more prominent over the last ten years. DiAngelo's own 2011 scholarly paper titled "White Fragility" helped expand upon existing notions of systemic racism, arguing that a degree of adverse emotional defensiveness is a necessary element for White people to accept that Whiteness is a system and racism is dyed into its very fabric.[74] She argues that "White Fragility is a state in which even a minimum amount of racial stress becomes intolerable, triggering a range of defensive moves" which are often intensely emotional, and that Whites have not built the cognitive and affective skills to develop the stamina required to accept the challenge to their sense of equilibrium.[75] Following her paper, DiAngelo focused her attention on articulating this particular take on systemic racism through pedagogical means that meet this White fragility resistance head on. At a 2014 conference on race and pedagogy in Tacoma, she worked with Heather Bruce and Gyda Swaney on a set of principles for confronting potential future students and trainees of this developing pedagogy, amongst which are, "No-one chose to be socialized into racism so no-one is 'bad,' but no-one is neutral"; "The question is not 'did racism take place?' but rather 'how did racism manifest in that situation?'"; "The racial status quo is comfortable for most whites. Therefore, anything that maintains white comfort is suspect"; and "To not act against racism is to support racism. The 'default' is racism." And, something that resonates with the latter half of this chapter: "Resistance is a predictable reaction to anti-racist education and must be explicitly and strategically addressed."[76]

The tone of DiAngelo's book *White Fragility* is markedly different from the standard academic prose of her 2011 journal paper. When her ideas were worked up into *White Fragility*, they took on the format of a self-help book (though nonetheless academically informed and practicing an activist pedagogy). As BLM protests arose in cities across the US, otherwise locked-down White liberals pushed *White Fragility* to the top slot on Amazon's best-seller list, and DiAngelo was inundated by urgent enquiries for corporate speaking engagements, including workshops and keynotes at Amazon, Nike, Under Armour, Goldman Sachs, Facebook, CVS, American Express, and Netflix. Katy Waldman says, "[o]ne has the grim hunch that such an approach has been honed over years of placating red-faced White people, workshop participants leaping at any excuse to discount their instructor."[77] DiAngelo makes it clear that she is speaking to a primarily *White*, politically liberal audience (American, she states, but applicable in other White settler societies such as Australia, Canada, and South Africa),[78] and the book maintains an oratory tone similar to that in online video recordings of DiAngelo addressing her mostly White workshop audiences. After years as a diversity trainer, she found participants' responses of anger, fear, anxiety, and discomfort to be so consistent and reliable that throughout the book she pre-emptively exhorts her readers to *breathe*.[79]

The Evergreen Affair

We shift focus at this point from contemporary art to the visuality of live video streaming on the internet, particularly YouTube and social media, and how it connects with mainstream news media, in this instance Fox News. The incident we choose to discuss has been an important rallying point for the conservative, right-wing ecosphere. It is the 2017 Evergreen Affair, a series of escalating events at Evergreen State College in Olympia, Washington State, centered around the conflicting perspectives on race and racism discussed above. The trigger for the controversy occurred only weeks after the *Open Casket* controversy, and so is similarly contextualized by the shock felt amongst the American Left of the triumph of Donald Trump in the 2016 presidential election. The Evergreen Affair demonstrates some key aspects of the Trump Effect. The flash point of the Evergreen Affair played out through hours of live-streamed videos on social media, many of which have entered the permanent archive of YouTube, and then the canon of the right-wing ecosphere. These videos capture Trump Effect politics both Left and Right: expressly performative, public, and declarative. They demonstrate to some extent the evolving character of culture war politics, occupying the mainstream public discourse and functioning as political conflict *as* culture. As we shall see later, aspects of these events become channeled into the paranoid style of politics that is a constitutive dimension of the Trump Effect. As with our discussion of *Open Casket*, it is not our intention to recount in great detail the events of the Evergreen Affair (which is multifaceted and complex), but rather to sketch out some of its key moments as they relate to our concerns.

A reasonable place to begin is a series of lectures and workshops at Evergreen State College from October 2015 to March 2016, called *Coming*

Together. The college had appointed a new president, George Bridges, in March 2015, and the workshops were aimed at creating action items for the college's administration and new leadership. The first workshop was a faculty staff forum titled *A Call To Action*, and it concluded with three visiting lectures by DiAngelo.[80] Indeed, at the faculty forum, an academic faculty member who had attended DiAngelo's 2014 workshop with Heather Bruce and Gyda Swaney had read out their proposed principles on race and pedagogy. Other faculty staff agreed upon a need for ongoing work and, following the *Coming Together* series, Evergreen formed an Equity and Inclusion Council to work on codifying some of these principles within a Strategic Equity Plan. At her *Coming Together* workshops, DiAngelo commended the formation of the Council, and suggested that as things progressed in the coming months,

> the racism that's imbed [sic] and will surface more and more . . . [T]he white people on campus are going to have to endure looking at the way we've been colluding and maybe not knowing it, and I urge us to put our efforts on not protecting each other's feelings but remembering "it is inevitable that I have been colluding."[81]

Throughout 2016, the Council worked on Evergreen's 2016–17 Strategic Equity Plan. The result was a run-of-the-mill equity plan in much the same model as those of many corporations and institutions. It does not use the language of critical race theory (the word "racism" appears only twice, and "White" or "Whiteness" not at all), but speaks in the corporate parlance of creating "a more student-ready college," by addressing "representation of underrepresented faculty and staff," "educational resources that are directed at closing equity gaps," and the college's leaders "demonstrating an awareness and a willingness to address equity issues."[82] The Strategic Equity Plan was dated November 11, 2016, and was to be launched at a special event on November 16.

However, to widespread shock, and very much to the horror of America's left-wing, liberals, progressives, and Democrats, on November 8, 2016, Donald Trump won the US presidential election. In the video of the November 16 Evergreen special event, titled *Equity and Inclusion Council: Community Report Back*, the shock is palpable. In his Indigenous welcome to the event, an American Indian faculty member began the meeting by acknowledging, "I know our Campus is under a little bit of chaos; our country is under a little bit of chaos."[83] The 90-minute session was facilitated by the co-chair of the council, who spoke slowly, with deliberation and gravitas, conveying the earnestness of the occasion. The first half of the meeting included speeches by faculty members. Following the speeches, the meeting switched gears. The facilitator asked the college's key stakeholders "to get on board our journey to equity," by boarding an imagined canoe at the front of the lecture theatre, in front of a video of a beach and the sound of crashing waves. One analysis of the video of the event says: "Due to its somewhat performative presentation, which concluded in a group exercise about a metaphorical canoe, the meeting became known to some documentarians and journalists as 'The Canoe Meeting'."[84]

In the video, the Canoe Meeting comes across as familiar milquetoast corporate role play, at least to anyone who has worked in a large white-collar organization. However, what retrospectively became an ideologically charged point of contention was that people of color, Black faculty and students, and council members were invited to board, while a number of White faculty had to make their case for being allowed to board. The intention seems to have been to "decolonize" the White space of the institution by emphasizing to White faculty that they did not have default access. It is a symbolic gesture typical of today's demonstrative politics across the political spectrum, also manifested in the affective tenor of the meeting which was both aspirational and deeply solemn.

The meeting was markedly performative, with contrite claims of privilege and declarations of oppression: very different from the humanist "kumbaya moment" in Rankine's quote from Baldwin at the Whitney event. The speeches evinced an underlying simmering anger; one Black woman talks of "grasping our identities, owning our power, loving our image and forcing others to respect us, being unapologetic." Another Black faculty member declared, "I stand here with my colleagues who are in the trenches, who are doing this hard work and who are tired of the load, and carrying the load alone. I am committed because I am." College President George Bridges responded, "I'm here and I commit the position of privilege in power I occupy as the President of this College, to invest in this council, its initiatives and its plans. I'm here because I was told by a high school counsellor I wasn't smart enough to go to college."[85] In the more impromptu "canoe" section of the meeting, a woman with Anishinaabe native American heritage spoke in trembling voice about her forced adoption. The affective intensity became gradually heightened throughout the Canoe Meeting.

Bret Weinstein

Bret Weinstein, at the time a little-known evolutionary biologist and White member of faculty at Evergreen State College, recounts feeling in the meeting "that something terrible is afoot."[86] Six months later on April 12, 2017—about a month after the *Open Casket* controversy—the college held its annual Day of Absence. On previous Days of Absence, staff and students of color had absented themselves from the campus to emphasize the importance of their place in the college. For 2017, this was reversed and White members were asked to be absent. Weinstein, seemingly already sensitized after the Canoe Meeting and other changes in policy, wrote an all-faculty, all-staff email that objected to the request on the basis of liberal humanist values.

with aligned beliefs that she characterizes as "fundamental biological differences between men and women. Free speech is under siege. Identity politics is a toxic ideology that is tearing American society apart. And we're in a dangerous place if these ideas are considered 'dark'."[101] Like most in the group, Bret Weinstein circulates around the other "intellectual dark web" channels, such as those featuring Rogan, Rubin, and Peterson, all echoing each other's arguments and talking points.

In June 2019, Bret Weinstein started his own YouTube channel called *Dark Horse*, and his first guest was Benjamin A. Boyce, a former Evergreen student who has his own YouTube channel (much of the Evergreen video footage still available on the internet is reposted by Boyce). Weinstein's early, little-watched *Dark Horse* videos focus on issues like "big tech's influence over censorship and free speech"[102] and the first impeachment of Trump.[103] However, when the COVID-19 pandemic hit America in March 2020, Weinstein's *Dark Horse* became a regular live-stream video podcast, often presented with his wife and fellow former Evergreen academic, Heather Heying. In their first live-stream the couple begin with their scientific credentials, Heying adding, "we're both PhDs in biology but we're not medical doctors, so we're going to be talking about the evolutionary implications of what we're going through, both biological and social, but we're not providing medical advice."[104] Despite this disclaimer, throughout the series Weinstein has increasingly joined the chorus of voices on the Right strongly suggesting the efficacy of unproven COVID-19 "treatment" Ivermectin, a horse de-wormer, and actively promoting suspicion and fear of the COVID-19 vaccines in videos that receive several million views. In his podcast episode titled "Spike protein is very dangerous, it's cytotoxic,"[105] he talks to Robert Malone, billed as "the inventor of the mRNA vaccine" (actually one of hundreds who worked on mRNA, to which Malone was an early contributor in the 1980s),[106] and Steve Kirch, an entrepreneur who wrongly claimed that the mRNA vaccines attack the ovaries and have little effect against the virus.[107]

The video stoked fears about the vaccines, mainly based on anecdotes, and was viewed around 4.5 million times in its first three months, before it was eventually deleted. It went viral amongst anti-vaxxers on social media, being reposted as "'Red Pilled' on Covid vaccines" on anti-vaxxer site Zeromandatoryvaxx.com.[108] Leslie Lawrenson, a 58-year-old British lawyer, posted a link to Weinstein's video on June 19, 2021;[109] then six days later he posted a video describing his worsening COVID-19 symptoms, saying "COVID-19, in my view, from what I've experienced so far, is nothing different [from a flu], but the potential dangers from taking the experimental jab for me are not worth that risk. I'd rather take my chances with my immune system."[110] He died on July 2. The connection, though not direct, is stochastic. On September 30, 2021, YouTube, after serving as a platform for Rogan, Weinstein, and the alt-right ecosphere of anti-vaxxers and COVID sceptics, announced that it will begin removing all anti-vaxxer material

(Weinstein's Robert Malone video amongst it). Rogan had already ditched YouTube at the beginning of the pandemic, signing a $100 million exclusivity deal with Spotify in May 2020.[111] However, following his December 2021 podcast with vaccine sceptic Dr Peter McCullough—sparking the withdrawal of Neil Young and Joni Mitchell from the platform in protest of misinformation, followed by a 10% hit to the company's share value in January 2022—Spotify deleted over forty *Joe Rogan Experience* episodes which included interviews with former alt-Right darling Milo Yiannopoulos and InfoWars conspiracist Alex Jones.[112]

Right-wing Liberalism

Running for re-election in 2020, Donald Trump addressed a rally in an airport hangar at Manchester, New Hampshire saying: "We stand for so much, including Martin Luther King's dream of a nation where our children are judged not by the color of their skin but by the content of their character."[113] Similarly, in his September 22, 2020 Executive Order banning diversity and inclusion training, Trump quoted both Abraham Lincoln and Martin Luther King Jr., stating his "dream that his children would one day 'not be judged by the color of their skin but by the content of their character'."[114] Throughout Fox News' critical race theory moral panic, King's "I Have a Dream" speech has been repeated, for example by Sean Hannity in arguing that America was founded on "personal freedom, not collective guilt, not judging people by the color of their skin but by the content of their character. What they are teaching and what they are preaching is the antithesis of what Martin Luther King dreamed of—that was a color-blind society."[115] Even on Fox's Business channel, viewers could find Ben Carson on Larry Kudlow complaining that "the focus has moved from equality to equity . . . instead of pursuing reverend Martin Luther King Jnr's ideal" and, almost inevitably, "what are we doing to our children?"[116] The MLK color-blind trope is found throughout influential and best-seller books of the last few years that pitch liberal humanism against the progressive Left. It has become something of a "gotcha" moment for commentators such as Douglas Murray (*The Madness of Crowds*, a *Sunday Times* Book of the Year in 2019),[117] Paul Embery (*Despised*),[118] and Helen Pluckrose and James Lindsay (*Cynical Theories*, which we discuss in our next chapter).[119]

Fox's frequent attacks on critical race theory characterize both the Democrats and critical race theory itself as racist for not being color-blind, and for betraying King's "Dream." It is a clever tactic. DiAngelo says, "[o]ne of the greatest social fears for a white person is being told that something that we have done is racially problematic."[120] And for most liberal White people, the very suggestion of being called a racist comes with fear of social devastation, for which DiAngelo says is a symptom of White fragility.[121] In her introduction to *White Fragility*, DiAngelo recognizes that the definition of "racism" in critiques of systems of Whiteness differs from that of "racism" in the Civil Rights frame: "if your definition of racist is someone who holds conscious dislike of people because of race," then "I am not using this definition of racism."[122] Eddo-Lodge, in *Why I'm No Longer Talking to White People about Race*, says that White people often quote King's apparent color blindness to her, suggesting that she is misguided. She says, "the intent of these messages suggests to me that these well-wishers believe that, in today's context, these words are best suited to mean that *white* people should not be judged on the colour of their skin. That the power of whiteness as a race should not be judged."[123] She points out that King, writing from his prison cell in Birmingham, Alabama in 1963, wondered if White moderates present a bigger stumbling block than the KKK because they are "more devoted to 'order' than to justice." The White moderate is one "who prefers negative peace which is the absence of tension to the positive peace which is the presence of justice; who constantly says 'I agree with the goal you seek, but I can't agree with your methods of direct action'."[124]

We cannot help but suspect a level of disingenuity in the many mentions by Fox News commentators of King's "color-blind" "dream"—not necessarily because Carlson and other commentators do not believe in that vision, but because it seems very much like trolling. To Fox's conservative audience, this point of divergence (whether or not one can be racist against the dominant group) between liberal humanism and the progressive Left appears as a collapse of logic on the Left. In these current debates, however, it does seem that many agitators in the arena—progressive Left, egalitarian Left, the media, the online Right—possess some comprehension of the slippage and resulting friction within the same terms, and that willfully disregarding the differences Black/White allows one position to accuse others of racism while claiming to be against racism. This accusation was exactly Trump's play at the first presidential debate in Cleveland, a week after signing the Executive Order banning critical race theory in federal agencies: "I ended it because it's racist."[125] The Executive Order itself proclaims to "combat offensive and anti-American race and sex stereotyping and scapegoating,"[126] as did his Proclamation for National American History and Founders Month which accused critical race theory of "promoting racial division and discrimination."[127] The accusation serves another function of the Trump Effect, which is to complicate the established political spectrum to the point of disorientation, performing aspects of a Gilroy-like liberal humanism while maintaining a steadfast core of conservativism.

This disorientation resonates with Steve Mickler's assessment of the Australian context in his book *Andrew Bolt, The Far Right and the First Nations*. The book focuses on Bolt, perhaps Tucker Carlson's antipodean spiritual twin, commentating on Sky News, Australia's version of Fox News. Mickler argues that Bolt's description of the Left

> as fascists has been sustained over quite a few years, such as to constitute a more serious effort to invert popular understandings of to whom and what the term fascism refers, and consequently to upset one of the givens of the so-called culture wars—the one that has the Left resolutely and unequivocally opposed to fascism.[128]

A similar sleight of hand allows Carlson to talk of critical race theory as "indoctrinating children with creepy and poisonous racial theories, master race stuff."[129] Critical race theory is, it would seem to Carlson's viewers, the ideology of "Commie-Nazis".

Amidst the Right's cartoonish rendering of the progressive Left are images of performative contrition amongst White liberals, a phenomenon which is perhaps borne out in reality. Among the many hours of live-streamed and recorded footage from Evergreen College's very public conflict, some moments call to mind DiAngelo's observation that White progressives can sometimes be the most difficult for her to deal with, "to the degree that we think we have arrived, we will put our energy into making sure that others see us having arrived."[130] Those moments of confessional contrition can be understood as what psychologist Matthew W. Hughey calls "stigma allure" in "white antiracist identity management."[131] Taking from Jack Niemonen, Hughey describes the antiracist movement as operating in confessional and redemptive modes that are commonly found in evangelical Protestantism,[132] centering much attention on "their own guilt, anger, and denial."[133] For all its well-intended earnestness, the tenor of Evergreen's Canoe Meeting managed to animate Hughey's characterization of "white antiracist meetings and workshops [which] serve as dramaturgical settings for profuse apology, relinquishment of authority, and the confession of 'bad deeds'."[134] Essential to confessing in this way is to "embrace stigma as markings of moral commitment and political authenticity";[135] that is, being stigmatized as guilty of racism, Hughey observes, is a desired characteristic of white antiracist identity. Reflecting on the sudden and urgent demand for diversity training during the 2020 Black Lives Matter protests, DiAngelo as well wondered if corporate America was not indulging in something "performative."[136] Whether or not we agree with Weinstein's position or his actions, the protests triggered by his refusal of Evergreen's Day of Absence bear out Hughey's argument that to not take on the stigma means to be stigmatized by the group, to paradoxically become a pariah of the group.

It has been intriguing to watch Bret Weinstein's rapid movement across the fractured political spectrum, from "deeply progressive" Bernie Sanders voter in 2017 to aligning with anti-vaxxer right-wing libertarians like Joe Rogan in 2020. It perhaps suggests that while the progressive Left reject liberalism for its dubious claims to universality and neutrality, and conservatives now move in on aspects of liberal humanism in order to frame the progressive Left as authoritarian, the egalitarian Left is losing its purchase on liberalism similarly to how it lost poverty and class to the

Trumpist reframing that we see demonstrated in Rufo's *America Lost*. Nancy Fraser's discussion of 1990s "third way" Blair and Clinton politics sees this as the rise of "progressive neoliberalism versus reactionary populism."[137]

Of course, as is the established wisdom since 2016, the rust belt that had grown out of Roosevelt's New Deal became a heartland of White resentment that tipped the Electoral College in favor of Trump. The political and philosophical corollary is the cleaving of the Left from liberal humanism, setting it adrift to be quickly pirated by what Blake Stewart calls "far-right civilizationism."[138] (Incidentally, as the article by Stewart, who is Canadian, demonstrates in its use of North American political nomenclature, referring to the Left as "liberals" seems to have served to have further confused the difference between the progressive Left and liberalism.) Stewart includes Murray's *The Madness of Crowds* as a recent example of right-wing civilizationism.[139] The blurring of aspects of liberalism and right-wing politics are also found in the IDW's Jordan Peterson's and Steven Pinker's pronouncements.[140] It seems that a secondary feature of the post-ideology politics of the Trump Effect has been a short-circuit between aspects of liberalism and right-wing politics under the guise of the "defense of Western Civilization." William Davies argues that Trumpism marks an erosion of liberalism and a diminished public trust in representative democracy, institutions of record, and expertise in favor of the "harnessing of emotional discontents."[141] Journalist Jef Rouner describes Weinstein as "a far right grifter,"[142] particularly regarding his promotion of Ivermectin and scaremongering about COVID-19 vaccines—yet Rouner then considers how a "left-leaning" liberal finds himself now aligned with the alt-Right. Rouner suggests that since around 2010, the Right have abandoned most of their values, except for low taxes, and that "especially since the election of former president Donald Trump, the one consistent right-wing position is 'whatever owns the libs.' One side of the political spectrum, especially at the regular citizen level, has firmly committed itself to eternal opposition for opposition's sake." Such are the troll-like politics of the Trump Effect. "Weinstein is a perfect example of how a 'liberal' can still become radicalized to the right," says Rouner. "[H]is story is actually very common." Rouner brings up other examples such as Laci Green, Candace Owens, and J.K. Rowling, each of whose "exile" was sparked by having clashed with an aspect of progressivism.[143]

Conclusion

Keith Whittington, Chair of the US Academic Freedom Alliance, is intellectually opposed to critical race theory but nonetheless concedes that the Right's "political discussion is less informed by engagement with serious scholarly works than by rumors of what is happening in corporate diversity training workshops."[144] Whittington draws a direct link between DiAngelo's work and Trump's Executive Order amidst the mid-2020 gear-change in the moral panic.[145] However, we must be clear that DiAngelo's notion of White fragility is not identical to critical race theory. It represents one manifestation of a field that emerged from poststructuralism fifty years ago and, like many academic fields of research around social justice, expanded into a vast, varied, and contentious intellectual space. Yet, in part due to the broad success of *White Fragility*, the persona of DiAngelo as public intellectual has emerged as the face of the field, to which numerous newspaper and online magazine articles attest. In June 2020, a month before Trump's Executive Order banning diversity and inclusion training in federal agencies in direct response to Rufo's Fox News plea, DiAngelo addressed a Democratic Caucus family discussion attended online by 184 members of Democrat Congress.[146] And Whittington—again, no fan of DiAngelo (lumping her amongst "popularisers and propagandists")—himself firmly warned against banning critical race theory, not merely because of the paradox of banning ideas in supposed defense of free speech. Amidst the 2021 panic he argued that "[w]hen professors and universities cancel entire classes dealing with the subject of race so as to avoid raising the ire of politicians, the educational mission of the university is potentially damaged. There is no reason to think that politicians can evaluate what work merits discussion on a college campus."[147]

America's Summer of '21 critical race theory moral panic is one component of a broader right-wing media scare around the "new authoritarian" Left. On Australia's Sky News, former Senator Cory Bernardi said of the Left, "these people are already rewriting history to suit themselves. They're poisoning our children's minds with harmful and damaging concepts about race and gender fluidity in schools." Bernardi warned, "for decades these totalitarians have been taking baby steps towards their final goal but now they're sprinting towards the finishing line, sensing that victory is near at hand."[148] At the same time, Tucker Carlson, in one of Fox News' numerous attacks on critical race theory, was making the off-the-cuff assertion that critical race theory "came from the universities, of course, like all bad ideas."[149] As Whittington notes in his article on critical race theory, universities have become an easy target for the Right in America: "Conservatives have often complained about the left-wing tilt of academia and been critical of universities, but in recent years they have shifted to thinking that universities are actively harmful to society."[150] In the next chapter, we will discuss the ways in which Trumpist anti-intellectualism is amplified by social media (particularly YouTube) beyond the United States, and we will turn our attention to our own local context of humanities faculties in Australian universities. Trumpism has had direct and catastrophic effects on humanities education in Australia, amidst mounting attacks by Sky News Australia, News Corp Press, conservative think-tanks, and the federal government itself. Kevin Donnelly, Senior Research Fellow at the

Australian Catholic University, warns that education "is being used to indoctrinate students with politically correct language, ideology and group think."[151] Jennifer Oriel, a regular columnist in Rupert Murdoch's *The Australian*, repeats the same MLK tropes as Carlson, with caricatures borrowed from Peterson's cast of bogeymen: "Neo-Marxists began their revolution in universities and socialism led by a new proletariat class: radical minorities . . . The left moved away from the aim of civil rights, which was equal treatment under law. Instead, it devised a system stacked against critics of the politically correct."[152] We will examine the direct and deep impacts of this toxic, anti-intellectualist perception of university education that holds enormous sway over Trumpism, and the ways in which the Trump Effect at the American "center" affects, and is in turn amplified by, the global "peripheries."

CHAPTER THREE

#cancel #woke #universities

"burn them down and start it all over again!"

A middle-aged, White American man in a hoodie appears in front of a television screen in a video overlayed with the text, "It's NOT just in colleges & university's *[sic]*." He gestures to the television behind him.

> Man: Hey guys, Dave Rubin from *The Rubin Report*—if you y'all don't follow him, y'all need to! Check this out, this is the best explanation I've seen yet!
>
> Rubin (on TV): . . .this slow march through the institutions, where they went to our colleges, our universities and they basically trained a generation of young people to believe that America is fundamentally evil. And then these ideas then leak out.[1]

This is a sixty-second TikTok video, surfacing amidst a seemingly endless stream of hyperstimulation—desperate Afghans clinging to the side of a moving US Air Force cargo plane at Kabul Airport, three young women posing for a video selfie on a night out, an angry antivax trucker in a video tagged #fuckyavaccine refusing the "poison" of the COVID-19 vaccines. The footage of Dave Rubin is from Fox News' *The Next Revolution w/Steve Hilton*, broadcast on April 5, 2021. In the full video on Fox's website, the focus of Hilton's interview with Rubin was critical race theory, discussed within a well-established Fox narrative around "wokeism's takeover of corporate America, Hollywood, Silicon Valley, and Democrat-run government at every level."[2] At that time in 2021, "woke" and "wokeism" had long since joined "political correctness" and "cancel culture" in the lexicon of the Right, and featured in a succession of moral panics around "cancel culture." A month earlier, Fox had stirred viewer indignation over the decision by the owner of the Dr. Seuss books to stop printing six of the titles. The decision was not the result of any public pressure or made by any authoritarian body; it was "a moral decision," says English professor Phillip Nel, "of choosing not to profit from work with racist caricature in it."[3] Fox hosts such as Sean Hannity nevertheless angled the story into a "cancel culture" narrative: "now the left is bent on canceling Dr Seuss. This woke cancel-culture fight-against-freedom is spiraling *way* out of control."[4]

And yet, Hilton and Rubin's warning registered as something of a shift in popular narratives around "wokeism" and "cancel culture," defining them as having diverged from the standard "canceling *Baa Baa Black Sheep*" trope[5] of which the Dr. Seuss story was an iteration. "Wokeism," warned Hilton, was "not some short-term fad . . . it's the culmination of a radical ideological movement that began in Germany in 1923, with the Frankfurt School of philosophers."[6] A few weeks later, when *Fox & Friends*' Steve Doocy interviewed parents at a school in Loudoun County, Virginia about their anger at critical race theory "infecting" their school, parent Elicia Brandy said, "I don't want critical *theory*—not just critical race theory, but critical *theory*—taught in our classrooms."[7] While Christopher Rufo had stirred up fear of critical race theory in mid-2020 with some highly-charged yet vague rhetoric ("destructive, divisive, pseudo-scientific ideology"; see also Chapter 2),[8] a year later Liz Wheeler, conservative YouTuber and former anchor of the right-wing One America News (OAN), could be heard discussing the Frankfurt School, Max Horkheimer, Antonio Gramsci, and Herbert Marcuse.[9]

To any academic scholar in a university humanities department, the mention of these names may well have seemed quite surreal. They are the names of thinkers that many of us know, whose ideas are amongst those we first learned about as undergraduates in the 1990s or earlier. For your authors, who studied art theory in Australia during the 1990s, and were fed a diet of MIT Press's *Semiotext(e)* Foreign Agent Series books by Jean Baudrillard or Paul Virilio and the now-defunct Australian art magazine *Art & Text*, critical theory was capital "T" theory. Indeed, for contemporary art internationally, *Art & Text* was important in connecting continental postmodern texts and ideas with art, with reviews of Michel Foucault's *The History of Sexuality Volume 1*,[10] Roland Barthes' newly published *Camera Lucida*,[11] and interviews with Barthes, Rosalind Krauss, and others. Importantly, it was instrumental in bringing translations of key critical theory to the English-speaking world, such as the first English language translation of Baudrillard's highly influential essay on postmodern visual culture "The Precession of the Simulacra."[12] In Australia, Baudrillard even became something of a rock-star theorist amongst artists and intellectuals, mobbed by hundreds at the 1984 Sydney *Futur*Fall* conference.[13] By the time your authors studied and researched art theory in the 1990s, post-structuralism, critical theory, and postmodernism were *the* established ideas in art theory, although we were also riding a wave of the backlash, following the rise of a return to the body and theories of affect following what Hal Foster in *Return of the Real* (1996) saw as signaling "dissatisfaction with the textualist model of culture."[14] As we grew tired of the 1980s obsession with appropriation, signification, simulation, and the death of originality—not to mention the bad pseudo-continental art writing that the original French texts inspired—critical theory became far less *de rigueur*. Yet, for artists and art theorists in the 1990s a passing knowledge of critical theorists, such as Michel Foucault, Jacques Derrida, and Jean-François Lyotard, was still deemed important. These days, these names arise only occasionally in academic discussions, and increasingly rarely over the last twenty or so years. They are, however, absolutely not names we would ever have expected to hear in the 2020s on Fox News.

Yet in 2021, the critical race theory moral panic had, for some key figures on the right, opened a pandora's box of ideas. For them, peering into the dusty library of twentieth-century critical theory may well have seemed like the thrilling uncovering of a sinister Marxist conspiracy going back a hundred years, a plan to take over the world. As Hilton explains it, introducing his Fox News interview with Rubin: "A central part of their success in capturing the levers of power, first in academia and now throughout our society, has been to capture our language. If you control language, you control thought and that is the ultimate power."[15] As an undergraduate's summary of poststructuralist critique, this would certainly rate a "pass."

Great Super-Genius

On social media, a chorus of contempt for university education has spread throughout the online right ecosphere, on YouTube and TikTok, propagating the anti-intellectualism that is a feature of Trumpist populism. And that position is met with retorts from the anti-Trumpist left, such as one American TikToker, whose personal narrative characterizes what he sees as the underlying thrust of this anti-intellectualism:

> [Trump supporters] have absolute disdain for the educated, and people that have credentials that know what they're actually talking about in [their] fields. They dream of a world where what they say matters just as much [as experts], when it doesn't. And it never has. The amount of visceral rage and this irritation I got from my family, country bumpkin relatives, whenever I graduated college you would have thought that I killed someone. "Aw, you think you're better, college boy?" Like, "no, I just know what I'm talking about in the field I studied in, whereas you don't." They dream of a world where what they have to say, without any

> knowledge, is relevant. And I hope we never get there. They're trying, they're trying so hard.[16]

While for Fox News fear has long been established as both a political radicalization model and a business strategy (as Nicole Hemmer says in *The New York Times*, "it keeps people watching"),[17] this strategy has also become important to social media. As Frances Haugen's whistleblowing on *60 Minutes* in October 2021 suggests, political radicalization is also the business model of Facebook.[18] TikTok's powerful and sophisticated algorithms take this attention economy to a whole different level, apparently favoring content that is more likely to provoke engagement, such as misinformation and dangerous content.[19] And YouTube is very much the home of the far Right and the "intellectual dark web," where Rubin, Joe Rogan, Ben Shapiro, and Bret Weinstein attract many millions of views.

Jordan Peterson is possibly one of the most influential figures of the "intellectual dark web." An "alt-right darling,"[20] he owes much of his international fame to attacking universities, particularly humanities disciplines, for being bastions of neo-Marxism and postmodernism. His video blog on YouTube has around 4 million subscribers and many of his videos have over a million views.[21] Even the 2017 video of his testimony to the Senate hearing for Bill C16 attracted millions of views.[22] The videos regularly highlight Peterson's disdain for academia, addressing topics such as "campus indoctrination,"[23] "the perilous state of the university,"[24] and "the end of universities."[25] Many of Peterson's guest interviewees are either vociferous critics of universities, such as Lindsay Shepherd and Yeonmi Park, or are drawn to comment on Peterson's characterization of universities as organs of indoctrination. At Peterson's provocation, journalist Rex Murphy, a guest in June 2021, decried, "the universities, *damn them* . . . At the humanities level, *from everything I read*, [they] are a disgrace." Railing against "postmodernism and deconstruction and all those attendant pseudo-philosophies," Murphy argued, "we've allowed secondary minds, political agents, propagandization as instruction; we have decimated the soul of the university . . . Burn them down and start it all over again!"[26] In the online right-wing ecosphere for at least the last five years, universities have been figured as dark actors in an insidious conspiracy theory.

Alternatively, Trumpism favors salt-of-the-earth, intuitive folk wisdom. In his account of the deep historical roots of this current disdain for university education, *Nervous States: How Feeling Took Over the World*, William Davies finds a strong anti-university, anti-higher-education ethos in the works of the "founding fathers" of neoliberalism, Friedrich Hayek and Milton Freedman.[27] In the neoliberal schematic, university book-learning is opposed to the honest, wholesome, and practical knowledge of the intuitive entrepreneur, which "doesn't consist of a set of findings or facts. It isn't a representation of the world, but an ability to manipulate it . . . a knowing *how*, not a knowing *that*."[28] This is an important facet of the Trump Effect,

FIGURE 3.1 During the COVID-19 outbreak, US President Donald J. Trump at the headquarters of the Centers for Disease Control and Prevention in Atlanta on March 6, 2020: "Every one of these doctors said, 'how do you know so much about this?' Maybe I have a natural ability." Photo: Hyosub Shin/Atlanta Journal-Constitution via AP via AAP.

which Trump himself frequently demonstrated throughout his presidency. For example, during his visit to the headquarters of the Centers for Disease Control and Prevention on March 6, 2020, as the COVID-19 pandemic was spinning out of control, the president boasted to the press:

> You know, my uncle was a great—he was at MIT, he taught at MIT for, I think, like a record number of years—he was a great super-genius, Doctor John Trump. I like this stuff. I really get it. People are surprised that I understand it. Every one of these doctors said, "how do you know so much about this?" Maybe I have a natural ability. Maybe I should have done that instead of running for President.[29]

This is, of course, the same president who a few weeks later promoted taking unproven pharmaceutical cures and treating COVID-19 by ingesting bleach, and who, when he had contracted the virus and recovered with the help of actual leading-edge treatments, further boasted "maybe I'm immune."[30] We have mentioned elsewhere that Bryan Walsh wrote in *Time* in 2017, "Trump's habit of making wild claims on Twitter could be especially dangerous in the event of a pandemic, when public confidence in government is critical to public safety."[31] When a pandemic did eventuate three years later, intuitive Trumpist gut wisdom evolved into global anti-vaxxer and anti-masker disinformation movements, variously denying the existence of SARS-CoV-2, denying the seriousness of COVID-19, and/or promoting horse de-worming medication as a cure, all of which have proven fatal for many of the movements' followers who were infected with the virus.

In Trump's America, public perceptions of the positive role of university education for the individual and for society saw a sharp *volte face*. Pew Research recently found that "there is an undercurrent of dissatisfaction—even suspicion—among the public about the role colleges play in society, the way admissions decisions are made and the extent to which free speech is constrained on college campuses. And these views are increasingly linked to partisanship."[32] In fact, Pew Research conducted a survey on perceptions on university education in 2015, and then a year into the Trump presidency in 2017. Amongst Republican-leaning voters, in 2015, 54 percent saw college education as positive and 37 percent as negative; whereas in 2017, 36 percent saw it as positive and 58 percent as negative, an almost complete flip between 2015 and 2017.[33] Pew notes, "[t]he increase in negative views has come almost entirely from Republicans and independents who lean Republican."[34] Moreover, 79 percent of Republicans "say professors bringing their political and social views into the classroom is a major reason why the higher education system is headed in the wrong direction," while only 17 percent of Democrats say the same.[35]

However, what we saw in 2021 was the development in the Right's narratives of a more sophisticated nexus between two well-established strands of the Trump Effect: the "anti-woke" and anti-university strands. The critical race theory moral panic drove significant elements of the "anti-woke" Right in America to take a deep dive into critical theory, evolving more sophisticated strategies beyond the rhetoric of "political correctness gone mad" and decrying "cancel culture." This growing awareness amongst the Right of critical theory is perhaps the biggest recent surprise of the Trump Effect. The increasingly sophisticated entwining of the dog-whistle narratives of "wokeism" and "harmful university education," both of which are products of the Trump years, have emerged very recently as conspiracy theory.

Of course, not far beneath the surface of the current debates is an age-old fear of intellectuals that has grown into a distrust of universities, and of the humanities in particular. We consider that the progressive Left's "wokeism," and the Right's caricature of it, owe far more to the degraded political discourse of 2020s social media (YouTube, TikTok) than to what actually occurs in university humanities departments, which, we argue, bears very little relationship to the popular narrative. This is an important aspect of the Trump Effect for us to consider in this book because, as we will argue, this degraded American culture-war politics has unwarranted and damaging impacts elsewhere in the world, far beyond the shores of the United States. The effects of Trumpism are global, and on the opposite side of the planet, in our own context of humanities in Australian universities, have led to misguided actions that have wrought significant damage.

"Woke"

"Woke" is a highly polarized term; even to use the term without scare quotes to describe contemporary social justice politics in culture implies a position in relation to, and suggesting opposition to, the progressive Left social justice movement. This has only recently become the case. In the pre-Trump world of the early to mid-2010s, "woke" was in popular use by the progressive Left in the US to self-describe a state of being aware of social injustice and actively resisting it. Yet, around the same time, the word "woke" was also emerging as an outright insult in online discussions that opposed the sometime performative expressions of social justice politics. Angela Nagle provides an account of this emergence in *Kill All Normies*, her book on online culture-war politics for a scholarly readership.[36] She cites two viral social media milestones by which this became apparent: the *Kony 2012* video about a Ugandan war criminal, and the 2016 killing of the gorilla Harambe in Cincinnati Zoo after a child had fallen into his enclosure. Cynical readings of the social media outrage focused on these incidents and others like them called into existence the pejorative terms "virtue signaling" and "clicktervism."[37] Thus, as public discourse degenerated into the polarized ideological conflict of a culture war in the early days of the Trump presidency, being "woke" rapidly transformed from an earnest call to resistance into a dog whistle for the online right-wing ecosphere.

The mass media of American movies and television series has been instrumental in the culture war around "woke" in recent years. YouTube commentators with considerable followings have launched "anti-woke" critiques of popular culture with underlying social justice messages or expressly racially diverse casts. It seems that the most inflammatory instances are those in which Hollywood has remade or reconstituted twentieth-century fan favorites in ways that seem to intentionally subvert the normativities of their original incarnations. For example, the most recent three episodes of the *Star Wars* saga were targets of the "anti-woke," particularly *Star Wars: The Last Jedi* (2017) and its character of Rose Tico, played by Vietnamese-American actor Kelly Marie Tran, the first woman of color to play a leading character in the entire series. Some attacks were unequivocally racist,[38] while others attacked what they saw as "woke" tokenism.[39] Similar criticisms have been made of other franchise reboots such as *Oceans 8* (2018), which has an all-female lead cast, and *Captain Marvel* (2019), in which the title character is played by a woman, Brie Larson, herself a frequent target of the "anti-woke." The first and one of the more notable of these attacks was the Twitter storm surrounding the 2016 remake of *Ghostbusters* with an all-female principal cast (the original 1984 version had an all-male cast). As Alissa Wilkinson notes in the left-leaning *Vox*, the casting of four women for some was "'SJW' [social justice warrior] capitulation to 'political correctness'," and the most vicious responses were reserved for African American actor Leslie Jones.[40] Indeed, it was this particular battle in the larger culture war that resulted in Milo Yiannopoulos, right-wing "provocateur" and supposedly "loveable rogue,"[41] trolling Jones to the point that Twitter permanently banned him from the platform.[42] Yiannopoulos had risen to prominence within the alt-Right in 2014 for his defense of the rightist libertarian "Gamergaters," fending off the "social justice extremism" of "woke" feminist critiques of gendered tropes in video games;[43] Wilkinson says the attacks on *Ghostbusters* were a furtherance of that fairly arcane culture battle into mainstream entertainment.

By early 2020, the word "woke" had completed its transformation in mainstream culture from an earnest awareness of social justice to a pejorative ironizing of that position. So, whereas in 2018 Tom Shillue on Fox News Radio struggled with the question of "what does 'woke' even mean?,"[44] by 2020 Tucker Carlson, Laura Ingraham, and other Fox anchors were routinely decrying "woke companies" like Disneyland "canceling" rides that relied on outdated cultural tropes. As Nick Bryant says, tracing the symbiotic evolution of the American Right since Ronald Reagan, there is a "feedback loop between the right-wing media and right-wing politics,"[45] which we see in Fox's fixation on being "anti-woke" as it likely fed into the 2021 Conservative Political Action Conference (CPAC) panel on "wokeism" in Dallas,[46] Republican Senator Josh Hawley's Tweeted "statement on the woke mob" at Simon & Schuster after they pulled out of his book contract, and Representative Matt Gaetz's Tweet "[w]e must defend our patriotic military service members against their woke leadership."[47]

One of the most important transformations during the Trump presidency was the shift of the Republican Party from a conservative establishment to a radical culture-war movement based on the organizing principle of being "anti-woke." Shortly after Trump left office, Ed Kilgore asked in *New York Magazine*, "Is 'anti-wokeness' the new ideology of the Republican Party?," quoting former Trump Press Secretary Sarah Huckabee Sanders' gubernatorial run in Arkansas in an advertisement in which she claimed she "took on the radical left, the media, and their cancel culture . . . and won!"[48] As Perry Bacon Jr. observed in the center-left *FiveThirtyEight*, "[t]alking about identity and racial issues in vague terms like cancel culture and woke is particularly important right now for the GOP."[49] In 2020, Steve Rose noted in *The Guardian* that "woke" had become weaponized by the right: "Criticising 'woke culture' has become a way of claiming victim status for yourself rather than acknowledging that more deserving others hold that status. It has gone from a virtue signal to a dog whistle. The language has been successfully co-opted."[50]

With the 2021 critical race theory moral panic, discussions around "woke culture" moved from *Star Wars*, *Dr Who*, and *Dr Seuss* to a higher-stakes game centering on the institutions of government, with Trump's executive order (see Chapter 2), and the military, with Matt Gaetz's criticism of its supposed "woke leadership." A YouTube video titled *The Origins of Woke Ideology*, released in July 2021, begins with the Thomas Sowell quote, "there are few things more dishonorable than misleading the young." A fast edited series of images is accompanied by a voiceover:

> Woke social justice ideology has turned into something like a new religious cult . . . It is common to believe that this is actually just a minor problem, and one we are now exaggerating. After all, aren't these just radicals in the university? Why should we be concerned about this ideology? Since about 2010, this new woke religion has spread into every corner of society, and started to change how we think and speak about many social issues. Woke social justice activists want us to reform the way we see every aspect of society and even reality itself.

The voiceover is interrupted with illustrative exemplars, such as footage of academic Angela Davis from UC Santa Cruz, and images of stacks of books that include Robin DiAngelo's *White Fragility* and Paulo Freire's *Pedagogy of the Oppressed*. Likening it to religion or cult, the voiceover argues that "woke" ideology has its sacred texts: "These texts, written by people like Judith Butler, Richard Delgado, Ibram X Kendi, and many more, act like scripture for the woke believers."[51]

In Australia in 2021, the book *Cancel Culture and the Left's Long March* assembled chapters by Australian Sky News pundits and right-wing populists including former Prime Minister Tony Abbott to attack "the 'quackademics' in education."[52] The book's editor, Kevin Donnelly, echoes Peterson's familiar refrain: "Education is being used to indoctrinate students with politically correct language, ideology and group think."[53] The book, however, also includes a reasonably considered brief primer on Frankfurt Marxism by Gary Marks, Marcuse, postmodernism, Hegel, dialectical materialism, and hermeneutics.[54] So, in what ways were the universities—long-established institutions of higher education and knowledge—supposedly misleading the youth?

Cynical Theories

The *Origins of Woke Ideology* video is in two parts, the first spoken by Helen Pluckrose and the second by James Lindsay (both are scripted by Travis D. Brown). Lindsay and Pluckrose, along with Peter Boghossian, have been instrumental in attacking critical theory in academia, which they see as not merely the underlying cause of "wokeism" but an existential threat to Western society and liberalism. The three were responsible for a coordinated hoax attack on humanities research in 2017 and 2018 which came to be known as the "grievance studies affair." They authored a series of bogus academic papers that "featured radically skeptical and standpoint epistemologies rooted in postmodernism, feminist and critical race epistemology rooted in critical social constructivism as well as psychoanalysis."[55] The papers were generally well-written and thoroughly referenced and demonstrated a reasonably sound understanding of across a range of fields, but the methodologies were often absurd and the interpretations and conclusions were deliberately outlandish and—being the main point—politically aligned with leftist critical theory. Importantly, Boghossian, Pluckrose, and Lindsay identify as "liberals" in the Civil Rights mould; *Areo* magazine, of which Pluckrose was editor-in-chief, says it is "committed to an ethos of universal liberal humanism" and it publishes articles that tend towards a small-L libertarianism from both the left and right sides of politics.[56] The papers they authored passed peer review in some of the top humanities academic journals, leading them to conclude that "something has gone wrong in the university—especially in certain fields within the humanities."[57] Paradoxically, as a searing critique of postmodernism, the exercise bore many of the characteristics of 1980s postmodernism in art: an ironic and bad faith appropriation of archetypes aimed at destabilizing their cultural hegemony through parody. It even mimicked the sneering, dry humor. Ultimately, however, the "grievance studies affair" was an in-joke that was so "in" that it would scarcely be understood by anyone outside of its targeted crowd of academics.

Perhaps it is for this reason that Pluckrose and Lindsay co-authored for a wider general readership *Cynical Theories: How Activist Scholarship Made Everything about Race, Gender and Identity—and Why This Harms Everybody*. Pluckrose and Lindsay make quite a considerable effort to map out for their intended "anti-woke" readership some of the complex conceptual architectures of critical theory (to which they give a capital "C" and "T"). There is a conflation between the terms "Critical Theory" and postmodernism, which is characteristic of the critiques by Peterson and Stephen R.C. Hicks that preceded *Cynical Theories*, echoed also in Douglas Murray's *The Madness of Crowds*. Nonetheless, Pluckrose and Lindsay demonstrate an impressive grasp of a vast field of theory that can be punishingly dense, and convincingly identify common structures underlying postmodernism and much of the critical theory they later discuss.[58] The book is clearly intended as a partisan and cynical reading of the historical development of critical theory, particularly with regard to language as the site of the social construction of identity for the maintenance of tyrannical power hierarchies in the more identitarian fields of critical theory that emerged in the 1990s.

Strangely and in spite of itself, *Cynical Theories* provides an excellent series of summaries of select domains of critical theory and select strands within them, expressed and structured with refreshing clarity. It is ironic that theorists whose writings are notoriously dense, convoluted, and difficult to read and comprehend, such as Jacques Derrida, are captured so succinctly and effectively in an attempt to read against them. It is one of the many ironies of *Cynical Theories* that, in intending to disarm French deconstructive theory through demystifying it, this partisan reframing re-presents many of its arguments with seductive clarity. Moments redolent of Stockholm syndrome briefly punctuate the book's reading-against-the-grain of critical theory. Any co-authored book (such as this one you are reading) tends to have inconsistencies in its voice and approach, and *Cynical Theories* betrays what seem to be Pluckrose's more sympathetic framings of critical theory and the more cutting and instrumental approach of Lindsay, a mathematics PhD.

In a nutshell, Pluckrose and Lindsay argue that the liberal/social democratic idea of social justice has given way to a capital "S-J-M" "Social Justice Movement" which is less concerned with tangible progress through liberal humanism than with engaging in performative, virtue-signaling, authoritarian "wokeism", wherein people are pilloried for minor missteps, problematic utterances, decade-old Tweets, or association with anyone already ostracized,[59] and wherein media and art are scrutinized for their discursive power dynamics.[60] Pluckrose and Lindsay declare their adherence to principles of universal humanism and liberalism,[61] while, they argue, "far-left progressive social crusaders portray themselves as the sole and righteous champions of social and moral progress."[62] *Cynical Theories* argues that "identity politics," "political correctness," and "cancel culture" are manifestations of the Social Justice Movement[63] and—using the same evocative word as does Rubin—all this has "leaked" out of the universities[64] where it originated, mutating from twentieth-century postmodern theory, or "Theory."[65] Postmodernism, they argue, has "given rise to one of the least tolerant and most authoritarian ideologies that the world has had to deal with since the decline of communism and the collapse of white supremacy and colonialism."[66]

A Caricature of Postmodernism

What do they mean by "postmodernism"? Specifically, they mean humanities critical theory that is built upon the mid-twentieth-century Marxism of Antonio Gramsci, Max Horkheimer and the Frankfurt School, and the New Left, that then later evolved through the social constructionism of poststructuralist thinkers, particularly Michel Foucault, Jacques Derrida, and Jean-François Lyotard. This period, Pluckrose and Lindsay argue, can be understood as the first wave of postmodernism, that sometimes playfully proposed that the self and the world it understands are ultimately constructed socially, primarily in language. They argue, quite correctly, that it is in the work of Foucault that "power and knowledge become inextricably entwined" as "power-knowledge."[67] Certainly, Foucault's thinking is vital in establishing the principle in much theory thereafter that power is not something one possesses, but that it operates within the social relationships between us. *Cynical Theories* reserves some begrudging veneration for Foucault.

tyrannical structure of the patriarchy army oppressors. It's, like, I'm not making this stuff up. It's embedded right in the theory."[81] Dion Kagan in *The Monthly* says, "*Cynical Theories* isn't quite Jordan Peterson-level caricature of postmodernism, but it is certainly fixated on the French deconstructionists. The likes of Wendy Brown, Nancy Fraser, Slavoj Žižek, Alain Badiou, and Giorgio Agamben, for example (and an entire generation of more recent thinkers who tend to argue for the existence of truth and whose work is deeply informed by postmodern ideas), don't rate a mention."[82]

In fact, the underlying architecture of both *The Madness of Crowds* and *Cynical Theories* echoes an earlier book which Peterson says he "liked quite a bit,"[83] and has clearly influenced his own understanding of postmodernism Stephen R.C. Hicks' *Explaining Postmodernism*.[84] Shuja Haider describes Hicks as "an acolyte of Ayn Rand,"[85] who remains a central thinker in the rightist libertarian canon. So, unsurprising Hicks provides a similarly cynical explanation of postmodernism that fixates on Foucault. Somewhat oddly, Hicks characterizes Foucault as a Marxist,[86] which also seeps into Peterson's understandings. Similarly, references to the work of Richard Rorty are another curious shared gene baked into the Hicks-derived caricature of postmodernism shared by Peterson, and Pluckrose and Lindsay. Rorty was important enough, but certainly not a central figure in 1980s postmodernism, and it is curious that he reappears time and again as one of the intellectual dark web's key po-mo villains. Haider has pointed out that Peterson's *12 Rules for Life* warns of the postmodern ideas of Derrida and Foucault, but "armed with this dubious secondary source [Hicks' *Explaining Postmodernism*], Peterson is left making statements that are not only mired in factual error, but espouse a comically reductive conception of how social life and history work."[87] We notice that echo chambers are not confined to social media.

Spreading the Word

At this point, a reasonable reader may wonder why should this arcane academic quarrel matter? What consequence could it possibly have for the *real* world beyond ivory tower navel-gazing?[88] The answer, for *Cynical Theories*, comes in its second to last chapter, with a foreboding echoed in Rufo's moral panic around critical race theory and Rubin's warning on Fox News that "these ideas then leak out."[89] "Theory has broken the bounds of academia," warn Pluckrose and Lindsay, "and exerts a profound influence on our culture."[90] Having carefully built the narrative that 2020s "wokeism" is the bastard child of Foucault, they promise that "we will endeavour to convince you that what is happening in universities is a genuine problem, that these [conflicts over academic theory] are impacting the real world."[91] And, what is "a good case study" to demonstrate this for *Cynical Theories*? It is the same "case study" to which Murray dedicates several pages in *The*

Madness of Crowds, and has been discussed at length on Peterson's YouTube channel: the Evergreen Affair.[92] We discussed the Evergreen Affair in Chapter 2, which has become something of an ongoing rallying point for the anti-university Right, thrusting Bret Weinstein center stage and a frequent topic on Weinstein's own *Dark Horse* channel.[93] So much raw video material is available on YouTube on the Evergreen Affair that it is a readily accessible *cause célèbre*. However, what to *us* appears primarily to be issues of institutional leadership and implementation of corporate human resources policy, functions as frequent culture-war cannon fodder to these aforementioned discussants. Apparently, Evergreen proves that "wokeism" and "cancel culture" have leaked like a virus from the perverse, experimental, social laboratory of universities: "There is a one-word answer to how this could have happened: Theory," *Cynical Theories* says.[94]

When *Cynical Theories* was initially published in early 2020, before Rufo began to harness Fox News conservatism into its campaign on critical race theory, it attracted the modest levels of interest that one might expect for a book about critical theory thirty years after its academic heyday. A potential scholarly audience might have regarded its topic as "old hat," while a potential general readership might have struggled with the arcane ideas of critical theory, had there been little to drive their desire to know more about it. Yet by July 2021 it was number 1 in Amazon's Best Sellers list in the category "Philosophy & Social Aspects of Education" (the audio book was number 2 and Kindle version number 11).[95]

At first publication, Pluckrose and Lindsay made some promotional appearances for the book on the rightist libertarian YouTube circuit—with Rogan, Weinstein, and the like—where it would no doubt find its most sympathetic hearing. However, as the 2021 critical race theory moral panic hit fever pitch, the right's eagerness to understanding this narrative gained sudden urgency and *Cynical Theories* found a new audience amongst the same readership who may well have also rushed to buy DiAngelo's *White Fragility* to read against-the-grain. On February 20, 2021, Lindsay appeared with Christopher Rufo and Allie Beth Stuckey on *The Rubin Report* on YouTube, discussing the "Critical Race Theory War" that was just starting to heat up.[96] By mid-2021 Lindsay, notably more so than Pluckrose, took to spruiking not just the arguments but the "anti-woke" cause of *Cynical Theories* on right-wing YouTube, such as on *Classically Abbey*, the channel of Abigail Shapiro (sister of Ben)[97] and on Tim Pool's *Timcast*.[98] When he returned to *The Rubin Report* in June 2021, Rubin praised him: "You seem to be the main guy covering critical race theory, you've been warning about it forever. You're taking the heat for doing so."[99] Lindsay's *New Discourses* podcasts and YouTube channel are also popular, a nearly four-hour podcast on the Hegelian Dialectic's relationship to "woke" culture has attracted hundreds of thousands of views.[100] Lindsay's April 2021 video "What is Critical Race Theory?" for the conservative YouTube channel PragerU received over 1.5 million views in its first three months.[101] In August 2021,

Lindsay was addressing the conservative Young America's Foundation national conference.[102]

Lindsay, a committed atheist and author of *Everybody Is Wrong About God* (2015), also made appearances on more niche Christian conservative channels such as Stuckey's *BlazeTV* podcast[103] and evangelist Pastor Rick Brown's YouTube channel in July 2021,[104] leading to a guest appearance at Godspeak Calvary Chapel in Thousand Oaks. Here, Lindsay warned:

> The way that they are going to achieve the infection of institutions is by, especially in the university, training people in critical consciousness to make them think this way—to think in critical theory—and then have them go out into institutions and slowly take positions of leadership, and slowly turn those things from within.[105]

Cynical Theories was thereafter cited in Christian sermons condemning critical theory:[106] "From start to finish critical theory is an unrelenting, unremitting attack upon all traditional institutions and traditional norms, as a result Marxist critical theory brings about much self-hate and cultural pessimism in the population that is under attack."[107]

The Woke Conspiracy

In considering the wider context of QAnon in Chapter 1, we discussed what Richard Hofstadter calls "the paranoid style" in American politics.[108] To reiterate, Hofstadter argues that paranoia about nefarious conspiracies is knitted into the fabric of American political life, since the very early days of the Republic. It persists as a cultural tendency in American politics and the basis of its worldview is that a hostile and often invisible enemy within is at work, "directed against a nation, a culture, a way of life."[109] Hofstadter says that "the feeling of persecution is central" to the paranoid style and that it "is indeed systematized in grandiose theories of conspiracy."[110] For the Trumpist Right, critical theory is driving the newly-uncovered "woke conspiracy," an existential threat to the United States and its way of life that has even America's military elite reading Marx and Mao. Whereas QAnons believe that "the world is run by Satanic pedophile cannibals who trade children as currency and literally skin babies to make shoes out of,"[111] the "woke conspiracy" thesis in books such as *Cynical Theories* and *The Madness of Crowds* argues that a cabal of academic evil geniuses are taking over America's culture and institutions by bending language to catch-out ordinary honest folk. In 2021, that fringe thesis went mainstream when Fox News' Steve Hilton cautioned his conservative audience about the "Frankfurt School of philosophers",[112] and Liz Wheeler likewise warned of the Frankfurt School and that critical theory "isn't really a *theory* at all, it's actually a tactic used, with the intention at least, to start a Marxist revolution."[113] The critical theory panic is yet another ideologically driven guided gamification, the Right's new "choose your own adventure" doomsday rabbit hole.

In 2021, the American Right's vague disdain for universities acquired a new sense of urgency, after seemingly lifting the thin veil of university education to reveal a festering, creeping, slow Marxist revolution that is finally reaching crisis point and about to upend traditional American values and common sense. And, just like revelations about satanic pedophiles secretly running Hollywood and the Democratic party, or conspiracy between Bill Gates and big pharma to inject the world's population with nanochips, the only way to reliably uncover the terrifying "truth" is to "do your *own* research" into this sinister critical theory.

In Chapter 1, we argued that QAnon's conspiracy theory formed through engaging a mega-archive of information with a "paranoid epistemology," in which official accounts, authoritative facts, and expert consensus are presumed by their very officiality to be suspect, while discredited evidence, random relationships, and outliers are presumed reliable due to their exclusion from officiality.[114] Peterson, Murray, Pluckrose and Lindsay engage in a different kind of paranoid epistemology: rather than privileging discredited outlier sources and disdaining experts, as QAnon does, the "woke conspiracy" thesis regards academics as secretive, duplicitous, and ultimately out to harm society. However, this "woke conspiracy" thesis likewise relies on a particular kind of apophenia, seeing meaningful conspiratorial connections within what is actually an almost-inconceivably expansive mass of critical theory literature developed over fifty years. Similarly to QAnon foot-soldiers, otherwise disempowered and disenfranchised patriots, armed once again with Google and YouTube, can connect the dots between Hegelian dialectics, Foucauldian analytics of power, Marcuse's repressive tolerance, DiAngelo's *White Fragility*, and the canceling of Dr Seuss and the all-female *Ghostbusters* movie, outsmarting and exposing the world's supposedly most intelligent and certainly diabolical Marxist elites, for no less a noble cause than to save America. And the world. But where exactly can good patriots fight this insidious invader from within?

Australia: Burning to Boredom

Kian Kogan notes that that the original subtitle of *Cynical Theories* (*How Activist Scholarship Made Everything about Race, Gender, and Identity—and Why This Harms Everybody*) was changed for the Australian market: "'Activist Scholarship' has been replaced with 'Universities'. It's a minor enough change, but it certainly makes it clear who is to blame."[115] In early 2021, an Australian book *Cancel Culture and the Left's Long March* was published, following very much in the footsteps of *Cynical Theories* a year before, which it cites.[116] *Cancel Culture* is an edited anthology of chapters by some of Australia's most prominent mainstream conservatives, many of whom are frequent commentators on the Rupert Murdoch-owned Sky News Australia. In Australia, Sky occupies a cultural and political space similar to Fox News' in the US. It does not have the reach into middle Australia that Fox does into middle America (although that is about to change with a syndication deal for regional television), but its on-screen stalwarts are important figures of the mainstream Right in Australian politics: Peta Credlin (former Chief of Staff to right-wing former Prime Minister Tony Abbott), Andrew Bolt (an anchor prosecuted in 2011 for breaching the Racial Discrimination Act), and until late 2021 Alan Jones (a former radio shock-jock with a decades-long track record of controversy, climate denial and, recently, COVID conspiracism).

Cancel Culture includes Credlin and Abbott, as well as many of Sky's guest commentators such as Kevin Donnelly (the book's editor), Jennifer Oriel, and Anthony Dillon, and it retains Sky's dogmatic tone. Donnelly claims that "[e]ducation is being used to indoctrinate students with politically correct language, ideology and group think";[117] Fiona Mueller asserts that "postmodernist literary theory, and writing instruction based on text types (genre theory), [are] just a few examples of the anti-intellectualism and duplicitous movements that found their way into schooling during the last century";[118] Oriel propounds that "[i]n the place of the civilising campus has come the banal, brutalising education of the revolutionary college."[119] *Cancel Culture* lacks the sophistication of *Cynical Theories*, and its earnest claims to a liberal humanist foundation, but the underlying message is the same in this Australian variant. "Cancel culture represents the consolidation of illiberal tendencies in Western universities, media and law," argues Oriel. "What began as political correctness in the 1990s has developed into the regime of thought control so oppressive that it is codified in law and higher education policy across the West."[120]

Cancel Culture's arguments echo Peterson's caricature of universities, using the terms "political correctness," "the cultural-left," "cultural Marxism," "neo-Marxism," and "postmodernism," and also in bemoaning the decline of the fineries of Western high civilization: "In today's postmodern, new-age classroom SMS messaging, graffiti, movie posters, and computer games are on the same footing as Shakespeare's plays and the novels of Jane Austen and David Malouf,"[121] in universities' transformation "from education to enstupidation," as Mueller puts it.[122] It is a familiar narrative, that "Neo-Marxists began their revolution in universities and socialism," devising "a system stacked against critics of the politically correct."[123] And as Oriel argues, of course, "the humanities was remade in the image of a new ideology called neo-Marxism."[124] The problem, we are told, is that the humanities and their century-long conspiracy of critical theory have cooked up Marxist ideas for manipulating culture to gain "total control of society," and the final process is now underway.[125] And the proof is in the parlous state of free speech on campuses in Australia, they argue.[126] Mueller quotes an Australian lecturer as saying, "[t]he idea that university campuses are places of free speech and robust debate is a joke."[127] So, what evidence is there of this?

In the UK, right-leaning libertarian website *Spike* published a UK Free Speech University Ranking from 2016 to 2019, ranking UK universities as "Red: has actively censored speech or expression," "Amber: has chilled speech or expression through excessive regulation," and "Green: has not restricted or regulated speech or expression."[128] Their 2018 audit, for example, found that 54 percent of universities were red, 40 percent amber, and only 6 percent green.[129] As Nesrine Malik says, with tongue in cheek, "[t]he only conclusion to be drawn from the data was that there was a plague of free speech suppression."[130] *Spike*'s audit of free speech was extremely misleading and its methodology dubious, basing a red or amber rating on the existence of run-of-the-mill corporate HR policies that seek to ban hate speech, which *Spike* frames as "excessive regulation."[131] It is a similar measure to that used by Oriel in *Cancel Culture* to argue that "[s]everal Australian universities regulate speech by providing language guidelines," such as "Curtin University in Western Australia provides Inclusive Language Procedures,"[132] in actuality a half-page policy document stating merely that staff and students take all reasonable steps to avoid bias and stereotyping.[133] The UK Government's fourth report on Freedom of Speech in Universities, covering the same period and under a Conservative government, suggests that *Spike*'s audit is "whipping-up 'moral panic'," and finds that the "widespread view [was] that free speech was not overly inhibited and that it was valued by students."[134] It concludes,

> press accounts of widespread suppression of free speech are clearly out of kilter with reality. During our inquiry, we have heard first hand from all the key players in the university setting, including students, student society and student union representatives, vice-chancellors and university administration staff. A large amount of evidence suggests that the narrative that "censorious students" have created a "free speech crisis" in universities has been exaggerated.[135]

Malik says of *Spike*'s audit, "the data simply does not hold up," citing examples such as a university being ranked "red" because it banned on-campus advertising to students of legal, yet usurious and exploitative, companies that trade in pay-day loans. Malik also points out that *Spike*'s audit received significant funding from the right-wing Charles Koch Foundation.[136]

Similarly to *Spike*, Australia's Institute of Public Affairs (IPA), a right-wing "think-tank," has published an annual audit in recent years, each authored by Matthew Lesh.[137] Each year it has used headlines such as "University Audit Finds Humanities Riddled with Critical Race Theory and Identity Politics"[138] and "Free Speech Crisis at Australia's Universities Confirmed by New Research" (referring in both cases to its own report).[139]

Large portions of the text from the 2018 "audit" are reproduced verbatim from its 2017 version: "Since the previous Audit, Monash University has become Australia's first to introduce trigger warnings in formal university policy, and there is growing usage of trigger warnings on official university websites"[140] appears in 2017 and 2018. In the 2018 audit, 12 of the 96 footnotes reference the author's own work or his media appearances on *The Alan Jones Breakfast Show* and Sky News Australia.[141] Just as lazily, the IPA's report reproduces *Spike*'s Red/Amber/Green ranking—predictably finding a paucity of "green" and a high yield of "red," since its measure of restricted speech is largely corporate HR policies like that of Curtin University, above. ABC Australia's Katharine Gelber points out that this measure is "unsupportable, especially when measured against the evidence of the extent to which universities do protect academic and intellectual freedom."[142]

The 2018 report is "error-ridden and incorrect,"[143] and ideologically loaded with US culture-war politics. Taking content directly from the US context of the "Chicago statement"[144] and the Goldwater Institute's "model legislation," the IPA makes recommendations to the Australian Government, such as to "require a university to have a standalone policy that clearly protects free expression, invalidating policies that limit free expression,"[145] and that this be directly linked to the government's support of universities.[146] The IPA audits are a clear example of the Trump Effect and the way it spreads and mutates in contexts outside of the United States, for instance in the dog-whistling in the following passage:

> A social justice university is one with a specific ideological purpose, to "improve" society towards a predefined outcome using certain methods. It is a university that tells students not to try to understand the world, but to be activists who try to change the world. From the social justice perspective, following in the footsteps of French social theorist Michel Foucault, knowledge is power and there is no objective truth.[147]

The Australian Government's commissioned *Report of the Independent Review of Freedom of Speech in Australian Higher Education Providers*, known as the French Review after its main author, Robert French, was clearly in response to the IPA, dedicating three pages in response to IPA audits.[148] As in the UK government's report, the French Review found that the handful of incidents reported by the IPA "do not establish a systemic pattern" by universities that is "adverse to freedom of speech," but conceded that "even a limited number of incidents seen as affecting freedom of speech may have an adverse impact on public perception of the higher education sector."[149] Evidently to appease the perception of a right-wing think-tank and commentators in the Murdoch-owned news media, the Review recommended codification of freedom of expression in a "model code."[150] In the Australian context, the call to "burn them down and start it all over again" seemed to have lost its edge and ended in the dreary, bureaucratic fizzle of individual university committees adopting aspects of the code into the existing policies.[151] That is, until the advent of COVID-19.

Defund the Thought Police

Since radical reforms to Australian tertiary education from the late 1980s into the 1990s, universities have shifted from following a free, public-good model to an increasingly corporate model. This has meant steadily decreasing Australian Government support for university places, students paying more and accumulating increasing personal debt, and institutions making up the shortfall by tapping into the lucrative "international student" market. In some Australian universities, international full-fee-paying students constituted 48 percent of the student body.

Then COVID-19 reached Australia. Those international students who had entered Australia before the commencement of the 2020 academic year were told by then Prime Minister Scott Morrison via a press conference to "go home,"[152] and Australia's border remained closed to international visitors for the next two years. The impact on Australian universities was devastating. Morrison, who leads the Australian Government via the center-right Liberal Party in coalition with the right-wing National Party, came to the rescue with the innocuous-sounding Higher Education Support Amendment (Job-Ready Graduates and Supporting Regional and Remote Students) Bill 2020. In Australian universities, a large portion of tuition fees are covered by the government, and these fees have generally reflected the cost of resourcing the different courses. However, the new Bill radically re-allocated the government portion, massively defunding degrees in the humanities, society and culture, and journalism—sending a "price signal." The Bill is now law, meaning that students gaining humanities degrees are saddled with more than double their previous debt.[153]

Only two years earlier, the same government had intervened to block eleven Australian Research Council (ARC) grants, all in humanities disciplines, worth A$4.2 million, the Minister Tweeting "I'm pretty sure most Australian taxpayers preferred their funding to be used for research other than spending $223,000 on projects like 'Post orientalist arts of the Strait of Gibraltar'."[154] And when the Australian Government proposed to defund degrees in the humanities, society and culture, and journalism, Adam Creighton at the Murdoch-owned newspaper *The Australian* wrote an article titled, "Want to study Foucault? Don't expect a cent," beginning with "[i]f tearing down statues is the thanks taxpayers get from tipping millions into critical theory courses, it's about time we stop chipping in," and including images of the statues of Captain James Cook and Robert the Bruce that were vandalized during Black Lives Matter protests.[155] Creighton repeats sentiments shared by Lindsay that humanities departments should actually be shut down: "These departments can continue to do what they want to do, but outside of the university system."[156] Creighton's article, triumphant at the government's plans to defund the humanities, suggests that "graduates in queer and diversity studies" struggle to get jobs and repay their student loans, and that humanities students "leave university angry, narrow-minded, and unemployed, and obsessed with viewing everything through the simplistic prism of race, sexuality and gender." He further repeats the now-familiar Hicks-Peterson-Murray-Pluckrose-Lindsay-Donnelly-Oriel refrain, "the Left lost the economic arguments comprehensively when the Soviet Union collapsed, but their rear guard action in the academy has been highly successful."[157]

In reality, the humanities departments in the universities in which your authors work produce research on topics as diverse as building environmentally sustainable living, understanding the cultures of online extremism that radicalize disillusioned young men to commit violent real-world acts, and implementation of audio-described television for the hearing impaired. Much of this research does draw on critical theorists—including Foucault—in ways that are widely divergent from the caricature of "neo-Marxism" and "postmodernism" propounded by right-wing pundits. Janna Thompson, discussing *Cynical Theories*, says that

> the most problematic aspect of Pluckrose and Lindsay's book is the blame it heaps on humanities departments of universities for stirring up a cancel culture and the culture wars. This gives ammunition to those who want to defund humanities and discourage students from taking humanities courses. It gives support to the position of the Australian Federal Education Minister, Dan Tehan, who thinks that Australian universities have succumbed to a left-wing culture that "cancels" conservatives and their opinions.[158]

Truly, while the culture war narrative about universities and "woke ideology" might feed into the "outrage" business model of Fox News and the attention economy models of Facebook, YouTube, and TikTok, monetizing contempt towards experts and university education and providing yet another conspiracy for the "anti-woke" Right to unpick in the next development of paranoid American politics, this bears little relation to what actually happens on university campuses. In the US, Keith Whittington, Chair of America's Academic Freedom Alliance, says:

> Unfortunately, universities have become an easy target for American conservatives. Conservatives have often complained about the left-wing tilt of academia and been critical of universities, but in recent years they have shifted to thinking that universities are actively harmful to society. Unsurprisingly, such attitudes tend to translate into public policy. Republicans have become increasingly bold in interfering with university governance and attacking university endowments.[159]

Similarly, Canadian academic Jeffrey Sachs, writing for the left-leaning libertarian Niskanen Center, says:

> Whipped up into a populist fervor, politicians from across the country [US] are rushing to pass ill-conceived bills that would restrict student protests, abolish tenure, and even cut off federal funding for specific universities. Coming at a time when public support for higher education is already low (both financially and in terms of popular approval), this is a distressing trend. Meanwhile, a new breed of grifters has emerged that only seem interested in campus free speech to the extent that it can be monetized, weaponized, or used to "trigger the libs".[160]

Far beyond the US, the sum effect in Australia is that humanities degrees have been priced out of reach of students from low-income families by a "price signal." At the same time, initiatives such as the Ramsay Centres are being established by private donations at some Australian universities for expressly conservative ideological purposes.

The Trump Effect

Again, this "woke" conspiracy narrative around universities illustrates a core aspect of The Trump Effect: how Trumpism resonates from its epicenter in the heartlands of the United States out towards the relative peripheries of the world, such as Australia. Like a global tsunami, it spreads outwards as well as draws back to the center; it transforms to fit the local political conditions of the peripheries, creating bewildering effects that precede any widespread knowledge at that periphery of the US culture war from which it has spread. As the Morrison government in Australia sent its "price signal" against the humanities, much of the Australian public who had not been paying attention to America's civil culture war were unaware of the specific politics being channeled into the local context. Meanwhile, Australian culture warriors, such as Senator Pauline Hanson, leader of the right-wing One Nation party, passed a motion with the support of the government calling for the government to eject critical race theory from the national education curriculum—even though CRT is not in the curriculum. The motion could have no actual effect but, as Kishor Napier-Raman writes in *Crikey*, it "was a valuable bit of culture war theatrics" at the periphery,[161] further reifying and reinforcing the "global spread" of Fox News' moral panic, lending the bogeyman ever-greater international substance. The Trump Effect is self-amplifying as it resonates from center to periphery and back again: the periphery is thus vital to the Trump Effect, both reflecting and producing its world-creating potency.

We have heard much about the supposed impact of the ideas of the Frankfurt School but little about the profound impacts of the Montpellier

Society on universities in Australia; and yet neoliberalism, which has turned universities from a public good to corporate enterprises, has most severely impacted higher education. Milton Friedman dedicates an entire chapter to education and universities in his highly influential 1962 book *Capitalism and Freedom*. He concludes that universities are good for "training youngsters for citizenship," but that governments should limit their subsidies to "a kind that is desirable to subsidize."[162] And as Davies suggests, appearing "implicitly in much of the Hayekian agenda is [the idea] that traditional universities are a type of cartel, which conspire against the public by asserting their right to control the facts."[163] Since the beginnings of neoliberalism, public funding of university education has been resented for going beyond technical training by aiming to develop critical thinking based on rational approaches to knowledge. It is a convenient extension of this narrative to position the criticality of universities as nefariously propagating ideological indoctrination. It is galling for academics that they are attacked for this supposed indoctrination at a moment when their jobs are more vulnerable than ever as a result of corporate austerity and forced redundancies "due to COVID-19." In our context in Australia, universities are operated as corporations, led by the American model.[164] Face-to-face teaching time has gradually reduced, and semesters have progressively gotten shorter, or become trimesters that allow students to complete a degree quicker by completing three "semesters" in one year. Academic staff experience increasing teaching, supervision, and administration demands on their time, with less time that can be allocated to researching and writing the kinds of papers that the "grievance studies affair" would suggest is central to what we do. In fact, since the heyday of poststructuralist theory in the humanities in the 1980s, humanities course content has tended less and less towards theory of any kind. The economic and time demands on students in their daily lives compete with study demands, and rather than the radicalized social justice warrior meme propagated by the right, students in the 2020s seem to be more disengaged with their tuition and spending less time on campus. The realities of universities and humanities departments would be unrecognizable to anyone watching Fox News, *Joe Rogan Experience*, or *The Rubin Report*. The Trumpist bogeyman of Marxist humanities academics engaged in a century-long march through the university, indoctrinating impressionable young minds with critical theory so that they can be deployed "undercover" in corporate America, Hollywood, Silicon Valley, government, and elsewhere is a paranoid conspiracy. Rather than a radicalization of academia and the humanities that has spread like a disease into mainstream society to erode its liberal fabric, Western societies have seen four decades of economic rationalism and smaller government.

In a 2020 paper, as "woke" was transforming into a pejorative term, Akane Kanai and Rosalind Gill discussed the relationship between "woke" and neoliberalism, using the term "'woke' to signify *the corporate extraction of value from the struggles for recognition led by historically oppressed populations*."[165] Kanai and Gill's twist on "woke" sees it as separate from social justice (as Pluckrose and Lindsay also see it), but also unrelated to scholarship; they focus on its more recent development as a public relations exercise and performance by "highly paid white men," creating "a veneer of radical politics, especially around gender, race and sexuality," which "is put to work through woke capitalism in the current moment as a response to capitalist crisis."[166] Drawing from Stuart Hall's analysis of Thatcherism, they argue "that much of the work of synthesising neoliberalism's contradictory elements must be done by subjects via affective attachments to particular identities,"[167] and that "a good neoliberal subject" foregrounds what they *feel* rather than *do*.[168] We, too, in our previous book, have explored these ideas in relation to "trauma art" and Slavoj Žižek's notion of the "interpassive." The performance of a political posture has an affective pay-off, more important than it effecting any actual change. This is the root of what many on the right condemn as "virtue signaling." Kanai and Gill do not use that term, but one example they cite is the 2018 Pepsi "protest" TV advertisement featuring Kendall Jenner. They conclude that "woke" capitalism essentially exploits historically marginalized populations by performatively raising their visibility without committing any action towards dismantling the actual oppressions they reference.[169]

A further step, perhaps to some extent in response to this phenomenon in broader culture, is the corporate HR manifestation of a "woke capitalism" of the kind that seems to have been at play in the Evergreen Affair (see Chapter 2). If it bore any relationship to activist scholarship it is now quite distanced from it, and its concepts and language have lost much in translation, becoming decomplexified and corporatized "weasel words." In this kind of misinterpretation, managerial classes refer to minorities as "diverse people"[170] as though individuals are themselves "diverse," rather than "diversity" actually meaning variations within a group. This corporate managerial "woke" terminology is neoliberal, pseudo-political corporate posturing. As the Evergreen Affair showed, universities can also be victims of this corporate simulacrum of social justice. If there is any substance to the notion that university curricula are becoming increasingly "woke," it is perhaps because administrators in leadership positions, who have usually chosen bureaucracy and policy over scholarship, are leading the charge. While some of the ideas and language may have once emerged from academic scholarship, they have long since mutated into box-ticking jargon of the managerial class.

This capture of "leftist" politics by neoliberal corporatism and managerialism is yet another instance within the broader frame of the Trump Effect: that is, post-ideological politics primarily focused on rhetorical posturing—a performance or wearing of politics as style, of politics *as* culture—comprising a culture war in the US which has spread throughout the world, and returns to the US further amplified. For academics in the humanities, what does it mean to have the conceptual tools for understanding culture enlisted into a culture war? How does it impact notions of discursive power, to have Foucault and his ideas as players within that discourse? For many theorists, there arises an urge to defend "postmodernism"—which would be more accurately characterize as poststructuralism—from the Right's attack, despite having long ago rejected it ourselves for a wholly different range of reasons. One final irony worth noting here is that the Right is affording these ideas far greater political meaning and influence than they ever had in academia. Possibly every academic harbors the narcissistic dream that their research will have "impact," that they are engaging not just in chin-rubbing theorizing but in boot-wearing praxis wherein new ideas will shake and shape the world. Finally, our message is out there, being widely misread.

CHAPTER FOUR

Our Past But Not Our Past

"Statue Wars" and Contemporary Art

The most recent episode of the "Statue Wars" began just months before Donald J. Trump announced his run for president, in 2015, with the *Rhodes Must Fall* movement at the University of Cape Town in South Africa, and the removal of a statue to British imperialist Cecil Rhodes.[1] A few months later, students at Oxford University in England demanded the removal of Rhodes' statue at Oriel College and changes to university curriculum that would move beyond the Western-centric canon. Yet it was 2020—the final year of the Trump presidency—that saw the climax of the "Statue Wars," the result of a world-wide movement centered on the performative removal of the public aesthetic expressions of Whiteness. As we discussed in Chapter 2, 2020 was a year in which history seemed to be unfolding—and unravelling—at a rapid pace, while the whole world was paradoxically being brought to a standstill with lockdowns and border closures to slow the outbreak of COVID-19. During 2020, sparked by the murder of George Floyd, the Black Lives Matter protests in the US highlighted the anachronism in the twenty-first century of maintaining monuments to White colonialists. Protests spread globally, often in open defiance of lockdown orders. In the US, statues of Christopher Columbus were beheaded, and others of confederate General Robert E. Lee were removed. In the UK, a statue of seventeenth-century slave trader Edward Colston was toppled by a crowd and thrown into the harbor in Bristol; this event grew into a "topple the racists" movement. Similar movements emerged in Canada, New Zealand, Germany, and Australia, where protesters were questioning whether colonial monuments—standing prominently in towns and cities—should remain.[2] Fierce debates surrounding historical representation and the troubling legacies captured in monuments highlighted the shifting public sentiments over monuments that symbolize the rhetoric of colonialism and white supremacy.[3] In the second decade of the twenty-first century, public monuments and statues have become lightning rods for significant political conflict.[4]

In our final three chapters, we pull focus from the broader visual culture of the Trump Effect to concentrate more directly on the ways in which contemporary art can re-conceptualize the present in ways that radically reframe the kinds of political deadlocks that feature in our first three chapters. In this fourth chapter, we consider recent works whose political and conceptual interventions draw our attention to deeper historical temporalities, yet bring us back to the present in ways that are sometimes jarring and disruptive. Moreover, each of the contemporary art examples we discuss includes varying degrees of performance and performative politics. Following this chapter, we discuss the notion of the political strongman authoritarian—personified by leaders such as Vladimir Putin, Viktor Orban, Recep Tayyip Erdogan, Xi Jinping, and Donald Trump—and the ways in which contemporary art works have adopted elements of performance in a strategic overidentification with the strongman. Our focus in that chapter is on Slovenia's Janez Janša, a conspiracy theorist and Balkan Trump. And in our final chapter we circle back to Capitol Hill on the afternoon of January 6, 2021, and our radical re-reading of the riot as a form of delegated performance. To reiterate the point, we made in our Introduction, we look to art not with the expectation that its public exhibition can intervene in some direct way, through mobilizing audiences to act; indeed, our previous book *Images of War in Contemporary Art* is resistant to that particular expectation of art. Rather, as we see in this chapter, contemporary art sometimes presents productively disruptive and counter-intuitive ways of conceptualizing the present.

In this fourth chapter, we address the ways in which contemporary art engages the complexities of the post-ideological condition of the Trump Effect through strategies that attempt to bring to account a deeper historical frame. The final year of the Trump presidency felt like a dangerous moment in which the true picture of the past emerged (how did we get here?) and human circumstances surged forward through the visible wreckage of our problematic histories in our public spaces. While the actions of the 2020 "statue wars" aimed to intervene in Western colonialism by stripping it down, the works we examine address the same impulse in more sophisticated ways. Monuments are time-keepers and time-dividers: material markers that divide time into "before" and "after" significant events. The tearing down of statues sometimes marks the event of tearing down a tyrannical regime, such as in the toppling of Nazi monuments at the end of World War II, of Apartheid era statues in South Africa, of Stalin's statue in Budapest in 1956, and of Lenin's statues across Eastern Europe in 1989.[5] It can sometimes mark an assertion of imperialism, as with US troops' toppling of Saddam Hussein's monumental statue in Baghdad in 2003. In the context of the 2020 "statue wars," in addition to re-interrogating the subjects of our monuments, we should also question how monuments themselves divide time and assign value.

In particular, we will ask what role monuments have played in the context of neoliberalism as a global economic and social framework from 1989 to 2020, and what insights to the "statue wars" can be provided by contemporary artists whose work deals with public monuments. We examine the work of artists as a way to provide a new perspective on the heated debates over the ownership and representation in public spaces: the work of Kara Walker and Raqs Media Collective addresses the colonial and racist legacies embodied by monuments, while that of Adrian Paci and Mladen Miljanović approaches monuments in relation to the post-socialist shifting of the historical horizon. Our intention is to frame the "statue wars" as symbolic of a shifting historical horizon in the present, reframed within the politics of the post-ideological condition of the world of the 2020s. 1989 was the last time this kind of convergence of big historical questions played out through debates over monuments. In the wake of the fall of the Berlin Wall in 1989, the monument emerged as one of the most prominent symbols of the demise of communism as an epitome of authoritarianism. Its symbolic end was reinforced by images of monuments pulled down, destroyed, and transported to peripheral areas.

1989, Monuments and Neoliberalism

In order to explain why so many controversies over monuments are happening right now, we need to consider them in the context of the "neoliberal episode" 1989–2020. We are using the term "episode" in order to highlight the way in which neoliberalism went from being the desirable destination in 1989 to an existential crisis in 2020. As previously argued, the fall of the Berlin Wall in 1989 not only symbolized the end of the Cold War and the dissolution of the so-called Soviet Bloc and state-based socialism,[6] it also represented the triumph of capitalist teleology and Western-style liberal democracy as the only and ultimate global destination. Captured in Francis Fukuyama's now-infamous "end of history" appropriation of Hegel, the event set the next decade's global free trade and liberal democracy as the drivers of progress and growth. The exuberance of the 1990s in the West set the tone for two decades of neo-colonial military interventionism in Iraq, Afghanistan, and Syria, creating the largest refugee crisis since World War II, rampant financial deregulation, and a globalization of capital which in turn created the market crash of 2008 and pushed economic inequality to levels never before seen. The past few decades have also witnessed the steady breakdown of international norms, the rise of illiberal democracy and re-entrenchment of authoritarian regimes, and the emergence of right-wing populism in the West leading to the populist nationalism of Brexit and the

Trump presidency. Meanwhile, the world faces the impact of decades of unchecked growth on climate change, with rising temperatures and quickening cycles of natural disasters that threaten new calamities every day. And all of this has so recently converged with the 2020 break-out of the COVID-19 pandemic.

In this context of two decades of disaster and a year of global pandemic confinement, representations of the past take on new significance and become political flash points. As people seek explanations for our present predicament, they find answers relating to the injustices of the past, which they now approach with different perceptions. For every group that sees colonialist statues as symbols of a racist past that continues to inform the present, there are many (White) people who come to the opposite conclusion: that the present is so difficult because "we" have strayed off the path of the post-1989 teleology. Mass populist movements like Brexit and Make America Great Again (MAGA) feed on nostalgia for the moral failures of the past (racism, colonialism, patriarchy, and so on). For their adherents, these institutions are social triumphs, and the difficult present is a result of disrespect to them. Statue wars embody the oppositionality of the worldviews, historical experiences, and perceptions of temporality of these two groups. The public clashes between them express civilizational and entrenched political differences that inform our present.

The responses to statue wars fall into three groups: groups who advocate for removal of offensive statues, street names, and signs; groups who advocate for modifications and changes to statues to reflect the changing perceptions and sensibilities around commemoration; and groups who argue that they should stay untouched. While your authors' political sensibility may be with the first group advocating for removal, in fact all three approaches are inadequate in moving the discussion forward. Leaving the statues might seem blatantly ignorant of the present and willfully hurtful to people protesting against them. Removing the statues would be symbolically significant but it would not remove the attitudes or structures of power that enabled their creation, and it would also risk enabling the forgetting of violence perpetuated in the name of ideas behind the statues. Modifying seems a reasonable position of compromise, yet the existing models of modification are insufficient: housing rejected confederate monuments in museums (re-institutionalizing them) risks reinforcing institutional racism by deferring historical capital upon them; proposals to move the statues to statue graveyards modelled after similar spaces in Hungary, Lithuania, and Estonia can be seen as just physically moving the problem around.[7]

Perhaps the solution is to think laterally, to ask the "what if" questions about what can be done with public monuments beyond the exiting models of compromise. This is the approach is evident in the following three artworks, in different ways. Tatzu Nishi's *Discovering Columbus* (2012) constructed a living room around the New York's Columbus statue (1892), which was accessible via six flights of stairs. By creating an intimate functional space at the height of 22 meters around a statue usually only visible as a silhouette against the sky, Nishi prompted viewers to reimagine our perspective on the statue.[8] Stefanos Tsivopoulos' *Lost Monument* (2009) is a short film featuring Athens' controversial statue of American president Harry Truman (which was subject to multiple attacks), in which the statue moves through situations and locations in which different ethnic and class groups interact with it.[9] Tsivopoulos imagines situations as a series of conversations about the meaning and usefulness of the statue relative to different groups. Christian Jankowski's *Heavy Weight History* (2013) is a film featuring Poland's professional weightlifters attempting to lift various statues off the ground. Staged as a sporting event—including an over-enthusiastic commentator cheering the athletes on—the film draws comparisons between nationalism in sport and perceptions of historical representation.

Or, perhaps another approach is to question the very validity of the perceived opposition between destroying and preserving troubling historical legacies. This is the strategy of the work that will be considered in this chapter, presented in two groups. The first discussion concerns artists who question the racism inherent in some public monuments: Kara Walker, Nicholas Galanin, and Raqs Media Collective. The second group of artists, Adrian Paci and Mladen Miljanović, approaches "statue wars" as a manifestation of a vanishing historical horizon.

Contextualizing the Art

There is a long history of artistic practices that address the political qualities of monuments, from modernist interventions in Man Ray's *Monument to de Sade* (1933), Marcel Duchamp's *Fountain* (1917), and Kurt Schwitters' *Merzbau* (1923–37), through postmodernist revisions in Claes Oldenburg's *Lipstick (Ascending) on Caterpillar Tracks* (1969), Christo and Jeanne-Claude's wrapped monuments, and Jochen Gerz's countermonuments, to more recent investigations of limits of public interactions with monuments in Thomas Hirschhorn's monument series.[10] Another way to position this work is within the field of practice concerned with monuments as symptomatic of modernism. Claire Bishop identifies "retrospectivity" as a mode of art concerned with quoting and appropriating modernist art, architecture, and design: utopian thinking "reformatted" by contemporary artists as a formal exercise.[11] Bishop is rightly critical of what she describes as turning history into images: practices that remove the early twentieth-century avant-garde and experiments from the 1960s from their original contexts. This gesture of retrospectivity works to rehabilitate the more problematic aspects of modernism (normativity, teleology) by focusing on formal or aesthetic aspects of historical works. But Bishop may be overstating the fascination with the formal aspects of modernism: a number of contemporary artists take this "removal" or "rehabilitation" as their departure point to contest versions of the past that have been instrumentalized in the name of power.[12]

It is more productive to place the work in relation to critical projects that seek to address the temporalization of modernism within larger frameworks of inequality. "Formering" is a term developed in a large-scale project that examined the post-1989 relationship between the Cold War divisions in approaches to contemporary art.[13] The departure point was the use of term "Former East" in reference to works from that ambiguous region, despite the presumed end of Cold War binaries. This project critically examined the ways in which these binaries continue to inform exhibition practices, debates, and perception of artworks from the "Former Easter Bloc." Specifically, it showed that the Western art world has been relatively uninterrupted throughout the tectonic global shifts that followed 1989, and it staked a claim against the West's continued hegemony in the global context. Formering the West critically reverses the term "Former East." Attached to the East, "former" qualifies a geographic space with a teleological temporality; the East which has liberated itself from communism, but not from its past. "Former" places the East in a scene of belated, non-historical present whose future is someone else's already existing reality, and whose past has become a burden with no inherent value.

The above artists engage with the instrumentalization of the past, aligning with the critical impetus of Former West to draw out how our thinking continues to be framed by problematic historical temporalities, and how this limits our ability to imagine different possibilities. Their approach highlights the duality at the core of monuments: that they are material forms intrinsically connected to the grand narratives of modernism, and that, because of this connection, they most clearly embody modernism's failures. In the works considered below, monuments represent something far more "ungrounded" than may be expected—not just the return of twentieth-century repression; they return as signifiers of our changed perspective on the past.

Decolonizing Monuments: Walker and Raqs

One of the most significant developments in contemporary art practices over the last decade has been the growing number of works that critically investigate the continuing presence of colonialism in public spaces. The next section will discuss the work of Kara Walker and Raqs Media Collective. Other artists who have created work during this decade that dealt with the colonial legacy in public sculpture include: Fernando Sanchez Castillo's *Swing* (2018) commissioned for the Shanghai Biennale, a bronze statue of an nineteenth-century male figure bending backward (in a limbo-like position) with a swing hanging from the body; Meekyoung Shin's renditions of public statues in soap; Tom Nicholson's poster project for *Comparative Monument (Palestine)* (2012), reflecting on the use of the word "Palestine" in Australian monuments to World War I; and Nicholas Galanin's work *Shadow on the Land, an excavation and bush burial* (2020) for the Biennale of Sydney, an excavation on Cockatoo Island of the shadow cast by the Captain Cook statue in Sydney's Hyde Park.

Walker's practice is the act of taking a highly recognizable public monument and rewriting it through the lens of race as identity. For Tate Modern's 2019 Hyundai commission *Fons Americanus*, Walker created a large-scale public sculpture in the form of a four-tiered fountain which references London's Victoria Memorial (1911) and the Trevi Fountain in Rome.[14] *Fons Americanus* takes one of the most identifiable celebrations of colonialism in London and changes the figures from symbols of White colonial history to figures of Black suffering and resistance. Walker presents an extended metaphor of the Black Atlantic, a term used to acknowledge how the legacy of the transatlantic slave trade has shaped the development of Black identity and culture in America and Europe; in this process, she also rewrites the Whiteness of art history. Her work conjures up an array of art historical references, from romanticist painting to the contemporary art of Damien Hirst. (She references Hirst's *The Physical Impossibility of Death in the Mind of Someone Living* (1991) in naming a section of her fountain *The Physical Impossibility of Blackness in the Mind of Someone White*.) She regards all these reference points through the lens of Blackness, each time asking the same question: "what would this work look like if it were framed around Blackness?" Walker suggests that her guiding principle is working back through history to locate her own place.[15] In each historical location is revealed an invisible support infrastructure for Whiteness. Each story and narrative that we know is shown to be underpinned by exploitation and dispossession—but also by creativity and resistance. The overall mood of the work is one of pride and defiance rather than of mourning. This sense of exploding history, of rewriting well-known stories to highlight the oppressed, the dominated, and the exploited takes shape through the mode of montage. Rather than a singular narrative, Walker's work takes the multiplicity of stories and weaves them together.

Restorative time travel through history also takes place in order to reclaim and reimagine colonial figures. In various places on the *Fons Americanus* fountain appear figures such as "Venus," "The Captain," and "Queen Vicky," symbolizing the transatlantic slave trade. "Queen Vicky," standing on the second tier, plays with the stern image of Queen Victoria; the queen is caught mid-laughter, holding a coconut at her breast. The figure of "The Captain," positioned at the front of the sculpture, is a composite of important Black individuals who rebelled against European colonial forces. At the very top of the fountain stands the figure of "Venus." Various references to this deity go as far back as Roman mythology. Walker's *Venus*

FIGURE 4.1 Fons Americanus, 2019, by Kara Walker © Kara Walker, 2019. Reproduced with the permission of the artist, courtesy of Sikkema Jenkins & Co. Photo: Tate (Matt (Greenwood).

stands at the summit of the fountain like a priestess of Afro-Brazilian or Afro-Caribbean religion.

In her critical approach to colonial history, Walker takes the position that *Fons Americanu*s is a gift to the dominion from one of her subjects. This is crucial because it establishes the gift economy at the center of the symbolic premise of the work. On one hand, a gift is considered a selfless act, one in which something is offered to another as a gesture of good will or reconciliation (in this sense, this artwork mimics the colonial practices of ceremonial gift-giving to the previous rulers, little more than ways of reinforcing existing inequalities). But on the other hand, a gift is a way to put the other in a position where they are expected to reciprocate. Discussing the reciprocity of exchange implicit in gift-giving, Slavoj Žižek argues that it assumes the "mystified" form of two consecutive acts, each of which is disingenuously staged as a free, voluntary display of generosity. The receiver encounters the paradox of forced choice: I have to do freely what I am expected to do. (Yet if, upon receiving a gift, I immediately return it to the giver, this direct circulation would amount to an extremely aggressive gesture of humiliation. It would signal that I refused the other's goodwill—unless the tenor is to recall such embarrassing moments as when elderly people might forget and give us last year's present back again.)[16]

A gift is thus the basis for establishing the terms of the exchange. Put differently, if this monumental fountain of Walker's is the gift from one of the colonial subjects, what should be the reciprocal gift from the dominion? Would it be the permanent construction of the monument? Would it be preserving it in a museum? Herein, the work displays a sense of self-awareness: Walker is aware that creating this piece in the context of a corporate-sponsored commission raises the specter of whitewashing history through art. So, in this sense, calling the work a gift is a way of acknowledging that the sacrifice of the subjects will never be repaid. Or rather, this gift is not just a mimicry of colonial gestures, it is also an active message. The original gift was the centuries of suffered dispossession and exploitation, which were visibly celebrated through public monuments and whitewashed histories. This monument is actually the returning of that "gift."

Fons Americanus continues Walker's long-established practice of taking familiar narratives or markers of history and rendering them in a new light by highlighting the violence at their core. Her celebrated silhouettes in *Insurrection! (Our Tools Were Rudimentary, Yet We Pressed On)* (2000) and subsequent works were visceral depictions of colonial violence rendered as shadow-play, drawing us in by recalling children's night-lamps which are meant to cast calming shadows on the wall. *Fons Americanus* does something similar with a public statue: it shifts it from invisibility (through familiarity) into visibility. Or to put it another way, it shifts it from complacent silence into non-silence. This is especially pertinent in relation to public monuments, whose familiar invisibility is based on silence about the history of violence that underpins them: "what appears to be an act of public storytelling is at least as much about silence as narrative."[17] (An example of this violence is the image of a tree with a noose hanging from a branch. It evokes the frequent lynching of African Americans by White supremacists, who were rising in number following the end of the American Civil War and the emancipation of enslaved peoples in the late nineteenth century.)

Another work that critically investigates the continuing presence of colonial symbolism in public monuments as symbols of hollow power is Raqs Media Collective's *Coronation Park* (2015). New Delhi-based artists Monica Narula, Jeebesh Bagchi, and Shuddhabrata Sengupta of Raqs Media Collective have been dealing with questions about time and history for several decades now, producing works that reconfigure normative conceptions of linear time. For their contribution to the 2015 Venice

FIGURE 4.2 Coronation Park, 2016, by Raqs Media Collective © Raqs Media Collective, 2016. Reproduced with the permission of Raqs and Firth Street Gallery, London. Photo: Raqs.

Biennale, Raqs presented *Coronation Park*, a series of nine sculptures installed in the Giardini. The title of the work refers to a public park built in 1877 on the outskirts of Delhi, where large sculptural monuments were installed to commemorate the British Raj in the nineteenth and early twentieth centuries. In *Coronation Park*, Raqs Media Collective displaced and re-imagined a selection of figures from this site, maintaining their authoritative postures and monumental scale but also drawing out their inherent incompleteness and impermanence. Closer examination of the sculptures revealed that certain faces, heads, torsos, and whole bodies were missing—lopped off, hollowed out, or left unfinished—in the midst of all the ceremonial formalities and pompous regalia that the former imperial power wanted to set in stone.

Narula describes the site of the original Coronation Park in Delhi as "a derelict quasi-ceremonial space, where relics of the British Raj are kept for the consideration of an absent public."[18] It was here, amongst the dilapidated and near-forgotten official commemorations, that Raqs experienced an epiphany "about the hollow interiority of all constituted authority; the constant panic at the heart of power considering its fraught, frayed and often fraudulent claims to legitimacy." This moment of revelation provided the impetus for the *Coronation Park* work, which they consider as "a provocation to think about the inner life of power, and its deepest anxiety: the inevitability of abdication."[19]

The materiality of the sculptures further draws out the sense of impermanence and inner fragility. Initially suggestive of classical sculptural materials like solid marble and polished granite, the partial figures are in fact cast in white fiberglass, with their lofty pedestals made from cheap plywood coated in bitumen. So, what appears at first to be solid, impressive, and lasting turns out to be flimsy, hollow, and always in the process of coming undone. Yet the temporality evoked is not simply that of entropy's irreversible arrow, of things moving incrementally towards ruin: power *is* inevitably eroded over time, but it is also inherently incomplete and always in the process of constituting itself. The sculptures' missing pieces suggest that they are either/both unfinished or undone, thus the time that is described in this work is both *not yet* and *no longer*.

This insistence on the multiplicity of narratives and temporalities is a central feature of Raqs' approach.[20] In *Coronation Park* we find a questioning of monuments' materiality and the notion of the journey. In an immediate sense, the work is about the symbolic affirmation and preservation of colonial power through the monumental form. In replicating the statues of the British Raj, Raqs is asking, "what is their meaning in the present?" But in presenting them in the context of Venice's Giardini, Raqs is asking about the relevance of the historical form of remembering associated with statues. They present the material reminders of the control one colonial power imposed over its "dominion," exhibited at the "ground zero" of another colonial power—in the garden which was built to celebrate the might of that colonial power and be a place where all nation-states came together to compete for influence. We might recall Michel Foucault's account of the garden as the heterotopia, as well as the intrinsic connection of the Venice Biennale to the nation-state. The event was modelled on world fairs, and it is one of the last remaining "dinosaurs" from that era: a relic of another time struggling for relevance in the twenty-first century.

The use of cheap materials and the journey of the statues Europe–India–Europe brings the work in line with Paci's thinking about cultural translation. The choice is pointed at the neo-colonial racism of treating products from Asia as inferior, while depending on the exploitation of cheap labor at their site of production. If China is the world's factory, India is considered the world's primary site for the outsourcing of service industries (call centers, publishing companies, etc.). Regarding the journey, it was often the case that colonial statues were built as replicas of existing statues around the empire, and also that old statues were shipped to be installed in new locations. This meant that the colonial power was symbolically supported by the network of statues that spanned continents and connected disparate locations under the British Empire. In this context, Raqs' "returning" the statues to the "center" (although not the British center) can be read as a gesture of haunting, or of returning a repressed message. The fact that the site is Venice not London means situates all colonialist endeavors on the same historical continuum of domination and exploitation. Raqs are returning the favor in treating all colonizers the same, much like all colonized were treated like children to be disciplined.

The incompleteness and imperfection of the statues in *Coronation Park* relates to ongoing efforts to 3D scan colonialist statues for preservation. This is the case across Australia and the UK, where we see the convergence of cutting-edge 3D technology with the desire to preserve colonial heritage. It is almost as if the former colonies are racing against time, trying to digitize their memories before they fall prey to "vandalism." In a telling incident in Sydney during the 2020 Australian BLM protests, a sizeable police force was posted in Hyde Park to protect a colonial statue against protesters. Barely a few weeks earlier, a mining company Rio Tinto had destroyed an ancient Aboriginal sacred site in their search for resources and profit.

Raqs' gesture of using cheap materials is thus given a new level of meaning in present decades, against the demands that these kinds of statues be removed from the public eye. The Giardini becomes the equivalent of *Memento Park* (1993) near Budapest where undesirable monuments and statues from Hungary's Communist period (1949–1989) were placed. The playoff between the familiarity of the statues (their invisibility) and their strangeness is created through their spatial and temporal displacement. They "look" like the don't belong in the present. This artistic estrangement of colonial artifacts (our past but not our past) reminds us of colonialism's ongoing presence in the public sphere (and our forms of remembrance) and of its global ubiquity. It also reminds us just how much our cognitive mapping of, or way of thinking about, the past still relies on these forms. It puts the colonial problem faced by societies like India on the same playing field as Europe's "monumental problem" of socialist statues after 1989. Europe dealt with its problem of "totalitarianism" by removing the statues, yet the colonial world is unable to do the same almost thirty years after 1989. It is this inability that becomes the symbol of the unfinished "revolution" at the post-1989 end of history. The works in the next section unpack the oppositional meanings of 1989 and of monuments as historical symbols. Artists Adrian Paci and Mladen Miljanović establish clashes of oppositional meanings as a way to demonstrate the shifting historical horizon.

Vanishing Historical Horizon: Catching up to Dafen

Paci's *The Column* (2013) is a video work featuring stone being extracted from a quarry in China and then carved into a column on a Chinese factory ship *en route* to an art exhibition in France. While the opening sequence shows artisans excavating a large piece of marble, most of the film shows the process of carving and shaping the column on the ship at sea. A ship on the sea as the location sets the themes of the work around trade and transport, transformation, and indeterminacy.[21] *The Column* moves slowly, matching the steady pace of the ship and the workers, the rhythmic sound of the water, the hum of the ship's motors, the sounds of drills and other mason tools, and the muffled conversations of the artisans.

The Column approaches 1989 through the metaphor of a journey, both a physical trip and a shifting historical horizon. In an immediate sense, *The Column* is about the factory ship as site of production. It explores production through this space in which production and distribution are simultaneous. Paci was fascinated with factory ships after hearing about them. These ships represent the next (mobile) stage of Special Economic Zones. As sites of offshore manufacturing in de-nationalized regions they are exempt from labor laws and environmental codes and populated by rural migrants seeking economic opportunities. The ship is the logical extension and intensification of these zones. The symbolism of the ship also connects the work to an array of histories (from colonialism and slave trading to migration, piracy, and viral contagion) which align with the emergence of global capitalism and trade. Thus, 1989 is the journey of the mobile Special Economic Zone as a manifestation of the triumph of exploitative, highly efficient capital.

"End of history" means the end of ideological divides and triumph of free market trade. "End of history" in *The Column* marks the beginning of the catch-up revolution. In the context of the post-1989 world, which forms the backdrop of much of Paci's practice over the last few decades, *The Column* is showing us the birth of the current nation-state, the construction of its foundations post-1989. A catch-up revolution emerged in the wake of 1989 as former socialist economies were steered onto the path toward free market democracy, undergoing the same historical processes as the developed West in order to "catch up." However, the last three decades have shown that, rather than having disappeared, communism has returned as the authoritarian framework for the most powerful and growing global economy, that of China. The journey of the ship in *The Column* reflects the returning of this return, and the clear allusion to slave-trade ships is significant. Just as the foundations of the European nation-states in the nineteenth century were built on colonial trade and exploitation of labor, and just as the cultural primacy of the West was built on cultural appropriation (and theft) from all over the world, the contemporary nation-state is built on the fluid and moving foundations of economic interests and global trade. The journey from China to the exhibition in Europe echoes journeys past, seen differently through our present circumstances.

Another version of 1989 as journey in *The Column* is the success of China's "catching up" and becoming the powerhouse of contemporary capitalism which is now exporting democracy to Europe. This is the past returning, but not in the standard way that return is understood in post-socialist transition. This is the return of tradition that underpins parliamentary democracy, but tradition that is produced anew by an economical super-force ruled by an iron-fisted communist party. This is capitalism that is much more dynamic and efficient that its Western counterpart, because has been divorced from its reliance on a parliamentary democracy. The premise of *The Column* is based on an inversion of the belief that the West has been exporting civilization to the rest of the world. It shows us a column, as the material foundation of "Western democracy," being imported back into Europe. The production of the column has been outsourced to China, the economic powerhouse of authoritarian capitalism, the ideology set to shape the next century much as democracy shaped the last. The work thus demonstrates that, post-1989, the West has failed to undergo its own revolution and is being left behind by China. It is being left behind in the race to find the most exploitative and profitable form of capitalism. In this sense, *The Column* does show us the world after the end of history, though not the one that we imagined: not global liberal democracy but the triumph of market-based economics reconciled with the primacy of an authoritarian state.

Monument as an idea in *The Column* also appears through a contrast between different versions of the installation. In the first version, the column is a symbol of European classicism and a foundation of modernism. It is the material support of democracy and tradition, associated with temples, museums, and parliaments. As an architectural object the column is also a symbol of Western colonialism, both in terms of historical projects of national expansion, and more contemporary economic and political relationships. The video is exhibited together with the manufactured column, which is placed outdoors, reclining on its side. To be horizontal undermines the column's powerful form, rendering it impotent. In this sense, the work becomes a powerful allegory about the outsourcing to China[22] of the foundation of the colonial nation-state.

The approach that *The Column* takes, outsourcing production to cheaper labor from China, recalls the phenomenon of that country's Dafen painters' village. *The Column* can be described as "Dafen on a boat," because it draws on many of the existing discussions around the Dafen painters' village and applies them to the production of a column.[23] A key aspect of Dafen present in *The Column* is that the artisans are at no point shown to be working from drawings or schemes or models. In other words, they are not using a "source image," but working entirely from memory. This suggests that they are highly skilled and experienced and have been doing the work for so long that they have memorized the scales and dimensions. (This is confirmed by footage of one artisan casually drawing decorative shapes to be carved out in the stone.) But it also raises questions of the opposition between "original" and "reproduction" that have been unavoidable since Marcel Duchamp, Andy Warhol, and Walter Benjamin asked them so publicly. Our curiosity—about Dafen, but also about *The Column*—wraps questions about economic and political competition from China in provocative questions about aesthetics and a thinly veiled air of condescension in their production. *The Column* asks: do China's highly productive uses of Western history and culture lay claim to an alternative modernist legacy, that of Western art history (or socialism, or capitalism) with Chinese characteristics? Or do they, in fact, represent a broader, even universal fulfilment of modernism's most avant-garde ideals?[24]

The other important relation to Dafen that needs to be mentioned is that in showing the next step of speeding up of production by placing "Dafen" on a boat, Paci is unmooring the "copy factory" from its location. If the phenomenon of Dafen raised the question of authenticity and authorship, it was nevertheless still anchored in a specific location, with all the cultural associations of that location. In Paci's work, "Dafen" becomes mobile, an unmoored signifier. It is easy to imagine a subsequent scenario wherein a fleet of factory ships simply move between locations, not governed by any labor protection laws. They transport the global precarious workers who circulate according to the needs of capital and the market. *The Column* suggests that economic models are more portable than political ideas (which are represented by the column): countries like China that have wholly embraced capitalism are thriving (by the West's own standards). It suggests that market-based economics have no problem accommodating any cultures or traditions, or being reconciled with an authoritarian state. No longer wedded to "Western cultural values" (egalitarianism, fundamental worker rights, universal welfare state), this is the triumph of capitalism.

FIGURE 4.3 The Column, 2013, by Adrian Paci, film still, HD Video projection, Color, sound, duration: 25.40 minutes, edition of three © Adrian Paci, 2013. Courtesy the artist, Galerie Peter Kilchmann, Zurich, and kaufmann repetto, Milan and New York.

FIGURE 4.4 The Column, 2013, by Adrian Paci, film still, HD Video projection, Color, sound, duration: 25.40 minutes, edition of three © Adrian Paci, 2013. Courtesy the artist, Galerie Peter Kilchmann, Zurich, and kaufmann repetto, Milan and New York.

A clash of multiple temporalities (manufacture time and maritime) and histories is shown in the final minutes of the video as an extended time-lapse sequence of shadows dancing through the belly of the ship. The column lies on its side under the roof of the upper deck, spotted with beams of light moving over its curves. In this striking final sequence, Paci is paying homage to the Italian masters, using chiaroscuro to accentuate the column's classical

FIGURE 4.5 The Column, 2013, by Adrian Paci, film still, HD Video projection, Color, sound, duration: 25.40 minutes, edition of three © Adrian Paci, 2013. Courtesy the artist, Galerie Peter Kilchmann, Zurich, and kaufmann repetto, Milan and New York.

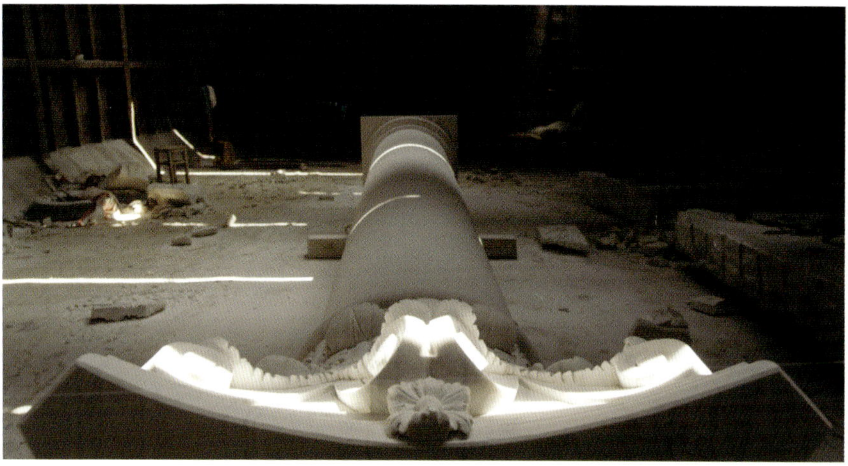

FIGURE 4.6 The Column, 2013, by Adrian Paci, film still, HD Video projection, Color, sound, duration: 25.40 minutes, edition of three © Adrian Paci, 2013. Courtesy the artist, Galerie Peter Kilchmann, Zurich, and kaufmann repetto, Milan and New York.

(Corinthian) features. Reference is made to the art of the Italian Renaissance in the composition, as the column is depicted throughout in linear perspective: positioned at the center of the frame, the ribs of the ship rise to either side of the column, its length receding into the space as though concentrating at a vanishing point.[25] The sequence features no people and uses time-lapse to accentuate the passing of time. Without any information given, we can speculate on its meaning. It could be confirming the efficiency of the work being done, suggesting it was completed ahead of time of arrival and delivery. It could also be articulating the "tradition" of the column being static while the world around it changes, and with that world, our perspective on it.

In the Meantime: *Draft for a 20-Minute Monument*

While Paci's work critically unpacks the teleology of modernist–capitalist production as progress, showing that the West has failed by its own standards and that Chinese copying is the truest fulfillment of modernist avant-garde principles, Miljanovic's work is about the proximity of production to nationalism. Miljanovic shows that extreme forms of nationalism such as that in Bosnia and Herzegovina (BiH), symbolized by hyper-production of monuments, are not an aberration of the post-socialist teleology of transition to peace, prosperity, and democracy, but that destructive nationalism is an inherent and necessary part of nationalism, albeit usually ascribed to underdeveloped peripheries like BiH. Miljanovic shows that the post-Dayton meantime of BiH—the feeling of being temporally stuck —has in fact become the global condition.

Miljanovic's *Draft for a 20-Minute Monument* (2019) is a video showing nine disabled war veterans sitting on a pile of discarded stones. The work features Bosniak, Croat, and Serb veterans, representing the three sides of the

FIGURE 4.7 Draft for 20-Minute Monument, 2019, by Mladen Miljanović, film still, duration: 21 minutes © Mladen Miljanović, 2019. Reproduced with permission of the artist.

war in BiH. They exhibit various levels of disability (such as having arms and legs missing), and slowly take up positions to sit on this pile of stones behind a stone factory. The work moves slowly with minimal action. The men shuffle in their spots, trying to find a more comfortable position on the hard and uncomfortable surfaces. Some engage in chatter about the surroundings, and a ringing mobile phone goes unanswered. Towards the end of the video, they stand up one by one and slowly move offscreen.

The work combines long-running themes in Miljanovic's work—his personal experience as a tombstone maker, his collaboration with veterans in BiH, his experience of war, and his army service—with a response to the political weaponization of monuments in BiH following the 1990s war.[26] This includes examining the changing meaning of the year 1989 as the symbolic end of state-based socialism, witnessed in BiH as a readymade, failed state of post-socialist and post-conflict transition.[27] *Draft for a 20-Minute Monument* suggests two versions of 1989.

In the first version, 1989 falls in line with the Fukuyaman narrative of the "end of history" and BiH as a readymade failure of transition, *not* catching up to the West. This failure is connected to the work's main theme of monuments and war veterans. *Draft for a 20-Minute Monument* is responding to the monument obsession and history wars in which BiH has been locked for more than two decades. Since the end of the 1992–5 war, over 2,100 monuments have been built in a country that remains one of the most divided twenty-first century post-conflict societies, with ethnic division enshrined in its constitution. Its contemporary social and aesthetic complexities around monuments—the high number built, the entrenched nationalism, the systemic denial of genocide and revision of history—resonates with the difficult political situation in the country. Since the signing of the Dayton Agreement in 1995 that marked the end of war, the country has remained mired in the "ethno-national identitarianism" of its two main constituent entities (the Bosniak-Croat Federation and the Serb-dominated Republika Srpska) and has charted a failed trajectory from violence to reconciliation. This post-conflict trajectory has been hampered by dispossession of social wealth and infrastructure, a labyrinthine system of government, and routine sequestering of political debate into nationalist rhetoric by the dominant ethno-nationalist parties. Consequently, BiH is confronted with the co-existence of three mutually exclusive "official" narratives, which dominate its culture of remembrance whilst simultaneously disputing each other's claims to ownership over the space and time of the country. In this context, it is difficult to understand BiH monuments as anything other than materializations of aggressive nationalist rhetoric, or the war veterans as anything other than living reminders of the continuing prevalence of that rhetoric.[28]

But *Draft for a 20-Minute Monument* also presents a second perspective on 1989, which questions the teleology of transition. By showing BiH as a failure, Miljanović is also showing transition as a failure (asking the question "transition to what?"), and suggesting that BiH is not the exception—or a failure—but representative of the current global condition. The hyper-production of monuments in BiH after 1996, whose leftovers are captured in the artwork, operates as a free market which validates the neoliberal–nationalist nexus as the sole mode of remembrance and identification. Whereas it is relatively easy to articulate the hyper-production of monuments in BiH as a manifestation of the dysfunction of an economically underdeveloped, socially dysfunctional, and politically corrupt periphery still dealing with unresolved historical legacies, this explanation ignores the fact that the very perception of BiH as stuck on the road to Europe accepts a neoliberalist–nationalist nexus as the inevitable and undisputable global order. Miljanović's work demonstrates how this nexus determines the experience of history and remembrance. On the one hand, this includes accounting for the continuing presence of Yugoslav socialism as a historical reference despite the demonization of the Yugoslav socialist system as undemocratic, the destruction of socialist monuments, and the rehabilitation of Yugoslav World War II fascists and collaborators. On the other hand, his work articulates the relation of monuments to historical revisionism and genocide denial. Historical experience in BiH has been relativized to the point where it functions like predatory capital: it permeates all aspects of the social sphere of everyday life, and relies on corruption and self-interest. Miljanović's work suggests that any critique of the conservative, religious, patriarchal, nationalist hegemony of the post-Yugoslav societies must also be a critique of the neoliberal capitalism that enabled that transformation.

To articulate the deployment of this critique in Miljanović's work, we can draw on the term "meantime" to capture the temporal experience of the last two decades in BiH. While 2020 has marked the intensification of the temporal sense of suspension (a feeling of intense stillness and simultaneous intense acceleration; tectonic shifts occurring across all aspects of life), this global sense of temporal displacement has been part of BiH's experience for a long period. The war in BiH has, in addition to the physical devastation of life and property, been a rupture in the experience of time, between pre-war "normality" (an idealized pn a) and a normative (or returned-to-normal) yet unattainable future in the EU. Memorial culture in BiH therefore not only reflects the past and present, it anticipates the future of Europe, much like the dissolution of Yugoslavia in the early 1990s anticipated many of the current events in Europe. The temporal suspension between a war that has not quite ended and a future that has not yet been embarked upon has been described as "post-Dayton meantime."[29]

Meantime plays out in *Draft for a 20-Minute Monument* across several registers, bringing up associations with waiting and the staging of an event. The work is a recording of a group waiting: but for what? The metaphor of waiting has been a powerful one for post-socialist artists, for example as used in early video works by Chantal Akerman such as *From the East* (1993), in which Akerman captures scenes of groups of people standing around waiting. Similarly, the trope of waiting and delay has often been used in critical writing that describes "the road to democracy" of post-socialist transition as a form of temporal delay: entire populations are expected to undergo a developmental phase until they are ready to re-join the EU community.[30] Miljanovic's work does not signal to anything in particular that these veterans are waiting for, but rather uses the powerful symbolism of their passive bodies to suggest that meantime is a global condition, one which determines the limits of our historical imagination.

If *Draft for a 20-Minute Monument* establishes a contrast between two versions of 1989 as symbol, the work takes a similar approach to monument as the conceptual and material embodiment of this shift. In the first version of its symbolism, monument is representative of the political staging of commemorative culture, or what has been described as dead body politics wherein death is instrumentalized for political purposes.[31] Here Miljanović acts as a director: his hand is visible in that the veterans slowly move onto the rocks and take their positions in a choreographed fashion. Their distribution across the representational plane recalls scenes of leisure activities such as picnics in nineteenth-century impressionist paintings. But the strongest indicator of staging is in the disparate casting of the veterans; Miljanović "uses" the veterans as stand-ins for the way in which BiH is routinely used in EU discussions to illustrate contemporary failures: an internally divided country with the highest EU level of migration (notwithstanding it supplies cheap labor to Germany). Miljanović inverts this "dead" "failure" to create a "draft" of a monument for the living: a temporary, ephemeral, staged monument which lasts for only 20 minutes.[32]

In the second version of the monument as symbol, *Draft for a 20-Minute Monument* shows people posing as monuments to themselves, reflecting on the broader culture of self-monumentalization. Miljanović's approach here operates as a critique of the narcissism surrounding the culture of self-memorialization. (The crucial difference, related to staging, is that these men were being directed to pose.) *Draft for a 20-Minute Monument* recalls a comedy sketch by *Top List of the Surrealists* (*Tol Lista Nadrealista*), a well-known television comedy show in the Former Yugoslavia in the 1980s. In this sketch, produced at the height of a mid-1980s unemployment crisis which in many ways led to the rise of nationalist tensions, a news crew visits a factory that has found an innovative solution to unemployment for young university graduates: they earn money by posing as living statues representing hard-working socialist laborers. The sketch is a parody of socialist failures and obsession with workers as symbols of (failed) progress. In Miljanović's work, we have a parody of participation, in which veterans become transformed into statues representing themselves: participating again in a history they have sacrificed their bodies to create, but that will never be fully theirs ("ours but not ours"). There is a clear sense that these men are "leftovers" of the war: discarded human fodder used in the nation-building war which has been forgotten by the political elites, but is periodically remembered in line with election cycles (such as in the opportunistic use of veterans by the parties to trot out announcements about increasing their pensions). Miljanović's men perform the stark contrast between the overwhelming commemoration of military personnel in monuments (there are almost no monuments to civilians in BiH), and their lived experience of being left behind. This is further reinforced by the pile of discarded stones: rejected parts of commemorative culture, left behind in the process of producing ideologically loaded remembering.

On the production of remembering, Miljanović's setting his video behind a privately owned tombstone factory is significant. The setting is a reference to what has been described as the privatization of commemoration.[33] At a time when production in BiH is generally in rapid decline—factories closing, skilled labor leaving the country by the thousands (only temporarily delayed by the COVID-19 pandemic)—monument construction is on the rise. In what seems like a weekly occurrence, there are reports of new monuments being constructed, and new controversies over commemorations of war criminals or fascist collaborators. In most of these cases, the monuments are the initiative of individuals or interest groups, yet the authorities do little to prevent, and often a lot to enable, their construction. The only construction in BiH that is seemingly happening at an even greater speed and intensity than that of monuments is that of neoliberal infrastructure. Even as its young people leave, the country is getting more (half-empty) shopping malls, more privatized highways, and more privately initiated nationalist monuments. This is the nationalist–neoliberal nexus: parallel economies of construction each determined by capital, both of which define the temporal axis of the present. Nationalist rhetoric is defining the unfinished history that is usurping the present, and neoliberal infrastructure is defining the movement towards the future of capital. This nexus hosts the temporal directionality of "Balkan nationalism" that is in the process of "becoming Europe" by being integrated, or dissolved, into the invisible global infrastructure of capitalist production. The reverse dynamic, as we described in the introduction to this book, is that developed democracies such as the US are now caught in a similar toxic nationalist–neoliberal manipulation of nationalist narrative to bolster big capital, which we call the "balkanization" of politics.

Conclusion

The ways in which these artists approach monuments can be explained through the phrase used by Miljanović to describe the relation of his work to the past: "our past but not our past." We can understand this phrase in two ways. First, it refers to a normative past that excludes us from its narratives; past as written by the presumed victors, post-1989. Second, it refers to our rejection of this past, refuting that it could be the only possible way to represent and explain how we got to the present.

The two understandings of this phrase articulate the ways in which this chapter's artworks engage with modernist aesthetics and the politics of temporal formations while focusing on contemporary failures of democracy. The works are giving us key moments in the production cycle of monuments: the creation of the monument, the modification of the monument, and the leftover scraps after the monument has been produced. They are sharply contrasted against the lived experience of excluded subjects. The works offer interesting perspectives on the present debates about monuments, including the question of what fills the representational void once a certain picture of the past, however problematic that picture was, is removed. The removal of colonial statues is an important symbolic and performative gesture that will move the discussion over our public spaces forward, but there is there is nothing to suggest this actually addresses the broader system of racism and discrimination that supports this form of public remembrance. It may remove the symptoms but not the disease. There is a risk that removing colonialist and Confederate statues may in fact create a vacuum and/or trigger forms of mythologizing and martyrdom that will continue to feed into right-wing narratives of self-victimization.

The artworks that we discuss in this chapter signal that in a shifting world—where the very temporal register we use to comprehend and experience the present is being upended—we don't only need new kinds of monuments, we need new ideas about monuments. Looking back upon history does not have to mean giving up the possibility of moving away from the current crisis, it could unveil the possibility of moving differently. Furthermore, in the order in which we have addressed these works—Walker, Raqs, Paci, and Miljanović—each makes increasingly clear that monuments possess a performative dimension that is often masked by their very static nature. In particular, in Paci's *Column*, the laborers toil, the ship cuts through the ocean; in Miljanović's *Draft for a 20-Minute Monument*, the assumed stasis and stability of meaning of war monuments is undermined by its subjects' shuffling, finding a comfortable position, chatter, the ringing mobile phone, standing up, and leaving the scene. These works draw attention to the underlying long-term instability of monuments. Similar to the aphorism that "all glass eventually breaks," all dominant regimes eventually end, and all monuments eventually fall. The act of toppling a statue, defiling a monument to a regime that has passed, whether tossing Colston's statue into Bristol Harbor or dragging the head of Stalin through the streets of Budapest, is one of the clearest performative expressions of shifting politics—often attendant at a riot or a revolution. We will return to the political performance of the riot in our final chapter.

CHAPTER FIVE

Overidentifying with the Strongman

Trump and the Capitol Hill Riot

A giant blimp of a baby wearing diapers, a collection of dildoes, a gaping mouth, a sculpture of a sagging overweight man with miniscule genitalia. These are the images that come to mind if we think about art that was produced during Donald J. Trump's presidency. It seems that no US president in recent memory has been the subject of so much artistic ire. Yet what is also striking about this body of work is how little distinguishes it from what could be considered promotional (propaganda) art; examples might be Annie Liebowitz's 2006 photograph of Donald and Melania posing before their luxury possessions, or Andy Thomas' painting of Trump playing cards with previous Republican presidents. If the first group aims at discrediting Trump by ridiculing his physical features and outbursts of sexism and misogyny, the second group celebrates his equally publicized narcissism and promotion of wealth. In different ways, both groups of works are reflections of a highly contentious and divisive populist politician that tell us very little beyond his public image. And one thing that is striking about Trump's public image is how much of it is the product of his campaign, or a direct reaction to it. In other words, what is decidedly missing from art produced during Trump's rule is anything that cuts through the public relations machinery.[1] Contrast this with the scenes from Capitol Hill on January 6, 2021: costumed protestors engaging in a violent, carnivalesque transgression and an attempt to overthrow the US Government. Trump supporters stormed the Congress, engaging in wanton violence that would ultimately leave five dead and many injured, and forced Trump to distance himself from them. The Capitol Hill riot managed to not so much cut through but to implode the Trump PR machine—which incited the riots—and show an ugliness lurking beneath that surprised even Trump.

FIGURE 5.1 Pro-Trump protestors at the Capitol Hill riot, Washington, D.C., January 6, 2021. Photo: AAP Image/SIPA USA/Chris Kleponis.

Following our broader discussion of the "statue wars" and the underlying performative dimensions of monuments, highlighted through certain contemporary art works, we now turn in a more direct way to one of the key ways in which the persona of Trump has been met by artistic resistances during his presidency. As one of the more divisive US presidents in recent memory, Trump has sharply polarized public debate. Since descending that golden elevator at Trump Tower on June 16, 2015, to announce his run in Republican presidential primaries, liberal and leftist creative practitioners have struggled for ways to resist Trump and his right-wing populist politics. Within the art context there has been consensus about the need to resist the inherent fascism of his politics,[2] but little serious consideration of or consensus on what forms artistic resistance should take. If art should be critical of the public landscape that has been left behind by Trump, what form might this critique take? In this chapter, we consider some ways in which contemporary art has responded to Trump, and the inherent limitations of those responses. Specifically, many artistic responses to Trump tend to adopt a transgressive approach that simply does not work against the already transgressive public persona of Trump. How can art begin to respond to Trump? It has been often noted that Trump was impervious to comedy,[3] so what does this mean for art as a form of critique that often uses strategies that overlap with those of comedic performances? Trump is now out of office (albeit with the possibility of running again in 2024), but "Trumpism" and the Trump Effect are here to stay. If contemporary artists intend to seriously resist the Trump Effect, rather than simply perform ineffective public gestures of resistance, we need to consider more sophisticated forms of critical resistance that will endure in the longer term.

What Is "Trumpism"?

In 2016 *The Financial Times*' Gideon Rachman suggested that the "strongman" style of macho leadership was on the rise across the world, from Russia, China, India, and Egypt to the United States.[4] Rachman's article was one of the first to articulate and name the broader authoritarian trend across the globe that included political leaders Vladimir Putin, Bashar al-Assad, Viktor Orban, Recep Tayyip Erdogan, Xi Jinping, and Trump. While all these politicians are known for their loose approach to truth, there is no recent example in a Western democracy of a political leader who lied as persistently and shamelessly as Trump, inventing a whole new vocabulary of double-meaning slogans in the process. He dismissed inconvenient or critical information as "fake news" and journalists or organizations who reported this information as "enemies of the people," and his electoral defeat in 2020 as "the big lie." Trump has not accepted his electoral defeat, and it is very likely that he never will. Trump's resistance to election results is part of his broader authoritarian practices during his presidency, including delegitimizing electoral process, interfering with judicial independence, and attacking independent media and opposition. Trump's use of ploys from the autocratic playbook throughout his presidency will have lasting consequences.[5] This behavior is reminiscent of leaders of countries that have what political scientists call "hybrid regimes," which have elements of democracy but in practice are not democracies.

Taking the position that the US political landscape after Trump is increasingly resembling pseudo-democratic "hybrid regimes" around the world, in this chapter we draw on the work of artists Sanja Iveković, Adrian Paci, and Janez Janša, Janez Janša, and Janez Janša to critically examine the "strongman" Trump. We will examine the Capitol Hill riot on January 6, 2021 through Iveković, Paci, and the Janšas' work to draw out unacknowledged aspects of the riot and Trump the strongman: the different ways in which Trump's political power enunciated itself through the riot, the way in which the Capitol Hill riot performed loss while attempting insurrection and, central to our argument here, the way in which the protesters overidentified with Trump's message. We are also interested in the role of Trump in triggering the riot. Our starting point is that the Capitol Hill riot was the defining moment of the Trump presidency: a choreographed public performance of Trump's public rhetoric by his followers—something we explore in further detail in our final chapter. But it was also something that seemingly happened without his knowledge, or at least he has been unwilling to accept any responsibility for the events. Trump's rhetoric is filled with half-truths and manipulative assertions, and the choreography of the protesters reflected this through overidentification. In this chapter and the next, we draw on ideas from contemporary art to argue that the Capitol Hill riot is the most successful subversion and critique of Trumpism so far.

While the Trump Effect is centered on the political persona—the political celebrity—of Donald J. Trump, his presidency is not the source of what we call the Trump Effect, but rather its most notable manifestation to date in the "Western" world. The conspiracist strongman archetype that Trump fulfils appeared in Eastern Europe many years before, such as in Slovenia's Janez Janša. As we argue in the first three chapters of this book, the Trump Effect is a global phenomenon that precedes the Trump presidency and that feeds its archetypes and its combination of conspiracism, paranoia, xenophobia, and culture war politics into Trumpism, resonating and self-amplifying back and forth from the American "center" to the "peripheries" such as Australia, Eastern Europe, and Russia.

For this reason, in this chapter we focus on works by non-US artists to make sense of Trump. In our Introduction, we borrowed Maria Todorova's term "balkanization" to characterize the "mismanagement, blurring of the competencies and borders in the order of law and much else."[6] Our use of this concept is intended to demystify the appearance and popularity of Trump, not as a US-centric phenomenon but as part of a broader global slide towards populist authoritarianism; Trump marks the balkanization of the US political mainstream. Our borrowing of this term recognizes that the US has only recently begun to slide towards an authoritarianism that has been manifesting in post-socialist societies for at least two decades. As we explain in this chapter, it is instructive to look towards Eastern Europe as a prime example of this autocratic global tendency. Dominic Boyer and Alexei Yurchak point out the growing number of similarities between late socialism and neoliberalism, such as the normalization, ritualization, and homogenization of public political discourse (the production of a formulaic language of political communication loaded with repetitive and coded phrases).[7] Boyer and Yurchak show the uptake of Eastern artistic practices in Western critical art post-1989; they notice in particular the strategy of overidentification. Articulated by Boyer and Yurchak—following Slavoj Žižek—as taking power literally at its word, overidentification means that we are caught in the web of power precisely when we maintain a critical distance from it. This is because this type of power encourages us to break the rules and keep a distance, but also does not take itself seriously. In our next chapter, we ask what would these insurrectionists have done if they had succeeded on January 6? Leading to that discussion, here we draw upon the idea of overidentification in the artwork by the Janez Janšas to reconceptualize the persona of Trump and actions of the Capitol Hill riot, and argue that perhaps the most effective way to subvert the populist Trump is not by mocking him, but by overidentifying with him to highlight his empty ideological core. This is what happened amongst the QAnon, "Q's, Boogaloo Bois, and Proud Boys that raided the

Capitol Building on January 6, 2021, and, paradoxically, may actually possess potential for resisting not only Trump, but the larger Trump Effect.

What Is a Strongman?

Although there is a trend of confrontational and abrasive strongmen appearing in political and public life, globally it is occurring in vastly different socio-political, historical, and cultural contexts. There is consensus in the literature about the key characteristics of the strongman,[8] which include: violations of human rights and international law and agreements through police and military violence, inflicted on domestic or international civilians; undermining and dismissal of democratic and critical institutions such as critical media (through media monopolization, and attacks on journalists and media organizations) and the judiciary system (through questioning judges, undermining the separation of powers, and dismantling processes of checks and balances); and using the language of populist nationalism in policy both domestic ("us versus them" narratives targeting migrants or "outsider" groups, and establishing the leader as the spokesman for "the people" and against other politicians and economic elites) and foreign (advocating protectionism, cutting foreign aid, and limiting movement of people and goods across borders).

For our purposes here, the most significant characteristic of strongman politics is the performance of vulgarity. This is because vulgarity establishes the form—or the spectacle of discourse—through which all the other characteristics are communicated to the public. While aspects of authoritarianism are not new on the political scene, the way in which they are being delivered and used to gain political advantage is a relatively new phenomenon. This phenomenon is connected to the Trump Effect's post-ideological fracturing of the left–right political spectrum (epitomized by Senator Josh Hawley's raised fist at the Capitol on January 6, 2021, the image of which began our Introduction) and the many examples we have discussed so far—of the shift in far-right and conservative politics towards co-opting "traditionally left" tactics, political ground and its cynical appropriation of color-blind liberalism.

Trump's performative vulgarity is aimed at creating a point of identification with the working-class voters and a point of differentiation against the elitist establishment liberals. In order to articulate this performance of vulgarity, we draw on Žižek's argument regarding Trump as the "obscene master."[9] Žižek's departure point is asking why each time Trump was exposed or called out for his use of obscenity—his sexist "grab them by the pussy" comments, his sexualized misogynist mocking of ex-FBI lawyer Lisa Page, his numerous racist or otherwise insensitive statements—did these events not spell his political end but increase his popularity. Žižek argues that this is because Trump is the emblematic figure of "obscene populist

FIGURE 5.2 The "Trump Baby" blimp, flown over Parliament Square, London, on July 13, 2018, during protests marking the state visit of the then-US President. The blimp was designed by Matt Bonner, and is now in the collection of the Museum of London. Photo: Matt Dunham via AP via AAP.

Master" through which we are witnessing the re-assertion of male authority through the use of obscenity. For Žižek, the obscene Master represents the inversion of the "traditional" figure of the leader, whose authority and dignity are inverted via obscenities. Žižek argues that we are at the opposite end of Stalinism, wherein the figure of the leader should be kept unblemished at any price. Being mindful of the power of appearances meant that the Stalinist leader behaved as if the smallest indecencies would destroy his power. While Žižek does not mention this, we can also imagine the 1960s sexual revolution and embrace of free love to be an example of opposing domination by embracing what was considered indecent at the time.

Žižek argues that the use of obscenities by a strongman is strategic populism designed for two main outcomes. First, Trump and other leaders like him, such as the UK's Boris Johnson, speak in this way to make themselves more relatable to the public. Their use of obscenities is intended to show them as ordinary human beings with flaws. Second, obscenity is used to generate a sense of solidarity with "ordinary people": the experience of bonding with a stranger by sharing a dirty joke. Third, the strategic use of obscenities functions as a diffuser of critique. In functioning as his own court jester, by supplementing public statements with dirty remarks, Trump narrows the space for comedy or parody to critique him. This point is illustrated if we survey the art that was produced during Trump's rule. Much

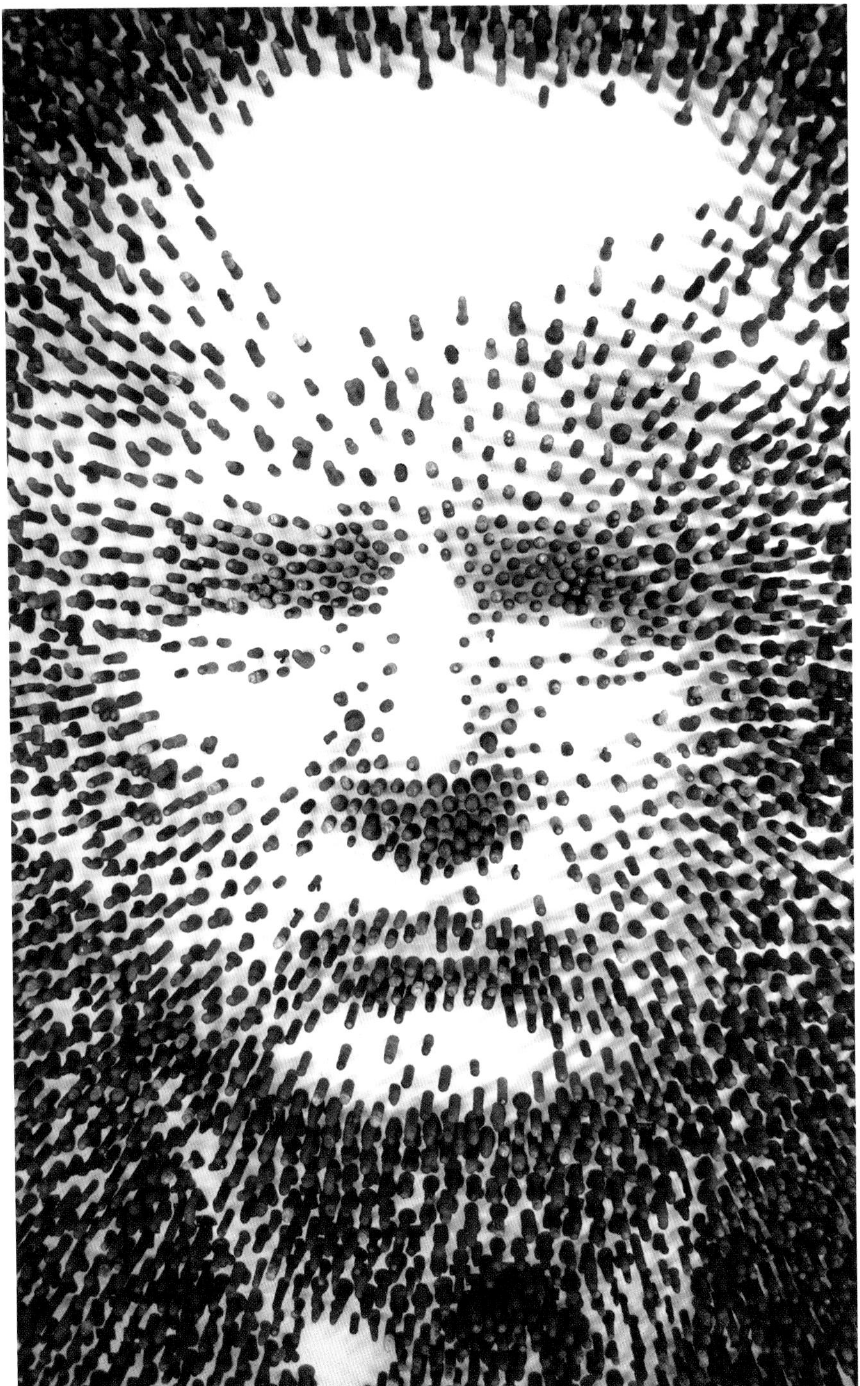

FIGURE 5.3 The Donald Mandala (THE DONGALD), 2020 by Stephen Manka, Manka Design Studio, installation © Stephen Manka, 2020. Reproduced with permission of the artist.

anti-Trump art has used taunting mockery to target Trump's physical features: a "Trump Hut" mocking his hair,[10] "Dump Trump" graffiti depicting him as giant feces,[11] a "Trump Baby Blimp" depicting him as a giant baby wearing diapers,[12] a painting of him naked with small genitalia (*Make America Great Again* by Illma Gore which led to the artist being physically assaulted),[13] naked statues of a castrated Trump (*Emperor Has no Balls*),[14] Stephen Manka's giant portrait using 2020 vintage metal dildos.[15] Other examples include the use of his open mouth by cartoonists and in memes,[16] and obscene jokes at the expense of Trump's appearance during the Women's March in January 2018.[17] This approach is also evident in less overt, less didactic anti-Trump art. Maurizio Cattelan's *America* (2016) featuring a solid-gold toilet preceded Trump's presidency,[18] however it was clearly aimed at the growing wealth disparity. The work did get embroiled in controversy involving Trump in 2017: following a request from the White House to the Guggenheim for a loan of a Van Gogh painting, head curator Nancy Spector replied with an offer of a long-term loan of Cattelan's toilet.[19] It is interesting to note that this was on the hundredth anniversary of Duchamp's *Fountain*, a work which must have inspired Cattelan's. Duchamp's work is a canonical example of modernist democratization of aesthetics, which worked by bringing everyday aesthetics into the sphere of high modernism (he placed a urinal on a pedestal to transform it into an object of art).

These listed artworks all reinforced Trump's message that the derisive liberal elite saw him, and by extension his supporters and their priorities, as a joke. However critical of Trump an artwork may have been, he still stood to benefit from its circulation: he looked like the everyman who made it to the top without ever being truly accepted by the elites.[20] Regular controversy was rewarded with a platform and publicity.[21] All these works failed to meaningfully attack Trump, or even illuminate anything about him, because they did not understand that Trump is an "obscene master."[22] Thus, they become almost indistinguishable from art that celebrates Trump, or from Trump's own one-dimensional strategies of body-shaming and taunting.[23]

Returning to Žižek's account of the obscene master, there are two main consequences of strategic use of obscenity. The first is that it marks the reversal of the public–private space distinction in the lives of political leaders. Just a few decades ago, the public lives of politicians were intended to be led with dignity and distinguished from their intimate or private lives which had the potential to destabilize their careers (the case of Bill Clinton would be a good example). However, today not only is media filled with increasingly intimate accounts of politician's dirty secrets—such as the 2021 scandal over masturbation on female MPs' desks by male staffers in the Australian Parliament—but politicians themselves often openly share such "secrets."

The second consequence is even more significant for our argument. Žižek argues that while Trump's strategic obscenities have become synonymous with his public persona, there is also a limiting point at which he intends to be taken seriously. When he is talking about "making America great again" or "enemies of the people," Trump means what he says. According to Žižek, this is why undermining Trump as obscene master must begin by treating these serious statements as obscenities: by ignoring his use of obscenity as a form of dismissing his opponents and focusing on the obscenity of his political decisions, such as dismantling important laws, racist deportations, and violations of human rights. Žižek's account helps us articulate the shift in perception of "strongman" political leadership in relation to critical art practices. The aim here is to look at works that take Trump (or rather, the working of power behind the performed vulgarity) seriously rather than openly mocking his body or obscenities. We can step through the argument by looking at works of artists who have addressed these different points of the public perceptions of political leaders. The point about using obscenity to challenge the traditional political leader by depriving them of dignity is the driving motivation behind Sanja Iveković's work *Triangle* (1979), which is where we begin.

Triangle

Triangle is a critique of the visual order of the socialist state, aimed at the pervasiveness of images of political leaders in the "socialist iconosphere."[24] Four photographs and text document the performance in Zagreb on May 10, 1979, the day of Yugoslav President Josip Broz Tito's visit to the city: Iveković sitting on the balcony overlooking the parade reading a book and making gestures as if she is masturbating, a member of the security detail on the nearby rooftop spotting her and notifying a police officer who comes to her door and orders her to leave the balcony.

The work is a triangulated interaction between Iveković and mechanisms of state power, which effectively critiques the public appearance and performance of ideology because it forces the socialist visual order to enunciate itself. It remains an open question whether this enunciation of the state (the reaction) was the result of Iveković being spotted on the balcony and thus deemed a security risk, or whether in fact it was her making "obscene" gestures of masturbation that forced the hand of the secret service. Nevertheless, it is precisely this use of sexuality to challenge political power in *Triangle* that makes it impossible and unimaginable in the present. From a security standpoint, it is impossible to imagine that an artist (or any anonymous civilian for that matter) would be so close to a head of state. From the standpoint of a critique of patriarchal state ideologies and rituals, the work looks almost quaint. Put differently, is it even possible to imagine a similar work being produced in the present? Or to be more crude, what would Trump—who is known for bragging about grabbing women "by the pussy"—make of a work like this? And what can we make of the work in response to Trump?

FIGURE 5.4 Sanja Iveković, Triangle, 1979. Four gelatin silver Digital (1)(A) prints and printed paper, frame: 20 × 24 × 1 in. (50.8 × 61 × 2.5 cm); each: 12 × 16 in. (30.5 × 40.6 cm). Committee on Media and Performance Art Funds. Acc. no.: 126.2011.a-e. New York, Museum of Modern Art (MoMA). © 2021. Digital image, The Museum of Modern Art, New York/Scala, Florence.

Insomuch as *Triangle* is about the public display of state power, it is in equal part about the performance of individuality juxtaposed against expectations of docile citizenship. *Triangle* has been read as an act of dissidence, where Iveković's drinking, smoking, reading, and masturbating stand in contrast to the expectation of citizens to dutifully participate in the parade.[25] *Triangle* operates through series of oppositions between Iveković and Tito along axes of power: man/woman, politician/artist, public/private, media image/snapshot. The intimate close-up of Iveković counterposes the wide-shot of Tito, establishing a contrast between the male statesman in a populist projection of his self onto the public and the female artist, inwardly focused and engaged in intellectual pursuit. While the private scene portrays the artist surrounded by props of sustenance, Tito is signified by the choreography of the motorcade, with the police and military in the background of the stationary body of citizens.[26] Tito is never actually shown, partly for logistical reasons (inability to see him from the balcony), but also recalling the intense censorship of images of Tito in the public sphere.

Retrospectively, *Triangle* has been understood as a signal of both the opening of Yugoslav socialism to a more liberal and tolerant version (which was happening since the 1970s) and the ultimate implosion of the country.[27] This gesture of opening is generated through Iveković's manipulation of the "triangle of sight" within the work: the shifting relation between the state (represented by the police), the citizens (represented by the crowd), and the artist. In forcing the hand of the state apparatus to enunciate itself and censor Iveković, it showed the state's ultimate weakness.

If we apply this triangle principle to the events on Capitol Hill on January 6, 2021, we can observe a shifting dynamic between state power, the crowd, and Trump. In the days leading up to the protests on January 6 and during his speech, Trump's approach was a public performance of standing against the "deep state." To his supporters, he resembled an outsider uncovering the superficiality and corruption of the state's trying to silence voices of dissent. To everyone else, he was a defeated megalomaniac stroking his own ego by inventing falsehoods about the outcome of election and declaring himself a victim of the system he represents and benefits from. Therefore, in the first triangle formation the state power announced itself against itself: a lame-duck sitting president railing against the stolen outcome of elections. It was this enunciation (repeated endlessly in the weeks leading up to January 6 and during the speech itself) that riled up his supporters.

But Trump's political power enunciated itself a second time during the Capitol Hill riot, and this time it was to retreat into plausible deniability in trying to distance himself from the protesters. As the crowds broke into Congress and the scenes of violence and death began, the triangle changed: Trump started enunciating respect for state law and order, and the crowd became the performance of his prior obscenity. They were no longer "the good protesters." We argue that this is because it became clear that the protesters believed and identified with Trump's words more than he did. *Triangle* helps us to understand the shifting power dynamic that underpinned Trump's rhetorical U-turn; Adrian Paci's *Interregnum* (2017) helps us to understand the split within the crowd that made the turn to violence possible.

Interregnum

Interregnum weaves together footage from state and national television archives to show the public performance of mourning surrounding the passing of communist leaders in China (Mao Tse-tung and Zhou Enlai), North Korea (Kim Il-Sung), the Soviet Union (Lenin), Yugoslavia (Tito), and Albania (Enver Hoxha). The work shows the suspension of everyday life with scenes of long processions of people on streets without cars. This sense of temporal suspension is reinforced by the work's title, describing the interval between the succession of two regimes of power. Paci references Antonio Gramsci's famous description of "interregnum" as a moment of crisis in which "the old is dying and the new cannot be born; in this interregnum a great variety of morbid symptoms appear."[28]

Using this idea of temporal suspension, we can read *Interregnum* as a study of the shifting relation between the leader and citizens. From the perspective of the leader, *Interregnum* is a study of the death of the patriarchal socialist cult of personality, and of the regime mourning itself in a permanent state of surveillance. Following the death of "fathers of the nation" figureheads, their regimes stage rituals of mass mourning, with the population performing the role of mourning children.[29] The absence of visible dead bodies of the leaders represents the sense of historical loss. In relation to the absence of the leaders' dead bodies in *Interregnum*, it is interesting to consider it together with Shen Shaomin's *Summit* (2009), which operates as a conceptual prequel of sorts. Featuring replicas of corpses of Mao Zedong, Vladimir Lenin, Kim II Sung, Ho Chi Minh, and Fidel Castro encased in glass coffins, *Summit* provides us with voyeuristic insight into what the crowds in *Interregnum* are waiting for: to ensure that their leaders are in fact dead.[30]

FIGURE 5.5 Interregnum, 2017, by Adrian Paci, Film still, Single channel video, colour, sound, 17.28 minutes, Ed. of 6 © Adrian Paci, 2017. Courtesy the artist, Galerie Peter Kilchmann, Zurich, and kaufmann repetto, Milan and New York.

This ambiguity about the motivations of the crowd holds the key to *Interregnum*'s insight into the Capitol Hill riot. The death of "fathers of the nation" is marked with appropriate emotional intensity and epic pathos performed by "the people." The close-ups show solemn grieving faces, and a woman in the Eastern European scenes wipes away a tear, acting as our emotional surrogate. This figure of an older woman crying is positioned as a symbolic vessel of pure grief, referencing traditions of mourning in many cultures. But the figure is also a reference to the tradition of hiring the service of "weepers" at funerals. Žižek picks up on the transactional aspect of weeping, suggesting that the employment of weepers enables families to outsource mourning so that they can get on with negotiating over the inheritances left by the deceased.[31] Seen in this context, *Interregnum* becomes less a moment of national loss than a performance of mourning, the citizens acting as "weepers" against the background of an ideological struggle to fill the power vacuum left behind by the dead leader.

What can we learn from *Interregnum* in relation to the attempted insurrection? The riot was a staged public performance split between the QAnon faithful, mourning the loss of their leader and their stolen enjoyment (Stop the Steal), and an armed right-wing militia attempting insurrection. The mourners at Capitol Hill on January 6 operated like weepers: they performed mourning for the stolen votes. And while they did this, the others went on with the business of planning the overthrow. This is reminiscent of ex-communist apparatchiks who mourned the loss of their "father" figures while plotting how to stay in power.

Triangle helped us articulate the enunciation of state power implicit in Trump's rhetorical shift during the Capitol Hill riot; *Interregnum* gives clarity to the different levels of meaning performed by the crowd. In the next section we will articulate the reason for Trump's retreat into plausible deniability. Drawing on the work of Janez Janša, Janez Janša, and Janez Janša we argue that the crowd overidentified with Trump's words, taking him more seriously than he took himself, and thus demonstrated the pragmatist superficiality of his position.

The Janez Janša Project[32]

In July 2007, three artists in Slovenia (Emil Hrvatin, Žiga Kariž, and Davide Grassi) changed their names to Janez Janša. The artists articulated their decision as a personal one and, following the change, continued with their daily lives and usual professional activities such as making work and exhibiting it, attending public events, and writing for newspapers, all under their new names. They created new meanings through open-ended and ongoing relationships and situations between individuals, institutions, and their representation in the media.[33] They came up with the concept of "collateral art" to describe this form of practice. In collateral art, meaning is not generated through direct production but through activating the process of production and then framing this process as art.[34] This update of the Duchampian readymade, which withdrew even further the agency of the artist, created an interesting effect on the public perception of the original Janez Janša as a political brand.

What is this brand? We can call it the transitional strongman. Janša started his political career in 1988 as a journalist for *Mladina*, when he was arrested under suspicion for stealing confidential military documents and disclosing of military secrets. He became a key figure in the Slovene struggle for independence from Yugoslavia, and a symbol of anti-war and anti-military politics in Slovenia.[35] In large part due to his role in the 1991 Slovenian "ten-day war" which led to Slovenia's independence from Yugoslavia, he became Minister of Defense in 1992. He lost the post in 1994 due to his involvement in an affair of illegal arms trading with Croatia and Bosnia and Herzegovina. Between 2004 and 2008, and 2012 and 2013, he was Premier of Slovenia. In 2011, he was charged with taking bribes from an arms manufacturer, in 2012 he was impeached, and in 2013 he was sentenced with a two-year prison term for corruption.[36] This ruling was overturned by the Constitutional Court of Slovenia in 2015, and he was released after serving only six months. Despite his party winning the 2018 Slovenian parliamentary election, Janša was initially passed over as a prime ministerial candidate because most parties refused to join a Janša-led government. However, Janša was selected as Prime Minister-designate in March 2020, following the resignation of Prime Minister Marjan Šarec, and served a third term as Prime Minister until he was voted-out in April 2022.

A communist in his youth, Janša's political stance has drifted rightward during the course of his political career, from a liberal, pro-democracy dissident to a right-wing hardliner whose politics have been compared to Trump's conspiratorial, paranoid populism.[37] Once he was in power, the former Marxist became a strident anti-Marxist, the former pacifist became the Minister of Defence who personally profited from arms sales, and the former fighter for free speech and democracy became the practitioner of unconstitutional mobbing of free media.[38] Janša has been called "mini Trump" because of his tendency to inflammatory and racist Tweets—often directed at journalists criticizing him, or minority groups in Slovenia—and because of his vocal support for Trump, which included congratulating Trump on an election victory in 2020 weeks after it became apparent that Biden had won.[39] But if he is "mini Trump," he has also been called "Marshal Tweeto." He is thus the synthesis of the authoritarianism of the traditional leader (represented in *Triangle* and *Interregnum*) and the empty ideological position represented by Trump. The 2020 "Marshall Tweeto" series of protests has of course also been decried by Janša as a smear campaign: the Slovenian PM is known for his extremely vocal attacks on socialist Yugoslavia and on communism more generally, prompting the protesters to mock him by reusing the socialist imagery.[40]

The activities of the three artists after the name change caused confusion, including: Janez Janša getting married with Janez Janša as the best man; media reports of Janez Janša directing plays, exhibiting artwork, and appearing simultaneously in multiple locations; a newspaper containing multiple columns and opinion pieces authored by Janez Janša; different Janez Janšas giving interviews to the media during the campaign for the 2007 election; the "wrong" Janez Janša (the politician) being sent court summons for offences committed by an artist; and the establishment of a crowdsourcing campaign, Free Janez Janša, for funding to complete a documentary about the project while the politician was in prison. Clearly, part of the project's creative strategy was to participate in the broadcast media in order to saturate its sphere with the name and confuse the message. This approach was reinforced in the documentary *My Name is Janez Janša* (2012), in which one scene features a number of people repeating the title in a mechanical fashion, rendering it empty of all meaning.

The significance of the name change by the three artists is in the short-circuits it creates in the media sphere where, through unexpected interactions, the message is often confused or subverted. In an era of media-savvy political sloganeering and targeted promotions, the name change takes the form of political manipulation. But there is another level at which this gesture taps into the working of political manipulation: the intentional misunderstanding of the political message in order to subvert it. Or rather, misunderstanding of the call of the political leader through overidentification. We can see this in the way the three Janez Janšas explain their reason for the name change. The only reason for the name change that the artists ever gave—in addition to the explanation that it was a personal and intimate act—is available in the letter that they sent to the politician Janša, in which they state that they were motivated by the motto of his political party: "The more of us there are, the faster we will achieve our goal."[41] So, the professed trigger for the work is an act of clever, subversive, overidentification with a political slogan. In Janša the politician's universe, "we" in the slogan refers to an ideal community, yet in this broadcast it is not based on the usual moral conservative values (family, virtue, tradition), but on simple multiplication. In other words, his slogan refers to little more than the securing of numbers, which will ensure gaining political influence and reaching "our" goal. The apparent cynicism openly acknowledges the complete absence of political orientation, exhibiting instead a ruthless pragmatism. In fact, rather than being an exception, Janša's sloganeering typifies a common practice in the contemporary politics that factors into the Trump Effect's post-ideology expediency, in which governments, in the firm grip of their political donors, routinely change or abandon their political platforms for pragmatics once they are in power.

Janša's "we" is the empty ideologic center that can be filled by whatever content is necessary or required. Janez Janša is the placeholder for an emptiness which is infinitely flexible and translatable. His personal story (rags–riches/power–imprisonment–more power) is one of political

Possibly inspired by Selak's sculptures of Donald and Melania Trump, in 2018, Berlin-based US artist Brad Downey commissioned Slovenian artisan Ales "Maxi" Župevc to create a sculpture of Melania Trump in the Slovenian village of Sevnica, near her birthplace. A local, self-taught woodcarver, Zupevc was commissioned because he was the same age as Melania Trump and born in the same local hospital when Slovenia was still part of Yugoslavia. The wooden statue was based on photographs of Melania from the inauguration of her husband. Being wooden, the statue was flammable, and on July 4, 2020, Župevc's sculpture of Melania Trump was set ablaze by unknown arsonists. While the Banja Luka episode enabled the media event in which "Trump fell but Putin remained," the episode in Sevnica generated headlines wherein "Melania was on fire." In almost a reverse of Colson's statue in Bristol, the destroyed wooden sculpture was then replaced by a bronze statue based on the original. In this Balkan context, Melania's public image is one of first being "de-balkanized"—a child from a working-class family leaves socialist Yugoslavia in search of a better life, tries her luck in Austria, changes her name from a "Slovenian sounding" Melanija Knavs to an "Austrian sounding" Melania Knauss, then marries rich in America, and then uses "chain migration" to help her parents move to the US (under policies that were later opposed by Donald Trump). Melania's transformation—the name change, the foregoing of socialist past and working-class roots—connects her and Trump's story to Janša. However,

FIGURE 5.7 A life-sized wooden sculpture of U.S. first lady Melania Trump is officially unveiled in Rozno, near her hometown of Sevnica, Slovenia, July 5, 2019. Photo: REUTERS/AAP/TPX IMAGES OF THE DAY/Borut Zivulovic.

once reinvented, Melania is "re-balkanised"—rendered as a turbo sculpture, destroyed and symbolically re-born in bronze, the wife of a "balkanized" American president, himself an echo of Slovenian president Janša. Župevc's statue overidentifies with the re-balkanized Melania, proudly reclaiming her as the Slovenian girl who left and did everything to forget her Balkan roots.

Conclusion

Janez Janša is "more Trump than Trump." He has outlasted him; he has been more successful using similar tactics. It would not be surprising if Trump started looking at Janša when plotting his possible second run at the presidency. We can use insights from Janez Janša, Janez Janša, and Janez Janša to examine the Capitol Hill riot through the lens of overidentification. Žižek's notion of overidentification articulates the way a performer identifies with an object to such a degree that it becomes impossible to tell whether it is a form of support, ridicule, or a combination of the two. Žižek's questions cynical distance and distrust as the standard positions against the dominant ideology.[46] Subversion and transgression have been embraced and diffused as virtues into the culture of postmodern capitalism. Žižek reverses the understanding of cynicism as critical distance, to ask whether it instead represents peak conformism by supplying the perception of critical distance. He argues that overidentification, the almost fanatical adherence to the rules of ideology, is the only way to frustrate the efficiency of the dominant ideology. By taking it too seriously, overidentification reproduces the authoritative discourse back to itself and demonstrates the working of its ideology.

We observe this relationship between Trump's inflammatory rhetoric and his followers at Capitol Hill, namely in how he riled them up only to backtrack as soon as it got serious. Michael Wolff's account of the events of January 6, 2021, from the perspective of Trump's inner circle, shows the extent to which even Trump himself felt that his supporters misunderstood him and took things too far.[47] Top of FormWolff says that Trump often expressed puzzlement about his supporters—about who these people were, with their low-rent "trailer camp" bearing and their "get-ups"; he once joked that he should have invested in a chain of tattoo parlors, shaking his head about "the great unwashed."[48] To Trump, the January 6 protest was secondary to his hope that Vice-President Mike Pence would reject the final tally of the November vote. Trump's speech reflected this:

> After this, we're going to walk down—and I'll be there with you. We're going to walk down. We're going to walk down any one you want, but I think right here. We're going to walk down to the Capitol, and we're going to cheer on our brave senators and congressmen and women. We're probably not going to be cheering so much for some of them because

> you'll never take back our country with weakness. You have to show strength, and you have to be strong.[49]

In his desire to rile up the protesters, Trump said he was planning to march to the Capitol with them. According to Wolff, shortly after the speech finished, one of his aides told the president that it would be impossible to organize him marching to the Capitol, to which Trump replied: "I didn't mean it literally."[50]

Trump's refusal to understand or acknowledge the mounting crowds, the breached barricades, and the protesters entering the Capitol continued for another two hours. According to Wolff, it was at 3 p.m. that Trump seemed to begin the transition from seeing the mob as people protesting the election to seeing them as not his supporters. This was most likely Trump's political self-preservation kicking in and him distancing himself from the protesters to ensure that he could not be held responsible for them. As Wolff describes it:

> the radically faithful had simply been concentrated. The merely eager party types, and the Las Vegas audience sorts, and the local business proprietors, and the family-outing Republicans, and the VFW-post members, and various church groups, the salt of the Republican earth, more or less in normal dress, all had mostly self-selected out, leaving what was generally, if abstractly, referred to in the Trump circle as the "hard core." But no one had ever come so clearly face-to-face with this pure hard core as was happening now and would happen, in video footage and in indictments, in the weeks to come. Even Trump himself, the clearest channel through to this fan base, was growing confused. "This looks terrible. This is really bad. Who are these people? These aren't our people, these idiots with these outfits. They look like Democrats."[51]

Wolff concludes that while disorder had always been Trump's element, it was now his followers', too. His followers misunderstood Trump by taking him too seriously. Such an overidentification can show the true face of Trump: not obscenity of the strongman, but political pragmatism weaponizing obscenity and doublespeak.

While the ideology of the Capitol Hill rioters is determinatively conservative, at a formal level their tactics follow a tradition that has a lineage going back to the modernist ethics of transgression and subversion (such as the counterculture of May '68).[52] On the one hand, this demonstrates that a formal transgression of the existing order does not necessarily move in the direction of emancipatory and progressive change. On the other hand, it also suggests that a formal transgression such as the Capitol Hill riot will give us valuable insight into how power enunciates itself. Both events were triggered by an answer to a call: the Janez Janšas changed their name in answer to Janša's call "the more of use there are. . ."; the rioters answered Trump's call to fight against the stolen election with the words "[y]ou will never take back our country with weakness."[53] It is interesting to compare the way in which this language was taken up: the Capitol Hill riot is almost the negative image of the Janša artwork. In both cases, actions and events resulted from misinterpretation of the leader's message. In both cases, the act of identification forced the cynical opportunism to enunciate itself: Jansa and Trump have no ideological ambition other than to rule. Contrary to popular thinking, Trump does not universally use inflammatory rhetoric. While he is well known for his social media posts, in official settings his language has been quite similar to that of other US presidents.[54] All of this brings us closer to unpacking the questionable the "leadership" (and responsibility) behind the event. In our final chapter, we extend from this discussion of overidentification and consider the relationship of the carnivalesque mob to its master.

CHAPTER SIX

Delegated Insurrection

An angry crowd storms the parliament building on behalf of a popular president deprived of his electoral victory through the political manipulations of a conspiratorial and secretive state. This sounds like a description of a people's uprising that happened somewhere far from Capitol Hill in Washington, D.C.—possibly in the Balkans—to which the US would send observers and peacekeeping troops to perform what we have previously described as militaristic humanism.[1] Viewed formally (that is, separated from its racist and nationalist politics), the storming of the Capitol Building by Trump supporters on January 6, 2021 appears as a direct expression of popular dissatisfaction with a corrupt electoral system—it seems an extension of similar popular uprisings and protests over the last decade: the Arab Spring, the Occupy movement, the BLM protests across the globe. Yet, the Capitol Hill riot could not be further removed from the political and social motivations behind these movements. Driven by a pro-White American racist vigilantism, the riot only shares its *appearance* with anti-establishment protests that have shaped recent years. In this sense, the participants in the insurrection were doing the right thing for the wrong reason.[2]

This chapter will explore the ambiguity inherent in interpretation of the Capitol Hill riot. In the aftermath of the event, most analyses have interpreted it as a riot, a protest, an insurrection, or a violent carnival, and the participants as mob, a crowd, or supporters.[3] Some responses questioned "did they really mean it?" by pointing out the difference between "mum and dad" Trump supporters and armed insurrectionists, while others questioned whether Trump, as the lead character of the event, meant what he said and stood for, or whether that was consistent with his performative presidency, full of proclamations about "fake" things that he disagreed with. These interpretations converge around the question of authenticity. The Capitol Hill riot brought us into proximity with a disturbing social reality of violent anti-democratic racists whose failure to follow through with the insurrection left a lingering unease about unforeseeable and unpredictable outcomes. It left us wondering, what would the insurrectionists have done if they had been

FIGURE 6.1 Protestors loyal to US President Donald J. Trump waving Trump banners and American flags storm the temporary Inauguration dais at the U.S. Capitol in Washington, D.C., attempting to prevent by force the democratic process. Photo: Mihoko Owada/STAR MAX/IPx, STAR MAX File Photo via AP via AAP.

successful at Capitol Hill on January 6, 2021? Would the mob have dragged senators to the steps outside the building and lynched them in view of the public? Would they have occupied the chambers and issued a statement of demands for political reform of the electoral and legal system? Would they have attempted similar actions in other locations around the US and initiated a civil war or violent overthrow of the government? These are disturbing questions with no clear answers, and they present a challenge to our standard ways of thinking about the events in Washington, D.C., on that day. But this ambiguity is also what brings the incompleteness of the *attempted* insurrection on Capitol Hill into the conceptual territory of the theory of delegated performance, allowing us to take another approach to its interpretation.[4]

In this chapter we pick up upon a theme that has percolated throughout the previous chapters: that across our fractured political spectrum, politics is now expressly performative, public, and declarative. Political subjectivity has become central to "our" culture, and to how we position and identify in that culture—politics *as* culture, politics *as* identity—precisely at a moment when political positionality is more fluid and harder to pin down; or, perhaps, political subjectivity is even amplified *because* of this fluidity. We argue that the widely differing levels of authenticity at the Capitol Hill riot can be approached through the fundamentally performative nature of the event. For instance, the Stop the Steal rally, and subsequently the riot, were seen by its actors as a way to gain support by performing for the cameras of the media and those of their own smartphones. Building on our previous chapter's discussion of Trump as an obscene strongman, we now examine the Capitol Hill riot as an unintentional work of performance art, through the theory of delegated performance art, and draw out its key themes in relation to analyses of Jeremy Deller's *Battle of Orgreave* (2001), Milica Tomić's *This Is Contemporary Art* (2001), and Vladimir Nikolić's *Death Anniversary* (2004).

This speculative chapter is intended as a theoretical experiment: the conceptual clash of a White nationalist, violent event and a socially progressive theory of performative art. In forcing an encounter between two things that seem incompatible, our analysis seeks to evaluate the continuing shift between strategies on the left and on the right. Through this encounter new understandings of the riot and delegated performance emerge: the Capitol Hill riot becomes a delegated performance that failed for the right reasons (it does not hold up to ethical standards but it shows the injustice and racism of the system of power and exploitation it represents), while delegated performance becomes a flawed approach to social relations that provides the right answers (performed social antagonism as the only way of showing injustice and exploitation). If this seems like a conceptual deadlock wherein we have extended ideas to their limit (revealing the limits of the current democratic system), a key aspect of our experiment is that the encounter between the Capitol Hill insurrection and delegated performance is viewed "from the periphery." It is framed through the cultural and historical experience of the mythical Balkans: the imagined space full of political manipulators, liars, and bloodthirsty mobs. This chapter "balkanizes" the performances of Trump and his rioting supporters at Capitol Hill to demystify his hold on the imagination of many Americans. We place Trump in the context of nationalist demagogues from the Balkans to show that his political strategy has clear precedents, and thus forms part of a longer and broader trend. We place his supporters in the context of turbo-culture from the Balkans to show that there are important historical lessons to be learned from the Balkans as a region with lived and historical experience of toxic nationalism.

Trump the Artist and his Performance at Capitol Hill

There are a few important clarifications that must be made regarding our approach to Trump as an artist and to the Capitol Hill riot as his delegated performance artwork. Regarding Trump as an artist, several scholars have identified his election campaign and presidency as performative.[5] Trump's inflammatory and racist rhetoric (about White nationalism, the US workers) and his political paraphernalia (MAGA hats, shirts, posters) have been analyzed as examples of performative "late fascism," which intensifies the aesthetic dimension of politics and regards the public as artistic material with which the leader can work.[6] We extend this argument to examine the Capitol Hill riot as the crescendo of Trump's political performance and choreography. We also understand that the participants of the riot engaged in a build-up of prior violent, racist protests such as that in Charlottesville in 2017 and earlier Stop the Steal rallies in Phoenix, Arizona, in which they rehearsed and tested their strategies.

We are not suggesting that there is an equivalence between the Capitol Hill riot and delegated performance, or that there was an intentional staging of the event as a delegated performance. Rather, we argue that there is a striking convergence between the formal approach of delegated performance and the dynamic between Trump, his supporters, and the public at Capitol Hill, which can be described through the term "accidental postmodernism." By this, we mean that the relation between the Capitol Hill riot and delegated performance is the same as the relation between postmodernism and the "accidental postmodernism" of turbo-architecture. Turbo-architecture is a phenomenon originating in 1990s Former Yugoslavia, where unregulated and illegal construction of houses, buildings, and shopping malls found aesthetic and formal similarity with the eclecticism of postmodernist architecture. The fact that the hybridity and pastiche of symbolism and design in buildings were not the products of architecture as a discipline or of architectural theory, but amalgams of systemic lawlessness and lack of regulation, made the similarity even more striking.[7] Drawing on this understanding of the relation between eclecticism and lawlessness, we argue that the accidental postmodernism at the Capitol Hill riot is not a result of an engagement in performance art or theory, but the embrace of transgressive style driven by the hyper-individualism of a failing state.[8] Calling the Capitol Hill riot accidental postmodernism enables us to draw attention to three key characteristics: we highlight that it is primarily a "style" (meaning it formally resembles postmodernism, rather than being developed in relation to it); we highlight that it is focused on debates and ideas from the critical Left from decades ago (see Chapter 3); and we highlight that it is the result of lack of regulation, that is, abandonment of all aesthetic and ethical rules.

The notion of the Capitol Hill riot as a manifestation of accidental postmodernism potentially equips us to reconceptualize and disarm the larger phenomenon of the Trump Effect. As we have demonstrated throughout this book, the Trump presidency is marked by ideological confusion, and contemporary visual culture is the place where ideological and iconological collisions take place. Similarly, at certain points, Trumpist transgression formally resembles avant-garde artistic practices. While the Trump Effect has in large part been marked by an uncanny resemblance between normative transgression and historical critical practices, our reconceptualizing here of the Capitol Hill riot also draws attention to another key aspect: here we draw on Stephen Eisenmann's approach to photographs of torture at Abu Ghraib prison that were leaked to the public in 2003. Eisenmann's approach to the disturbing photographs—and to the broader apathy in the public and political response to the images which he describes as the "Abu Ghraib effect"—is to locate them in the context of art history.[9] As Eisenmann argues, while these Abu Ghraib photographs were never intended to be seen as artworks, they should not be excluded from a comparison with works that belong to the history of art.[10] Eisenmann's approach helps us to position the Capitol Hill riot within the same genealogy as the Abu Ghraib photographs: as a seemingly unprecedented eruption of images of violence that is "at once disturbing and familiar in their form and content, demanding yet somehow denying interpretation."[11] Our aim is to interpret the Capitol Hill riot, not to render its disturbing logic somehow "artistic" but to critically unpack its seeming familiarity and normality. Following Eisenmann, we will position the Capitol Hill riot in relation to a set of performance artworks by Deller, Tomić, and Nikolić. These works contain themes, subjects, and performative approaches that will help us to better understand the violent performance of the Capitol Hill riot and to counter its effect of normalizing (and making appealing) White supremacist violence as a legitimate form of protest.

The seeming normality and familiarity of the January 6, 2021, violence is evident in some of the other aesthetic reference points through which it has been interpreted so far. These include the pseudo-fascist "blood and soil" choreography of the protesters mixed with populist macho-vigilantism in films such as *Fight Club* (1998), and discussions of the riot at Capitol Hill as a carnival. Trump's election success in 2016 and his entire presidency have been attributed to his anti-establishment, carnivalesque appeal;[12] so, following the attack on the Capitol Building, several authors described it as a carnival.[13] Understanding the insurrection as a carnival relates to the understanding of carnival as a populist outburst of energy. Mikhail Bakhtin's *Rabelais and His World* (1965) positioned the medieval carnival as a moment of rupture and renewal in popular culture. It is a loose repertoire of feasting, eating, dancing, play, and spectacle. It has been taken up as a protest aesthetic identifiable in artistic and social movements from the Situationist International, through Carnival Against Capital (1999), to the Pussy Riot protests.[14] But some major critiques of the political efficacy of the carnival are that there is no way to determine its political orientation[15] and that the permissiveness of authorities towards carnival is an effective way for them to defer genuine upheaval.[16] Specific to our purpose here, the idea of carnival does not address the symbolic exchange that took place at Capitol Hill between Trump the artist, his supporters the performers, and the audience. Neither does it address "the day after" this exchange took place.

Indeed, the question "what happens after the Capitol Hill riot?" got an answer almost the next day. Shortly after the event, a group of curators and conservationists were dispatched to assess the damage. But even before they arrived, cleaners and maintenance workers were deployed to the Capitol

FIGURE 6.2 Pro-Trump protestors at the Capitol Hill riot, Washington, D.C., January 6, 2021. Photo: AAP Image/SIPA USA/Lev Radin.

Building to clean the site. Given the White supremacist tone of the attack, it was striking that most of the cleaners were people of color.[17] This connects to a question that we have always had about the carnival, for which there is no clear answer in the literature from Bakhtin onward: who does the cleaning up after the party is over? So, regardless of the long-term effects of the Capitol Hill riot on the political landscape of the US, immediately the scene defaulted back to its class- and race-based system of exploitation. White racists destroyed and defaced; workers of color cleaned up the mess.

The Capitol Hill Riot as a Delegated Performance

Since the early 1990s there has been a broader discussion about the emergence of artistic practices which use social relations and situations as material for their work. This period saw the rise of performances that feature activities that would traditionally be peripheral to fine art: preparation and consumption of a meal, casual conversations or fierce disagreements, members of the public dancing. Nicholas Bourriaud identified this trend through the term "relational aesthetics," and his short book framed the conversation about performance art for the better part of a decade.[18] Claire

Bishop's intervention into this conversation was to question the frequently uncritical celebration of social relations (the "relationality") as something that was inherently ethical and contrary to the rampant commodification of art. Providing an alternative genealogy of socially-engaged performance, Bishop argues that there has been an emerging trend in performance art since 1990 of "delegated performance":

> the act of hiring non-professionals or specialists in their fields to undertake the job of being present or performing at a particular time and a particular place on behalf of the artist, and following his/her instructions.[19]

Her approach is to provide an alternative account to Bourriaud's relational aesthetics. Rather than celebrating the "relationality" of social practice performance, Bishop provides a more contractual understanding of social relations in this kind of work. In being a mimicry of delegation and outsourcing in post-1989 capital, this work can present a powerful critique of social relations and commodification of art. Bishop argues that

> delegated performance produces disruptive events that testify to a shared reality between viewers and performers, and which defy not only agreed ways of thinking about pleasure, labour and ethics, but also the intellectual frameworks we have inherited to understand these ideas today.[20]

Bishop's analysis created a powerful effect and drew criticism, some of which was justified. But she made an important point in demonstrating the proximity of critical artistic practices to both growing exploitation of workers and diminishing quality of workers' rights (through outsourcing), and she effectively highlighted commodification and exoticization in contemporary art (here, a search for authenticity in the post-1989 world finding new "others").

This approach of looking at artistic practices that mimic forms of oppression and exploitation in order to critique them has historical precedents, including works by NSK and Laibach. It has often created powerful works which continue to resonate, but it has most always had an implicit understanding that the provocation and antagonism created in the works by mimicking exploitation or injustice is motivated by progressive politics. Even when it flirted with symbols of totalitarianism, even when it replicated processes of exploitation, the provocative or antagonistic work was defensible because it was assumed to be progressive. Our post-1968 legacy of defying social rules and norms as the default left-wing position begs the lingering question of what will happen if the forces of conservatism draw upon those same strategies, as demonstrated by the Trump presidency and its performative crescendo at Capitol Hill.

How can we understand the Capitol Hill riot as a delegated performance? How do we determine its success or failure, or evaluate its aesthetic and

trade unions that enabled the introduction of the program of free trade in the UK. It thus represents the last gasp of class struggle in the UK, where the working class was suppressed by the right-wing state. Deller's re-enactment, however, featured not only the former miners (in some cases playing themselves; in some cases switching roles to play policemen), but also members of re-enactment societies, who had no personal connection to the event. So, rather than a therapeutic re-enactment of the traumatic event, the performance hovers between "menacing violence and family entertainment," in which still-resentful working-class miners participated alongside middle-class re-enactment enthusiasts for whom it was a stylized performance.[25] As Bishop explains, "it took place in circumstances. . . akin to a village fete," with live music, food stalls, and cavorting children.[26]

Bishop concludes that the reason *Battle* is one of the earliest and highest profile examples of participatory art is that Deller reorganized the traditional expression of leftist politics in art.

> Rather than celebrating the workers as an unproblematically heroic entity, Deller juxtaposed them with the middle class in order to write a universal history of oppression, therefore disrupting not only the traditional tropes of leftist figuration but also the identificatory patterns and tonal character by which these are habitually represented.[27]

The ambiguity of violence mixed with entertainment in *Battle* was also on display at the Capitol on January 6, 2021. We witnessed the disturbing footage of violent clashes between protesters and the police, threats of lynching, and even the death of Ashli Babbitt. These images were interspersed with shots of costumed protesters looking like extras from a comedy skit, reports of protesters smearing feces on the walls of the building, and images of protesters taking selfies behind Nancy Pelosi's desk as if they were posing behind a presidential desk display at Madame Tussaud's waxworks museum.

Another way to frame this ambiguity is in terms of class identity, which was on display at the Capitol as much as it was in *Battle*. We can see this if we examine who was in the crowd, and what their actions were. The storming of the Capitol Building provided a negatively charged image of the multitude: a simultaneously frightening and ridiculous display of the different social and economic groups who answered Trump's call and behaved in a range of ways once they were inside the building. There were people who behaved like tourists on a tour of the building, taking photos and staying within the marked areas, and there were armed vigilantes in tactical gear (including current and former agents of the state) who engaged in direct confrontations with police.[28] Perhaps the most surprising group were members of the petite bourgeoisie, for instance a CEO of a Chicago company,[29] a Texan woman who flew in on a private jet in a bachelorette-style outing,[30] a Baltimore man who wore his work nametag during the attack,[31] and an academic and former member of Pennsylvania state legislature.[32]

The most disturbing and violent protestors were the armed vigilante groups such as the Proud Boys, who fought police but also formed alliances with police during the attack.[33] The most violent and destructive acts—assaulting officers, spitting on officers, teargassing, using bear-spray, shouting racial slurs—were committed by this group. It was the petite bourgeoisie who supplied some of the more ridiculous images from the attack. Aaron Mostofsky, the son of a Brooklyn Supreme Court judge, can be seen descending steps wrapped in fur and a bulletproof vest, armed with a large wooden stick and a police shield. This cosplaying insurrectionist looks like a fusion between an overgrown character from the *Lord of the Flies* and the sidekick to Lord Humungus from *Mad Max: Road Warrior* (the one who gets his fingers sliced off by a boomerang). The eclectic mix of vigilante apocalypticism with cosplay-worship of popular icons of masculinity was best expressed by Jacob Chansley, aka Jake Angeli. Bare chested with an American flag painted on his face, wearing a fur hat with horns, Angeli's widely circulated image became one of the most recognizable from Washington, D.C., on January 6, 2021. Characters like Mostofsky and Angeli brought a sense of upper-class frat-boy masculinity and entitlement to the riot. This was epitomized when Angeli went on hunger strike after he was imprisoned because the prison did not serve organic food.

FIGURE 6.4 Aaron Mostofsky, right, was indicted on eight charges, including Assaulting, Resisting, or Impeding Certain Officers, Theft of Government Property for taking Police body armor and riot shield, and Disorderly and Disruptive Conduct in a Restricted Building or Grounds. He pleaded not guilty to all 8 counts. Photo: Manuel Balce Ceneta via AP via AAP.

Over the course of the day, these different groups could be seen variously fighting with the police, stalking the halls of Congress, and posing for photographs on social media. What separated them was delegation between different aspects of the attack, from violent attack to tourist strolling through the building. What united them is that they were engaged in a delegated performance that failed for all the wrong reasons.

How did the Capitol Hill riot fail as a delegated performance? First, Trump didn't give up any of his power or privilege in the exchange with the protesters, he simply made it seem like he did.[34] Second, the social reality of protesters reaffirmed their and Trump's position in relation to the law. If the protesters were delegated the dirty work of insurrection (overt racism, violence, destruction, murder), their carrying out of the work was a transgression that violated the law but left it untouched. Given the severity of repercussions for the protesters (imprisonment, investigations, FBI calling for public to identify them), their transgression even reasserted the "law and order" through transgression. In provoking the state into action, they demonstrated that it works. And third, the protesters did not give Trump any of their social reality, which would have meant being accountable when breaking the law. The performers' fundamental difference to the "artist" was not only preserved but even increased. The Capitol Hill riot as a delegated performance seen in the context of *Battle of Orgreave* reaffirmed class difference as difference between transgression with and without consequences.

FIGURE 6.5 Jacob Chansley, aka Jake Angeli, aka the QAnon Shaman, at the Capitol Building during the riot on January 6, 2021. Chansley carries a spear with an American flag attached. Photo: Chris Kleponis/Sipa USA via AP via AAP.

The Failed Encounter in *This Is Contemporary Art* (2001)

In 2001, artist Milica Tomić staged a performance in a Vienna gallery with a popular Serbian vocalist from the 1990s, Dragana Mirković. Entitled *This Is Contemporary Art*, the event featured Mirković performing a six-song set in the gallery performance space, accompanied by a dance group. In addition to the standard greeting of "good evening ladies and gentleman," Mirković's performance opened with the declaration, "this is contemporary art." On the surface, the event was a manifestation of a broader trend of the commercialization and diversification of exhibition spaces across the globe, wherein additional income revenue for cultural institutions is generated by hiring out their exhibition spaces to the public. Celebrations, social gatherings, and private events are routinely held in art galleries, being seen by the galleries as a way to raise funds while introducing new audiences and demographics to gallery spaces. It is in this introduction of groups not usually seen in or identified with galleries that the work can provide insight into the Capitol Hill riot.

Tomić's collaboration with Mirković within the gallery space represented the introduction of turbo-folk music and its highly charged cultural and political history into the sphere of contemporary art.[35] Turbo-folk is high-energy dance music with melodies based loosely on traditional Balkan folk music. Originating in Serbia, it peaked in popularity during the 1990s at the time of the civil wars in Bosnia and Croatia, and at the time of international sanctions against Serbia that caused hyperinflation and a steep decrease in living standards there. Turbo-folk's populist celebration of hedonism and consumerism provided an escape from grim reality, while also aligning with the interests of Serb nationalists. Yet, despite its proximity to nationalist violence and crime, turbo-folk has survived the political fall, incarceration, and death of Slobodan Milošević and the North Atlantic Treaty Organization (NATO) bombing of Serbia; not only that, it has also risen in popularity, crossing ethnic boundaries throughout Bosnia, Croatia, and Slovenia.

How can we understand this early example of delegated performance in relation to our discussion of the Capitol Hill riot? Tomić's performance enables us to examine the riot as a (failed) encounter between the different groups. What is striking about Tomić's work is the way in which it anticipates the importing of a toxic cultural and political phenomenon (mixing of populism and nationalism/racism) into the cultural sphere, where strategies of "radical art" become indistinguishable from the alt-Right. While Tomić was not the first artist to bring turbo-folk into the context of contemporary art,[36] her positioning of this encounter beyond the borders of the Former Yugoslavia highlighted the role and perception of participants. In this sense, the work raises the question of delegation and outsourcing of authenticity through cultural processes of exclusion: through the question of who or what is "contemporary art" in the work.

Many of these questions are raised in a text by Belgrade-based art theorist Branislav Dimitrijević, which uses Tomić's work as a departure point to discuss the encounter between different social groups. Dimitrijević's text about the performance is one of the earlier attempts to grapple with the question of the relation of turbo-folk to contemporary art, and to articulate the delegation in the performance even though he never quite uses that word.[37] His discussion predates Bishop's articulation of delegated performance by almost a decade and anticipates many of the questions with which she grapples. Dimitrijević's discussion pivots around three key issues which we will consider below in relation to the Capitol Hill riot: the speech act of Tomić's work in her performer announcing "this is contemporary art"; turbo-folk as a cultural phenomenon which mimics global trends, yet is perceived as their anathema; and Tomić's event as a "failed encounter" between two socioeconomic groups.

Regarding the speech act in Tomić's work, Dimitrijević argues that the enunciation "this is contemporary art" is the only act through which the artist became visible/audible in the performance.

> The utterance we are dealing with here becomes a speech event, a form of action that is not the act of speaking, but an act performed by speaking. This is a constative that becomes a performative, at least through the act of naming. The event, i.e. the performance, is named contemporary art. Its performativity makes it not a simple tautology. Its illocutionary force, naming as doing, includes not only the act of uttering but the act that the speaker (the singer) performs in saying the words. If a turbo-folk singer names her concert "contemporary art", this is both false and communicative.
>
> What we saw on the stage in Vienna is another woman who belongs to a cultural sphere that is far remote from the established art context. This woman, the singer Dragana Mirković, does not act in the performance but performs her standard act taken from some other context where the turbo-folk music is consumed. Neither her act nor her body are shaped for the occasion, they are taken as a package, as a ready-made. And ready-made in an original Duchampian meaning: "object from life" that is placed in a gallery context puts the observer in the position of reconsidering his own views of the relationship of the quotidian and the artistic, while the object itself becomes the "focus of a meditation on the relation between external things and our perception of them".[38]

We can draw an analogy between the enunciation of "this is contemporary art" and of "Stop the Steal." While on the one hand "Stop the Steal" was Trump's political sloganeering (which predated January 6, 2021, and his presidency), on the other hand there was a purely performative element to the phrase. In this sense, turbo-folk as contemporary art in Tomić's performance and Trump's grievance with the US electoral system both represent forms that mimic broader trends but are presented and understood as opposed to them. Dimitrijević argues that the radical potential of turbo-folk is that it mimics global trends in popular culture but is treated as if it is opposed to those trends. He sees the Tomić work as an attempt to bring this tension into the space of the gallery and contemporary art. In this respect, the work (and Dimitijević's discussion) anticipates not only the clash between ideas that played out at the Capitol on January 6, but also the reactions to them.

We have previously demonstrated that turbo-folk operates less as a genre and more as a conceptual device used to negatively label phenomena.[39] In this sense, it should not be seen as a definition of a genre, but more to identify something as kitsch and corrupt: turbo-architecture, turbo-politicians. Trump is the perfect candidate for a turbo-politician. This became most evident in the months following his electoral loss and the Capitol Hill riot, when two jokes appeared online. The first joke featured Pope Francis, Donald Trump, Barack Obama, and a little boy, crossing the Atlantic together on an airplane when the engines fail. They find three parachutes. Trump grabs the first parachute and jumps out of the plane saying, "the world needs my leadership!" Obama grabs a parachute and says, "I need to help make choices for our world," then also jumps out of the plane. At this point, the Pope says to the boy, "take the last parachute, I am too old and I'm going to die one day soon." The little boy says, "actually there are two left. Donald Trump took my backpack." The second joke was a balkanized version of the first one, featuring Trump, Putin, and Bosnian Serb politician Milorad Dodik on a plane when the engines fail, and they find only one parachute. They decide to vote; whoever wins the most votes will get the parachute. Dodik wins, and quickly grabs the parachute and jumps out. A perplexed Trump, looking after him, says, "I don't understand how he managed to win by fifteen votes, when it was just us and the pilot on the plane." While the first joke talks about Trump's ineptitude, the second reframes this in terms of development as a political villain. Trump is an aspirational turbo-politician who is unable to properly cheat in the elections and is forced to embarrass himself with fake insurrections.

Regarding the third point Dimitrijević makes about Tomić's work as a failed encounter, towards the end of the text Dimitrijević remarks in a footnote that, despite seeing the potential of *This Is Contemporary Art* as a "radical gesture" bringing the discourse of turbo-folk into the space of the gallery, he nevertheless has "many problems with the work," such as "the failed attempt to bring together turbo-folk audience and exhibition-goers in Vienna."[40] While the details of this failure are never clearly articulated by Dimitrijević, we can speculate that he means the failure to bring together the working-class migrants with the middle-class and petite bourgeoisie art audience. Mirković's performance in the gallery represents the cultural experience and identity of Former Yugoslav migrant "guest workers" (*gastarbeiten*) communities in Western European countries. Even though turbo-folk was closely identified with Serbian nationalism, xenophobia, and war, it also crossed boundaries and became a form of transnational solidarity through hedonism and enjoyment of music. In including this in the space of a Viennese gallery, Tomić's work sought to draw attention to the "invisible" status of the ex-Yugoslav guest worker community in the eyes of the larger community in Vienna. Vienna has one of the largest ex-Yugoslav migrant populations, and is one of the cultural capitals of Mitteleuropa. The setting of the artwork in this context, and in a contemporary art gallery, frames the performance with questions of cultural exchange.

The performance was complemented by the audience's enthusiastic and energetic response to the music, which is typical of turbo-folk concerts. This response was strengthened because the audience was comprised not only of the usual art gallery crowd but also of Yugoslav migrant workers in Vienna. The documentary photographs of the event, available on Tomić's website, testify to this "clash of cultures," with images juxtaposing the art crowd's "black-on-black" outfits with the ex-Yugoslav migrants' golden crosses and leather jackets.

A "failed" encounter in Tomić's work refers to the absence of any meaningful connection between the turbo-folk audience and the contemporary art audience. Seemingly, the event staged a situation in which a readymade crowd of Balkan *gastarbeiten* entered the gallery space, enjoyed the performance, and left at the end. For their part, the art audience enjoyed the spectacle of Balkan exotica usually seen in clubs on the periphery of Vienna. While Tomić claimed that she wanted to make visible the invisible migrant community, it is more accurate to say that she made it visible in an art gallery only.

With regard to the failure of the encounter, Dimitrijevic's critique was correct, but he was talking about the wrong day. Given that a large majority of migrants work in cleaning and maintenance, their encounter with the work would have been the following day while cleaning the space after the performance. In a similar sense, the truth of the Capitol Hill riot was visible the day after the uproar, when cleaners (most of whom were people of color) were dispatched to clean up after the White supremacist protesters. Tomić's work helps us to illustrate the weaponization of populism and the failed encounter at the Capitol. In her work, these questions pivot around the relationship of "Balkan exotica" to the European center. In the next section, we will further "balkanize" Trump and the Capitol Hill riot by discussing the work of Vladimir Nikolić.

Balkanizing the Hero in Death Anniversary *(2004)*

For *Death Anniversary* (2004), Nikolić employed a Balkan professional weeper and visited the gravesite of Marcel Duchamp in Rouen, France, on the thirty-sixth anniversary of Duchamp's death.[41] The video features footage of Nikolić somberly standing over the tombstone while the weeper wails a mournful dirge about Duchamp's legacy.[42] According to Nikolić, his intention was to take "a true Balkan artist" to "the wrong place": to stage an encounter between the irreducible cultural difference of the shepherdess from Montenegro performing an archaic social ritual and what Nikolić describes as "the ultimate point of art universality" symbolized by Duchamp, the "Godfather" of European modernism.[43] The weeper is included distinctly strategically: she is outsourced affective labor of mourning for Duchamp. The weeping acts as an exotic distraction in the work, allowing Nikolić, having delegated the emotional labor of art, to remain preoccupied with the "proper" art business of presenting cultural capital to gain recognition internationally.

Death Anniversary is ostensibly about the European perception of art from the Balkans. The work uses an idiosyncratic cultural form as a strategy to make visible the identity-branding engaged in by artists seeking visibility on the global art circuit. Nikolić deploys the cultural specificity of his work to create a symbolic universe that "balkanizes" Duchamp by acknowledging him—and his legacy—through the cultural lens of the "dark side" of the civilization he represents. *Death Anniversary* operates a triple parody: of the role of the international art circuit in the production of mythologized Balkan identities; of the veneration of Eurocentric heroes of modernism; and of nationalist populism as reinforced through tradition. Nikolić intentionally selects a highly idiosyncratic and archaic form of "communicating with the dead" to parody the vocabulary of epitomized national identity as performed through the dead body. In *Death Anniversary* he uses his position of the artist "with a geopolitical burden" to reflect on the strategies of self-exoticization often used to gain visibility on the international art circuit. The work is a powerful critique of art with an ethnographic impulse, wherein artists use carefully selected cultural forms to represent an aspect of their local identity. In this context, art functions as a passport to international exhibitions such as Biennales, allowing artists from the global periphery access to the center, albeit for a limited time. *Death Anniversary* is a direct response to this cultural game of inclusion and exclusion, repurposing self-exoticization to highlight the inherent inequality. Nikolić "balkanizes" his work, intentionally framing it as a historically frozen and culturally backward response to European universality. Here, as previously, we use the term "balkanization" in the sense articulated by Maria Todorova: an act of creating a negative and exclusionary stereotype about people and cultural phenomena from the Balkan region.[44]

Nikolić's strategic usage of "self-balkanization" in *Death Anniversary* enables us to shift the discussion about the exchange of authenticity at play in delegated performance. Nikolić outsources authentic social reality to the weeper in *Death Anniversary*, even as he sources a readymade stereotype that undermines and reverses the premise of the work. Rather than bringing us closer to a perception of the center—represented by Duchamp's universality—the work exposes a strategy of manipulation of cultural difference that aims to move its proponents closer to the center. *Death Anniversary* shows us the *effect* of delegation, which is also at play in the Capitol Hill riot.

Rather than giving up any control of the work, this artist becomes a master manipulator. In performing a version of Balkan tradition designed to catch the eye of international tastemakers, he is also referencing the political choreography of populist politicians in the Balkans who "perform" traditions.[45] Rather than performing her social reality, the weeper is performing a business transaction masked as a traditional ritual. Nikolić's employment of the weeper is a tactical use of tradition, a reinvention of an established tradition of delegation into a cultural-financial transaction for the present. In Balkan societies that still use weepers at funerals, the service is first and foremost a business transaction. Weepers often have a repertoire of mourning songs from which some are chosen in discussion with the customer. As discussed in Chapter 5, Slavoj Žižek picks up on this aspect of weeping when he humorously remarks that the employment of weepers in a "traditional" sense enables families to outsource mourning, so they can get on with negotiating for the fortune of the deceased.[46]

We have previously established the way in which Trump cynically manipulated his supporters and stood by as they rampaged through the Capitol Building. Here we can add that in doing so, Trump "balkanizes" himself, joining the ranks of political manipulators from the Balkans. In particular, Trump's grandstanding can be compared to the political theater employed by Serb far-right politician Vojislav Šešelj, who in 2003 voluntarily surrendered to the International Criminal Tribunal for the Former Yugoslavia (ICTY) in the Hague in order to use it as a stage for his message.

Šešelj's trial for war crimes, which began in 2007, was a calculated political performance. Šešelj made demands of the court and went on hunger strikes until they were met, he disclosed identities of protected witnesses, and he routinely insulted the judges.[47] Even though Šešelj was found guilty of instigating deportations of Croats and sentenced to ten years in prison, he was released because his trial lasted for almost twelve years. In a sense, Šešelj's performance in court was a critique of the inherent problems with ICTY: from accusations of politically motivated decisions to procedural errors and long delays in trials. But in another sense, Šešelj was appropriating the tribunal as a platform for national myth and group making.[48] Šešelj was delegating the performance of justice to the ICTY, while he could get on with generating nationalist mythology about a martyr hero and collectivizing the blame for war crimes. There was also a second delegation: the public watching the spectacle would discuss how Šešelj was "doing the right thing for the wrong reason"—he was uncovering the truth about the corrupt ICTY even while he was a nationalist war criminal—while he appeared to be their victim, and was using the performance to generate publicity in the run up to the 2014 elections in Serbia.

FIGURE 6.6 Serbian ultranationalist Vojislav Šešelj during his initial appearance at the Yugoslav war crimes tribunal in The Hague, February 26, 2003. The tribunal acquitted Seselj in 2016 of all nine counts alleging that he was responsible for, or incited, atrocities by Serbian paramilitaries in the wars in Bosnia and Croatia in the early 1990s. Photo: Toussaint Kluiters via AP via AAP.

To frame Šešelj's performance in terms of the ambitions of *Death Anniversary*: upon initial inspection, ICTY is like Duchamp (the epitome of the universal discourse which excludes a local/national peripheral group), and Šešelj is like the artist (the singular martyr taking on the challenge of fighting the international art circuit/international justice). The performance of the legal trial creates a crucial shift where the target of the performance becomes the instrument of the performance: the corrupt ICTY becomes the weeper performing the protracted process, while in *Death Anniversary* the delegate is not the target of critique.

Trump's performance on January 6, 2021, and in the months after becomes the American version of Šešelj and the ICTY. Trump's challenge to the US electoral and legal systems becomes a performance in which the system is the weeper (or perhaps the "Veeper," personified in Vice President Mike Pence, who was expected to take his procedural role seriously and "challenge" the electoral outcome). A crucial part of this "artwork" is production of the myth that it is an act of defiance against entrenched injustice embedded in an institutional framework. In reality, however, it is not an act of defiance but a reinforcement: the performance is done in conversation with the institution. Šešelj's mythology was built in conversation with the "imperial West" in a collective narrative that contests the legitimacy and intention of The Hague while disguising individual responsibility. Trump's mythology was built around refuting and shaming the same imperial West, even though he is its clearest beneficiary.

> Trump has never drawn a distinction between these two: the organizational performance of his brand and his constant cultural performance of himself.[52]

The Capitol Hill riot on January 6, 2021, was an attempt to corporatize antagonism: to delegate an overthrow of government. Trump incites, rioters fight, Republican senators agitate, lawyers initiate lawsuits. This was based on Trump's belief that delegation of performance "works"; that it results in outcomes quantifiable in corporate terms. But delegated performance works through unexpected outcomes, which do not translate into measurable outcomes but raised critical awareness. Therefore, while the Capitol Hill riot failed on Trump's terms, it succeeded as a delegated performance because it demonstrated that the true losers in the event were the Trump supporters, and it was they who paid the price.

Conclusion

In the six chapters of this book, we have attempted to characterize the ways in which the Trump effect has resonated throughout aspects of visual culture since the mid-2010s: in the aesthetics of the paranoid epistemology of QAnon, in the conflicting representations of racial politics both on the Left and the Right, and in the conspiracist anti-intellectualism at the heart of the ongoing ideological and financial attack on universities. We have also considered ways in which contemporary art can open conceptual ground for reframing the role of monuments on our shifting post-ideological sands, undermine the authoritarianism of the strongman, and claim the attempted insurrection of the Capitol Hill riot as a delegated performance. Each of the chapters addressed to varying degrees the four key features we identified as the Trump Effect in our Introduction: that it is a global phenomenon that though embedded in the US precedes the Trump presidency and resonates with culture-war politics at the global "peripheries," which resonance is vital to its amplification; that it is characterized by a post-ideology politics, highly dependent on visual culture, that fragments old definitions of left and right politics; that it is a "balkanization" of American politics which, in turn, resonates back from the Balkan periphery; and that it is fundamentally paranoid and conspiracist. However, another underlying theme haunts our concerns and those of many of the artists we discuss, and this is "democracy."

On election night in 2020, as Trump addressed his inner circle of supporters and the world media, he spent seven minutes running through a cherry-picked list of vote tallies before declaring:

> This is a fraud on the American public. This is an embarrassment to our country. We were getting ready to win this election. Frankly, we did win this election. We did win this election. So, our goal now is to ensure the integrity, for the good of this nation, this is a very big moment, this is a major fraud on our nation, we want the law to be used in a proper manner, so we'll be going to the US Supreme Court. We want all voting

> to stop. We don't want them to find any ballots at four o'clock in the morning and add them to the list.

In that moment, the Trump Effect was fully realized: an attempted coup of a democratic election in the United States, in the name of democracy, in the name of the American public—an echo of Belarus' Alexander Lukashenko only weeks earlier, and based on conspiracy theory worthy of Slovenia's Janez Janša. Ultimately, the Trump Effect heralds the erosion of democracy in the twenty-first century. Against the historical backdrop of the emphatically ideological twentieth century, twenty-first-century politics is shaping up to be a contest of passions and competing post-truth live action role play games. The aim of Trumpism is to deploy emotions and the conspiracist imagination towards undermining the consensus of credibility that has ambiently held in place the most concrete of representative systems of government and knowledge. The objective is the consolidation of power.

Three weeks after the inauguration of US President Joe Biden, at the end of the Trump administration, the UK's BBC released *Can't Get You Out of My Head: An Emotional History of the Modern World*, a six-part documentary by British filmmaker Adam Curtis.[1] Curtis' *Can't Get You Out of My Head* may well give its audience a stultifying sense of overwhelmingness, of the confounding tsunami of information, fragmented narratives and disorienting politics, which has also characterized Trumpism and the global Trump Effect. The style of Curtis' documentaries—streams of moving images drawn from decades of television archives, structured around thematically interwoven narratives broken by occasional and often enigmatic captions of white block capital sans serif text—predate the Trump era. However, with their hypnotic, bleak atmosphere of foreboding, low-fidelity audio, slow-tempo repetitive sequences of minor-key music, droning discordant notes, and nostalgic pop songs, they articulate something of the political tenor of the 2020s. Curtis' disembodied BBC-English voiceover frequently evokes dark forces, strange twists, and the impending destruction of democracy. The combination of the familiar, uncanny, and occasionally violent images is purposely both unsettling and stimulating, possessing an addictively mesmeric appeal. Never quite reaching a climax or resolution, *Can't Get You Out of My Head* maintains a rhizomatic quality, which can leave the viewer with a pervading sense of all not being right in the world while maintaining an undulating near-sameness of mood that suspends time in a stasis of suspicion and intrigue, never resolved.

Like many of Curtis' epic documentaries, *Can't Get You Out of My Head* touches upon many themes, but its narratives converge around the topic of conspiracy theory: the Illuminati, the JFK assassination, Kerry Thornley's Discordianism, and "Operation Mindfuck" amongst many other threads. In interviews, Curtis elaborates on his focus on conspiracism, expanding from Richard Hofstadter's "paranoid style" idea that Americans brought with them from Europe "a suspicion that there might be corruption coming to haunt them. . . constantly aware that the old forces of corruption might have come with them in some way."[2] Curtis' hypnotic aesthetic of intertwined narratives, connections, and patterns echoes conspiracy documentaries like *Out of Shadows* and *Plandemic*, and employs many of the same atmospheric devices, such as company logos, Ken Burns effected photos, long-range telephoto aerial shots of corporate skyscrapers and government buildings, fast-paced montages of often disparate images, archival and news footage, ominous droning, and disembodied voiceover.

After nearly eight hours, *Can't Get You Out of My Head* settles on two conspiracy theories of the Trump era: the Cambridge Analytica data scandal and QAnon. Of Cambridge Analytica Curtis says,

> the liberal opposition became lost in an endless conspiracy theory, constantly searching for hidden clues, links and fragments of evidence to prove that really Vladimir Putin and firms like Cambridge Analytica had orchestrated Brexit and the election of Donald Trump. It was a mood of hysteria that ran out of control.

Of QAnon, he flatly says, Trump's supporters "had their own conspiracy theory, QAnon, that explained why nothing was happening. Trump was being stopped by a secret cabal of pedophiles in Washington."[3] To anyone paying attention to either "conspiracy," Curtis' off-hand flattening of them may be jarring. Cambridge Analytica stole the personal data of millions of Facebook profiles and subsequently misused it to micro-target content to foster voter suppression, and spread fake news and political advertising in order to tilt the 2016 US presidential election.[4] It was investigated by a US Congressional hearing, for which Facebook founder Mark Zuckerberg gave evidence, and in the UK resulted in the 2018 *Parliamentary Digital, Culture, Media and Sport Committee's Inquiry into Disinformation and "Fake News,"* which concluded that the UK's "electoral law is not fit for purpose."[5] Facebook agreed to pay a £500,000 fine in the UK as a result of the Cambridge Analytica controversy.[6]

Pervading Curtis' conspiracism theme is the broad thesis that politics in the twenty-first century has run out of ideas: that in every powerful country across the world those in power have no "idea of an alternative better future."[7] *Can't Get You Out of My Head* suggests that, in the politics of the post-ideological condition of the world of the twentieth century, conspiracism has taken the place of "real politics."[8] And, cleverly, after eight mesmeric hours of its mega-archive of suspicion, it delivers to its audience a post-ideological non-conclusion, dedicating only a few dispassionate seconds each to Cambridge Analytica and QAnon, both treated with innocuous neutrality. This curiously understated twist, withholding any substantial conclusions, reflects and articulates something important about the now substantially evolved, fractured politics of the twenty-first century upon which the documentary comments and which it also performs. It is perhaps a bleak realization that Curtis' *Can't Get You Out of My Head* may articulate the shape of post-ideological politics of the twenty-first century: a politics primarily aesthetic and, as our previous book has argued, affective and ontological, and ultimately concerned with holding onto power even if it means destroying democracy.

Democracy

Anne Applebaum's book *Twilight of Democracy: The Failure of Politics and the Parting of Friends* is part memoir and part political analysis, similar to Peter Pomerantsev's *Nothing is True and Everything is Possible*, which we quoted in our Introduction.[9] Applebaum begins with her New Year's Eve party in Poland on December 31, 1999, at the very beginning of the twenty-first century. She was living in Poland with her husband, at the time a Polish government minister. The party was largely attended by European, British, and American friends and professional associates, who were generally socially liberal, politically centrist, and economically neoliberal. She then chronicles the multitude of relationships with these people that, over twenty years and mostly the last ten, have shattered beyond repair as a consequence of those friends being swept up in the rise of strongman ethnonationalist politics and corrupt regimes. Hers is just one account, but it is fascinating because (like Pomerantsev) she paints a very vivid picture of Eastern Europe at the end of the 1990s, ten years after the fall of the Berlin Wall in 1989, and the optimism of the former Eastern Bloc as it sought to adopt a free-market economy and replicate Western European liberal democracy. In her recounting, Eastern Europe aspired to meritocracy yet quickly descended into nepotism, cronyism, and paranoid conspiracism under the leadership of populist nationalists such as Viktor Orbán in Hungary and the Law and Justice party in Poland, which Applebaum characterizes as angry, vengeful, and resentful.[10] From her account, it seems that during the communist era in Eastern Europe loyalty to the single Party, demonstrated through public displays of enthusiasm, was rewarded with positions and privileges without any measures of competence.[11] And while a neoliberalist, meritocratic ethos dominated for almost twenty years, faith in universalistic liberalism rapidly waned, and since then the communist era structures have resurged, except that the "Party" is now nation and ethnicity. With it has gone the taboo against political violence.[12]

What is most interesting about *Twilight of Democracy* is the way in which, by Applebaum's account, the conservatism of the "new Right" is "more Bolshevik than Burkean."[13] That is, the regimes that have arisen throughout Eastern Europe, as well as in the Trumpist US and Boris Johnson's UK, are less concerned with conserving the status quo and resisting social change than they are with destruction of systems of government. Steve Bannon, Trump's 2016 campaign manager and 2017 senior aide, and former executive chairman of Breitbart and former vice president of Cambridge

Analytica, famously identifies himself as a Leninist, which seems a curious political alignment for a man dedicated to engaging in culture war on behalf of the far Right. However, for Bannon, to fundamentally change society "you have to break everything."[14] Applebaum notes that, "[t]he language used by the European radical right—the demand for 'revolution' against 'elites', the dreams of 'cleansing' violence and an apocalyptic cultural clash—is eerily similar to the language once used by the European radical left."[15] This is very much the language of Trump, his acolytes, and his mass of followers, and this is what we have throughout this book articulated through the aesthetics and iconology of the Trump Effect. We have referred to it sometimes as "ideological confusion," however it would be more accurate to say it is the fungible rhetoric of a performative radicalism that historically belonged to leftist struggles for equality and justice and has been appropriated by post-ideology politics. Its effect is multifarious, but most importantly it renders unusable the ways that the Left once articulated its egalitarianism; in turn, it further fractures the political spectrum.

Arguably, the Trumpist right have even appropriated progressive left-wing arguments around epistemic justice. Whereas deeply pluralist progressivist scholars posit that dominant Western liberal systems of representation and knowledge enact epistemic oppression on local forms of knowledge, the Trumpist Right (more intuitively than scholarly) argue that the regime of expertise (big pharma, big government, "woke" corporations, and government institutions) is dominating and oppressing their own local forms of knowledge. This structure has been clear in the COVID-19 anti-vaxxer movement. Their repeated urging to "do your own research" and the QAnon demand to "join the dots" are an assertion of outlier local knowledges. Indeed, much of what we have discussed in this book suggests that epistemology is a conflict zone of The Trump Effect. We are no longer in the 2017 world of "alternative facts," but the 2020s world of incommensurable systems of knowledge, in which the very ways in which we establish fact are systematically divergent. C.J. Polychroniou writes, in the Foreword to Noam Chomsky's *The Precipice* (2021):

> And here is the trouble. Trump may be out of office, but Trumpism is still very much alive and kicking in the "land of the free and the brave." The Republican Party is Trump's party, and followers of the MAGA movement live in an entirely different galaxy than the rest of the population. To be sure, the United States remains most likely the most divided and polarized nation in the world. The differences among the citizenry are not merely political or ideological, they are epistemological.[16]

Worse still, more critical research epistemologies inherited from the Enlightenment stand as increasingly outmoded in opposition to ontologically based paranoid epistemology. Within the longer timeframe of this decade, paranoid epistemology may become established as the new political norm.

Privileging outlier, non-expert, and non-consensus sources of information, it aligns with the rightist libertarianism of Trumpism: consensus is to be distrusted because it represents the collective and, so the logic goes, is communistic.

In the first year of the Trump administration, British philosopher A.C. Grayling responded with his book *Democracy and Its Crisis*, which considered the threat to democracy through big data manipulations, such as that by Cambridge Analytica, and the rampant spread of misinformation. His discussion of the Trump era refers back to the earliest European discussions of democracy in the work of Plato.[17] Famously, Plato raised the dilemma of democracy, rule by the *demos* (the people), descending into ochlocracy (mob rule). He argued that direct democracy is always at risk of collapse into tyranny, because the *demos* is prone to the seductions of demagoguery, of manipulations of crowds by strongman tyrants by means of emotion and prejudice: "generally speaking, when politicians claim to know or be acting on behalf of 'the will of the people' one should be reaching for a thousand-liter tank of skepticism."[18] As early Enlightenment thinkers such as Thomas Hobbes, John Locke, and Jean-Jacques Rousseau developed the modern notion of democracy, notions of the "general will" of "the people" transformed into structures of government with layers of codified and conventional checks and balances. Thus, after America declared its independence, James Madison, Thomas Jefferson, and others designed its systems of representative democracy with three branches of government and checks such as the Electoral College and other systems through which governments gain "consent of the governed" while short-circuiting any single claim to a direct popular mandate.[19] These arguments are well-known, but Grayling's *Democracy and Its Crisis* emphasizes that in systems of representative democracy reliable information is vital. He says, "no form of democracy can protect itself from degenerating into ochlocracy or being hijacked by hidden oligarchy. . . unless the enfranchised are informed and reflective."[20] A political order that subverts democracy through manipulating the electorate with misinformation is not a democracy.[21]

In democracies in which the sources of vast amounts of information are the internet and social media, we have gone well beyond the potential problems of poor and unverified information. During the Trump 2016 US presidential campaign, Cambridge Analytica spent US$85 million on Facebook advertisements.[22] Without user consent, the company gained the personal information of 87 million Facebook users[23] it identified as "persuadables" in electoral precincts in swing states. This is not really political advertising or even propaganda, but rather directly targeting specific messages to specific people, something that Cambridge Analytica specialized in and that had proven effective in other foreign elections.[24] In 2021, "Facebook whistleblower" Frances Haugen warned on America's *60 Minutes*:

> when we live in an information environment that is full of angry, hateful, polarizing content it erodes our civic trust, it erodes our faith in each

> other, it erodes our ability to want to care for each other. The version of Facebook that exists today is tearing our societies apart and causing ethnic violence around the world.[25]

Nearly two billion people use Facebook daily.[26] Haugen joined Facebook in 2019 on condition that she could work against misinformation, having lost a friend to online conspiracy theories.[27] Many of us have lost friends and family: people who are still living but locked inside paranoid alternative realities, aping YouTube demagogues, spreading misinformation on TikTok. What can art do? How can the slow burn of contemporary art and the complexity of its ideas make a difference in the face of this tsunami of social media misinformation?

The contemporary art we have discussed suggests that it does have potential to intervene, offering different approaches to thinking through some of the ideas propagated by the Trump Effect, grappling with the slipperiness of the visual culture that gives it potency. We will offer one final example. The Trump era *per se* really began on June 16, 2015,[28] when Trump announced, "I would build a great, great wall on our southern border," and first declared, "we will make America great again." The day before Trump's announcement was the 800th anniversary of the Magna Carta, one of the most significant historical documents that sought to establish in England the rule of law and a suite of rights and protections, and limitations to the autocratic power of the sovereign, King John of England. Leading up to 2015, Cornelia Parker, an artist whose work has at times considered democracy and who would be appointed Britain's election artist in 2017, was working on an epic and collaborative object titled *Magna Carta (An Embroidery)*.[29] We can read Parker's pre-Trump *Magna Carta (An Embroidery)* as the converse of articulation of the Trump Effect in Curtis' *Can't Get You Out of My Head* documentary. While in Curtis' *Can't Get You Out of My Head* conspiracy reigns but is never resolved, Parker's collective and collaborative *Magna Carta (An Embroidery)* optimistically performs a cooperative and directly democratic endeavor, centered around the rule of law and not-insurmountable tensions over factual details.

Magna Carta (An Embroidery) is the depiction of a screenshot of the Wikipedia English language article on the Magna Carta, screen-captured on June 15, 2014, its 799th anniversary. Parker printed the image onto a piece of fabric 1.5 meters high by 13 meters wide, then cut it into fifty strips that were distributed to over two hundred people who spent the following months embroidering their portion of the fabric.[30] The contributors were prisoners, lawyers, civil rights campaigners, aristocrats, Members of the United Kingdom's Westminster parliament, and other contentious figures such as Julian Assange and Edward Snowden. Parker says, "I like the idea of other people's hands" having made the work.[31] Parker's collaborative process is very much a delegated performance of the kind we discussed in Chapter 6, and Parker's underlying message is that this document, a 1215 royal

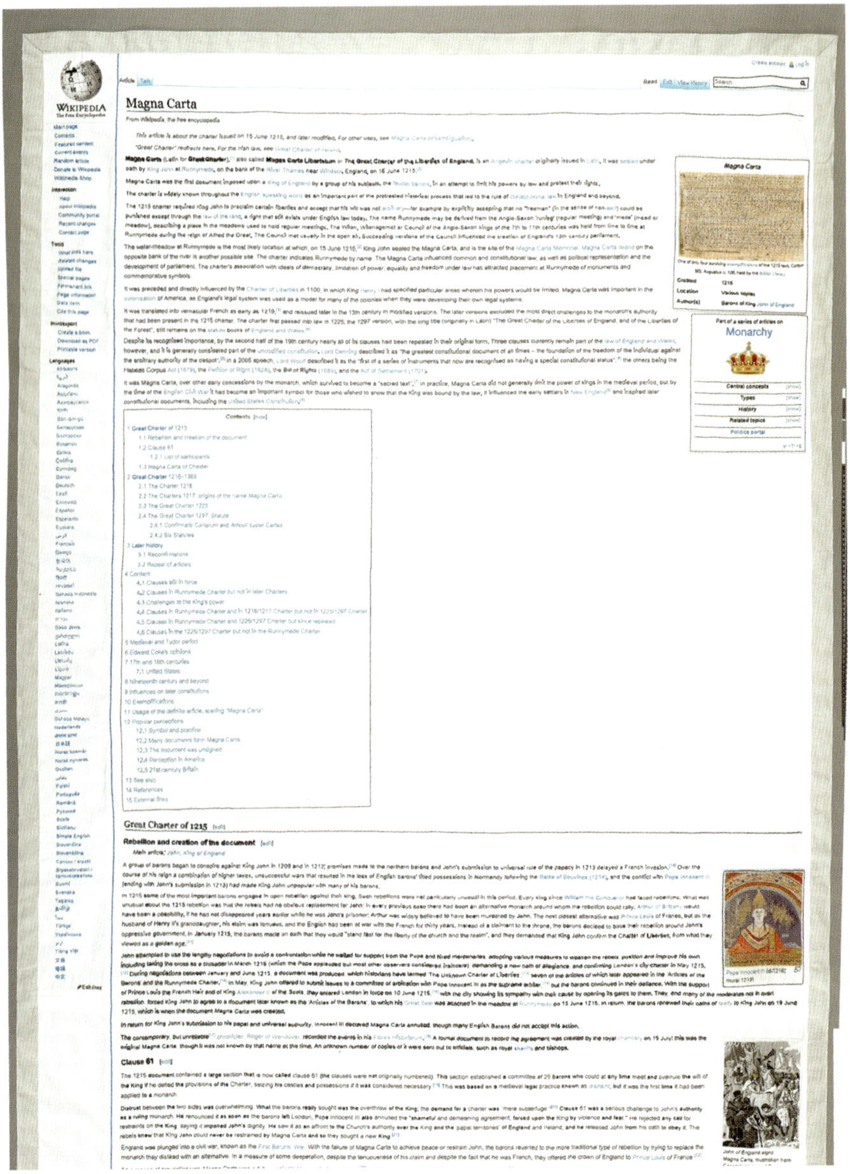

FIGURE 7.1 Cornelia Parker, Magna Carta (An Embroidery), 2015, half panama cotton fabric, pearl cotton thread and other media, embroidered by over 200 individual contributors, Image courtesy the artist, British Library and Frith Street Gallery, London. © the artist, © British Library Board.

agreement between a people and a king, is now available and distributed throughout the globe through the democratizing power of the internet.

Of course, Wikipedia is an important source of encyclopedic knowledge in the internet age. It is crowd-sourced and, in that sense, highly democratic, engaging in the kind of direct democracy we optimistically witnessed blooming in the early days of social media. As we signed up on Facebook, Twitter, and YouTube, it seemed that we were all granted the power of a public voice hitherto preserved for those with the privilege of passing the gatekeepers of knowledge—journalists, writers, celebrities, intellectuals, authors. In 2011, Heather Brook wrote optimistically about the revolutionary potential of social media, of a "New Enlightenment," "discovering truths about the way we live, about politics and power."[32] Suddenly we were content creators as well as consumers. In the 2011 Occupy Movement, the Arab Spring, and the campaigns of Anonymous and Wikileaks, social media seemed to be realizing the democratizing force of the internet.[33] However, as with all social media, the democratic aspect of Wikipedia (drawing on the

FIGURE 7.2 Cornelia Parker, Magna Carta (An Embroidery), 2015, half panama cotton fabric, pearl cotton thread and other media, 1236 × 157 cm. Courtesy the artist and Frith Street Gallery, London. Magna Carta (An Embroidery) was commissioned by the Ruskin School of Art at the University of Oxford in partnership with the British Library and in association with the Embroiderers' Guild, Fine Cell Work, Hand & Lock and the Royal School of Needlework. © the artist, © British Library Board. The commission was supported by Arts Council England and the John Fell OUP Research Fund. Installation View Portals, Hellenic Parliament + NEON. Photography © Natalia Tsoukala, Courtesy NEON.

"hive mind" of crowd-sourced knowledge) is also its greatest weakness. Any information on the site is highly unreliable precisely because of its directly democratic model. Wikipedia frequently becomes a site of conflict, in which not only different versions and perspectives on events and facts are contested, but even epistemological tensions are played out.

Yet, Parker's role in the work functions analogously with the notion of representative democracy, aggregating a mass into a consensus. The materiality of Parker's embroidery is also significant. It locks the ever-changing information (June 15, 2014) into a semi-permanent fabric. It can be amended, but that would require coordinated and carefully unpicking the fabric, a job more onerous than editing the Magna Carta Wikipedia page which is no doubt different now to how it appeared at the time of Parker's screenshot. In *Images of War in Contemporary Art*, we began to consider the ways in which contemporary art potentially arrests, or at least slows, the temporal loops that dominate the present political paradigm. In that work, it was the popular and well-established fixation of the temporal suspension of affect and the repetition of trauma that we sought to address. In this book, it is against the emerging tendencies of the Trump Effect, which will likely dominate the 2020s, that we suggest potential ways in which to weaponize art. Works such as *Magna Carta (An Embroidery)* effectively resists the tendencies and temporalities of the internet and social media age that we have discussed here, of YouTube, TikTok, Facebook, and Wikipedia, resituating social relations along non-virtual lines and geographical materiality and, overall, slowing down the rapid flow of "fast knowledge," rendering more palpably quantifiable the mega-archive of the internet.

NOTES

Introduction

1 Olivia Rubin, Lucien Bruggeman, and Will Steakin, "QAnon emerges as recurring theme of criminal cases tied to US Capitol siege," *ABC News*, January 20, 2021 https://abcnews.go.com/US/qanon-emerges-recurring-theme-criminal-cases-tied-us/story?id=75347445 accessed March 11, 2021.

2 Eden Gillespie, "How Republican Josh Hawley became one of America's 'most despised men' after the Capitol siege," *SBS News*, January 12, 2021 https://www.sbs.com.au/news/how-republican-josh-hawley-became-one-of-america-s-most-despised-men-after-the-capitol-siege accessed July 15, 2021.

3 Francis Cheung, "Photo shows Hawley giving fist pump to Trump supporters before Capitol violence," *KSDK*, January 7, 2021 https://www.ksdk.com/article/news/politics/national-politics/senator-josh-hawley-photo-capitol-trump-supporters/63-3b5d7611-9d07-41bd-8113-a9ccf74ebb68 accessed July 15, 2021.

4 Elizabeth A. Harris and Alexandra Alter, "Simon & Schuster cancels plans for Senator Hawley's book," *The New York Times*, January 7, 2021 (updated January 15, 2021) https://www.nytimes.com/2021/01/07/books/simon-schuster-josh-hawley-book.html accessed July 15, 2021.

5 Josh Hawley, "Josh Hawley, @HawleyMO, My statement on the woke mob at @simonschuster," *Twitter*, 7:42am, January 8, 2021 https://twitter.com/HawleyMO/status/1347327743004995585/photo/1 accessed September 14, 2021.

6 Maria Todorova, *Imagining the Balkans* (Oxford: Oxford University Press, 2009). We mean "balkanization" in the sense that Todorova uses it in her book.

7 Richard J. Hofstadter, "The paranoid style in American politics (1964)," in *The Paranoid Style in American Politics and Other Essays* (Cambridge, MA: Harvard University Press, 1996), 7 n: "Conspiratorial explanations of Kennedy's assassination have a far wider currency in Europe than they do in the United States, but no European, to my knowledge, has matched the ingenuity of Professor Revilo P. Oliver of the University of Illinois, who suggests that while Kennedy had performed many services for the Communist conspiracy, he was falling behind in the schedule for the 'effective capture of the United States in 1963' and was 'rapidly becoming a political liability.' He therefore had to be shot. *The New York Times*, February 11 1964."

8 Uroš Čvoro and Kit Messham-Muir, *Images of War in Contemporary Art: Terror and Conflict in the Mass Media* (London: Bloomsbury, 2021) 13–15.

50 Ibid., 8.

51 Ibid., 6.

52 Ibid., 14.

53 Ibid., 9.

54 Knight and Geddes, *QAnon and The Great Awakening*, 57–9.

55 Hofstadter, "The paranoid style in American politics (1964)," 21.

56 Matthew Hannah, "Qanon and the Information Dark Age."

57 Ibid.

58 Clarke, "Conspiracy theories and conspiracy theorizing," 132.

59 William Davies, *Nervous States: How Feeling Took over the World* (London: Jonathan Cape, 2018), 40–48.

60 Ibid.

61 Michael Deacon, "Michael Gove's guide to Britain's greatest enemy . . . the experts," *The Telegraph*, June 10, 2016 https://www.telegraph.co.uk/news/2016/06/10/michael-goves-guide-to-britains-greatest-enemy-the-experts/ accessed April 18, 2019.

62 Finlay Grieg, "Jeremy Vine: Brexit was no surprise to Radio 2 listeners," *iNews*, October 3, 2017 https://inews.co.uk/culture/radio/jeremy-vine-brexit-radio-2-listeners/ accessed April 18, 2019.

63 John Clarke and Janet Newman, "'People in this country have had enough of experts': Brexit and the paradoxes of populism," *Critical Policy Studies* 11, no. 1 (2017): 100.

64 Donald Trump, "Let me ask America a question," *Wall Street Journal*, 7:18 p.m. April 14, 2016 https://www.wsj.com/articles/let-me-ask-america-a-question-1460675882 accessed April 18, 2019.

65 Jon Cohen and Martin Enserink, "False positive," *Science* 333, no. 605023 (2011): 1694–1701.

66 Davey Alba, "Virus conspiracists elevate a new champion," *The New York Times*, May 9, 2020 https://www.nytimes.com/2020/05/09/technology/plandemic-judy-mikovitz-coronavirus-disinformation.html accessed March 26, 2021.

67 "Plandemic: The hidden agenda behind Covid-19," 2020 https://plandemicseries.com accessed March 26, 2021.

68 Cohen and Enserink, "False positive."

69 "Plandemic indoctornation," 2020 https://plandemicseries.com accessed March 26, 2021.

70 Michael A. Peters, "On the epistemology of conspiracy," *Educational Philosophy and Theory* 52 (2020): 1.

71 614Patriot, "Biden loses his head due to CGI (m.youtube.com)," *The Great Awakening: Unite World Wide*, March 18, 2021 https://greatawakening.win/p/12hl0TShYQ/biden-loses-his-head-due-to-cgi/c/ accessed March 26, 2021.

72 TheHenchman, "This is 100% CGI/deep fake of Biden. Please watch and keep your on the mask movement as he speaks. This is without a doubt fake. (youtu.

be)," *The Great Awakening: Unite World Wide*, March 18, 2021 https://greatawakening.win/p/12hkmYabhv/this-is-100-cgideep-fake-of-bide/c/ accessed March 26, 2021.

73 "President Joe Biden visits the NIH campus", *NIH Videocast*, YouTube, March 12, 2021 https://youtu.be/CDYCpPAnRaw?t=18 accessed March 26, 2021.

74 Peters, "On the epistemology of conspiracy," 1–2.

75 ZeroDeltaTango, "DAILY REMINDER."

76 Peters, "On the epistemology of conspiracy," 1.

77 *Out of Shadows: The Documentary*, dir. Mike Smith, 2020 https://www.outofshadows.org accessed March 16, 2021.

78 "OUT OF THE SHADOWS | OFFICIAL DOCUMENTARY. FULL.", thrEdward Grana, YouTube, Apr 16, 2020, https://youtu.be/IRt5cnQGPC4 accessed 16 March 2021

79 Paramount Theater, photo by J. R. Eyerman/The LIFE, Getty Images Editorial #: 50611221.

80 Hofstadter, "The paranoid style in American politics (1964)," 11.

81 Sarah Polus, "Chrissy Teigen fights back after Twitter user drags her into the false 'Pizzagate' conspiracy theory", *The Washington Post*, 12:25 a.m. January 2, 2018 https://www.washingtonpost.com/news/reliable-source/wp/2018/01/01/chrissy-teigen-fights-back-after-twitter-user-drags-model-into-the-false-pizzagate-conspiracy-theory/ accessed March 16, 2021.

82 Tami Katz-Freiman, "Biljana Đurđević," in *Aesthetics of Violence Three Solo Exhibitions: AES+F Group, January 24–June 20, 2009* (Haifa: Haifa Museum of Art, 2009).

83 Khan Do, "BUSTED! POOL PARTY PODESTA Favorite artist: Biljana Djurdjevic is exploiting kids (THE PROOF)," *YouTube*, March 7, 2018 https://youtu.be/i4u68UI_F3U accessed March 15, 2021.

84 Ibid., comments under video.

85 Benjamin Lee, "Marina Abramović mention in Podesta emails sparks accusations of satanism," *The Guardian*, November 5, 2016 https://www.theguardian.com/artanddesign/2016/nov/04/marina-abramovic-podesta-clinton-emails-satanism-accusations accessed March 16, 20201; Lee's article includes a link, no longer active to, Alex Jones, "Sprit cooking Clinton campaign chairman invited to bizarre satanic performance," *InfoWars*, 2016, https://www.infowars.com/spirit-cooking-clinton-campaign-chairman-invited-to-bizarre-satanic-performance/.

86 Andrew Russeth, "Marina Abramovic on right-wing attacks: 'It's absolutely outrageous and ridiculous'," *Art News*, November 4, 2016 https://www.artnews.com/art-news/news/marina-abramovic-on-right-wing-attacks-its-absolutely-outrageous-and-ridiculous-7255/ accessed March 16, 2021.

87 Alex Marshall, "Marina Abramovic just wants conspiracy theorists to let her be," *The New York Times*, April 21, 2020 (updated April 23, 2020) https://www.nytimes.com/2020/04/21/arts/design/marina-abramovic-satanist-conspiracy-theory.html accessed March 16, 2021.

88 Rice, "The rhetorical aesthetics of more," 33.

89 Arthur Delaney, "Tony Podesta has a party pooper", *Huffington Post*, March 18, 2010 (updated May 25, 2011) https://www.huffpost.com/entry/tony-podesta-has-a-party_n_333819 accessed March 27, 2021.

90 Alan Smithee, "Macaulay Culkin: 'Satanic' Hollywood execs wear shoes made from dead children," *New Punch*, December 12, 2017 https://newspunch.com/macaulay-culkin-hollywood-shoes-dead-children/ link no longer active; archived at http://archive.is/ekumf accessed March 27, 2021.

91 Reuters staff, "Fact check: Macaulay Culkin quote about child sexual abuse is fabricated," *Reuters*, 11:19 p.m. July 23, 2020 https://www.reuters.com/article/uk-factcheck-culkin-quote-idUSKCN24O28C accessed March 27, 2021.

92 "Macaulay Culkin EXPOSES the 'Red Shoe Men'—Episode 1," *Dropping Truth Bombs*, YouTube, September 2, 2019 https://youtu.be/9Zx3OaK4Mf0 accessed March 27, 2021.

93 Knight and Geddes, *QAnon and The Great Awakening*, 53–6.

94 Reed Berkowitz, "A game designer's analysis of Qanon: Playing with reality," *medium.com*, 2020 https://medium.com/curiouserinstitute/a-game-designers-analysis-of-qanon-580972548be5 accessed January 21, 2021.

95 Ibid.

96 Klaus Conrad, *Die beginnende Schizophrenie; Versuch einer Gestaltanalyse des Wahns* (Stuttgart: Thieme, 1958).

97 Peter Brugger, "From haunted brain to haunted science: A cognitive neuroscience view of paranormal and pseudoscientific thought," in eds. Houran J. and Lange R. *Hauntings and Poltergeists: Multidisciplinary Perspectives* (Jefferson, NC: McFarland & Co., 2001).

98 Ibid.

99 Ibid.

100 Melissa Rein Lively, quoted in "Former QAnon follower: This is what people need to understand," *CNN*, March 2, 2021 https://edition.cnn.com/videos/business/ 2021/03/02/qanon-followers-coronavirus-voter-panel-sot-vpx.cnn accessed March 11, 2021.

101 Brugger, "From haunted brain to haunted science."

102 Jan-Willem van Prooijen, Karen M. Douglas, and Clara de Inocencio, "Connecting the dots: Illusory pattern perception predicts belief in conspiracies and the supernatural," *European Journal of Social Psychology* 48, no. 3 (2018): 320–35.

103 Ibid., 326.

104 Ibid., 328.

105 Ashli Babbett, quoted in Lois Beckett and Vivian Ho, "'She was deep into it': Ashli Babbitt, killed in Capitol riot, was devoted conspiracy theorist," *The Guardian*, January 9, 2021 https://www.theguardian.com/us-news/2021/jan/09/ashli-babbitt-capitol-mob-trump-qanon-conspiracy-theory accessed March 31, 2021.

106 Bubba1776, "The next 48 hours will be glorious," *greatawakening.win*, January 18, 2021 https://greatawakening.win/p/11S0uRqRqZ/the-next-48-hours-will-be-glorio/ accessed March 31, 2021.

107 Reuters, "Fact Check—Claims Trump will be reinstated on August 13 stem from debunked conspiracy theories," *Reuters*, July 20, 2021 https://www.reuters.com/article/factcheck-trump-reinstated-idUSL1N2OV1W3 accessed September 18, 2021.

108 Knight and Geddes, *QAnon and The Great Awakening*, 196.

109 Rothschild, *Q: The Storm Is Upon Us*, 85.

110 Hofstadter, "The paranoid style in American politics (1964)," 29–30.

111 Tucker Carlson, quoted in Philip Bump, "Tucker Carlson's 'we could not find' QAnon comment was worse than it appears," *The Washington Post*, February 24, 2021 at 9:50 am EST https://www.washingtonpost.com/politics/2021/02/24/tucker-carlsons-we-could-not-find-qanon-comment-was-worse-than-it-appears/ accessed January 25, 2022.

112 *US DOMINION, INC., DOMINION VOTING SYSTEMS, INC., and DOMINION VOTING SYSTEMS CORPORATION, Plaintiffs, v. FOX CORPORATION and FOX BROADCASTING COMPANY, LLC, Defendants*, Superior Court, State of Delaware, EFiled: Nov 08 2021 03:25PM EST, Transaction ID 67077140; Case No. N21C-11-082 EMD.

113 Keith Kloor, "The #MAGA Lawyer Behind Michael Flynn's Scorched-Earth Legal Strategy," Politico, January 17, 2020 https://www.politico.com/news/magazine/2020/01/17/maga-lawyer-behind-michael-flynn-legal-strategy-098712 accessed January 25, 2022.

114 Donald J. Trump quoted in "President Trump joins 'Sunday Morning Futures'," *Fox News*, November 29, 2020 https://video.foxnews.com/v/6212917383001# sp=show-clips accessed January 26, 2022.

115 *DOMINION v. FOX*, 3.

116 Donald J. Trump (@realDonaldTrump), *Twitter*, November 12, 2020 https://twitter.com/realdonaldtrump/status/1326910770194632704 now deleted.

117 *DOMINION v. FOX*, 3.

118 Rudy Giuliani quoted in "Giuliani returns to court to argue Trump campaign's election case," *Fox News*, November 19, 2020 https://video.foxbusiness.com/v/6210778333001?playlist_id=933116636001#sp=show-clips accessed January 25, 2022.

119 Ibid, 71.

Chapter 2

1 Christopher Rufo, "Critical race theory has infiltrated the federal government | Christopher Rufo on Fox News," *The Heritage Foundation*, YouTube, September 3, 2020 https://youtu.be/rBXRdWflV7M accessed June 11, 2021.

2 Rufo, "Critical Race Theory Has Infiltrated the Federal Government."

3 Ibid.

4 Donald J. Trump, "Presidential documents: Executive Order 13950 of September 22, 2020 combating race and sex stereotyping," *Federal Register* 85, no. 188, September 28, 2020 https://www.govinfo.gov/content/pkg/FR-2020-09-28/pdf/2020-21534.pdf accessed June 18, 2021.

5 "Debate transcript: Presidential debate at Case Western Reserve University and Cleveland Clinic in Cleveland, Ohio," *The Commission on Presidential Debates*, September 29, 2020 https://www.debates.org/voter-education/debate-transcripts/september-29-2020-debate-transcript/ accessed June 18, 2021.

6 Donald J. Trump, "Proclamation 10110 of October 30, 2020; National American History and Founders Month, 2020; By the President of the United States of America," *Federal Register* 85, no. 215, Presidential Documents 70419, 70420, November 5, 2020 https://www.govinfo.gov/content/pkg/FR-2020-11-05/pdf/2020-24739.pdf accessed June 18, 2021.

7 Lis Power (research contributions by Rob Savillo), "Fox News' obsession with critical race theory, by the numbers: Fox has mentioned 'critical race theory' over 1,900 times in the past 3.5 months," *Media Matters* 15, June, 2021 https://www.mediamatters.org/fox-news/fox-news-obsession-critical-race-theory-numbers accessed July 21, 2021.

8 Donald J. Trump (@realDonaldTrump), *Twitter*, July 10, 2020 https://twitter.com/realDonaldTrump/status/1281616586273468416 no longer available, quoted in Tyler Olsen, "Trump threatens tax-exempt status, funding for universities and schools over 'radical left indoctrination'," *Fox News*, July 10, 2020.

9 Keith Whittington, "The trouble with banning critical race theory," *Areo Magazine*, June 16, 2020 https://areomagazine.com/2021/06/16/the-trouble-with-banning-critical-race-theory/ accessed June 23, 2021.

10 Adam Harris, "The GOP's 'critical race theory' obsession: How conservative politicians and pundits became fixated on an academic approach," *The Atlantic*, May 7, 2021 https://www.theatlantic.com/politics/archive/2021/05/gops-critical-race-theory-fixation-explained/618828/ accessed June 12, 2021.

11 Arizona, Texas, Tennessee, Florida, Arkansas, Oklahoma, New Hampshire, Indiana, and Idaho.

12 "Virginia parents push back against critical race theory, 'won't stand for lowering education standards'," *Fox News*, May 14, 2021 https://video.foxnews.com/v/ 6254192917001#sp=show-clips accessed June 24, 2021.

13 Ibid. Emphasis is spoken.

14 Tucker Carlson, "Parent arrested during school board meeting 'chaos' speaks out on 'Tucker'," *Fox News*, June 24, 2021 https://youtu.be/lB9p4ERQszE accessed June 24, 2021.

15 Harris, "The GOP's 'critical race theory' obsession."

16 Rufo, "Critical Race Theory Has Infiltrated the Federal Government".

17 Hofstadter, "The paranoid style in American politics (1964)."

18 Donald J. Trump, "Read Trump's Jan. 6 speech, a key part of impeachment trial," *NPR*, February 10, 2021 https://www.npr.org/2021/02/10/966396848/read-trumps-jan-6-speech-a-key-part-of-impeachment-trial accessed June 13, 2021.

19 Aruna D'Souza, *Whitewalling: Art, Race & Protest in 3 Acts* (New York: Badlands Unlimited, 2018), 16.

20 Ibid., 16–17.

21 Ibid., 16.

22 Ibid., 37.

23 Ibid., 24–6.

24 Precious Okoyomon, quoted in "Offence, power and progress," *BBC Radio 4*, November 26, 2017 https://www.bbc.co.uk/programmes/b09fy1qp accessed June 20, 2021.

25 Howardena Pindell, quoted in Kymberly N. Pinder, "Missus Kara E. Walker: Emancipated, and on tour," *The Art Bulletin* 90, no. 4 (December 2008): 645.

26 David D'Arcy, "Kara Walker kicks up a storm," *Modern Painters* (April 2006): 59.

27 Kara Walker, quoted in Helen Stoilas, "Controversy over Emmett Till painting at Whitney Biennial goes beyond art world," *The Art Newspaper*, March 24, 2017 https://www.theartnewspaper.com/2017/03/24/controversy-over-emmett-till-painting-at-whitney-biennial-goes-beyond-art-world accessed September 29, 2021.

28 Coco Fusco, "Censorship, not the painting, must go: On Dana Schutz's image of Emmett Till," *Hyperallergenic*, March 27, 2017 https://hyperallergic.com/368290/censorship-not-the-painting-must-go-on-dana-schutzs-image-of-emmett-till/ accessed September 29, 2021.

29 Whitney Museum of American Art, "Perspectives on race and representation: An evening with the Racial Imaginary Institute: Sun, Apr 9, 2017, 7:30pm," *Whitney Museum of American Art*, April 9, 2017 https://whitney.org/events/perspectives-on-race-and-representation accessed June 29, 2021. A full video of the event can be found at https://whitney.org/media/1493.

30 Adam Weinberg, quoted in Whitney Museum of American Art, "Perspectives on race and representation."

31 Christopher Y. Lew, quoted in Whitney Museum of American Art, "Perspectives on race and representation."

32 LeRonn P. Brooks, quoted in Whitney Museum of American Art, "Perspectives on race and representation."

33 D'Souza, *Whitewalling*, 32.

34 Whitney Museum of American Art, "Perspectives on race and representation."

35 Christina Sharpe, quoted in Whitney Museum of American Art, "Perspectives on race and representation."

36 Ibid.

37 Lyle Ashton Harris, quoted in Whitney Museum of American Art, "Perspectives on race and representation."

38 D'Souza, *Whitewalling*, 42.

39 Randy Kennedy, "White artist's painting of Emmett Till at Whitney Biennial draws protests," *The New York Times*, March 21, 2017 https://www.nytimes.

com/2017/03/21/ arts/design/painting-of-emmett-till-at-whitney-biennial-draws-protests.html accessed September 29, 2021.

40 D'Souza, *Whitewalling*, 37.

41 Josephine Livingstone and Lovia Gyarkye, "The case against Dana Schutz: Why her painting of Emmett Till at the Whitney Biennial insults his memory," *New Republic*, March 23, 2017 https://newrepublic.com/article/141506/case-dana-schutz accessed June 25, 2021.

42 Ibid.

43 Robin DiAngelo, *White Fragility: Why It's So Hard for White People to Talk About Racism* (London: Penguin, 2018), 131–8.

44 Ibid., 132.

45 Sheila Weller, "How author Timothy Tyson found the woman at the center of the Emmett Till case," *Vanity Fair*, January 26, 2017 https://www.vanityfair.com/news/2017/01/how-author-timothy-tyson-found-the-woman-at-the-center-of-the-emmett-till-case?mbid=social_twitter accessed June 25, 2021.

46 DiAngelo, *White Fragility*, 133.

47 DiAngelo, *White Fragility*, 136.

48 D'Souza, *Whitewalling*, 44.

49 Ibid., 42.

50 Ibid., 38.

51 Ibid., 15.

52 Ibid., 37.

53 Ibid., 15.

54 Nancy Fraser, "Progressive neoliberalism versus reactionary populism: A Hobson's choice," in *The Great Regression*, ed. Heinrich Geiselberger (Cambridge: Polity, 2017), 41.

55 Press release from the National Republican Congressional Committee (NRCC), quoted in Fox Nichols, "Helms ups the ante," *New Art Examiner* (October 1989): 20.

56 DiAngelo, *White Fragility*, 40.

57 Paul Gilroy, *The Black Atlantic: Modernity and Double Consciousness* (London: Verso Books, 1993.)

58 Paul Gilroy, *Against Race: Imagining political culture beyond the colour line* (Cambridge MA: Belknap, 2000) 28.

59 Ibid.

60 Yohann Koshy, "The last humanist: how Paul Gilroy became the most vital guide to our age of crisis," *The Guardian*, August 5, 2021 https://www.theguardian.com/news/2021/aug/05/paul-gilroy-britain-scholar-race-humanism-vital-guide-age-of-crisis accessed February 2, 2022.

61 Frank B. Wilderson III, "Close-Up: Fugitivity and the Filmic Imagination: Social Death and Narrative Aporia in 12 Years a Slave," *Black Camera, An International Film Journal* 7, no. 1 (2015): 134–149.

62 Ibid., 135.

63 Kevin Lawrence Henry, Jr. and Shameka N. Powell, "Kissing Cousins: Critical Race Theory's Racial Realism and Afropessimism's Social Death," in *The future is Black: Afropessimism, fugitivity, and radical hope in education*, (eds.) Carl A. Grant, Ashley Woodson, and Michael Dumas (New York, NY : Routledge, 2021) 81.

64 Frank B. Wilderson III, *Afropessimism* (New York: Liveright, 2020) xi.

65 Ibid., 15.

66 Henry and Powell, "Kissing Cousins," 80.

67 Wilderson, *Afropessimism*, 225. Emphasis in original.

68 Paul Gilroy quoted in Koshy, "The last humanist."

69 Vinson Cunningham, "The Argument of 'Afropessimism'," *The New Yorker*, July 13, 2020 https://www.newyorker.com/magazine/2020/07/20/the-argument-of-afropessimism accessed February 3, 2021.

70 Reni Eddo-Lodge, *Why I'm No Longer Talking to White People About Race* (London: Bloomsbury, 2017).

71 DiAngelo, *White Fragility*.

72 Robin DiAngelo, *Nice Racism: How Progressive White People Perpetuate Racial Harm* (London: Allen Lane, 2021).

73 Daniel Bergner, "'White fragility' is everywhere. But does antiracism training work?," *The New York Times Magazine*, July 15, 2020 https://www.nytimes.com/2020/07/15/magazine/white-fragility-robin-diangelo.html accessed June 18, 2021.

74 DiAngelo, *White Fragility*, 54–70.

75 Ibid., 57.

76 Heather Bruce, Robin DiAngelo, and Gyda Swaney, with Amie Thurber, "Between principles and practice: Tensions in anti-racist education. 2014 Race & Pedagogy National Conference," *Collins Memorial LibraryPLUS*, 2014 https://vimeo.com/ 116986053 accessed June 18, 2021.

77 Katy Waldman, "A sociologist examines the 'White fragility' that prevents White Americans from confronting racism," *The Atlantic*, July 23, 2018 https://www.newyorker.com/books/page-turner/a-sociologist-examines-the-white-fragility-that-prevents-white-americans-from-confronting-racism accessed June 21, 2021.

78 DiAngelo, *White Fragility*, xi.

79 Ibid., 3.

80 The lectures were conducted in 2016 on January 25 (https://youtu.be/4xeVKcduyP0), February 22 (https://youtu.be/E2-4PTo4Krk), and March 7 (https://youtu.be/wVddM1hzmvI). Evergreen State College, "Coming Together. The 2015–16 Coming Together Speakers Series focused on addressing many of the problems and challenges that face the students, faculty and staff of color at the Evergreen State College," *Evergreen State College website*, https://www.evergreen.edu/equity/coming-together accessed June 21, 2021.

81 Robin DiAngelo, in Evergreen State College Productions, "Coming Together Speaker Series: Dr. Robin DiAngelo," *YouTube*, March 10, 2016 https://youtu.be/wVddM1hzmvI accessed June 22, 2021.

82 Evergreen State College Equity & Inclusion Council, "2016–2017 Strategic Equity Plan," *Evergreen State College website*, https://www.evergreen.edu/sites/default/files/equity/documents/FINAL%202016-17%20Strategic%20Equity%20Plan%20--%20FOR%20CAMPUS-1.pdf accessed June 21, 2021.

83 John Edward Smith, quoted in Benjamin A. Boyce, "Evergreen's LEGENDARY canoe meeting (FULL VIDEO)," *YouTube*, May 12, 2020 https://youtu.be/IHM7SUFIE8w accessed June 22, 2021.

84 Shaun Cammack, "The Evergreen Affair: A social justice society," paper submitted in partial fulfillment of the requirements for the Master of Arts degree in the Master of Arts Program in the Social Sciences, University of Chicago, August 2020, 68.

85 Benjamin A. Boyce, "Evergreen's LEGENDARY canoe meeting."

86 Bret Weinstein, quoted in Mike Nayna, "PART ONE: Bret Weinstein, Heather Heying and the Evergreen Equity Council," *YouTube*, January 18, 2019 https://youtu.be/FH2WeWgcSMk accessed June 22, 2021.

87 Susan Svrluga and Joe Heim, "Threat shuts down college embroiled in racial dispute," June 2, 2017 https://www.washingtonpost.com/news/grade-point/wp/2017/06/01/threats-shut-down-college-embroiled-in-racial-dispute/ accessed June 22, 2021.

88 Tucker Carlson, quoted in Fox News, "Professor objects to no white people on campus demand," *YouTube*, May 27, 2017 https://youtu.be/_j9nFced_eo accessed June 22, 2021.

89 Cammack, "The Evergreen Affair." Videos, such as Benjamin A. Boyce, "Evergreen's LEGENDARY canoe meeting," were accessed through the Freedom of Information Act and uploaded to YouTube by Boyce (at the time a student of Evergreen who opposed the protestors' position), along with his own video documentation. Furthermore, videos of workshops are still available on Evergreen State College's YouTube channel.

90 Carlson, in "Professor objects to no white people on campus demand."

91 Carlson, in "Professor objects to no white people on campus demand."

92 The Rubin Report, "Evergreen State College racism controversy | Bret Weinstein | ACADEMIA | Rubin Report," *YouTube*, streamed live on May 31, 2017 https://youtu.be/-fEAPcgxnyY accessed June 22, 2021.

93 Bret Weinstein, quoted in Benjamin A. Boyce, "The complete Evergreen story (18)," *YouTube*, Feb 14, 2020 https://youtu.be/Z6Oj-tDr07M accessed June 22, 2021. Emphasis is spoken.

94 The Rubin Report, "Evergreen State College Racism Controversy."

95 PowerfulJRE, "Joe Rogan Experience #1006—Jordan Peterson & Bret Weinstein," *YouTube*, streamed live on September 2, 2017 https://youtu.be/6G59zsjM2UI accessed June 22, 2021.

96 Anonymous, quoted in Craig Sailor, "Man arrested for June 1 threat to 'murder as many people . . . as I can' at Evergreen," *The Olympian*, July 4, 2017 (updated July 5, 2017) https://www.theolympian.com/news/local/crime/article159596399.html#storylink=cpy accessed June 22, 2021.

97 Vice News, "Campus argument goes viral as Evergreen State is caught in racial turmoil (HBO)," *YouTube*, June 16, 2017 https://youtu.be/2cMYfxOFBBM accessed June 22, 2021.

98 Bari Weiss, "Meet the renegades of the intellectual dark web," *The New York Times*, May 8, 2018 https://www.nytimes.com/2018/05/08/opinion/intellectual-dark-web.html accessed June 24, 2021.

99 The video shown was The Agenda with Steve Paikin, "Genders, rights and freedom of speech," *YouTube*, October 27, 2016 https://youtu.be/kasiov0ytEc accessed June 29, 2021.

100 Lindsay Shepherd, quoted in *No Safe Spaces*, 2019, dir. Justin Folk (USA: Atlas Distribution Company).

101 Weiss, "Meet the renegades of the intellectual dark web."

102 Bret Weinstein, "Steven Crowder & big tech influence on free speech | Bret Weinstein," *YouTube*, June 20, 2019 https://youtu.be/RGvI0O82fF0 accessed September 20, 2021.

103 Bret Weinstein, "Bret Weinstein on Trump impeachment with John Wood Jr.," *YouTube*, October 5, 2019 https://youtu.be/HiwU20fxF1o accessed September 20, 2021.

104 Bret Weinstein, "Bret and Heather 1st in a series of live streams: Tests, masks, and more—DarkHorse Podcast," *YouTube*, March 25, 2020 https://youtu.be/ym-WGOq96G0 accessed September 20, 2021.

105 Bret Weinstein, "Spike protein is very dangerous, it's cytotoxic (Robert Malone, Steve Kirsch, Bret Weinstein)," *YouTube*, June 14, 2021 https://youtu.be/Du2wm5nhTXY accessed September 30, 2021.

106 Elie Dolgin, "The tangled history of mRNA vaccines," *Nature*, September 14, 2021 https://www.nature.com/articles/d41586-021-02483-w accessed September 30, 2021.

107 "COVID-19 vaccines don't affect ovaries or fertility in general; the vaccines are highly effective at preventing illness and death," *Heath Feedback*, June 24, 2021 https://healthfeedback.org/claimreview/covid-19-vaccines-dont-affect-ovaries-or-fertility-in-general-the-vaccines-are-highly-effective-at-preventing-illness-and-death/ accessed September 30, 2021.

108 "'Red pilled' on COVID vaccines," *Zerimandatoryvaxx.com*, https://zeromandatoryvaxx.com/2021/red-pilled-on-covid-vaccines/ accessed September 30, 2021. Video on website deep linked from https://youtu.be/Du2wm5nhTXY is no longer available.

109 Leslie Lawrence, *Facebook*, June 19, 2021 https://www.facebook.com/leslie.lawrenson.5/posts/10227381202375191 accessed September 30, 2021.

110 Lawrence, *Facebook*.

111 Anne Steele, "Spotify Strikes Podcast Deal With Joe Rogan Worth More Than $100 Million," *WSJ*, May 19, 2020 https://www.wsj.com/articles/spotify-strikes-exclusive-podcast-deal-with-joe-rogan-11589913814 accessed February 3, 2022.

112 Anna Nicolaou and Alex Barker, "Spotify warns it is 'too early' to calculate impact of Joe Rogan row," *The Financial Times*, February 2, 2022 https://

www.ft.com/content/df1437bc-ded5-491e-b320-2dcc93f8f3a9 accessed February 3, 2022.

113 Donald J. Trump, quoted in "Campaign 2020: President Trump speaks in Manchester, New Hampshire," *C-SPAN*, August 28, 2020 https://www.c-span.org/video/?475119-1/president-trump-speaks-manchester-hampshire accessed 1 October 1, 2021.

114 Trump, "Presidential documents: Executive Order 13950."

115 Sean Hannity, "Hannity: Democrats think they're immune to racism," *Fox News*, June 24, 2021 https://youtu.be/SzZxSML7W8c accessed June 25, 2021.

116 Ben Carson, quoted in "Ben Carson on critical race theory: What are we doing to children?," *Fox Business*, May 8, 2021 https://youtu.be/p3yKcamADZI accessed June 25, 2021.

117 Douglas Murray, *The Madness of Crowds* (London: Bloomsbury, 2019), 122.

118 Paul Embery, *Despised: Why the Modern Left Loathes the Working Class* (Cambridge: Polity, 2021), 98.

119 Helen Pluckrose and James Lindsay, *Cynical Theories: How Universities Made Everything about Race, Gender and Identity—and Why This Harms Everybody* (London: Swift Press, 2020), 258.

120 DiAngelo, *White Fragility*, 40.

121 Ibid., 120.

122 Ibid., 12.

123 Eddo-Lodge, *Why I'm No Longer Talking to White People About Race*, 100. Emphasis in original.

124 Martin Luther King Jr., quoted in Eddo-Lodge, *Why I'm No Longer Talking to White People About Race*, 101.

125 "Debate transcript: Presidential Debate at Case Western Reserve University and Cleveland Clinic in Cleveland, Ohio."

126 Trump, "Presidential documents: Executive Order 13950."

127 Ibid.

128 Steve Mickler, *Andrew Bolt, the Far Right and the First Nations* (Perth: UWA Publishing, 2019), 1–2.

129 Tucker Carlson, "Parent arrested during school board meeting 'chaos' speaks out on 'Tucker'," *Fox News*, June 24, 2021 https://youtu.be/lB9p4ERQszE accessed June 24, 2021.

130 DiAngelo, *White Fragility*, 5.

131 Matthew W. Hughey, "Stigma allure and White antiracism identity management," *Social Psychology Quarterly* 75, no. 3 (2012): 222.

132 Jack Niemonen,"Antiracist Education in Theory and Practice: A Critical Assessment," *The American Sociologist* 38 (2007): 159–77.

133 Ibid.

134 Ibid.

135 Ibid.

136 Bergner, "'White fragility' is everywhere."

137 Fraser, "Progressive neoliberalism versus reactionary populism."

138 Blake Stewart, "The rise of far-right civilizationism," *Critical Sociology* 46, no. 7–8 (2020): 1207–1220.

139 Ibid.

140 James A. Smith, "Steven Pinker and Jordan Peterson: The missing link between neoliberalism and the radical right," *Open Democracy*, November 1, 2018 https://www.opendemocracy.net/en/steven-pinker-jordan-peterson-neoliberalism-radical-right/#ftnt1 accessed October 6, 2021.

141 William Davies, *Nervous States: How Feeling Took Over the World* (London: Jonathan Cape, 2018), xiv.

142 Jef Rouner, "How self-identified 'Liberals' get radicalized to the far right," *Houston Press*, July 7, 2021 https://www.houstonpress.com/news/why-bret-weinstein-is-part-of-the-right-even-if-he-says-he-isnt-11597786 accessed October 5, 2021.

143 Ibid.

144 Keith Whittington, "The trouble with banning critical race theory," *Areo Magazine*, June 16, 2020 https://areomagazine.com/2021/06/16/the-trouble-with-banning-critical-race-theory/ accessed June 23, 2021.

145 Ibid.

146 Bergner, "'White fragility' is everywhere."

147 Whittington, "The trouble with banning critical race theory."

148 Cori Bernardi, "Slowly but surely, the people will wake up and that's what these plutocratic elites fear the most," *Sky News Australia*, July 11, 2021 https://www.skynews.com.au/details/_6258355702001 accessed June 13, 2021.

149 Tucker Carlson, "Trump: Time to stop indoctrination sessions," *Tucker Carlson Tonight (Facebook)*, September 8, 2021 https://www.facebook.com/TuckerCarlsonTonight/videos/2696598097262791/ accessed June 18, 2021.

150 Whittington, "The trouble with banning critical race theory."

151 Kevin Donnelly, "School education," in *Cancel Culture and the Left's Long March*, ed. Kevin Donnelly (Melbourne: Wilkinson Publishing, 2021), 34.

152 Jennifer Oriel, "Universities," in *Cancel Culture and the Left's Long March*, ed. Donnelly.

Chapter 3

1 Larry Andres (@justtheretolaughpatriot) and Dave Rubin, "#stevehilton #MERICA #wokeism #moderndayracism #🇺🇸 #border #wethepeople #TEXAS #daverubin," *TikTok*, April 5, 2021 https://vm.tiktok.com/ZSJWefeCQ/ accessed August 16, 2021. Video no longer available.

2 Steve Hilton, "Will free speech survive the 'cancel culture' movement?" *Fox News: The Next Revolution w/Steve Hilton*, April 5, 2021 https://video.foxnews.com/v/6246628645001#sp=show-clips accessed August 16, 2021.

37 Ibid., 8–9.

38 David Moye, "Kelly Marie Tran of 'Last Jedi' facing racist, sexist comments online. Online trolls invaded the actress' fan page but social media users clapped back," *Huffington Post*, December 27, 2017 (updated December 28, 2017) https://www.huffpost.com/entry/kelly-marie-tran-racists-last-jedi_n_5a4400fee4b06 d1621b6b2bb accessed July 21, 2021.

39 For an example of criticism about "woke" *Star Wars* episodes 7, 8, and 9, see The Dave Cullen Show, "The vandalization of Star Wars," *YouTube*, January 2, 2018 https://youtu.be/K-GxIoQPXPg accessed July 21, 2021.

40 Alissa Wilkinson, "In 2016, the Ghostbusters reboot didn't change movies. But the backlash was a bad omen," *Vox*, December 30, 2019 https://www.vox.com/culture/2019/12/30/21037815/ghostbusters-backlash-decade-black-panther-captain-marvel accessed July 20, 2021.

41 John Carucci, "Milo Yiannopoulos on Trump, Ariana Grande, and Russia," *The Seattle Times*, July 21, 2017 https://www.seattletimes.com/nation-world/milo-yiannopoulos-on-trump-ariana-grande-and-russia/ accessed May 5, 2020.

42 "Abuse of Ghostbusters' Leslie Jones leads to Twitter ban for Milo Yiannopoulos," *ABC News*, July 20, 2016 https://www.abc.net.au/news/2016-07-20/twitter-bans-milo-yiannopoulos/7644668 accessed May 5, 2020.

43 Kevin McDonald, *Gamergate: First Battle of the Culture War* (United States: independently published, 2019), 8.

44 Tom Shillue, quoted in "What does 'woke' even mean," *Fox News*, August 2, 2018 https://video.foxnews.com/v/5817262219001#sp=show-clips accessed July 16, 2021.

45 Nick Bryant, *When America Stopped Being Great: A History of the Present* (New York: Penguin Random House, 2020), 143.

46 "Panel on 'Wokeism' at CPAC," *C-SPAN*, July 10, 2021 https://www.c-span.org/video/?513283-112/panel-wokeism-cpac accessed July 21, 2021.

47 Rep. Matt Gaetz, *Twitter*, June 23, 2021 https://twitter.com/mattgaetz/status/1407796912309342214 accessed July 21, 2021.

48 Ed Kilgore, "Is 'anti-wokeness' the new ideology of the Republican Party?" *New York Magazine*, March 19, 2021 https://nymag.com/intelligencer/2021/03/is-anti-wokeness-the-new-ideology-of-the-republican-party.html accessed July 13, 2021.

49 Perry Bacon Jr., "Why attacking 'cancel culture' and 'woke' people is becoming the GOP's new political strategy," *FiveThirtyEight*, March 17, 2021 https://fivethirtyeight.com/features/why-attacking-cancel-culture-and-woke-people-is-becoming-the-gops-new-political-strategy/ accessed July 13, 2021.

50 Steve Rose, "How the word 'woke' was weaponised by the right," *The Guardian*, January 21, 2020 https://www.theguardian.com/society/shortcuts/2020/jan/21/how-the-word-woke-was-weaponised-by-the-right accessed July 16, 2021.

51 Travis D. Brown (spoken by James Lindsay), quoted in The Signal Productions, "Episode Two—Origins of woke ideology Part 2," *YouTube*, July 2, 2021 https://youtu.be/4dcw29urMTs accessed July 16, 2021.

52 Fiona Mueller, "From education to enstupidation—teaching English language and literature in Australia," in *Cancel Culture and the Left's Long March*, ed. Kevin Donnelly (Melbourne: Wilkinson Publishing, 2021), 68.

53 Kevin Donnelly, "School education," in *Cancel Culture and the Left's Long March*, ed. Donnelly, 34.

54 Gary Marks, "The origins of cancel culture and the Left's long march," in *Cancel Culture and the Left's Long March*, ed. Donnelly, 13–31.

55 James A. Lindsay, Peter Boghossian, and Helen Pluckrose, "Academic grievance studies and the corruption of scholarship," *Areo*, February 10, 2018 https://areomagazine.com/2018/10/02/academic-grievance-studies-and-the-corruption-of-scholarship/ accessed August 20, 2021.

56 "About," *Areo*, 2020 https://areomagazine.com/about/ accessed August 20, 2021.

57 Lindsay, Boghossian, and Pluckrose, "Academic grievance studies and the corruption of scholarship."

58 Helen Pluckrose and James Lindsay, *Cynical Theories: How Universities Made Everything about Race, Gender and Identity—and Why This Harms Everybody* (London: Swift Press, 2020), 31. Pluckrose and Lindsay identify a "postmodern knowledge principle" and a "postmodern political principle" as well as four major themes: 1) blurring of boundaries, 2) power of language, 3) cultural relativism, and 4) loss of the individual and the universal.

59 Ibid., 222.

60 Ibid., 224.

61 Ibid., 251.

62 Ibid., 12.

63 Ibid., 14.

64 Ibid., 220.

65 Ibid., 47.

66 Ibid., 13.

67 Ibid., 35.

68 James Lindsay, "Marcuse's subverting forces in transition," *New Discourses,* August 19, 2021 https://youtu.be/9ju2BGLAi9A accessed August 26, 2021.

69 Pluckrose and Lindsay, *Cynical Theories*, 45.

70 Ibid., 43.

71 Ibid., 181.

72 Ibid., 182.

73 Ibid., 260.

74 Ibid., 72.

75 Ibid., 189.

76 Ibid., 190.

77 Ibid., 198–207.

78 Ibid., 199.

79 Lindsay, "Marcuse's subverting forces in transition."

80 William Davies, "*The Madness of Crowds* by Douglas Murray review—a rightwing diatribe," *The Guardian*, September 19, 2019 https://www.theguardian.com/books/2019/sep/19/the-madness-of-crowds-review-gender-race-identity-douglas-murray accessed July 25, 2021.

81 Jordan B. Peterson "Identity politics and the Marxist lie of white privilege," *YouTube*, November 14, 2017 https://youtu.be/PfH8IG7Awk0 accessed 15 June 2021 accessed June 15, 2021.

82 Dion Kagan, "Cancel the woke: 'Cynical Theories'," *The Monthly*, November 10, 2020 https://www.themonthly.com.au/blog/dion-kagan/2020/10/2020/1604981911/cancel-woke-cynical-theories#mtr accessed July 9, 2021.

83 Jordan B. Peterson, "Modern times: Camille Paglia & Jordan B. Peterson," *YouTube*, October 3, 2017 https://youtu.be/v-hIVnmUdXM accessed September 1, 2021.

84 Stephen R.C. Hicks, *Explaining Postmodernism: Skepticism and Socialism from Rousseau to Foucault* (Tempe/New Berlin/Milwaukee: Scholargy Publishing, 2004).

85 Shuja Haider, "Postmodernism did not take place: On Jordan Peterson's 12 rules for life," *Viewpoint Magazine*, January 23, 2018 https://viewpointmag.com/2018/01/23/postmodernism-not-take-place-jordan-petersons-12-rules-life/ accessed July 29, 2021.

86 Hicks, *Explaining Postmodernism*.

87 Haider, "Postmodernism did not take place."

88 Indeed, as Boghossian, Pluckrose, and Lindsay similarly asked in relation to "grievance studies," why should any of this "obscure academic squabble of little relevance to the real world" matter: Lindsay, Boghossian, and Pluckrose, "Academic grievance studies and the corruption of scholarship."

89 Larry Andres (@justtheretolaughpatriot) and Dave Rubin, "#stevehilton #MERICA #wokeism #moderndayracism #🇺🇸 #border #wethepeople #TEXAS #daverubin," *TikTok*, April 5, 2021 https://vm.tiktok.com/ZSJWefeCQ/ accessed August 16, 2021.

90 Pluckrose and Lindsay, *Cynical Theories*, 213.

91 Ibid., 215.

92 Ibid., 231; Douglas Murray, *The Madness of Crowds* (London: Bloomsbury, 2019), 137; Jordan B. Peterson and Bret Weinstein, in "Minefields and the new political landscape | Bret Weinstein—Jordan B. Peterson Podcast S4 E10," *YouTube*, March 16, 2021 https://youtu.be/2O_gW4VWZ5c accessed September 1, 2021.

93 Such as in Bret Weinstein, "DarkHorse Podcast with Douglas Murray & Bret Weinstein: View from an outpost of the American Empire," *YouTube*, October 23, 2020 https://youtu.be/E7LMSZ2xsRs accessed October 6, 2021.

94 Pluckrose and Lindsay, *Cynical Theories*, 232.

95 Amazon, "Amazon best sellers: Best sellers in philosophy and social aspects of education," *Amazon website*, July 14, 2021 https://www.amazon.com/gp/bestsellers/books/266129/ref=pd_zg_hrsr_books accessed July 15, 2021.

96 The Rubin Report, "Critical race theory war: James Lindsay, Allie Stuckey, Christopher Rufo | ROUNDTABLE | Rubin Report," *YouTube*, February 20, 2021 https://youtu.be/q-z_ZrxP9hI accessed July 16, 2021.

97 Classically Abbey, "The AMAZING story of how James Lindsay met his wife! ‖ Get to know the EXPERT on critical theory," *YouTube*, June 18, 2021 https://youtu.be/nIs-jy9YZFM accessed July 13, 2021.

98 Timcast, "Timcast IRL—Minneapolis to fund Antifa autonomous zone eith $500k w/James Lindsay," *YouTube*, March 13, 2021 https://youtu.be/K8ZXzSADXjE accessed August 13, 2021.

99 The Rubin Report, "Exposing useful idiots & the lies Liberals told me | James Lindsay | ACADEMIA | Rubin Report," *YouTube*, June 20, 2021 https://youtu.be/Dx1ZruoTnrg accessed June 16, 2016.

100 James Lindsay, "Hegel, wokeness, and the dialectical faith of Leftism," *YouTube (New Discourses)*, May 29, 2021 https://youtu.be/uf4R0gX7g3w accessed September 2, 2021.

101 James Lindsay, "What is critical race theory?," *YouTube (PragerU)*, April 26, 2021. https://youtu.be/8Zy6DQoRYQw accessed July 16, 2021. The video had 1,648,611 views as of October 6, 2021.

102 Emma Parker, "Freedom reigned at YAF's 43rd Annual National Conservative Student Conference," *Young America's Foundation*, August 12, 2021 https://www.yaf.org/news/freedom-reigned-at-yafs-43rd-annual-national-conservative-student-conference/ accessed September 2, 2021.

103 Allie Beth Stuckey, "It's vital that Christians understand this about critical theory | Guest: James Lindsay | Ep 431," *YouTube*, June 3, 2021 https://youtu.be/1xhxIt XRPf0 accessed October 6, 2021.

104 Pastor Rick Brown, "Critical race theory with DR JAMES LINDSAY, AUTHOR OF CYNICAL THEORIES | part 1," *YouTube*, July 5, 2021 https://youtu.be/CYWXK9-CMoY accessed July 9, 2021.

105 Godspeak Calvary Chapel, "Critical race theory | James Lindsay (9AM)," *YouTube*, June 27, 2021, https://youtu.be/JA0kD4p7Nsk accessed November 26, 2021.

106 For example: Evidence and Answers, "Critical critique of critical theory," *YouTube*, July 8, 2021 https://youtu.be/4IkxjmQg5OQ accessed July 21, 2021.

107 Sensus Fidelium, "Critical theory vs Catholicism," *YouTube*, July 10, 2021 https://youtu.be/_0FQbKGwk_M accessed July 21, 2021.

108 Richard J. Hofstadter, "The paranoid style in American politics (1964)," in *The Paranoid Style in American Politics and Other Essays* (Cambridge, MA: Harvard University Press, 1996).

109 Ibid., 4.

110 Ibid., 4.

111 ZeroDeltaTango, "DAILY REMINDER—TRUMP WON—WE WERE ROBBED—OUR VOTE DOESNT COUNT UNTIL THIS GETS FIXED," greatawakening.win, March 10, 2021, https://greatawakening.win/p/12hkmRkJVb/daily-reminder--trump-won--we-we/ accessed March 11, 2021.

112 Hilton, "Will free speech survive the 'cancel culture' movement?"

113 Wheeler, "Is critical race theory Marxist?"

114 Keith Harris, "What's epistemically wrong with conspiracy theorising?" *Royal Institute of Philosophy Supplement* 84 (2018): 235–57; Brian Keeley, "Of conspiracy theories," in *Conspiracy Theories: The Philosophical Debate*, ed. David Coady (Farnham: Ashgate, 2006), 45–60.

115 Kagan, "Cancel the woke: 'Cynical Theories'."

116 Marks, "The origins of cancel culture and the Left's long march," 27.

117 Donnelly, "School education," 34.

118 Mueller, "From education to enstupidation," 66.

119 Jennifer Oriel, "Universities," in *Cancel Culture and the Left's Long March*, ed. Donnelly, 54.

120 Ibid., 53–4.

121 Donnelly, "School education," 34.

122 Mueller, "From education to enstupidation," 65.

123 Oriel, "Universities," 58.

124 Ibid., 57.

125 Mueller, "From education to enstupidation," 68.

126 Ibid., 68.

127 Ibid., 69.

128 "Free Speech University Rankings 2018: Results summary," *Spike*, 2019 https://media.spiked-online.com/website/images/2019/02/21153835/FSUR-PACK-2018.pdf accessed September 3, 2021.

129 Ibid.

130 Nesrine Malik, *We Need New Stories: Challenging the Toxic Myths Behind Our Age of Discontent* (London: Orion, 2019), 119.

131 "Free Speech University Rankings 2018."

132 Oriel, "Universities," 60.

133 Curtin University, *Inclusive Language Procedures* (Perth: Curtin University, 2020) https://policies.curtin.edu.au/local/docs/policy/Inclusive_Language_Procedures.pdf accessed September 3, 2021.

134 *Freedom of Speech in Universities: Fourth Report of Session 2017–19 (HC 589, HL PAPER 111)* (London: The House of Commons and House of Lords, 2018), 18.

135 Ibid., 19.

136 Malik, *We Need New Stories*, 120.

137 Matthew Lesh, *Free Speech on Campus Audit 2017*, Institute of Public Affairs, December, 2017 https://ipa.org.au/wp-content/uploads/2017/12/IPA-Report-Free-Speech-on-Campus-Audit-2017.pdf accessed September 25, 2019; Matthew Lesh, *Free Speech on Campus Audit 2018*, Institute of Public Affairs, December, 2018 https://ipa.org.au/wp-content/uploads/2018/12/Free-Speech-on-Campus-Audit-2018.pdf accessed September 25, 2019.

138 Bella d'Abrera, "University Audit Finds Humanities Riddled With Critical Race Theory And Identity Politics," *Institute of Public Affairs*, 16 January 2021 https://ipa.org.au/publications-ipa/media-releases/university-audit-finds-humanities-riddled-with-critical-race-theory-and-identity-politics accessed September 3, 2021.

139 Evan Mulholland, "Free speech crisis at Australia's universities confirmed by new research," *Institute of Public Affairs*, August 31, 2019 https://ipa.org.au/publications-ipa/media-releases/university-audit-finds-humanities-riddled-with-critical-race-theory-and-identity-politics accessed September 3, 2021.

140 Lesh, *Free Speech on Campus Audit 2017*; Lesh, *Free Speech on Campus Audit 2018*.

141 Harry Kalven, *Kalven Report: Report on the University's Role in Political and Social Action* (Chicago: University of Chicago, 1967).

142 Katharine Gelber, "Is there a 'free speech crisis' in Australian universities?" *ABC*, July 15, 2020 https://www.abc.net.au/religion/katharine-gelber-free-speech-crisis-in-australian-universities/12459718 accessed June 14, 2021.

143 Ibid.

144 John Ellison, quoted in Richard Pérez-Peña, Mitch Smith, and Stephanie Saul, "University of Chicago strikes back against campus political correctness," *The New York Times*, August 26, 2016 https://www.nytimes.com/2016/08/27/us/university-of-chicago-strikes-back-against-campus-political-correctness.html accessed September 25, 2019.

145 Lesh, *Free Speech on Campus Audit 2018*.

146 Ibid. "Recommendation 2: Introduce a policy that protects intellectual freedom, as mandated by the Higher Education Support Act 2003."

147 Ibid.

148 Department of Education and Training, *Report of the Independent Review of Freedom of Speech in Australian Higher Education Providers* (Canberra: Department of Education and Training, 2019).

149 Ibid., 217.

150 Ibid., 230–6.

151 Sally Walker, *Review of the Adoption of the Model Code on Freedom of Speech and Academic Freedom* (Canberra: Department of Education, Skills and Employment, 2020).

152 Jano Gibson and Alexis Moran, "As coronavirus spreads, 'it's time to go home' Scott Morrison tells visitors and international students," *ABC News*, April 3, 2020 https://www.abc.net.au/news/2020-04-03/coronavirus-pm-tells-international-students-time-to-go-to-home/12119568 accessed November 26, 2021.

153 Jon Piccini and Dirk Moses, "Simon Birmingham's intervention in research funding is not unprecedented, but dangerous," *The Conversation*, October 26, 2018 https://theconversation.com/simon-birminghams-intervention-in-research-funding-is-not-unprecedented-but-dangerous-105737 accessed September 3, 2021.

investigate the relation of nation-state formation to modernist monuments include Stefanos Tsivopoulos' *Lost Monument* (2009) and Manaf Halbouni's *Monument* (2017).

13 *Former West: Art and the Contemporary After 1989*, ed. Maria Hlavajova and Simon Sheih (Cambridge and London: MIT Press, 2017).

14 Michael Glover, "Kara Walker's monument to monstrousness," *Hyperallergic*, October 5, 2019 https://hyperallergic.com/520353/kara-walkers-monument-to-monstrousness/ accessed June 29, 2020.

15 "Kara Walker's *Fons Americanus*: Delve deeper into 2019's Hyundai Commission by Kara Walker," *Tate Modern*, 2019 https://www.tate.org.uk/art/artists/kara-walker-2674/kara-walkers-fons-americanus accessed June 29, 2020.

16 Slavoj Žižek, *In Defense of Lost Causes* (London: Verso, 2009), 25.

17 Zadie Smith, "What do we want history to do to us?" *The New York Review of Books*, February 27, 2020 https://www.nybooks.com/articles/2020/02/27/kara-walker-what-do-we-want-history-to-do-to-us/ accessed June 29, 2020.

18 Amelia Groom, "RAQS Media Collective: Epiphany and escape," *Neue Luxury* 2, https://www.neueluxury.com/feature/raqs-media-collective/ accessed June 16, 2020.

19 Ibid.

20 The "shared inhabitation of time," as Raqs Media Collective articulate, "leads one to think of different registers of temporal existence" because, contrary to the assumption "that contemporaneity has a certain single direction and a certain single velocity," it may be possible "to think of these inhabitations of shared moments of time leading to movements in very different directions and at different speeds." See: Raqs Media Collective, R. Sundaram, and D. Zyman, "The And: An expanded questionnaire on the contemporary: Has the moment of the contemporary come and gone?" *Asia Art Archive: Field Notes* 1 (2012), http://www.aaa.org.hk/FieldNotes/Details/1192 accessed July 13, 2020.

21 Sarah Messerschmidt, "The aesthetics of labour: Beauty and politics in Adrian Paci's 'The Column'," *Burlington Contemporary* 2 (November 2019): 5.

22 Another example of works addressing cross-cultural outsourcing of monument production is Onejoon Che's three-channel video *Mansudae Master Class* (2013). It documents the labor of North Korean sculptors constructing colossal sculptures in Africa, revealing that monumental commissions can transcend isolationist politics.

23 In this sense, Paci's work should be aligned with that of other artists who have dealt with this subject matter, such as Christian Jankowski's project *China Painters* (2008), for which the artist collaborated with Dafen painters.

24 This question is explored in relation to Dafen painters in: Winnie Won Yin Wong, *Van Gogh on Demand: China and the Readymade* (Chicago: University of Chicago Press, 2014).

25 Ibid., 6.

26 Mladen Miljanovic, *Aperta Fenestra* (Banja Luka: Kamena Kuca Banski Dvor, 2019).

27 On Bosnia and Herzegovina as a readymade failed state, see: Uroš Čvoro, *Post-Conflict Monuments in Bosnia and Herzegovina: Unfinished Histories* (London: Routledge, 2020).

28 For a discussion of post-1996 monuments and commemorative culture in BiH, see: Čvoro, *Post-Conflict Monuments in Bosnia and Herzegovina*.

29 For an articulation of the concept of meantime, see: Stef Jansen, *Yearnings in the Meantime: "Normal Lives" and the State in a Sarajevo Apartment Complex* (New York: Berghahn, 2015), 457. It is also important to acknowledge the relation of meantime to Antonio Gramsci's concept of the interregnum as an in-between period of crisis where "the old is dying and the new cannot be born." While Gramsci's concept captures the sense of a stunted passage, his concept nevertheless relies on a sense of temporary suspension which will inevitably result in something new. Meantime much more effectively captures the sense of exacerbation of present conditions with an uncertainty about what is waiting on the other side. See: Antonio Gramsci, *Selections from the Prison Notebooks*, ed. and trans. Quentin Hoare and Geoffrey Nowell Smith (London: Lawrence & Wishart, 1971).

30 For discussion of the use of metaphors of journey and family in discussions of EU ascencion, see: Tanja Petrović, *Yuropa: Jugoslovensko Nasledje I Politike Buducnosti u Postjugoslovenskim Drustvima* (Beograd: Fabrika Knjiga, 2012).

31 Katherine Verdery, *What Was Socialism and What Comes Next?* (Princeton, NJ: Princeton University Press, 1996), 185.

32 Here we can also recall Krzysztof Wodiczko's project *Monument for the Living* (2020), which used projections to engage with existing monuments as ways to open them up to conversations about the past. See: Caroline Goldstein, "We have to help them be useful': Artist Krzysztof Wodiczko explains how existing monuments can be made to speak for the voiceless," *Artnet*, March 19, 2020 https://news.artnet.com/exhibitions/art21-krzysztof-wodiczko-1808949 accessed July 19, 2020.

33 Čvoro, *Post-Conflict Monuments in Bosnia and Herzegovina*.

Chapter 5

1 One notable work that drew attention to the violence and racism of Trump's immigration policies is *Teeter-Totter Wall* (2019): a see-saw installed on the US–Mexico border by artists Ronald Rael and Virginia San Fratello with Colectivo Chopeke.

2 See Angela Dimitrakaki and Harry Weeks (ed.), *Third Text* "Anti-fascism/Art/Theory" 3 (May 2019): 158.

3 Throughout Trump's presidency, it was consistently asked why so much of the critical comedy that was directed against him "failed." It seemed that a range of comedians—from Baldwin's on-point impersonations of Trump to Borat's reappearance in 2020—tried to parody or mock Trump only to come up short in the face of his real-life stunts.

4 Gideon Rachman, "Trump, Putin, Xi and the cult of the strongman leader," *Financial Times*, October 31, 2016 https://www.ft.com/content/39da343a-9f4b-11e6-891e-abe238dee8e2 accessed May 25, 2021.

5 This was already evident in May, 2021 with the continuation by the Republican Party of Trump's claim that the election result was a "big lie." See David Smith, "Trump's grip over Republicans hardens as party cleaves to election 'big lie'," *The Guardian*, May 10, 2021 https://www.theguardian.com/us-news/2021/may/10/republicans-trump-election-big-lie accessed May 24, 2021.

6 Maria Todorova, *Imagining the Balkans* (Oxford: Oxford University Press, 2009), 33, 35.

7 Dominic Boyer and Alexei Yurchak, "American Stiob. Or, what late-socialist aesthetics of parody reveal about contemporary political culture in the West," *Cultural Anthropology* 25, no. 2 (2010): 179.

8 Ivan Krastev, *After Europe* (Philadelphia: University of Pennsylvania Press, 2017); Ian Bremmer, "The strongman era: How tough guys came out to rule the world," *Time*, May 14, 2018, 29–31; Madeleine Albright, *Fascism: A Warning* (London: William Collins, 2018); Yascha Mounk, *The People vs Democracy: Why Our Freedom is in Danger and How to Save It* (Cambridge: Harvard University Press, 2018).

9 Slavoj Žižek, "Appearance and obscenity: Five reflections," *The Philosophical Salon*, June 22, 2020 https://thephilosophicalsalon.com/power-appearance-and-obscenity-five-reflections/#_ednref4 accessed April 19, 2021.

10 Maddie Crum, "Now you can protest Donald Trump's wealth in this luxury art hut: Orange you glad you can now live inside a life-size replica of the Donald's hair?," *Huffp*ost, July 29, 2016 (updated July 30, 2016) https://www.huffpost.com/entry/trump-hut-protest-art_n_579a6915e4b0693164c06f59 accessed April 6, 2021.

11 Priscilla Frank, "'Dump across America': A street art project devoted to taking down Trump," *Huffpost*, February 26, 2016 https://www.huffpost.com/entry/donald-trump-is-a-steaming-pile-of-sht-according-to-street-artists-campaign_n_56d08be8e4b0bf0dab31e7cb accessed April 6, 2021.

12 Hakim Bishara, "Trump Baby Blimp has entered the Museum of London collection," *Hyperallergic*, January 18, 2021 https://hyperallergic.com/615315/trump-baby-blimp-has-entered-the-museum-of-london-collection/ accessed April 6, 2021.

13 Rain Embuscado, "Illma Gore's censored portrait of naked Donald Trump heads to London gallery," *Artnet*, April 7, 2016 https://news.artnet.com/art-world/naked-donald-trump-gallery-show-469016 accessed April 6, 2021.

14 Elizabeth Garber-Paul, "Naked Trump statues: Meet anarchist artists behind 'Emperor Has No Balls'," August 19, 2016 https://www.rollingstone.com/culture/culture-features/naked-trump-statues-meet-anarchist-artists-behind-emperor-has-no-balls-249522/ accessed April 6, 2021.

15 Sarah Rose Sharp, "SCROTUS: An artist created a giant portrait of Trump using vintage dildos," *Hyperallergic*, September 10, 2020 https://hyperallergic.com/586808/trump-dildo-portrait-cleveland/ accessed April 6, 2021.

16 Daniël de Zeeuw, "The gaping mouth: Trump and the carnival in power," *A*Desk*, May 18, 2020 https://a-desk.org/en/magazine/the-gaping-mouth-trump-and-the-carnival-in-power/ accessed April 6, 2021.

17 Anne Graefer, Allaina Kirby, and Inger-Lise Kalviknes Bore, "Unruly women and carnivalesque countercontrol: Offensive humour in mediated social protest," *Journal of Communication Inquiry* 42, no. 1 (2018): 1–23.

18 Nancy Spector, "Maurizio Cattelan's Golden Toilet in the time of Trump," August 17, 2017 https://www.guggenheim.org/blogs/checklist/maurizio-cattelans-golden-toilet-in-the-time-of-trump accessed April 6, 2021.

19 Brian Boucher, "Sit on this! The Guggenheim basks in the reflected glory of its golden riposte to Trump's Van Gogh Request," *Artnet*, January 25, 2018 https://news.artnet.com/art-world/maurizio-cattelan-guggenheim-trump-gold-toilet-1207634 accessed April 6, 2021.

20 This was not the only time Cattelan's work intersected with Trump: his famous sculpture *Him* (2001), featuring a small figure of Adolf Hitler kneeling in prayer, was appropriated into a kneeling Trump figure and quietly installed at the 2016 Art Basel fair. While the maker of the sculpture remains unknown, it drew significant connections between discussions of Trump and Hitler.

21 A similar criticism can be made of Andres Serrano's 2019 exhibition *The Game: All Things Trump*, which showed $200,000 worth of Trump and MAGA memorabilia. The exhibition did not reveal anything we didn't already know about the presidency or Trump. It also featured Serrano's 2004 portrait of Trump, raising the question of the artist's complicity in creating the cult of personality which he seemingly criticized. It was a gesture of excess—of spending so much money—to make an obvious point. See Zachary Small, "There's ego aplenty in Andres Serrano's exhibition on Trump," *Hyperallergic*, May 23, 2019 https://hyperallergic.com/495006/theres-ego-aplenty-in-andres-serranos-exhibition-on-trump/ accessed April 6, 2021.

22 They operated on the principle of "dethroning the king": pulling back the perceived veil of deception to show the obscene underside of power. We are not suggesting that this is only applicable to Trump protesters. We can see a similar dynamic playing out in FEMEN protesters baring their breasts at Putin in 2013 and basically being congratulated by Putin. Rather than take offense, he enjoyed it. See Daniel Alan Kennedy, "Putin unfazed by topless protest in Hannover," *Global Voices*, April 11, 2013 https://globalvoices.org/2013/04/11/putin-unfazed-by-topless-protest-in-hanover/accessed June 28, 2021.

Similarly, Italian artist Gianni Motti made *Clean Hands Berlusconi Soap* (2005), a bar of soap which he claimed was made from the fat of former Italian Prime Minister Silvio Berlusconi. Motti claimed that Berlusconi underwent liposuction at a Swiss clinic, after which the artist collected the fat from an employee. The title of the work is a reference to the investigation into the 1990s corruption (Mani Pulite), and Berlusconi's alleged connections to corruption and the mafia. The work uses body humor aimed at Berlusconi who, according to many, provided the political blueprint for Trump: he assumed the premiership without having held any prior government or administrative offices; his political style was based on his populism and brash personality; his tenure was filled with accusations of nepotism and conflicts of interest; his is_Contemporary_Art_Turbo_Folk_and_its_radical_potential_2001_ accessed June 28, 2021.

39 Čvoro, *Turbo-folk Music and Cultural Representations of National Identity in Former Yugoslavia*.

40 This note is available in an early draft of the text which has been republished many times. This version of the text was published in *The Real, The Desperate, The Absolute*, ed. Marina Gržinić (Graz/Celje, 2001).

41 The discussion of Nikolić's work in this section draws on Chapter 4 of Uroš Čvoro, *Transitional Aesthetics* (London: Bloomsbury, 2018).

42 The video of the work is available on Nikolić's website. *Death Anniversary*, http://www.vladimir-nikolic.com/death_anniversary.html accessed August 12, 2021.

43 Vladimir Nikolić, "About Death Anniversary 1968–2004," 2007, 24, http://www.vladimir-Nikolić.com/foto/about%20death%20anniversary.pdf accessed August 12, 2021.

44 Maria Todorova, *Imagining the Balkans* (Oxford: Oxford University Press, 1997).

45 For discussions of political performances of "traditions" in the Balkans, see Katherine Verdery, *The Political Lives of the Dead: Reburial and Postsocialist Change* (New York: Columbia University Press, 1999); *Horror Porno Ennui: Kulture Prakse Postsocijalizma*, ed. Ines Prica and Tea Skokić (Zagreb: Biblioteka Nova Etnografija, 2011).

46 Slavoj Žižek, "Will you laugh for me please," *Lacanian Ink*, http://www.lacan.com/Žižeklaugh.htm accessed August 12, 2021.

47 Even a cursory search of YouTube will find numerous videos of Šešelj's antics in the courtroom.

48 For an analysis of Vojislav Šešelj's performance of national mythology at the ICTY, see Izabela Stefija, "The production of the war criminal cult: Radovan Karadžić and Vojislav Šešelj at The Hague," *Nationalities Papers* 46, no. 1 (2018): 52–68.

49 Guy Richards Smith, "When your protest art gets coopted," *Hyperallergic*, May, 2021 https://hyperallergic.com/649525/when-your-protest-art-gets-coopted/ accessed August 4, 2021.

50 As Miller argues about Bishop's account of Sierra, "a second order ethical imperative for critical awareness trumps any first-order ethical concerns about the nature of aesthetic relations." Miller, "Activism vs. antagonism," 173.

51 "We made a mistake": Dark Mofo pulls the plug on "deeply harmful" Indigenous blood work' *The Guardian*, 2 March 2021 https://www.theguardian.com/culture/2021/mar/23/we-made-a-mistake-dark-mofo-pulls-the-plug-on-deeply-harmful-indigenous-blood-work accessed August 4, 2021.

52 Christopher Grobe, "The artist is President: Performance art and other keywords in the age of Donald Trump," *Critical Inquiry* 46, no. 4 (Summer 2020): 764–805. Grobe provides a summary of accounts of the Trump presidency as a form of performance on pp. 797–8.

Conclusion

1 "Documentary film: *Can't Get You Out of My Head,*" *British Broadcasting Commission*, 2021, https://www.bbc.co.uk/iplayer/episodes/p093wp6h/cant-get-you-out-of-my-head accessed March 31, 2021.

2 Adam Curtis, "Adam Curtis interviewed by Simon Mayo and Mark Kermode," *Kermodeandmayo*, YouTube, Jan 30, 2021 https://www.youtube.com/watch?v=5eRrZif FkHA accessed March 6, 2021.

3 Adam Curtis, "*Can't Get You Out of My Head* (2021)—Part 6: Are We Pigeon? Are We Dancer?" *British Broadcasting Commission*, February 14, 2021 https://youtu.be/yv7NFn95R0s accessed March 11, 2021.

4 Christopher Wylie, quoted in "'Cambridge Analytica planted fake news'—BBC News," *BBC News*, March 20, 2018 https://youtu.be/mjtR3W3eAFU accessed October 7, 2019.

5 *House of Commons Digital, Culture, Media and Sport Committee: Disinformation and "Fake News': Final Report* (London: House of Commons, 2019), 60.

6 "Facebook agrees to pay Cambridge Analytica fine to UK," *BBC News*, October 30, 2019 https://www.bbc.com/news/technology-50234141 accessed March 30, 2021.

7 Curtis, "Adam Curtis interviewed by Simon Mayo and Mark Kermode."

8 Peter Pomerantsev, *Nothing is True and Everything is Possible: Adventures in Modern Russia* (London: Faber & Faber, 2017), 6.

9 Ibid., x.

10 Anne Applebaum, *Twilight of Democracy: The Failure of Politics and the Parting of Friends* (London: Penguin, 2021), 58.

11 Ibid., 24.

12 Ibid., 36.

13 Ibid., 20.

14 Steve Bannon, quoted in Chris Wylie, *Mindf*ck: Inside Cambridge Analytica's Plot to Break the World* (London: Profile Books, 2019), 132.

15 Applebaum, *Twilight of Democracy*, 58.

16 C.J. Polychroniou, "Foreword," in Noam Chomsky, *The Precipice: Neoliberalism, the Pandemic and the Urgent Need for Radical Change* (London: Penguin, 2021), viii.

17 A.C. Grayling, *Democracy and its Crisis* (London: OneWorld, 2017), 2.

18 Ibid., 73.

19 Ibid., 83.

20 Ibid.

21 Ibid.

22 *House of Commons Digital, Culture, Media and Sport Committee*, 40.

23 Cecilia Kang and Sheera Frenkel, "Facebook says Cambridge Analytica harvested data of up to 87 million users," *The New York Times*, April 4, 2018

https://www.nytimes.com/2018/04/04/technology/mark-zuckerberg-testify-congress.html accessed November 26,2021; Wylie in "Cambridge Analytica Planted Fake News."

24 Paul Hilder, "'They were planning on stealing the election': Explosive new tapes reveal Cambridge Analytica CEO's boasts of voter suppression, manipulation and bribery," *Open Democracy*, January 28, 2019 https://www.opendemocracy.net/en/dark-money-investigations/they-were-planning-on-stealing-election-explosive-new-tapes-reveal-cambridg/ accessed November 26, 2021.

25 Scott Pelley, "Whistleblower: Facebook is misleading the public on progress against hate speech, violence, misinformation," *CBS News*, October 4, 2021 https://www.cbsnews.com/news/facebook-whistleblower-frances-haugen-misinformation-public-60-minutes-2021-10-03/ accessed October 11, 2021.

26 "Facebook reports second quarter 2021 results," *Facebook Investor Relations*, 2021 https://investor.fb.com/investor-news/press-release-details/2021/Facebook-Reports-Second-Quarter-2021-Results/default.aspx accessed November 26, 2021.

27 Pelley, "Whistleblower."

28 Of course, Trump displayed some nascent aspects of the Trump Effect during the Obama years, for instance with the "birther" conspiracy that asserted without evidence that Barack Obama was born outside the United States and was thus ineligible to be president, which would of course render his entire administration illegitimate.

29 "Cornelia Parker's Magna Carta and Alice in Wonderland at 150 celebrated at British Library, 3 December 2014," *Artlyst*, December 3, 2014 https://www.artlyst.com/news/cornelia-parkers-magna-carta-and-alice-in-wonderland-at-150-celebrated-at-british-library/ accessed October 8, 2021.

30 Cornelia Parker, "Magna Carta (An Embroidery), 2015," in *Cornelia Parker*, ed. Rachel Kent (Sydney: Museum of Contemporary Art Australia, 2020), 61.

31 Cornelia Parker, quoted in "Cornelia Parker in conversation with Rachel Kent," in *Cornelia Parker*, ed. Kent, 9.

32 Heather Brook, *The Revolution Will Be Digitised* (London: William Heinemann, 2011), ix.

33 Michael Conover, Emilio Ferrara, Filippo Menczer, and Alessandro Flammini, "The digital evolution of Occupy Wall Street," *PLoS ONE* 8, no. 5 (2013): 1.

BIBLIOGRAPHY

"'America Lost' premiering tonight on PBS World." *Discovery Institute*, October 27, 2020 https://www.discovery.org/a/america-lost-premiering-tonight-on-pbs-world/ accessed July 5, 2021.

"Cornelia Parker's Magna Carta and Alice in Wonderland at 150 celebrated at British Library, 3 December 2014." *Artlyst*, December 3, 2014 https://www.artlyst.com/news/cornelia-parkers-magna-carta-and-alice-in-wonderland-at-150-celebrated-at-british-library/ accessed October 8, 2021.

"COVID-19 vaccines don't affect ovaries or fertility in general; the vaccines are highly effective at preventing illness and death." *Heath Feedback*, June 24, 2021. Accessed September 30, 2021. https://healthfeedback.org/claimreview/covid-19-vaccines-dont-affect-ovaries-or-fertility-in-general-the-vaccines-are-highly-effective-at-preventing-illness-and-death/

"Free Speech University Rankings 2018: Results summary." *Spike*, 2019. Accessed September 3, 2021 https://media.spiked-online.com/website/images/2019/02/21153835/FSUR-PACK-2018.pdf.

"Plandemic indoctornation." 2020. Accessed March 26, 2021 *https://plandemicseries.com*

"Plandemic: The hidden agenda behind Covid-19." 2020. Accessed March 26, 2021. *https://plandemicseries.com*

"'Red pilled' on COVID vaccines." *Zeromandatoryvaxx.com*. 2021. Accessed September 30, 2021. https://zeromandatoryvaxx.com/2021/red-pilled-on-covid-vaccines/

@dstew79. "David Smith · 5d ago #stitch with barrister424 #liberal #Democrat #education #antiintellectualism #voteblue #biden2020 #vetsagainsttrump #veteran." *Tiktok*, September 10, 2021. Accessed September 16, 2021. https://www.tiktok.com/@dstew79/video/7006369471870881030

1776Mogul. "CRITICAL THINKING—Fundamentals: Introduction to critical thinking for normies (www.youtube.com)." *greatawakening.win*, February, 2021. Accessed March 25, 2021. https://greatawakening.win/p/12hRQGKH6S/critical-thinking--fundamentals-/c/

60 Minutes. "Facebook whistleblower Frances Haugen: The 60 Minutes interview." *YouTube*, October 4. Accessed October 6, 2021.2021 https://youtu.be/_Lx5VmAdZSI

614Patriot. "Biden loses his head due to CGI (m.youtube.com)." *The Great Awakening: Unite World Wide*, March 18, 2021. Accessed March 26, 2021. https://greatawakening.win/p/12hl0TShYQ/biden-loses-his-head-due-to-cgi/c/

ABC News. "Abuse of Ghostbusters' Leslie Jones leads to Twitter ban for Milo Yiannopoulos." July 20, 2016. Accessed May 5, 2020. https://www.abc.net.au/news/2016-07-20/twitter-bans-milo-yiannopoulos/7644668

ABC News. "Donald Trump says he ordered slowdown in coronavirus testing in speech to rally in Tulsa, Oklahoma." 9:10 a.m. June 21, 2020, updated 1:56 p.m. Accessed March 25, 2021. https://www.abc.net.au/news/2020-06-21/donald-trump-says-ordered-slowdown-coronavirus-testing/12377556

ABC News. "TikTok: Eating disorders, racism, censorship and distorted realities | Four Corners." *YouTube*, July 28, 2021. Accessed October 6, 2021. https://youtu.be/Rwu5C8JWO_k

Afrasiabi, Kaveh L. "Trump's Bakhtinian moment." *Eurasia Review*, 8 January 2021. Accessed July 19, 2021. https://www.eurasiareview.com/08012021-trumps-bakhtinian-moment-oped/

Alba, Davey. "Virus conspiracists elevate a new champion." *The New York Times*, May 9, 2020. Accessed March 26, 2021. https://www.nytimes.com/2020/05/09/technology/plandemic-judy-mikovitz-coronavirus-disinformation.html

Albright, Madeleine. *Fascism: A Warning*. London: William Collins, 2018.

Aly, Waleed. "How liberalism's blind spot let cancel culture bloom." *The Monthly*, November 2020. Accessed July 13, 2021. https://www.themonthly.com.au/issue/2020/november/1604149200/waleed-aly/woke-politics-and-power#mtr

Amazon. "Amazon best sellers: Best sellers in philosophy and social aspects of education." July 14, 2021. Accessed July 15, 2021. https://www.amazon.com/gp/bestsellers/books/266129/ref=pd_zg_hrsr_books

Andres, Larry (@justtheretolaughpatriot). "#stevehilton #MERICA #wokeism #moderndayracism #🇺🇸 #border #wethepeople #TEXAS #daverubin." *TikTok*, April 5, 2021. Accessed August 16, 2021. https://vm.tiktok.com/ZSJWefeCQ/

Annear, Judy. "Book Reviews: Beatrice Faust, Women, Sex & Pornography, Melbourne House, Melbourne, 1980; Michel Foucault, The History of Sexuality Volume 1: An Introduction (translated by Robert Hurley), Random House, New York, 1978." *Art & Text*, Issue 4 (1981): 55–61.

Applebaum, Anne. *Twilight of Democracy: The Failure of Politics and the Parting of Friends*. London: Penguin, 2021.

Argentino, Marc-André. "QAnon and the storm of the U.S. Capitol: The offline effect of online conspiracy theories." *The Conversation*, 4.39 p.m. AEDT January 7, 2021. Accessed 12 March 2021. https://theconversation.com/qanon-and-the-storm-of-the-u-s-capitol-the-offline-effect-of-online-conspiracy-theories-152815

Australian Government. "Unit of competency details: CHCDIV001—Work with diverse people." 2015 Accessed September 11, 2021. https://training.gov.au/training/details/chcdiv001

Bacon Jr., Perry. "Why attacking 'cancel culture' and 'woke' people is becoming the GOP's new political strategy." *FiveThirtyEight*, March 17, 2021. Accessed July 13, 2021. https://fivethirtyeight.com/features/why-attacking-cancel-culture-and-woke-people-is-becoming-the-gops-new-political-strategy/

Baudrillard, Jean. "Precession of the Simulacrum." Translated by Paul Foss and Paul Patton. *Art & Text*, Issue 11 (1983): 2–47.

BBC. "Documentary film: Can't Get You Out of My Head." 2021. Accessed March 31, 2021. https://www.bbc.co.uk/iplayer/episodes/p093wp6h/cant-get-you-out-of-my-head

BBC News. "'Cambridge Analytica planted fake news'—BBC News." March 20, 2018. Accessed October 7, 2019. https://youtu.be/mjtR3W3eAFU.

BBC News. "Facebook agrees to pay Cambridge Analytica fine to UK." October 30, 2019. Accessed March 30, 2021. https://www.bbc.com/news/technology-50234141

BBC News. "Trump on coronavirus: 'People are really surprised I understand this stuff'." March 9, 2020. Accessed September 16, 2021. https://www.bbc.com/news/av/world-us-canada-51761880

BBC News. "Trump says 'maybe I'm immune' after White House return." October 6, 2020. Accessed November 25, 2021. https://www.bbc.com/news/av/election-us-2020-54429222

BBC Radio 4. "Offence, power and progress." November 26, 2017. Accessed June 20, 2021. https://www.bbc.co.uk/programmes/b09fy1qp

Beauchamp, Zack. "The 'Grievance Studies' or 'Sokal Squared' hoax aimed to discredit gender and critical race studies. Did it work?" *Vox*, October 15, 2018. Accessed July 5, 2021. https://www.vox.com/2018/10/15/17951492/grievance-studies-sokal-squared-hoax

Beckett, Lois and Vivian Ho. "'She was deep into it': Ashli Babbitt, killed in Capitol riot, was devoted conspiracy theorist." *The Guardian*, January 9, 2021. Accessed March 31, 2021. https://www.theguardian.com/us-news/2021/jan/09/ashli-babbitt-capitol-mob-trump-qanon-conspiracy-theory

Benjamin A. Boyce. "Evergreen's LEGENDARY canoe meeting (FULL VIDEO)." *YouTube*, May 12, 2020. Accessed June 22, 2021. https://youtu.be/IHM7SUFIE8w

Benjamin A. Boyce. "The complete Evergreen story (18)." *YouTube*, Feb 14, 2020. Accessed June 22, 2021. https://youtu.be/Z6Oj-tDr07M

Bennett, Jill. *Practical Aesthetics: Events, Affects and Art after 9/11*. London & New York: IB Tauris, 2012.

Bergner, Daniel. "'White fragility' is everywhere. But does antiracism training work?" *The New York Times Magazine*, July 15, 2020. Accessed June 18, 2021. https://www.nytimes.com/2020/07/15/magazine/white-fragility-robin-diangelo.html

Berkowitz, Reed. "A game designer's analysis of Qanon: Playing with reality." *Medium.com*, 2020. Accessed January 21, 2021. https://medium.com/curiouserinstitute/a-game-designers-analysis-of-qanon-580972548be5

Birmingham, Simon (@Birmo). *Twitter*, October 26, 2018. Accessed September 3, 2021. https://twitter.com/Birmo/status/1055586252244713474

Bishara, Hakim. "Trump Baby Blimp has entered the Museum of London collection." *Hyperallergic*, January 18, 2021. Accessed April 6, 2021. https://hyperallergic.com/615315/trump-baby-blimp-has-entered-the-museum-of-london-collection/

Bishop, Claire. "How did we get so nostalgic for modernism?" *Fotomuseum Winterthur*, September 14, 2013. Accessed June 12, 2020. https://www.fotomuseum.ch/en/explore/still-searching/articles/26960_how_did_we_get_so_nostalgic_for_modernism.

Bishop, Claire. *Artificial Hells*. London: Verso, 2012.

Blackson, Robert. "Once more . . . with feeling: Re-enactment in contemporary art and culture." *Art Journal*, vol. 66, no. 1 (2007): 28–40.

Bobic, Igor. "Pro-Trump mob chases lone Black police officer up stairs in Capitol—video." *The Guardian*, January 7, 2021. Accessed November 24, 2021. https://www.theguardian.com/us-news/video/2021/jan/07/pro-trump-mob-chases-lone-black-police-officer-up-stairs-in-capitol-video

Boghossian, Peter, James A. Lindsay, and Helen Pluckrose. "Academic grievance studies and the corruption of scholarship." *Areo*, February 10, 2018. Accessed August 20, 2021. https://areomagazine.com/2018/10/02/academic-grievance-studies-and-the-corruption-of-scholarship/

Bote, Joshua. "An ex-Oakland cop and veteran was part of D.C.'s pro-Trump mob. He defended the Capitol siege." *SF Gate: San Francisco Chronicle*, January 7, 2021. Accessed July 28, 2021, https://www.sfgate.com/bayarea/article/dc-trump-protests-former-oakland-cop-jurell-snyder-15853235.php

Boucher, Brian. "Sit on this! The Guggenheim basks in the reflected glory of its golden riposte to Trump's Van Gogh Request." *Artnet*, January 25, 2018. Accessed April 6, 2021. https://news.artnet.com/art-world/maurizio-cattelan-guggenheim-trump-gold-toilet-1207634

Bourriaud, Nicolas. *Relational Aesthetics*. Paris: Les Presses du réel, 2009.

Boyer, Dominic and Alexei Yurchak. "American Stiob. Or, what late-socialist aesthetics of parody reveal about contemporary political culture in the West." *Cultural Anthropology*, vol. 25, no. 2 (2010)

Brasher, Jordan and Derek H. Alderman. "A Confederate statue graveyard could help bury the Old South." *The Conversation*, July 26, 2019. Accessed June 12, 2020. https://theconversation.com/a-confederate-statue-graveyard-could-help-bury-the-old- south-118034

Bremmer, Ian. "The strongman era: How tough guys came out to rule the world." *Time*, May 14, 2018.

Bret Weinstein. "Bret and Heather 1st in a series of live streams: Tests, masks, and more—DarkHorse Podcast." *YouTube*, March 25, 2020. Accessed September 20, 2021. https://youtu.be/ym-WGOq96G0

Bret Weinstein. "Bret Weinstein on Trump impeachment with John Wood Jr." *YouTube*, October 5, 2019. Accessed September 20, 2021. https://youtu.be/HiwU20fxF1o

Bret Weinstein. "DarkHorse Podcast with Douglas Murray & Bret Weinstein: View from an outpost of the American Empire." *YouTube*, October 23, 2020. Accessed October 6, 2021. https://youtu.be/E7LMSZ2xsRs

Bret Weinstein. "Minefields and the new political landscape | Bret Weinstein – Jordan B. Peterson Podcast S4 E10." *YouTube*, March 16, 2021. Accessed September 1, 2021. https://youtu.be/2O_gW4VWZ5c

Bret Weinstein. "Spike protein is very dangerous, it's cytotoxic (Robert Malone, Steve Kirsch, Bret Weinstein)." *YouTube*, June 14, 2021. Accessed September 30, 2021. https://youtu.be/Du2wm5nhTXY

Bret Weinstein. "Steven Crowder & big tech influence on free speech | Bret Weinstein." *YouTube*, June 20, 2019. Accessed September 20, 2021. https://youtu.be/RGvI0O82fF0

Brook, Heather. *The Revolution Will Be Digitised*. London: William Heinemann, 2011.

Brown, Rick. "Critical race theory with DR JAMES LINDSAY, AUTHOR OF CYNICAL THEORIES | part 1." *YouTube*, July 5, 2021. Accessed July 9, 2021. https://youtu.be/CYWXK9-CMoY

Bruce, Heather, Robin DiAngelo, and Gyda Swaney, with Amie Thurber. "Between principles and practice: Tensions in anti-racist education. 2014 Race & Pedagogy National Conference." *Collins Memorial LibraryPLUS*, 2014. Accessed June 18, 2021. https://vimeo.com/116986053

Brugger, Peter. "From haunted brain to haunted science: A cognitive neuroscience view of paranormal and pseudoscientific thought." In *Hauntings and Poltergeists: Multidisciplinary Perspectives*. Edited by J. Houran J. and R. Lange. Jefferson, NC: McFarland & Co., 2001.

Bryant, Nick. *When America Stopped Being Great: A History of the Present*. New York: Penguin Random House, 2020.

Bubba1776. "The next 48 hours will be glorious." *greatawakening.win*, January 18, 2021. Accessed March 31, 2021. https://greatawakening.win/p/11S0uRqRqZ/the-next-48-hours-will-be-glorio/

Buden, Boris. *Zona Prelaska: O Kraju Postkomunizma*. Beograd: Fabrika Knjiga, 2012.

Bump, Philip. "Tucker Carlson's 'we could not find' QAnon comment was worse than it appears." *The Washington Post*, February 24, 2021 at 9:50 am EST. Accessed January 25, 2022. https://www.washingtonpost.com/politics/2021/02/24/tucker-carlsons-we-could-not-find-qanon-comment-was-worse-than-it-appears/

Burke, Kelly. "'We made a mistake': Dark Mofo pulls the plug on 'deeply harmful' Indigenous blood work." *The Guardian*, 23 March 2021. Accessed August 4, 2021. https://www.theguardian.com/culture/2021/mar/23/we-made-a-mistake-dark-mofo-pulls-the-plug-on-deeply-harmful-indigenous-blood-work

C-SPAN. "Campaign 2020: President Trump speaks in Manchester, New Hampshire." August 28, 2020. Accessed 1 October 1, 2021. https://www.c-span.org/video/?475119-1/president-trump-speaks-manchester-hampshire

C-SPAN. "Panel on 'Wokeism' at CPAC." July 10, 2021. Accessed July 21, 2021. https://www.c-span.org/video/?513283-112/panel-wokeism-cpac

Callaghan, Greg. "Right-winger? Not me, says alt-right darling Jordan Peterson." *The Sydney Morning Herald*, April 19, 2018 (updated April 21, 2018). Accessed August 17, 2021. https://www.smh.com.au/world/north-america/right-winger-not-me-says-alt-right-darling-jordan-peterson-20180417-p4za14.html

Cammack, Shaun. "The Evergreen Affair: A social justice society." Paper submitted in partial fulfillment of the requirements for the Master of Arts degree in the Master of Arts Program in the Social Sciences, University of Chicago, August 2020.

Carlson, Bronwyn. "Friday essay: taking a wrecking ball to monuments—contemporary art can ask what really needs tearing down." *The Conversation*, June 12, 2020. Accessed March 15, 2021. https://theconversation.com/friday-essay-taking-a-wrecking-ball-to-monuments-contemporary-art-can-ask-what-really-needs-tearing-down-140437

Carucci, John. "Milo Yiannopoulos on Trump, Ariana Grande, and Russia." *Seattle Times*, July 21, 2017. Accessed May 5, 2020. https://www.seattletimes.com *The* / nation-world/milo-yiannopoulos-on-trump-ariana-grande-and-russia/

CBS Baltimore. "Maryland man fired after seen wearing work badge in photo of him storming Capitol'." January 8, 2021. Accessed January 31, 2022. https://baltimore.cbslocal.com/2021/01/08/maryland-company-navistar-fires-employee-who-went-to-u-s-capitol-riot-wearing-work-badge/

Chadury, Amit. "The real meaning of Rhodes Must Fall." *The Guardian*, March 16, 2016. Accessed March 15, 2021. https://www.theguardian.com/uk-news/2016/mar/16/the-real-meaning-of-rhodes-must-fall

Cheung, Francis. "Photo shows Hawley giving fist pump to Trump supporters before Capitol violence." *KSDK*, January 7, 2021. Accessed July 15, 2021. https://www.ksdk.com/article/news/politics/national-politics/senator-josh-hawley-photo-capitol-trump-supporters/63-3b5d7611-9d07-41bd-8113-a9ccf74ebb68

Chomsky, Noam. *The Precipice: Neoliberalism, the Pandemic and the Urgent Need for Radical Change*. London: Penguin, 2021.

Cineas, Fabiola. "Donald Trump is the accelerant." *Vox*, January 9, 2021. Accessed May 29, 2021. https://www.vox.com/21506029/trump-violence-tweets-racist-hate-speech

Clarke, John and Janet Newman. "'People in this country have had enough of experts': Brexit and the paradoxes of populism." *Critical Policy Studies* vol. 11, no. 1 (2017).

Clarke, Steve. "Conspiracy theories and conspiracy theorizing." *Philosophy of the Social Sciences*, vol. 32, no. 2 (2002): 131–50.

Classically Abbey. "The AMAZING story of how James Lindsay met his wife! || Get to know the EXPERT on critical theory." *YouTube*, June 18, 2021. Accessed July 13, 2021. https://youtu.be/nIs-jy9YZFM

Christopher F. Rufo. "Homelessness." *YouTube*, December 15, 2020. Accessed July 5, 2021. https://www.youtube.com/watch?v=essjVcdPuFk

CNN. "Former QAnon follower: This is what people need to understand." March 2, 2021. Accessed March 11, 2021. https://edition.cnn.com/videos/business/2021/03/02/qanon-followers-coronavirus-voter-panel-sot-vpx.cnn

Cohen, Jon and Martin Enserink. "False positive." *Science*, vol. 333, no. 605023 (2011): 1694–1701.

Commission on Presidential Debates. "Debate transcript: Presidential debate at Case Western Reserve University and Cleveland Clinic in Cleveland, Ohio." September 29, 2020. Accessed June 18, 2021. https://www.debates.org/voter-education/debate-transcripts/september-29-2020-debate-transcript/

Conover, Michael Emilio Ferrara, Filippo Menczer, and Alessandro Flammini. "The digital evolution of Occupy Wall Street." *PLoS ONE*, vol. 8, no. 5 (2013): e64679.

Conrad, Klaus. *Die beginnende Schizophrenie; Versuch einer Gestaltanalyse des Wahns*. Stuttgart: Thieme, 1958.

Cornelia Parker. Edited by Rachel Kent. Sydney: Museum of Contemporary Art Australia, 2020.

Creighton, Adam. "Want to study Foucault? Don't expect a cent: If tearing down statues is the thanks taxpayers get from tipping millions into critical theory courses, it's about time we stop chipping in." *The Australian*, June 19, 2020. Accessed September 3, 2021. https://www.theaustralian.com.au/commentary/uni-fee-shakeup-explosion-of-degrees-has-sapped-their-value/news-story/86cee36cb7a65ddc1e79a4dbf2ceaaff

Crum, Maddie. "Now you can protest Donald Trump's wealth in this luxury art hut: Orange you glad you can now live inside a life-size replica of the Donald's hair?" *Huffpost*, July 29, 2016 (updated July 30, 2016). Accessed April 6, 2021. https://www.huffpost.com/entry/trump-hut-protest-art_n_579a6915e4b0693164c06f59

Cunningham, Vinson. "The Argument of 'Afropessimism'." *The New Yorker*, July 13, 2020. Accessed February 3, 2021. https://www.newyorker.com/magazine/2020/07/20/the-argument-of-afropessimism

Curtin University. *Inclusive Language Procedures*. 2020. Accessed September 3, 2021. https://policies.curtin.edu.au/local/docs/policy/Inclusive_Language_Procedures.pdf

Curtis, Adam. "Can't Get You Out of My Head (2021)—Part 6: Are We Pigeon? Are We Dancer?" *YouTube*, February 14, 2021. Accessed March 11, 2021. https://youtu.be/yv7NFn95R0s

Čvoro, Uroš. *Turbo-Folk Music and Cultural Representations of National Identity in Former Yugoslavia*. Farnham: Ashgate, 2014.

Čvoro, Uroš. *Transitional Aesthetics: Contemporary Art at the Edge of Europe.* London: Bloomsbury, 2018.

Čvoro, Uroš. *Post-Conflict Monuments in Bosnia and Herzegovina: Unfinished Histories.* London: Routledge, 2020.

Čvoro, Uroš and Chrisoula Lionis. "When the periphery laughs: Humor and locality in contemporary art from Greece and Bosnia and Herzegovina." *Cultural Politics* vol. 15, no. 2 (2019): 223–43.

Čvoro, Uroš and Kit Messham-Muir. *Images of War in Contemporary Art: Terror and Conflict in the Mass Media.* London: Bloomsbury, 2021.

d'Abrera, Bella. "University Audit Finds Humanities Riddled With Critical Race Theory And Identity Politics." Institute of Public Affairs, 16 January 2021. Accessed September 3, 2021. https://ipa.org.au/publications-ipa/media-releases/university-audit-finds-humanities-riddled-with-critical-race-theory-and-identity-politics

D'Arcy, David. "Kara Walker kicks up a storm." *Modern Painters*, (April 2006): 59.

D'Souza, Aruna. *Whitewalling: Art, Race & Protest in 3 Acts.* New York: Badlands Unlimited, 2018.

Dave Cullen Show. "The vandalization of Star Wars." *YouTube*, January 2, 2018. Accessed July 21, 2021. https://youtu.be/K-GxIoQPXPg

Davies, William, *Nervous States: How Feeling Took over the World.* London: Jonathan Cape, 2018.

Davies, William. "The Madness of Crowds by Douglas Murray review—a rightwing diatribe." *The Guardian*, September 19, 2019. Accessed July 25, 2021. https://www.theguardian.com/books/2019/sep/19/the-madness-of-crowds-review-gender-race-identity-douglas-murray

Deacon, Michael. "Michael Gove's guide to Britain's greatest enemy. . . the experts." *The Telegraph*, June 10, 2016. Accessed April 18, 2019. https://www.telegraph.co.uk/news/2016/06/10/michael-goves-guide-to-britains-greatest-enemy-the-experts/

Delaney, Arthur. "Tony Podesta has a party pooper." *Huffington Post*, March 18, 2010 (updated May 25, 2011). Accessed March 27, 2021. https://www.huffpost.com/entry/tony-podesta-has-a-party_n_333819

Department of Education and Training. *Department of Education and Training, Report of the Independent Review of Freedom of Speech in Australian Higher Education Providers.* Canberra: Australian Government, 2019.

Department of Education, Skills and Employment. *Review of the Adoption of the Model Code on Freedom of Speech and Academic Freedom.* Canberra: Australian Government, 2020.

de Zeeuw, Daniël. "The gaping mouth: Trump and the carnival in power." *A*Desk*, May 18, 2020. Accessed April 6, 2021. https://a-desk.org/en/magazine/the-gaping-mouth-trump-and-the-carnival-in-power/

Dezeuze, Anna. *Thomas Hirschhorn: Deleuze Monument.* London: Afterall, 2014.

DiAngelo, Robin. *White Fragility: Why It's So Hard for White People to Talk About Racism.* London: Penguin, 2018.

DiAngelo, Robin. *Nice Racism: How Progressive White People Perpetuate Racial Harm.* London: Allen Lane, 2021.

Dimitrakaki, Angela and Harry Weeks (eds.), *Third Text*, Anti-fascism/Art/Theory. vol. 33, issue. 3, no. 158 (2019): 271.

Dimitrijević, Branislav. "Ovo je savremena umetnosst: Turbofolk kao radikalni performans." (This is contemporary art: Turbofolk as a radical performance). Prelom 2–3, Belgrade, 2002.

Do, Khan. "BUSTED! POOL PARTY PODESTA Favorite artist: Biljana Djurdjevic is exploiting kids (THE PROOF)." *YouTube*, March 7, 2018. Accessed March 15, 2021. https://youtu.be/i4u68UI_F3U

Dodge, Robert. "Stockholders of Lykes, LTV back merger." *The Washington Post*, December 6, 1978. Accessed July 5, 2021. https://www.washingtonpost.com/archive/business/1978/12/06/stockholders-of-lykes-ltv-back-merger/3cb3ad0e-a3ef-43f5-98d6-5ab965587fb3/.

Dolgin, Elie. "The tangled history of mRNA vaccines." *Nature*, September 14, 2021. Accessed September 30, 2021. https://www.nature.com/articles/d41586-021-02483-w

Donald Trump. "Let me ask America a question." *Wall Street Journal*, 7:18 p.m. April 14, 2016. Accessed April 18, 2019. https://www.wsj.com/articles/let-me-ask-america-a-question-1460675882

Donnelly, Kevin (ed.) *Cancel Culture and the Left's Long March*. Melbourne: Wilkinson Publishing, 2021.

Dropping Truth Bombs. "Macaulay Culkin EXPOSES the 'Red Shoe Men'—Episode 1." *YouTube*, September 2, 2019. Accessed March 27, 2021. https://youtu.be/9Zx3Oa K4Mf0

Eagleton, Terry. *Walter Benjamin or Toward a Revolutionary Criticism*. London: Verso, 1981.

Ebner, Julie. *Going Dark: The Secret Social Lives of Extremists*. London: Bloomsbury, 2020.

Eddo-Lodge, Reni. *Why I'm No Longer Talking to White People About Race*. London: Bloomsbury, 2017.

Ehrenreich, Barbara. *Dancing in the Streets: A History of Collective Joy*. New York: Holt Paperbacks, 2006.

Eisenmann, Stephen. *The Abu Ghraib Effect*. London: Reaktion, 2007.

Embery, Paul. *Despised: Why the Modern Left Loathes the Working Class*. Cambridge: Polity, 2021.

Embuscado, Rain. "Illma Gore's censored portrait of naked Donald Trump heads to London gallery." *Artnet*, April 7, 2016. Accessed April 6, 2021. https://news.artnet.com/art-world/naked-donald-trump-gallery-show-469016

Evergreen State College. "Coming Together. The 2015–16 Coming Together Speakers Series focused on addressing many of the problems and challenges that face the students, faculty and staff of color at the Evergreen State College." 2016. Accessed June 21, 2021. https://www.evergreen.edu/equity/coming-together

Evergreen State College Equity & Inclusion Council. "2016–2017 Strategic Equity Plan." 2016. Accessed June 21, 2021. https://www.evergreen.edu/sites/default/files/equity/documents/FINAL%202016-17%20Strategic%20Equity%20Plan%20--%20FOR%20CAMPUS-1.pdf

Evidence and Answers. "Critical critique of critical theory." *YouTube*, July 8, 2021. Accessed July 21, 2021. https://youtu.be/4IkxjmQg5OQ

Facebook Investor Relations. "Facebook reports second quarter 2021 results." 2021. Accessed November 26, 2021. https://investor.fb.com/investor-news/press-release-details/2021/Facebook-Reports-Second-Quarter-2021-Results/default.aspx

Fisher, Mark. "Exiting the Vampire Castle." *Open Democracy*, 24 November 2013. Accessed 24 January 2022. https://www.opendemocracy.net/en/opendemocracyuk/exiting-vampire-castle/

Flisfeder, Matthew. "Trump"—what does the name signify? or, Protofascism and the alt-Right: Three contradictions of the present conjuncture." *Cultural Politics*, vol. 14, no. 1 (2018): 38–56.

Forest, Benjamin and Juliet Johnson. "Confederate monuments and the problem of forgetting." *Cultural Geographies* vol. 26, no. 1 (2019): 127–31;

Foster, Hal. *Return of the Real: The Avant-garde at the End of the Century*. Cambridge, MA: MIT Press, 1996.

Fox Business. "Ben Carson on critical race theory: What are we doing to children?." May 8, 2021. Accessed June 25, 2021. https://youtu.be/p3yKcamADZI

Fox News. "Giuliani returns to court to argue Trump campaign's election case." November 19, 2020. Accessed January 25, 2022. https://video.foxbusiness.com/v/6210778333001?playlist_id=933116636001#sp=show-clips

Fox News. "Hannity: Democrats think they're immune to racism." June 24, 2021. Accessed June 25, 2021. https://youtu.be/SzZxSML7W8c

Fox News. "Media uproar over Dr. Seuss." March 7, 2021. Accessed March 15, 2021. https://video.foxnews.com/v/6237761356001#sp=show-clips

Fox News. "Parent arrested during school board meeting 'chaos' speaks out on 'Tucker'." June 24, 2021. Accessed June 24, 2021. https://youtu.be/lB9p4ERQszE

Fox News. "President Trump joins 'Sunday Morning Futures'." November 29, 2020. Accessed January 26, 2022. https://video.foxnews.com/v/6212917383001#sp=show-clips

Fox News. "Professor objects to no white people on campus demand." *YouTube*, May 27, 2017. Accessed June 22, 20212017 https://youtu.be/_j9nFced_eo.

Fox News. "Virginia parents push back against critical race theory, 'won't stand for lowering education standards'." May 14, 2021. Accessed June 24, 2021. https://video.foxnews.com/v/6254192917001#sp=show-clips

Fox News. "What does 'woke' even mean." August 2, 2018. Accessed July 16, 2021. https://video.foxnews.com/v/5817262219001#sp=show-clips.

Fox News. "Will free speech survive the 'cancel culture' movement?", April 5, 2021. Accessed August 16, 2021. https://video.foxnews.com/v/6246628645001#sp=show-clips

Fracanzani, Edoardo M. *Lives of Donald Trump and Silvio Berlusconi*. Alresford: Zero Books, 2021.

Frank, Priscilla. "'Dump across America': A street art project devoted to taking down Trump." *Huffpost*, February 26, 2016. Accessed April 6, 2021. https://www.huffpost.com/entry/donald-trump-is-a-steaming-pile-of-sht-according-to-street-artists-campaign_n_56d08be8e4b0bf0dab31e7cb

Fraser, Nancy. "Progressive neoliberalism versus reactionary populism: A Hobson's choice." In *The Great Regression*. Edited by Heinrich Geiselberger. Cambridge: Polity, 2017.

Freedland, Jonathan. "Trump may be fading away, but Trumpism is now in the American bloodstream." *The Guardian*, August 6, 2021. Accessed August 12, 2021. https://www.theguardian.com/commentisfree/2021/aug/06/trump-trumpism-american-presidential-run-republican

Friedman, Milton. *Capitalism and Freedom*. Chicago: University of Chicago Press, 2020.

Fukuyama, Francis. *Identity: Contemporary Identity Politics and the Struggle for Recognition*. London: Profile Books, 2018.

Fusco, Coco. "Censorship, not the painting, must go: On Dana Schutz's image of Emmett Till." *Hyperallergenic*, March 27, 2017. Accessed September 29, 2021. https://hyperallergic.com/368290/censorship-not-the-painting-must-go-on-dana-schutzs-image-of-emmett-till/

Gaetz, Matt. *Twitter*, June 23, 2021. Accessed July 21, 2021. https://twitter.com/mattgaetz/status/1407796912309342214

Gamboni, Dario. *The Destruction of Art: Iconoclasm and Vandalism Since the French Revolution*. London: Reaktion, 1997.

Garber-Paul, Elizabeth. "Naked Trump statues: Meet anarchist artists behind 'Emperor Has No Balls'." *Rolling Stone*, August 19, 2016. Accessed April 6, 2021. https://www.rollingstone.com/culture/culture-features/naked-trump-statues-meet-anarchist-artists-behind-emperor-has-no-balls-249522/

Gaufman, Elizaveta. "The Trump carnival: Popular appeal in the age of misinformation." *International Relations*, vol. 32, no. 4 (2018): 410–29.

Gelber, Katharine. "Is there a 'free speech crisis' in Australian universities?" *ABC*, July 15, 2020. Accessed June 14, 2021. https://www.abc.net.au/religion/katharine-gelber-free-speech-crisis-in-australian-universities/12459718

Gibson, Jano and Alexis Moran. "As coronavirus spreads, 'it's time to go home' Scott Morrison tells visitors and international students." *ABC News*, April 3, 2020. Accessed November 26, 2021. https://www.abc.net.au/news/2020-04-03/coronavirus-pm-tells-international-students-time-to-go-to-home/12119568

Gillespie, Eden. "How Republican Josh Hawley became one of America's 'most despised men' after the Capitol siege." *SBS News*, January 12, 2021. Accessed July 15, 2021. https://www.sbs.com.au/news/how-republican-josh-hawley-became-one-of-america-s-most-despised-men-after-the-capitol-siege

Gilroy, Paul. *The Black Atlantic: Modernity and Double Consciousness*. London: Verso Books, 1993.

Gilroy, Paul. *Against Race: Imagining political culture beyond the colour line*. Cambridge, MA: Belknap, 2000.

Glover, Michael. "Kara Walker's monument to monstrousness." *Hyperallergic*, October 5, 2019. Accessed June 29, 2020. https://hyperallergic.com/520353/kara-walkers-monument-to-monstrousness/

Godspeak Calvary Chapel. "Critical race theory | James Lindsay (9AM)." *YouTube*, June 27, 2021. Accessed November 26, 2021. https://youtu.be/JA0kD4p7Nsk

Goldstein, Caroline. "We have to help them be useful': Artist Krzysztof Wodiczko explains how existing monuments can be made to speak for the voiceless." *Artnet*, March 19, 2020. Accessed July 19, 2020. https://news.artnet.com/exhibitions/art21-krzysztof-wodiczko-1808949

Gounari, Panayota. "Authoritarianism, discourse and social media: Trump as the 'American Agitator'." In *Critical Theory and Authoritarian Populism*. Edited by Jeremiah Morelock. London: University of Westminster Press, 2018.

Graefer, Anne, Allaina Kirby, and Inger-Lise Kalviknes Bore. "Unruly women and carnivalesque countercontrol: Offensive humour in mediated social protest." *Journal of Communication Inquiry*, vol. 42, no. 1 (2018): 1–23.

Gramsci, Antonio. *Selections from the Prison Notebooks*. Edited and translated by Quentin Hoare and Geoffrey Nowell Smith. London: Lawrence & Wishart, 1971.

Grant, Melissa Gira. "This isn't an insurrection. It's an alliance." *New Republic*, January 7, 2021. Accessed July 29, 2021. https://newrepublic.com/article/160816/congress-mob-law-enforcement-alliance

Grayling, A.C. *Democracy and its Crisis*. London: OneWorld, 2017.

Green, Charles. *Peripheral Vision: Contemporary Australian Art 1970–1994*. Roseville, NSW: Craftsman House, 1995.

Grieg, Finlay. "Jeremy Vine: Brexit was no surprise to Radio 2 listeners." *iNews*, October 3, 2017. Accessed April 18, 2019. https://inews.co.uk/culture/radio/jeremy-vine-brexit-radio-2-listeners/

Grindon, Gavin. "Carnival against capital: A comparison of Bakhtin, Vaneigem and Bey." *Anarchist Studies*, vol. 12, no. 2 (2004): 147–61.

Grobe, Christopher. "The artist is President: Performance art and other keywords in the age of Donald Trump." *Critical Inquiry*, vol. 46, no. 4 (Summer 2020): 764–805.

Groom, Amelia. "RAQS Media Collective: Epiphany and escape." *Neue Luxury*, Issue 2, Accessed June 16, 2020. https://www.neueluxury.com/feature/raqs-media-collective/

Gržinić, Marina (ed.) *The Real, The Desperate, The* Absolute. Graz: Celje, 2001.

Haider, Shuja. "Postmodernism did not take place: On Jordan Peterson's 12 rules for life." *Viewpoint Magazine*, January 23, 2018. Accessed July 29, 2021. https://viewpointmag.com/2018/01/23/postmodernism-not-take-place-jordan-petersons-12-rules-life/

Hannah, Matthew. "Qanon and the Information Dark Age." *First Monday*, vol. 26, no. 2 (February 1, 2021). Accessed November 25, 2021. https://firstmonday.org/ojs/index.php/fm/article/download/10868/10067

Harris, Adam. "The GOP's 'critical race theory' obsession: How conservative politicians and pundits became fixated on an academic approach." *The Atlantic*, May 7, 2021. Accessed June 12, 2021. https://www.theatlantic.com/politics/archive/2021/05/gops-critical-race-theory-fixation-explained/618828/

Harris, Elizabeth A. and Alexandra Alter. "Simon & Schuster cancels plans for Senator Hawley's book." *The New York Times*, January 7, 2021 (updated January 15, 2021). Accessed July 15, 2021. https://www.nytimes.com/2021/01/07/books/simon-schuster-josh-hawley-book.html

Harris, Keith. "What's epistemically wrong with conspiracy theorising?" *Royal Institute of Philosophy Supplement*, vol. 84 (2018): 235–57.

Hawley, Josh. "Josh Hawley, @HawleyMO, My statement on the woke mob at @simonschuster." *Twitter*, 7:42 a.m., January 8, 2021. Accessed September 14, 2021. https://twitter.com/HawleyMO/status/1347327743004995585/photo/1

Helmore, Edward. "'It's a moral decision': Dr Seuss books are being 'recalled' not cancelled, expert says." *The Guardian*, March 7, 2021. Accessed March 15, 2021. https://www.theguardian.com/books/2021/mar/07/dr-seuss-books-product-recall-cancel-culture

Henry, Jr., Kevin Lawrence and Shameka N. Powell. "Kissing Cousins: Critical Race Theory's Racial Realism and Afropessimism's Social Death." In *The Future is Black: Afropessimism, fugitivity, and radical hope in education*. Edited by Carl A. Grant, Ashley Woodson, and Michael Dumas. New York, NY : Routledge, 2021.

Hicks, Stephen R.C. *Explaining Postmodernism: Skepticism and Socialism from Rousseau to Foucault*. Tempe/New Berlin/Milwaukee: Scholargy Publishing, 2004.

January 16, 2021. Accessed May 29, 2021. https://theconversation.com/how-trumps-language-shifted-in-the-weeks-leading-up-to-the-capitol-riot-2-linguists-explain-152483

Lawrence, Leslie. Facebook, June 19, 2021. Accessed September 30, 2021. https://www.facebook.com/leslie.lawrenson.5/posts/10227381202375191

Lee, Benjamin. "Marina Abramović mention in Podesta emails sparks accusations of satanism." *The Guardian*, November 5, 2016. Accessed March 16, 2021. https://www.theguardian.com/artanddesign/2016/nov/04/marina-abramovic-podesta-clinton-emails-satanism-accusations

Lesh, Matthew. "Free Speech on Campus Audit 2017, Institute of Public Affairs." Institute of Public Affairs, December, 2017. Accessed September 25, 2019. https://ipa.org.au/wp-content/uploads/2017/12/IPA-Report-Free-Speech-on-Campus-Audit-2017.pdf

Lesh, Matthew. "Free Speech on Campus Audit 2018, Institute of Public Affairs." Institute of Public Affairs, December, 2018. Accessed September 25, 2019. https://ipa.org.au/wp-content/uploads/2018/12/Free-Speech-on-Campus-Audit-2018.pdf

Livingstone, Josephine and Lovia Gyarkye. "The case against Dana Schutz: Why her painting of Emmett Till at the Whitney Biennial insults his memory." *New Republic*, March 23, 2017. Accessed June 25, 2021. https://newrepublic.com/article/141506/case-dana-schutz

Liz Wheeler. "Is critical race theory Marxist? | Liz Wheeler & Marc Lamont Hill." *YouTube*, July 11, 2021. Accessed July 15, 2021. https://youtu.be/0sVIS9n4KZU

Lowe, Mike. "Chicago area residents arrested, lose jobs after riots at U.S. Capitol." *WGN9*, January 7, 2021. Accessed July 28, 2021. https://wgntv.com/news/chicago-area-residents-arrested-lose-jobs-after-riot-at-u-s-capitol/

Lukan, Blaž "The Janez Janša project." In *Name Readymade*. Moderna Galerija Ljubljana, 2008.

Luke, Timothy W. "The ambiguities of memory and ambivalences of monuments: Confederate memorials in America." *Telos*, Issue 181 (2017): 218–22.

Luthar, Oto (ed.) *The Land Between. A History of Slovenia*. Frankfurt am Main: Peter Lang Verlag, 2013.

Macauley, Melissa. "To understand Trump's GOP, we need to look to Lenin and Mao." *The Washington Post*, November 1, 2020. Accessed September 14, 2021. https://www.washingtonpost.com/outlook/2020/11/01/understand-trumps-gop-we-need-look-lenin-mao/

Malik, Nesrine. *We Need New Stories: Challenging the Toxic Myths Behind Our Age of Discontent*. London: Orion, 2019.

Marković, Anđelka. "Trumpova frizura preživjela orkan, Chuck Norris neuništiv." *N1*, December 13, 2017. Accessed April 6, 2021. https://ba.n1info.com/vijesti/a232308-trumpova-frizura-prezivjela-orkan-chuck-norris-neunistiv/

Marshall, Alex. "Marina Abramovic just wants conspiracy theorists to let her be." *The New York Times*, April 21, 2020 (updated April 23, 2020). Accessed March 16, 2021. https://www.nytimes.com/2020/04/21/arts/design/marina-abramovic-satanist-conspiracy-theory.html

Mayer, Jane. "The making of the Fox News White House: Fox News has always been partisan. But has it become propaganda?" *The New Yorker*, March 4, 2019. Accessed March 15, 2021. https://www.newyorker.com/magazine/2019/03/11/the-making-of-the-fox-news-white-house

McDonald, Kevin. *Gamergate: First Battle of the Culture War*. United States: independently published, 2019. 8.

McDonough, Katie. "Die laughing at the Capitol." *New Republic*, January 11, 2021. Accessed July 28, 2021. https://newrepublic.com/article/160846/die-laughing-capitol

McIntyre, Lee. *Post-Truth*. Cambridge Massachusetts: MIT Press, 2018.

McQuinn, Brian and Laura Courchesne. "Strategic extremism: 4 insights on the U.S. Capitol siege from established insurgencies." *The Conversation*, May 19, 2021. Accessed August 4, 2021. https://theconversation.com/strategic-extremism-4-insights-on-the-u-s-capitol-siege-from-established-insurgencies-158747

Messerschmidt, Sarah. "The aesthetics of labour: Beauty and politics in Adrian Paci's 'The Column'." *Burlington Contemporary*, Issue 2 (2019).

Mickler, Steve. *Andrew Bolt, the Far Right and the First Nations*. Perth: UWA Publishing, 2019.

Mike Nayna. "PART ONE: Bret Weinstein, Heather Heying and the Evergreen Equity Council." *YouTube*, January 18, 2019. Accessed June 22, 2021. https://youtu.be/FH2WeWgcSMk

Miljanović, Mladen. *Aperta Fenestra*. Banja Luka: Kamena Kuca Banski Dvor, 2019.

Miller, Jason. "Activism vs. antagonism: Socially engaged art from Bourriaud to Bishop and beyond." FIELD: *Journal of Socially Engaged Art Criticism*, Issue 3 (Winter 2016).

Mounk, Yascha. *The People vs Democracy: Why Our Freedom is in Danger and How to Save It*. Cambridge: Harvard University Press, 2018.

Moye, David. "Kelly Marie Tran of 'Last Jedi' facing racist, sexist comments online. Online trolls invaded the actress' fan page but social media users clapped back." *Huffington Post*, December 27, 2017 (updated December 28, 2017). Accessed July 21, 2021. https://www.huffpost.com/entry/kelly-marie-tran-racists-last-jedi_n_5a4400 fee4b06d1621b6b2bb

Muksati, Alem. "Janez Jansa, Slovenia's paranoid Marshal Tweeto." *Balkan Insight*, November 11, 2020. Accessed November 19, 2020. https://balkaninsight.com/2020/11/11/janez-jansa-slovenias-paranoid-marshal-tweeto/

Mulholland, Evan. "Free speech crisis at Australia's universities confirmed by new research." Institute of Public Affairs, August 31, 2019. Accessed September 3, 2021. https://ipa.org.au/publications-ipa/media-releases/university-audit-finds-humanities-riddled-with-critical-race-theory-and-identity-politics

Murray, Douglas. *The Madness of Crowds*. London: Bloomsbury, 2019.

Nagle, Angela. *Kill All Normies: Online Culture Wars from 4chan and Tumblr to Trump and the Alt-right*. Alresford: John Hunt Publishing, 2017.

Napier-Raman, Kishor. "Government backs Hanson's critical race theory culture war. The question is: why?" *Crikey*, June 22, 2021. Accessed September 10, 2021. https://www.crikey.com.au/2021/06/22/government-backs-hansons-critical-race-theory/

New Discourses. "Hegel, wokeness, and the dialectical faith of Leftism." *YouTube*, May 29, 2021. Accessed September 2, 2021. https://youtu.be/uf4R0gX7g3w

New Discourses. "Marcuse's subverting forces in transition." August 19, 2021. Accessed August 26, 2021. https://youtu.be/9ju2BGLAi9A

Ng, Lynda. "Where have all the surpluses gone?" *Overland*, September 1, 2020. Accessed October 6, 2021. https://overland.org.au/2020/09/where-have-all-the-surpluses-gone/

Nichols, Fox. "Helms ups the ante." *New Art Examiner*, (October 1989).
Nichols, Tom. *The Death of Expertise: The Campaign Against Established Knowledge and Why It Matters*. Oxford: Oxford University Press, 2019.
Nicolaou, Anna and Alex Barker. "Spotify warns it is 'too early' to calculate impact of Joe Rogan row," *The Financial Times*, February 2, 2022. Accessed February 3, 2022. https://www.ft.com/content/df1437bc-ded5-491e-b320-2dcc93f8f3a9
Niemonen, Jack. "Antiracist Education in Theory and Practice: A Critical Assessment." The *American Sociologist*, vol. 38 (2007): 159–77.
NIH Videocast. "President Joe Biden visits the NIH campus." *YouTube*, March 12, 2021. Accessed March 26, 2021. https://youtu.be/CDYCpPAnRaw?t=18
Nikolić, Vladimir. "About Death Anniversary 1968–2004." 2007. Accessed August 12, 2021. http://www.vladimir-Nikolić.com/foto/about%20death%20anniversary.pdf
No Safe Spaces, 2019, directed by Justin Folk. USA: Atlas Distribution Company.
Noack, Ruth. *Sanja Iveković: Triangle*. Cambridge, MA: MIT Press, 2015.
NPR. "Read Trump's Jan. 6 speech, a key part of impeachment trial." February 10, 2021. Accessed June 13, 2021. https://www.npr.org/2021/02/10/966396848/read-trumps-jan-6-speech-a-key-part-of-impeachment-trial
Olsen, Tyler. "Trump threatens tax-exempt status, funding for universities and schools over 'radical left indoctrination'." *Fox News*, July 10, 2020. Accessed January 31, 2022. https://www.foxnews.com/politics/trump-threatens-to-remove-tax-exempt-status-of-universities-and-school-systems
Out of Shadows: The Documentary, dir. Mike Smith, 2020. Accessed March 16, 2021. https://www.outofshadows.org
Pabst, Adrian. *Postliberal Politics*. Cambridge: Polity, 2021.
Parker, Emma "Freedom reigned at YAF's 43rd Annual National Conservative Student Conference." *Young America's Foundation*, August 12, 2021. Accessed September 2, 2021. https://www.yaf.org/news/freedom-reigned-at-yafs-43rd-annual-national-conservative-student-conference/
Peiser, Jaclyn and Justin Jouvenal. "Woman fatally shot as pro-Trump mob stormed the Capitol identified as Air Force veteran." *Washington Post*, January 7, 2021. Accessed July 28, 2021. https://www.washingtonpost.com/nation/2021/01/07/ashli-babbitt-dead-capitol-riot/
Pejić, Bojana. "Metonymical Moves." In *Sanja Iveković: Is This My True Face*. Edited by Tihomir Milovac. Zagreb: Museum of Contemporary Art, 1998.
Pelley, Scott. "Whistleblower: Facebook is misleading the public on progress against hate speech, violence, misinformation." *CBS News*, October 4, 2021. Accessed October 11, 2021. https://www.cbsnews.com/news/facebook-whistleblower-frances-haugen-misinformation-public-60-minutes-2021-10-03/
Pérez-Peña, Richard, Mitch Smith, and Stephanie Saul. "University of Chicago strikes back against campus political correctness." *The New York Times*, August 26, 2016. Accessed September 25, 2019. https://www.nytimes.com/2016/08/27/us/university-of-chicago-strikes-back-against-campus-political-correctness.html
Peters, Michael A. "On the epistemology of conspiracy." *Educational Philosophy and Theory*, vol. 52 (2020: 1413–17.
Petrović, Tanja. *Yuropa: Jugoslovensko Nasledje I Politike Buducnosti u Postjugoslovenskim Drustvima*. Beograd: Fabrika Knjiga, 2012.
Pew Research Center. "The growing partisan divide in views of higher education." January 30, 2019. Accessed June 11, 2021. https://www.pewresearch.org/social-trends/2019/08/19/the-growing-partisan-divide-in-views-of-higher-education-2/

Piccini, Jon and Dirk Moses. "Simon Birmingham's intervention in research funding is not unprecedented, but dangerous." *The Conversation*, October 26, 2018. Accessed September 3, 2021. https://theconversation.com/simon-birminghams-intervention-in-research-funding-is-not-unprecedented-but-dangerous-105737

Pinder, Kymberly N. "Missus Kara E. Walker: Emancipated, and on tour." *The Art Bulletin*, vol. 90, no. 4 (December 2008): 640–8.

Pintilescu, Corneliu and Attila Kustán Magyari. "Soros conspiracy theories and the rise of populism in post-socialist Hungary and Romania." In *Conspiracy Theories in Eastern Europe: Tropes and Trends*. Edited by Anastasiya Astapova, Onoriu Colăcel, Corneliu Pintilescu, and Tamás Scheibner. New York: Routledge, 2021.

Pluckrose, Helen and James Lindsay. *Cynical Theories: How Universities Made Everything about Race, Gender and Identity—and Why This Harms Everybody*. London: Swift Press, 2020.

Polus, Sarah. "Chrissy Teigen fights back after Twitter user drags her into the false 'Pizzagate' conspiracy theory." *The Washington Post*, 12:25 a.m. January 2, 2018. Accessed March 16, 2021. https://www.washingtonpost.com/news/reliable-source/wp/2018/01/01/chrissy-teigen-fights-back-after-twitter-user-drags-model-into-the-false-pizzagate-conspiracy-theory/

Pomerantsev, Peter. *Nothing is True and Everything is Possible*. London: Faber, 2020.

Power, Lis and Rob Savillo. "Fox News' obsession with critical race theory, by the numbers: Fox has mentioned 'critical race theory' over 1,900 times in the past 3.5 months." *Media Matters* 15, June, 2021. Accessed July 21, 2021. https://www.mediamatters.org/fox-news/fox-news-obsession-critical-race-theory-numbers

PowerfulJRE. "Joe Rogan Experience #1006—Jordan Peterson & Bret Weinstein." YouTube, streamed live on September 2, 2017. Accessed June 22, 2021. https://youtu.be/6G59zsjM2UI

PragerU. "What is critical race theory?." YouTube, April 26, 2021. Accessed July 16, 2021. https://youtu.be/8Zy6DQoRYQw

Prica, Ines and Tea Skokić (eds.) *Horror Porno Ennui: Kulture Prakse Postsocijalizma*. Zagreb: Biblioteka Nova Etnografija, 2011.

Qanaut. "A dig into Q Post 4281: How about a nice game of chess? . . . Do emotions affect critical thinking? . . . 'At this time'." *greatawakening.win*, March 15, 2021. Accessed March 25, 2021. https://greatawakening.win/p/12hkrFFIjm/a-dig-into-q-post-4281-how-about/

Rachman, Gideon. "Trump, Putin, Xi and the cult of the strongman leader." *Financial Times*, October 31, 2016. Accessed May 25, 2021. https://www.ft.com/content/39da343a-9f4b-11e6-891e-abe238dee8e2

Rangelov, Iavor. *Nationalism and the Rule of Law: Lessons from the Balkans and Beyond*. Cambridge: Cambridge University Press, 2013.

Raqs Media Collective, R. Sundaram, and D. Zyman. "The And: An expanded questionnaire on the contemporary: Has the moment of the contemporary come and gone?" *Asia Art Archive: Field Notes*, vol. 1 (2012). Accessed July 13, 2020. http://www.aaa.org.hk/FieldNotes/Details/1192

Rasmussen, Mikkel Bolt. "The estheticization of late capitalist fascism." *Third Text*, vol. 35, no. 3 (2021): 341–54.

Reuters. "Fact Check—Claims Trump will be reinstated on August 13 stem from debunked conspiracy theories." July 20, 2021. Accessed September 18, 2021. https://www.reuters.com/article/factcheck-trump-reinstated-idUSL1N2OV1W3

2021. https://www.theartnewspaper.com/2017/03/24/controversy-over-emmett-till-painting-at-whitney-biennial-goes-beyond-art-world

Stuckey, Allie Beth. "It's vital that Christians understand this about critical theory | Guest: James Lindsay | Ep 431." *YouTube*, June 3, 2021. Accessed October 6, 2021. https://youtu.be/1xhxItXRPf0

Sunstein, Cass R. and Adrian Vermeule. "Conspiracy theories: Causes and cures." *Journal of Political Philosophy*, vol. 17, no. 2 (2009): 202–27.

Svrluga, Susan and Joe Heim. "Threat shuts down college embroiled in racial dispute." *The Washington Post*, June 2, 2017. Accessed June 22, 2021. https://www.washingtonpost.com/news/grade-point/wp/2017/06/01/threats-shut-down-college-embroiled-in-racial-dispute/

Tate Modern. "Kara Walker's Fons Americanus: Delve deeper into 2019's Hyundai Commission by Kara Walker." 2019. Accessed June 29, 2020. https://www.tate.org.uk/art/artists/kara-walker-2674/kara-walkers-fons-americanus

The Agenda with Steve Paikin. "Genders, rights and freedom of speech." *YouTube*, October 27, 2016. Accessed June 29, 2021. https://youtu.be/kasiov0ytEc

The Heritage Foundation. "Critical race theory has infiltrated the federal government | Christopher Rufo on Fox News." *YouTube*, September 3, 2020. Accessed June 11, 2021. https://youtu.be/rBXRdWflV7M

The House of Commons and House of Lords. *Freedom of Speech in Universities: Fourth Report of Session 2017–19 (HC 589, HL PAPER 111)* (2018).

The Rubin Report. "Critical race theory war: James Lindsay, Allie Stuckey, Christopher Rufo | ROUNDTABLE | Rubin Report." *YouTube*, February 20, 2021. Accessed July 16, 2021. https://youtu.be/q-z_ZrxP9hI

The Rubin Report. "Evergreen State College racism controversy | Bret Weinstein | ACADEMIA | Rubin Report." *YouTube*, streamed live on May 31, 2017. Accessed June 22, 2021. https://youtu.be/-fEAPcgxnyY

The Rubin Report. "Exposing useful idiots & the lies Liberals told me | James Lindsay | ACADEMIA | Rubin Report." *YouTube*, June 20, 2021. Accessed June 16, 2016. https://youtu.be/Dx1ZruoTnrg

The Signal Productions. "Episode Two—Origins of woke ideology Part 2." YouTube, July 2, 2021. Accessed July 16, 2021. https://youtu.be/4dcw29urMTs

TheHenchman. "This is 100% CGI/deep fake of Biden. Please watch and keep your on the mask movement as he speaks. This is without a doubt fake. (youtu.be)." *The Great Awakening: Unite World Wide*, March 18, 2021. Accessed March 26, 2021. https://greatawakening.win/p/12hkmYabhv/this-is-100-cgideep-fake-of-bide/c/

Thompson, Janna. "Friday essay: a new front in the culture wars, Cynical Theories takes unfair aim at the humanities." *The Conversation*, November 6, 2020. Accessed July 2, 2021. https://theconversation.com/friday-essay-a-new-front-in-the-culture-wars-cynical-theories-takes-unfair-aim-at-the-humanities-148524

Timcast. "Timcast IRL - Minneapolis to fund Antifa autonomous zone eith $500k w/James Lindsay." *YouTube*, March 13, 2021. Accessed August 13, 2021. https://youtu.be/K8ZXzSADXjE

Todorova, Maria. *Imagining the Balkans*. Oxford: Oxford University Press, 2009.

Trump, Donald J. "Presidential documents: Executive Order 13950 of September 22, 2020 combating race and sex stereotyping." *Federal Register* 85, no. 188,

September 28, 2020. Accessed June 18, 2021. https://www.govinfo.gov/content/pkg/FR-2020-09-28/pdf/2020-21534.pdf

Trump, Donald J. "Proclamation 10110 of October 30, 2020; National American History and Founders Month, 2020; By the President of the United States of America." Federal Register 85, no. 215, Presidential Documents 70419, 70420, November 5, 2020. Accessed June 18, 2021. https://www.govinfo.gov/content/pkg/FR-2020-11-05/pdf/2020-24739.pdf

Trump, Donald J. (@realDonaldTrump), *Twitter*, July 10, 2020. https://twitter.com/realDonaldTrump/status/1281616586273468416 [NOTE: the @realdonaldtrump account has since been permanently suspended from Twitter].

Trump, Donald J. (@realDonaldTrump), *Twitter*, November 12, 2020. https://twitter.com/realdonaldtrump/status/1326910770194632704 [NOTE: the @realdonaldtrump account has since been permanently suspended from Twitter].

Tucker Carlson Tonight. "Trump: Time to stop indoctrination sessions." *Facebook*, September 8, 2021. Accessed June 18, 2021. https://www.facebook.com/TuckerCarlsonTonight/videos/2696598097262791/

Turrill, Katrina. "Melania Trump: Move over Ronaldo, the First Lady's newly erected statue is JUST as bad." *The Express*, June 6, 2017 https://www.express.co.uk/life-style/life/813570/donald-trump-melania-statue accessed April 6, 2021.

u/wreck2009. "NWO Guide." *Reddit*, accessed March 12, 2021. https://www.reddit.com/r/coolguides/comments/fgcm3m/nwo_guide/

Valasik, Matthew and Shannon Reid. "After the insurrection, America's far-right groups get more extreme." *The Conversation*, March 15, 2021. Accessed August 4, 2021. https://theconversation.com/after-the-insurrection-americas-far-right-groups-get-more-extreme-156463

van Prooijen, Jan-Willem, Karen M. Douglas, and Clara de Inocencio. "Connecting the dots: Illusory pattern perception predicts belief in conspiracies and the supernatural." *European Journal of Social Psychology*, vol. 48, no. 3 (2018): 320–35.

Verdery, Katherine. *The Political Lives of the Dead: Reburial and Postsocialist Change*. New York: Columbia University Press, 1999.

Verdery, Katherine. *What Was Socialism and What Comes Next?* Princeton, NJ: Princeton University Press, 1996.

Vice News. "Campus argument goes viral as Evergreen State is caught in racial turmoil (HBO)." *YouTube*, June 16, 2017. Accessed June 22, 2021. https://youtu.be/2cMYfxOFBBM

Vladisavljevic, Anja. "'it'll be bloody': Under Jansa, troubled times for the Slovenian media." *Balkan Insight*, April 28, 2020. Accessed November 19, 2020. https://balkaninsight.com/2020/04/28/itll-be-bloody-under-jansa-troubled-times-for-slovenian-media/

Waldman, Katy. "A sociologist examines the 'White fragility' that prevents White Americans from confronting racism." *The Atlantic*, July 23, 2018. Accessed June 21, 2021. https://www.newyorker.com/books/page-turner/a-sociologist-examines-the-white-fragility-that-prevents-white-americans-from-confronting-racism

Walker, Shaun. "Slovenia's PM Janša channels Orbán with attacks on media and migrants." *The Guardian*, May 4, 2020. Accessed November 19, 2020. https://www.theguardian.com/world/2020/may/04/janez-jansa-new-pm-slovenia-in-mould-of-orban

Walsh, Bryan. "The world is not ready for the next pandemic." *Time*, May 4, 2017. Accessed April 24, 2020. https://time.com/magazine/us/4766607/may-15th-2017-vol-189-no-18-u-s/

Weiss, Bari. "Meet the renegades of the intellectual dark web." *The New York Times*, May 8, 2018. Accessed June 24, 2021. https://www.nytimes.com/2018/05/08/opinion/intellectual-dark-web.html

Weller, Sheila. "How author Timothy Tyson found the woman at the center of the Emmett Till case." *Vanity Fair*, January 26, 2017. Accessed June 25, 2021. https://www.vanityfair.com/news/2017/01/how-author-timothy-tyson-found-the-woman-at-the-center-of-the-emmett-till-case?mbid=social_twitter

Whitney Museum of American Art. "Perspectives on race and representation: An evening with the Racial Imaginary Institute: Sun, Apr 9, 2017, 7:30pm." April 9, 2017. Accessed June 29, 2021. https://whitney.org/events/perspectives-on-race-and-representation

Whittington, Keith. "The trouble with banning critical race theory." *Areo*, June 16, 2020. Accessed June 23, 2021. https://areomagazine.com/2021/06/16/the-trouble-with-banning-critical-race-theory/

Wilderson III, Frank B. "Close-Up: Fugitivity and the Filmic Imagination: Social Death and Narrative Aporia in 12 Years a Slave." *Black Camera, An International Film Journal*, vol. 7, no. 1 (2015): 134–149.

Wilderson III, Frank B. *Afropessimism*. New York: Liveright, 2020.

Wilkinson, Alissa. "In 2016, the Ghostbusters reboot didn't change movies. But the backlash was a bad omen." *Vox*, December 30, 2019. Accessed July 20, 2021. https://www.vox.com/culture/2019/12/30/21037815/ghostbusters-backlash-decade-black-panther-captain-marvel

Willingham, AJ and Carma Hassan. "People at the US Capitol riot are being identified and losing their jobs." *CNN*, January 9, 2021. Accessed July 28, 2021. https://edition.cnn.com/2021/01/07/us/capitol-riots-people-fired-jobs-trnd/index.html

Wolff, Michael. "Donald Trump's January 6: The view from inside the Oval Office." (book excerpt). *New York Magazine*, June 28, 2021. Accessed June 29, 2021. https://nymag.com/intelligencer/article/michael-wolff-landslide-final-days-trump-presidency-excerpt.html

Wong, Winnie Won Yin. *Van Gogh on Demand: China and the Readymade*. Chicago: University of Chicago Press, 2014.

Wood, Michael J., Karen M. Douglas, and Robbie M. Sutton. "Dead and alive: Beliefs in contradictory conspiracy theories." *Social Psychological and Personality Science*, vol. 3, no. 6 (2012): 767–73.

Wylie, Chris. *Mindf*ck: Inside Cambridge Analytica's Plot to Break the World*. London: Profile Books, 2019.

ZeroDeltaTango. "DAILY REMINDER - TRUMP WON - WE WERE ROBBED - OUR VOTE DOESNT COUNT UNTIL THIS GETS FIXED." *greatawakening.win*, March 10, 2021. Accessed March 11, 2021. https://greatawakening.win/p/12hkmRkJVb/daily-reminder--trump-won--we-we/

Žižek, Slavoj. "Why are Laibach and NSK not fascists?" *Maska* vol. 21, no. 3–4 (2006 [1993])

Žižek, Slavoj. *In Defense of Lost Causes*. London: Verso, 2009.

Žižek, Slavoj. "Appearance and obscenity: Five reflections." *The Philosophical Salon*, June 22, 2020. Accessed April 19, 2021. https://thephilosophicalsalon.com/power-appearance-and-obscenity-five-reflections/#_ednref4

Žižek, Slavoj. "First as a farce, then as a tragedy? Denying US divisions perpetuates Trumpism's delusions." *ABC Religion & Ethics*, 22 January 2021. Accessed July 19, 2021. https://www.abc.net.au/religion/slavoj-zizek-first-farce-then-tragedy-inauguration/13084544

Žižek, Slavoj. "Will you laugh for me please." *Lacan.com*. Accessed July 19, 2021. https://www.lacan.com/zizeklaugh.htm

INDEX